"A lot of writers invent a fake world, maybe because the real world isn't worthy of them. This writer focuses on the real world and allows the reader to lose herself in the beauty and breathtaking quality of real life. Because real life is beautiful, even if it has rough edges."

—Reader S.

Praise for The Dad Who Stayed
AND OTHER STORIES

"New and full of surprises."
—2025 Utah Book Awards

"*The Dad Who Stayed* depicts with hilarity and deep compassion the inner world of a kindergarten-age boy beginning to navigate the outer world. Every emotional payoff, whether flash-of-lightning funny or tearfully joyful, is earned through a rich depth of honesty that is the polar opposite of sentimentalism."
—Darrin McGraw, co-author of Animal Future

"*The Dad Who Stayed* brought to my mind memories of my own experiences and things I'd never thought about them before."
—Reader L.

"David Rodeback deals with difficult subjects with grace and humor. These stories . . . will make you laugh, break your heart, and enrich your soul."
—Reader S.

Praise for Poor As I Am

AND OTHER STORIES AT CHRISTMAS

"Utterly charming . . . clever and kind."
—2025 Utah Book Awards

"Christmas stories with wonderfully dry humor and heart. . . . Some made me laugh, some made me cry."
—Reader C.

"Like sitting by a fire with a warm mug: nostalgic, sincere, quietly moving . . . moments of unexpected depth . . . really captured the spirit of the season without falling into cliche."
—Reader G.

"Loved these stories a whole bunch. My only problem was that my eyes kept leaking."
—Reader S.J.

"Richard Paul Evans has some competition."
—Reader J.

Also by David Rodeback

The Dad Who Stayed and Other Stories
Poor As I Am and Other Stories at Christmas

Hearts Together

David Rodeback

60 East Press
867 N 60 E
American Fork, UT 84003
60eastpress.com

LCCN: 2025917920
Trade Paperback ISBN: 979-8-9883510-4-7
eBook ISBN: 979-8-9883510-5-4

Printed in the United States of America

No part of this book's text was written by or with the direct assistance of generative artificial intelligence (AI), including large language models (LLMs).

Book cover by BookCoverZone

To the many who taught me to believe

Blessed are they who see beautiful things in humble places where other people see nothing.

Camille Pissarro

We do too much watching of our neighbor's garden, too little weeding in our own.

William George Jordan

Dancing

1

Happy New Year

THE LAST SONG FADED away. The scoreboard on the church gym wall counted down to midnight—a minute nineteen, eighteen, seventeen seconds. I wondered what a good New Year's resolution would be, and if there was any point.

I tried to sound official in my head, but I couldn't get past the first five words: "I, Jenny Miller, hereby resolve . . ."

Resolve what? To be normal? I might as well resolve to be willowy.

Resolve not to be ignored at dances in the new year? If that were up to me, boys wouldn't have ignored me, mostly, at dances in the old year. Including tonight.

The DJ announced that she had noisemakers up front for anyone who didn't get one when they passed them out. I turned mine over in my hand. The scoreboard clock said 54 seconds.

Weren't New Year's resolutions supposed to be achievable, as in realistic? Realistically, if I resolved to get better at denial and distraction, I might notice the aching emptiness less often.

I could resolve to avoid dances henceforth and forever, but that felt like giving up, and I didn't want that.

I could reach for the stars and resolve (realistically) to be okay with the fact that boys weren't interested in me. But if there wasn't a rule there should have been: never resolve to feel okay about something that will never feel okay.

My best friend Nikki—whose real name, to her dismay, was Veronica—collapsed onto a folding chair next to me. A guy I didn't know had asked her to dance, and she'd been gone for a while.

I tried to sound cheerful. "How'd it go? Who was that guy?" Then I saw her deep frown and my heart sank. "What's wrong? What happened?"

Her mouth barely moved. "Later?"

"Thirty seconds!" called the DJ. "Count down with me, everybody!"

Others joined in, but we didn't. Nikki leaned forward and buried her face in her hands. I put my arm around her waist and worried.

Our other best friend returned. Jack was all girl but liked the nickname. She'd just danced with a boy who looked twelve but probably wasn't, since the minimum age for our church dances was fourteen. She caught my gaze, shook her head, and sat next to Nikki.

Fourteen seconds.

Jack looked at Nikki, then turned to me with raised eyebrows.

"Later," I mouthed.

"Four!" yelled the crowd.

"Three!

"Two!

"One!

"Happy New Year!"

Boys and girls all around us cheered, blew their noisemakers, high-fived, hugged, and danced around. A few couples kissed, and I envied them. Nikki didn't move. Jack and I winced at the heavy metal version of "Auld Lang Syne" which began to pound our skulls.

I produced a wry smile and raised my green plastic noisemaker for one half-hearted blow. Before it reached my lips, I changed my mind.

The New Year's Eve dance and midnight breakfast were an ancient tradition. My parents had done the same thing at church when they were teenagers. Different music, different hairstyles, same giant bags of pancake mix we'd seen on the way in.

Same noisemakers too, probably. Blow into one end, noise happens, garishly colored paper thing unrolls. Stop blowing, it rolls back up. Some kids near us blew them in each other's faces. I set mine on the empty chair beside me.

Maybe it was time for the whole tradition to die.

The brutal song finally ended, the lights went up, and about 200 kids began to turn a big gym from a dance hall into a banquet hall. Adult volunteers were cooking our breakfast in the kitchen, and the scent of bacon must have cut at least five minutes off the setup time. The din of unfolding tables and a lot more chairs being put up so quickly was only slightly less deafening than "Auld Lang Syne" had been.

Long food lines formed, and we joined one. Jack looked at me in surprise. "You should sit. We'll save your place."

"I sat enough tonight," I said. "I'll be okay."

I'd been sitting all evening, as usual, but this was different. I didn't want to be sitting over there, when Nikki needed us over here. She was quiet and listless. We'd wait for some privacy to question her, but we'd stay with her in the meantime.

I sat a lot, not just at dances. It was safer. My legs worked, and I could walk and even run. But if I was vertical when I had a seizure, the only questions were, which parts of me would hit what on the way down, and how hard?

So if a boy asked me to dance, which happened sometimes, I'd thank him, tell him I couldn't, and ask him to sit with me instead. He'd agree—they always did—and we'd make awkward conversation for a few minutes. I might tell him why I couldn't dance, if he didn't know. Either way he'd probably never sit with me again.

Two lines over, an enormous, bearded boy stomped up to an equally large, clean-shaven boy, flexed his massive arms, and roared, "Bacon! Need bacon! Must have bacon! Where is bacon?" They growled and butted heads, and some boys around them cheered. I didn't see any girls cheering.

Our line was tamer. Just ahead of me were two younger girls who looked barely fourteen. One exulted to the other, "I love that you did your hair the way I said. It's so pretty!" They giggled and hugged, and I tried not to roll my eyes.

Ahead of them, a blonde girl and a blond boy held hands. She asked him if he wanted her pancakes, which he did. "If there's any food left by then," he grumbled. There were still at least thirty people ahead of them in our line.

"We never run out of food at church activities," she said.

"We ran out of peanut butter at Scout camp two years in a row," he said. "Bread too. Does that count?"

She put an arm around his waist and leaned in. "Does this feel like Scout camp?"

He squeezed her shoulders. "Nope."

"Good," she said.

In the line next to ours, two girls argued just loudly enough that I could listen.

"I don't see the problem," said one. "I wish a boy wanted to kiss me for New Year's."

The other was deadly serious. "I'm saving my kisses, among other things, for my future husband, whoever he is. You should do that too."

"You are so not my mother. Anyway, it's just kissing, not sex."

"Don't say that word in a church! Besides, if they kiss like that here, they probably go way past kissing when nobody's watching. But they'll be in church Sunday anyway, acting like they didn't."

"Wow. Judgy much?" asked the first. "You don't know they're doing anything bad. And it's just kissing I want. The other stuff can wait for my honeymoon, after my temple wedding. There's nothing wrong with kissing until then."

I glanced at my friends, but they weren't listening. Nikki stared blankly into space. Jack had her phone out.

"We shouldn't even think about that yet," said the serious one.

"Pretty sure you think about it too."

"When I start to, I stop myself and repent. That would be a good New Year's resolution for you. You know, repenting."

"Oh, lighten up, you little prude!"

"If it's wrong to do, it's wrong to think about. Not as wrong as doing it, but wrong enough. Do you even have a testimony at all?"

"Better than yours. Here's my real New Year's resolution. This year I will kiss and be kissed. No matter what my super-righteous little sister thinks. Wish me luck?"

They were sisters. No surprise there.

"You know what?" asked the younger sister. "I'm not talking or listening to you for at least two minutes, starting now. And I'm telling Mom and Dad you're thinking about having you-know-what."

"I want to be there, okay? When you tell them? You realize Mom and Dad sometimes, well, I don't know how often—"

"Shut up!"

"And the older, wiser sister wins again. Will you be starting your two minutes soon?"

When we reached the food, we had to wait, while the servers replaced empty pans of scrambled eggs with full ones. I scanned the line ahead, all the way to the drinks. One boy, six girls—and every girl had long, blonde hair. Five wore it perfectly straight. One had a little wave. They were all skinnier than me, except the one with the wave.

The blonde girl who had offered the boy her pancakes leaned on him, looking tired but content. He idly wrapped a lock of her hair around his finger. I didn't even know their names, but something in me yearned to take her place.

Maybe I should resolve to grow my black hair longer and dye it blonde. It was already straight. And I could lose a few pounds.

When the server asked, "One pancake or two?" I said two.

We took our food to the corner farthest from the serving lines. Jack and I sat across from each other at the end of a long, rectangular table, with Nikki between us on the end. The next few places were empty.

"Time to compare notes," Jack said. We usually did that on the way to my house for late-night, after-dance smoothies.

I turned to Nikki. "Who was that guy? What happened?"

Her gaze moved to me, then to Jack, then back to her plate. "Could one of you go first?"

"I will," said Jack. "Two eighth-graders and a ninth-grader who skipped a grade. He wanted me to know that. Without girls' choice I wouldn't have danced with a high school boy at all. Nothing special there either. I went for cute and got cute-but-stupid. Not my best dance ever. Or my worst, I guess. Who's next?"

"I'll go." Nikki pushed her paper plate away but kept staring at it. She hadn't touched her food. "Except for those two girls' choice songs, I only danced with that subhuman at the end. He's a future state champion wrestler. So he says, and I kind of believe him. He really, really wanted to wrestle tonight." She shivered. "Seriously, before that much of a boy touches that much of me, shouldn't I want it too?"

Her voice trembled, and a tear rolled down each cheek. Her hands were fists. "Why does the first high school guy who ever told me I was pretty have to be a total creep?"

She looked up. "He said I move like a dancer. I mean, duh. I am a dancer. And he likes brunettes." She touched her hair. "Yay for me."

"What did he do?" asked Jack. "Did he hurt you?"

"The fast dance was okay, but we're barely into that slow song, and he pulls me way too close and says he wants to kiss all my freckles, one by one, for a New Year's countdown. I doubt he can count backwards correctly all the way from 29—that's my latest count—but I didn't ask. And where he put—" She folded her arms and shivered again. "I need a long, hot shower."

I could have enjoyed dancing close, I thought, or dancing at all, and kisses counting down to the New Year. But not with some random creep who just assumed I was into him, when I wasn't. Or didn't care if I wasn't.

She groaned, and Jack and I shared a look. Was this about to get worse?

"I put up with it at first, a little," Nikki said. "Didn't want to make a scene in the middle of everybody. Thought maybe he'd get that I wasn't into, you know, wrestling with him. Then he lifted my chin and started moving in for a kiss. I think that's what he was doing. Nowhere near a freckle, either. I pushed him away and told him not to touch me again. Ever. I might have smelled alcohol."

Her face looked ready to crumple, but she squared her shoulders and composed herself. "At least he let me go without a struggle, and maybe he was a little embarrassed. I don't know. I ran away to the restroom for the last few songs. When I came out, I saw him leaving with some other guys. I made sure he didn't see me."

I was a bad, selfish friend. I should at least have wondered why she'd been gone so long, or maybe even noticed when she left the dance floor alone in the middle of a song. I should have worried about her instead of myself a lot sooner.

She'd been crushing a napkin in her fist. Now she set it on the table and tried to smooth it out. Her eyes met mine, and she sighed. "Your turn to complain," she said. "Did a boy even talk to you tonight?"

I knew Nikki didn't mean her question to be a gut punch. This was just what we talked about after a dance. The thing to do was get past it quickly, and her question had pretty much answered itself anyway. "No," I said. "That's my whole complaint, I guess."

"Boys suck," she said.

Jack frowned. "We need to find the boys who don't."

Nikki asked my question for me. "Does that kind come to dances?"

"The problem," Jack explained, "is that guys who don't know us can't just look at us and see our delightful personalities."

"Delightful for introverts," said Nikki with no trace of a smile.

Jack nodded. "I know, right? I also realize we're not blondes." She corralled a stray lock of wavy red hair. "And we don't want to be. But we're reasonably cute. We shouldn't have to wait for guys to discover how amazing we are on the inside before at least a few of them"—she glanced at Nikki—"the fully human ones—notice us at dances. But even guys who know us already mostly ignore us. We need different guys."

Nikki put my doubts into words again. "What can we do that we're not doing?"

We exchanged blank stares. Then we all had the same idea: focus on breakfast. Even Nikki picked up her plastic fork.

After a few bites I reached for my juice, took a sip, and cringed. It was fake juice, almost the right shade of orange but sickly sweet, and the texture was kind of gross. I doubted any part of it had ever been inside a fruit.

Before I could complain, Jack broke our silence. "New Year's resolution for me: eat thick-cut pepper bacon more often. This is amazing."

"Is that a metaphor?" I asked. "Or are you talking about actual bacon, when we're trying to talk about boys?"

"Metaphors are more your thing," she said. "You're the writer. Right now, my thing's bacon. So finish yours or give it to me."

I broke my last strip and gave her the bigger half. She took a bite and talked around it. "Thank you! A gift from a true friend."

She swallowed, then beamed at Nikki with exaggerated hope. "Equally true friend, I could help with your bacon too."

Nikki's eyes twinkled, and I was relieved. She was starting to cheer up. "No, thanks," she said.

"Back to boys, then," said Jack.

I tried to sound innocent. "You mean, how do we attract perfectly cooked, thick-cut pepper bacon and repel that bland, paper-thin stuff they serve at free hotel breakfasts?" I held up my fake juice. "Also, does it mean anything, metaphorically, when they go all-out for fantastic bacon at a church breakfast, and they even add some vanilla to the pancake mix from the giant bag, but they give us this extreme-fructose abomination to drink?"

Jack grinned, and Nikki smiled faintly. They were used to big words from me. They spent a lot of time at my house, around my parents, the writer and the English professor. We used big words for fun.

Jack put on a businesslike face. "We're officially ignoring your second metaphor. Too deep for 12:46 a.m. And because we're such good friends, we'll try to forget you just referred to boys as meat."

Nikki smiled grimly. "Sliced pig meat. So how do we attract thick-cut pepper bacon?"

"I have an idea," Jack said.

So maybe there was a spark of hope, or at least the possibility of a good joke. We leaned in.

2

Desirables

"**L**et's be more scientific," Jack said. "More organized, anyway."

Jack's two superpowers were science, especially chemistry, and playing the oboe. We were only sophomores, but she already had college scholarship offers for both.

"Obviously, two of us need less attention from the wrong boys," she said. "We all need a lot more attention from the right boys, whoever they are. Agreed?"

We nodded.

"I get that a lot of guys from our school don't know us yet. Thank you, crazy high school boundary change."

"At least they didn't split us up," I said.

"Tragedy averted," Jack said. "Anyway, I know that school where we thought we'd be this year is now dead to us, but the big church dances are for both high schools, and that's hundreds more boys our same age or a year or two older, and some of them even know us.

"I'm guessing, but if a third or a half of the boys from both schools show up at dances at least sometimes, and ten percent of those, or even five percent, are the right kind of guy, that's dozens of guys we could attract. And maybe what attracts them will discourage some of the other ninety percent."

"If we knew how to attract them," I said, "we'd be doing it."

"She's right," said Nikki.

"I know," said Jack. "That's what we have to figure out. Anything else we want from guys depends on meeting them, and meeting them, at least at dances, mostly depends on attracting them."

"That's obviously true," I said. "So?"

"So . . ." Jack hesitated. "So let's say it aloud, just to be thorough." She looked at me expectantly. "What do you really want from guys? While we're in high school."

Nikki looked expectant too but less cheerful.

I put my elbow on the table and my chin on my hand and just looked at them. If I said something about wanting guys to see me as a normal girl, they'd shower me with kind and reassuring words, which wouldn't change anything, and which I didn't want to hear again right now. Besides, normal wasn't the only thing I wanted.

"We're not boy crazy," I finally said. "I don't think we are. We know what that looks like."

We remember what it felt like, I could have said, and it didn't feel like this. This was down deep, steady and real, a quiet emptiness that didn't have to be filled today but ached to be filled someday.

Knowing the right words was easy. Saying them aloud was a little harder. "What I want . . . Eventually, I want to be in love with a good boy who's in love with me."

Nikki nodded. "Me too. Different boy."

"Me three," said Jack.

"Until then, and for however long it takes," I said, as if being a freak didn't disqualify me already, "I want plenty of good guys around us, guys who want to spend time with us, so we actually have a social life."

The rest of it just spilled out. "I don't know what to do about that, especially at dances. Just sitting and hoping hasn't worked. I want to do something. I can be patient for the results, if I have to, but I want to do something."

I began fiddling with my hair, winding some of it around my finger, then letting it go and winding it again, which wasn't like me. "What's your idea?" I asked Jack, moving my hand away from my hair.

"If we want to be in love with boys who are in love with us," she said, "and if we want a social life in the meantime, we need to swim in a big pool filled with our kind of guys." She pointed at me with her fork. "There's your metaphor. Here's another one: if we want that anytime soon, we don't have time to search under every rock.

"What I mean is, if we have to get acquainted with ten or twenty guys to find one good guy for the pool, either it'll take forever, or we'll have to be incredibly lucky. So here's what I'm thinking. Instead of finding them, mostly, we need to help them find us."

This was Jack, so I didn't have to be psychic to see a list coming—a list that wouldn't help, except as a diversion while we made it. A happy little fantasy.

"Let's make a list describing our kind of guy," she said. "In writing, this time. Maybe we've overlooked something. Then we try again to figure out how to attract them."

While I tried to find some optimism, she pulled a pen from her jeans pocket and helped herself to one of Nikki's spare napkins. "So. Our kind of guy. Go."

"His parents should have raised him to be a gentleman," Nikki said. "Successfully," she added bitterly.

"Gentleman," Jack said, and wrote on the napkin. "Straight would help. And high school, not junior high." She kept writing.

"If possible, he should like to dance," I said—mostly for Nikki, but a girl could dream. "Like a gentleman, not a creep."

Nikki's smile was sweet and sad. "If possible." Her voice trembled again. "Could we do this later? Maybe tomorrow? I guess that would be today already. Maybe this afternoon? I just want to go home."

Jack's face changed from focused energy to gentle compassion. "Sure. Let's check in later today and see if we're all in the mood by then. We can do it at my house, if you want."

⋘◆⋙

I slept until almost noon, then texted Nikki. "Are you okay after last night?"

She replied immediately. "Mostly, I guess. He didn't hurt me, at least not physically."

"We don't have to get together and talk about boys today," I wrote. "It can wait."

"We kind of do. We have to do something."

"It doesn't have to be today."

"It's the first day of the year. Good day to start whatever this is," she wrote. "I'll be okay. I'll be fine."

That afternoon, when the three of us met on Skype, Nikki was more cheerful and energetic, and Jack was just as eager as before. I was well rested but still, in the final analysis, a freak.

"We already listed four things," Jack said. "I started a Word doc."

"I have two more," Nikki said. "Prefers smart girls and has enough social skills and brainpower for long conversations without sounding awkward or stupid."

"Those make the pool a lot smaller," Jack said. "I'm shrinking it again. They should look us in the eye, not the chest. Speaking of last night's eighth graders."

I felt myself blush.

Nikki snorted. "Not just eighth graders," she said. "I have less to stare at than you two, but seriously, most guys? I also want to say, no hands below the waist during slow dances, but just write that their hands shouldn't wander."

"Hands . . . don't . . . wander. Done. What else?"

"Kindness and respect," I said. "For everybody, not just girls they like."

"Good ones," said Nikki. "There should be something interesting about them, and they should be interested in us, not just themselves."

"Interesting and interested," Jack echoed. "Shall we say no jocks? And no clarinet players?"

"I don't mind an athlete," Nikki said, "if he fits our other things. What's wrong with clarinet players?"

It felt like a setup, but Jack's poker face didn't twitch. "It's mostly the section leaders in the Wind Symphony," she said. "Two senior boys with big, fragile egos. Damaged egos, lately."

I smiled in spite of myself. "How did you damage them?"

"I didn't. Well, I did, but not directly. Before Christmas we read some pieces Mr. Lim was considering for district and state. Half of them featured your favorite oboe player, which is pretty good for a sophomore. Only one had a clarinet solo, and it was short and kind of boring. They thought it wasn't fair. So they called me names in whispers and bumped my stand whenever I had a solo, to throw me off. Lim ended up choosing a gorgeous piece with three long solos for me. They complained to him in class, in front of everybody."

"Losers," Nikki said.

"I know, right? They went to him after class and complained again. They're seniors, blah, blah, blah. He told them, when you have one of the best oboes in the state, you feature her, not some talented but unmotivated clarinet players who need to practice more, if they want to stay section leaders. I didn't hear what they said to that. I was overcome with girlish modesty, and I slipped out the door."

"I believe the best and the door," Nikki said. "Not so much the modesty."

Jack just smiled.

"I wouldn't mind a non-loser clarinet player," I said. "If he's nice."

"Assuming good grooming and personal hygiene," Nikki added.

"And grammar," I said.

"Grooming, hygiene, grammar," Jack repeated. "Got them. And we won't exclude jocks and clarinet players after all. I'm thinking, if we each made our own list, they might be a little different, but you know what? If you two don't like a guy, I don't want him."

"Friends first," Nikki declared. "Then guys. If our kind of guy actually exists in nature."

"Friends first," I said. "So if—I mean when—things start to go really well for one of us, probably one of you, no being jealous by the other two." I forced a wan smile. "That might be hard for me, but I can do it. Friends first."

"Friends first," Jack said. "And really, our kind of guy should like any one of us more because our friends are so amazing. Any religious requirements?"

I didn't hesitate. "No."

Nikki looked surprised. Jack looked thoughtful. We were all pretty devout, and at church they said, among many other things, to date only guys who shared our faith, which most of the guys at our school did.

"We're looking for dancing and dates here, not husbands," I said. "If they respect our beliefs and standards, I'm okay with religious differences. You can be a good person and not be a Latter-day Saint."

Nikki nodded seriously. "You can be a good Latter-day Saint wrestler and not be a good person."

"Then we agree," Jack said without cracking a smile, so we had no warning. "To be a fun date, a boy doesn't have to be prime breeding stock."

Our wide eyes and our blushes, if she could see those over Skype, were her reward.

"Okay," she said. "I'm adding respect for our beliefs and standards. And just to be clear, no pressure for snugglebunnies."

Nikki giggled. "Is that your latest way to say hooking up?"

"Is it a person or an activity?" I asked, remembering the couple from last night's food line. "I can see myself as someone's snuggle bunny. I could totally do that."

Jack grinned. "I think it's an activity. *The* activity. I saw it in an old comic strip my dad likes. One word, plural, snugglebunnies. What else?"

"Maybe that's enough," I said, "or the pool really will be empty."

"Good thought," said Jack, "but one more question. How handsome do they have to be?"

"Not super handsome," Nikki said, "but decent-looking, so we can enjoy the view."

"Not obsessed with their looks," I added.

"Amen," said Jack. "Decent-looking or better. And not . . . is *preening* a good word?"

"Perfect," I said.

"Okay, I'm sharing my screen. Any tweaks?"

We read through the list and changed nothing.

"Give me a minute," she said, and we waited. "Okay. There's a PDF in the chat, suitable for printing, if not framing. I'll save the Word doc for future revisions." She unshared her screen, so we could see each other again. "Now's the hard part. How do we attract them?"

"If they exist in high school," Nikki repeated.

"We have to assume they do," Jack said. "We also assume enough of them go to dances. Any ideas?"

I thought I saw Nikki shrug. Then there was silence.

Before long, Jack said, "I hate to say it starts with how we look, but it does. Unless a guy already knows us, all we are to him is what he sees.

Can we dress a little older somehow? More grown up? Maybe that would attract the desirables."

"And repel the undesirables," Nikki added. "Maybe even the creeps."

I smiled, and I sort of meant it. "I like it. Desirables. Even a pool of potential desirables would be amazing. Make that probationary desirables."

"Last night was casual, so jeans," Nikki said, "but we could have dressed up a little. Skirts, dresses, nice pants at least."

"Tell us more," Jack said. "You're the clothes expert."

Which was true for our little circle, but mostly Nikki was a dancer and a math whiz, with a logical mind to rival Jack's. Her mom was a lawyer, like Jack's, so it was probably hereditary.

"It's stuff we already know," she said. "I mean, think about last night." She closed her eyes, and I imagined her scanning the gym. "Subdued colors, nothing really bright." She winced at something. "No neon anything. Subtle patterns. No large polka dots or animal prints. No glitter."

She stopped and scowled. "You know what? Forget all that. We shouldn't dress for guys anyway."

"That's what Mom tells me," I said.

"Maybe we just go for classy and avoid cute," she continued. "And we don't do boring, especially not the same boring everybody else does. We do us."

"We do us? What does that mean?" I asked too aggressively. "I'm already doing me, and it's not working."

"Yeah, my question too," Jack said gently. "We kind of have our own styles already, and that's what's not working."

Nikki took a moment to think before answering. "I guess I'm saying we should upgrade our own styles. It might take a while to figure out, but we can help each other." She hesitated. "To start, I think we try to go classy, like I said, and we mostly avoid cute, and we see what works and what doesn't."

"She's making a lot of sense, Jenny," said Jack.

"That's her style," I deadpanned.

"Good one," Jack said. "Okay, what about hair?"

"Jenny, you're there already," Nikki said. "Straight, anti-blonde, shoulder-length or a little longer, not all the way to your waist. It's classy."

If I was there already, shouldn't it be working? Maybe if I weren't a freak.

"I guess I could avoid ponytails," she added.

"You're cute in a ponytail," Jack said.

"Exactly," said Nikki. "Time to try something else. But they're so easy."

"I could do better at containing the ginger explosion," Jack said. "Cut some of it off, maybe put the rest up in a bun. Should I mask my freckles sometimes?" For every freckle Nikki had, Jack had hundreds.

Nikki was firm. "No. They're awesome. They're you. Besides, you'd have to do your arms too, or wear long sleeves. And your shoulders, when you show them."

Church and school both had dress codes for dances, so she wouldn't show much shoulder at those. I pictured us in bathing suits instead and mentally recoiled. It wasn't my best look.

"Besides how we look," Nikki said, "we could ask potential desirables to dance even when it's not girls' choice."

I made a face, not too sour. "You two could."

"Sorry," said Nikki. "No, wait. You can invite guys to sit with you."

We'd been through this before, but this time I added a number. "Even if I weren't timid, there's like a ninety percent chance that, if I ask someone I don't know, I'll get an undesirable. A little less, if I avoid stoners and guys in sports jerseys that need laundering."

"And guys who dance like they're already groping you in the parking lot," Nikki said, "where none of us has ever been for that purpose, I know."

"Let's make a New Year's resolution," Jack said. "We will all look classier and more grown up at dances this year, to help us attract the right kind of guys, for social purposes and possible romance. If it works at dances, we'll try other places too."

"If it works at dances," Nikki said, "we may not need other places."

Jack smiled. "True. Sorry to sound like my marketing class, but our key metric could be the number of songs we spend dancing or sitting with our kind of guy. We should track that."

"We all got zeroes last night," Nikki said, "unless I got a negative number. And we don't need boyfriends right away, just a large, interested pool of desirables who could become boyfriends."

"True," Jack said. "Do we agree on the resolution?"

I tried not to sound too skeptical. "Tell me again, why do we think this will attract better guys—or any guys at all?"

"Maybe it won't," Jack said. "But all we have with guys who don't know us is what they see. Plus we need boys who already know us to see us differently. So that's what we change. If it doesn't work, we try something else."

It probably wouldn't work for me, but it might for them, so I nodded. "If you're both in, I'm in."

"We're in," they said in unison.

"This will be good," Nikki said. "Let's talk to our moms too. And let's watch some films with classy women and see what they do that might work for us. Maybe something old with Audrey Hepburn." Nikki loved Audrey Hepburn, and she sort of looked like her.

I started to shake my head but stopped myself. Movies might help somehow, even if comparing real girls to fictional characters in movies probably wouldn't help anything at all.

"What's our next step, if this works?" I asked.

"Enjoy it," Jack declared. "We'll work out the rest as we go."

And when it doesn't work? I thought.

If it doesn't work.

⸺◦⸺

I printed our list on baby blue paper and stuck it on my mirror. Not twenty-four hours passed before Mom stood in my doorway and asked, "Are you sure you're a teenager?"

"You were there at my birth, I think."

"True." She pointed toward my mirror. "'Our Kind of Guy, by Nikki, Jenny, and Jack.' I think I was in college before my taste in guys was so sensible. We must be raising you right." She smiled impishly. "Have any candidates?"

I played it straight. "None of us does."

"I'm sure they'll turn up sooner or later," she said reasonably.

"We're hoping for sooner. What?" Her smile had faded. "Why do you look worried?"

"I hope it still works," she said. "Boys, girls, dating."

"So do I. Wait, what?"

"I teach college kids, right? They should be dating, practically all of them, but mostly they're not. The ones who even want to date don't know how to connect with people in real life, and the dating apps aren't helping. When they meet someone, let's just say they don't know how to build a healthy relationship, if they even know what that looks like. Sorry, stepping down from my soapbox."

I tried to square what she said with what I saw and heard at Lakeside High. "I don't think your collegiate dystopia has infected my high school yet."

She gave me a wry smile. "I hope it doesn't." She nodded toward my mirror. "It's a good list."

—◆—

We did some research on the Internet and compared notes. We talked to all three moms too. I was pretty sure they didn't think our New Year's resolution would help, and they were just humoring us. But none of them said that, and they all seemed pleased that we wanted to consult them.

On Saturday we watched films together, modeled outfits, and experimented with our hair (but not very much with mine). Even after all that, the changes we planned seemed awfully small for the large effect we wanted them to have.

The second Saturday after New Year's, we had our first opportunity to test our resolution at a dance.

3

Sitting

T HE WELCOME BACK TO Winter dance at school wouldn't have been my first choice for starting our plan, and it wasn't going brilliantly, even though we looked good—and a little older.

Jack's red hair was up in a bun. Her simple, dark green dress was the perfect setting for her hair and her mischievous eyes, especially in the subdued lighting of the dance. She stood out, but not too much. A lot of the girls were in pants, and most of those were in jeans.

We'd worked on Nikki's French braid for twenty minutes, after practicing twice in the past week. She was in a navy-and-white embroidered top, skinny light blue cropped pants, and navy ballet flats. She looked like a dancer who was there to dance.

I wasn't sure I looked like a sitter who was there to sit, but I did like my outfit. My skirt made me feel almost overdressed, which was what we wanted, but it hadn't helped at all. It was too soon to declare failure, but the air smelled of disappointment, a familiar mix of body sprays and nervous teenager sweat.

I'd have been more comfortable at a church dance. A lot of the same kids went to those, but being in a church seemed to dull the sharp edges of school world and smooth its abrasive surfaces a little too.

Not that school world wanted anything to do with me on this wintry Saturday night. There was less than an hour left, and it was pretty crowded. But none of the boys I knew had even said hi, and the dress-a-little-older version of me hadn't attracted any boys I didn't know. No desirables at all. No undesirables either—which would have been partial success for Jack and Nikki. It was just more failure for me.

They had done no better. Now they were in the restroom, adjusting Nikki's braid. I sat with two empty folding chairs on one side and four on the other, missing my friends, who'd been gone all of three minutes, and even my dog, Zeus, who was almost always with me, except at dances.

I wanted to slump my shoulders and stare vacantly at the floor, or maybe at something on my phone, but I knew better. I sat straight, slightly forward in my chair, and looked toward the dancers in front of me. One of my hands lay lightly on the other in my lap. I crossed my ankles and kept my knees together but angled them slightly to one side, which both Mom and Nikki said looked older and more feminine. I smoothed my skirt, a heather gray midi I liked a lot, and tried for a Mona Lisa smile, pleasant but reserved. A girl sitting alone at a dance shouldn't look too happy about it.

For a lot of boys, sitting and talking with a girl who wasn't gorgeous should have been less scary than dancing, which should have made the chair next to me a little busier. Maybe conversation scared more high school boys than I thought. Maybe my medical thing scared them. Maybe they just didn't like me that much. But a dance was the wrong place to ponder the reasons. I needed to smile, and for that I needed happier thoughts. I began to write a story in my head.

My imaginary heroine was having a much better evening. She wasn't the prettiest or most popular girl at the ball, but she was pretty enough when she smiled. She didn't need to be the center of everyone's attention, but she wasn't invisible, and she didn't just sit.

I imagined her on the dance floor in the arms of a handsome boy who adored her. They glided and turned as one, rising slightly on their toes for the second and third beats of each waltz measure, seeming to hesitate without breaking tempo, then taking a bold, perfectly synchronized step on each downbeat.

Her cheeks flushed with more than the exertion of the dance, and her smile was radiant, because she adored him too. She didn't need anyone else's attention when she had his.

When the song ended, they didn't use words to thank each other for the dance. He reached down, and she reached up, and they shared a quick, tender kiss. They glowed at each other for a beautiful moment, then walked away, hand in hand, to find a place to sit and talk.

It was my story to invent, so they always behaved themselves together, even after a romantic Saturday evening of dancing. She tried not to imagine doing passionate, physical things with him, because daydreaming about forbidden activities would be wrong too. She mostly succeeded. When her thoughts and wishes strayed, she did her best not to dwell on them.

So no matter how much they liked each other, she'd sit in church tomorrow with her family, as always, and sing and pray and worship God with a joyful heart and a clear conscience. In the boring moments, she'd think of her boyfriend, gently smile, and maybe blush a little.

It wasn't a complete story; for that she needed to change somehow. If this was the beginning, she needed unfulfilled desires and intentions, and things had to get in the way, obstacles for her to overcome. Things would have to fall apart somehow, get worse before they got better. She needed a character arc. Mom, Dad, and Mrs. Tornow, my writing teacher, would all agree on that. Or this could be her happy ending, after all the trouble.

I couldn't wait for my own character arc. I needed happy now. I pushed aside the thought that my fictional heroine's fictional life was better than my real one in every way that really mattered to a girl, and I focused on her joy.

I might have been smiling already, when an actual boy approached. He was tall and good-looking, with short, light brown hair and a lean face. He wore khakis instead of jeans, and a long-sleeve shirt with an open collar and cuffs rolled partway up his forearms. The light blue fabric had a handsome crosshatch pattern.

He was smiling too—not a lot, but enough to look pleasant.

He was looking *toward me* and smiling. A nervous thrill raced through me, and I took half a second to convince myself he hadn't just spilled out of the story in my head. Then I worried that shock might have replaced my own little smile for a moment. I couldn't be sure.

He stopped abruptly, maybe five feet away, furrowing his brow but still faintly smiling. A shorter, younger boy passed absently between us, enthralled by a colorful game on his smart phone. I wondered how he could see his screen through the dark, longish hair which hid his face.

My suitor, if that was the right word, waited for the phone zombie to pass, then took the last step or two toward me.

"Hi. I'm Troy." His voice was warm and confident, and I might have seen a twinkle in his eye. "Welcome to the mobile gamers convention. We have dance music."

I chuckled, which calmed my nerves a little. "I'm Jenny. Hi. Nice to meet you."

I knew Troy was on the basketball team, because they'd introduced the players at an assembly. He was a junior, a year ahead of me. And they might have said he moved from Texas over the summer, unless that was somebody else.

We'd never spoken, and I couldn't remember that our eyes had ever met. Yet he knew what to ask.

"May I sit this one out with you?"

"Sure."

As he sat, he slid his chair a few inches further from mine—but he used the extra space to angle it toward me. I had his full attention, and he wanted me to know it.

I was glad but suspicious. Jocks, especially handsome, older jocks, didn't sit by me at dances or anywhere else, if they had a choice. New Year's resolution or not, I wasn't the kind of girl they noticed.

The odds were slim that he was our kind of guy, but it was possible. I had to try something, and I knew what it was. I had to become Bold Jenny. I couldn't be shy or afraid. I didn't get second chances with boys, and I didn't get many first chances either. By the end of the song, he had to be enjoying my company enough to stay longer, or at least to remember me and come back later. There was no time for nervous small talk or awkward silences.

Be bold, Jenny, I thought, and plunged ahead.

"I guess someone told you I don't dance." My voice came out more confident than I expected, with no nervous tremor at all.

"No, I sort of figured it out," he said.

My eyes narrowed. "You've been watching me?"

"At that children's choir concert before Christmas, the others stood, but you had a chair. At the end you picked it up and walked off. That was you, right?"

I nodded.

"Saw you with a service dog later," he said.

"Zeus," I said.

"Pardon me?"

"Zeus. That's my dog's name." I took a deep breath. "So I sit when other people stand, but I can walk. And I have a service dog, but I'm not blind. All of which adds up to . . ."

"Wasn't going to ask."

"Nobody told you?" We were both at a new school, but it was already January. Then again, why would anyone tell someone like him about someone like me?

"Didn't ask," he said. "Like to learn about people firsthand."

Which was too perfect, but at least he was a boy, and he was sitting and talking with me. Apparently at least one boy knew how to meet a girl, despite Mom's pessimism.

My hands wanted to fidget in my lap. I had to squeeze them together, but maybe he wouldn't notice. Nikki said boys were bad at reading body language.

Be bold, Jenny.

"I have epilepsy," I said, and watched for his reaction.

He nodded slightly. "Figured it was something like that."

"It's not contagious. And it's not too bad. But I mostly sit, and I have Zeus to look after me." My hands relaxed a little.

"Where is Zeus?"

"He doesn't like dances. I come with my girlfriends, and my parents text me every hour, to make sure I'm okay. They let me come, and I agree to, you know." I gestured toward my lap with both hands.

He smiled gently. "Sit? Instead of dancing?"

"Dancing or standing around." That was popular at our dances too.

He tilted his head slightly. "May I ask a personal question?"

I noticed things like *may* instead of *can*. I inherited that from my parents. Proper English was a good way to get on their good side. And mine.

"I've been giving you personal answers," I said.

"Do you sit here and watch everybody and wish you could dance?"

"Yes, but not necessarily like that." I pointed toward the dancers in front of us. Most of them moved awkwardly—some barely moved at all—to the beat of a song that was little more than a beat. Hardly anyone our age bothered to learn how to dance.

Not that I had any room to talk.

"How do you want to dance?" he asked.

"I guess that would be nice too, but since I'm wishing, I wish I could waltz."

"Too bad they never play anything in 3/4," he said. "I love to waltz." Which was either a happy coincidence or too much of a coincidence.

"Where did you learn?" I tried not to narrow my eyes, because he could have been telling the truth. I wanted it to be the truth.

"Social dance classes at church in the summer on Thursday afternoons. But that was Texas, not here."

"Sounds fun," I said. "I don't know of any dance classes at church here, unless the single adults have some. Is something wrong?"

He studied his hand, first the palm, then the back. When he held it up, I saw a dark smear along the side, from the base of his pinkie to his wrist.

"Is that blood?" In the dim light I couldn't be sure.

He rubbed at it with his thumb. "No. Grease, maybe? Wait." He sniffed at that thumb, then touched it to the tip of his tongue, raised his eyebrows, and put it in his mouth halfway to the first knuckle. He pulled it out with a barely audible smack. "Chocolate. Saw some frosted brownies. Don't remember touching any of them."

While I wondered if identifying mysterious, dark substances by taste was one of those boy things I'd never understand, he checked his shirt and pant leg. "Better take care of this before it gets on my clothes. Excuse me, please."

"Of course." I wondered if he planned to come back.

"Save my seat?"

I couldn't help myself. I glowed at him. "Sure."

I watched him walk away and enjoyed the thought of him returning. Jack and Nikki might be back before he was, but they'd happily make room.

For the next few minutes I thought of things to say, depending on where the conversation went. Then he was back.

I told myself to be bold again. "May I ask you a personal question?"

"Sure," he said.

It came out bolder than I intended. "Why were you at my concert? You're not stalking me, are you?"

He smiled. "That's two questions."

"So you can count, not just waltz." I was trying to be witty, but I sounded a little snotty.

"If I couldn't count all the way to three, I couldn't waltz," he said. "Mom and Dad were looking for a children's choir for my little sister. They heard yours is the best."

"I think it is. High school's pretty old to be saying I'm in a children's choir, but I love it."

"Only too old if you're a boy, right?" he asked. "How old can the girls be?"

"I turned sixteen in October, so this is my last year." Good for him to know I'm sixteen, I thought.

"How many years?"

"Going on seven."

"Long time. It's a great choir. Lily starts in August, I think."

"Thanks for the compliment," I said. "I hope she likes it. And you've answered my first question."

"Noticed you first because you were sitting. Already said that."

"That's why everyone notices me," I said. If they notice me at all, I thought. "That and my dog."

"I've seen people sit in other choirs."

"Do you sing or just go to choir concerts a lot?"

"I'm in the men's chorus here," he said. "Last year I was in a musical at my old school in San Antonio. I was Mordred."

"The bad son in *Camelot*?"

"Cool that you know that."

"There's a solo, right?" I asked.

"'The Seven Deadly Virtues.' Got to use words like *ennui* and *ghastly* and *Beelzebubble*." He said "ghastly" with a British accent: "*gaw*-stly."

"Two of those are words," I said, channeling Professor Mom. I tried to look serious, but my eyes and the corners of my mouth betrayed me.

He grinned. "*Beelzebubble*'s a word too. I've started using it sometimes." His grin disappeared, and he spoke in a deeper, dramatic tone, using the British accent again. "It helps me hold back the ghastly ennui."

I smiled, and he continued in a normal voice. "My old choir teacher always told us to notice singers who look connected with the music. 'Authentically expressive,' he said. So I watched you. You look like a singer when you sing, not a robot or a mime or whatever."

"Thank you." I hurried ahead, before I could worry about sounding self-centered or insecure. "So watching me sing that night was somehow enough that, when you saw me here, you remembered me and wanted to sit here not dancing with me?"

He'd been relaxed and confident so far. Any girl who ever took a quiz on the Internet knew what that meant: the boy didn't really like you. Now he blushed slightly and looked down, before he found my eyes again.

"Might have been enough," he said softly.

"Was there more?" I asked.

My question was calmer than I was.

Because there was more. I could feel it.

4

Hopes, Suspicions

T ROY HESITATED, THEN ANSWERED my question. "There was more. I'm not just flattering you."

"Flattering me?"

"Spent part of the concert . . . I was . . . Sorry, this sounds, I don't know, shallow. I was picking the three or four prettiest girls in the choir. Just the older girls."

I could see where this was going. He was playing me. He had to be. And he was so good at it that he looked and sounded completely sincere.

I stared at my hands. "And you thought I was one of them? Is that what you're trying to say?"

When I looked up, there was color in his cheeks. "Yeah. Well, not exactly."

It wasn't like he slapped me or something, and I wasn't going to believe whatever he said now anyway. And I had no business expecting any guy to think I was one of the prettiest girls in my choir. But his words hurt me all the same. Not exactly? Why would he say that?

His eyes widened with alarm. "Wait, said that wrong. Wanted . . . wanted to say . . . you're . . ."

There was something earnest in his eyes. Did I dare to trust it?

My brain kept moving my mouth. "Third or fourth would be good in that choir," I said reasonably. "Or sixth or seventh. Even tenth," I added for my own benefit. I could be tenth. It wasn't that big a choir.

"A lot of the girls are pretty," I added.

"Yeah," he said. "I'm trying to say you were the prettiest. You're beautiful."

My insides cartwheeled—awkwardly, of course—and I blushed, which made me flustered. Then I remembered Nikki's wrestler. But Troy wasn't acting like him, was he? Except for saying I was beautiful?

The only thing I could say was exactly what I was thinking. "You are either the most dangerous boy I've ever met or the sweetest. You think I'm . . . ?"

He nodded solemnly. "Watched you for a while at the concert. Then I saw you here tonight. So I don't think I'm stalking you. I do think you're beautiful."

Undesirables might tell Nikki she was beautiful. Desirables too. No boy ever said that of me. But part of me stopped thinking I was being played. It wasn't just my wanting to be beautiful to a handsome basketball player. I didn't fully trust the feeling, but I felt like it might be the real Troy talking, not some fake version trying to impress a girl.

Either way, I was beyond impressed. My head and heart together had built a thousand daydreams, imagining such moments in lovelier places than a school gym. They all paled next to an actual boy sitting beside me on a folding chair and saying what Troy had just said twice. If he didn't mean it, it was the most intoxicating fiction my heart had ever encountered. If he meant it . . .

If he meant it, my whole world was new and brighter. Was our New Year's resolution working for me after all? I felt like it might be—but maybe not. According to Troy, this had started before Christmas.

"Thank you," I said. "You really thought I was . . . ?"

"Still do," he said seriously.

I tried to turn my biggest reason for doubting him into a wry joke. "It couldn't have been my hourglass figure. I was wearing a choir robe."

I didn't have an hourglass figure, and Regular Jenny was beside herself that Bold Jenny would mention my figure at all.

"Saw your face and your hair," he said. "Watched you sing. Saw you smile."

I might have been wiser not to smile so warmly at him just then, but what if he was for real?

"That was all I needed to see," he said.

Be bold, Jenny.

"Seeing me up close tonight hasn't changed your mind?" Seeing me without the choir robe, I thought but didn't say.

I might have seen a twinkle again. "Nope," he said. "Plus I get to see your blue eyes."

It made no sense to ask him, "What if they're green?"—because they weren't. But that's what I asked.

He smiled. "Lights aren't that low. Your eyes are blue." So were his, and now I was sure about the twinkle. Maybe the hard part was over for him.

"You're too good at this," I said. "You must do it a lot."

"Do what a lot?"

"Tell a girl she's beautiful."

"Not really. My sisters, sometimes, or a date."

"A brother who tells his sisters they're beautiful? You're from what planet again?" I'd heard brothers call their sisters lots of things, but never beautiful.

Three guys greeted him as they walked by, which gave me time to notice that we'd been together through at least four songs already. *Bold was working.* I wondered where Jack and Nikki were, but I didn't mind them staying away. Even if Troy turned out not to be for real, having fun with a boy at a dance was way better than pretending to have fun without a boy.

If he was for real, I needed to fix something. When he turned back to me I said, "So you wanted to meet the choirgirl with the pretty smile, and I turned out to be suspicious and a little snotty. Sorry."

He looked wary, or maybe puzzled, and spoke slowly. "I wanted to find out about you, so you're right about that. But we just met. You probably should be suspicious."

"And snotty?"

"Must have missed that part," he said.

Whether he actually had missed it or was just being kind, I was relieved. The next thing slipped out before I could stop it. "You really think I'm . . . ?"

"Yeah."

Bold Jenny summoned all her courage. "I like your smile." I sounded timid, not bold. I wanted to say he was handsome, which he was, but I couldn't.

"Thanks," he said. "Was saying something like that as hard for you as it was for me?"

I smiled sheepishly and noticed my heart melting. "It didn't seem hard for you."

He shook his head. "You kidding? Had to go through that whole story. It's true, but I was too much of a coward just to say what I wanted to."

"You said it eventually. So it's a good story, with a happy ending for me."

There might be another happy ending here, I thought. A boy who told me I was beautiful was a boy I could ask to sit with me at dances—especially if I got his phone number, so I could invite him from a distance by text message.

My hands were squeezing each other again.

Be bold, Jenny.

I didn't get the chance.

"I should go," Troy said in the middle of what was probably the next-to-last song of the evening. "Promised someone the last dance. Guess I should find her."

Sometimes my mind knew a thing to say, when my heart had no words. "You should keep your promise," I said, attempting a smile. "Thanks for sitting with me."

His smile was more successful. "Thank you. It was fun."

He wasn't two steps away when a girl named Audrey appeared at his side. She was a junior and a cheerleader, a relatively nice one. At that moment she was also the most gorgeous girl I could imagine.

"Ready?" she asked him.

"All yours," he said.

She took his arm just as the DJ broke in to tell us it was the last dance and we should drive home safely. In the seconds before the music resumed, I heard her ask, "Did Maddi find you?"

"Haven't seen her," Troy said.

"Her loss," she said over the first piano chords of the last song. "Oh, I love this one! And it's long."

"From *Twilight*?" he asked.

They walked off together, and I didn't hear her answer, but yes, it was from *Twilight*, and it was lovely. I watched them for a moment, then looked away—and saw someone else watching them. Maddi Burke was a cheerleader too. She was nearly as pretty as Audrey in a platinum-blonde-from-a-bottle way, but now her face and shoulders drooped.

She pressed her lips together so they nearly disappeared, then turned and walked away. She never even glanced toward me.

I forced myself not to watch Troy dance with Audrey and hoped for Jack and Nikki to return. Sometimes, when we weren't dancing, we left during the last song.

The song finally ended, the lights went up, and Jack and Nikki appeared, both smiling.

"You were dancing?" I asked.

"Seniors," Nikki said.

"We bumped into them on our way back from the restroom," Jack explained. "So we asked them."

"She asked them for both of us," Nikki said.

"Desirables?" I asked.

"Not sure," said Nikki.

"They were nice enough," Jack said, "and it's not like they smelled bad."

"Or let their hands wander," Nikki added.

They told me the boys' names, which I didn't recognize. "Maybe it's working," I said.

Jack's smile brightened. "For you too, right?"

"Was that Troy Pullman?" Nikki asked.

Their questions came too fast for me to answer.

"How long did he sit with you?"

"What did you talk about?"

"Isn't he gorgeous?"

"He's from Texas, right? Does he have a sexy drawl?"

"Did you tell him why you don't dance?"

They stopped and looked expectant.

I managed a smile. "Maybe five or six songs. He seems nice. He talks, which I really like, and he listens. Handsome, but I wouldn't say gorgeous. Very slight drawl. Occasional fake British accent."

Jack's eyes twinkled. "Desirable?"

"I don't know." I fixed my eyes on Nikki. "He said I'm pretty, but that could be bad, right?"

Nikki's smile faded. "You are pretty. He's in one of my classes this semester. He seems like a good guy. Good manners?"

"Better than good. Maybe a Texas thing?" I looked from one friend to the other. "I don't know what to think. Or feel."

I knew what I wanted to feel.

"Did you ask about his religion," Nikki asked, "even if we left that off our list?"

"I should do that," I said. "Even if it's not a requirement, I do kind of prefer a nice Mormon boy."

"You like him," Jack said.

"It probably doesn't matter." I told them about Audrey and the last dance.

"Maybe he'll sit with you again sometime soon," Jack said.

"Maybe." I started to say, "Boys don't come back to me," but my friends were happy for me, and I preferred that to pity, so I kept it to myself.

———◆———

At my house, over after-dance fruit smoothies, Jack and Nikki evaluated our New Year's resolution.

"Progress is progress," Jack pronounced, "and we all made progress. It was a good dance for us."

That thought kept me optimistic until I fell asleep for the night.

———◆———

Late Sunday morning, when I awoke, I was less optimistic and more realistic. Progress was only progress if it continued, I told myself as I dressed for church, which wasn't likely in my case.

In my Young Women meeting that afternoon, they said to be sure and reread the Church's standards on dating and sexual purity in the next few weeks, as preparation for a "very special lesson" coming in February. I forced myself not to shake my head at that.

First of all, we had that "very special lesson" three or four times a year. Second, a lot of us already had those pages of our little standards booklet more or less memorized. And third, you don't need the rules if you'll never have a decent opportunity to break them.

By evening I felt completely realistic about Troy, and not optimistic at all. In our Skype call Jack and Nikki stubbornly insisted that I should go back to optimism, because I'd done the best among the three of us last night. I had to admit they were right.

I admitted that to myself over and over again through the following week. At worst, that night at the dance, I'd sat and talked for quite a while with a boy who seemed nice, and maybe he really was. Or not. At best, I'd found a desirable for our pool—he'd found me, which was how we wanted it to work—and maybe he'd sit with me again.

If he did reappear, I'd have to choose between happy and suspicious. I didn't like being both. Troy was a handsome jock who told a girl like me that she was beautiful. He resembled Nikki's wrestler that far. But he hadn't even hinted at wanting to wrestle. We'd just talked, and it was nice. And his manners really were excellent.

Then again, manners weren't character. One could be good and the other bad.

Then again, both could be good.

Then again, we were talking about Jenny Miller and a handsome, popular athlete. Even if he was a good guy, I'd be a fool to get my hopes up.

"Wait and see," I told myself over and over again—which felt sensible but never worked for very long. Watching for him in the halls at school didn't work at all.

5

Just a Wallflower

THREE DANCES IN THREE weeks was a lot, but there was a big church dance every month for kids from all across town, and we didn't even consider skipping this one. All day Saturday, I bounced between eager hope that Troy would be there, whether he was a Church member or not, and gnawing dread that, if he was there, I'd have a front row seat while he danced with the gorgeous, popular girls who obviously liked him.

I liked him too, and my lingering suspicions had mostly faded. He had seemed to like me, but maybe not quite enough.

Evening finally came. For a while the dance was like all the others, except we were dressed better than most of the other girls again. The sameness dashed my hope more than it calmed my dread.

My phone vibrated, and I pulled it from the pocket of my skirt. It was my parents' hourly check-in. This one was from Dad.

"Don't look now," Jack said as I sent Dad a thumbs-up emoji. "There's good news and bad news."

I took a deep breath and didn't look. "Start with the good news."

"Troy's here."

My hope and dread both sprang to attention.

"What's the bad news?"

"You should just look," Nikki said.

Troy and Audrey weren't right in front of us, but they were in plain view, dancing to a fast song. They moved gracefully to the beat. She said something to him, and he smiled. He said something to her, and she laughed and touched his arm.

He really was handsome, and she was gorgeous. She had perfect brunette hair with perfect highlights, framing her perfect eyes and perfect skin. She lit up Troy with her perfect, movie star smile, but not so constantly that she seemed like a perfect airhead. Her stylish pink top and white jeans effortlessly flattered her perfect figure.

So of course he smiled at her. No boy could help himself. But it was worse than that. She really wasn't an airhead. She was smart enough to interest guys who might care about more than her looks. Guys like Troy.

They stayed together for a slow song. She slipped her arms around his neck, and I couldn't watch anymore. I thought about texting Dad to come and take Lonely Jenny home early.

"Are you okay?" Jack asked in her gentlest voice. "Dancing with her now doesn't mean he won't sit with you later."

Nikki put her arm around me. She was between me and Jack. "He probably will."

I shrugged, and it was a lie. It said I didn't care very much. "Boys don't come back to me."

"This one might," Nikki said. "He sat with you for a long time last Saturday, and he's a non-wrestler who thinks you're beautiful."

I shrugged again. "Are wrestlers and basketball players different?"

"Why do you think he won't?" Nikki asked.

"The way they talk to each other, they're either already a couple or about to be. That's just how it is. Some girls get the guys they want, no matter who else wants them."

"But Jenny . . ." Nikki didn't finish. I didn't look, but I knew her eyes were full of pity.

I was an object of pity. Again. Including my own.

Jack and Nikki kept watching them. "That's just rude," Jack said after a minute. "She's all over him."

"Rude," Nikki echoed.

I looked silently at Jack.

"Sorry," she said. "Not helping."

I dropped my gaze to a point on the floor about three feet in front of me—and a bit to the right, since the dancers I cared about were to our left.

"Oh, crap," Nikki muttered just above the music. I looked up. Her cheeks were flushed and her lips were a thin line.

I followed her gaze. "Is that—?"

"Yes," she hissed.

A sandy-haired boy with a muscular build stopped in front of her. His dark eyes darted to Jack, then to me, then back to Nikki. We all glared, and he frowned.

"Nikki, I . . . uh . . . I need to apologize . . . for New Year's Eve."

She kept glaring and said nothing.

"I think I hurt you. I'm sorry."

She didn't move.

He was sweating this. Literally. "If it's okay, I was hoping we could finish our dance. I could show you I'm not always a jerk. Then I'll never ask you again, unless you want me to."

"No, thank you," she said.

"I'm not like that. I had a drink with my friends before the dance, which I never did before. I'll never do it again either. It was stupid. Not much of an excuse."

"It's no excuse at all," she said firmly. "You wouldn't do those things when you're drunk, if you weren't enough of a creep to do them when you're sober."

Nikki was officially my hero.

"I'm not sure it . . . I only had . . . I wasn't . . ." His shoulders slumped, and his frown twitched. "I'm really sorry. And you look really great tonight."

She nodded slightly. "Thanks for the apology."

"You sure we can't—"

"We can't."

"Okay." He exhaled loudly. "See you around, I guess."

He trudged away. When I turned back to Nikki, her head was in her hands. We both put an arm around her.

"You were awesome," Jack said. "How do you feel?"

Nikki looked up, and her voice shook. "I feel violated all over again. I mean, it's good that he apologized, I guess. But he makes my skin crawl."

"Of course he does," Jack said. "You were in an abusive relationship with him that night for a few minutes, in the middle of the dance floor." She stood and reached for Nikki's hand. "Let's go. Chocolate chip cookies. We all need them. Jenny, we'll be right back with mood-altering refreshments."

"Restroom first, okay?" Nikki asked. "I need a mirror again."

While they were gone, I stared at nothing and tried not to look like I felt sorry for myself. At first I mostly hurt for Nikki, but soon I mostly hurt for me.

I tried to be happy that our New Year's resolution might be working, even if it wasn't helping tonight. I failed.

I tried to revive the story I composed last Saturday in my head, but something essential in my writer's brain was off duty for the night, and I failed at that too.

I scanned my end of the gym for something to think about. Something besides the fact that I was just one more wallflower among dozens. Something besides sitting and feeling lonely in a crowd.

It wasn't one of the fancier dances like Valentine's Day, where they insisted on skirts and neckties, and the dance committee used enough decorations and floor lighting that you could almost forget you were sitting on folding chairs around the edges of a gym. We had dressed up a little, but jeans were allowed, if they weren't torn or badly faded. T-shirts were still out.

Most of the lights were down, but not enough to make a gym look like something else. At least the basketball things were folded up against the ceiling.

There was a gym in almost every Latter-day Saint church building. A lot of adults called it a "cultural hall," and sometimes that's how the doors were labeled. There was always a stage along one side. But it was still a gym, with painted lines on a polished hardwood floor, painted cinder block walls, and a small electronic scoreboard near the ceiling at one end.

Tonight, as usual, more kids milled around than actually danced, and a lot of those had their phones out. Fortunately, the music wasn't painfully loud, and the ventilation system worked, so it wasn't stuffy and hot. A girl could sit and be lonely in reasonable comfort.

Or a girl could think about something else. "You're in charge of your thoughts," my parents liked to proclaim. I closed my eyes and leaned back slowly—which was good. I'd forgotten what was just behind my chair.

I rested the back of my head against the hard, cool wall of the gym.

I could think about walls. That might work. The cinder block walls at church were a lot like the ones at school. Six days a week, or seven if I went to something on Saturday, I spent at least a few hours encased in cold, hard cinder blocks. They were almost always painted white.

Sure, at school they were broken up by banks of locker doors or striped with long swaths of pastel colors someone probably chose for their cheering and soothing effects on teenage barbarians. But the colors were less a remedy than a confession that the walls were what they always were, cold and hard.

Here in a church, the block walls in the halls and foyers came with framed paintings—scenes from scripture, mostly happy things from the New Testament. Lots of lambs and children and Jesus, not so much leprosy or crucifixion. But the dance and I were in the gym, where the cold, hard walls were dimly lit, had no inspiring paintings, and were adorned with wallflowers like me.

I opened my eyes and contemplated my outfit. My lavender top was like the cheerful, soothing pastels at school—but the wall was still hard and cold, and I wasn't cheered or soothed. I was lonely, and the boy I'd met last time and started to like, who was fun to talk to and thought I was beautiful, was dancing and laughing—again—with a gorgeous and relatively nice cheerleader who apparently liked him and wasn't shy about draping herself all over him in front of everybody at a dance.

So much for thinking about something else.

"All yours." That's what Troy had told Audrey. And Jack and Nikki hadn't seen him push her away or whatever else a boy did, if he didn't want a girl dancing too close.

I couldn't compete with her. She'd already won. She got her boy, a really nice boy. Handsome too. I got an empty chair.

From the beginning Jack and Nikki had offered to ask boys to sit with me, when there were girls' choice songs, but feeling like a charity case was worse than being ignored. Now I knew something even sadder: hitting it off with a nice guy, then seeing him prefer someone prettier and more popular.

I couldn't expect boys to ignore every other girl and sit with me the whole time, once they sat with me at all. But it hurt to watch that boy dancing with that girl.

I wanted to go home.

Maybe I'd tell Mom and Dad they'd been wise to worry, more than two years and maybe thirty dances ago, that I'd be more miserable sitting at dances than not going at all. I'd begged and cried and persuaded—I sort of made them miserable—until I got my way. But maybe they'd been right.

I shook my head. I was so done with this dance. Maybe all dances. I could text Dad for a ride, then try to enjoy the cookies with Nikki and Jack until he arrived. My hand went to my skirt pocket for my phone.

"Jenny, are you okay?" someone asked.

I started, but the voice was familiar. I looked up.

6

One, Two, Three . . . Boys

I LOOKED UP AT Troy and smiled. "Hi. I'm okay."

It wasn't a lie, because suddenly I was okay. I was better than okay. My heavy heart was light again, and my head gleefully rounded up all my sad little thoughts and pushed them off the nearest mental cliff. I'd been wrong. Wondrously, deliciously wrong. He came back to me!

My phone stayed in my pocket.

"Good," he said. "Looked a little sad or something."

"Just distracted for a minute. Please, have a seat."

He had a plastic cup in each hand. "Didn't know which you'd want, so I brought water and punch. I'm happy with either one—or both, if you don't want anything."

He wasn't just back. He was thoughtful and sweet.

"I think . . . punch. Thank you." I reached for the cup he offered. Somehow my hand was steady.

He'd thought of napkins too, and he gave me one with my drink.

"You're welcome," he said. He sat and started to say more, but the music suddenly got a lot louder, as if someone had bumped the volume control. It was too loud to talk. He shrugged and smiled.

We sipped our drinks, watched the dancers, and stole sideways glances. Once we caught each other's eyes and traded smiles. Mine felt shy.

I saw Jack and Nikki returning with cookies, but they spotted Troy and stopped several paces from us. They beamed, and Nikki gave me a little wave before they slipped away.

I suppressed a giggle. Maybe I wouldn't need cookies at all.

The loud song ended, and a softer, slow song began. Couples on the floor reached for each other. Some got closer than others.

Troy shook his head slightly. He seemed to be watching one of the nearby couples. I'd seen the girl around school, but I didn't know the guy. Their version of slow dancing was the kind where chaperones would quickly intervene, if they saw it.

Cautious Jenny checked that Troy really was watching that couple—and didn't look jealous. Then Bold Jenny spoke. "In the absence of a chaperone, perhaps a well-aimed bucket of ice water?"

It worked. He smiled at me. "Good idea."

"They seem . . . well acquainted," I said. "Do you know them?"

"He lives on my street. Just moved in the day after New Year's, so it's hard to imagine they're well acquainted. Looks embarrassed."

"Maybe she's marking her territory," I said, hoping for another smile. I didn't get one.

"What if he doesn't want to be her territory?"

"Maybe she wants to change his mind."

"You think it's about his mind?" he asked skeptically.

"Some girls care about that."

I ached to know what he thought of Audrey. It took me about three seconds to find her on the dance floor, maybe thirty feet away. She wasn't glued to her partner this time, and she wasn't looking toward us. But Troy must have followed my gaze. Now he was watching her too.

He turned to me. "I was thinking about something while I danced with Audrey. Would you be able to dance with me—I guess it would have to be a slow dance—I mean, if I promise not to let you fall, if . . . something . . . happens?"

When I realized my mouth had fallen open, I closed it, but I couldn't help my wide eyes.

"It's okay to say it," I said softly. "If I have a seizure." At least I had that to say, while I processed the idea that I might dance—and the even happier thought that, while he danced with her, he thought about me.

There was an opposing thought, my own bucket of ice water. My deal with my parents from two years before was clear: I could come to dances if I sat. Sitting was safer.

"If you have a seizure," Troy said seriously.

My brain had a weird moment, but it wasn't a seizure. It was my friends' voices in my head.

"Nikki, check my math," said Imaginary Jack. "Given the gravitational acceleration of an atonic Jenny, and the likely neuromuscular response of an attentive Troy—"

Imaginary Nikki jumped in. "He should be holding her pretty tight already."

Whatever he saw on my face just then got me a wary look. "Would dancing be okay?" he asked. "Don't want to get you in trouble. Did you really promise your parents you wouldn't?"

Two years had blurred my memory just enough. "I don't remember promising them I would never dance ever. I did promise to sit instead of dancing, but I don't sit the whole time either. I walk in and out, for example. And they haven't mentioned it in a while."

"Is it scary? Dancing? Because . . . seizures?"

Be bold, Jenny.

"Just walking down the hall at school is a little scary. I've had seizures there. I hate making a scene anywhere."

My hands squeezed each other in my lap. Then his hand was on top of them, and I was half-thrilled, half nerves. No, all thrilled, all nerves.

"It's okay," he said lightly. "If you decide to dance, we'll dance. But no pressure. Sitting and talking is good."

I searched his face for any sign of disappointment, but he just looked . . . kind. "Thank you," I murmured.

He moved his hand away, and my hands missed it, but the effects lingered.

We talked until his phone made a weird sci-fi sound. "Sorry," he said. "Doing something at 10:00."

"Rendezvous with the mother ship?" Bold Jenny thought his alarm tone made it an obvious question. Regular Jenny hoped he wasn't meeting another girl again.

"Ship comes at the end," he deadpanned, and I made a mental note to tell Jack and Nicki we should add a sense of humor to our list. "Meeting some guys from the team. We're picking wallflowers for a while."

"The basketball team?"

"Yeah. Should have said, dancing with wallflowers."

"I like a good metaphor. Why do you do that?"

"We meet nice girls, and they usually like being asked. Also reminds certain girls they don't own us, but that's not why we do it."

I didn't want to ask, but I really did want to ask. "Am I part of your wallflower project? It's okay if I am."

"Hey, that's actually what we call it. And you're not. But you'd be a great reason to have it, if you were a wallflower. Excuse me. I'll be back."

For a moment I was speechless. *If* I were a wallflower? What else would I be?

"I'll be here," I murmured, but he was gone. "Along the wall. Flowering."

I tingled with excitement and watched for Jack and Nikki to return for another report, because I had a good one.

One song became another, and a much taller boy appeared. Will was a junior too, and even I knew he was our basketball star, not just an ordinary player. He was also one of the good guys, and everybody knew it. Maybe our resolution was working after all—for Jack and Nikki too, I hoped.

"Can I sit with you?" His voice was deep, and everything but his dark hair seemed long: nose, face, arms, legs, fingers, feet. He wasn't as handsome as Troy, but he wasn't bad. He was so tall that, when he sat, the chair looked too low for him.

After maybe thirty seconds of small talk I asked, "Am I part of your wallflower project? It's okay if I am."

He did a double-take. "You know about that?"

"Troy told me. He does it with you, right? Sorry, is it a secret?"

He smiled. "Can't really keep it a secret, but we don't advertise."

"Since I already know, would you tell me more?"

He said he and his friends started it in junior high. Troy was a more recent addition. I wanted to thank him and tell him how it felt to be ignored at dances, but I changed the subject to something that wasn't so obviously about me.

"How's basketball going?" I asked. "That's where you put the round ball in the round hoop, right? You play indoors, I think?" I wasn't really that ignorant. Just almost.

"We lost Wednesday in overtime. Won last night, but it was ugly."

"I'm sorry. Were they just two bad games in a good season?"

"I think we're good. We'll know for sure next week. Fairview's coming on Friday, and they're number one in the state. Could be a big win for us. Or we could get killed. You should come."

"I should?" No athlete had ever suggested to me personally that I should attend a game. And I had never wanted to. Until now.

"If you can." His eyes widened, and he lifted a big hand, then let it drop. "Sorry, I didn't mean . . ."

"No worries," I said. "Maybe I will. Aren't you supposed to be more optimistic than 'we might get killed'?"

That got me an intense look. "They're going down."

I smiled. "That's more like it."

"Varsity tips at 8:00. Troy plays in the JV game at 6:00."

"Good to know, thank you. What's he like?"

"Good on defense, quick, works hard, great rebounder for a point guard, picking up the offense really well. Almost laid out a couple of guys last night with hard picks." He smiled. "It was great. But he's not dirty."

"Thanks," I said, "but that's not what I meant. And I didn't understand most of it."

"Sorry. He's a really good guy. I think he misses Texas a lot, but he doesn't talk about it. Anyway, yeah, I'd let my sister go out with him." He smiled wryly. "I said that wrong."

"What do you mean?"

"If she heard that, she'd be in my face, telling me she doesn't need me to *let* her do anything." He tilted his head and looked at me thoughtfully, as if sizing me up. "Not sure you qualify for the wallflower project, if Troy was sitting with you."

It was bizarre from Will too. "I almost always qualify. Tonight's unusual. Did he send you to sit with me?"

"No."

The song was ending. My cheeks warmed, anticipating what I was about to say.

"Thanks for sitting with me. You could stay for another song, and I could try to persuade you I'm an authentic wallflower." I wanted bold to keep working.

His cheeks might have reddened slightly just then. "I would, but it's three dances with three different girls, then we meet and report. I'll sit with you again sometime, if that's okay."

I tried to pretend this was routine. Two boys. Two *desirables*. Both said they would come back. "I'll look forward to that. Good luck Friday."

"Thanks. You should come cheer for us."

Will had barely left when Landon, the resident math genius, asked if he could sit. He wasn't on the basketball team, and I wondered again if our resolution was working. Or was a girl just more interesting to boys, when other boys were interested?

Landon was a fellow sophomore. We'd had at least one class together almost every semester since we started junior high. A year or two ago—the first and last time he'd sat with me at a dance—he'd been a shorter, pale, pudgy kid with bad acne and sorely neglected hair. Now he was as tall as Troy but almost frail. He was still pale, but his acne was mostly gone. He'd obviously started caring about his hair, which was still unruly, but now it was clean and it worked. He wasn't bad to look at.

We had enough in common that conversation shouldn't have been a struggle, but the first awkward silence began when he sat down. I broke it by talking about the senior classes we were in as sophomores—Advanced Writing for me, BC Calculus for him. That worked for maybe half a minute.

After the next awkward silence, I tried talking about Nikki. He'd hovered around her off and on for years, and they were in the same BC Calc class this semester. He said she was nice, I said she was amazing, and we fell silent again.

I asked him how he liked the dance. He said it was okay. I said I felt odd going places without Zeus. He confessed he was terrified of dogs, and there was another gap in the conversation.

I finally got him talking about the college math he'd studied over the summer. It was over my head, but at least he was enthusiastic. He talked through the end of one song, then another. He finally wound down as our fourth song together was ending, and he awkwardly excused himself.

I shook my head at the relief I felt, watching him go. An hour earlier, four songs' worth of advanced math and awkward silences would have made my week. It really was a new and brighter world.

7

A Song and a Question

Troy returned soon after Landon left. My heart beat faster, but I tried to sound casual. "Did you meet charming wallflowers?"

"Always do."

"Good," I said. "While we're on the subject, why did you say I'm not a wallflower?"

"I said that?"

"You said, if I were a wallflower, I'd be a good reason to have your project."

He nodded soberly. "See what you mean."

"I've always been one. I fit your project perfectly."

"Okay, but that's the past."

My heart may have stopped then. My brain nearly did. I couldn't keep my nerves out of my voice, and I needed to breathe. "An hour ago . . . it was the present."

"Sitting with a guy is like dancing for you, right? And it's not just me. Will sat with you, and that other guy after him, who's not part of our project, by the way. You're not a wallflower tonight."

I took a deep, not-very-calming breath, and my happy eyes met his. "Did Will say anything about me? Or is that confidential?"

"Said you're cute, smart, and fun to talk to, which I already knew."

My cheeks tingled, and I looked down at my hands. "You're both very kind." I smoothed my skirt, which didn't need it, and looked up at him. "He talked about you for a minute. Because I asked him. He said you miss Texas."

"Yeah. I mean, nothing against Utah, but yeah."

"He also said you're a good basketball player. I think that's what he said. I didn't understand all of it. And he may want you to date his sister." I struggled to keep a straight face.

"Abby?"

"He didn't say her name."

"Only has one. She's in college on a volleyball scholarship. She's taller than me and a lot cuter than Will. He wants me to date her?"

I felt my face color. "I more or less asked him if you're a good guy. He said he'd let you date his sister."

Troy laughed. "Nice."

I seized the first new topic that came to mind. "You're not scared of dogs, are you?"

"No, just girls. Why? Oh, Zeus?"

"The boy I sat with after Will is scared of dogs. He's also a math genius, even more of a geek than I am. He'll talk forever about math, if you can get him started, but not much else. Are you good at math?"

"I do okay. Want to talk about math?"

"Only if you really want to. Number theory sounds fun, from what he said, but group theory sounds pretty weird."

"Never even heard of those. Is your math genius Landon?"

"You know him?"

"We have BC Calc together. He does the teaching when there's a sub."

"I'll bet. He's really more my friend Nikki's math genius than mine."

I wondered if Jack or Nikki was dancing, so I scanned what I could see of the dance floor. I didn't see them, but I saw a lot of others dancing while I sat, as always. I really wanted to dance with Troy. I probably wouldn't have a seizure right then. Even if I did, he promised not to let me fall, and maybe I really wouldn't.

Be bold, Jenny.

"I've been thinking about what you asked me," I said.

He perked up. "Dancing?"

"I'll do it."

His face broke into a smile. He'd been smiling a lot. "Excellent. What about your parents?"

"I'll have to tell them. I'm terrible at keeping secrets from them. Maybe it's an only child thing." I tried to look sheepish, but I was too happy. "Just don't let my head hit the floor."

"Okay. Have you ever danced before?"

"Socially? Only in my daydreams." I felt strangely comfortable mentioning something so personal as daydreams.

"We need a slow song," he said. "They're not playing very many."

Regular Jenny reddened slightly, but Bold Jenny ignored her. "It's a church dance. They probably want it as unromantic as possible."

He chuckled. "Just in case, what if you save the last dance for me?"

"You may have any slow dance you want, anytime," I said. "There's very little competition for me." I was stating a fact, but it sounded like self-pity, so I hurried to add, "I like sitting and talking with you."

"I like it too," he said seriously.

My heart was rapidly melting. My brain was still suspicious—and dazed enough to say the quiet part out loud. "I'm seriously wondering if you're too kind to be real," I said. "Or too smooth."

He cocked his head and looked at me. His eyes looked . . . hurt? I turned cold. Had my big, bold mouth just ruined everything?

"Too smooth? I don't—"

I couldn't wait. "Can we pretend I never said that? Please?"

He looked into my pleading eyes. He didn't say anything, and he didn't smile. But he didn't get up and leave. Finally he asked, "What shall we pretend you said?"

It felt like a reprieve, or at least my chance to earn one. I concentrated on using the right words this time. "You're really good at just sitting and talking with a girl. Better than any other boy I know." I looked up, feeling bold and timid at the same time. "I'm pretty much convinced you're real. Genuine, I mean."

The corners of his mouth turned upward. "If dancing goes well, maybe we could talk some more after that."

I relaxed. It was behind us. "That will be nice. But define 'goes well.'"

"You don't have a seizure, and I don't drop you? I could take you safely home at the end, if you want."

My newly-chastened, now-cautious brain overruled my eager heart. "Thanks, but maybe sometime after you meet my parents."

"Deal," he said. "If they don't ground you for dancing."

"Raising parents is hard, isn't it?" I deadpanned.

He laughed. "It's not so bad. But I guess you're doing it alone, and I have three sisters to help me."

The DJ announced a girls' choice dance, and when it proved to be a fast song, I didn't hesitate. "Since it's girls' choice," I said, "would you care to sit this one out with me?" I was proud of my steady voice.

He smiled warmly. "Yeah. Thanks. More punch first?"

"Maybe just water, please?" I handed him my cup. It was empty, so he might not have noticed that my hand was less steady than my voice.

"Water it is."

He said he'd be right back, and he was. That was four times he'd come back to me, including last week. Four times. Audrey probably couldn't say that. I was warm all over, from the inside. Warm and light. I could have floated away.

"What happens when you have a seizure?" His eyes were all concern. "Do I call an ambulance or maybe your parents? After I catch you?"

I wrenched my soaring mind back to practical things. "Are you an Eagle Scout?" Dad was a Scoutmaster when I was little, so I knew about Boy Scouts. I also knew you couldn't swing a dead cat at a church dance without hitting some Eagle Scouts. If you were Huckleberry Finn and they let you in with a dead cat in the first place.

"Yeah. Why?"

"You know those *grand mal* seizures you learned about in first aid, with convulsions and foaming at the mouth?"

"Sure. Never saw one."

"Mine are less dramatic. They're called atonic. I just fall down, because all my muscles go limp. After 10 or 15 seconds I'm okay again, as long as I didn't hurt myself on the way down. If I'm sitting in a chair, Zeus can keep me from falling. If I'm hurt, he can get help. Plus my parents say he's 'a constant reminder to be sensible.' That's a direct quote."

Troy grinned. "Do you need constant reminders to be sensible?"

I smiled in response. "Not like I used to. I got him when I was eight. Before that I wore a little helmet everywhere, which pretty much marked me as a total freak."

"Must have been hard."

I pretended to misunderstand. "It was softer than you might think, and smaller than a football helmet. And no face mask. I had four colors, so I could coordinate."

"Didn't mean the helmet was hard."

There was something gentle about him that made it okay to talk about uncomfortable things. His eyes, maybe, and his voice.

"I know." I took a deep breath and let it out. "You're right. Being the girl who wore a helmet was hard. When Zeus arrived, that was a good day. I was old enough to be more careful, and we phased out the helmet, so I was less of a freak. Less obviously, at least. How much of this do you want to hear?"

"As much as you want to tell me."

I took a moment to study this boy who wanted to listen. "Okay. So. At first they didn't think it was epilepsy, because patients with atonic seizures 'usually don't present with normal intellectual function,' as my pediatric neurologist put it. Even a seven-year-old remembers a phrase like that, if she hears it a few times and it's scary enough. Not that I really understood it. There were lots of tests for a while, starting with some cardiac stuff. I don't remember it being a lot of fun."

He still looked interested, so I dug deeper. "I was sure I was going to die soon, and they just kept saying I had to stay in the hospital for tests."

"Scary," he said.

"I thought it was the end. I panicked, and I think they had to sedate me at first. I was six, and they were connecting all these wires to me, and tubes and machines and everything. Well, six, then seven."

"You were there for your birthday?"

"They made it into a thing. If I hadn't been sure it was my last, I'd have enjoyed it. Everybody kept insisting I'd be okay. I tried to be calm and polite, like a big girl, every time I told them I knew their secret. I was never going home, because I was going to die."

"Wow," he said—and kept listening.

"I was there almost three weeks, and there were outpatient tests after I went home. Finally Mom and Dad, my doctor, and a child psychologist named Jane sat me down and told me I'd been very brave for all the scary tests, and they were ready to tell me everything, even if it took a long time. Which it did."

He smiled. "Bet they didn't call the tests scary before you had them."

"And the dentist says I won't feel a thing. They went through every test, how it worked, what it tested for, even a lot that were negative. They'd explained most of it before, but it helped that they put it together. They showed me models and diagrams and numbers and charts. It was all in a big binder they made for me. When I didn't understand something the first time, they explained again and wrote more notes in the binder. The less scared I got, the more questions I had."

He nodded solemnly. "I'm that way at dances. You may have noticed."

I smiled, which was probably what he wanted. "They told me what they found and how they would treat it, and what I could do to live with it. And how it might go away in early adulthood, which seemed impossibly distant and kind of still does. I kept asking, 'So I'm not going to die soon?' They kept saying no and explaining, and when they were done, I believed them. Which I guess was mostly the point."

This was more than I'd ever told anyone except Jack and Nikki. Something in my head said it was too much, too soon, but my heart disagreed. Besides, I'd already said it. My cheeks flared, and I looked away. Then I needed his eyes again.

"I'm sorry for talking so much. Long story short, they eventually figured me out, and I didn't die. As you may have noticed."

He nodded slowly. "Don't be sorry. Good stuff to know about you. How often does it happen? If you don't mind my asking."

"The seizures? I don't mind," I answered honestly. "I had one at the movie theater just before Christmas. We were in our seats—Jack and Nikki and I—so it wasn't a big deal, except I spilled half the popcorn."

"Free refill?" he asked.

"Yeah. Anyway, it's been every week or two, mostly. Hardly ever twice in the same day. A little less often lately." I pushed back a few strands of hair. "If I weren't allergic to a certain medication, I could drive. Assuming it worked."

"Are there warning signs?" he asked.

I shook my head. "No. Haven't found any triggers either."

"Like flashing lights or something?"

"Or stress, lack of sleep, low blood sugar, something I ate," I said. That time of the month, I didn't say. "It's different for everybody, and for me we just don't know."

"So all I have to do is not drop you?" he asked.

"Even if I trip over my feet, please, which is more likely than a seizure."

"Do my best." He thought for a moment. "We should be careful walking out onto the floor, right?"

"If you don't mind. But people will talk, if you have your arm around me before we start dancing." Even Bold Jenny blushed to share that thought.

His eyes twinkled. "There's the fireman's carry, if you don't mind me throwing you over my shoulder."

"Sure, because nobody would talk about that, or think we were drunk or anything." I heard my own merry laughter and realized my doubts about him had faded. I was growing fond of the twinkle in his eyes—and his eyes seemed fond of me.

"Okay, maybe not that," he said. "My arm will be happy to serve. We just need a slow song."

"While we wait," I said, "tell me your favorite song from my concert, if you remember. If you had one."

"Your small group. Nine of you, right? Was it 'Open My Eyes'? A cappella, and I'm sure it's pretty hard, but you made it sound easy."

"Thank you. You were close. 'Open Thou Mine Eyes' by John Rutter. I always like Rutter."

"Tried to remember the words later." He shrugged. "Could have checked the Internet."

"I can tell you the words." I recited from memory, trying to do justice to the poetry, the way Mom and Dad had taught me. It was a prayer that God would help me see and desire what I should, and help me serve him and obey his commandments.

Troy watched my recitation with new intensity. When I finished, he seemed to relax. "I like that," he said. "Liked watching you sing it." He tensed again and shifted in his chair. "Are you—"

Possible questions danced through my mind. Was I dating anyone? (No.) Was I busy Friday night? (No.) Next Saturday night? (No.) Would

I like to go out with a kind, handsome, talkative junior who played basketball, sang in a school choir, and knew more math than I did? (Yes!)

When he didn't continue, I prompted him. "Am I . . . ?"

He visibly deflated. "Never mind. Too personal."

I really wanted to hear his question.

Be bold, Jenny.

"You should ask me. If I don't want to answer, I won't. And I might blush. But you already know my medical history, at least the highlights, and you've seen me blush. How bad could it be?"

He looked at me soberly. "Is that who you are? Who you want to be, at least?"

I forgot to breathe. "I'm . . . not sure . . . what you mean."

He looked toward the dance floor. "Are those just the words of a song your choir sings, or do you mean it?" He met my eyes again. "Because at the concert you looked like you meant it. And when you told me the words just now, it was like you were praying, almost."

I stared at him with wide eyes. This was like no conversation I'd imagined with any boy ever.

The tremor in my voice was small, but it was there. "You're asking if I want to obey God? And serve him like the song says, in public and private, in body and spirit and word, and so on?"

"Yeah, don't answer that." He looked away. "Shouldn't have asked."

"It is . . . personal," I said slowly and more calmly. "Why did you ask?"

He turned back to me. "Wanted to know. Let's talk about something else."

Be bold, Jenny.

"I'll answer your question," I said. "If you'll answer mine."

"What's yours?"

"I haven't asked it yet. I do want to be that person," I said. "Most of the time, I try."

He nodded silently.

"Are you that kind of person?" I asked. "Is that who you want to be?"

"Same question?"

"Same reason too."

He nodded again. "Same answer. On my good days."

"Okay," I said.

8

Not a Waltz, but . . .

W E WATCHED THE DANCERS without talking for a while. I didn't try to imagine Troy's thoughts. I was too busy noticing that something in me wanted a boy I'd met just a week ago to ask me deeply personal questions, and I ached to answer them, and for him to answer too.

The song ended, and he leaned toward me. "Didn't wear a helmet to school, but I was a freak for a different reason."

Was he trying to rescue me from the inner scars of my helmet-wearing childhood? "You're very kind," I said. "Freakishly kind, almost."

"Thanks, but it wasn't that. It was being a Mormon kid in Texas public schools."

"What's that like? My schools have been mostly Mormon. I mean Latter-day Saint. Much like myself." I flashed a silly smile.

He chuckled, then spoke seriously. "Bible Belt, right? Some kids thought I wasn't Christian. They heard that at church and maybe at home. They thought I worshipped Satan, which bugged me, especially when I told them it wasn't true and they wouldn't believe me. I mean, it's right there in the name: The Church of Jesus Christ of Latter-day Saints. Pretty hard to miss. Told them we believe in the Bible, and the Book of Mormon's all about Jesus too, but they didn't care.

"They didn't beat me up at recess or try to burn me at the stake after school. Just wouldn't play with me, some of them, or even talk to me if they could avoid it."

He leaned forward, resting his forearms on his knees. I tried to keep listening, while I admired his broad shoulders. My head was a jumble of happy thoughts. It was like nearing the climax of a great book, a captivating film, and a moving piece of music all at once. I instinctively searched for the right word.

Ecstatic? Too much, maybe.

Exhilarated? Yes, but with a bit of silliness. More than a bit.

"Try *giddy*," said Mom's voice in my head.

Yep, I was giddy. And I liked it.

"If they got to know me," Troy was saying, "then we were okay, unless their parents found out they were friends with that Mormon boy. If that happened, they might come back with a pamphlet from their pastor about how evil my religion is and how I should accept Jesus Christ—their way, not ours—and be saved. Guess that doesn't happen much here, but I wonder if it happens in reverse sometimes."

I hadn't seen Mormon kids proselyting non-Mormons at school, but it could have happened. "Maybe," I said. "I don't know."

"Later it was the fact that I wouldn't even try alcohol or drugs," he said.

"I know there's some of that here."

"Not as much, I think. Then there were a couple of girls who liked me but wouldn't believe I liked them—because I wouldn't date until I was sixteen, and then I wouldn't . . . fool around."

He turned to me, and he might have been blushing slightly. The thought that he felt comfortable enough with me to say such things lifted me and swept me along, like an ocean wave rolling toward the little beach I loved to visit every summer in Maine.

What came after giddy? Giddier? Giddiest? Afloat in a welcoming sea of magical happiness bubbles? I gave up trying to describe the atmosphere of this strange, invigorating world and just breathed it in.

By the time I realized he was waiting for me to say something, I needed a moment to remember what he'd just said.

"I understand there are girls like that here too." I was pleased with myself for not sounding flustered.

"Found that out pretty quickly." He sat up and exhaled. "Couldn't believe they were so insecure or whatever, even girls from church. I don't know. Maybe they didn't want proof that I liked them. Maybe they just want to fool around. But my sister told me something. She said, whether

I knew it or not, I'd never met a teenage girl who wasn't insecure about almost everything. Not in Texas, not here. No offense."

Be bold, Jenny.

"Troy?"

"Yeah?" He looked at me.

"She was right." I reached for even bolder. "And you still haven't met one."

He absorbed that, then shrugged. "Okay," he said, and an unexpected wave of relief lifted me higher still. "Guys have insecurities too."

"That's good to know," I said. "Like what?"

"Lot of the same ones, I think."

That was when bold, giddy, crazy Jenny tumbled out of control. Before I knew it, I was saying in my most innocent voice, "You worry about your bra size too? I wouldn't have guessed."

My timing was terrible. He was swallowing a sip of water when he exploded into laughter, and that made him cough.

My question was terrible too. Jack could talk to a boy like that without dying of shame, maybe, but I couldn't. I hid my face in my hands and invented a new shade of red.

I had to speak before he did, or it might actually kill me. "I'm so sorry. I can't believe I said that." I'd meant to look up just long enough to tell him that, but then I couldn't look away.

His eyes were full of mirth. His face was red, and his whole body shook, more with suppressed laughter than with coughs, I thought. I had to change the subject.

"So . . . what part do you sing in your choir?" My voice was a timid disaster.

He said he was a second tenor. I wanted to thank him for letting me change the subject, but I said I was a second soprano instead. We'd just discovered that we planned to audition for the same school choir next year, when he noticed something I didn't.

"I think this is our song. Sure it's okay?"

I smiled and nodded, eager both to dance and to get as far as possible from what I'd said.

He stood and held out his hand, bowing slightly. He was hamming it up, but it was chivalrous and charming. "In that case, my lady, would you honor me with this dance?"

I tried to answer in kind. "With pleasure, sir, and I thank you." I took his hand and stood. Having my hand in his made me shaky inside. So did the prospect of dancing.

I'd always thought it looked nice when a girl took a boy's arm on the way to the floor, except when it was Audrey taking Troy's, but that wouldn't keep me from falling if I had a seizure. He put his right arm firmly around my waist and held my left hand in his. We walked side by side, like a promenade. He felt strong, and it thrilled me. I felt safe and comfortable.

We didn't slow dance like most kids, just swaying in a little circle, with my arms on his shoulders or around his neck and his hands at my waist—or around my waist, like the friendlier couples. We used a ballroom dance position instead. Troy said the proper "closed position" was with his right hand near my shoulder blade, but I'd be hard to catch that way, so he put his hand firmly behind my waist.

The song was something about running away together, but I couldn't spare much attention for the words. Being in his arms was disorienting, and all my daydreaming about dancing wasn't the same as knowing how. He took small steps, and my part should have been simple enough, or at least possible, but I stumbled and stepped hard on his toes.

"Sorry," I said, and just stopped. "Help? I don't know where to put my feet."

He grinned. "No problem. First thing, my trick for not stepping on your normal feet with my giant ones is not to pick them up that much. Slide your feet just above the floor, and you might bump into my toes, but you won't step on them. If you do, I'll be okay. I really will."

"Where do I slide my feet?"

"When I step forward with my left foot, you step back with your right. Then I step forward with my right, and you step back with your left. Let's try it."

We did that a couple of times.

"Good," he said. "Here's what we do next."

The song was still going by the time we were actually dancing—he said it was a basic foxtrot step—but there was a new problem. The first beat of every measure was clear, but the other three weren't. Then I discovered on my own that I could just follow his lead. I was less awkward after that, and I started to enjoy it.

The song faded away, and I beamed. Now I was ecstatic. *Bold. Jenny. Just. Danced.*

"Thank you," I said. Two words didn't feel like enough.

"Thank you," he said, and smiled.

"Sorry I was so clumsy."

"You did fine. I'm honored to be your first cavalier." He let go of me for a moment, except my hand, so he could bow slightly. He was still hamming it up, and it was still charming.

My happy smile felt new. My eyes were big, and my face tingled. All of me tingled. I managed a single word. "Cavalier?"

"Shall we?" He put his arm around me again, and we walked off the floor. "My little sisters do ballet. They say the principal ballerina's partner is a cavalier. Thought it would sound cool. May I sit with you again, if you're not tired of talking?"

That won him another smile. "I hardly ever get tired of that. If they play another slow song, could we dance again? It worked once," I said hopefully.

"Let's do it."

In the next moment I realized what I'd done. I'd asked a boy to dance, sort of, and he'd agreed. It was spontaneous, or I'd have been terribly nervous. I'd also assumed he intended to continue sitting with me—which he apparently did.

Then came an even warmer thought. I liked having his arm around me even more than dancing. Was it because he was a boy or because he was this boy? Either way, I thought he held me longer than necessary for safety's sake, when we reached our chairs. I so didn't mind.

And: *our* chairs. That was a happy thought too.

When we were seated, with Jack and Nikki nowhere to be seen, I asked, "Do you mind if I send a quick text to a friend?"

"Go for it," he said. "If it's about me, do I get to read it?"

"It's not."

I showed him my message to Nikki anyway: "Landon said you're nice. You should ask him to dance. Don't talk about dogs. I'll explain later."

When they played another slow song, we danced again. I was less clumsy, and I enjoyed it from beginning to end. I hoped in vain for another one after that, mostly so he'd put his arm around me again. Then maybe he could forget to remove it when we sat down. Wanting that had me on pins and needles, but I still liked sitting and talking with him.

Until I remembered my embarrassment.

"Troy," I said timidly, "may I ask a big favor?"

"Sure."

"That thing I said before, could we keep it just between you and me?"

"About obeying God?"

Was he teasing me? "No, that other thing. The one I can't remember without blushing again?" Please don't make me say it, I thought.

"Oh, our, uh, mutual insecurity?" He grinned mischievously—but I gave him full credit anyway, for diplomacy and because his eyes didn't wander.

"Please?"

"So I'm supposed to tell my friends and my parents about this beautiful, smart, funny girl I sat with—and danced with—but not how you made me laugh so hard that water came out my nose? That's a pretty big favor."

I looked at him, silently pleading.

He nodded. "Okay. Just between us. Should I not mention it to you in the future either? At least not very often?"

"Please. Thank you." I smiled gratefully. "I owe you a pretty big favor." Then I realized he'd hinted at a future with us together in it, and my head and heart started to float away again.

Because giddy had gone so well last time, I thought wryly, and pulled myself back to Earth.

"You could smile at me a couple more times, and we could call it even," he said. His eyebrows were slightly raised, and his eyes were very, very blue.

When his eyes saw an even warmer smile from me, they twinkled like a whole skyful of stars.

"Yeah," he said. "Like that."

During the last song, which wasn't a slow dance, we exchanged cell phone numbers and promised to run into each other at school. It was the first time I saw him look at his phone.

I thanked him for a fun evening, and he thanked me too. I thought we'd just say good night after that, but he seemed to want to say more. His cheeks flushed, and his faint, self-conscious smile would have been utterly disarming, if there'd been anything left of me to disarm.

"Was there something else?" I thought I sounded encouraging.

"Just . . . I like talking with you," he said. "This was really fun. Dancing with you too."

My eyes said what my words couldn't, and he seemed to understand. But I still wanted to say something, even if I didn't quite know what or how.

"You already know . . . the feeling is . . . mutual . . . right?" It was terribly awkward, and it made my face hot, but it was honest.

"Yeah," he said, regarding me with happy, beautiful eyes for another moment. "See you at school?"

I nodded eagerly.

"Good night," he said softly.

"Good night," I murmured automatically.

He waved, hesitated, and turned away. I watched him disappear through a doorway. Then I watched a little longer, before floating away to find Jack and Nikki.

On our way out to Jack's car I said to myself, maybe that's why most of us keep going to dances. One of them—but we never know which one—might turn out to be wonderful.

9

Aftermath

O N T H E W A Y H O M E I told Jack and Nikki almost everything. I left out the part which began with Troy's favorite song at my concert and ended with me hiding my face in shame. Some of it I wanted to ponder on my own for a while, and some of it would have been too embarrassing, when Jack and Nikki told Mom and Dad.

Which they totally would have. I couldn't expect them to pass up a story like that, if they knew it.

We debated whether our New Year's resolution had anything to do with my amazing evening. It hadn't done much for them this time.

I'd forgotten to count the songs I spent sitting or dancing with—now I thrilled at the word—*desirables*. In the end, all we knew for sure was that something worked beautifully for me, and being a little dressed up made us all feel a little older again, which we liked.

At my house they came in, as usual. After-dance smoothies were my way of thanking them for hauling me around—and a fun ending, when we needed one, for downer evenings spent being invisible to boys at dances.

Sometimes Mom or Dad joined us, or both. Last week, after the dance where I met Troy, Mom was in bed already, and Dad was fading fast, he said, so we were on our own. I hadn't even mentioned Troy. This time they were in their matching blue cable-knit sweaters, snuggling on the family room sofa and watching a video, as they often did when I went to a dance. If they had dozed off, I was to wake them, so they could join us for smoothies, and so they'd know I was home.

They were awake, but they didn't jump up to play the gracious hosts. Jack and Nikki were more like family than guests. Dad smiled and waved with the arm that wasn't around Mom. She didn't lift her head from his shoulder. She just said, "Hi, girls. This is almost over. Why don't you get started? The fruit's on the counter."

Soon we were all in the dining room with our smoothies, at the polished mahogany table that could seat at least ten. I could hardly wait for Mom to ask what she always asked. Finally she did.

"How was the dance?"

Usually there wasn't much to say, but this time I knew we'd talk about my answer for a while.

"It was the best dance ever," I said. My heart fluttered, and I remembered feeling Troy's arm around me and drinking in his smile, and the look in his eyes when—

This was a bad time to be giddy.

"Do tell," said Mom. My parents said lots of things usually found only in books.

Be bold, Jenny.

"I danced two slow dances. I hope that's okay. We were careful. He promised not to drop me, if anything happened."

"Who's he?" she asked.

Jack answered before I could. "She scored with two basketball players, Will and Troy, and one math genius, Landon."

Jack liked drama—and Mom knew Jack. I mentally sighed with relief that only Troy and I knew the embarrassing part.

Mom asked calmly, "Scored, Jenny?"

Nikki jumped in. "Will—he's varsity—sat with her once. Troy—he's JV—danced with her twice and sat with her until the dance was over. He sat with her last week at the school dance too. Landon, the math genius, sat with her tonight too, for a while."

Mom turned to me with a gentle smile. "You were busy. Tell us about Troy," she said reasonably.

Jack said, "He's new this year, from Texas. He's tall—well, not super tall for a basketball player—and handsome and smart. He's a junior."

"Last week, he told her she's beautiful about three times in the first ten minutes," Nikki said. "He stalked her at the children's choir Christmas concert."

"Actually," I said, "he was there with his family. His little sister's joining the choir. He saw me and thought I was pretty." My cheeks were hot again, and I struggled to focus. "He's in the men's chorus at school, so he's more than a jock. He's a year ahead in math, so he's smart. And he's fun to talk to. His manners are excellent. So's his grammar. He was too good to be true."

I was still pretty sure I'd met the real Troy, but I thought Mom and Dad would welcome some skepticism at first.

"Definitely too good to be true," Mom echoed.

It was already enough skepticism. "That's what I thought at first," I said. "Later I thought, maybe he's real after all. I'm sure he's not perfect. But he seemed like he was being himself, not just trying to impress a girl. He was even shy sometimes."

"He's in my calculus class," Nikki said. "He's not rude or crude or anything, and he dresses neatly."

I looked gratefully at Nikki, but she was already looking at Jack. I caught them exchanging slight but mischievous smiles.

"I wish he had a twin brother," Nikki announced.

"Two twin brothers," said Jack. "Triplets. Whatever. I'd like mine to be a fellow redhead. Better odds of redheaded children."

Part of me wanted to change the subject. It briefly overwhelmed the part that didn't. I turned to Nikki. "Speaking of boys in your calculus class, did you dance with Landon?"

She scowled. "No. I asked him, but he said he doesn't dance. He wouldn't even try, not even for me. So I'm officially uninterested." She grinned again. "And I'm changing the subject back to you and Troy."

Jack turned to Mom and Dad. "Your honors, we have just a few questions for this witness."

Mom looked curious and mildly amused.

Dad smiled like he was about to laugh. "This should be good."

All eyes were on me.

Jack asked, "Did he put his arm around you or hold your hand?"

"Only between our chairs and the dance floor. For safety."

"Right," said Jack, and I blushed.

"Did he try to kiss you?" Nikki asked solemnly.

"No," I said. I was trying for matter-of-fact, but I sounded defensive.

Nikki was unfazed. "Would you have let him?"

I sipped my smoothie and summoned Bold Jenny. "Yes. Maybe."

"Seriously?"

"No. I'd have to know him a lot better and a lot longer." I thought I sounded serious and sensible. Then I deadpanned dreamily, "Another half hour at least. When's the next dance?"

Jack took over. "We'll ask the questions. Did he offer to take you home? And if so, to your home or his?"

"I assumed he meant mine."

"Of course. Did he use any fancy words? For example, did he happen to call himself your cavalier?"

I nodded. "Yes."

Mom looked amused. Dad was actually laughing quietly. "Sometime soon," he said, "we should meet this cavalier of yours."

"First let's see how he treats me at school," I said, trying to sound more philosophical than I felt. "Or if he notices me at all. Maybe he won't think I'm beautiful by daylight."

Dad frowned at that, but he let it go until later.

After we cleaned up, Jack and Nikki left for home, and Mom went upstairs. Dad asked if I felt like talking. I invited him to my room, and we sat on my love seat. He put his arm around me, and I nestled my head on his shoulder. His sweater was wonderfully soft.

He spoke quietly. "I'm not surprised a boy enjoys your company and thinks you're beautiful. You're smart and fun to talk to, and you look like your mom. She's beautiful. Do the math."

I tried to believe him. "Thanks, Dad."

"If he had dropped you on the dance floor . . ."

"I told him. We danced with his arm around my waist. And only slow dances, just in case." I looked up for his reaction.

He raised both eyebrows. "Sounds friendly."

"We were trying to be careful. I may not have danced before, but I have tried concussions."

"Okay." He seemed to relax, and I eased my head back onto his shoulder. "So you like him?" he asked.

"I think I do." Exhaustion closed in, bringing doubts, as usual—about myself or whatever else was in my head. "Dad, what if he's just a jerk who's really good at charming lonely girls at dances?"

"Lonely? Where were Jack and Nikki?"

I hesitated. "Lonely for a boy. What if he isn't real? Or what if there's also an ugly side, and I just haven't seen it yet?"

"You'll find out soon enough. Will you be heartbroken?"

I nodded. "Probably."

"What if he really is a good guy?" he asked. "Some of us are."

I could believe he was a good guy and still doubt myself, among other things. "I'm sixteen. I'll probably get my heart broken either way, right?"

"Good chance," he said. "Doesn't mean you shouldn't live. Broken hearts mend, especially when you're young. But Jenny?"

"Dad?"

"It's late, and you're tired, and that makes somber cowards of us all. Do you know what I'm about to say?"

He'd said it often enough. "Dad, you know Stonewall Jackson owned slaves, right?"

"I do know that. But besides being a brilliant military mind, he was right about one other thing, at least."

I looked into his eyes, put my hand on his bearded cheek, smiled, and recited the familiar words. "Never take counsel . . ."

His hand covered mine.

". . . Of my fears," I said. I settled onto his shoulder again. "I was a little bit brave tonight. I didn't quote Stonewall Jackson to myself, but I did keep telling myself to be bold."

"It must have gone well."

"I was still nervous, and I said the wrong thing a few times, but I didn't let my shy self get in the way of my talkative self. Is it okay that I danced with him, instead of just sitting?"

"Sounds like you were smart about it. I'm glad you got to dance."

"Is it okay with Mom?"

"I think so. We didn't expect our original agreement about dances to last forever."

I stared at him. "What? Really? Were you ever going to tell me?"

He regarded me with mild amusement. "Didn't think we'd need to. We were right, of course."

"Of course," I murmured. "I know Troy and I just met last week, but we had about five dates' worth of good conversation tonight." I looked up. "I'm a little giddy." A tired, happy fog had settled over my brain.

Dad was tired too; I could see it in his smile. "I'm a little scared."

I grinned. "'Don't take counsel of your fears.' That's what my daddy would say."

"Wise man. Keep us posted, okay?"

"You know I talk to my parents."

"We love that about you."

"Do you think it's because I'm an only child?" I asked.

"I'm sure that's part of it, but do you remember Jane, the social worker?"

"Of course I do."

"She said children who've had serious health challenges tend to be closer to their parents. I hope that continues when the health challenge ends, assuming it does."

"So do I," I said.

After he went up to bed, I sat a while longer, comparing what I knew about Troy to the list taped to my mirror. He did really well.

Dating

10

Research

J UST AFTER NOON ON Sunday, as I got ready for church, my phone
vibrated on my bathroom counter. I glanced at the screen and nearly
dropped my hairbrush. It was a text from Troy.

The preview alone made me tingle all the way to my toes. "Hi Jenny. Last night was fun. Thanks again."

My three hours of church meetings hadn't begun, but his had just ended. "Church was boring today," his message continued, "so I sat there wishing we didn't have a no-texting rule for church. Wanted to say hi." He ended with a smiley.

As I told Zeus, how cool was it that he texted me—or thought about me at all?

I rewrote my response twice before sending it. "Hi! I had fun too. Same rule here, but we go at 1:00. Nice to hear from you."

Typing the last five words made my hand shake. I needed three tries to hit the send button.

His reply arrived seconds later. "1:00? Bummer!"

I typed more calmly, "I don't mind sleeping late." I didn't tell him I'd slept until nearly noon and wasn't dressed yet. I pressed the send button more carefully. The sooner he got my message, the sooner he'd reply.

Seconds felt like minutes.

"Bump into you at school, if that's still okay," he wrote.

Everything that was tingling started to melt. "Looking forward to it."

"Cool. Dad and I are going home teaching. Then we're all off to somebody's house for dinner. Have a great day!" Home teaching was another church thing, and I was already having a great day.

"You too!" I spelled it out. U2 was a really old band my parents liked, not a proper abbreviation for literate girls writing text messages.

I scrolled blissfully through our chat, savoring every line. Then I finished brushing my hair and took a moment to appreciate it in the mirror. It was naturally straight, with a slight curl at the bottom, depending on the humidity. Today it framed not the bleary face of a plain girl who was barely awake at midday, but an uncommonly happy smile, cheeks flushed with excitement, and blue eyes that were shining.

Maybe a boy really could think I was pretty.

I pulled on some navy tights and a navy wool blend dress that reached below my knees. I wanted to be warm for the walk to church, and the building itself was sometimes chilly.

When Zeus and I met Mom and Dad at the front door, Dad smiled. "You look radiant, not to mention well rested. Still aglow from last night?"

"Yup." Bold Jenny could do parents too. I added a kiss on his cheek to the usual hug. Mom got the same greeting, with an air kiss to protect her makeup. I caught them sharing a look as we walked out the door.

I looked forward to the weekly walk to church because I actually walked. It was less than a block, and it was probably no more dangerous for me than walking from the parking lot if we drove. I'd never had a seizure walking to church, but I'd had a few in parking lots, and I'd hit my head on a parked car or two on the way down. One of my concussions happened that way.

On this Sunday afternoon, I kept my distance from cars parked along the sidewalk, as usual, but mostly I tried to suppress the new bounce in my step, so Mom and Dad wouldn't feel the urge to comment.

Soon I was sitting in sacrament meeting, the service at the beginning of our three-hour meeting block. I sang, prayed, and worshipped God with a joyful heart—except it probably didn't count as worship, because I mostly thought about a boy.

Then again, a boy who thought about me while he was in church, then texted me about it, was a lot like a miracle, so it wasn't the complete opposite of worship.

I read through our messages a few more times during the meeting. After the benediction Mom turned to me. "Reading scripture on your phone?" Her tone said she knew better.

"Not scripture." I showed her the texts. She read them, then asked with a look and a gesture if she could show Dad. I nodded. It was nice of her to ask.

He read them, smiling faintly, then looked up. "Someone won't hear much of her Sunday School or Young Women lessons today."

Someone smiled and shook her head.

Mom frowned. "What happened to not texting in church?"

"Look at the time stamps," Dad said. "Two hours ago."

"That explains some things," she said. "What are we going to do with her?"

He gave me my phone. "We will trust the daughter."

"The daughter is so twitter-pated she'll get lost going to class." Mom's words were dismissive, but she smiled a little.

I didn't think my own smile was confused or empty. But I hadn't stopped smiling, and I wasn't talking much, and I was kissing my parents and saying things like "yup."

Dad nodded. "For that, my dear, we trust the dog."

⸺◦⸺

School felt different on Monday. Mom and Dad might have called it sociology, but to me it was geometry. It was all about circles.

I had my small circle of friends, with Jack and Nikki permanently in the center. Our circle overlapped other circles—but not the circle we called the beautiful people.

This was high school, not junior high, so the beautiful people were mostly interested in themselves. If we peasants made it difficult for them to ignore us, they might lash out, but otherwise we weren't important enough for them to mean us actual harm. They just didn't want our circles colliding with theirs.

In the cafeteria there was space for circles to keep to themselves. In classrooms mixing was inevitable but well supervised, and it mostly happened peacefully for an hour and a quarter at a time. But in the crowded, chaotic halls between classes, looks and words were sometimes harsh. Zeus and I mostly kept our heads down, figuratively, and tried not to collide with anyone.

Today hope replaced caution, and I scanned the halls for Troy. He was out there somewhere, well beyond any circle of mine.

If he watched for me, we both watched in vain.

I could have looked near the gym, between school and basketball practice, but even Bold Jenny wasn't comfortable going there. Instead I met Jack and Nikki, as usual. They hadn't seen him either.

"He probably has early lunch and lots of junior classes," Nikki said. We were on late lunch, and the two shifts didn't overlap.

"So here's how we're helping you," Jack said. "We know he has calculus with Veronica the Brainiac." Nikki glared, but Jack could call her that—because she was just as smart and because she was Jack. "Tomorrow we'll get his whole schedule. If you still don't see him, on Wednesday you can be where he can bump into you."

"I could just text him. 'Long time, no see,' or something like that. Or I could help you."

"First rely on your experts," said Nikki.

"That's us," said Jack.

"Yeah, me and Jacqueline here," Nikki said drily.

Jack grinned. "I deserved that."

<hr>

When school let out on Tuesday, I still hadn't seen or heard from Troy. I tried not to worry that he'd lost interest.

As usual, Nikki and Jack drove Zeus and me to my weekly children's choir rehearsal after school. As soon as we were in Jack's car, away from listening ears, they began their report. Just hearing them talk about Troy gave me hope.

His schedule was filled with serious classes like Honors Junior This and AP That, including the calculus class he had with Nikki. He had seminary during fourth period on A days. That was released-time religious instruction, held just off campus at a classroom building the Church owned. Most Latter-day Saint kids went. I had the same teacher before lunch on B days.

Before and after school were basketball practices and workouts. Then he ate dinner with his family and usually studied all evening, unless he had a game or something.

"He's in bed by 11:00," Nikki reported, "so he can get up at 6:00. Coach Witt insists on seven hours of sleep, minimum."

I turned to Zeus with a hopeful smile, but he was looking out the window. "No wonder I haven't heard from him. He's too busy. Thanks for being my detectives."

"We're not finished." Jack's eyes caught mine in the rearview mirror. "The Pullmans moved from Texas in August. His dad's an airline pilot. My dad knows him a little.

"The older sister's at some college in Texas. Two little sisters are in eighth grade and third grade. His mom's an accountant, mostly works from home. Why do people in gigantic Buicks drive twelve miles below the speed limit?"

Jack drove like her dad, the pilot. She never yelled, cursed, or made rude gestures, and she didn't tailgate, honk, or flash her lights at the slow-moving behemoth in front of us.

"He's been out with several girls this year," Nikki said. "Only once each, we think, and they do some of the asking. He's not dating anyone in particular, but at least one cheerleader wants to change that."

"He's on Facebook and Instagram," Jack added, "but he obviously doesn't spend any time there. You two have that in common. We didn't find him on Twitter, and we wouldn't know about Snapchat. He's on the JV basketball team as a junior, for leadership and to get lots of playing time in the system. Next year he'll probably start at point guard for the varsity."

"What's a point guard?" I wondered.

"We didn't ask," Jack said.

Nikki turned in her seat. "Some of the girls on the dance team say he's stuck up, but—"

I blanched. "You asked the dance team?"

"No," Nikki said. "They were talking about him, and I listened."

"Considering some of the sources," Jack said, "'stuck up' might just mean he's not into tarts."

Every time Jack visited her brother and sister-in-law in England, she came back with more British vocabulary: *loo, lift, boot, torch, zed*. A party was a *do*, a shopping cart was a *trolley*, sometimes she said *ring* instead of *call*, and certain girls were *tarts*.

"As I was saying," Nikki continued, "they think he studies too much, but duh! He was on the high honor roll last semester."

Jack said, "The beautiful people saw you together on consecutive Saturday nights. If it keeps happening, they may have to hate you."

It would be worth it, I thought. "Ladies, it's scary how good you are at this. I'm concerned about one thing."

"Changing the phenomenon by trying to measure it?" Jack asked. It was a very Jack-the-science-geek thing to say.

"Something like that."

"We were careful. Mostly we just let people talk, and they hardly knew we were there. As usual."

I decided to believe them and not worry about it.

We pulled up in front of the community center where my choir rehearsed. "One more thing," Nikki said, "in case you want to run into him tomorrow. The team leaves during late lunch for a game about three hours away. I forget where."

◆◇◆

Bold Jenny decided to be Patient Jenny, or maybe I was Shy Jenny, for one more day. If we still hadn't met, I could text him after his game and ask how it went.

He didn't come to me or text me Wednesday, so after school I texted him. It was either that or sink into a sad, familiar feeling of being passed over. Again.

"Good luck tonight!" I wrote.

He didn't reply, and I slowly sank after all.

After dinner, I reasoned that the JV game had to end before the varsity game began, so I pinned my hopes to 8:00 p.m. But 8:00 p.m. came and went, then 8:30.

Finally my phone pinged. "Thanks! We won."

I smiled and sent a fireworks emoji.

He replied with a basketball emoji.

"Good luck to the varsity," I wrote.

He liked my message, but that was all. It felt like a sign-off. I waited a few minutes before I got on Skype with Jack and Nikki to report, hoping there was more, but there wasn't.

◆

At lunch on Thursday, Jack, Nikki, and I sat at one of the round tables with actual chairs, as always, because the long, folding cafeteria tables with long, folding benches were awkward for Zeus. He was partway under the table with his water dish.

We'd finished eating when Jack said, "Don't look now. Cute Texas Boy at your six o'clock, inbound."

It was all I could do not to look.

Nikki snorted.

Jack turned to her. "What?"

"We're talking about a cute boy and Jenny's six o'clock."

They giggled, and I tried to glare, but I was too happy.

Jack stood. "Our six o'clocks are outta here."

11

Cute Texas Boy

J ACK, NIKKI, AND THEIR trays were long gone, when Cute Texas Boy appeared beside me. I had dialed back my smile as much as I could, so I wouldn't look like a complete fool—but then I looked up at him.

He wore jeans and a burgundy polo shirt, and he looked really good. He smiled, said hi, and asked if he could join me.

I blushed and babbled like an idiot. "Hi. Please. Yes. Have a—. Yes." I nodded desperately.

He sat so that Zeus was between us, and I tried to settle down. It helped to look at Zeus instead of Troy.

"Troy, this is Zeus. Zeus, Troy." Saying a few normal, non-idiotic words helped too.

"May I? When he's working?"

"Sure." I still couldn't quite look him in the eye. Not again. Not yet.

He knew how to meet a dog. He didn't stare into Zeus's eyes or lean over him. He let him sniff his closed fist, then his open hand.

I said, "Shake his hand, Zeus," and Zeus lifted a paw.

Troy grinned and shook it. "Pleased to meet you, Zeus. Heard good things about you. Heard anything about me?" He patted Zeus's neck.

Zeus was silent, but I could tell he liked the attention by how he held his head and twitched his tail.

When Troy turned his eyes and smile to me, I didn't look away, and three and a half days of watching and wondering were totally worth it. My insides skipped tingly and went straight to melty.

"German shepherd, right?" he asked, as if this were an ordinary conversation on an ordinary day. "Not a golden retriever?"

It took a moment to switch my brain from melty to small talk. I hoped he couldn't hear how hard I was trying to sound calm and matter-of-fact.

"Golden retrievers make great service dogs, but they're too big, they shed too much, and not one of them is Zeus. You know dogs?"

He chuckled. "Mostly I know Wikipedia, and I try to be prepared for a first interview."

"With me?"

"With Zeus."

"Right. What does Wikipedia say?"

"German shepherds are popular service dogs, after golden retrievers, and most of them look like Zeus. Lots of brown, with black on their backs and faces."

"There was red in the brown," I said, "but it faded. He's not so young anymore."

"Also says they're intelligent, curious, and very protective."

Zeus didn't like me getting mushy with him, so I just patted the side of his neck. "That's my Zeus." I looked up. "You should stay on his good side. That protective thing is for real."

"Good to know. Can he tell when you're about to, you know?"

"No. I've heard that works for some epileptics and their dogs, but not for all of us. Good question, though."

"Okay that I asked?"

"Ask whatever you want," I said. "I think that's our rule now."

He smiled. "Okay, next question. Who are your friends? Only saw their backs."

"Nikki's the brunette. Isn't she in your math class?"

"Yeah, okay. She's smart. Kind of quiet."

"Except with friends. So's Jack. She's the redhead. Her dad's a pilot. I think he knows your dad."

Oops. Too much information.

"They've been asking people about me, but you probably already know that," he said pleasantly.

I nodded, relieved that he wasn't annoyed or angry. "Sorry. Not as noble as learning about people firsthand."

"I don't mind. Kind of says interested. How much did they learn?" The twinkle I'd enjoyed at the dance was back.

"They learned a lot." I tried to twinkle too, but it must have gone badly, because he said, "Hey, don't worry about it. I learned some things about you."

"That kind of says interested." Those words came out on their own, and I tried even harder to feign a calm I didn't feel. "What did you learn?"

"Learned by watching for you that we don't have classes in the same part of the school at the same time."

I wanted to stop and enjoy the thought of him watching for me, but I couldn't. "You're a junior. I'm a sophomore," I said. "You're an athlete, and I am so not."

"You're a writer. Saw you in Advanced Writing when I walked by. You must be good to take a senior class as a sophomore."

"I do okay," I said. Would he realize I was quoting him? His little smile said yes.

"Also learned you have late lunch," he said.

"Speaking of which, shouldn't you be in class right now?"

"Finished a test early. Asked Mrs. Hepworth if I could leave to take care of something. She said okay."

Bold Jenny took over. "Did she know 'something' meant meeting a girl at late lunch?"

"Might have let me anyway, but no. Need the office too."

My cheeks warmed again, and I made the understatement of the hour. "I'm glad you found me."

"So am I," he said. "Been hoping to run into you, but obviously that's going to be a challenge."

Going to be? Trying to be calm was a lost cause. My nerves buzzed, and my heart did something I couldn't name. Then Bold Jenny, who still felt a little hurt from three days of his silence, said the unsayable. "I was starting to think you didn't enjoy Saturday night that much after all."

His smile faded. "Don't think that. Been trying to find time for something." Now he sounded nervous. He looked down at Zeus, smiled wryly, and shook his head. "I should just say it."

He looked up. "I want us to get together this week. If you want to. But I can't do Saturday, and Friday's a game, and tonight I have to study."

I tried to appear calm, but I had no calm words. I raised my eyebrows and hoped he had a solution.

"Here's what I'm thinking," he said. "Tomorrow we're at home. I play the JV game. Then I have to stay and watch the varsity, which I would anyway. Thought maybe we could watch them together, if you don't have plans. If you want to. You could bring Zeus. Thing is, I can't leave to pick you up, so we'd have to meet there. And I don't even know if you like basketball, or if you want to go out with me. Guess one or the other might be enough."

I liked how he babbled when he was nervous, just like me. It was oddly calming. And of course I wanted to go out with him. But why did it have to be a basketball game?

"I've never been to a game before," I said.

"Medical reasons? We can find something else."

"No, just . . . I don't like sports."

He smiled, but maybe he was just hiding his disappointment. "If you've never been to a game, how do you know you don't like it?"

"I was bad at almost everything in gym class. I was terrible."

His smile grew. "Almost everything? What were you good at?"

"Worksheets. Walking too, I guess."

He chuckled. "Not asking you to play, just watch some guys play. But we can find something that's not sports." His eyes twinkled again. "Or find a worksheet for the game. You like food?"

"Who doesn't like food?"

"Might be surprised. Anyway, I'll buy you a hot dog. Or nachos. Or both. We can do ice cream somewhere later. Crap!"

My eyes went wide.

He pointed to the wall clock. "Lost track of time. Better hit the office before the bell, or I lied to Mrs. H. Gotta run. Bye, Zeus. Bye, Jenny. Think about it and text me, okay?"

He was gone before I could say anything, and Jack and Nikki were back.

"He looked nervous," Nikki said. "Did he ask you out?"

I nodded.

"Yes!" Jack pumped her fist. "A date with Cute Texas Boy."

I looked at her soberly and shook my head.

She was stunned. "You said no?"

I shook my head again.

"What's going on?" Jack demanded. "You like him, right?"

"Tell us everything," Nikki said. "Are you sad? You almost look sad."

After I explained, Nikki said, "Don't make him wait. Text him now. Tell him you'd love to watch the game with him, and you're sorry for being a dip for a minute."

"Which I am," I confessed. "Sorry and a dip. I do like him."

"You need to try to like at least one sport," Jack said. "Want some help with your text?"

I smiled faintly. "No. I'll do it now."

"Good," said Nikki. "See you later." She pulled Jack away with her.

There was no time to agonize through four drafts and still get to class. "Troy," I wrote, "I'm sorry for being a dip for a minute. I'd love to watch the game with you. Yes to food, and thanks."

I tapped the send button. Then I had another thought.

"Dad can bring me to the JV game and start explaining basketball. He's tried before with games on TV, but this time I'll listen. After your game, you can meet him, and he can leave." The rule said parents should meet your dates. It said nothing about them accompanying you.

Zeus and I made it to class on time. I spent part of the hour worrying that Troy might decide a dippy girl who didn't like sports wasn't worth his trouble after all. In between I wondered, did my second text message look too eager? I'd heard that a girl shouldn't send a second text until the guy replied to her first.

Just after school, my phone pinged. "Yay! Text you after practice."

I updated Jack and Nikki, then took a city bus to visit Grandpa for half an hour, then rode another bus home. They were happy bus rides. Then I sat in my room, alternately poking at my homework and hoping I could be good company at a game and even like basketball a little too, not just the boy.

I gave up on studying in my room, grabbed a book I had to read, and went to the kitchen. It was Mom's night to make dinner, and if I couldn't help her, I'd try to read there.

Mom and Dad were working at the dining room table, Mom with her laptop and Dad with a fat manuscript, likely his own, and a red pen. "I got dinner in the oven late," Mom said, "and I forgot to thaw the lasagna so it cooks faster. Probably 7:30 or a little later. Grab something if you're starving."

I wasn't starving. I joined them at the table. It was easier to force myself to read when they were there to notice if I wasn't turning pages.

Mom was taking the foil off the lasagna for the last ten minutes in the oven when my phone pinged again. It was Troy. "Finished dinner cleanup. You and your parents okay if we don't double or whatever? If it's just you and I?"

I was glad he cared about the rules but also distracted by how he asked. He not only knew to use "I" instead of "me" there, but he also cared enough to do it. I smiled broadly. Mom and Dad would appreciate this feat of grammar. If I told them.

"In a gym full of people," I wrote, "no problem. Afterward, they'll feel better if we're not completely alone, especially on a first date. So will I."

"Sounds good," he replied. "Time for homework. Tomorrow!"

Over dessert, which was leftover chocolate cake, I told Mom and Dad, "I have a date tomorrow night. I'm meeting Troy after his JV basketball game, and we're watching the varsity game."

"Sounds fun," Mom said with a smile.

"Sounds shocking," Dad said. "You realize that's a sporting event?"

I didn't take the bait. "I was hoping you could take me to the JV game and explain how basketball works. Then you can meet Troy and leave."

"So after all my failures, all it takes is a boy," Dad mused. "I'm in. Thanks for not being embarrassed to be seen with your dad at school. Before your date, not during it. I know my place." He started to sob, but I knew he was faking it.

12

The Date

D AD EXPLAINED IN A mock-tearful voice that he had dreamt of taking his little girl to a basketball game since before I was born. After all the negative things Mom and I had said to him about sports in the past, I took my medicine without protest. Besides, I enjoyed his ham acting.

He tried to persuade Mom to join us. "Honey, didn't you say recently that you'd go to a monster truck rally or watch paint dry or even attend a country music concert, if it meant spending time with me?"

"O-kay," I said slowly. "This is a side of my parents I don't need to see."

"You're not seeing it," Mom said. "That was, what, fourteen years ago? It was Valentine's Day, as I recall, and he'd just come home after being away for three weeks. He brought flowers, chocolate, and a romantic movie. We were all younger and dumber then."

"Jenny," Dad said with big, sad eyes I didn't believe for a second, "you're old enough to know Mom just stays married to me for the kids. I mean the kid. And the dog. And the occasional pun."

Mom couldn't keep a straight face. She laughed softly and reached for his hand.

I tried to look skeptical. "Really, Mom? Monster trucks? Country music? I'm so disillusioned."

"We never actually did those things," she said. "And there's nothing wrong with country music. It's just not to my taste."

"That doesn't help very much," I said.

"I'd love to meet Troy sometime," Mom said. "But one parent is plenty before your date and one too many during it, which is why he won't stay, even if it's a basketball game." She gave Dad an expectant look. He just smiled.

My phone vibrated. Dinner was over, so I could check. It was Troy again, and I had to smile, even if Mom and Dad were watching.

"Why was Cinderella bad at basketball?" he asked.

"She lost her shoe?"

"She ran away from the ball."

I sent a laughing smiley.

"And she had a pumpkin for a coach," he added.

I laughed softly and sent, "LOL. Literally."

"Something to share?" Mom already looked amused.

"Troy sent me a riddle."

Mom guessed the shoe. Dad guessed running from the ball, then laughed about the coach.

"See you tomorrow," Troy wrote.

"Good luck in your game," I replied, adding a smiling, black-haired girl emoji and a four-leaf clover. He sent a thumbs-up, a basketball, a hot dog, and ice cream.

"He makes you laugh," Dad said as I set down my phone.

"As you see." I said bookish things too, especially at home.

"An admirable quality in a young man."

"It's a requirement, Dad. It's like they say in Young Women and seminary. Any fool can know the gospel's true. Moroni promised that, right there in the last chapter of the Book of Mormon. But God either gave you a sense of humor or he didn't."

Mom tried to look serious. "They teach you that?"

"The testimony part, not in so many words. The rest is just obvious." I held her gaze and tried to look just as serious.

Dad turned to her. "Our comic theologian has a boy who likes making her laugh. How will it end? My daughter is scaring me."

She had her poker face working again, and she had his number too. "I don't remember telling you she's your daughter. I don't recall that you ever asked."

He exploded with laughter, and I laughed too. She finally smiled. She really was pretty, especially when laughter danced in her eyes—and when she looked at Dad.

Do the math, he had said. She was pretty, and I looked a lot like her.

Her face was thinner than mine, and there were subtle wrinkles at the corners of her mouth and eyes. She kept her hair shorter, and her eyes were green. But otherwise I had her face, her smile, and her hair. I had her blush too, and I used it more.

I wondered if she thought Dad was handsome. He worked out every day, between writing sessions, so he was fit. I was fond of his neatly trimmed beard, which he wouldn't have had if she didn't like it. It was gradually turning gray, like what was left of his blond hair. The effect was dignified and somehow comfortable.

So maybe he was handsome. But mostly he was Dad. And I definitely had his eyes.

⸺◆⸺

On Friday after school, Jack and Nikki came over to help me dress for my date. I was nervous, but they were stressing out. They debated what I should wear, as if the fate of nations hung in the balance. When I laughed, they stopped arguing and looked at me.

"Enough already," I said. "Nikki, what are you wearing tonight?"

"A nice school tee and skinny jeans, but—"

"You're the only one here who can wear skinny jeans," Jack said.

"She asked what I'm wearing." Nikki turned to me. "You could wear regular jeans. You'll be cute."

"Jack," I asked, "what are you wearing?"

"Jeans and my pep band shirt. It's basketball, not the New York Phil."

We settled on a nice pair of jeans that fit, but not like a coat of paint, and a red school t-shirt I'd worn only once before. It was one size too big, but I liked that. Snug t-shirts didn't flatter me like I wished they did.

They helped me with some subtle makeup. I wore my hair down and straight, as always, but we gave it a little more inward curl at the bottom.

⸺◆⸺

At the JV game Dad and I sat six rows up, near the middle, behind what Dad called the scorer's table. I'd been in the main gym before, at school assemblies, but I'd never sat higher than the second row, in case I had a seizure at just the wrong time. Dad said we could see the game better if we were higher, and he'd make sure I didn't fall.

I'd also never seen the gym so empty. There were barely 150 people there, including the players. Dad said JV games were like that when he played in high school.

He explained that the home team usually wore white, and the visiting team wore its colors—in this case, green—which I had already figured out. I liked Troy in his white uniform, with its red and black numbers and trim. He didn't look as skinny as most of the other players. He was more muscular and a little shorter. He subtly waved at me during his warm-ups before the game and after halftime.

Dad said he played well. "Watch how hard he works on defense. He's always between his man and the ball, unless his man has the ball. Then he's between the ball and the basket. His stance and his footwork are excellent. He's aware of the whole floor, and he's good at help-side defense. Now watch—right there—when somebody shoots, he blocks out before he goes for the rebound."

"Dad, I left my sports dictionary in my other life."

"Rebounding is getting the ball after a missed shot," he explained. "Before you go for the ball, you get in the way of the opponent nearest you, so he can't get to the ball. That's blocking out. It's a big part of the game. Nice pick!"

What I saw was Troy standing in the way of the opponent who was guarding another of our players, who had the ball. Their guy ran into Troy pretty hard, and our guy got away and scored.

"Isn't that a foul?" I asked. "On Troy? For getting in the way? Or the other guy for running into him?"

"It's a contact sport," Dad said. "And there's nothing cooler than picking someone really hard."

"Which one was picking?"

"Troy was. It means setting a screen. Getting in the way of the opponent who's guarding one of your guys. That way, maybe your guy gets loose and scores."

"It still looks like a foul."

"If Troy's still moving when the guy hits him, it's a foul on Troy," he said. "It's a foul on the other guy, if he hits Troy too hard or pushes him at all. That's the basic idea."

At the other end of the floor, a visiting player ran over Troy on the way to the basket, knocking him onto his back.

"Ooh, Dad!" I worried that Troy was hurt, but he bounced right up. A referee blew his whistle, used his fingers to signal a number to the scorer, then put both hands on his hips for a second. Troy scowled.

"What does that mean?"

"Blocking foul on Troy," Dad said, just before the announcer said it.

"Their guy knocked him over!"

"Troy moved into him with his hip and knee. It's the right call."

It was a lot to learn about something that was just a game, but I did my best. Troy was worth it. I hoped.

Later he got run over again. He took a few seconds to get up, but this time he smiled. The referee gave a different signal and pointed dramatically to the other end of the court. Troy's teammates on the floor high-fived him, and the guys on the bench stood and cheered.

"Now that was a charge," Dad said. "Nicely done!"

"Why is that a good thing?" I demanded.

"They don't score, we get the ball back, and the other guy gets a foul. Five fouls and he's out of the game."

"He could've been hurt. They both could've." I heard the distress in my own voice. Dad heard it too.

"Relax, okay? Basketball players are tougher than they look."

I took a deep breath. "You guys like doing this?" I asked. "This is fun for you?"

"Some girls like it too. It's a lot of fun. Much safer than football."

"If you say so." I'd never been to a football game, but I knew they wore helmets and lots of padding, and played on grass, not a hardwood floor.

We won the JV game, and the gym filled up quickly. I wasn't sure how long Troy would take to shower and dress. I was on pins and needles, watching Will and the varsity team warm up, and for whole first quarter of their game.

When Troy appeared, he smiled at me, and my nerves mostly went away. His hair was damp, and he looked great in his official red polo shirt and khakis. His upper lip was noticeably swollen.

"Hi, Jenny. Mr. Miller. It's a pleasure, sir." He shook Dad's hand. "And Zeus. Shake my hand?" Zeus lifted his paw.

I wondered if Troy would wait for me to extend my hand before offering his. His manners were that good. Remembering his quaint gallantry at the dance, I offered him my fingers with my palm down, instead of a regular handshake. I was pretty sure my twinkle was working.

So was his. He squeezed my fingers gently, and I knew instantly what Bold Jenny would do. Holding his happy gaze with mine, I closed my hand over his fingers and squeezed them for a second or two. His smile grew, and my twinkle felt like it turned into an all-out sparkle.

We let go, and he sat next to me, on the opposite side from Dad. Dad leaned forward and turned to him. "Great game tonight. You play smart, and you work hard."

"Thank you, sir. I'm just glad we won."

"Always more fun to win. Well, dads don't belong on dates, so I will take my leave." He offered to take Zeus home, and I agreed.

"Is 11:00 p.m. okay for you kids?" he asked.

"Yes, Dad."

"On second thought, make it 11:30," he said.

"Mr. Miller, you could stay and watch the game," Troy said. "Biggest home game of the year, probably."

"I love a good basketball game," Dad said. "But I'd rather my daughter were still speaking to me after tonight. She can tell me all about it when she gets home."

Like I could explain a basketball game.

"I don't mind if you stay a while," I said. It was almost true.

Dad glanced at the scoreboard. "Tell you what. We're halfway through the second quarter, almost. I'll watch until halftime. Nobody tell Mom. Then Zeus and I will magically disappear."

Teams kept calling time out, so the half lasted a while. Dad let us talk, except for asking two or three questions about the offense, which Troy answered in terms I mostly didn't understand. Having both of them there wasn't terrible, and they got along well.

The clock ran out, the horn sounded, and Dad stood up. "Time for us old farts to fade away. Great meeting you, Troy. You kids have fun. See you by 11:30."

I was already glaring at him for saying "farts." Mom and I did that a lot with certain words. I glared harder when he said 11:30 again. The time was fine, but repeating it in front of my date was too much.

I had to let him off the hook. "Thanks for explaining everything," I said. And not embarrassing me or my date too much, I didn't say. He didn't need the encouragement.

"You're welcome. It was the most I could do. Come on, Zeus."

13

The Real Date

Troy turned to me as Dad left with Zeus. "Hot dog and a drink? I'll get them, and you can sit."

"Yes, thank you. But first let's watch the dance team. I've never seen Nikki do a halftime show before." The pep band was just finishing a song. "It's fun to hear Jack in the pep band too," I said.

"What does she play?"

"Usually oboe, but not for pep band. Flute or clarinet mostly, I think, or whatever they need. She's that good."

After the dance team, which we both applauded enthusiastically, he went for food and drinks. Jack appeared next to me, and Nikki joined us few minutes later, after she'd changed out of her halftime outfit. I told them my date was going even better, now that Dad was gone and the real date had begun.

Troy appeared with the food. "Hi, Nikki," he said, "and it's Jack, right? Hi."

They said hi and smiled. They seemed shy, but I knew that wouldn't last.

He turned to me. "Got four hot dogs, in case we're hungry, but we could share instead."

I nodded, and he turned to Jack and Nikki. "Want one? Sorry, no extra drinks."

They each took a hot dog, and he displayed a collection of sauce packets. "Mustard? Ketchup? Relish?"

"Mustard and relish," Jack said. "Thanks." Her smile was already less shy.

Nikki blushed slightly. "Ketchup, please?"

While we ate, the teams came out to warm up, and soon it was time for Jack and Nikki to return to their duties. "Nice to meet you, Troy," Jack said. "Please have Jenny home by 11:00."

Nikki giggled, smiled, and gave a little wave.

"Trying for 11:30," Troy said.

The second half began, and we watched the game while we talked.

"I like your dad," Troy said.

"You're not just saying that?"

"Nope. He knows basketball. He's fun to talk to, like you. And he's good at not making your date uncomfortable."

"He didn't have to say 11:30 twice."

"Hey, he just met me, and I'm on a date with his daughter. So how's basketball so far? What you expected?"

"More or less," I replied. "Knowing a player or two helps. The strangest thing is all the shoes squeaking on the floor."

"Interesting. I don't even notice that."

"I'm not used to that loud horn yet, either. The hot dog's good."

"Was one enough?"

"Yes, thank you. It was nice of you to share. Was one enough for you?"

"According to my mom, no amount of food is ever enough. I'll probably grab something later. I usually do anyway. Were you disappointed that your dad stayed a while?"

"A little, but I got over it. Did you want him to stay, or were you just being polite?"

"We like people to watch our games, and I didn't want to look eager to get rid of him. Plus, if he stays, he gets to know me and maybe starts to trust me around his daughter and reports good things to your mom."

My eyes might have gone wide just then. "That's a lot of strategy for one date," I said. It was getting harder to tell Bold Jenny from Regular Jenny.

He smiled and turned back to the game. "Yup."

"If a girl were suspicious, she might wonder—"

Troy winced. "Oh, ouch. That's not good."

"What's not?" I worried that I shouldn't have said . . . something.

He pointed. Will was leaning on another player and limping off the court in obvious pain. "Looks like Will turned his ankle again."

"I guess he's done for tonight," I said.

"Maybe not. They'll probably just retape it. But I'm sorry. You were talking about a girl being suspicious." I glanced at him and saw a twinkle.

"Oh, yes. A girl might suspect you, uh, scored well in strategic thinking on the vocational aptitude test." I struggled to keep a straight face.

"Right," he said with a knowing smile and turned back to the game. "Actually, I did. So now that I've met your dad, what's your mom like?"

"A lot like Dad. Smart. Easy to talk to. Fun sense of humor. Nervous about the daughter dating, but she tries to hide it, like Dad. She's a great mom."

"Cool."

"On a good day, she might be cool," I said, in what I realized was a Mom-like tone.

He gave me a patient look.

"Okay, so most days with Mom are good days," I said.

He turned back to the game. "Are you a lot like her?"

"Dad says I am. I just caught myself sounding like her. I look a lot like her, except I have Dad's blue eyes. Hers are green."

"So she's beautiful," he said, still watching the game. "Gotta love genetics."

I didn't even try to hide my delight.

Will was back in the game a few minutes later, and he wasn't limping. Troy said he wasn't moving as well as usual, but he was too good to leave on the bench if he could play.

"I don't understand why you do this," I said. "You work for hours and hours, year after year, just to play for a few minutes twice a week. You get run into and run over and hurt, and sometimes that's supposedly a good thing. You must really love it."

"Yeah, we do." He turned to me with a one-sided smile. "Plus it helps us get girls."

I didn't know whether to be shocked or amused. I was a little of both. "I don't know about that."

"For example, at least tonight, basketball helped me get the girl."

His smile was playful, but there was something else in his eyes. The word *fondness* popped into my head. I didn't know what to do with that either.

"Okay, but I never saw myself as the kind of girl basketball would help someone get."

"That was before you got to know the handsome, charming gentlemen who play it."

"Some are more handsome and charming than others," said Bold Jenny.

"I'm taking that as a compliment," he said.

I tried for an innocent smile. "Your choice."

The game was close at the end. The crowd stood and chanted and cheered and stomped on the bleachers. I was uneasy with the bleachers shaking beneath us, but I seemed to be the only one.

I was more nervous about standing, but if I sat, I couldn't see.

Be bold, Jenny.

I wasn't bold enough to reach for Troy's arm and pull it around my waist—or just ask him to put it there. Maybe if his arm had been at his side. But his fists were up near his shoulders, and it would have been awkward.

He got more and more animated. We made a shot, which put us ahead by one point, and he raised one fist above his head. "Yes!"

He pulled it down and started almost chanting to himself, as the other team moved the ball up the court. His voice got steadily louder. "Get a stop, get a stop, get a stop, switch, help, switch, help, watch the roll . . . No! Yes! Yes! Yeah, Will!" He raised both fists high.

There was a timeout, and it was loud. Everyone clapped and stomped to the pep band's music. The tension and excitement affected me less than others, I thought—unless that's why I stayed standing like everyone else.

I noticed that cheerleaders had a purpose after all. They told us when to yell, "Go, Tigers!" or whatever, and the crowd fed off their energy, as they bounced and flipped across the floor and tossed each other into the air. It was so far beyond what I could do that they might have been a different species.

"Two seconds," Troy said, turning to me and smiling eagerly. "We get the ball inbounds, we beat the number one team in the state."

Which we did, so we did. The horn sounded, and everybody in the stands and on the floor went crazy, except the other team. Some of them hung their heads.

And except me. I started to clap.

Troy's face held pure joy. "Come with me!" He grabbed my hand, and by the time I realized I was living even more dangerously by just dashing down the steps, we were part of the celebration on the floor.

I'd never done anything like that, or wanted to. I saw high fives and fist bumps all around me, and people jumping into each other, which also looked dangerous. I noticed glares from a cheerleader or two, but I didn't care—especially when I realized Troy was treating me like a normal girl, not the girl with epilepsy.

He leaned down and said in my ear, "Let's find Will."

Will was on the team bench, leaning back and fist-bumping random students, with a big grin on his face and an even bigger ice pack on his knee.

Troy said, "You were awesome! That block at the end was highlight reel!"

It seemed wrong of Troy to care about wins more than wounds.

Will turned to me and held up his fist. It took me a second to realize he was offering me a fist bump. I aimed my fist carefully.

"Jenny, glad you came. Did you like it?"

"Big win, right?" I sounded stupid, but saying nice things about sporting events was new to me.

"Huge." He was much too happy for a star player with an injured knee.

"Will you be okay?" I asked.

"I'll be okay for next week."

"I'm glad. Does it hurt?"

"Yeah, but you know what?" He fist-bumped two more students.

"You love it? And it's a contact sport?"

"Yeah, it is, but the way Troy plays, he's in some pain too, even if he didn't sprain anything."

I looked at Troy. "You're in pain?"

He shrugged. "Have any ibuprofen? Forgot to take it before I came out and found you."

"Sorry, I don't." I liked that meeting me made him forget something.

"We can stop by the locker room."

I nodded. "Sooner than later, if you're in pain."

We said goodbye to Will. On our way out of the gym, Troy asked, "Ever been in a boys' locker room?"

I grimaced melodramatically—except I wasn't faking it. "No. Eww!"

He laughed. "Don't worry. Won't happen tonight either. I'm trying to make a good impression, not a disgusting one. Besides, girls aren't allowed."

"This girl's content to wait outside. Upwind, if possible."

"You're funny. And I know the perfect place."

In the hall near the locker room were some benches. Before I sat down, he said, "I owe you an apology."

"For what?"

"If you'd had a seizure anytime since the game ended, I couldn't have caught you. I'm glad you didn't, but I was pretty careless. Sorry."

"When we were going down the bleachers, that would have been a bad time for a seizure. But you can't hold me up all the time. Zeus doesn't. Besides, you hit the floor a few times tonight yourself."

He really had forgotten for a while that I wasn't a normal girl. For that, I looked him in the eyes and smiled. Really smiled. Which probably made the next thing worse, because people were watching us.

Well, not people so much as cheerleaders.

14

There's A Girl on It

T ROY EXCUSED HIMSELF TO go to his locker, and I sat on the bench in the hall. Two cheerleaders stalked by, with their red-and-white uniforms and their long, unnaturally straight hair in different shades of blonde. I tried to remember whether their hair had been down for all the bouncing and flipping, but I couldn't. They both glared at me.

One of them was Maddi. She spoke loudly as they walked away. "I can't believe Troy's with *that* again."

"It's just a service project," said the other. "Maybe he wants to be seminary president next year, and he's trying to impress people. He'll check the box and move on."

I pondered that for a minute. Nothing Troy had said or done suggested I was just a project for him. And I could almost hear my parents saying, "Consider the source."

Troy returned and sat beside me before I could stand. "Miss me?"

"Only a little." I was careful to sound unconcerned. I wanted to tell him about the cheerleaders, but I didn't want him to ask what they said.

The other school's cheerleaders walked by in green warm-ups, chatting quietly. One looked like she'd been crying. Two of the others smiled at us—probably at Troy, but he was looking at me.

"Thanks for coming tonight," he said. "I know basketball's not your thing."

"It's definitely new, including being on the floor after the game. Did I see chest bumping? Is that what it's called?"

"Probably did. Everybody was pretty happy."

"Happy's good," I said. "So where do you hurt?"

"Here and there." He extended one arm and winced. "Want the whole list?"

"As much as you want to tell me."

He leaned back and closed his eyes. "Neck's kind of stiff. Left shoulder feels a little strained. Bruised both elbows again, not too badly. Head hurts from hitting something, but the ibuprofen should kick in soon."

"Maybe it hit the floor," I said.

"Then I'm lucky I don't have a concussion."

"I've had concussions," I said. "Not recommended."

"I'll bet. Okay, what else? Tweaked an ankle, and my tailbone hurts. All that should be better by Monday. No jammed thumbs or fingers this week. Those can last a while."

"Your upper lip is swollen," said Bold Jenny, apparently unembarrassed at having noticed his lips.

"Yeah." He touched it gently. "Caught an elbow, maybe. Might have been my own guy, by accident. Anyway, elbows have done worse. No stitches, no missing teeth, no big deal."

"Troy! Now I'm imagining you spitting out teeth after the next game. Or during it."

"We wear mouth guards."

"Good." I reached for a more pleasant thought. "Dad liked talking basketball with you. There's literally no one at home to do that with him. He should have had a son."

"Instead of a daughter? No way."

All I could do was smile.

"So we could go for ice cream with some of the gang. Or I could just take you home, but don't pick that one, please."

"I vote for ice cream. I think it's unanimous."

At the concrete steps outside, he put his arm firmly around my waist. He kept it there all the way to his car.

"You said you'll be better Monday?" I asked as we walked. "Not tomorrow or Sunday?"

"Pretty sore tomorrow. Same on Sunday, but less."

"This is normal after a game?"

"I'm lucky. I play a lot," he said. "Oh, there's something going on with my arm too."

"Bruise, sprain, floor burn?" I knew all about floor burns from gym class.

I didn't see it coming.

"Not exactly," he said. "Just looked at it again, and there's a girl on it."

Regular Jenny wanted to swoon. "I noticed that too." Then Bold Jenny took over. "Do you think it's serious?"

"Not sure it's a problem. If it gets painful, I can have it removed."

A younger version of me had wished for a brother I could tease, who would tease me back without hurting me. This was better.

"Tell you what," I said. "If it gets painful, we'll get Jack to remove it for you. She's good at dissecting things. Nikki will gladly assist." I waited a second, because timing matters. "Oh, wait, you meant just the girl, not the whole arm?"

He grinned. "Kind of asked for that, didn't I?"

I nodded. "Kind of."

"Been friends a long time?"

"Inseparable since sixth grade. They've been great about my dog and my sitting all the time. And not driving. They're practically members of the family, and they're talented and smart. They're also really good at not making me feel like they're having less fun because I'm with them."

"Hanging out with you is more fun, not less," he said. "Even I know that."

I hadn't seen that coming either. I said something Mom-like again. "I've been told it offers some occasional, small pleasures."

His reply was perfect, a compliment but not overdone. "Yeah. It does."

Then came another first: I got into a car alone with a boy I liked as more than a friend.

I texted Mom and Dad about where we were going and told them we won the game. Dad replied that we should wear our seat belts. When I told Troy, he was suddenly very serious. "Always."

On our way to the ice cream place I asked, "Is the reason you love basketball so much because you like being on a team?"

I saw a smile by the dashboard's glow. "Probably the biggest reason. That and the competition."

His phone made the sci-fi sound again, and he handed it to me. "PIN's 2846. Check the message?"

"Someone named AJ says Frozen Paradise is too crowded," I reported. "Everybody's going to Granny's instead. There's a link with an address."

"That okay with you?"

"Sure."

We got there first and decided to wait for the others before ordering. The only place we weren't in the way was near a cooler full of beautiful ice cream cakes, so we admired those for a couple of minutes.

I admired them, at least. Troy looked tired or worse, especially around his eyes. I finally asked, "Are you okay? You look tired."

"I'm okay." He seemed to be forcing his smile.

"Are you in more pain than you said? The ibuprofen should kick in soon, right?"

"Something like that."

"We can order now and get you home a little sooner," I said.

"You're not about to suggest we skip ice cream and get me home a lot sooner, are you?"

"Not my first choice," I said.

He looked me in the eye. "I'm okay."

On the way home he said out of the blue, "I kind of lied to you. I'm sorry."

"About being in pain?"

"Can I tell you something sad?"

"Sure."

"Sad is not what I want you to remember from our first date."

Our future again! "I promise to have happy memories," I said.

"Sorry it took me until Thursday to see you again."

"You were busy, right?"

"Was busy Thursday too."

"What are you trying to tell me?"

"Went to somebody's house for Sunday dinner. Texted you about that."

"I remember."

"They had a nice ice cream cake for dessert."

"Okay," I said, when he didn't continue immediately.

"I think it gave me an old nightmare that night. Monday and Tuesday nights too."

"I don't understand."

"Sorry. In Texas . . . well, a guy I knew. Older than me, but I knew him pretty well. Anyway, one Saturday he met a girl he really liked at a church dance. A few weeks later they were picking up an ice cream cake together for somebody's birthday. He was driving, and they were in an accident. Bad one."

Hearing about bad accidents while I was riding in a car was almost as scary as seeing one, but my fear only lasted until Troy glanced at me. There was pain in his face, a pain that ibuprofen couldn't help, and I started to feel it too.

"She died at the scene," he said. "He died a few days later. Not their fault, or his, and they had their seat belts on. Some guy in a truck."

"Troy, I'm so sorry! He was your friend?"

He hesitated, then nodded. "Knew her a little too. She was nice."

"I'm so sorry. Then tonight, you and a girl you met at a dance just spent a few minutes at Granny's looking at ice cream cakes."

We pulled into my driveway, and he turned off the ignition. "Place in Texas was Granny Mae's."

"That's terrible! You and I should never go to Granny's again. We should never even go near Granny's again."

He shrugged. "Sorry to end on such a downer. The rest of tonight was really fun."

"I'm sorry I gave you nightmares. I'm the girl of your nightmares."

I was serious, but he gave me a faint smile. "You're not."

"Would you tell me if I were?"

"Don't know. Maybe. Probably. Feel like I want to tell you things."

"I'm glad you told me." Which might have been true. At least I was glad he wanted to tell me. "I'm glad you asked me out. Thank you."

I wanted to tell him things too. I took a deep breath. "By Thursday I thought you probably weren't interested after all."

"Wasn't that," he said. "Can we go out again soon? I'll be happier. I promise."

I didn't make him wait. "Yes."

"Thanks, Jenny." He seemed to mean more than just thanks for agreeing to another date.

"Thank you," I said, and I meant more too.

Before I fell asleep, and the next morning when I awoke, I worried about him having nightmares again, and it being my fault. He hadn't told me many details, and I was glad I hadn't asked.

I eventually noticed that he'd texted me just after 7 a.m., two hours before I was even awake: "Good morning. No nightmare. Thought you might worry about that. Kinda sore, but I'll stretch. Price of playing. See you soon."

I dressed for the day but sat a while in my room. I compared how nervous I felt before our date with how comfortable we were together by the end—so comfortable that we would say the things we'd said, especially what he'd said. I tried to identify a point during the evening when everything had changed for us, but I couldn't. I just knew that I liked him, and he liked me, and he trusted me, and I liked who I was when I was with him. We fit together—like old friends, but different.

The next week, Troy's games were both at home. On Wednesday and Friday he drove Zeus and me home from school, because he didn't have to be on a team bus to somewhere. Jack and Nikki took me to the JV games and watched them with me. Then Troy and I watched the varsity games together, and I kept learning about basketball.

Those were our only chances to be together. We filled the gaps with text messages and a few Skype calls. In between, I sometimes caught myself staring into space, wishing for hours to shrink magically into minutes, and minutes into seconds. It never worked.

Jack and Nikki tried to persuade me that our difficulty getting together just made everything more romantic. I said they'd never convince me that being apart was more romantic than being together.

I didn't tell them about Troy's nightmare or the story behind it.

They debated whether our New Year's resolution had worked for me. Jack thought it hadn't, because Troy first noticed me in my choir robe at my concert, not dressed up for a dance. Nikki thought it had, because

I dressed up for the dance where he introduced himself, and he kept coming back. I was glad there was something to debate.

That Friday, he made sure Jack and Nikki, not just his friends, were part of a group that gathered at his house for pie and ice cream after the game. He acted like including my friends wasn't a big deal, but it was to me.

There were ten of us there for pie, but only one was nervous about meeting his parents. They hadn't been at his last two games, so I hadn't met them there. I might have seen them at this one, but I didn't know who they were, and they'd left after the JV game, before he could introduce me. I wondered if they'd seen me.

15

To Pie and Beyond

M Y FIRST IMPRESSION OF Troy's home was the tantalizing smell from the kitchen. His mom baked pies every Friday afternoon, and this time she made three extra for the postgame crowd. Troy said she hurried home after his game to bake them, so they could cool.

His parents were still in red Lakeside High sweatshirts, which was less weird than Mom and Dad wearing matching movie night sweaters. They were friendly and gracious, and maybe a bit shy or nervous at first.

I tried to be as comfortable as Troy had been with Dad, but I felt like I was on trial. I wondered what he'd told them and what they would think of me. Would they think I was good enough to date their son?

It helped to realize that their nerves—if that's what I saw—probably meant they wanted to impress me too, at least for Troy's sake. I was still glad I wasn't the only guest.

I mostly watched and listened to the chatter around the dining room table, while Troy and his dad served pie and ice cream to the girls, then the boys. Will talked with Jack and Nikki. I wondered if helping them feel comfortable outside our circle was something he did spontaneously, or if Troy had asked his best friend to help my best friends feel at home. Either way, it worked.

I was two glorious bites into my peach pie and French vanilla ice cream, when I felt a tap on my shoulder. It was a little blonde girl with eyes like Troy's and a red school t-shirt.

"Hi. My name is Lily Pullman. Nan and I—she's the middle sister—want you to sit with us for a while, if that's okay. You can bring—" She corrected herself. "You *may* bring your pie. We're not allowed to eat there, but you are. Plus we already ate ours, and we can't have seconds, because Mom said we made our firsts too big. Come with me, please."

I excused myself from the table, trying not to look as amused as some of the others.

Lily escorted me to a sofa in an alcove at the end of the dining room and introduced me to the girl who was already there.

"This is Nan. She's in eighth grade. You should sit between us. You can put your pie and water on the coffee table. We don't drink coffee, but that's what we call it."

Nan was a few years older than Lily, but their hair, eyes, and shirts matched. Her build reminded me of Nikki. Troy had said his sisters were dancers.

I smiled at her. "Hi, Nan. It's nice to meet you. And thank you, Lily."

Nan smiled too, and her cheeks colored a bit. "Nice to meet you." Her voice was lower than Lily's and a little breathy.

I sat between them.

"Troy's right," Lily said. "You're pretty. He says you're smart and funny too. Is he in love with you? Is black your real hair color? I like it."

Nan leaned forward and frowned at Lily, shaking her head. Lily stuck out her tongue. I smiled and answered the less exciting question. "Thank you, Lily. Black is my natural color. And Troy's very kind. Is he a good brother?"

She nodded vigorously. Then they—mostly Lily—asked me one question after another about myself, my family, Zeus, and my choir.

Troy pulled up a chair and listened for a minute, pie in hand. Then he told them it was their turn to tell me about themselves, so I could eat before my ice cream melted. They were self-conscious, and he had to coax them. It was adorable.

"You should meet our sister Beth," Lily said. "She's at college, and she knows almost everything. She's really nice, except when she's not. She's pretty too." She looked past me to Nan. "Beth is pretty, isn't she?"

"Just like you," Nan said.

Lily beamed.

Before long, Nan took Lily off to bed, and Troy and I rejoined the others for a raucous game of *Apples to Apples*.

By 11 p.m. the others had left, including Jack and Nikki. Ten minutes would get me home, which left twenty minutes for Troy and me to spend with his parents.

Be bold, Jenny, I thought.

Not too bold, I thought.

I began helping Troy rinse the dishes and load the dishwasher, but his mom took me gently by the arm. "Thank you for wanting to help, but Troy can handle this, and you're a guest. Why don't we sit and get acquainted? He won't be long."

Mrs. Pullman was two or three inches taller than me. She seemed young for the mother of a college student and trim for a mother of four. Her blonde hair barely touched her collar. Her smile looked a lot like Troy's.

She sat beside me on the sofa in the alcove, and Mr. Pullman joined us too. He was about Troy's height, with a similar athletic build but a little heavier. His hair was a darker brown and tipped with gray on the sides. He could have been on an airline pilot recruiting poster.

He pulled up a chair for himself, as Troy had earlier, leaving a place for Troy next to me on the sofa. His smile matched his wife's, so maybe Troy's came from both parents.

They said they'd enjoyed meeting Jack and Nikki. Then we learned things firsthand about each other that we already knew secondhand. When I mentioned that Mom was an English professor and Dad was a writer, Mr. Pullman said, "I understand you're a writer too. What do you like to write?"

"Besides very literate text messages," Mrs. Pullman added.

I smiled shyly. Enough parents, including mine, claimed the right to read their teenagers' text messages that I had never assumed Troy would be the only one seeing mine. I wondered if they'd read them all.

"I enjoy almost everything, so I guess I don't know yet."

"There's no hurry, is there?" she asked.

"I'm only a sophomore."

"A sophomore who writes well enough for advanced senior English," said Mr. Pullman.

"It's probably hereditary," I said.

Mrs. Pullman smiled. "Speaking of offspring, you held your own with Lily and Nan. They can be a handful. Especially Lily."

"It was fun to meet the sisters Troy told me about," I said. "In some ways it was like talking to him."

"Did I hear my name?" Troy landed on the sofa beside me.

I tried not to look or sound relieved. "We were comparing you to Nan and Lily."

"How'd I do?"

"We decided you're different, but we like you anyway."

I wondered if his parents were smiling at what I said, how I said it, how I looked at Troy when I said it, or how he looked at me, which had me melting again.

When it was time for him to take me home, I tried again to hide my relief. His parents had been gracious, and I liked them, but meeting them was still an ordeal.

I was two or three steps from the sofa, automatically keeping the best distance I could from hard furniture, when something crunched softly under my foot. I felt it more than I heard it—and it was pie. The crunchy part was a bit of crust, but there was part of a peach too, which I had just smashed into their carpet.

"What's wrong?" asked Troy's mom.

"I'm so sorry. I think I just ground some pie into your carpet." I looked at Troy. "I'll clean it up, if you—"

"Troy, please bring us two damp rags and that orange spray bottle of carpet cleaner," said his mom.

I looked at her sheepishly. "I wasn't watching where I put my feet. It was probably my pie, too. I'm the only one who ate in here. I'm sorry."

"Trust me," she said. "This carpet has already seen much worse."

Troy reappeared.

"You do the shoe, Troy," she said. "I'll get the carpet. You two are on a clock, right?"

Before I knew it, she was on her hands and knees with the spray bottle and one of the rags, scrubbing at the little mess I'd made.

"Sorry," I said to Troy.

He was smiling. "Why don't you take off your shoe and hand it to the guy with the rag?"

I cocked my head and reached for the rag. He pulled it away and raised his eyebrows. I made an embarrassed little noise, steadied myself with a hand on his arm, lifted my foot, pulled off my shoe, and handed it to him.

When I looked down to slip it back on, I saw the gaping hole in the toe of my sock. By then Troy and his mom must have seen it too. I slipped my shoe back on and suppressed a frown.

"We should go," Troy said.

"Mrs. Pullman, I'm really sorry about the carpet," I said.

She smiled. "It'll be fine. You two should hurry—but not speed, Troy."

On the way home I tried not to stew about the pie, the carpet, and the sock. We were halfway to my house, pulling up to what we knew was a long red light, when he interrupted the story he was telling about his sisters. "Jenny, would you mind if I held your hand?"

What I should have said without hesitation was, "I'd like that." I couldn't form the words.

My brain took off on its own. Why did he think he needed to ask? He'd held my hand before. Was he timid? Or trying to be respectful? Was this time different?

It was different. He wasn't walking me onto a dance floor or pulling me down from the bleachers for a victory celebration. The only reason for him to hold my hand now was . . . to hold my hand.

My heart thumped its approval—not that he could hear it—while I tried to regain my power of speech. Wondering what he was thinking and feeling, while his question hung in the air, just made it worse.

If I couldn't say something, I had to do something. His right hand was on the gear shift lever between our seats, but he wouldn't need to shift for a while. I reached out, and our fingers somehow automatically intertwined.

My heart danced; it might have been a waltz. I looked up at his gentle smile, then down at our joined hands resting on my leg, and wondered at how well they fit together, when his was so much larger than mine. Then I knew what to say.

"Turns out I don't mind at all." I looked up and smiled ruefully. "I'm sorry I left you hanging while I tried to think of what to say. I wasn't deciding whether I wanted this or not."

He squeezed my hand. "I was a little worried."

After that, it was good that he knew where I lived. All I knew for the next five minutes was that we were holding hands, and I was happy.

He had to let go to shift into Park, walk around, and open my door, but our hands found each other again, and I wished the walk to my front door were a lot longer.

⸺◆O◆⸺

The next morning, Troy picked me up on his way to do a little shopping, just so we could spend some time together. On our way home he said his family had talked about me over breakfast. "They all like you," he said, grinning mischievously. "So far."

"What else did they say?" Had anyone mentioned my embarrassments as we were leaving?

"Dad said you're smart and sweet. Mom said you're genuine, and she really likes that. So do I."

"I was genuine?" It didn't feel like much of a compliment. "So I'm genuinely a girl who babbles nervously when she tries to have a conversation, a klutz who grinds homemade peach pie into a nice carpet, and a dork who can't be bothered to check her socks for gaping holes?"

Troy frowned. "That's not what she meant. Why do you do this?"

"Do what?"

"Mom said something really nice about you, and she meant it. I asked her to explain, and she said you don't put on airs. You're not wearing a mask. You're just you. No façades, I think she said. But you take a really nice compliment and act like it's a bad thing, and pile more bad things on top."

"I thought about this last night," I said. "I'm genuinely bad at having a social life."

"What are you talking about?"

"Think about it. The first time you asked me to dance, I really wanted to, but it took me half an hour to say yes. When you met me at lunch to ask me out, I wanted that too, but I couldn't give you a straight answer until after you had to go. Last night, I wanted you to hold my hand, but I still left you hanging for a minute. And that was after the pie on the carpet and the hole in my sock."

I ignored the color high on his cheeks and the angry set of his mouth. "So, yes, I'm genuine," I said. "That's genuine Jenny."

He sighed loudly and shook his head. "Why do you do this? Why can't you think good things about yourself?"

We pulled into my driveway. I was speechless, reeling from his questions.

He filled the silence. "When I say you're beautiful, do you tell yourself you're not? Geez, Jenny, do I have to stop saying it, so you won't do that?"

I looked into his eyes for a minute, and my chin started to tremble. "Sometimes I do that," I said softly. "Not always. Please don't stop saying it."

His gaze softened. Then a tear ran down my cheek, and he instantly looked distressed. "I'm sorry I made you cry," he murmured.

"I'm not sure it was you." I willed my gathering tears to keep their places. "It probably wasn't."

"My parents like you," he said. "They don't care about the carpet. Even if they did, it turned out fine. They didn't mention the hole in your sock. And Mom says you being genuine is a welcome contrast to some other girls I've taken home. She's not wrong."

I tried to smile, but it didn't go well.

"Could you do something, please?" he asked. "For me, if not yourself?" He still sounded upset.

"Okay."

"Stop beating yourself up inside your head."

I stared at my feet, nodded slightly, and said, "I'll try." I hesitated, then looked up at him. "I'm sorry."

"Just stop doing it, okay? You deserve better."

⸺◆⸺

Our conversation ate at me all day. It stung, even after I realized Troy had loyally defended me against myself. More than that, he was genuine, and that was one of my favorite things about him. Getting upset that his mom called me genuine made no sense.

I wasn't sure I deserved better, like he said, but the part of me he didn't like was a part I didn't like either. So I resolved not to be that way—and when I failed at that, which I would, I could do better at keeping it to myself.

Our next Skype conversation felt awkward at first. So did the next time we saw each other in person. But I did better at keeping certain thoughts unspoken, and things between us went back to being amazing.

Week followed week. I savored our new routine and the completely unexpected fact that a nice boy liked my hand in his—and liked talking with me and listening to me. Even looking at me.

More than once I smiled and shook my head at a stranger thing. After several basketball games filled with explanations, I'd developed unimaginable skills, like telling a man-to-man defense from a zone.

Nikki and Jack kept asking me when Troy and I would finally get around to Defining The Relationship. I said I was in no hurry to Define anything. We were friends—okay, good friends who held hands, gazed happily into each other's eyes, and spent every spare minute together, which wasn't a lot. I didn't need any more Definition than that. Not yet.

Either that didn't satisfy Nikki and Jack, who had only slightly more experience than I had with boys—before I met Troy—or they just liked talking about it. The DTR question came up almost daily in one form or another.

One Saturday in my room, it was Nikki saying dreamily, "On Valentine's Day, maybe he'll kiss you and ask you to be his girlfriend." Then she came down to earth rather abruptly, I thought. "Would you let him kiss you? Do you want him to? Would you kiss him back?"

"Yes, yes, and yes," I said, "but what if I'm terrible at it? I've never had a boy to kiss."

"Neither have I," Jack said. "Neither has Troy, we hope. Nikki had one once."

I looked at Nikki expectantly. "I didn't know that."

She blushed. "Third grade. It was over almost before it began, and it was, I don't know, dry and weird. He smelled like school lunch pizza. It would probably be better now. I hope."

"It was Timmy Wells," Jack said. "He moved away at the end of the year, because she wouldn't agree to marry him when they're older."

"His dad changed jobs," Nikki said. "But it's true I've already refused a marriage proposal. And that's still my only kiss, which is rather sad."

All of which was interesting, but less so in that moment than my question. "What if I'm terrible at it?" I repeated.

Nikki furrowed her brow.

Jack cocked her head to the right and pushed out her lips a little, as she often did when concentrating. Then she produced a mischievous smile. "Get him to practice with you until you're good at it."

For such a logical thought, that did a pretty thorough job of making me blush. My heart beat faster, and my stomach got all . . . something. Fluttery, maybe.

"Kissing can't be difficult," Jack said. "There are billions of people on the earth. They all had to be born, so they all had to be conceived. Kissing probably preceded that in most cases. So pretty much anyone can figure it out."

"Kissing and other activities," Nikki said.

I tried not to visualize any other activities. "I'm thinking aloud here. Some couples are more serious than others, right?"

"Sure," Nikki said. "You mean more physical?"

"Not really. I mean, obviously that's true. But some kids have a girl-friend or boyfriend just for the sake of having one, right? And maybe some light hand-holding and a kiss or two?"

"Or endless hours of NCMO," Jack said.

I made a face. I'd never liked that acronym. It sounded coarse.

"What are you asking?" Nikki said.

"I guess I'm saying I don't want that kind of boyfriend, and I don't want to be that kind of girlfriend."

Jack spoke up again. "You want Committal Making Out, without the Non?" Her eyes twinkled proudly.

I blushed again. Because I did want that. Sort of. Eventually. Within limits. "What I'm trying to say is, a boy should want me for his girlfriend because he likes me personally, not just the idea of having a girlfriend, and not just the possibility of exploring whichever body parts I'll let him touch. The very few parts I'll let him touch. I want him to like spending time with me and talking with me. And vice versa. I want to build a relationship, not just hang out for a few days or weeks until one of us gets bored or distracted and moves on. That stuff is so high school."

"We're in high school," Jack said. "But I get it. You want a boyfriend who's a good friend and wants to stay a while, not some horndog who just hangs around to see if you'll eventually let him go biological."

I moved my mouth, but no sounds came out. *Go biological?*

Jack grinned. "You don't like NCMO. We need a new term."

"I don't know why you're worried," Nikki said. "You want a boyfriend who likes you the way Troy likes you, and vice versa. And you want it to last a while. You're practically there already."

"That's a happy thought," I said.

It was a warm, energizing thought. Valentine's Day couldn't come soon enough.

16

My Valentine

As Valentine's Day approached, I complained. A lot. To Mom, Dad, Jack, Nikki, and especially my captive audience, Zeus. Troy had an away game that night, which was unusual for a Thursday, and it was something like 83 miles from home. I probably could have found a ride to the game, but I had a checkup with my neurologist late that afternoon, and those were nearly impossible to reschedule. But it was bigger than that.

For once I had a boy who liked me, and I liked him, and we'd barely see each other on the most romantic day of the year. What kind of sociopath scheduled basketball games on Valentine's Day?

I finally complained to Troy, but more gently, as he walked me to my locker one morning. He put an arm around my shoulders and squeezed. "Yeah, it stinks. Amazing girl here. Boy who likes her, hundreds of miles away."

He liked me enough to sound sad about it, which made me sort of cheerful. "We'll make the best of it," I said. "It's not really hundreds of miles."

"Might as well be. What do you have in mind, valentine?"

I beamed at him. No boy had ever called me his valentine before. Then I told him the truth. "Nothing," I said. "I've been too busy complaining, but I can be done with that. I'll take good care of my long-distance valentine."

As he would for his, he said.

First thing on February 14, I sent Troy a text message. "Good morning! Happy Valentine's Day! (This is only the prelude.)"

He replied, "Happy Valentine's Day! Wish I didn't have a game tonight. Not sure I ever wished that before."

"Patience," I wrote. He sent back a smiley.

When I opened my locker before lunch, my books had been re-arranged to make room for a vase with four roses: white, pink, lavender, and red.

Leaning against the vase was a lilac envelope with my name in a familiar hand. The card inside was homemade, with a colored pencil drawing on the front. A brown-haired boy and a black-haired girl smiled and held hands. My fingers trembled as I opened it.

I read softly to Zeus. "Dear Jenny, I can't decide whether you're as pretty as flowers, or flowers are as pretty as you. Wish we could dance tonight. I'll be thinking of you.

"Have a wonderful day, Valentine! —Troy

"PS: Nan hopes you like her drawing. I commissioned it."

I was still standing there a minute later, warm on the inside, smiling dumbly on the outside, looking from my card to my flowers and back again, when Jack and Nikki came by. They both acted surprised, but no one else knew my locker combination.

Lunch was next, but before I could eat I had to text Troy, so he'd see my message before he left for his game.

"Troy, thank you! The flowers are beautiful. So's the card. Nan's an artist, and you're sweet. On the bus, please remember not to think about me until after the game. You have a job to do. We'll both be patient. Good luck!"

I tapped the send button just as Nikki said, "Got it," and looked up from her own phone.

Jack swallowed a bite of pizza. "Got what?"

"What we need to decode the bouquet."

I was pretty sure my eyes were sparkling. I knew what the red rose meant, even if we weren't saying it in words yet.

"There's nothing ambiguous about red," Nikki said. "According to this it means love. And longing." She smiled mischievously. "And desire."

I turned my own lovely shade of red and said nothing.

"White is for purity, chastity, and innocence, so you can stop blushing. No, don't. It's also for weddings. Do we need to remind you that high school is far too young to get married?" Her eyes sparkled too.

"Yes, because she doesn't have parents, after all," Jack said drily. "Or a brain. Weddings in general? Or just first-time, virginal weddings?"

I uttered a meaningless syllable and hid my flaming face in my hands.

"Sorry," Jack said, but there was laughter in her voice.

My hands muffled my words. "No, you're not. But that's okay." I composed myself and looked up. They were watching me and grinning. "We're officially going with purity, chastity, and innocence," I said. "What about pink?"

"Friendship, admiration, and/or happiness," Nikki said.

"Perfect," I said. "Lavender?"

"Lavender's big. Enchantment, fascination, adoration, and—wait for it—love at first sight."

"Wow," I said, because it was all I could say. It wasn't just the lavender rose or even the red one. It was the whole bouquet. The boy who gave it to me and wrote the note. And how I'd felt with him, and about him, since we met.

"How did this happen?" I asked. "I never imagined our New Year's resolution working faster for me than for you."

"It's working for us too," Nikki said. "Something is. We've met some pretty nice guys, mostly by hanging out with you and Troy."

"Okay, but how am I suddenly the one with the amazing boyfriend?"

"Had to happen sooner or later," Jack said. "We know you're amazing, and a great guy just discovered it too. He's probably not the last. If you have any extras, don't discard them too cruelly, please. One of us might want them."

Nikki giggled.

"Do you think he knows what the colors mean?" I asked. "Maybe he picked a random bouquet he thought I would like."

Nikki said, "Everybody knows red and probably white, and anyone with half a brain can interpolate pink. Lavender's the giveaway. This is not a random grocery store bouquet. Not that there's anything wrong with those."

"But he's a boy. He may not even know the color lavender."

"He has a mom and sisters. And the Internet," Nikki replied. "Maybe he asked the florist. Anyway, you have a totally smitten boyfriend, and it was pretty close to love at first sight."

"Not officially a boyfriend," I said. "Not yet."

"It looks almost official," Nikki said.

"Wow," I repeated.

Before fourth period I tried to text Troy again, but I didn't know what to say. I had thoughts I couldn't send.

"Re: flowers. Message received. I love you too"? Maybe someday.

"Yes, I'll officially be your girlfriend. Please ask me soon"? Not that either.

"My heart is yours. Keep it as long as you want. Forever would be nice."? Yes, but no.

"I'm so happy! You know what all those colors mean, right?" A definite no, in case he didn't.

Just before I had to give up and turn off my phone for class, he replied to my earlier text. "Glad you like them. Jack and Nikki sent a candid of you at your locker. Very cute. Wish I could have been there. About the bus ride: I will obey. Won't be easy."

I hastily sent him a heart. A red one. I wondered if Valentine's Day made that ambiguous. Then I wrote, "I didn't know there's a picture. Do I look as giddy as I feel?"

⸺◆⸺

At my appointment my neurologist said I looked unusually happy. Did it have something to do with Valentine's Day? I said yes, and she said, "He must be a young man of taste."

The medical part of the visit was routine, but I was her last appointment, and we spent an extra ten minutes talking about Troy. I told her about the card and the flowers, and what I had planned for him later, even though we'd be miles apart.

I realized too late, as Dad drove me home, that I'd been self-centered. I hadn't thought to ask about her Valentine's Day.

⸺◆⸺

I could hardly wait for evening—7:45 p.m., give or take.

Will had enlisted the JV team manager to deliver two things for me after Troy's game: an envelope and a gift-wrapped water bottle with the colors and logo of Troy's favorite NBA team, the San Antonio Spurs. Over and over I imagined him opening the envelope, removing the card, and reading what I'd written—what Bold Jenny had written after discarding drafts for about a week. It wasn't a masterpiece, but it was as much of me as I could stuff into an envelope.

"Dear Valentine—calling you that makes me happy—I wish you didn't have to be far away tonight, doing glorious battle for the honor of our school. I hope you played well and won and didn't get hurt. When you read this, I'll be getting ready for tonight's dance.

"Here are two photos of me in my dark green dress, which I'm wearing to the dance. One's a close-up, so you can see my smile when I think of my distant but gallant cavalier and point guard.

"Look at my hands in the other one. They'll wish you were holding them tonight, instead of, say, a water bottle.

"I probably won't dance without you, but I like sitting and thinking of you. If any boys come by, I'll be friendly and try to concentrate on them until they leave. Then I'll go back to thinking of you.

"Now that your duty is done, I hope you'll think of me once or twice. Could you please smile when you do? I'm fond of your smile.

"Happy Valentine's Day. —Jenny

"PS: Go, Spurs! Tigers too, of course."

His text came at 7:53. "Thank you! Love the card, read it three times already. The water bottle's perfect. You're beautiful, and my hands are lonely too. I'll think of you only once tonight, starting five minutes ago and ending when I'm home and unconscious and can't think anymore. We won, and I did all right."

He wrote "all right" correctly, as two words.

I replied, "You should see my smile right now."

"Could I see it in person tomorrow?"

"I'll trade it for one of yours. Gotta run. Jack and Nikki are here to whisk me away to the ball."

"Have fun," he wrote. "I know you don't do selfies, but you could hand your phone to Jack or Nikki. Can't text you during the varsity game. No service in the gym. I'll check in at halftime."

That would be less than an hour. "I can hardly wait."

Jack and Nikki spent at least five minutes with me when we got to the dance, trying different settings, poses, and expressions, before they had two photos they thought were just right. They added captions: "Jenny thinking of Troy" (I had a happy smile) and "Jenny at the Valentine's dance without Troy" (I looked pouty and sad). I added only, "Photos and captions by Nikki and Jack," and sent them.

After that I had a lot less time to miss him than I expected. Boys kept coming to sit with me. Four were fellow sophomores. Two were seniors from my writing class. There was one brave freshman, who was too young to be a desirable, technically, but he was okay.

For a few minutes it was two boys at once, with me in the middle. My phone vibrated, then vibrated again. I wanted to excuse myself, but I couldn't be that rude.

Another boy came as they left. When I could finally check my phone, I had three messages from Troy, and in a way it was too late.

The first one said, "Beautiful! Thanks!"

The second said, "Here's a photo." He was in front of a "Happy Valentine's Day" sign at the other school, smiling, waving, and holding up his new water bottle. I wanted to melt. I wanted him with me, to melt me in person.

His last message said, "Must be busy. That's good. Miss you tonight."

I stared at the photo, missing him, until I thought I'd better reply while I could. At least he'd have a message from me after the varsity game.

"Sorry! Lots of boys tonight, but no you. Thanks for a wonderful Valentine's Day. Have a safe trip home."

Another boy approached.

⋅⋅◆⋅⋅

It was a school night, so the dance ended early. When I pulled my coat from the back of my chair and put it on, I found something new in one of the pockets. It was from Troy. I thought Jack or Nikki must have delivered it, but they said they hadn't.

It was my favorite Lindt chocolate bar, with a handwritten note attached in a small envelope. "Jenny, is it too late to wish you a happy Valentine's Day one more time? I thought you could share this with Jack and Nikki or your Mom and Dad. I have another for us to share later. Hope the dance was fun. Was my messenger charming? Miss you. —Troy"

I had no idea which boy was his messenger, if it even was a boy.

It was just after 10 p.m., so I couldn't text him to say thanks. We'd made a rule for ourselves, at our parents' suggestion. We didn't text, call, or e-mail each other after 10 p.m., unless we were somewhere together and got separated. We hadn't thought to add an exception for being far apart on Valentine's Day, on a bus and at a dance.

Jack, Nikki, and I headed home. There wouldn't be smoothies on a school night, but we split half of Troy's chocolate three ways while we compared notes. Jack and Nikki had attracted some desirables too. Something was working.

I finally tuned out their chatter, melted into the back seat, rehearsed all the sweet things Troy had written to me that day, and tried to remember the feeling of his arms around me.

At home I shared the rest of the chocolate with Mom and Dad and told them about my day. They thought one of the two boys who sat with me at the same time might have been Troy's messenger, with the other one there to distract me during the delivery.

"Or vice versa," Dad said.

17

Outside the Lines

O N THE SUNDAY AFTER Valentine's Day, a tall girl named Britney conducted our Young Women opening exercises to begin the third hour at church. We always met together for a hymn, a prayer, and announcements before splitting into three classes by age group.

She said the Beehives—the twelve- and thirteen-year-olds—would meet in their regular classroom for their lesson, while the two older groups stayed together. That wasn't unusual. Either we were missing a teacher or we older girls were having a lesson which didn't suit the younger ones.

The Beehives and their advisors left, and Sister Alberson stood to begin our lesson. She was the youngest of our adult leaders and advisors. She was only 24, and some of the older girls called her by her first name, Cori. The rest of us called her Sister A.

She worked at a bank, but she should have worked on the women's floor of an expensive department store. She always looked amazing, from her straw-colored, shoulder-length hair to her generous collection of tasteful but fashionable shoes. This time she wore a simple navy ankle-length dress with a tie at the waist, and a pair of caramel-colored dress sandals some of the girls had admired before the meeting.

We knew she cared about us, and being a newlywed gave her added credibility, but her teaching didn't thrill me. She often didn't think things through before she said them, so she didn't always make sense. She could speak with great conviction, even when she contradicted what she'd said a minute earlier, also with great conviction.

As she stood to begin her lesson, I reminded myself not to laugh sarcastically, which I wouldn't anyway, and not to get frustrated, which

I probably would, and not to raise my hand to hint at some problem in her lesson.

She said, "What we're talking about today is super important. We'll be walking on sacred ground. I need you to remember that."

The first thing I wanted to say, but didn't, was that our lessons were nearly always religious, so walking on sacred ground wasn't unusual. I reminded myself to keep my mouth shut, or at most speak only when spoken to.

"As you know," she said, "if we want to live eternally in the celestial kingdom with God and the Savior and our eternal families, we have to obey God's laws. Our lesson today is on dating and the law of chastity. If you're like me, this time of year is a great time for this topic, because our heads are filled with romantic thoughts."

She glanced at her notes, then looked up and smiled sweetly. I wondered if her notes said to do that.

"Our physical bodies are sacred gifts from God. So is the power in them to procreate."

She looked toward the back row. "Hallie, thank you for raising your hand. Do you have something to contribute?"

Hallie was fourteen. She could be pretty funny, and she didn't always wait to be called on. A few months earlier, in our last lesson on this topic, she'd asked, "Is 'procreate' different from 'create'? Will we be doing it professionally?"

Almost everyone had laughed, including me—but not that day's teacher or Hallie's older sister, Megan, who was mortified, as usual.

Today Megan was on the front row, two seats from me. She cringed when she heard her sister's name, before Hallie could say anything cringeworthy.

"Wouldn't the Sunday before prom be the best time for this lesson?" Hallie asked. "Then we could have a lesson on repentance after prom, for anyone who didn't listen well enough the week before."

Some of the girls snickered. Megan turned and delivered a death glare.

Sister A smiled even more sweetly. "Why do you think that, Hallie?"

Now I cringed. How dumb did Sister A have to be to ask her that?

Or maybe she wasn't dumb, because Hallie was suddenly flustered. "Well, you know. Prom. And . . . you know."

Sister A nodded. "I see what you mean. Maybe we'll talk about this again before prom. But I went to prom every year, and I always liked my date, and we never got involved in any 'you know.'" Her eyes twinkled. "Speaking of which, who can define the law of chastity for us?"

No one raised a hand. Which meant I was about to hear my name, because I was reliable and safe—as long as she couldn't read my mind.

"Jenny, how would you define the law of chastity?"

I knew one way to say it without blushing. "Abstinence before marriage. Fidelity in marriage."

She nodded. "Perfect. Can you say it in smaller words?"

My cheeks warmed. "No sexual activity outside of marriage."

"Good job. Anything you'd like to add?"

"Not really. I'm not married."

I was pretty sure the snort behind me came from Hallie—and that Megan was about to be mortified again.

Sister A's eyes went a little wide, and she scowled in Hallie's general direction. "Sacred ground, remember, Hallie? Please?" She held her pose for a moment, probably waiting for a sign of surrender from Hallie. Finally she glanced down at her notes.

"Okay, moving on. The law of chastity is a big commandment, one of the most important, which you know, because we've been telling you since you were twelve. Breaking it is a big-time sin with serious consequences. You won't have the Spirit of God with you, and that's really bad. There are some obvious physical risks and some emotional risks too. And while it's true that you can repent and be forgiven, it's also true that breaking the law of chastity can jeopardize your opportunity to serve as a missionary after high school. And if you want to marry in the temple for eternity, which we all should want, and I highly recommend it, you'll have some serious repenting to do before that's possible."

She checked her notes again.

"To keep us out of big trouble, as you know, we have lots of little commandments. That's good, because if you obey the little ones, you'll never get close to breaking the big one. On the other hand, lots of little sins usually precede the big ones. So what are some of the smaller commandments?"

Any of us could have answered, but none of us did.

"I'll use different words, while you think for a minute," she said. "Hardly anyone commits that big sin without first committing a lot of smaller, related sins. We have lots of smaller commandments designed to keep us out of situations where we might break the big one. What are they?"

Still she got no response.

"Okay," she said, "let's open *For the Strength of Youth*." That was the Church's booklet of moral and behavioral standards for youth. We all had our own copies, either tucked into our scriptures or buried in a drawer at home.

We were supposed to know it inside and out, and we did. We'd had lessons on each of its topics at least twice a year since I was twelve. I'd listened to the chastity lessons eagerly at first, but not recently—partly because they were all pretty much the same, and partly because no boys were interested enough in me that I needed to worry about it, and there hadn't been much hope of that changing anytime soon. Guys didn't exactly flock to epileptic girls who sat too much.

Now a boy was interested, but he was a good boy, so the rules still weren't a problem.

It helped that they were pretty sensible.

Don't date before you're sixteen.

When you date, activities with other couples are safer.

Make sure your parents meet your dates and know where you're going, who you'll be with, and when you'll be back.

Don't stay out too late.

Always have something planned to do. After that, the date is over.

No bedrooms together.

Then it struck me, just before Sister A read it aloud—a rule Troy and I were already breaking. They taught us to avoid frequent dates with the same person—but Troy and I were together at least twice a week and trying for more.

We were on our way to breaking another rule. She read that one next: avoid serious relationships until we were old enough to consider marriage. For the boy, at least, "old enough" was sometime after his two-year mission for the Church. It certainly wasn't while we were both in high school.

I saw myself as a person who obeyed rules, and I didn't want to do anything seriously wrong. But Troy and I were happy together, and we were getting more serious, and we would both want that not to be wrong.

Something my parents said popped into my head, and I raised my hand—because Sister A asked for questions before we moved on.

"Yes, Jenny?"

"You said all these rules are little commandments which keep us far away from breaking a big commandment. I get that the big one's a commandment, and breaking it is a serious sin. But the little ones aren't commandments, are they? Aren't they more like wise counsel or helpful guidelines? Don't we all have to decide which ones apply to us and how? Individually, I mean."

Her eyes went wide again. She glanced at the other adult leaders in the room, but no one rescued her.

"That's a good question," she said. "I think we should treat them as commandments, because they come from the inspired leaders of the Church. That would be safe. But maybe I need to understand what you're asking a little better."

I scrambled for an example. "This didn't happen to me, but if a good guy asked me out a week before I turned sixteen, and my parents said it was okay, would it have been a sin to go on a date with him? Is the boy sinning by taking me out, or even asking, if he knows I'm not sixteen yet? Are my parents sinning if they let me? What if I don't meet his parents until our third date?"

"Well, maybe no one is sinning, exactly." Her deer-in-the-headlights look didn't inspire confidence.

"Okay. Suppose I meet a boy somewhere for a date, instead of him picking me up, so he doesn't meet my parents—but they know where I'm going and with whom. Are we okay, if they meet him when he brings me home? Are we sinning until they actually meet him?"

"I guess it's not a sin," she said. "If it's okay with your parents. It's risky, maybe." She sighed. "Hallie?"

This time, it was Hallie's serious voice. I wondered how long that would last. "If a boy asks me out, but no other boys want to ask a girl and go with us, because we're going to a women's soccer game or something, and his friends think that's stupid, which it's totally not, do I have to tell him no, because it's not a double date? When I'm old enough to date, I mean. Can it count as a group date anyway, if there are other couples on dates in our section of the stadium?"

"I guess . . ." Sister A sounded overwhelmed. "I guess those are questions for your parents. But it's still best not to single-date when you're young."

"So Jenny's right. That's not a commandment either!" Hallie sounded triumphant.

Sister A turned to me. "What did you call it, Jenny? Helpful counsel?"

I nodded. "Something like that."

"So let's call these little rules wise, helpful counsel. But it's still better to obey them. It's better to be wise than unwise. And the law of chastity is still absolutely a commandment," she said more firmly. "Not just good counsel or a wise suggestion. Anything else before we move on? Libby?"

Libby was visiting from California, so I didn't know her at all. The one thing I'd noticed when she introduced herself at the beginning was her hair: a short, curly, brown bob that was cute with her round face.

"My parents won't let me go on two dates in a row with the same boy," she said, "even if they're a month apart. They only let me date boys from the Church, and only one of those ever asks. He's a good guy, but I'm not allowed to go out with him again until I've gone out with someone else. But no one else ever asks!

"Mom and Dad say their rules were good enough for my older sisters. They both got married in the temple last year, which no one will let me forget for five seconds. They say it wouldn't be fair to my sisters if I get to break rules they had to obey. What am I supposed to do? I'm not popular like they were, but I want to go on dates with boys."

Sister A spoke slowly. "I think it's important to obey your parents. One of the Ten Commandments is about that. But I don't have any firsthand experience with this situation. Anyone?"

Someone suggested that Libby could ask guys out, without waiting for them to ask her. She said she'd have to hide it from her parents, because they thought girls asking guys on dates was too forward, unless it was officially girls' choice, like Morp or Sadie Hawkins.

Someone else said she could ask a guy to ask her out. Or the guy who wanted to ask her out again could have one of his friends ask her out in between. That sounded like some of the novels I'd read. And it probably wasn't fair to the other guy.

"Jenny?" Sister A's tone made me wonder if she was about to punish me for derailing her lesson earlier, or maybe for getting Hallie involved.

She was. "You started this topic. What would you do if your parents had the same rules and refused to bend them? You've dated some, right?"

I told myself to be calm and not squirm. And think before I talked.

"My parents don't have those rules," I said, "and they wouldn't, unless I'd been getting into trouble already." I turned to Libby. "I'm not saying you've been getting in trouble, or that your sisters did.

"I'd probably beg and cry and plead with them until they were way past wanting to hear about it. That works with other things sometimes. If it didn't, maybe the guy who liked me could persuade them. But I'd probably just have to get someone else to ask me out. Which is easy to say, I guess."

The discussion moved in another direction after that, but my thoughts didn't follow. I was stuck on the rule Troy and I were already breaking and the one we might start breaking soon.

Sister A had said what I wanted to hear about those rules, but was she right? Was I right? Was it really not a sin to break some little rules, if you didn't break an actual commandment? Was it ever safe and right to disobey something they taught us at church? I couldn't remember any church or seminary lesson telling me it might be, unless this one counted. Otherwise, home was the only place I heard that.

Some of the rules were broken a lot, I knew. For example, there were plenty of teenage couples with Latter-day Saint kids in them. They didn't all get in trouble, did they?

I'd have to think through this, and soon. Could it really be okay to break two rules they taught us at church, as long as we didn't mess around with any commandments?

Decision

18

My White Board

ONE FRIDAY EVENING AFTER a game, there wasn't room for all of us to sit together at the ice cream place, so, after we ordered, Troy and I happily found a tiny table for ourselves.

We talked, held hands, and totally forgot to listen for them to call Troy's name when our order was ready. Before we knew it, Will towered over our table, clearing his throat dramatically.

"They called your order twice, so I grabbed it. I realize ice cream's not the first thing on your minds." He set it on our table, along with napkins and spoons. The ice cream was at least three inches taller than the cup. "Enjoy."

"Thanks, man," said Troy.

"Thanks, Will," I added.

"My pleasure." He grinned—mostly at me, I thought—and slipped away.

We dug in with our long plastic spoons. After two fabulous bites, I glanced toward Will and the others. They were a few tables away. "Will—"

Troy spoke at the same instant. "Will—"

We traded smiles.

"You first," Troy said.

"Will is very kind."

We each took another bite.

"Will thinks you walk on water," Troy said.

I beamed. "I think he does. Have you ever seen him unkind to any-one?"

"Nope."

"Some of the other guys are nice too," I said. "I thought you jocks were supposed to be jerks." I smiled again to soften the blow.

"Some of us are. Mostly we're like brothers. One guy's friend is everybody's friend."

"I would have liked having brothers." It wasn't a new thought.

"We're not so bad," he said. "Brothers, I mean." I thought I heard a note of sadness, so maybe he'd wished for brothers too. Then it was gone. "Ever want sisters?" he asked.

"I wanted a twin sister."

"Bad idea." He tried to look serious but failed. I loved that look. "One of the guys would have to date her," he said, "and we'd all be confused."

"We wouldn't have to be identical," I said. "We could be fraternal. She could be a knockout. And taller. Maybe even blonde. Nobody would believe we were twins. Let's give her three inches and say five-foot-eight, if she'd be dating anyone taller than a point guard. She'd be jealous of me for dating you, but she'd get over it quickly."

"Why quickly?" he asked with an exaggerated pout.

"We'd be sisters. She would love me."

He laughed. "Sometimes when we talk, it gets weird really fast."

I nodded seriously. "Jack and Nikki are a weird influence on me. Always have been."

His eyes were at full twinkle. "Must be it."

I shivered, and we weren't half-finished with the ice cream. I pushed the cup toward him and put down my spoon. "You should finish this, or I'll freeze. But thank you for buying me ice cream."

"You're welcome." If he was trying to warm me with his eyes and smile, it was working.

"I meant to thank you for helping me with my writing exercise today," I said.

"You're welcome again. How'd I help?"

"Mrs. Tornow had us pick three objects in the classroom, then think of someone we know now but didn't know six months ago. The exercise was to figure out how that person resembles the objects, and maybe the comparison would teach us something. We can do the same thing to make our characters more interesting when we write fiction."

"You picked me?"

"Of course. My objects were a wastebasket—which sounds terrible, but we picked them before we knew why—and the white board across the whole front wall, and Mr. Cain. He was observing today."

"He might not like being an object, but I won't tell. How am I like the wastebasket?"

"You take everything I throw at you, even the silly stuff, and contain it, so it doesn't make a mess. Then you carry it away and come back for more."

"This taught you something you didn't know about me?"

"It made me more grateful for what I already knew, including how you keep coming back."

He smiled. "Yeah, I do. How about the huge white board?"

"No matter how many words I throw at you, there's always room for more. And I go through a lot of words. Far too many words."

"You say things like that a lot. Why do you think you talk too much?"

It was a fair question. "I guess I just like to talk."

"Sorry," he said. "I meant, why do you think it's too much? You're smart and funny, and you have things to say. I like it when you talk."

That earned him a self-conscious smile. "Maybe because I spend more time sitting and less time doing things than other people, and all there is to do when I sit is talk."

"You do plenty of stuff. You sing in two choirs. You're a great student. You read books. You've even been learning about basketball. And you write. I still want to read some of your writing."

"Which you can, but isn't writing just another way of talking?"

"Jenny, you don't talk too much. I should know by now, right?"

"I guess so. If I ever do, will you stop me? Please?"

He grinned. "I can try. How am I like Mr. Cain?"

"This one helped me see you more clearly. You like rules. You can hardly bear to break one. If there isn't a rule for something, you'd be happier if there were."

"That's good for an English teacher who mostly teaches grammar," he said. "Not so good for a basketball player."

"Basketball has lots of rules."

"It's not that. When I run the offense, I'm good at knowing where everyone's supposed to be, and when they're supposed to get there.

When things break down, which happens a lot if the defense is good, I don't improvise well."

"Okay," I said, "but this rules thing is good in a friend or a date. It makes me feel safe, and it helps my parents trust you. I told you Dad's a writer and Mom's an English professor, right?"

"You saying they like rules too?"

"Yes. But they also say rules are tools, and breaking one is the right tool sometimes. Or you may need to break a rule to obey a more important rule. Mom quotes George Orwell, something about breaking any of his other writing rules rather than saying something barbarous."

"The *Animal Farm* guy?" Troy asked. "Some equals are more equal than others?"

"Very good. What else?"

"*1984*, right? War is really peace, or maybe I have it backwards. Freedom is actually slavery. Ignorance is strength."

"You get an A for the day. Don't forget Big Brother."

"To some people at home, I am Big Brother," he said ominously, pointing at me with his spoon.

I giggled. "You sure can sweet-talk an English professor's daughter."

"I can bring it. I was going to say, my parents don't like breaking rules. That's probably good in a pilot and a tax accountant. But all those objects fit you too. You're my wastebasket—which still sounds bad—and my white board."

"A smaller white board. You talk less than I do." I smiled." Even if I don't talk too much."

"You don't talk too much. And you're just as much into rules as I am, Ms. Cain."

"Why do you say that?"

"The way you handle your illness and your meds. The way you mostly get along with your parents, instead of fighting a lot against their rules. The way you don't text me after 10 p.m., even on Valentine's Day, and you're okay with me not texting you, because we made our own rule. Oh, and your practically perfect grammar."

"Yes, my grammar," I said. "When I was a little girl, before my bedtime prayer, Mom would say, 'Jenny, darling, if you study hard and say your prayers every night, someday a man will come along who will be attracted to your excellent grammar. He'll hold your hand and say sweet, grammatical things to you on Friday nights over ice cream.'"

He laughed. "Did she really say that?"

"Of course not. Why would an English professor who married a writer ever imagine a boy and a girl attracting each other with good grammar?"

He looked at me, then smiled and shook his head.

"What?" I asked.

"I understood every word you said, and I'm less certain of the answer now than I was before I asked. How do you do that?"

I smiled triumphantly. "I'm an ironic woman in an ironic world. You may have to live with some uncertainty. Did I mention we studied irony last week in my writing class?"

He was still smiling. "I'm glad you broke your parents' rule and danced with me that night."

"After you asked me to, even though you already knew their rule. Then you went out of your way to work out the details of my disobedience. But they were fine with it, when they found out we were careful."

"Sometimes breaking a rule is the right thing to do," he said. "Heard that somewhere."

My Young Women lesson flashed through my brain, and I wondered how Sister A would have responded if I'd said what Troy just said. "We need a new rule," I said. "Jenny gets to dance. Preferably with someone strong enough to bench-press her, so she doesn't fall and crack her skull."

"Not the muscle group I'll need, mostly. You know about bench pressing?" he asked.

"I learned about things in PE. I just didn't learn to be good at any of them. You could bench press me, right?"

"If you don't squirm too much. Are you ticklish?"

I wasn't ready to admit it. "Ticklish is so not the point," I said. "How can you be sure, when you don't know my weight?"

"You weigh less than I do, and I can bench press my own weight."

"How much do you weigh?"

"I can't ask you, but you can ask me?"

"I'm the girl. I thought you'd noticed that already," I said with a mischievous thrill.

"I've noticed. I like noticing. I'm noticing right now."

I smiled. And blushed. At least he was looking me in the eyes.

"About 185," he said. "So you're safe? Sorry, not supposed to ask."

"Plenty safe. Very . . . safe." I took a deep breath and tried to stop blushing, which never worked, but that never stopped me. "I know we have to go, but next time we get a chance to talk, I have a question for you. I promise to be more serious, at least for a few minutes."

"You mean 'Can you bench press me?' wasn't serious?" He smiled for maybe the hundredth time that evening.

I couldn't see him smiling at me and not smile back. "Not entirely, no."

"Could ask me now."

"No." I shook my head. "It'll take too long to ask, and it might take even longer to answer. It can wait."

19

Baggage

O N Sunday, as my Young Women meeting ended, Troy sent a text. "It's a beautiful, sunny day for another hour or two. Have time to walk around a lake?"

A few seconds later, another text arrived. "Technically, it's a pond."

I had time, as long as I was home for dinner at 6:30.

Zeus and I hurried home ahead of Mom and Dad. I traded my church clothes for jeans, thick socks, sneakers, and a sweatshirt. I pulled my navy blue parka from the coat closet, along with a medium blue ski cap made from yarn that would sparkle in the sun. I liked how it highlighted my eyes. I tucked thin gloves into my pockets but didn't plan to use them. I had a boy to keep my hands warm.

Zeus was due for a good walk, but Dad agreed to take him.

Troy appeared at the door in a dark gray coat with a fur-lined hood he wasn't using. His black, white, and silver ski cap had a little basketball on it, with "Spurs" in big letters across the front.

I stopped on the porch to pull on my hat, then looked up to see a smile.

"Your eyes are amazing," he said.

I glowed. "I think it's the hat. And the sun."

"I think it's your eyes."

A winter walk around a lake was far outside my routine. I found myself enjoying things I didn't usually notice. The sky was blue and clear, the air was still and winter-crisp, and the lake was a mirror.

There was snow on the grass and trees. The paved asphalt trail was wet and steaming in the sun. We walked hand in hand, chattering about this and that.

Troy asked, "Is this a good time for your serious question?"

"It's a great time," I said. "There's a long introduction, so be my white board for a minute?"

Just off the trail ahead was the perfect place to sit. Another couple was just leaving. I turned to Troy. "Care to join me on the sunlit bench?"

He cared to.

Even in the sun it was cool enough to give us an extra excuse to snuggle. I leaned on him, and he put an arm around my shoulders. "Big whiteboard at your service," he said.

I took a deep breath. "Okay, here goes. You know about my epilepsy. I try to have parts of a normal life, and sometimes it works out. When it doesn't, I try not to blame God or the universe or my parents or my neurologists. Or myself. Or Zeus. But it's not fair. Why can't I be normal? That's not today's big question.

"You haven't seen it, but sometimes I wallow in self-pity for hours or days. I get discouraged and depressed and angry—not as much as I used to, but sometimes. I take it out on other people, even Zeus, which is rotten of me.

"And I know you don't think I talk too much, but you can see I'm content to handle entire conversations by myself. I don't know whether I'm too self-centered or—sorry—just talk too much.

"I'm usually much better at talking to adults than to random kids our age, which is a nicer way of saying I'm a social misfit. And I'm more comfortable in class or doing homework than I am in social situations. You're dating a geek, maybe even a nerd."

"Are we doing this again?" he asked. "Let's not do this again."

"We're not," I said gently. "Though, as we've seen, I also say negative things about myself. And think them. But this is different. And I'm almost finished."

"Okay."

"Where was I? So here you are, the hardest-working teenager I know. You get up early every morning and work hard until bedtime, and I am so not like that. I love to sleep in. Almost noon today, which is not unusual with afternoon church. So I think I must be lazy, compared to you."

After all that, I still needed to stop, take another deep breath, and muster my courage.

"Here's my question. You already knew some of my baggage, and now you know more. What's yours?"

He was silent for a few seconds. "You want to know my baggage?"

That's when I realized my question might make him think about his dead friend again, and I didn't want that. "There must be things I still don't know. For example, if you're a seventeen-year-old serial killer or a registered sex offender, I'd like to know sooner rather than later." I smiled. "See how I helpfully made your baggage look not so bad already?"

He laughed quietly. "You really are a writer. It's like you think a few speeches ahead, when you write our dialogue."

I overreacted a little. "I'm so sorry. Don't ever let me put words in your mouth."

He looked me intently, as if trying to sort out the muddle in my head. Then a little smile appeared. "I like the story. I like my character. And I like dating my writer."

That set me aglow inside. He'd called me *his* writer. I must have glowed on the outside too, because he said, "You look happy again. Something I said?"

I nodded—and hesitated. To explain would be to open my heart to him even more. Which I wanted to do. It just felt new and . . . intimate. Then again, asking about his personal baggage was pretty intimate.

"You called me your writer," I murmured. "*Your* writer."

He squeezed my hand. "So, if I understand *my* writer correctly, *my* writer wants me to add depth to my character?"

His writer melted more but managed to nod.

"Okay," he said. "There's baggage. Won't impress a girl's parents."

He held my hand in one of his, stroking it lightly with his other index finger. He ran his finger slowly across the back of my hand, out to my fingertip and back again, all the way to my wrist. He did the next finger and the next, and when he finished, he turned my hand over and did more of the same. The warmth he created was like the winter sun on my face, but it came from inside me. I could have sat there until we had to leave, saying nothing, hearing nothing, not thinking at all, just lost in his gentle touch.

He stopped abruptly. "I'm forgetting to talk."

"I forgot to listen." I turned my smile to him. "I like how you keep me warm on a winter afternoon."

He kept holding my hand, but he put his other arm around me again and squeezed. I rested my head on his shoulder. That way, he could talk, and I could listen.

"I have no idea what I want to be when I grow up," he said, "or what I do well enough to turn it into something. I don't want to be a pilot like Dad or an accountant like Mom." He exhaled loudly. "Just don't know."

"What do your parents say? What does the school counselor say?"

"Not to worry yet. But we're talking about who I'm going to be for most of my life. Shouldn't I be working on that?"

"You probably are, without knowing it," I said. "Brains, hard work, solid academic skills."

"I feel like I should try to be good at something specific, but I don't know what I even care about that much. Dad knew he wanted to be a pilot when he was three. By the time he was my age, he had his first license. How long have you wanted to be a writer?"

"Long time."

"See?"

I nodded. "I wish I had a serious suggestion. All I have is a silly one."

"Tell me, and I'll tell you more baggage."

"Okay. You're amazing at making girls feel good about themselves, and you treat people really well. You could make a fortune giving seminars on how guys should treat girls, and how girls should expect guys to treat them. Think of the good you could do. Fewer girls would put up with jerks, so there might be fewer jerks. Girls wouldn't end up marrying and divorcing abusive losers, then single-parenting 4.7 children in poverty until they'd rather just drop dead from exhaustion. There should be a market for that. It's a big problem, to hear my parents talk.

"You could have a YouTube channel, even do a TED Talk. Obviously, you'd write some bestsellers. And rich parents might pay you astronomical fees to coach their daughters privately—take them on long walks, dance with them, show them how gentlemen treat ladies."

"O-kay," he said slowly. I looked up and saw a grin. "I'll be a well-mannered, book-writing gigolo specializing in rich girls with low self-esteem.

I'll get paid by their parents and do seminars and videos. School assemblies too?"

"You'd be a very chaste gigolo," I said. "And something like 'social coach' would look better on your website." I put my head on his shoulder again. "I told you it was silly. Sounds like a really stupid movie."

"Just figured out how some of our conversations get weird so fast," he said.

"It's really not Jack and Nikki. I'll be serious again." I snuggled closer, and he squeezed.

"Okay, more baggage. Tell me something," he said. "What kind of person do your parents think I am? What kind of person do you think I am? What do Jack and Nikki think?"

I looked up. "That's three somethings. Maybe more." I was echoing the night we met, and he knew it. I got another squeeze.

"It's a winning combination in a girl," he said. "A pretty smile and basic counting skills."

My head returned to its happy place. "We all think you're one of the good guys. Like that Scout Law thing, plus smart and handsome. And warm. And cuddly. The last two are just from me."

He laughed. "Thought you were going to be serious."

"I am serious. I'll try again. Like the Scout Law, plus smart and handsome."

"I'm glad people think that about me—especially you—but here's a big piece of baggage: I feel like I'm faking it, at least some of it. I pretend a lot, so people will think I'm better than I am."

"I don't understand. What are you faking?"

"Lots of things. I get up and go to church on Sunday, like I actually want to, but I usually don't. Today, for example."

Some part of my brain thought I should worry about that, but I felt the same way often enough. I just listened.

"Gets worse. I'm planning a mission, but not for the right reasons, mostly. Big reason is what people will think of me for the rest of my life if I don't. People in general, I guess, but especially all the good Latter-day Saint girls who want future missionaries now and returned missionaries later. Including you, right?"

I nodded. He wasn't exaggerating the expectation. Every able boy was supposed to serve a two-year full-time mission for the Church after high school—at his own expense, wherever the Church sent him in the world. Lots of boys put part of their allowance into mission savings, as soon as they had an allowance. By high school they had summer and after-school jobs to earn more of the money they'd need.

We girls were welcome to serve too, if we wanted, but there wasn't the same sense of obligation. What we were expected to do was encourage the boys to serve—and help them behave so they wanted to and could. We were supposed to want to marry returned missionaries—RMs—eventually. Most of us really did want that.

"It's not just because they tell us to prefer RMs," I said. "There are actual reasons."

He nodded. "Yeah. Putting something ahead of myself for two years, being serious about my religion. And they say guys grow up a lot in those two years, which we would probably do anyway."

"Mom and Dad are both RMs," I said. "They say people go on missions for lots of reasons, and what really matters is why you stay and finish."

"I've heard that too. But it's not just the mission. Guess I'm saying, a lot of times, when I act good, it's mostly so people will think I'm good."

"Are you just pretending to believe in God?" I asked. Maybe being happy to go to church every Sunday wasn't that important, but this was.

"That's not pretending."

"Good. What about wanting to be obedient?"

"Sometimes I want that. Most of the time, at least I want to want that."

"Doesn't everyone who wants to be good try to act better than he is?" I asked. "That's not hypocrisy. It's trying to improve. Is that different from what you're saying?"

"I'd feel better if I were just trying to be a better person, if I didn't care so much what people think. I don't run around paralyzed with fear that people will discover I'm not who they thought I was. Okay, running around paralyzed sounds weird. But when I should be thinking about how I can do something better or help someone more, I'm thinking, how can I make this look good, and make sure people see it?"

"So what is that?" I asked. "Pride? Hypocrisy? A lack of integrity?"

"Or not being genuine?" he asked. "Don't know. Don't think it's good."

I looked up. "I have a selfish question."

"Maybe that's what I am, selfish. What's your question?"

"Where do I fit into all this pretending you're doing?" I almost said, "All this pretending *you think* you're doing," because he was much too hard on himself. But I didn't want to dismiss his concerns that way.

"You mean, am I pretending to like you for some reason? Trying to think why a guy would do that. So people see me with a girl and think I'm cool? To make another girl jealous? To discourage a girl who has a crush on me? So people think I'm a good person, because someone like you hangs out with me? Or like you're some sort of charity case or something? Maybe you're a decoy, so my parents won't suspect I'm hooking up with some skank on the side."

"I hadn't thought of some of those." I let my head nestle back onto his shoulder. I trusted him enough not to fear his answer, but I wanted to hear it.

He took a deep breath. "When I'm with you, I don't feel like I have to pretend to be someone I'm not. And you like me anyway."

I processed that and felt happy and warm. "I thought you were pretending at first. You were too perfect. Too polite, too charming, too interested."

"What convinced you?"

"To get over it? The more we talked, the more I though you were being yourself, not just trying to impress a girl. Which impressed a girl."

He gave me a squeeze. "When I'm with you, it's like the real me is okay. And I want the real me to be good."

Knowing he liked me was one thing. I was getting used to that. Hearing him explain left me speechless for a moment. Finally I could say, "Now you've made me even happier." I tried to snuggle closer, in case that was possible. "I think you're too hard on yourself. We have that in common, apparently."

"Maybe. Anyway, there's lots of little baggage." He sounded less serious, and I smiled in anticipation. "I'm a slob sometimes. I try to show you the less disgusting version of the real me, but you should see my room or my basketball locker. Or my car, if you didn't ride in it. I have trouble getting dirty socks all the way to the laundry—just ask my mom. And sometimes I burp long and loud, mostly to bother my sisters, but also just for the joy of it. Want to hear?"

I giggled. "No, thank you. That's definitely baggage."

He smiled briefly. Then he was serious again. "Sometimes I swear, usually when no one's around. I also waste a lot of time on the computer. Not during basketball season. Just games, and nothing too gory. Mostly a waste of time, though."

"I guess I believe you, but you waste less time than any high school kid I know."

"Thanks." He hesitated. "There's another big one. Might give you second thoughts about me."

I doubted that. "You don't have to tell me."

"I want to. I like that about us."

To show him I wasn't worried, and just because, I did my best to melt into him, despite the two winter coats between us. "Then I will try very hard to keep liking you. I plan to succeed. Tell me your thing."

20

More Baggage

T ROY LOOKED OUT OVER the lake. "It's getting harder to go to church," he said. "Some people would say that means I don't have faith or a testimony, but I do. I think I do. And I still go. But we barely sing the hymns, and most of the prayers sound half-hearted and lazy, and I wonder, what's the point? I know, I'm terrible, saying people's prayers are lazy. Not sure how mine would be any better, if I were offering the prayer.

"The sacrament isn't lame, and I like blessing it, when it's my turn. But then we sit through half-baked talks by people who obviously don't want to be at the pulpit. Then we go off to our half-baked lessons and raise our hands when we have to and give all the right half-baked answers we've known since we were nine, and then we go home. We avoid hard questions like they scare us. New thoughts too. And anyone who doesn't fit in makes us squirm.

"It's not like I have urgent life-and-death questions. But I wonder what things mean and how they fit together. And sometimes it just doesn't make sense. I want to ask about stuff, but even my seminary teachers act like you can't be good and have faith and still ask serious questions.

"It feels like there should be more at church than there is, more of something. Sometimes it's better, so better's possible. Kind of painful in between.

"And it's not that they're always hammering on moral purity or the Word of Wisdom or whatever. God gives us commandments; we have to teach them. I'm all for being good and obedient, and I don't want to be out there smoking and drinking. Or sleeping around.

"But even I know there's more to the gospel than that. A lot more. We're children of God. That's pretty big. We have a Savior. Without him, keeping the commandments wouldn't matter much.

"We have prophets and scriptures and lots of glorious music. You'd think we'd sing hymns with, I don't know, some passion, maybe? But we usually don't. You'd think we'd put in some effort and insight when it's our turn to speak. Maybe even some fire. Instead we just fill the time, and everyone sits and yawns occasionally and says amen at the end.

"Maybe I'm not being fair. Maybe I'm exaggerating, but I feel like we're missing something big. Or I am." I felt him look down, and I saw his breath in the air. "If I say any of this at church, they'll think I'm ungrateful and unkind and don't have a testimony. Or worse."

He blew out a breath. "What do you think?"

I didn't look up. "I think, don't you love how a testimony explains every problem? You don't want to get up for Church? It can't be just working hard all week, or you're tired or sick. You must have a weak testimony, even if you get up and go anyway. You stayed home from an activity to catch up on your homework? Must be losing your testimony—or if you aren't already, you will. Sunday school bored you today? Or upset you or didn't make sense? Must need some work on that testimony!

"But I can know there's a God and Jesus is the Savior and the Church is true, and it still won't make my dull teacher exciting or my pillow less comfortable on Sunday mornings. Or magically turn sloppy thinking into divine wisdom. Was church any better in Texas?"

"Think so," he said. "Don't know if it was just different people or not being around Mormons much, except at church. Maybe converts from other religions make it livelier."

"Do your parents feel the same way?"

"They don't complain, even when I do, but they wouldn't. They'll be there every Sunday, no matter what, even if they don't always like it. Don't know if that's good or bad. Probably, they're good and I'm bad."

I pondered that. "What if it's not a case of good and bad? Maybe it's two different goods."

Troy took a deep breath, then another. "Did you say that to make me feel better, or do you really think that?"

I looked up and told the truth. "I started saying it to make you feel better, but I think I believe it. It's good that they go every week, because they're supposed to. It's also good to see how things could be better, even if it makes you impatient with how things are."

He didn't smile, but I couldn't miss the warmth in his eyes.

"What?" I asked softly.

He didn't answer right away. If anything, his eyes grew warmer. Finally he said, "Know how I said I can be myself with you?"

"And I still like you? And think you're a good person?"

"Yeah."

"I really do. But . . . what?"

"That."

I wished I could see my own eyes, because now the warmth was in them too. It felt new, like it existed only for him. For us.

I couldn't put into words what his heart had just said to mine. My head found his shoulder again—not so I could avoid his gaze, but because I needed to be closer to him, as close as I could get.

"That's my baggage," he said. "Glad it doesn't push you away."

"Mine hasn't pushed you away," I said. He couldn't see my smile, but it was in my voice too. "Thanks for telling me yours. I haven't seen you carrying it around, so I wondered. I'm glad you're not a registered sex offender or a teenage serial killer." Maybe the moment had passed, because I could look up, pretend to be concerned, and say, "Don't become a gigolo just to please my parents, okay?"

He laughed long and hard. But the moment hadn't passed, because he still held me tightly, and the warmth from his eyes was still in his voice, even when he asked, "Think anyone ever said that before, in the whole history of the English language?"

We sat in comfortable silence, an oasis of warmth, until the sun began to slip below the horizon and the air turned colder. It was time to finish our stroll.

"I have church baggage too," I volunteered as we walked. "Some of it's like yours."

I wanted him to know I had similar thoughts. Even more, I wanted to be the one who understood him best, or at least tried hardest to understand.

"Anything to do with helmets and dogs?" he asked.

"Some of it. When I was little, the other kids didn't know what to do, so they mostly avoided me. They usually weren't mean, but I was a misfit, even at church. Adults were too indulgent, as if I were helpless, which really bugged me. Both those things still happen, but less than they used to, I think. Anyway, I used to be a lot sadder and angrier than I am now. And a lot more often."

"I can understand that, I think."

"Can you understand I was angry with God too? I mean, obviously he can heal people. Jesus ran around healing everybody. Why wouldn't he heal me? Was that such a big thing to ask? All those New Testament miracles made me cry. Sometimes I went home after church and threw a tantrum.

"Other times, especially lately, my problems look pretty small. Plenty of people need a much bigger miracle and don't get it. God could have healed my grandma. We must have prayed for that a thousand times, but she had a long, painful exit, and now she's gone. I know she's in a better place. At least I believe it. But when she was here, this was a better place. I miss her.

"I don't know if Grandpa was ever angry with God, like I was. I know he missed her a lot. We used to sit under his tree, eating ice cream, while he told me stories about her."

I paused to let Troy get a word in, but he just looked at me soberly, so I continued.

"Once I got so angry when we were reading at home that I threw my Bible at the wall. That was bad."

"Sounds human," Troy said. "Kind of hard on the Bible though, and maybe the wall. What happened?"

"The wall was okay. Dad said I should be glad about that. Kind of messed up my Bible. Sometime after that, I decided I was tired of being a bad person who was angry with God and hated the scriptures. I tried to be good all the time. You know, remember my prayers, brush my teeth, not fight with my parents, pay attention at church, always tell the truth, do my chores and homework without complaining, all that stuff. Not throw my scriptures at the wall."

"So God would like you, and you could deserve your own miracle?"

I nodded. "You can probably guess where that led."

"To walking by the lake with my arm around you?"

I drew in a quick, surprised breath and beamed. "What a happy way to say I still have seizures. Thank you!"

I wanted to kiss him.

I *really* wanted to kiss him.

I couldn't kiss him. I just kept beaming.

He smiled faintly. "Let me guess. You decided to read the scriptures a lot, especially the Gospels, because you thought you could force yourself to love them. But it just got worse. And even though you tried really hard, you couldn't be good enough. So you thought you were a bad person after all, not the kind of girl God would love. You got discouraged because you thought he was angry and punishing you, but by then you weren't even sure for what."

I stopped short, and he stopped with me. I didn't smile when I looked him in the eye. He was stirring painful memories. My chin trembled. "How do you know all that?"

He held my gaze for a moment, then looked down. "Don't have to be sick to think he's angry with you. I try to force myself to love going to church." He blew out a long breath. "And there's always someone who needs a miracle and doesn't get one." He met my eyes again. "I was right?"

We rounded a bend, turning our backs to the lump of fire that lingered on the horizon. It cast long shadows ahead of us. Troy and I together made a single shadow, and as far as I could see, I couldn't see the end of us. I'd want to remember that.

"Was I right?" he asked again.

"Sorry, enjoying the view. Yes, except I never had any trouble doing naughty things. Nothing really bad, but when you think you have to be perfect for God to love you, even getting snippy with your Mom feels unpardonable."

I stared at our endless shadow. "Things were bad for a long time, not just church. The few things I didn't hate back then were all escapes: lots of novels and videos, mostly really good ones, and some parts of school that were okay. And my choir."

"You're happier now?"

"I am. I still do bad things."

"Yeah, you're a terrible sinner." He grinned, then looked serious again. "How'd you get past all that?"

"Time, I guess. Maybe growing up a little. Mom and Dad helped, when I let them. One Sunday afternoon we were reading aloud in John. Chapter Four, I think. There's a long story about a woman at a well, but after that, this nobleman begs Jesus to come and heal his dying son. When it was my turn to read aloud, I refused.

"We ended up having a long talk. I cried some and yelled a little, I guess, but Mom cried too. Even Dad got teary-eyed. I'd never imagined them having some of the same struggles, when they learned everything wasn't quite right with their first and only child, and might never be. And other times with other things."

Troy's eyes were sad, or maybe just kind and concerned—and still warm, which took some of the sting out of my memories.

"I asked them how they got over all that, and what I was doing wrong, because obviously they didn't have my trouble with those New Testament stories. They like reading that stuff and discussing it at dinner. What they said was totally something a writer and an English professor would say."

"What'd they say?"

"I was reading it wrong. I was reading the Gospels like they're about me, but they're not. They're about him."

"I like that," Troy said after a moment. "They always tell us to see ourselves in the scriptures, which makes sense, but this is kind of the opposite. So it helped?"

I nodded. "Once it sank in. I hate to admit it sometimes, but my parents are pretty smart. And I'm pretty stubborn. Anyway, now I love to read the Gospels, because I love to read about him. Mom and Dad said, when I knew him well enough, I'd start to understand myself."

"So you understand Jenny Miller now? I've been working on that too. Any tips?"

I had to smile. "Sorry. I'm still working on him. But I like it now. There's kind of a downside, which I think you'll understand. It's like they say at the airport. Many bags look alike."

"Already don't understand. What about the airport?"

"My church baggage looks a lot like yours. I get impatient with talks and lessons, even angry sometimes, or sad. We talk so much about all the little details and all the little rules, including some I think we just make up." And some we should probably ignore, I thought but didn't say. Like the one about how Troy and I shouldn't see each other so much.

"We don't talk enough about what Jesus did and who he was," I said. "And who he is. Like you said, he's kind of the point."

"Yup."

"It's like we think, if we can just get all the details lined up exactly right and keep them that way, he'll love us and save us from all our troubles, and everything will turn out perfectly in the end and be mostly wonderful along the way.

"But even the best people have troubles. He did. And the details never stay lined up, if they ever get there at all. Grandpa would say it's like herding cats. So no matter how hard we try, we fail. Then, instead of realizing we were never supposed to be able to do it on our own, we look for even more details we can get right, and it gets even more impossible than it was before. Does that make any sense?"

"Makes a lot of sense," he said.

"The big thing is, I'm pretty sure he loves us even when we're a total mess. And he doesn't wait to help us until we're practically perfect on our own, not that we ever could be. So it would help people if we talked about that more often. It would help me. People would be happier. I would have been happier. So anyway, I see wasted opportunities at church, and I get grumpy. Then I feel guilty for not liking church."

"Glad it's not just my ward," Troy said. "Maybe I'm not. I don't know."

"It's definitely not just your ward. Today in Young Women, the teacher was talking about the Word of Wisdom. Coffee, tea, alcohol, illegal drugs, tobacco, vaping. I'm fine not doing any of those. But then she railed against things that aren't forbidden, like chocolate, white flour, refined sugar, anything with MSG in it, cola drinks, white rice, high-fructose corn syrup. I probably missed a few.

"I was pretty frustrated. I wanted to ask, 'Could you please stop wasting our time? Maybe talk about the Savior, if you can't think of anything else that's actually part of the gospel?' I raised my hand, but I can only be that snarky in my head. When she called on me, I just said, 'Sorry, never mind.'"

We walked silently for a minute.

"Think I understand," said Troy.

"I think you do." I summoned my courage. What I wanted to say next had every nerve jangling.

21

We Should Go

OUR WALK AROUND THE lake was a lazy stroll, despite the falling temperature and deepening twilight, but mentally I needed a deep breath or two.

I squeezed Troy's hand. "By the end of junior high—not all that long ago—I was a lot less miserable. Lately I'm pretty happy." I looked up at him. "You've helped that a lot."

His smile was tender and warm. He started to say something, then stopped, then started again. "Been thinking how to say this. It's like I found a door someone left closed, and I opened it and let all the amazing out into the light."

I wanted to thank him—for saying that and for opening the door. I needed to tell him about the thrill that was engulfing me, but I had no words for it. No words for anything.

"That's all I did," he said. "Now I hang around to enjoy it."

We hugged the side of the trail, while an older, spandexed couple speed-walked past us.

"Believe me," he said. "I'm enjoying it."

We were fifty yards from the parking lot, then twenty, then five. I finally spoke. "Can you see that from my perspective? The door thing?"

We arrived at his car, but he didn't reach for the handle to open my door. He turned to me, his head slightly tilted. I watched his face light up. "I opened the door and let the light in?"

I nodded. "That's how it feels to me."

"I'm happier too, thanks to you," he said.

"What were you unhappy about?"

"New state, city, school, neighborhood, coach. New everything, al-most. Missing Beth a lot, because she stayed in San Antonio for school.

Missing . . . well, people and things we left behind. Lived there my whole life, until August. Mom says it was partly culture shock."

A slight breeze blew a few strands of hair across my face. He carefully brushed them away, his fingers warm against my cheek.

"Also," he said softly, "hadn't met you yet. Spend less time missing Texas now."

In the movies we might have kissed then, but apparently we were still too shy. We hugged instead. Hugging in winter coats wasn't ideal, and I couldn't hold him as tightly as he was holding me anyway, but I loved feeling his strength. Then a new thought struck, and I loved it too.

As strong as he was, he held me like he wasn't afraid to break me. Like I was strong too.

The breeze blew colder, as if to remind us not to stand there forever in the fading twilight. It took a few rounds of "I guess we should go" and "yeah, it's getting late" and "we probably shouldn't stand here all night," but we eventually got into his car and headed home.

He was so quiet as he drove that I asked if he was okay.

"Long day," he said. "You're the best part."

"You're sweet. What happened to you today besides me?"

"Back hurt last night. Better now, but didn't sleep enough. Had a 6:30 meeting this morning at church, with Dad sitting next to me to keep me awake, and me sitting next to him to keep him from snoring. Kind of been dragging all day." He squeezed my hand and smiled a little, without taking his eyes off the road. "Glad we did this."

"So am I," I said. "Thanks for helping me feel safe doing so much walking. It was so beautiful."

"You're welcome," he said. "Still spent most of the time sitting."

"Sitting was beautiful too." I hesitated. "I really do have seizures. It's not just an excuse to have your arm around me."

He smiled. "Never thought it was. Had one lately?"

"Last week, in the car. Dad was driving me to school. That's about as safe as it gets. I wasn't just sitting; I was strapped in. But you see why I can't have a license."

"As long as one of us can drive. Thanks for sitting and talking with me. And listening. You're really good at that."

That evening, before our electronic curfew, I composed a message. "Thanks again. I smiled all through dinner. I'm still smiling. I shared only one piece of your baggage with Mom and Dad, about not knowing what you want to be when you grow up. They don't seem worried. Probably helps that I left out my gigolo idea.

"No, wait, it was two things. I mentioned the burping, which I said I've never heard. They said you're a boy, so burping is pretty much assumed, which I guess I'd know if I had a brother. I still don't need to hear it. Good night. See you soon!"

I sent the message, then wrote one more line—but deleted it instead of sending. It was too soon. Then I wrote it again. And deleted it again.

"Someday, ask me about a beautiful shadow I saw tonight."

22

Pondering

ALL DAY MONDAY, I smiled inside. Troy and I had met only a few weeks ago, but he already knew—and cared and understood—what was in my head and my heart better than anyone besides Jack, Nikki, and my parents. And Zeus, maybe. I knew what kind of boy he was, what he cared about and worried about, and the kind of person he aspired to be—and he wanted me to know all that. We made each other laugh too. We'd been good at that from the start.

We didn't just like each other. We belonged together.

I brooded off and on over the rule we were breaking and the rule I was ready to break, but mostly I had happier thoughts. I felt like I was finally becoming the person I was always supposed to be—always had been, maybe, but I didn't see it until Troy helped me open my eyes. Rules or not, that had to be good.

All day, every time I thought things through, they got clearer. By the time I sat down at the dining room table with my homework after school, I was confident, not just happy. Troy and I felt right—to my mind and my heart.

Sure, a couple who really liked each other could misbehave and turn a good thing very bad—but that didn't mean it wasn't good before they ruined it. It meant we shouldn't ruin it.

If what was happening with Troy and me was too good to ruin by misbehaving, it was also too good to ruin because of a few lines in a booklet that wasn't scripture—lines which could be wise counsel generally without applying to us specifically. Counsel wasn't commandment. I'd heard Mom and Dad say that often enough.

When that was settled in my head, I found the next thing to worry about. If Troy considered the rules and thought what I was pretty sure we both wanted was wrong . . .

I didn't think I could bear to be just friends with him.

I stared at my math homework without seeing it and considered the possibilities. If he thought being a serious couple was wrong, would he still do it? For me? Would it be right to ask him? Or let him? What if he was right about that, and I was wrong? What if he wasn't sure? Could I persuade him? Would I be wrong to try?

Did the fact that we were so good together mean he was okay with it, and I was worrying over nothing? Or did he already feel guilty for breaking one rule and maybe wanting to break another, but he hadn't found a way to tell me yet?

What if we both thought it was right, and we were wrong? Would that mistake be small, medium, or huge?

Every path led to the same wall: I knew Troy's thoughts about lots of things, but not this. And he didn't know mine.

Over dinner Mom and Dad said they had no specific plans for our family home evening, so I boldly said I had a topic we could discuss. I didn't say what, but they agreed.

I figured they could reassure me that I was thinking straight, though I was pretty sure already. Plus I wanted them to agree. I needed them to agree. And talking through it with them might help me talk through it with Troy in a way that would reassure him or even persuade him, if necessary.

For generations our Church leaders had counseled families to reserve Monday evenings for family activities. We almost never missed a family home evening, even if it was sometimes planned at the last minute, over dinner. In a given week it might be a religious lesson, a work project at home or elsewhere, a cultural activity we enjoyed together, or just a video or a board game. The important thing was doing it together.

When the dishes were done, we situated ourselves comfortably in the family room and prayed together. That's how we usually started, when our lesson or activity was at home. Then Dad asked, "What's our topic?"

I was nervous about Mom and Dad after all. What if they didn't agree? Would they have said something already? They definitely would have—unless they were waiting for an opportunity like tonight.

They often said we accept counsel if it's wise for us and fits our situation, but commandments we simply obey. They also said not to judge others' decisions harshly, because everyone's circumstances are different. I'd heard them complain about people they called modern Pharisees, who loved having lots of little rules and using them to judge and condemn others. So in theory they should be on my side.

Be bold, Jenny.

"I have some questions," I announced. "When is it okay not to follow counsel from church? And how can you be sure you're rejecting it for the right reasons?"

"Interesting," Dad said gently. "Is this about you and Troy?"

I blushed. "Mostly, and I guess there's a third question. How can something feel right and still make me wonder if it's wrong? Maybe this is a lot bigger than me and Troy."

"I love a smart daughter," Dad said.

"What do you mean?"

Mom answered for him. "He means it is a lot bigger. People in the Church disagree about this. Lots of adults struggle with it."

My look said, "Tell me more," even if my voice didn't.

"We've seen friends leave the Church in both directions," Mom said. "Some decide even commandments are optional, and the Church has no business telling people how they should live their lives. Others conclude that the Church or some part of it has lost its way, because it doesn't emphasize or try to enforce some commandment or counsel the way they think it should. Once in a while you see someone completely give up on religion, because of counsel she mistakes for commandment, which she doesn't even suspect was never meant for her. There's a certain logic to that: if I'm expected to obey every little thing I hear at church, but that's impossible, and any imperfection is failure, why kill myself trying?"

Mom looked expectantly at Dad. He said, "There are good people who think every word of counsel from a church leader is a commandment and try to obey all of it without thought or question. Eventually, a lot of them can't handle the contradictions anymore, or the harm from following counsel that doesn't apply to them. Some leave the Church, as Mom said. Some stay but quietly give up hope for themselves. Some end up in chronic depression—which has a bunch of other causes, I know, but I think that's one. Some people, maybe most, finally learn to distinguish counsel and commandments, in practice more often than in theory. So it really is a lot bigger than you and Troy."

"Consider this," said Professor Mom. "At his last Passover Jesus told the apostles that one of them would betray him. Do you remember what they said?"

"Not really. Please pass the unleavened bread?"

"Maybe that too." She smiled, and then she was serious again. "One by one, they asked him, 'Lord, is it I?' When Judas asked, Jesus answered, 'Thou hast said,' or essentially, 'Yes, it's you.'"

"I remember now, and I'm sure there's a point here," I said, "but I think I'm missing it."

"Two points," she said. "First, each apostle listened to what the Savior said and considered whether it applied to him. Our attitude should be like theirs, 'Lord, is it I?' When we're given counsel, we should weigh the possibility that it's a message from the Lord that may apply to us. If it does, we should have in our hearts and minds the desire and intention to obey. That's completely different from seeking excuses or loopholes to justify disobedience.

"Second—we mention this less often—for Judas the answer to 'Lord, is it I?' was yes, but for the others it was no. If we humbly consider the possibility that some piece of counsel may apply to us, we also have to realize it may not. It may never apply to us, or it might apply later in life but not now. It may be harmful in our present circumstances, even if it's important guidance or protection for someone else right now. Or there may be a true principle in it that applies to us in a different way.

"All of that assumes the speaker or teacher said more or less what the Lord wanted said, and that we understood it properly. You know that doesn't always happen. We're imperfect humans speaking imperfect languages. Even when God inspires the speaker and the listener, things can go wrong.

"Sometimes we feel something is true and important long before we understand it. We struggle to discern what the Lord's message really is, before we can decide whether it applies to us and how. That's one reason we need the Holy Ghost—to help us communicate beyond the limits of language and understand spiritual feelings that don't come packaged with explanations."

Dad had been watching Mom with a gentle, appreciative smile, but now he turned to me. "She's really good at this. She should be a college professor or something."

Mom and I didn't roll our eyes, but I could see she wanted to as much as I did.

"In the end," Dad said, "we have to ponder carefully and honestly and make our own decisions. It's like what Joseph Smith said about teaching the people correct principles and letting them govern themselves."

"This sounds too much like adulthood," I said with only half a smile, since I was only half-kidding.

Mom smiled wryly. "You'll end up preferring adulthood, most days. And it's time for your dad to give us a good example of all this."

Dad's phone buzzed, and he checked the screen. "Sorry, this one's urgent. Editor on a deadline. Let's take a break. I'll be back in a few." He left the room.

Mom regarded me with a little smile, but said nothing.

"What?" I asked.

"What do you mean what?"

"Why are you smiling?"

"I'm your mom. I'm allowed to look at you and smile. But if you must know, are you sure you're a teenager?"

"We've been through this. You were there for my birth."

"True. I think it's brave and grown-up of you to sit us down and ask what you're asking, given the emotional stakes."

"I'm just trying to make sense of everything. And make sure my parents are on my side, I think."

"We're always on your side. Are you confident we see this the way you want us to? What if we don't?"

Uh-oh.

Something inside me dropped a foot or two and landed hard. It might have been my heart. What if Mom and Dad saw it differently?

23

Getting it Right

"S ORRY," DAD SAID, RETAKING his place next to Mom on the sofa. He'd been gone just long enough for Mom to worry me, whether she meant to or not. "I owe you an example."

He put his arm around Mom and gave her a squeeze. A certain boy giving me a squeeze would have been really comforting right then.

"Here's one," he said. "Since before I was born, the prophets have counseled us to reserve Monday evenings for family home evening, which we do religiously in our family."

Mom and I had heard that pun a dozen times or more. She smiled faintly and shook her head. I glared but kept listening.

"When I was your age, we had enough chores and activities and home-work that giving up Monday evenings became a hardship. Dad—Grand-pa—had to work late some Mondays too. So during the school year we had family home evening on Sundays instead. We did things that were appropriate for the Sabbath—my parents' sense of appropriate. You already know everyone has a slightly different version of that.

"There are very strict parents who won't let their kids do anything that requires any Monday evenings away from the family. Maybe they'd say my dad should have found a job that never interfered with Monday evenings, if he really had faith and a testimony and wanted to be obedi-ent. Maybe they thought we were less righteous than they were.

"But my parents saw the principle behind the counsel, that families need to plan and do things together regularly, and they applied it to our circumstances. I think we obeyed the prophets faithfully and wisely. We wouldn't have tried to adapt the law of tithing or the law of chastity or 'Thou shalt not steal.' Those are commandments. But, as we keep saying, there's a difference between counsel, even inspired counsel, and commandments.

"But this is your discussion," he said. "Are we talking too much?"

"No," I said. "Don't stop."

Mom and Dad shared a look. Mom said, "Obedience matters, and God and prophets and commandments are real. But just because God inspires someone to say or write something doesn't mean it applies in the same way to everyone who ever hears or reads it. Often it does, but often it doesn't. That seems logical to us, but some people consider it heresy or apostasy. Unfortunately, whatever you choose in these situations, some people at church may think you're wrong. They may try to correct you—sometimes publicly."

Dad said, "Sometimes the people who disagree are your Church leaders. That can be unpleasant. But we don't abandon the Church. We're in it to worship and serve the Lord, not for people to agree with us about everything or look at us and judge that we're wonderfully righteous."

He leaned forward slightly and pointed toward me with both index fingers. "I know we've said this before, but here's the key thing to remember. You have two conduits for wisdom and guidance from heaven. One is other people—at Church, at home, and elsewhere, including dead prophets in the scriptures. The other is your own direct connection to God. You know you can study, ponder, pray, and listen, when you need an answer. Don't ever let anyone—teachers, leaders, friends, boyfriend, husband, even your parents—don't let anyone disrupt that direct connection or try to pull rank on it. For your personal life, no one has that right. That's between you and your Father in Heaven."

"Dad's right," Mom said. "Ideally what you get through both channels is much the same, and each channel is a good check on the other. When the messages are different, things get harder. You try to figure out why, and what the truth is, and in the meantime you have to be more careful and more courageous. More independent too. And humbler, because you could be wrong. You know, 'Lord, is it I?'"

"So in the end," I said soberly, "I have to decide what to do, and good people may think I'm wrong. And they may be right."

Mom nodded. "Well said. And you don't get to decide what's true and what's false—whether God exists, for example. That's not up to us. He doesn't cease to be God if we stop believing. Truth doesn't stop being truth if people reject it.

"And if you decide it's right to violate a basic commandment, say, reducing your tithing to three percent, or ignoring the Sabbath, or having a sexual relationship outside of marriage, you're wrong, even if you think and feel that you're right. But those are commandments. Most of what we're told is just counsel. A lot of that counsel is good, but you still have to decide for yourself what applies to you, and how and when. You can talk to people you trust, and we love that you still talk to us, but the decisions have to be yours."

"What if I decide wrong?" I asked. "That seems like a real possibility. In general, if not now."

Dad laughed darkly, which was a little jarring. "Why should you be any different? You'll make mistakes. Sometimes you'll reject counsel you should obey, or vice versa, or expect others to obey what isn't for them. Sometimes you'll know what God wants you to do, and you'll be right, and you'll try to obey but make a mess of it. We all do that. Sometimes we do it in groups. But as long as you're doing your best to be wise and obedient, and you're willing to learn, and you genuinely care about the people around you, and you keep your brain switched on, you won't go far astray. God has ways of correcting us and warning us away from serious danger. Of course, we have ways of ignoring him."

I nodded slowly. "So I have to know the difference between warnings from God and warnings from people who just think I need a warning."

"True," Dad said. "Sometimes the best you can do is say your prayers and follow your instincts and your best judgment. And keep listening. And keep your heart engaged and your brain switched on. Or vice versa."

"I guess I can deal with all that," I said. "But why does this feel like a friendlier version of the gospel than I get from church and seminary?"

Professor Mom tossed my question back to me. "You tell us."

I thought for a moment. "Maybe some leaders and teachers haven't learned the difference yet—between counsel and commandments, I mean. Most of them probably have. Maybe they worry that, if they teach us to make our own decisions about all the counsel we hear, we'll take it as permission to disobey actual commandments we don't like."

"You may be right," Mom said. "But let's move past theory. Are you wondering if it's okay to go steady with Troy, even though the Church teaches to date different people and avoid steady relationships until you're older?"

My cheeks flushed, but not too much. "Yes, but I don't think we call it going steady anymore."

"Being boyfriend and girlfriend? Being a couple?"

"Something like that. Am I that predictable?"

Mom smiled. "We're not blind. And the counsel was essentially the same when we were teenagers."

Dad turned to Mom. "I wish I'd known you then. I could have fallen in love with you sooner."

"Could have?" Her smile for him was radiant.

"Would have."

"I think I *would have* liked that." She reached for his hand and held it between both of hers. He looked boyishly happy.

I had to smile at them, but they didn't see it. They seemed pretty relaxed for Latter-day Saint parents discussing their sixteen-year-old daughter and her boyfriend. Which made my next question easier to ask, when they turned back to me.

"So what do you think about Troy and me possibly being serious about each other, if we behave ourselves?"

Mom's eyes darted to Dad's, before she spoke. "We've asked ourselves the same question. Have you discussed it with Troy?"

"Not yet. First I wanted to know what I think. And what you think."

"You first," she said with a twinkle.

I didn't mind admitting that some of what was swimming around in my heart or head or wherever was new and disorienting. And I knew the feelings which help us judge right from wrong are easily confused with other feelings. But nothing inside me seemed to be saying it would be wrong for us to be together—if we behaved. I told them it felt right to me, besides feeling good in other ways.

"Do you think I'm getting it right?" I asked.

They shared another wordless look. Dad said, "We like Troy. You're both smart. You both want to be good. Granted, a lot of this is new—to him too, if I'm not mistaken. But we'll trust you."

"Both of you," Mom said.

Dad nodded. "Both of you. If you trust and care about each other enough that you want to be a couple, we'll support that, as long as we can see that you're behaving yourselves."

This was too good to be true, said my head. Too good not to be true, said my heart. "You're both okay with me having a serious boyfriend despite all the dire warnings in seminary and Young Women?"

"Suppose you tell us exactly what you mean by serious," Mom said.

I'd expected that question sooner. "We care about each other, not just the status or thrill of being with someone. We don't date other people. We spend lots of time together and get to know each other really well, and we help each other when we can. I don't mean we'll be secretly engaged, or engaged to be engaged, or planning our future together already. And we won't do anything physical that we shouldn't. So I guess serious means more serious about each other than some high school couples, and better friends than some, but not getting ourselves into serious trouble. Or any trouble."

Dad nodded. "Good answer."

"Eminently reasonable," Mom said. "You already behave yourselves, right? All the time, not just most of the time?"

"Yes."

"Then if the rest of the rules are enough, we won't sweat the ones you're ignoring. It helps that your decision process is careful and intelligent—and collaborative—not purely hormonal."

My blush deepened. "Thanks. But I think that other stuff is happening too." I couldn't say *hormonal* to my parents. Not when we were talking about me and a boy.

Mom smiled. "If it weren't, would we be having this conversation? Think about this. One helpful rule is waiting until you're sixteen to date. It's important to be grown up enough to date responsibly, and sixteen is a good general guideline. But there's nothing magic about your sixteenth birthday. You're not suddenly filled with self-control and mature judgment when you blow out sixteen birthday candles.

"We know parents who won't relax that by one day, even for something big, like prom. But if you'd come to us and told us some nice boy had asked you to the homecoming dance a week or two before your sixteenth birthday, we'd have let you go with him, if you wanted to. You were grown up enough by then."

"Wow, Mom, if only I had known!" Not that anyone had asked.

Mom read my mind. "If only some nice boy had known. By the way, if we'd let you date a little early, we certainly would have warned you not to feel free to ignore any other rules. Given the circumstances, I think your dad wants to talk about that right now."

He looked at her, eyebrows raised, then turned to me. "I do. Maybe you don't need us to repeat this, and you probably don't want us to, but if you're going to be serious about a boy, even an excellent boy, we're telling you anyway. There are rules you must follow strictly. You already know them, but let's review the high points."

I steeled myself for the high points.

"It's not okay to grope each other before you're married, as long as you keep your clothes on; or get naked together, as long as you don't go all the way; or have sex, as long as you don't get pregnant or pick up a disease. This you know."

I did know. But my whole head felt like it was under a heat lamp. I stared past them at the wall, tried not to visualize anything, and waited for it to be over. Because I was pretty sure it wasn't.

"As we've discussed before," Mom said, "you need to be careful with kissing—who kisses what and how and how much and how often. We'll definitely talk about that again. And we're sorry to embarrass you, but you picked the topic. If you intend to ignore a few of the safety rules, you have to be more careful about the rest."

I managed to speak. "We haven't kissed yet, but I want to." I smiled faintly. "Thanks for talking about all this. Most of it. I think it helps."

"So you've made a decision?" Dad asked.

I nodded. "Thanks for testing it with me. And trusting us."

"And?" Mom was smiling again.

"If Troy's in, I'm in." I smiled in relief at my own words. "We'll be careful. We already are."

I leaned back in my chair. My parents were with us—if we decided to be *us*. I could worry about his parents later.

24

Rebounding

ON THURSDAY AFTERNOON TROY met me as I left last period. I took his hand and smiled like a girl who couldn't quite believe her good fortune.

"No game 'til next Friday," he said, "so Coach cancelled practice today and tomorrow. Wants us to work on getting our grades up."

"Are your grades down?"

"Nope."

"What are you doing instead? Besides this." We walked toward my locker.

"He said, if our grades are good and our assignments are in, we can shoot around for half an hour. Want to do something after that? If Mom hasn't started dinner, we could go to my house and make pizza."

"I wish I could, but I visit Grandpa every Thursday."

"Oh, right. Where does he live?"

"An Alzheimer's place across town. Zeus and I take the bus."

"Want a ride? I'll go with you."

"Thanks," I said automatically, "but we're fine on—"

I stopped midsentence and my eyes went wide. "Brain cramp! We'd love a ride, thank you. If we go after your shoot-around, we might still beat the bus."

"Cool," he said. "What if you two wait for me in the gym, if that's not too boring?"

"I thought you weren't supposed to bring girls to practice. Or dogs, probably."

"It's not practice. Just me shooting around. Maybe a couple other guys." He smiled. "Come on. New experience."

Two rows of bleachers were out on one side of the gym, so Zeus and I sat there. Troy went to dress down. He came back with a player I didn't know and started shooting. One would shoot ten times from a spot, while the other rebounded and passed him the ball. Then they'd switch.

I tried to keep my nose in a textbook, so it didn't look like I was there to adore basketball players. But Troy looked good, and most of his shots went in. I was happy that he wanted me there, and that he was content to visit Grandpa with me on his afternoon off, instead of trying to talk me into something more fun. He didn't argue that missing one visit wouldn't matter, or that Grandpa had Alzheimer's and wouldn't know the difference anyway.

I'd used those arguments myself, but not recently, and I rarely missed a Thursday visit. Even if Grandpa might forget me before I reached the elevator, he was happy while I was there. Today I'd be happy that Troy was there.

I was texting Mom and Dad about Troy taking me to Grandpa's, so I didn't notice the coach until he was already standing next to Zeus. When I saw him, I started.

He smiled. "Sorry to startle you. Hi. I'm Dale Witt. People call me Coach. You must be Jenny Miller."

"Nice to meet you, Coach." I extended my hand, and he shook it firmly. He was about Troy's height, but more muscular, middle-aged, and with no trace of hair anywhere on his head, except his eyebrows. I knew from games that he could look angry and intimidating, but he was smiling now, and he seemed friendly. And I knew Troy liked him.

"My pleasure," he said. "Join you for a moment?"

"Of course."

He sat. "Are you waiting for Troy?"

"Is that okay? He thought it would be."

"It's fine. You're a sophomore, aren't you? I've seen you and your dog around school this year."

"Yes, I am. This is Zeus."

"Okay if I touch him?" he asked.

"He'll let you know if it isn't."

He chuckled. "Troy mentioned your wit." He got acquainted with Zeus for a minute. Zeus didn't seem to mind.

Then Troy came over, but not for me. "Hey, Coach, Kaden has to go. Do you mind rebounding for a few minutes?"

"I can, but shouldn't I be your second choice?" Coach turned to me. "Jenny, can you rebound?"

My eyes got big, and my heart skipped a beat. "No."

"Sure you can," Troy said. "Great idea, Coach."

"I'll teach you," Coach said. "If it's okay."

I looked at Coach, then at Troy. "Are you sure?"

"Come on. New experience," Coach said. I was hearing that a lot lately.

I had the perfect excuse to stay where I was, but I agreed to try it. I sat Zeus beyond the end line, and Coach showed me where to stand near the basket, so I could usually get the ball, whether Troy's shot was good or not. He showed me what to do and gently corrected some mistakes.

I settled into a rhythm. I tried to catch the ball, fumbled it once or twice, picked it up, made a weak and poorly aimed pass to Troy, said "sorry" when it was off the mark, waited for him to shoot, and started over again.

"Don't worry," Coach said cheerfully, as Troy chased an especially bad pass. "You'll get the hang of it. And please stop apologizing for every pass."

"Even that one?" I frowned and pointed to the other end of the gym, where Troy was just picking up the ball.

Coach laughed. "Maybe for that one. But bad passes are good practice for him."

"Why?"

"Against a defense, it's harder to make good passes. When the pass isn't good, it's harder to shoot with form and rhythm. That's why, if it's a good pass, he usually goes straight up and shoots. If it's not, he takes a dribble or does something else first, to get in rhythm."

I hadn't seen him just shoot at all, after one of my passes. All bad, then. No surprise there. "What does a good pass look like again?"

"Right here." He held his hands in front of his chest, as if catching the ball. "From here he can dribble, shoot, or pass. You're putting it in the right place sometimes, but it needs to be harder, so it's easier to catch."

"Harder is how the ball got over there." I pointed.

He laughed again. "Tell you what. New drill. You rebound and pass to me, and I'll pass to him."

As far as I could tell, Coach's passes were all perfect. Sometimes he hardly even caught the ball, before it flew hard and fast to Troy's waiting hands.

Finally Troy was finished, long after my arms were tired. He thanked us both.

"Looking good, Troy," Coach said. "Your follow-through's more consistent lately. Good work, Jenny."

I frowned again. "No, it wasn't, but thanks for helping me." I gave Zeus the silent "come" signal, and he jumped up and joined me.

Troy went to dress, but Coach lingered. "You were fine," he said. "Besides, I think he likes you."

"Not for my basketball skills." My left elbow hurt more than my right, from all the passing, so I rubbed it gently.

"There may be other reasons. I see you with him at our games. Are you a basketball fan or just a fan of Troy?"

I shrugged. "Mostly Troy. There's hardly time for us to do anything else."

"Season's like that, especially for him. He splits practice time between JV and varsity, and he's a serious student with hard classes. But the season ends eventually. Are you going somewhere to celebrate no practice?"

"We're visiting my grandpa. I go every Thursday after school."

"That makes Grandpa happy."

"He doesn't remember me, but he likes the visits," I said.

"Alzheimer's?"

I nodded.

"Tough duty," Coach said. "My mom had it for the last few years. She passed away in September."

"I'm sorry."

"Thank you," he said.

Coach was easy to talk to, like Troy. "Grandpa's gentle and kind," I said. "He just asks my name every few minutes."

"Sounds like Mom. Still sad to watch."

"Yes, it is." It was time to switch elbows.

"His granddaughter writes a memorable valentine."

I froze. He saw Troy's valentine?

"Troy showed me on the bus that night," he explained. "Thanks for having it delivered after his game. I tell the guys not to let girls distract them too much during the season, especially on game days. Appreciate the help."

I nodded. "I'm trying to distract him just enough."

Coach smiled broadly. "I think it's working. His grades are great, and he's focusing well on the court. Workouts too." He stood. "Jenny, Zeus, it's been a pleasure. Three things before I go. Four things. Have a good visit with Grandpa. You have excellent taste in young men. If you stretch your arms and shoulders gently for a while before bed tonight, they'll be less stiff in the morning, after all that passing. And thanks for coming to our games."

On the way to Troy's car, with his arm around me as usual, I said, "I thought Coach was loud and angry, but he's really nice."

"One of the best men I know," he said. "He yells at us, and he obviously loves to win. But it's pretty clear he cares about us more than the scoreboard."

"He reminds me of you," I said.

"Jenny, that's maybe the nicest thing anybody ever said to me."

I smiled, but only for a moment. "Did you pass around my valentine that night?" He must have heard the new tremor in my voice.

"Showed it to Will and two other guys. And Coach. That was all. Am I in trouble?"

"I'm thinking."

"While you think, I'll tell you more. Coach said, 'That girl can really write.'" He smiled cautiously. "All started when Will asked me why I looked so happy on the ride home. Are we okay? There's more if I need it."

"Assume that you do," I said, but only because I wanted more. I was more flattered than embarrassed.

Which he must have heard in my voice. We reached his car, and he turned to me with a knowing smile. "The guys said other girls should take valentine lessons from you. One of them asked if you have a sister or a cousin he could date. Should have thought of Jack and Nikki. Am I in trouble?"

"Were they really that nice to me?" I asked.

"They like you."

"You're not in trouble. But you could have been."

⸺◆⸺

On our way to Grandpa's we got stuck in construction zone traffic. A police officer walked from car to car, telling everybody there was a four-car accident ahead, but nobody was seriously injured, and things would be moving again in 15 or 20 minutes. We were in a single lane between concrete barriers, with no room to turn around, and they didn't want everyone trying to back up half a mile to get out.

I didn't mind the delay. It was Troy time for me, and Grandpa wasn't going anywhere.

The sun was warm enough that we wouldn't need the heater, so Troy turned off the car. Then he turned to me. "May we talk about something?" He sounded nervous, which made me nervous.

"You don't have to ask. And you're really not in trouble."

He nodded slightly, but then he was silent—for what felt like minutes to me.

I waited, but not patiently. Then I couldn't wait anymore. "Have we finally run out of things to talk about?"

"No," he said, but it was another long moment before he continued. "I like you, Jenny, but . . ."

My heart sank. *But*? Was he friend-zoning me? He might be, now that he'd seen how inept I was at the gym.

"I'm sorry I embarrassed you," I said. "I've never been any good at sports."

"You didn't—"

"Which I've told you before, I know, but demonstrating it is so much worse." I shook my head. "Especially in front of your coach."

"I'm so bad at this," he said.

I almost asked, "At friend-zoning a girl?" But I just asked, "At what?"

"You know what you're really bad at?" he asked.

I stared at him for a moment. "Besides sports?"

"Believing good things about yourself."

"Troy, I . . . Never mind. I don't know what I was going to say."

He sighed. "I'm sorry. Can we rewind and start over? Please?"

"Good idea," I said. But was it really?

It started the same way the second time: with silence. Finally he spoke.

"I like you a lot, Jenny."

I nodded without smiling. "But?"

"But what?" he asked.

"That's your next word. From before. 'I like you, Jenny, but . . .'"

He winced. "This is what I'm bad at."

I said it out loud. "Friend-zoning a girl?"

For a moment he just stared at me—and my hoping for a twinkle in his eye to hint that I was wrong . . . didn't mean I saw one.

"I like you, Jenny," he said, "but . . . but it's more than that. I haven't gone out with anyone else since we met. Haven't wanted to. Never met a girl like you before. You're amazing. And you're good." He'd grown more animated as he spoke, but then his voice went flat. "The friend zone?"

"Not my first choice," I said weakly. I was a little off balance. "I like you too. I even like watching basketball, if you're with me. Or playing. How did that happen?"

He smiled nervously.

I couldn't wait. "Is this about officially being a couple? Is that what you want to talk about? Is that what you want?"

His eyes went wide, but he nodded eagerly. "Yeah. If you want it too. Before you tell me, you should know I don't want a girlfriend just to have one. I want you. I want to be serious about you. If you want that too."

My heart was fully recovered and ready to leave my chest. My mind was being weird about it. "Have you talked to Jack or Nikki about this?"

"No. Why?"

"Never mind. I . . ." I wanted to say it. Could I say it? I had to say it. "I want it too. I want to be serious about you."

His nervous face began to relax, and I began to melt. "I feel pretty serious about you already," I said.

He smiled again, but less than he might have. "Then there's something we should talk about."

"I know." I took a deep breath. "What do you think about the rules?"

25

Visiting Grandpa with My Boyfriend

I WANTED US TO be a couple, and Troy wanted it too. There in his car, stopped in traffic on the way to Grandpa's, I needed only one more thing, and I would be being absolutely liquid with delight.

He was about to tell me what I'd most wanted to know for days. Was he was as comfortable as I'd decided to be with breaking two of the rules, if we obeyed all the others? If he was, assuming his parents would allow it, this would be wonderful.

"I like that we both want to be good, not just be together," he said. "I know there's a rule, but I'm already okay with frequent dates with the same person. Kind of looks like you are too. And the one about avoiding serious relationships for now, well, I don't want to avoid this one. I think we can be good and be together. We have plenty of other rules. Can even add some if we need to."

I leaned back and sighed in relief. I hadn't realized I was holding my breath. Then I turned to him with a smile, which he answered with his own. "It's a bit like my dancing after all, as long as we're careful," I said.

"Yeah, it is. So be my girlfriend, please? And I will be your very lucky boyfriend."

"Okay," I said. It was that simple, and I was happy in a way I couldn't remember feeling before.

"Thanks, Jenny." he said after a moment that didn't feel silent. "I talked to my parents about this. About us."

"I talked to mine. Are we weird?"

"Maybe. What did yours say?"

"It's not like I've been seeing you secretly," I said. "They like how you treat me. And them. They said they trust both of us to make good decisions—as long as we make good decisions."

"Your parents are cool," Troy said.

"I should tell you what else they said. It was a whole family home evening, which was actually my idea. One advantage of being an only child." I told him about counsel, commandments, Pharisees, and both sides of "Lord, is it I?" Then I asked with less than perfect confidence, "What about your parents?"

"They're not Pharisees," he said. "They say they're willing to trust us, as long as we don't look like we're about to do something stupid."

My heart didn't fit in my chest anymore, but that was okay. I wanted him to have it.

"Doesn't sound romantic," he said, "but they talked about managing risk. Mom said the only way to be sure Dad's plane will never crash is never to leave the gate, but that's not what planes are for. So you fly but you manage the risks. So far, Dad always comes home. We still worry sometimes."

"Here's a coincidence," I said. "Professor Mom sent me a quotation yesterday. Something about ships being safe in the harbor, but that's not what ships are for."

Troy inclined his head and smiled. "So our moms are encouraging this, not just tolerating this?"

"My dad too," I said. "And Jack and Nikki."

"And Nan and Lilly," he said. "And Will. And my dad."

"Even Coach," I said. "According to him, I have great taste in young men."

"Must be true, if Coach said it. What about everybody else?" he asked.

"I'm trying not to care what anybody else thinks. Easy to say."

There were plenty of others whose opinion shouldn't bother us, but that wouldn't keep them from having one. Some of them wouldn't be pleased, and it wasn't just adults. Some kids were certain that whatever any Church leader said—or whatever any official Church manual, pamphlet, poster, video, website, Facebook status, e-mail, tweet, press release, or television commercial said—was the voice of God speaking absolute truth to the entire human race with perfect clarity. After all, wasn't every word approved in advance by Church leaders? Or at least it was inspired by God, who seemed likely to agree with himself.

When they saw us ignoring two well-known rules, which they might mistake for commandments, they'd think we were foolish, rebellious, or blinded by teenage lust. Or all of the above. Or lacked strong testimonies of the gospel, which really was some people's explanation for anything they didn't like about other Church members' lives. But we could worry about those people later.

"Hey, I just realized something," Troy said. "You told me what you want, but not what you think. Are you sure we're not rationalizing a mistake we'll feel guilty about eventually, but we really want to make it anyway?"

"That's the right question," I said.

"What's the right answer?" He sounded almost nervous again, but I knew what to do.

"Yes, we're in high school," I said. "I mean, I'm only a sophomore. Are you out of your mind? Don't answer that." I grinned and slipped my hand into his, wondering why it wasn't there already.

"Yes, we really like each other. I'm way beyond fluttery about that. So yes, it makes me happy. Yes, you're going on a mission, and even if you weren't, yes, we'll both be smart and obey the commandments. Some people will think we can't be good and be together, but yes, I think we can."

"I'm hearing a lot of yes," he said. He relaxed against the back of his seat, gave me a dreamy smile, and squeezed my hand.

"Yes, I think it's okay if we're a couple," I said. "And I already said yes, I'll be your girlfriend, and yes, I want you for my amazing and very lucky boyfriend."

His smile grew. "Very lucky boyfriend," he echoed.

I had to work at it, but I put on a serious face. "Now that we're official, would you like the list of things to which I won't say yes? Mom and Dad reviewed it with me. They were rather explicit." I was totally kidding. I didn't want to give him the list, and I hoped he knew it.

He blushed less—and less often—than I did, but now he turned crimson. "What if we assume I got the same speech and leave it at that?"

Traffic started to move, and he had to drive with both hands. I watched him and couldn't restrain my smile. Or my heart.

"You really feel good about this?" he asked after a minute. I thought we'd settled that, but maybe he wanted to hear me say it again, because it made him happy. Or because it made me happy.

"It feels right to me," I said. "Not just good."

"Me too. Not reckless or evil?"

"No, or I'm pretty sure you wouldn't want it either."

"I'd still want you," he said. "Even if I had to try not to. That would hurt."

How was a girl supposed to breathe? "Thank you for not friend-zoning me because of two rules," I said. "Speaking of pain."

"Not sure I could do that," he said. "Look, with some kids, being together is stupid and risky. So's just dating, when they're not serious. But we're not stupid. We'll be careful."

"We're already careful," I said.

He glanced at me, then turned back to the road. "Never had an official girlfriend before."

"I've only been one in my daydreams. What if we don't like it?" I could hear my poker face crumbling.

He grinned. "We like it."

I hadn't paid enough attention to where we were going, as I realized a few seconds too late. "Uh, boyfriend?"

"Girlfriend?"

"That was our turn. Sorry. I forgot to tell you."

We went around the block and tried again.

On our way in to see Grandpa, I held onto Zeus with one hand and kept my other hand in Troy's. Even more than before, it felt like it belonged there.

None of the rules from church said we shouldn't hold hands.

———◆———

Grandpa was in his recliner as always, in gray khakis and a flannel shirt. We knocked on his open door.

"Welcome. Please come in."

He looked down, displaying the thinning white hair atop his head, while he concentrated on pulling himself up and standing as straight as he could. He forgot almost everything, but never his manners. He always stood to greet visitors, even the staff.

He looked at us without recognition. It was his old man face—mouth hanging open and eyes wide, as if searching for something.

"Hi, Grandpa," I said.

"Hello. Thank you for coming. Do I know you two?"

"You know me. I'm Jenny, your granddaughter. My dog is Zeus, and Troy is my boyfriend." I glowed at Troy. "May I hug you, Grandpa?"

Mom said hugs were good for Alzheimer's patients. They were good for granddaughters too.

"That would be very nice." He reached out, and I gave him a long hug. Then Troy shook his hand.

"Please have a seat," said Grandpa. He sat carefully.

"Have you had a good week, Grandpa?"

"I believe so. Did you visit me last week?"

"Zeus and I did. This is Troy's first time."

"Oh, okay. Tell me about yourself, young lady."

"I'm a sophomore in high school. I write. I sing in two choirs."

"Who are your parents?"

"I'll show you." On his shelf was a framed family picture I always showed him when he asked that, which he always did. "My mom's your daughter."

"A beautiful family. Oh, that's you. You have a pretty smile."

"She gets that a lot, sir," Troy said.

"And what is your name, young man?"

"Troy, sir. I'm Troy."

"Are you this beautiful girl's boyfriend?"

"Yes, sir."

"Are you being good to each other?" he asked.

"Always, Grandpa," I said.

"Yes, sir," Troy said firmly.

"Excellent. And what is your name?"

Troy's eyes darted to me.

"My name is Troy, sir."

Grandpa nodded.

"Troy's a junior," I said. "He's on the basketball team. Troy, Grandpa played basketball in high school too. I've seen pictures." I opened my purse. "Grandpa, I brought us some of those Key lime chocolates you like."

I helped him close his bony, mottled, arthritic fingers firmly enough around a chocolate that he wouldn't drop it on the way to his mouth. We had lots of practice with chocolates.

I gave one to Troy and considered the hands I now loved to hold. A few years ago, Grandpa's had been strong and capable too.

We stayed for half an hour, until Grandpa started to get tired—or I did. He stood when we stood to leave, and he shook Troy's hand and even remembered his name.

I said I'd visit him again next week, and Mom would see him tomorrow. He asked my name again, and I told him.

"Jenny," he said thoughtfully, as if hearing it for the first time. "It's a pretty name. You have a lovely smile."

Troy was quiet and sober, as he drove me home through rush hour traffic, and I knew why. I could usually keep my spirits up with Grandpa for half an hour, but not after I left.

"Don't take this wrong," he finally said, "but that's the saddest thing I've seen in a long time."

"I know what you mean. It's pretty much the same visit every week. You were good for some variety, though. I'll be telling him about you every week, so I'll need a good picture, preferably of us together."

I hoped for a smile, but he just nodded. "Did you know him before Alzheimer's?"

"This is just the last few years."

"You're so kind and patient with him."

I blushed a little. "What else can I do? He's my grandpa. You see how gentle and sweet he is."

"Was he always like that?"

"As long as I've known him. Mom would say the same."

"Did it bother you when he remembered my name at the end, but not yours?" he asked.

"That's just how it works. Next time he'll remember Zeus, maybe."

A hint of a smile appeared. "He knows a pretty girl when he sees one."

I had to smile too. "You men are all alike. Or as Dad would say, 'He may be old, but he ain't dead.'"

Troy's laugh was nice while it lasted, but then he looked serious again and shook his head. "Some of the guys were making Alzheimer's jokes in the locker room the other day. Won't laugh at those anymore."

"I can't either, but you should know something about Grandpa. He'd make Alzheimer's jokes about himself, if he could remember that he has it. He was a real wit." I managed a faint smile. "I miss that."

"I'll bet. If you want, after the season, I could come with you on Thursdays."

"I want! Have I ever told you you're the best boyfriend I've ever had?"

As we sat in rush hour traffic, I realized two things. First, my weekly sadness from visiting Grandpa had already turned back to delight at being with Troy. And second, slow rush hour traffic had become a welcome thing. It was official boyfriend time now, and the more I could get of that, the better.

Traffic started to move, and he had to drive again. I leaned back in my seat and squeezed his hand. Life was good.

"It's nice that we both had the couple conversation with our parents already," he said.

It was only a small step from happy to giddy, and I was there. I saw an opportunity for mischief and pounced.

"I don't know. That could have been fun. 'Mom, Dad, this may disturb you, but we really like each other, and we think we can be a serious couple without getting too much into the groping, fornicating, pregnant, high school dropout, buying diapers at Walmart on Troy's employee discount thing. Otherwise, we wouldn't want to stay together, and we know you wouldn't want that either.'"

While I reeled from the thought that I had just mentioned making a baby with Troy—or not making one, which was sort of the same—he glanced at me with wide eyes, then looked back at the road.

"So yeah," he said. "Good thing."

He sounded amused, not horrified, so I pressed ahead, trying for a sultry voice.

"Are you a threat to my virtue, sir? Any straight, non-comatose, non-quadriplegic, post-pubescent human male is, right?"

After a moment he asked seriously, "Doesn't your virtue come from your own choices?"

"Well, aren't you the modern Mormon boyfriend!"

"Yes, I am. Officially. Very happy about that. I'd like to believe I can spend lots of time with a girl I'm attracted to and not be a threat."

We pulled into my driveway.

"Same here," I said to the boy who was attracted to me. "You know what I mean. A guy. One specific, very attractive guy."

26

Giddy

I STOPPED US ON my the front porch just long enough to get a grip on my dangerously giddy self. Then Troy came in for a minute, as my parents expected, whenever a boy picked me up or brought me home.

Dad was there to greet us. "This is unusual for a Thursday. Did you two have fun?"

"Yes, sir," said Troy.

I had no warning.

"No practice today," he continued, "so we parked somewhere until the police told us to move. It was only twenty minutes, but that was okay. Windows were starting to fog anyway. Then I took her to see her grandpa." He put his arm around my waist and pulled me firmly to him. I was too stunned to enjoy it—or resist.

Dad and I stared at each other with matching wide eyes, then turned to Troy. If anything, he looked too innocent, too sincere.

Seconds passed. Dad said warily, "I think a parent might have cause for alarm, if all that were true."

I watched Troy's face for the slightest hint of a smile but saw none. I glared at him. "It's all true, Dad. The rest of the truth is, we were stuck in traffic behind an accident. The police said it would be 15 or 20 minutes, so he turned off the car to save gas. And the planet." I turned to Dad. "He's trying to be funny."

"He's succeeding," Dad said with a straight face. "Good thing I'm not a kill-the-boy-now, ask-questions-later sort of dad."

"Now you're trying to be funny," I said.

"He's succeeding," Troy deadpanned.

Dad relaxed and smiled. "There you have it. The deadpan comedy team of Troy and Dad, appearing for limited Thursday engagements. We find ourselves hysterical."

"Da-ad!"

He mimicked me. "Da-ad what?"

"Is this really the behavior you want to encourage in the boys I bring home? Or your impressionable teenage daughter?"

He turned to Troy. "She has a point. I might have had my own point before that."

"Understood, sir," Troy said. "And understood, sir."

"Understood what?" I demanded. "I don't speak man-code."

"Troy can explain later," Dad said. "In the meantime, let me just say, aren't men wonderful?"

I tried to sound businesslike. "Troy, thank you for taking me to see Grandpa. I'm glad we got to talk. And now, fond as I am of you both, I should take care of Zeus."

Just before disappearing, I added, with what I hoped was a radiant, innocent smile, "Bye, boyfriend."

⋯◆⋯

Dinner was ready, and we started without Mom. She was at a meeting.

Dad said, "I thanked Troy for taking you to see Grandpa. I'm afraid something he said will damage your humility. Shall I tell you anyway?"

I gave him a patient look.

"He said you were cheerful, kind, and patient with Grandpa. Like an angel, he said."

I blushed like Troy was there, saying it himself.

"I told him I've seen you at work. You get it from your mom."

My quiet smile felt like Mom's would have looked, if she had been there. "Thanks, Dad."

"I'm going to assume he's willing to joke about parking and making out because he's clever, not because you'll be doing it anytime soon."

"That's a very safe assumption," I said.

"Then I like his wit. Slightly edgy. I imagine you said something to deserve it."

"Yes." No way would I tell him what, because what did it say about me that I'd been giddy enough to joke with Troy about unplanned pregnancies and changing diapers? "He didn't say what, did he?"

"He did not. Should I ask?"

"No, probably not."

After dinner I texted Troy to ask what Dad said after I left.

He replied immediately. "Said you're a fun daughter with a quick wit. Praised me for holding my own. Also said he likes seeing you happy. Man-code for, I should treat you right and not hurt you. Did he tell you what he showed me in his study?"

"No."

"Have now read The Outdoor Adventures of Z-Dog. Twice. Pretty cool!"

I had written Dad a fictional story with terrible illustrations, starring a dog who resembled Zeus, as a Father's Day gift when I was eleven. He'd framed all four pages and hung them in his study, along with an award certificate I won with it in a contest at the public library. I didn't want him to, but he said they were a gift, so they were his now, and it wasn't up to me. I hadn't made a gift of my writing since. He'd seen a lot of it, but he couldn't claim any of it belonged to him and put it on his wall.

"There's a whole series he doesn't know about," I wrote.

"Can I read more sometime?"

"The series?"

"Anything," he wrote. "Already a big fan of your valentine cards."

"Most of it's not good."

"I get it. Anything you want me to read, anytime, I want to read. Doesn't have to be now. Or soon."

"I'll remember that. Thanks for understanding." My brain was a little skittish about this, but my heart was melting again. "I'll have some things I want you to read. I promise." I wanted to add a big, red heart emoji, but I felt it too much to be able to send it just then.

I also had text messages from Jack and Nikki. They always checked in with me on Thursdays—Nikki after her dance class and Jack after her oboe lesson at the university—because they knew visiting Grandpa made me sad.

Once they learned my happy news, they had to come over and hear it all in person. Our excuse was studying English, but we didn't expect much of that to happen, unless speaking English counted.

Nikki arrived first. I asked her what she thought about serious couples in high school. She and Jack had heard all the same lessons in church and seminary—but they'd cheered me on from the beginning with Troy, never hinting that a relationship with him might be wrong. We had thoroughly analyzed everything else together, but I hadn't asked them about this. Now I wanted to hear them agree with me, and I wanted their reasons why.

Nikki said, "You should behave yourself and have a relationship with that boy. You're amazing together. Can we find me an equally fabulous boyfriend? Jack too, of course."

"Will's available," I said. "Shall I drop a hint?"

"No. He's nice, but math and computer geeks are more my thing. Some of them are sweet, and they're going to be rich, and I don't have to compete with cheerleaders or sports. I can totally compete with video games."

Jack arrived. I wanted her opinion even more than Nikki's. She was like a philosopher. She thought carefully and came up with things others didn't.

She raised one eyebrow. "Are you asking if it's a sin to love Troy? Up close and personal, not from afar?"

"That's one question."

"How can it be a sin? You're perfect for each other. Are you supposed to pretend you never met?"

"It doesn't feel wrong," I said. "I'm a better person with him than without him."

"Okay. Are you asking if two high school kids can be in love without falling into bed together, even when they're warm for each other's form?"

"Ew. But that too." The word *love* did fluttery things to my heart and brain.

Her slight pout meant she was thinking hard. "If it's impossible, then no one is really morally good. We just lack opportunities to commit certain sins." She gave me an inquiring look. "Is that what you think?"

"No, but strong people have weak moments, right? King David, for example?" In seminary we'd thoroughly analyzed his troubles with Bathsheba and her husband.

"My parents would say, can you keep your weak moments out of dangerous times and dangerous places?"

"We think we'll be okay, if we're careful," I said.

"Then be in love with him. Are you? Is he in love with you?"

Judging by the cloud I was on, we were getting there. "For now, we're just girlfriend and boyfriend, and there's a lot of liking going on. And handholding."

"*Just* girlfriend and boyfriend? This is huge! I'm so happy for you!"

"Me, too," said Nikki. "Plus a little jealous. I guess we still don't know whether our New Year's resolution helped anything."

"Wait," said Jack. "We forgot Zeus. What does he think?"

I grinned. "He heard the whole DTR discussion today from the back seat and didn't object once, during or after."

"I almost forgot something else," Jack said. "I have historical artifacts to help us celebrate. First let's open our English books, so we look like we're studying. Then I brought three noisemakers." She pulled them from her backpack. "These are from the New Year's dance, the ones we never used. Thought we might want them someday. Jenny, green was yours. Nikki, yours was yellow. Blue for me."

We made noise like it was New Year's, and Jack and Nikki danced around.

Mom and Zeus appeared in the open doorway. Zeus cringed at the noise. Mom smiled and shook her head. Seconds passed before Jack and Nikki noticed and stopped dancing.

"Hi, Dr. Miller," said Jack. "English is fun."

Our open books were unconvincing, I thought.

"I love it too," Mom said. "Never celebrated quite like this. What are we reading?"

"Something new," Jack said. "It's kind of a romance."

"I hope it's a clean romance. What's it called?" Mom was still smiling.

Jack smiled too. "*Cute Texas Boy*. It's squeaky clean so far."

Nikki blew her noisemaker in Mom's direction. Jack blew hers at Nikki. Mom and I shared a look, and I tried not to laugh.

"I heard something about that," Mom said. "Is it long?"

"We don't know," Jack replied. "We're celebrating the beginning."

Nikki blew her noisemaker too hard, so it squawked. Then she did it again. She was wired.

"I'll get back to work," Mom said. "But I'm leaving Zeus to supervise. He's not crazy about the noisemakers."

"We'll stop," said Nikki. "For Zeus."

"I'm sure he thanks you. Enjoy discussing the cute Texas boy." Her eyes twinkled.

I gave Zeus a signal, and he joined me. Mom disappeared. Nikki did a little happy dance, then fell into her chair. Jack watched and grinned.

We analyzed my cute Texas boy for another hour, almost. When they left, I kept my noisemaker. I knew the perfect place for it: in the pocket of another historical artifact, the heather gray skirt I wore to meet Troy.

◄O►

On Friday my boyfriend had teammates to rebound for him. His giddy girlfriend sat and watched. Then my boyfriend and I went to my boyfriend's house to make pizza and salad for my boyfriend's family.

My. Boyfriend.

On the way there, I spoke a crazy thought. "After the season, will you still do shoot-arounds? Could you use a bad rebounder on Thursdays, before we go to Grandpa's?"

Troy sounded surprised but looked pleased. "You really want to? You don't have to."

"As long as you're not just humoring me. I'll try to be better than I was yesterday."

"That was your first day. Now you have experience and some good coaching. You sure it's safe enough?"

"There's always a chance I'll collapse," I said, "but even if I do, when it's just the floor and there's nothing to hit on the way down, I'm usually okay."

We stopped for a red light, and he turned to me. "Wouldn't mind reliving yesterday afternoon every week. That'll be fun."

"Don't think I told you," Troy said after dinner, as we sat in his living room. "I'm speaking in church Sunday morning. You can sit with my family, if you want to come."

Sacrament meeting speakers were usually ordinary members. Most Sundays, there was a youth speaker or two, then a couple of adults. From age twelve to eighteen, you could count on being asked to speak for three-to-five minutes at least once a year. More often in my case.

"Of course I want to come. Will I make you nervous?"

"Better than missing you," he said earnestly.

I struggled to focus. "What's your assigned topic?"

"Give you one guess," he said drily.

"Ah, the usual." I switched to an extra-deep voice. "Brother Pullman, pick something from *For the Strength of Youth*. Or one of the Young Women Values. Oh, but you're not a young woman. Maybe something from the *New Era*." That was the Church's monthly youth magazine.

I returned to my normal voice. "It's like they actually prefer boring and impersonal."

"I'm ignoring them this time," Troy said. "Want to hear my rant? Been working on it since seminary."

"Sure. May I keep holding your hand, or do you need it to talk?"

A playful smile flashed across his face. "We'll see. Anyway, it's like you said. We get up and read something that's not scripture, usually in a monotone. Everybody's bored, and nobody has to think, especially the speaker. If we try to be funny, it's even worse.

"The standards are good, okay? And the magazine's fine. But why don't they tell us to use our own thoughts and experiences and, you know, the scriptures? Why not talk more about Jesus himself? All that other stuff only matters if it leads to him.

"What's more important, mercy and grace, or whether some girl's skirt is half an inch too short, so all of us helpless boys have impure thoughts? Like we wouldn't have any, if her skirt were half an inch longer. Or her legs were shorter."

I grinned. "Where'd that come from?" Mom and I complained about those same attitudes. Troy had never heard us, but he had a mom and sisters.

"Seminary today. We talked about ways to serve God. At first it was pretty good. Then this girl said the best way she knows to do that is make sure her dresses and skirts cover her entire knees at all times, even when she's sitting, and to keep her necklines high enough that seeing her doesn't make even the weakest future missionary have impure thoughts. Then her friends raised their hands and said the same things in different words and told each other how spiritual they are. By the time Brother Stickinger could rein them in, the bell rang."

It had to be said, so I said it. "I guess we'll never see for ourselves, if she always dresses like that. But she must have incredibly erotic knees. Is that a thing?"

His big smile and burst of laughter fed the mischief in my heart.

"Too bad I'm not in a skirt. We could check my knees. Do you think they might . . ." I probed my kneecap through my jeans, like I was studying its shape and size, then looked up at him. "No, probably not."

Now he convulsed with laughter, while I beamed.

"Sorry, I interrupted your rant," I said, when he had mostly settled down. "That wasn't the end, was it?"

"It was worth it. Where was I? Oh. I know the booklet doesn't actually say how long skirts should be. Or how high necklines should be."

I reached for my neckline, to adjust my modest scoop neck half an inch downward—not enough to matter, just enough to fluster him. But I stopped. Knees were one thing . . .

His eyebrows arched. Had he read my mind? He smiled faintly and his cheeks colored a bit. So did mine.

"It's more sensible than that," he continued. "But there sure are a lot of people who know exactly what God thinks about every little thing. Seriously, how stupid are we, if we judge how good a person you are by half an inch more or less of cloth in your clothes?"

He sighed. "That's the whole rant, unless you have a ruler I can break for effect. You've been a beautiful, incredibly distracting audience."

I shifted so I could rest my head on his shoulder. He squeezed, and I purred.

I forced myself to focus. "It was a fine rant, and I totally agree. What will you talk about?"

"Doing what Jesus would do, if he were here. And something he did when he was."

"How can I help?"

"Give me permission," he said. "I want to tell four quick stories, one from the New Testament and one from kindergarten. Two from yesterday, Coach teaching you to rebound and you visiting your grandpa. That's why I need permission."

Troy wanting to use something about me in his talk thrilled me, but what I said was, "My two stories seem pretty ordinary."

"Not to me. I won't embarrass you. I'll just call you my friend and not mention your name, unless you want me to."

"You have my permission."

My phone vibrated. I checked the caller ID and sat up. "Excuse me. I should get this."

27

Speaking in Church

MY CALLER WAS BISHOP Savage. He'd been the leader of our congregation—ward—for years. He'd been a family friend even longer. I grinned mischievously at Troy. "This will be fun."

We said hello. Then I asked, "Checking up on your youth on Friday night again?" I'd never heard of that happening, but you could have fun with my bishop. "Here's my report."

I scooted half an inch closer to Troy, if that was possible. "At the moment, Bishop, I'm exactly zero inches from the nearest boy. His name is Troy. We were holding hands earlier. His parents are in the kitchen, cleaning up after the dinner we made them. We offered to help, but they wouldn't let us. His little sister keeps peeking around the corner to see if we're making out, but we're totally not. He's telling me about his sacrament meeting talk for Sunday morning.

"Dessert is next. His mother makes carnal, sensuous, and devilish pies on Fridays. Gluttony is one of the seven deadlies, right? That's my sin for tonight. Then maybe Troy will take me home, so he can concentrate on his talk, which so far really needs the work. This concludes my report."

Bishop Savage laughed so loudly over the phone that I thought Troy's parents might hear him in the kitchen. Troy's face was red, and he looked like he might explode with laughter again. Or hurt himself trying not to.

"Jenny," the bishop finally said, "thanks for your report. It's a first for me." He laughed again.

"It's all true."

"I believe you," he said. "I'm sorry to ask at the last minute"—I gave Troy an amused look—"but would you speak in sacrament meeting on Sunday? I know you'll do well on short notice."

"Sure, Bishop, I can speak Sunday," I said for Troy. "Which part of *For the Strength of Youth* shall I read from the pulpit?" Troy snorted softly. "Dating, perhaps? I've been doing that. Sexual purity? We're for that, right, and Satan's against it? Or we haven't heard anything from the copyright page lately, or the inside of the back cover. We're so blessed to have a reliable resource for our talks, so we don't have to struggle with the scriptures or have our own insights, like they did in the old days."

Troy was dying beside me, almost quietly.

The bishop laughed again. "Any gospel topic you choose will be fine, and I'll look forward to it. You know the drill. Three to five minutes. Seven or eight, if you want, since you're the only youth speaker. Sit on the stand if you can. We'll get out that tall stool for the pulpit."

I was tempted to say I'd stand at the pulpit like everybody else, but I'd be nearly surrounded by hard things I shouldn't hit on the way down. I was bold but not stupid, and the stool was tall enough that it was almost like standing anyway. I just said, "Thanks."

"Thank you, Jenny. Fun talking to you. Give my best to Troy. I want to meet him sometime."

After the call ended, Troy said, "I can't believe you talk to your bishop that way." He wiped tears from his eyes. "Can't believe he's okay with it."

"He's a good guy," I said. "Mom and Dad like him a lot. So do I."

"Used to think you were timid and shy," he said. "You're actually very bold."

Bold Jenny's heart swelled with pride. "Maybe even crazy?" I asked.

"Maybe a little. But it's a really good crazy." He grinned and shook his head.

"I'm not that bold. Just with people I know, like Bishop Savage. I'll admit just a bit of crazy." When I'm giddy enough, I didn't add.

"If I'm ever a bishop, I want all the young women in my ward to be just like you," Troy said.

"You can barely handle one of me," I said without thinking, then blushed slightly at my choice of verb.

"I'll learn. There's time."

I liked his hint at having a future together, if that's what it was. But now I had writing to do. "We could work on our talks together tonight,"

I said, "but we wouldn't get much done." I reached for his hand. "On our talks."

"I'll take you home after pie, so you won't have lied to your bishop," he said. "May I come hear you speak?"

"Of course."

"Won't make you nervous?"

"A little nervous. A lot happy."

Before we said goodbye at my front door—quite a while after pie—I gave him a line from an old talk Dad sometimes played for us, from 1980 or so. He laughed and said he'd use it.

⸺◆⸺

When Troy appeared at my door at 8:30 a.m. on Sunday, he was in his gray suit again, with a blue tie I loved because it matched his eyes.

I liked to be warm in cold chapels, so I wore an emerald green, leaf print jacket over a black midi dress with a round neckline. Dad said I looked "quite grown up." Mom confessed to buying me the jacket at a secondhand store mostly so she could borrow it.

Troy said I was beautiful. "Nice outfit too," he added.

When it was his turn at the pulpit, he began with my contribution. "I want to quote something President Gordon B. Hinckley said long ago, then follow his example. This is what he said: 'I've been assigned a topic, which I'm going to avoid.'"

His delivery was just right. People laughed, and my bishop would have, but Troy's didn't. He was a tall, dignified-looking man with a few wrinkles and a full head of salt-and-pepper hair. When he produced a faint, polite smile, the effect was austere.

Troy said, "After his resurrection, Jesus asked the Nephites, 'What manner of men and women'"—Troy added the women—"'ought ye to be?' Then he answered, 'Even as I am.'"

Troy said he had three examples of people he had seen being Christlike.

The first was from kindergarten in Texas. One day at recess, a girl in his class announced that she was making the Club of Kids Who Are Saved by Jesus and Don't Worship Satan. Everyone could be in it except Troy.

The way to join was to tell Troy, out loud and in front of everyone, "Get behind me, Satan."

In my mind I saw a little, blue-eyed Mormon boy on a school playground, listening to all his not-very-Christian classmates call him Satan. Tears pooled in my eyes.

The last boy, Troy said, was Philip. He wouldn't say it. He looked Troy in the eye and said, "Let's go play catch." Which they did.

I'd have cried at little Philip's courage and loyalty even if I hadn't known Troy. I dried my eyes and saw Troy's mom drying hers. She noticed me noticing and smiled self-consciously.

Next he told of a friend rebounding for him at the gym the other day, while he practiced shooting. The friend wasn't athletic and struggled just to catch the ball, let alone to make good passes. Coach wasn't critical or impatient, just helpful and encouraging.

It seemed like a small thing, Troy said, but a lot of important things are small. He quoted the Book of Mormon again, a verse from Alma this time, about great things coming out of small things.

Then he described how I'd treated Grandpa during our visit.

I liked thinking of myself as a little bit Christlike, and I liked Troy seeing me that way. But my visiting Grandpa wasn't a heroic sacrifice. It was once a week for half an hour. Mom visited him almost every day. But maybe that was Troy's point. The small things.

Finally he told the New Testament story of Zacchaeus, who climbed a tree to see Jesus over the crowd. Jesus didn't care that people hated Zacchaeus for being a tax collector for the Romans. He said he'd eat at Zacchaeus' home that day.

I only half-listened to Troy's conclusion. I was still thinking about a brave little kindergarten boy. When he was done, I turned to Troy's mom and whispered, "That was amazing."

She beamed. "People listened," she whispered. "I'm so proud of him."

I was proud of him too.

"When we heard what happened at recess that day," she whispered, "we went to see Philip's parents and told them, so they could be proud of their son."

I liked sitting with Troy's family at church. The congregational singing in their ward really did sound weak and half-hearted, but the Pullmans sang like they meant it. I happily joined in.

At home I learned that Mom and Dad had been there too, somewhere in the back, just long enough to hear Troy. They said he did very well, and they weren't surprised.

❦

I rehearsed my talk for maybe the twentieth time—this time just in my head—on the stand before my own ward's sacrament meeting that afternoon. I sat in the first row behind the pulpit, where leaders and scheduled speakers always sat, facing the congregation. Zeus sat on the floor beside me. There were three empty rows of seats behind us, because the choir wasn't singing that day. The soft organ prelude almost balanced the hum of baby noises and subdued chatter from the gathering congregation.

I looked down to where Mom and Dad usually sat, in one of the shorter pews along the sides of the chapel. I expected to see Troy, Jack, Nikki, and my parents. They weren't there, but it took only a moment to find them. They were just getting settled in a longer pew in the center section, the front one that was often empty. The reason they needed a longer pew made me more nervous.

Troy's parents and little sisters were with them. Lilly and Nan sat between Jack and Nikki, who was next to Dad. All four were conversing in whispers. Our moms sat together, between our dads, and Troy was at one end. I hadn't known Troy's family was coming. I didn't know why our parents wouldn't like each other, but what if they didn't?

When Troy saw me looking at him, he gave me a big smile and a small wave. I looked at our families with concern, then back at him. He nodded subtly in their direction and gave me a discreet thumbs-up. I went back to being nervous about my talk.

At the pulpit, half an hour later, I had to force myself not to be distracted by the whole row of smiling people just in front of me. Troy's smile was the brightest. Jack's had the most mischief in it. When she saw me looking, she waggled her eyebrows. I looked toward the back of chapel and focused.

I had to focus for another reason too. Remembering a time just before my seizures began stirred all sorts of emotions.

"When I was a little girl," I began as calmly as I could, "my family and some other families went to Wyoming for three hot, windy days and two chilly nights on the Mormon Trail. At night we slept in tents. During the days we pulled handcarts. They told us the real pioneers' handcarts were loaded with several hundred pounds each. Ours were almost empty.

"For breakfast they served us some water and a quarter-cup of flour. That's how much some of the handcart pioneers had to eat, when they ran into trouble. We mixed the water and flour together to make what they called 'skilly.' I tried to eat it. I was so hungry I cried.

"Later, unlike those pioneers, we had a good lunch and a big, hot dinner around the fire, instead of another quarter-cup of flour. And as much as I didn't like the wind, at least we weren't in a blizzard, freezing while we starved to death.

"I think about that sometimes, when my life feels hard. I think how hard life was for two famous companies of handcart pioneers.

"I remember stories of mothers going hungry, so they could feed their children a little more—stories often told by the children, because sometimes, eventually, the price of a child's life was a mother's death.

"I remember hearing of fathers who struggled to dig graves in the frozen earth, to bury a wife or child or someone else who'd died during the night. Then they pulled those handcarts as far as they could through the blizzard, and even a little farther—until some of them finally sat down beside the trail, in exhaustion and despair, and died in the bitter cold.

"Others somehow kept pulling their handcarts up Rocky Ridge in the snow and freezing wind. When their strength failed, their handcarts didn't stop moving or roll backwards. When they turned to see who was helping, they saw no one. It must have been unseen angels who pushed them along.

"Then I remember an old promise the Lord had made again to those pioneers, and I wonder if they thought of it then: 'I will go before your face. I will be on your right hand and on your left, and my Spirit shall be in your hearts, and mine angels round about you, to bear you up.'

"Then I cannot help but think of the Savior, the perfect Son of God, as his terrible suffering began, praying that the bitter cup might pass from him—if it was possible. But it wasn't possible, as he already knew. He was sent to save us, because no one else's agony and death could bring us life. So he did the Father's will and bled from every pore in Gethsemane, then hung for hours on the cross at Calvary by nails the Romans pounded through his hands, wrists, and feet. He died and was placed in a borrowed tomb. Soon he would rise again, appear to many who believed, and show them the wounds he chose to keep.

"Then I remember what he told his people from heaven, through a prophet, centuries before that awful night and day, speaking as if his future sacrifice had already happened: 'Yet will I not forget thee. . . . I have graven thee upon the palms of my hands.'

"I think of his promises to each of us, that he will remember us, be with us, help us, redeem us, and finally bring us home to himself and our Father. I think about the times when I can't pull my own life's little cart by myself, and I think about the angels, seen and unseen, who come to my aid and push.

"The angels in my life—the ones I know about—are ordinary people. Some of them are here today. They do God's work. They are his angels sent to help me, as he promised.

"I think about the help he sends us and his promises to everyone, and I want to thank him, love him, praise him, obey him, and serve him even more."

I didn't try to speak dramatically, just clearly and without sounding like I was reading. I couldn't claim I wasn't trying to impress anyone, because I was, a little. But I tried not to think that way. Mostly I had something to say, something important, at least to me. So I did my best and hoped it would matter to some of the people who listened.

When the meeting ended, Bishop Savage got to me first, before I left the stand. He was only a few inches taller than me, and his round face had a radiant smile. He shook my hand and said, "You were the highlight of my entire week. Thank you." He asked more softly, "How many hours to prepare that?"

"Since Friday evening?" I paused to count. "Eight, maybe nine."

"Thanks for giving us half your weekend," he said. "I certainly asked the right youth speaker."

When I left the stand, more than a dozen people were waiting to thank me and compliment me. I was embarrassed and delighted.

Mom and Dad had a class of five-year-olds to teach, so they couldn't wait for the people who got to me before them, while they chatted with Troy's parents. They just smiled and waved from ten feet away, then left for their class. But I already knew they liked my talk. Mom had texted me, "Beautiful. Powerful. Dad says you're still his favorite daughter."

One very old lady took my hand in both of hers. I had to lean down to hear her. She said I'd reminded her of her late husband's favorite hymn, "Come Unto Jesus," where it asks, "Know you not that angels are near you?" I told her I wished I'd thought of that.

Troy's sisters hugged me. Nan said, "I really liked your talk."

Lily said, "We all liked it. We even listened. Mom cried."

His dad shook my hand and said I did very well, and his mom hugged me and said my words were beautiful. So maybe they weren't too worried about the time I was spending with their son.

"That was so good," Nikki said as she hugged me.

Jack hugged me, then grinned. "A boy brought his family to hear you, and they sat with your family. What must people be thinking?"

For an instant I wondered if we'd just invited a lot of judgment, especially if people saw Troy with me at church in the future. Then he wrapped me in a hug, and I decided I wanted people to see us at church together as often as possible.

"Told you my girlfriend's amazing," he said. "You blew Mom and Dad away. Did you see me feeling my knee when you started?"

"No," I gasped. "Jack making faces was bad enough."

Too late I remembered wanting him to meet someone. Bishop Savage had left for his next meeting.

Together

28

Insecurities

E VEN BEFORE TROY AND I were official, three cheerleaders—all juniors like Troy—started saying hi to me in the halls at school. They weren't being friendly.

One would say, "Look! It's Troy's little service project," and they'd smile and wave. If a certain boy was with them, he'd add an obscene gesture. It happened almost daily, but never when I was with Troy, which wasn't often at school, or with Jack or Nikki, which was about half the time.

The ringleader was Maddi Burke. She was the perfect stereotype of a cheerleader. In two-inch heels she was about my height, but slim and enviably proportioned, with a pretty, oval face, big hazel eyes, and a perfect smile. Her platinum hair was artistic—every day. She probably spent more time on it in a day than I spent on mine in two weeks. She was also athletic enough to look natural when she bounced, flipped, and cartwheeled during timeouts at basketball games.

Sometimes she added a nasty flourish to their greetings. She'd say to the others, loudly enough for me to hear, something like, "It's so cool of Troy to be nice to the project, when he's allergic to its dog." (I knew he wasn't allergic to Zeus.)

Or: "She should stick to her own species." (The ones that were just mean were the easiest to ignore.)

Or: "Troy and Becca were so cute together at lunch. He deserves a normal girlfriend." (I knew he thought Becca was vacuous—our slightly nicer word for *airhead*.)

Or: "If she really loves him, she should set him free and see if he ever comes back, which he won't." (This one tickled somehow, but I kept my smile to myself.)

It was never the same twice, and some of her jabs seemed clever. Maddi was no airhead. She just wasn't smart enough to be kind.

I didn't tell Troy what was happening, or Jack or Nikki or my parents. I didn't want them making a big deal out of it, and most of the time I didn't give the haters a second thought.

Most of the time.

The Wednesday after we Defined The Relationship started badly. By second period I wondered if I was coming down with something. By lunchtime I was sure, but I didn't go home early. I didn't want to miss Advanced Writing or Troy. He had an away game, but we'd have a few minutes after school, before the team bus left.

On my way to meet him, I wished selfishly that basketball would just end, so we could spend more time together. That reminded me of Maddi's morning jab: "Troy says his little project is only until basketball's over. Then he'll have time for a real girlfriend."

I sat on a bench in a small common area between the locker rooms and the doors which led to the team bus outside. Zeus and I were early. I wasn't thinking straight, or I wouldn't have done something totally stupid while we waited. I wouldn't have thought for five seconds, let alone five minutes, about Troy dumping me for "a real girlfriend" after basketball.

I didn't notice him until he asked softly, "Are you okay?" He sat next to me, holding his gym bag in one hand and a hanger with his basketball uniform in the other.

I didn't even try to smile. "Not really."

"What's wrong?"

I meant to tell him I was sick and to keep a safe distance, but something else came out. "Troy, you've been good to me, and it's been fun, but I don't want to be your project anymore."

He furrowed his brow. "I'm sorry. What?"

I focused on the opposite wall. "I don't want to be your service project anymore."

I was certain he was about to say, "Okay," then stand up and walk out of my life, probably without looking back.

His tone was serious but gentle. "Somebody at lunch today said you're getting that in the halls. Wanted to ask you about it." He blew out a long breath. "I probably can't make them stop. Wish I could." Then there was a new tremor in his voice. "Maybe I can't stop you from saying it either. But I never said it. Never even thought it. It's not true."

Awkward seconds crawled by. I still didn't look at him. "I'm not your project?"

"No! Why would you—" He wasn't yelling, but he sounded more and more upset. "I like you. I like myself better when I'm with you. I thought you knew that. What part of that says project to you?"

I mostly heard his hurt, angry tone. A hot tear rolled down my cheek. "I don't know. None of it?"

"Then what—"

"I'm sorry! I'm sick, and Maddi said . . . and . . . I don't know." The tears dripped in earnest now, and I hid my face in my hands. "They usually don't bother me. I'm sorry. I'm having a bad day." Which was now a worse day for both of us, thanks to me.

He set down his things, eased my hands away from my face, and held them. His hands were gentle but his face wasn't. His cheeks were flushed, the mouth that smiled so often was contorted into a frown, and his eyes flashed. He was angry, and I deserved it.

"Sorry you're sick," he said. "But this is crazy. What are you thinking?"

I focused on our hands—it helped a little—and tried to explain my dark thoughts. "I was thinking, not for the first time, that you're this handsome, popular athlete, and I'm just the plain girl with epilepsy who sits and watches life go by. Why would a boy like you go to all the extra trouble to be with a girl like me, unless I'm some sort of project, like they say?" I glanced up at him, then back down. "Some way to get whatever it is that you want."

"Jenny, look at me. Please?"

He was still squeezing my hands. I slowly met his eyes.

"Those jerks are jealous and cruel, and they're wrong. When you say it, you're wrong too. And you're not plain." He glanced toward the doors, shaking his head. "Sorry. I have to get to the bus."

He let go of my hands and gathered his things, then turned back to me. "I'm not pretending to like you. I'm not using you to get what I want. I want you."

His words should have filled me with joy. They should have taken my breath away. But they didn't. My voice was unsteady, and I had to force my eyes not to look away. "I'm sorry. For what I said, and for ambushing you with my self-pity. Is there any way I can make it up to you?" I desperately wanted him not to be upset with me.

"Yeah, there is," he said more sharply than I expected. "Stop believing jerks who say you're my project. Please!"

The bus's horn sounded outside the doors. Two other players raced past us. "I have to go," he said, and he went.

"Good luck tonight," I croaked too softly for him to hear, as he disappeared through the door. "I'll text you," I whispered. I was on the verge of sobbing. "If you still want me . . . if you still want me to."

Zeus and I stayed until the bus pulled away. I felt like dirt. I'd let them hurt me. Then I hurt him. I wanted to resent his anger, but it was my fault. I'd been unkind, unfair, and selfish. He'd been loyal and sincere.

I could hardly wait to disappear into my bedroom and cry.

⸻◄O►⸻

I waited to text him until I thought the JV game might be over and he could turn his phone back on. But I didn't really wait. I spent a long time trying to get it right.

I finally gave up and sent what I had. "Troy, I've been imagining how what I said to you would have hurt me, if I were in your place. I didn't plan to say it. It just popped out. But I shouldn't even have thought it. I know you're not that guy. Wallowing in my self-pity is so selfish. I'm sorry. How can I make it up to you? PS: Did you win? I hope so."

I sat and waited for his reply—and waited and waited. Maybe there was overtime or bad cell phone reception at the other school. But what if he broke up with me because I lost my mind and accused him of using and deceiving me?

I wished Mom and Dad were home to hear my troubles, but it was their night teaching classes at the community college. I thought about texting Nikki and Jack. On the way home I'd only told them I was sick. Now I didn't feel up to explaining everything in text messages or talking on the phone with my sore throat. I didn't complain to Zeus either. He'd heard it all as it happened.

I wanted to let go and cry some more, but crying would make me cough, which would make my head and throat hurt worse. So I sat at my desk in my bedroom, motionless, head in hands, staring through half-closed eyes at the phone sitting between my elbows.

The watched pot finally boiled.

Once it arrived, I was only a little bit afraid of Troy's text message. The preview didn't say, "We're done. Leave me alone." It wasn't the beginning of something like, "If you don't trust me, then you were right. We should break up."

It said, "Sorry, two overtimes. Pretty exciting. We won."

It took my unsteady fingers almost forever to get to the rest of it.

"You're not a project or a burden," he wrote. "Don't listen to the haters. Try to think of some reasons why I like being with you."

He'd listed some reasons, when I was too upset to appreciate them. "I'm not too much trouble?"

"I spend some extra time with my arm around you," he wrote. "How is that bad for me?"

"It's good for me. I feel safe, not just physically." I almost added something about feeling warm and fluttery when I was with him, but I felt too rotten to multiply words. "I'm sorry I hurt you today. I was awful. Forgive me?"

When he didn't reply immediately, the knot in my stomach tightened again. What if he didn't want to forgive me? Or couldn't?

My phone's vibration was the one thing I was waiting for, but it startled me anyway.

"Hours ago. You weren't yourself. You're sick. Forgive me?"

The knot relaxed and I sat back, weak in my relief, until I realized he was waiting for my reply.

"There's nothing to forgive," I wrote.

"I was angry, and I'm sorry," he wrote. "Should have thought more about you than myself. Now I'm just angry at the jerks. Wish I knew how to make them stop. Anything we can do will just make it worse. Anything that might work, we can't do."

"That sucks," I wrote.

"Does your mom know you use such language?"

I tried to smile. "Yup. She disapproves."

"Any ideas?"

A thought popped into my head. "I can't have you beat them senseless, and you shouldn't anyway, so all I have is this: if we can't stop them, we have to keep them from getting between us again, like I let them do today."

"Like we both let them do. I'm in," he said. "They're out."

I hesitated. "We're okay, right?"

"You were never my project. You're my friend and my girlfriend."

"Thanks. I have a really good boyfriend."

"Who wishes you were here."

"You're thinking of Healthy Jenny. Sick Jenny's a real pill. Probably contagious too. I hope I didn't infect you. I washed my hands on my way to meet you." I stopped typing and wiped my nose with a tissue, then waited for a sneeze that didn't come. "Have a safe trip home. I'm going to bed early. I'm glad we're okay. Thank you for—"

The sneeze came, then another. I reached for a clean tissue and used it on my phone screen this time. I finished my abandoned sentence, wished the varsity luck, and said good night.

"Good night, beautiful Jenny," he replied. "Feel better."

I put my head down on my desk, weak with relief. We were okay. I hadn't ruined us. I breathed deeply and tried not to sob. That worked for a minute, maybe. Then my breath caught, and I fell apart.

Sure enough, sobbing made me cough and sneeze, which at least cut short the sobbing. When I was past all that, I read Troy's last message again, checked the clock, took another dose of cold medicine, and slowly got ready for bed. I smiled, sort of, at my puffy face and disheveled hair in the mirror. Good thing the boy who thought I was beautiful couldn't see me now.

I lay on my side with an extra pillow under my head and imagined him sitting with me—not in my bedroom—holding my hand, kissing me on the cheek, telling me about his game and what we'd do when I was better. That kept me awake and not too miserable, until Mom and Dad got home.

I told them for the first time about the haters at school, and how I let them get to me, and how I accused Troy of using me and faking his affection for me. "He basically had to defend me against myself," I croaked. "He shouldn't have to do that."

"Sounds like he did a good job," Dad said.

Mom smiled. "I think he likes you. You patched things up?"

"We texted some. I think we're okay. My throat hurts." I closed my eyes. "Is it still okay that I suddenly have a boyfriend?"

"As long as you're being good and sensible together," Mom said.

"Seems to me he's good for you," Dad said. "And good to you."

I decided my eyes were closed for the night. "I wasn't good for him today."

"You fixed it," Mom said. "Tomorrow's another day."

They kissed me goodnight and left me to sleep.

※

There was no JV basketball tournament after the regular season, so Troy practiced with the varsity. He'd dress for their tournament games, but he didn't expect to play much.

Early on the eve of his first-round game, we connected on Skype. I noticed his new black eye immediately.

"Troy, are you hurt?"

"Oh, this?" He pointed to his eye. "Sort of got into a fight today at practice."

I tried to be calm and collected, but the thought of him fighting scared me in about three different ways. I felt like I'd been startled out of a deep sleep: trembling, heart pounding, halfway to panic.

"Are you okay?" I asked.

"Just this shiner."

"Does it hurt?"

"Yeah. Does it look bad?"

"Yes. Sorry."

"I'll be okay," he said.

I was still on edge, and my voice shook. "I don't usually think of you as a boy who gets into fights."

"Don't usually get into fights."

"What happened? With whom?"

He smiled gently. "Such good grammar."

"Don't change the subject, boyfriend. What happened? With whom did you fight?" I'd show him grammar.

"Doesn't matter."

It did matter. "It was about me, wasn't it? Was it Skyler?" He was dating one of the toxic cheerleaders, and he liked to flash his middle fingers at me.

"Yeah."

"Did he punch you?"

"No."

"Did you punch him?"

"Not exactly."

"Did you break his middle fingers?"

"No. Good idea, though."

"Tell me what happened."

"We were scrimmaging, and things got rough in the middle. I gave better than I got."

"Over something he said?"

"I'm not telling you what he said."

"I'll hear it somewhere," I said at too great a volume and too high a pitch.

"Not from me."

I put my hands on my desk, palms down, and took a deep breath. "Okay. Did he start it?"

"He said some stuff. I gave him a few hard forearms in the back, when I was guarding him in the post after a switch. Then I put him on the floor when he tried to cross the key. No punching or tripping, just a lot of hip and some shoulder. Next chance he got, he threw an elbow and gave me this beauty. Didn't realize it was so colorful until later. I'll show you."

His black eye filled my screen. I gasped, winced, and looked away.

"Sorry," he said.

Still looking away, I attempted a wry smile. "Could I see the other eye instead?"

"Like this?" He was too close to the microphone, so his voice was distorted. His good eye was weirdly large.

"I think I prefer your whole face. Is Skyler hurt?"

He backed away from the webcam. "Nothing this obvious. Some bruises, I hope."

"Are you in trouble with Coach? This could be bad."

"Don't think so."

"Is he?"

"Don't know. Think he's in trouble with some of the guys, though. He had a tough scrimmage after he did this."

"They're very good to us." I smiled faintly. "Thanks for defending me."

He smiled. "Thanks for being the girl I defend."

"I'm not kidding. Thank you."

"You're welcome."

"I wish I didn't have a choir rehearsal tonight," I griped. "I miss you."

"Miss you too."

I sighed and changed the subject, sort of. "I'm sorry I can't go to your game tomorrow. When does the bus leave?"

"Nine. Game tips at noon. I won't play much, if I play at all. If we win, maybe you can come Friday."

"That's my plan. So win."

After we signed off, I should have had compassionate thoughts about his painful black eye. What I did wasn't very mature. I spent the rest of the evening—even my rehearsal—basking in the glow of having a boyfriend who fought for me.

⸻ ◆ ⸻

They announced our tournament victory at school before Troy could text me the news. He said he played a little but didn't score.

I went to the next game with Troy's family. Jack and Nikki were there too, with the pep band and the dance team. Troy played a few minutes in both halves and did fine, as far as I could tell, and Will scored a lot of baskets, but we lost by two points. Everyone was bummed, including me.

Troy and I had a few minutes after the game. We planned to go out for ice cream when the team bus got back to the school, but it broke down. At least they were allowed to use their phones on the way home.

"They say after midnight," Troy wrote. It was 9:52 p.m., eight minutes before our electronic curfew. "So much for ice cream with my girl. Was looking forward to it."

"To me or the ice cream?" Maybe teasing would cheer him up.

"Both."

"We're a lot alike, ice cream and I. We both start to melt when we see you."

"No melting tonight," he wrote—not very playfully. "Sorry."

I started to write that he had ways of melting me remotely, and "my girl" was one of them, but I deleted that and tried for something less self-centered. I was running out of minutes to cheer him up.

"I'm sorry too. But watching you play was nice, and we had a few minutes afterward. And we're chatting now."

I kept typing. "May I show you a good time tomorrow? I'll take the whole afternoon, if I can get it. Then I'll go with you to the game you wanted to play in, if you want to see it for research or whatever. Or because it's basketball. Hot dogs are on me."

"You got it," he replied. Then he added, "Thanks, Jenny."

It was 10:00 p.m., so our chat was over. There was no time to say good night, but maybe he wasn't quite so glum.

Impromptu smoothies at my house with Jack and Nikki didn't keep me from missing him, but tomorrow would be fun.

29

Surprises

THE NEXT MORNING, AS I lounged in my room, reading in my pajamas, Mom poked her head in. "You should get dressed. I know your plans are later, but Troy's picking you up at 9:30. Don't ask what for. I'm sworn to secrecy."

"You'll keep secrets from your only daughter, just because some boy wants you to?"

She smiled. "Dress casual but nice, and leave Zeus home."

Twenty minutes later, Troy arrived in his dad's mid-size SUV. He was perfectly willing to explain that. His usual car wouldn't start. But he wouldn't tell me where we were going—not when I answered the door, not as we backed out of my driveway, not when I tried to guess from our route. He just smiled.

We were well on our way to wherever when he finally said, "This morning we learn to waltz."

My heart did a handspring. "Really? Where?"

"I have these neighbors, the Hills. They're dance teachers. They run a Saturday morning class for single adults at a church across town. Today's the waltz, and they said we could sneak in. It's the older singles, so we may be the only ones under thirty."

"This is amazing! How long have you been planning this?"

"Since I found out I don't have a game tonight."

"I'm still sorry about that," I said.

He shrugged. "Next year. Look what I get to do instead."

"You're already more cheerful than last night."

"Ready for some fun that isn't basketball," he said.

"You're tired of basketball? Who are you, and what have you done with my point guard?"

He chuckled. "No, still love it. But now we can do other things, like learn to waltz."

"I'll learn," I said. "You already know how."

"I'm not that good. I'll learn too."

"You're very gallant, sir."

"Just honest." He shook his head. "Speaking of honest"—he glanced at me, then turned back to the road—"someone cornered me yesterday between classes. Said she hopes I'll make time for her when basketball's over, because she really wants to make time for me."

Somehow I took it calmly. "Make time *with* you, I think. Which gorgeous female was it?"

"Doesn't matter. Told her I'm flattered, but I'm with you. She asked me what I could possibly see in someone like you." He shook his head again.

"It's a fair question," I said.

"No, it's not."

"I understand her interest."

"Only interest I care about is yours."

My heart did another handspring. "And vice versa. What if I'm a slow learner this morning?"

"Then we practice a lot."

I watched him drive and savored the moment. Amazing boyfriend, holding his hand, about to learn to waltz. Pretty close to perfect.

"Want to know how this could have been perfect?" I asked.

"Not talking about another girl hitting on me?"

"Having my dancing shoes. But I can dance in sneakers. If they squeak too much, I'll show off my fuzzy red socks."

"It's pretty great that you have dancing shoes."

"Thanks to you." I smiled, but he was watching the road. "Here's what's not so great. Mom is now willing to keep your secrets—from me, her only daughter." I sighed melodramatically. "I don't know what to do with that woman."

He grinned. "I'm glad she likes me."

"She really does. I think the parents are relieved to see me having a social life. You make it easier for them to let their sick little daughter grow up."

His grin disappeared. "You're not a sick little girl who needs my help growing up."

"I'm a happy girl. Tell me more."

"We're careful," he said, "but otherwise it's not even like you're sick. I mean, I know in some ways your epilepsy's a big deal, and I'm not saying it isn't. But if you had my cousin's strawberry allergy instead, we'd still go out for ice cream. We'd just avoid strawberries. You and I do a few things to keep you from cracking your head against sidewalks and dance floors, but they're little things, and we like them. So no big deal. Is that bad to say?"

He had me all fluttery again.

"No, it's completely wonderful. I never told you, but one of my favorite things about our first date was how you forgot to treat me like the girl with epilepsy for a while. You apologized, remember? But I loved it."

We arrived at a large, red brick church and parked. When he opened my door, he said, "Keep your seat, please. I have a surprise."

"Okay." The SUV sat high enough that our eyes were at almost the same level. I liked the view, despite his black eye.

"Need you to turn your legs toward me and close your eyes."

I obeyed. I couldn't help smiling.

"Thank you," he said.

Nothing seemed to happened for several seconds. Then he spoke. "You have pretty eyes, but you're pretty when they're closed too."

"Does this have something to do with my surprise?" I asked.

"Just enjoying the view."

"Are you trying to distract me from something?"

"You trust me enough to close your eyes. Now trust me enough to be patient. I'm removing your shoes." He untied my sneakers and pulled them off. "Now I'm admiring your fuzzy red socks."

"This is about my socks?"

"No. And I promise not to tickle your feet."

I considered that possibility. I wasn't sure it would be a bad thing.

"Almost ready," he said. "Don't move. And don't open your eyes."

I heard him open the back door and rustle a plastic bag.

"Putting something on your feet now."

It was shoes, and I thought I knew which ones.

"Now you may look."

I opened my eyes and looked down at my feet, then up at Troy's expectant gaze.

And burst out laughing.

Troy looked surprised and a little hurt. "What's so funny?" he asked.

"You're sweet to bring my dancing shoes, but there's a problem."

"They don't go with jeans?"

"Almost anything goes with jeans. It's the socks. They're too thick for these shoes." I giggled. "They're like fuzzy red muffin tops."

He didn't say anything, so I kept explaining.

"Flats go with no socks, or thin socks that don't stand out, or very short ones that don't show." I lifted one foot and mostly stifled another giggle. "See how these kind of spill out of the shoes?"

"Okay. So what now?" His eyes were dull, and he quirked a corner of his mouth into . . . something. Not a frown, exactly, but definitely not a smile.

"Mom gave you my shoes, right?"

"Yeah."

"See if she put socks in the bag. If not, I'll do without. But socks will be better for dancing."

The plastic shopping bag rustled. "Didn't see these before. These are socks?"

"Perfect," I said. "They're no-shows."

"Well, they showed up this morning." He sounded like a boyfriend trying to be cheerful after his girlfriend laughed at his nice surprise.

He held them out to me, and I took them. "I'm sorry I laughed," I said. "You didn't ruin the surprise. It's really nice." I looked down at his sneakers. "So while you put on your dancing shoes, I'll change my socks."

"How do you know I brought dancing shoes?"

"You only wore sneakers because you didn't want to give it away."

When we were ready, he helped me down and put his arm around me for the walk to the church doors.

I put my arm around him and tried to melt into his side. "My kind, thoughtful, scheming boyfriend. I'm glad you're not tired of me," I said, as we turned up the sidewalk toward the doors.

"I'm really not," he said. "You thinking about that other girl?"

"Maybe a little."

"Ready for more honesty?" he asked.

"Should I worry?"

"Nope."

"Then I'm ready."

"Took her to an after-game dance once. We ran out of things to talk about in the first ten minutes." He smiled. "Maybe five. Long evening."

The church doors were locked. "Are we that early?" I asked. I'd finally noticed there were no other cars parked on our side of the building. "Maybe they're all on the other side."

He checked his phone. "Only nine minutes early. Hope I got the right place. Let me check their email." He poked at the screen. "Okay, I goofed. Right place, but 10:30, not 10:00. We're early. Sorry about that."

I took one of his hands in both of mine. "I'm not sorry. The sun's out. It's almost warm. I feel a walk with my boyfriend coming on. Change back into our sneakers?"

He smiled. "Sure. First I'll set an alarm, so we don't forget to come back."

We strolled hand in hand around the edge of a softball field next to the church. The dirt infield looked muddy, but there were a few young boys in the outfield, kicking a soccer ball on the gray-brown grass.

"Want to know my favorite thing from our first date?" Troy asked.

I looked up. "What was it?"

"You."

I drew in a surprised, blissful breath.

"You should see your eyes sparkling," he said. "You never cared about basketball before, or went to a game, or wanted to, but you let your Dad and me explain, and you listened and asked questions and tried to understand. Like you thought I might be worth the trouble. And the way you smiled at me out in the hall after the game, that was magic. Totally addictive."

"I remember a pretty big smile. You deserved it." I stopped, reached for his other hand, and pulled him around to face me. He was like a mirror. The warmer my smile, the warmer his eyes became. I couldn't tell how long the moment lasted. I had to hug him, and he hugged me back. I took a deep breath and let it out as a happy sigh. Then his phone alarm pinged.

He blew out his own breath. "Beautiful Jenny, we have a problem."

We didn't let go, but I looked up. "We have to go to waltz class now?"

His eyes twinkled. "Like I said, we have two problems."

"What's the other one?"

"How can I dance? You smile like that and my knees go weak."

I didn't even try to stop smiling. "You'd better man up, boyfriend. Besides dancing with me, if I'm half as pretty as you think I am, you may have to defend me from desperate thirty-something single males. Let's go change into our dancing shoes."

I grabbed his hand and pulled, but he didn't move. "Need to tell you something first," he said.

"Can you tell me and walk at the same time? Or do my blue eyes need to gaze fondly into your blue eyes?"

"Easier to remember what I'm saying when your blue eyes aren't doing that. Easier to walk too."

We started toward the church, hand in hand.

"Last night on the bus," he said, "I was thinking, how could I thank you for putting up with basketball for the last few months?"

"It was fun. You don't have to thank me."

"You were a good sport when I didn't have time for other things, like last night. So learning to waltz this morning and going out to a nice lunch is me thanking you. Hope you like it." He shrugged. "Just wanted to say that."

30

Whispers and Waltzes

T ROY INTRODUCED ME TO the Hills, a trim thirty-something couple who looked like dancers. They moved with poise and grace,
and even in the morning they were dressed for dancing. He wore black
slacks and a white, long sleeve shirt that might have been tailored. She
wore an elegant, knee-length, sleeveless blue dress with an enviably small
waist and a modest neckline.

He had receding, short brown hair and a thin face with sharp features.
Without his neatly trimmed beard and mustache, he might have looked
stern and severe.

She'd have looked severe too, without her friendly smile. Her blonde
hair was in a tight bun, highlighting her high cheekbones and perfect
eyebrows. She might have been a magazine cover, until she smiled, spoke,
and offered her hand. Then she was the girl next door, all grown up and
dressed for dancing.

One thing still intimidated me: her dancing shoes had three-inch
heels. I'd be lucky not to fall off my flats.

Troy and I found an open space on the gym floor and stood side by
side, held hands, and waited for the class to begin.

Be bold, Jenny.

I reached up to whisper in his ear. "That was a really nice walk. I'm still
melting inside."

"Tell me more," he whispered.

"I hardly have the words."

"Aren't you the writer?"

"I'll try." Thinking in words was harder than usual. "How about this?
Your knees weren't the only weak ones."

I glanced up long enough to see a little smile.

"Also, what's my name again?"

His laugh was as soft as our whispers.

"You probably already know this," I said, " but when you hold my hand or hug me, or even when you look at me and smile, I get all melty and fluttery inside."

Standing in the middle of a church gym, surrounded by two or three dozen adults who had nothing to do but look around, make small talk, and wait for a dance class to begin, struck me as a safe place for a girl to whisper such things to a boy.

He tilted his head toward me. "I like having that effect on you."

"Sometimes all it takes is a few words in a text message," I said.

I wanted to appear casual to the strangers around us, but my face was hot, and I could only imagine its color. There was bold, and then there was this.

"Good to know," he said neutrally. He was silent for a moment, then he asked, "Want to know what makes me feel that way?"

I couldn't look. I could only give him a little nod and listen.

"I told you about your smile. There's the way your eyes look at me sometimes. I like when you take my hand, and when I put my arm around you and you lean in. When you hug me like we're the only two people in the world. When you write me a beautiful valentine. When we stand in a crowd of people and whisper like it's an ordinary conversation, but it's totally not."

I looked up and said far less than I felt. "I'm liking that last one too."

"Know what else?" he whispered after I looked away. "I like how much we need the rules."

It took a moment to sink in. Then I was awestruck. Eight ordinary words, one syllable each—and they had me practically swooning.

Troy was physically attracted to me. Which I already knew, but it was still wondrous.

I was physically attractive—to him.

"We wouldn't be much of a couple if we didn't need the rules," I whispered.

"Must be a very good couple," he said.

I put my arm around his waist and leaned in. He squeezed my shoulders. Then we slipped back behind our casual façade.

"Are we doing this wrong?" I whispered. My question was less serious than it sounded.

"What do you mean?"

"In books and movies I swoon because we waltz, not before we waltz."

"Haven't actually swooned yet."

"Getting close," I whispered.

"Jenny?" he said after a moment.

I looked up. His face was serious.

"Nothing about this feels wrong to me."

"Me neither," I said.

"But I definitely need the rules," he said.

His words sent another thrill through me, leaving warmth in its wake. "So do I." I wanted to tell him things I didn't know how to say. But just then the Hills welcomed everyone and started the class.

It lasted an hour, and it was challenging enough that I had to concentrate. They taught a basic step and we practiced, first by ourselves, then with our partners, sometimes to music and sometimes not. They corrected some mistakes, we practiced again, and then we moved on to another step.

Troy and I really were the only ones under thirty. Some of the singles looked at least seventy. The ones wearing wedding rings were probably widows and widowers, I thought sadly.

There were exactly as many men as women. That must have been unusual, because the Hills congratulated the ladies on their effective recruiting.

We changed partners every ten minutes or so. I lived dangerously—and nervously—not telling them I might collapse and they'd have to catch me. Nothing like that happened, and I did my best to be friendly and graceful with several older men, all of whom waltzed better than I did. From what I overheard, Troy charmed his older partners.

For the last few minutes they put on fresh music and turned us loose to dance. One of my earlier partners, a dignified, soft-spoken, gray-haired man in jeans and a tweed jacket, was moving toward me, when suddenly my hand was in Troy's.

"May I have this waltz?" Troy asked.

I felt a brief flash of guilt for thinking he was rescuing me. Then we waltzed together, not too clumsily, and it felt less like a class in a church gym and more like my dream coming true.

When it was over, we went to thank the Hills again and ended up talking with them. They asked about me, told me they enjoyed having the Pullmans as neighbors, and asked Troy about his tournament.

We offered to help them pack their sound equipment and carry it out, but they had a better idea. When everyone else had gone, they invited us to stay for another half hour, so we could dance and they could coach us individually. When they danced too, it was distractingly beautiful.

It was the perfect end to a wonderful morning, even if my legs ached. I thought about Troy changing my shoes for me and wondered if he would enjoy massaging my aching calves as much as I'd enjoy him doing it, but that seemed like an activity we should avoid and a thought I should keep to myself. It took me a while to get past it.

He bought me lunch at a cute café with soft chairs, glass tables, and hanging plants, where they didn't hurry and we didn't have to. I had to keep reminding myself to stop smiling and eat.

As the server left with our dessert order, I remembered something I'd planned to tell Troy, before walking and whispers and waltzing wafted me away. "You liked being in *Camelot* last year, right? At your old school?"

"Loved it," he said.

"You should try out for *Fiddler on the Roof*. Auditions are a week from Monday."

He shrugged. "Thought I might skip the musical this year and do it next year."

"If you want a good role next year, shouldn't you be in it this year?"

"Mostly want to hang out with you, now that the season's over. But yeah, maybe. Think I should?"

"If you want to."

"I'll think about it," he said.

Our enormous death-by-chocolate brownie arrived, and we ate more than we talked. Finally he set down his fork, wiped his lips with his napkin, drank some water, and said, "Thought about it. I'll do it." He grinned. "If you will."

I shook my head. "I don't see Zeus and me onstage."

"Do something offstage. Be a prompter. You can sit, and we can hang out between scenes."

"Prompt people when they forget their lines?"

"You'd be great. For performances you'd sit just offstage, out of sight. For rehearsals, maybe the front row. Key word is *sit*."

The way this day was going, I might have tried out for the basketball team if he wanted me to. But this one actually made sense. "The key word is *Troy*. If you do it, I'll do it."

"Cool. Help me with my audition?" he asked.

"If I can. How?"

"Let's watch *Fiddler*. I'll find a role I like and use it. You can coach me on my lines and read the other parts. I may not get that role, but it won't hurt."

I changed my plans for our cheerful afternoon to watching *Fiddler on the Roof*, which we had at home on a disc. We'd had an amazing day already, so a sad, dark film would be okay. I'd seen it years before and hadn't loved it, but watching it with Troy would be good.

When we told Mom and Dad what we were doing, they asked if they could join us. I wondered if they saw us all aglow and thought we needed chaperones.

They made popcorn while we cued up the film. We took the love seat and left them the sofa, and we didn't change our behavior at all. Most of the time, I sat with Troy's arm around me and my head on his shoulder.

I watched them, off and on, but they watched the film, not us. They snuggled more than we did, and I caught them sneaking little kisses.

The film was captivating, with joy and humor to balance the darkness I vaguely remembered. As the closing credits rolled, I said to Troy, "What an amazing, sad, funny movie!"

"Hated it when I was little," he said. "Loved it when we watched it for a class last year."

"I have my role picked out," I announced, as Dad collected the empty popcorn bowls and Mom left to find a script in her library.

"Which one?"

I sat up with a silly grin. "Tevye, of course. He's clever, complex, profound, good-hearted—"

Troy chuckled. "Bearded. Male. That is so wrong. Your voice isn't low enough, and you're too pretty to be an old Jewish milkman."

"Oh." I feigned disappointment. "You could be Tevye."

"Won't get the lead. I'm thinking, Motel the Tailor. I'd have my own sewing machine," he said with a twinkle.

"I'll be your practice Tzeitel, if you want me."

"If?"

"I'm pretending to give you a choice," I said. "Did you have a fake beard for Camelot?"

"Yeah, why?"

"Then I have a deeply personal question. Real is better, right? Can you grow a decent beard in five or six weeks?"

31

Practice Tzeitel

Troy went home for dinner and chores before our evening of watching other teams play basketball. Over dinner at my house, I told Mom and Dad selected highlights from my morning.

"So the surprise worked?" Mom asked.

"It worked," I said. "Were the shoes his idea or yours?"

"They were his before they were mine," she said.

"He didn't notice the no-shows at first. He put my flats on over my fuzzy red socks."

Mom's eyes twinkled. "Sounds like something your dad would do."

Dad shrugged. "You let him change your socks and shoes?"

"Not my socks." I blushed, and a question popped out. "Would that be wrong?"

"Not necessarily," Mom said. "As long as occasional, small, harmless physical intimacies don't lead to greater ones."

That was good for another shade of red. "They won't." I hesitated. "Later we agreed that it's really nice to need the rules."

Mom and Dad both smiled at that, which seemed odd. It was past time to turn the tables. "Speaking of Troy and me, I thought we behaved well during the movie, even when we saw some married people kissing. Do you suppose they forgot we were there or just didn't care?"

Both parents were still smiling. I was on a roll.

"If you're curious, I'm still sweet-sixteen-and-never-been-kissed, I hope not for long. But I remember our little talks, and I'm sure we'll have more, and that's sort of okay."

I wondered if I'd said too much or said it too lightheartedly, and Mom and Dad would get stern. But I only wondered for a moment.

Dad turned to Mom. "You know I'm here for you, anytime I can help with your footwear. Or anything else."

The corners of Mom's mouth turned up in a closed smile that highlighted her lips.

Dad was to her left. She reached up and pushed back her hair on that side. She casually stroked her exposed neck with her fingertips as her hand came back down, and pulled her collar a bit lower in the process. Then she subtly licked her lips. Her eyes didn't leave his, and his were locked on her.

I was stunned. And fascinated. Had Mom flirted with him like this before, in front of me, and I was only now learning to see it? Was this for my benefit or just for him?

Watching them started to feel like an intrusion. "Excuse me," I said quietly. "I'll leave you two alone and start the dishes."

"We can help," Mom said brightly.

"No, it's okay. You look busy."

They both got up to help.

"Sorry if we made you uncomfortable," Mom said a few minutes later, while Dad took out the trash.

I kept my face serious. "I just watch and learn."

The stove clock said Troy was due in ten minutes. I wondered if I could tell him about the flirting. Or not tell him and demonstrate.

⸻◈⸻

On Thursday, while Zeus and I visited Grandpa after school, Troy had a team meeting, then a dentist appointment. Our postseason plans for Thursday afternoons had to wait a week.

Earlier than usual that evening, he texted me. "Skype date tonight? Miss your pretty face."

"I miss your scruffy face. You're not too numb to talk?"

"Might drool. Should be done with math by 9:30."

That was an hour away. "Okay, but 9:29 would be better."

He called at 9:29.

"All done," he said. "And you're beautiful. Are you free for the next few Saturday afternoons?" Some of his consonants were muddled.

I checked the family calendar on my phone. "Yes. Why do you ask?"

"Here's a clue. Nice casual. Leave Zeus home. Bring your dancing shoes. Pick you up at 1:45, if that works."

I forgot to talk and just beamed.

"So it's okay with you if we have private waltz lessons with the Hills on Saturdays for a while?"

"You know it is. Thank you!"

His grin was oddly lopsided. "You're welcome. Not bad for a scruffy boyfriend who's half a numbskull, right? Oh, and this Saturday, after our lesson, they'll coach me for my audition, if you can stay."

"Of course I'll stay. But Troy?"

"Yeah?"

What I wanted to ask was, if I wore my sneakers and brought my dancing shoes, would he be interested in changing my socks? I chickened out. "Nothing. Just thank you. This will be fun!"

•◦•

On Saturday I was in my dancing shoes when he picked me up. I hadn't seen him in person for a couple of days, and I was glad he finally looked like a guy who was starting a beard, not a guy who forgot to shave. I wasn't impressed yet, but there was potential. It was coming in a shade or two darker than his hair, which Dad said was common.

The Hills had a home studio with a polished hardwood floor, bright lights, mirrored walls, a sound system, and video. We'd learn International Style, they explained, because the couple never breaks the closed position, which might be safer for me.

After our hour-long waltz lesson, we spent an hour on Troy's audition. They coached him through a bit of choreography for one of the excerpts he'd prepared, then worked on his song. Sister Hill was a good pianist, and she'd offered to play for his audition.

Troy was nervous singing to me, but he got over it. I liked his warm tenor and his good sense of pitch.

They talked him through the dancing audition, where a bunch of kids would be on the floor or the stage together, trying to learn and perform a bit of choreography, while the directors watched how well they took correction, how quickly they learned, how well they remembered, and how gracefully they moved.

"It probably won't be long," Brother Hill said. "Sixteen measures is usually more than they need. You'll do well. All that attention to footwork in basketball and waltzing should pay off. Let's try it. You too, Jenny."

Troy learned quickly and remembered well. I thought he moved well too. I was a klutz, but the prompter didn't have to dance.

On Sunday evening he came to dinner. Then we worked his lines together until they sounded natural every time. Reading the other roles was real work for me. I had to get them right for him, especially the timing.

On Monday after school, we reported to the auditorium. I was a bundle of nerves. It was his audition, not mine, and I'd have a script, but what if I messed up and hurt his chances?

As we waited offstage, my thoughts turned completely inward. What if I was too nervous to speak at all?

"Jenny?"

He was facing me. I'd been looking at him without seeing him.

"What if I ruin it for you?" I asked.

He took my script and set it on a chair, then lifted both his hands to my face. I covered his with mine.

"You won't. Pretend you're talking in church."

"This is not that. It's your audition."

"We'll be great," he said.

I wanted to believe him. "What if—"

"No more what-ifs. I'm ready. We're ready. Think about the scene. Boy likes girl. Girl likes boy. We hardly even have to act."

I tried to smile.

"They're not looking for perfection," he said. "Take a deep breath. Then take another one."

I obeyed.

"Good. Can you talk?"

I nodded.

"Can't hear you."

"I can talk."

"Just get into the role, Tzeitel. Have fun. When we're on stage, try to match my volume. That'll help. You'll be amazing."

My smile pushed my cheeks against his hands. "Okay."

They called the student before us. Troy let go of me and gave me my script. "On deck. Game face?"

I squared my shoulders, looked out onto the stage, and nodded. I was getting better at navigating sports metaphors.

"Girlfriend, you have the prettiest game face. Let's whisper our first two or three lines right now, a couple of times, so they're in our heads and we don't freeze up when we go on."

I could totally see why they'd wanted Troy on the JV team for leadership. And reviewing the first few lines helped. On stage, once we were that far into it, I didn't sound nervous anymore, at least not to myself.

We started with dialogue from a scene where Tzeitel begs Motel to ask her father's permission to marry her. I managed not to get distracted, and I didn't mess up any of my lines. Then Troy sang part of "Miracle of Miracles," from a later scene. As he sang, he danced with me, then in joyful circles around me, like Motel does in a grassy field in the movie. I ended up standing in the middle of the stage, trying to look like a love-struck fiancée. It wasn't that much of a stretch.

Troy had warned me that they might stop him in the middle of something and ask him to do it differently, or move to the next thing, or thank him and send him on his way without doing the rest, any of which might be good or bad. But none of that happened.

"Thank you, Troy," said the drama teacher, when we were finished. "And Jenny, right? You signed up to be prompter?"

"Yes, sir."

"Excellent. Check the callback list in the morning, please, and the casting list on Thursday. Next!"

In Tuesday's callbacks they wanted Troy as Motel again, in a dramatic scene with the boy they cast as Tevye. I got to watch. Troy was good, and Tevye blew me away.

They put Troy in the first scene from his audition, this time with a girl they were considering for Tzeitel. Troy said they were looking for chemistry.

I'd enjoyed helping him, even on stage, but I was relieved just to sit with Zeus and watch. Their Tzeitel was far better than me. She was prettier, and she seemed perfectly natural when she talked and moved onstage. I wasn't sure what chemistry looked like in high school theater, but I thought I saw some—which I could worry about later, if they both got the parts. I wondered how hard I'd have to try not to be jealous. I didn't want to be the jealous type. I wanted to be a better girlfriend than that.

On Thursday morning the list came out. Troy was Motel the Tailor. I was Jenny the Prompter. And Jordyn, the girl who'd worked with Troy at callbacks, was Tzeitel.

Starting the next Monday, rehearsals would be after school every weekday except Thursday, when they'd be in the evening. I'd miss a few children's choir rehearsals on Tuesdays, but I could still do Troy's shoot-around and visit Grandpa on Thursday afternoons.

32

Black, Red, Green

O N THE DAY THEY posted the *Fiddler* cast, I worried more about rebounding for Troy after school. I wanted more time with him, but I was also insane. I'd make a fool of myself and waste his practice time, even if he'd be too kind to admit it.

Jack and Nikki took me shopping the night before, so I could at least look the part. Our school colors were red, black, and white, so I came home with red knee-length gym shorts, a reversible black and gray practice jersey, and some white gym socks. I already had sneakers.

The jersey was a tank top like Troy wore for practice, but with no number on the back. I didn't think I could bring myself to wear it without a shirt underneath, but I modeled it that way in my room.

"Wow!" Nikki exclaimed. "You look like—"

"The girl who embarrassed herself in junior high gym classes," I griped. Those memories were getting harder to repress by the minute.

"That's one opinion," Jack said.

I turned my frustration on her. "Oh? What's yours?"

"Come here," she said patiently, planting me in front of my full-length mirror. "Look at yourself."

So I looked. Then I kept looking. I might have been staring at a bad accident on the freeway. The sick feeling in my gut was about the same. The memories had taken over.

In gym classes I always had permission to sit out whatever the class was doing, if I or the teacher thought it would be dangerous for me. I avoided basketball, gymnastics, and anything else with a higher risk of hitting my head on something hard if I had a seizure. On those days I read a book, walked laps with Zeus on the track, or graded health class worksheets.

I only excluded myself when I thought I had to. I hated not fitting in—which was why I was in gym class in the first place, when the school counselor offered to waive the requirement.

The biggest embarrassment wasn't sitting out some things. It wasn't having a locker on the main aisle, so I could mostly stay away from hard benches that might slow my head on the way to the floor. It wasn't even group showers with girls who mostly were thinner and prettier. Maybe most days weren't terrible, but the worst memories came from participating.

In seventh grade we did soccer for a few weeks, weather permitting. I was useless at every other part of the game, so I volunteered to stand in front of the goal. But I was a bad goalkeeper too. I didn't just give up goals. I actually scored two or three for the other team. And when I had to kick or throw the ball, it never went very far, and rarely in the right direction. I remembered the other girls being kinder to me than I deserved, which helped a little.

I was also an automatic out in softball. I couldn't do more than two or three real push-ups, no matter how much the teacher and some of the girls encouraged me. And when we ran a lap around the track, I finished far behind most of the girls.

I logged every seizure, except for any I might not have noticed because I was asleep. I had three of them in gym class that year. One happened out on the track, when only Zeus was with me. The hoodie I wore against the cold breeze prevented some scrapes, so I was just a little bruised. Zeus didn't panic, and after a minute or so I got up and kept walking. Another happened on the grass in front of the soccer goal. The teacher stopped play, came to check on me, determined that I wasn't hurt at all, and helped me up when I was ready. She didn't even suggest I see the school nurse. She just asked if I could keep playing, and I did. The third one happened in the locker room, which could have been bad, but I was sitting on a bench tying my shoe, not standing, so I just slumped off the bench and onto the floor. The two girls who saw me did just what the teacher had done when we were playing soccer, and I was glad they'd seen her example. They helped me up and we all went off to class.

I stubbornly refused the waiver for eighth grade too. I thought it might be better. It was bad in the same ways, plus some mean girls who mostly ignored the rest of us, but not always. I had two seizures in gym class that year, one of which landed me in the nurse's office for some minor first aid.

Now, two years later, I stood in front of my mirror in gym clothes. My pasty-white shoulders contrasted starkly with my black jersey and black hair. I was a freak. I belonged in a circus. With my gym shoes, which always looked weird on me with white socks, all I needed was a big red nose, and I could be . . .

I sighed. "I see a clown."

"You're not a clown," Jack said. "You're cute. Maybe even sexy, but a guy should judge that."

"I don't see it."

"Look with the eyes of a boy who adores you."

Jack turned me to one side, then the other. Finally I said, "It's not working. I'm a high-contrast clown with comically pale skin. I just need to attach my giant round nose and paint on a big, stupid smile."

"Tell her, Nikki," Jack said.

"Girl," Nikki said, "you're actually kind of hot in this tank top. It's not super revealing, but if you show him this much shoulder and neck tomorrow, he won't be able to shoot straight. Has he ever seen this much of you?"

Before I could answer crossly that there were good reasons why he hadn't, and some of them were aesthetic, Jack added, "Pull your hair off your neck and into a ponytail, and he may not be able to shoot at all."

"That would be bad," I said. I took off the jersey, pulled on a red t-shirt that matched the shorts, and put the jersey back on. "Is this more businesslike?" I didn't look in the mirror again. I was so done with junior high.

"Sure, if that's what you want," Jack said.

I looked down at my outfit. The shirt covered a lot of pale skin, and maybe my gym shoes weren't that bad. "I look like less of a clown."

A less amazing boyfriend would not have been worth it.

After school on Thursday, Troy went to dress down, and I met Nikki in the girls' locker room. She had her own locker from being on the dance team, and she was happy to let me use it.

I hurried, because, if I stopped to think about what I was doing, I'd get nauseous or maybe run away. I tried to envision Troy's smile when he saw me, not the well-deserved ridicule I'd get, if the wrong people caught me impersonating an athlete.

Nikki helped me change and said she'd hang out with Zeus until I was ready to get dressed again. I chose the black side of the jersey to go over my red tee, and she agreed. She wanted to pull my hair back into a ponytail, but I stopped her. She pouted, and I let her do it.

When that was done, she turned me around to face her, put her hands on my shoulders, and looked at me seriously.

Almost seriously.

"Miller, you're going out onto the floor with a handsome boyfriend who dances with you and tells you you're beautiful and funny and smart and amazing, and it's all true, and he means every word. That boyfriend is relying on you"—she pointed at my nose—"to rebound and get the ball back to him, so he can shoot. Don't worry about the shooting. That's his job. Don't worry about the crowd. Zeus and I may be the only ones there anyway. Concentrate on the ball. Grab it and pass it to him. You can do this. He's counting on you. Zeus and I are counting on you. Young lovers everywhere are counting on *you*. Now let's go!"

In the gym, Nikki and Zeus headed for the bleachers. I strode as confidently as I could toward Troy. He was in a gray t-shirt and black shorts, warming up with layups. When he saw me, he stopped and held the ball. "You look great!"

Nikki's pep talk had already stopped working. "I look like a clown," I said dourly.

"You look like you belong here."

"Wait 'til I try to do something."

His smile faded. "You don't have to do this if you don't want to."

I tried to smile. This was my boyfriend, not a gym class. "I want to. I'm ready if you are."

Even at the beginning, it was better than the first time. Experience helped, but the right outfit seemed to help too. He only had to chase the ball across the gym once, and then only halfway. Sometimes he shot as soon as he caught my pass, which meant the pass was okay.

Nikki sat in a corner of the gym with Zeus and her calculus book. Except for them, we had the gym to ourselves, until a couple of Troy's teammates came to shoot. One was black, one was white, and both were lanky, tall, and dressed like Troy. It took me a few seconds to remember their names—one surname and one nickname, actually.

"Hi, Jenny." Ford waved. Then he turned to Chevy. "How come he gets a pretty rebounder, and I get you?"

"Hashtag bite me," said Chevy.

They moved on.

Afterward, at her locker, I thanked Nikki again and hugged her. She said Troy was a lucky boyfriend. She also said his girlfriend was cute in gym clothes, but I was unconvinced.

In our spare time Troy and I worked his lines. We practiced cues, timing, and intonation, to sound authentic instead of rehearsed. He memorized relentlessly. He wanted to be off book before he did any scene in rehearsal, so he could concentrate on everything else he needed to master.

Jordyn was part of his motivation. She was an experienced actress and maybe the best singer and dancer in the cast, and most of his scenes were with her. "Want to look like I belong on the same stage," he said.

She worked hard too. She only needed lines from me once in rehearsal, and that was after she'd tripped, fallen hard, and worried everybody by taking a while to get back up.

I tried not to be jealous of her onstage romance with my real-life boyfriend. I did pretty well for a while. Then, one Thursday evening, I watched the light in Tzeitel's eyes when she thought Motel was about to ask her father, Tevye, for her hand. I saw her tender expression even after he couldn't summon the courage that day. Everything I felt for Troy was in her face and eyes and voice. I struggled to remember she was acting, and she was good at it.

Then difficult became impossible. After Motel finally asked Tevye's permission, and Tevye bellowed for a while, then agreed to the marriage,

I watched and listened as Troy—Motel—held her face in his hands, glowed at her, and sang about the miracle of God giving her to him.

Her, not me.

But Jordyn wasn't herself; she was Tzeitel. And Motel wasn't Troy. He was awkward, neurotic, fawning, cowering.

But those were the eyes that adored me and the hands that caressed my face. That was the voice that said sweet things to me and made me laugh. Those were the arms which had fit around me since the evening we met.

Me. Not her.

But they were acting, I thought again and again. It was going well, which was a good thing.

They were just acting.

Acting.

During a break I confessed to Troy. We sat by ourselves, halfway back in the auditorium. I needed to tell him, even if I felt stupid. He listened patiently, then said, "There is zero chance of Jordyn stealing your boyfriend. Don't worry."

"I try not to," I said weakly. "You two are good together. On stage."

"Thanks," he said. "Offstage I'm not interested, and I'm sure the feeling's mutual."

"Did she tell you that? Why would she tell you that?"

"Jenny," he said seriously, "don't be jealous. And yes, she told me. It was after the first rehearsal. She had a whole little speech for me."

He imitated her normal voice and her wide-eyed, dramatic facial expressions. "'I did a play over the summer, and one of the guys thought I was in love with him offstage, just because I was in love with him onstage, and he drove me crazy, and I broke his heart. Please don't be that guy. Remember, we're acting. It's not real. And I don't actually think you'll fall in love with me, but in case you think you might, just don't.'"

I almost laughed.

He continued in his own voice. "She also said she doesn't steal other girls' boyfriends."

His remedy for my jealousy was mostly effective, but not totally so. "I just think any girl who knows you should want you."

"Not every girl has your incredible taste." He grinned. "You've spoiled all other human females for me. Totally eclipsed them. They barely even exist. Sometimes on stage I pretend she's you, just so I'll see someone there to talk to."

I managed to keep a straight face. "Don't overdo it, boyfriend."

His eyes twinkled. "Why not, girlfriend?"

I finally smiled too. My jealousy was gone for the moment. "I can't think of a single reason. Go ahead. Overdo it."

They called us back to work.

33

Real Waltzes

I N OUR SATURDAY WALTZ lessons we worked on turns, a spinning turn, a whisk, and a chassé, and putting everything together smoothly on the dance floor. We were serious students. We practiced enough during breaks at *Fiddler* rehearsals that we could mostly stop thinking about where to put our feet. That's when you really start dancing, said the Hills.

When I asked Troy if we shouldn't be paying for our dance lessons, he shrugged. "Yeah, probably."

I saw a twinkle, which meant he wasn't telling me everything. I stared at him, considering the possibilities. "You are paying for them. How much? Or is it gauche to ask?"

"They get yard work and snow shoveling. I get to waltz with you."

That won him a hug and three words: Best. Boyfriend. Ever.

⚬

After a few lessons, he took me to a family dance at his ward on a Saturday night. The rest of his family went too, but he said his parents were just there to socialize, and only because Nan and Lily insisted.

Dress was casual, and a lot of people were in jeans. I even saw cowboy boots. I wore the same lavender top and heather gray skirt I'd worn the night we met. He was in khakis and the same long-sleeve shirt—in case it was now his lucky shirt, he said.

For the first hour, when he wasn't dancing with me, he danced with his sisters. They loved dancing with him, and it was fun to watch.

As he and I danced for the third time, Bold Jenny spoke up. "We should ask your parents to dance. What would they say?"

His eyebrows arched. "Let's find out. Next slow song."

When we asked, they reluctantly agreed. It was awkward at first, and Lily declared it "Gross!" But it was okay. Later they danced with each other, and we were proud of ourselves for getting them started.

His family went home early, as planned, while he and I stayed for the last hour. It was mostly couples by then, and mostly adults, and more people danced than not.

Troy excused himself for a few minutes. When he came back, he said, "They're playing a song for us, an old one my parents like. It's in 3/4."

"We can waltz!"

"Yup. Tempo's a little slow, but it'll work."

Several minutes later, the DJ's voice came over the speakers. "Ladies and gentlemen, we don't take dedications, and we usually don't take requests, but we do take bribes. So here's an old song in three by the Commodores, called 'Three Times a Lady,' for those of you who love to waltz. It's the long version from the album, for those of you who love the one you're waltzing with."

Maybe it was that last part that made me tremble, as Troy led me onto the floor for our first real waltz, but my nerves disappeared when we started dancing.

To waltz well, the Hills had explained, you had to be so close that dance etiquette required the man's key ring not to be in his right-front pocket, where it might bruise the woman's left hip. We didn't mind close.

At least a dozen other couples were dancing, but it was as if we had the floor to ourselves. We didn't speak. We just smiled. It was a six-and-a-half-minute dream.

When the song ended, some of the dancers applauded. I'd never seen that at a dance with recorded music. I'd only seen it for live bands, which I'd only seen in movies and on TV. Apparently we weren't the only ones who loved to waltz.

My heart thumped and my cheeks were flushed, and I probably couldn't have stopped smiling to save my life.

"You look happy," Troy said. So did he.

"I am happy. My first real waltz! Thank you!" I paused to breathe. "How can I thank you?"

His smile grew. "Seeing you so happy is pretty good."

"Then I guess you don't need the hug I was about to give you."

"Wouldn't say that."

We hugged until the next song started. I didn't care if anyone was watching.

At youth dances they never played two slow songs in a row, but this wasn't a youth dance. The next song was a sad, quiet ballad I knew, called "The Love I Meant to Say." As a plaintive male voice began to croon over an acoustic guitar, we went from hugging to dancing gently and close. We weren't indecent, but it wasn't that much of a transition.

Troy spoke softly. "Remember the first time I visited your grandpa?"

"I remember that whole wonderful afternoon," I said. "Why?"

"You gave him a big hug, and I was jealous."

I tried to look concerned. "Remind me next time. After I hug him, I'll say, 'Grandpa, Troy wants to hug you too, if that's okay.'"

He laughed. "What if it's you I want to hug?"

"Then Grandpa is technically optional."

"Good to know," he said.

The song was winding down. I'd just made plans for the last few bars—plans that didn't involve dancing. "Let's stop, okay?"

He looked puzzled, but we stopped.

"Come here." I didn't so much pull him to me as pull myself to him. I wanted to melt into him, and I felt as if I almost could. His strong arms held me close.

This was more than pure happiness, I thought, but it was as close as I'd ever been to that. It was more than gratitude. It was more than physical attraction, but knowing that was mutual was more than a little thrilling.

I knew what this was. I'd read about it in hundreds of books. Most of my favorite movies were about it. I'd dreamt about it and hoped for it and made a New Year's resolution about it, even as I feared it would never happen to me.

I knew the perfect little word for it. Someday we'd say that word aloud to each other for the first time. For now, I squeezed him a little more tightly, and he held me a little more tightly, and the only people in the whole, blissful world were a girl and a boy in each other's arms, and somehow, miraculously, I was the girl.

The next song started loud and fast and broke the spell, but not completely.

We took our seats and held hands and talked about this and that for a while. I told him I enjoyed watching him dance with his sisters, and I thought he was a really good brother. I said, "Dad thinks girls learn how boys should treat them from their brothers. It'll be hard for guys to impress your sisters, thanks to you."

"Good," he said. "But you don't have a brother. Where'd you learn?"

"I guess from watching how Dad treats Mom and me. And from books and old movies. And you."

That made him smile.

"You worked pretty hard on my dream of waltzing," I said. "Thank you. I'll never forget this dance."

"More fun than work."

"Snow shoveling and yard work are fun?"

"I don't mind anyway, and it's for you. And us. I have a scripture about this."

"How spiritual of you," I teased.

"Maybe, maybe not. Genesis says Jacob worked seven years for Rachel, 'and they seemed unto him but a few days.' A few hours of yard work is like a few minutes, if it's paying for waltz lessons with you."

When I could speak again, I asked, "Is this going to be a habit for you, making my dreams come true?"

"If you'll let me. What's next? I'll get started."

I couldn't tell him I'd been daydreaming of my first kiss, and more kisses after that, so I told him something equally true. "This is all the dream I need tonight."

I leaned on him, while we watched other couples dance. When I was thinking at all, I thought that this one evening more than made up for the grief we got at school for being together.

Later he excused himself to visit the restroom. I pulled out my smart phone to look up a certain passage in Genesis. I thought there might be more to the story.

I found the place in Genesis 29 where Jacob met Rachel at the well. She was the beautiful sister and "well favored," whatever that meant. Jacob loved her—my heart got all fluttery—and offered to serve Laban seven years for his daughter's hand.

"And they seemed unto him but a few days . . ." When I saw the rest of the verse, my heart's fluttering turned to dancing. ". . . For the love that he had to her."

I stared wide-eyed at the screen. I wanted to cry and laugh and sigh and cheer. Was Troy thinking about that part too? Was he trying to say something without actually saying it yet?

When he returned, I saw nothing subtle or expectant in his face. Just a relaxed, happy boyfriend. So no intentional message, maybe. I had a new favorite scripture anyway.

I pressed the off button before he could see my screen.

"Are you blushing?" he asked.

"Must be warm in here." I breathed deeply and changed the subject. "Remember how Mom and Dad used to text me every hour at a dance, to see if I was still okay?" I held up my phone. "They stopped doing that."

The DJ was on his microphone again. "Thanks for having us this evening. We hope you've enjoyed yourselves. Some of you said you'd stay to the very end if we'd play more songs in 3/4, which seems like a fair trade. So the last three songs are in 3/4."

There was scattered applause from the eight or ten couples still on the floor, plus a whoop that got some laughter.

"We'll do something different for this one, so if everyone who wants to dance will come to the floor, I'll explain. Do you all have a partner? Good. You can save the last two dances for that special someone. For this one, I want you to find another couple and trade partners. Make it someone you haven't danced with yet tonight. Introduce yourself if you have to. Don't put the moves on anyone else's honey, but don't be shy. You'll be back to your main squeeze in three and a half minutes."

One or two couples stuck together, but the rest obeyed. Troy and I traded partners with the Hills. The song was "Jean," which Brother Hill said was from the 1960s. It was faster than "Three Times a Lady," which made it even more fun, especially with a really good partner.

He and I had danced together at our Saturday lessons, so I was comfortable with him. He didn't try any steps I hadn't learned, and he must have known the song, because he slowed us down and sped us up at exactly the right times. At the end, I surprised him with a quick hug. I told him he and his wife were kind and patient teachers, and I was grateful. Then he went back to her, and I went back to my Troy.

The DJ asked, "Who remembers Anne Murray or a movie called *Urban Cowboy*?" There was scattered applause again. "You may remember this country waltz. It's the next-to-last dance, so enjoy."

I didn't love country music, but waltzing with Troy to a song that kept asking, "Could I Have This Dance for the Rest of My Life?" was just fine.

I smiled up at him. "It's fun to dance with other guys sometimes, but I prefer my main squeeze."

He chuckled. "In case this really is the 1980s, I like being your main squeeze. So I didn't put the moves on Brother Hill's honey. I did thank her for teaching us."

"I thanked him too," I said. "I even hugged him. Didn't I used to be shy? I mean, I still am. But what a night!"

After that song the DJ said, "This old classic is the last dance. Enjoy it with that special someone. Thanks again for inviting us to spend the evening with you. If you're driving home, don't forget those seat belts and your turn signals."

I recognized the song from the first several notes: "Moon River" from the old Audrey Hepburn film.

"Special Someone," Troy asked, "are you too tired to turn it up a notch?"

I wanted to try. "Let's find out."

So we danced the last dance like an exhibition. We'd practiced a routine in our last two lessons, combining the steps we'd learned. We danced even closer, with bigger steps and bolder turns, and used more of the floor, like a satellite orbiting the couples grouped in the middle. The only other couple in orbit was the Hills.

I was breathless when we finished, and my legs were weak. Troy said I glowed. As we returned to our chairs for our coats, a graying lady in a floral blouse and bright green pants told us we were a lovely couple, and it was nice to see young people who could dance beautifully. Troy seemed to know her.

At first I was glad not to have noticed people watching us. Then I thought I wouldn't have cared. I was too happy. Either way, I didn't need anyone else's attention, when I had Troy's.

She offered to take our picture, so we gave her our phones and stood in front of a blank section of wall. She had us pose as if we were waltzing again. After she said good night, we stood there a while, admiring the photos.

When I slipped my phone back into my skirt pocket, my fingers touched something I'd put there weeks before. I pulled out my noise-maker from the New Year's Eve dance.

"What's that?" Troy asked.

"According to Jack, a historical artifact." I spent most of the drive home explaining, including our New Year's resolution.

"Dressing up a little could work," he said. "I liked your outfit then too, but I'd have wanted to meet you anyway."

"We wondered."

"I made a New Year's resolution too," he said. "Little early, though. I think it was over Thanksgiving."

"What did you resolve?"

"I resolved to find a girl I liked to listen to, not just look at, who liked to listen to me, even if it took all year or longer. So we could talk a lot."

"I'll bet she's glad you found her so quickly," I said.

He smiled. "That's when I made a new resolution."

I heard it coming. It was in his voice. "Keep her," he said.

"I can help with that," I murmured.

For a while we just glowed at each other. Then he nodded toward the noisemaker, which was still in my hand. "Planning to use that?"

"Too loud. What I want is to hug you. For longer this time."

A lot longer, I didn't say. As it turned out, I didn't have to.

At home we checked in with Mom and Dad, who paused the film they were watching but didn't get up. Then we retreated to the entryway to "break the four-minute hug," as Troy said when we were out of parental earshot.

It might not have been four whole minutes. I couldn't be sure. But my arms got tired and started shaking. His didn't.

He said good night in a voice that was soft and deep and slipped out the door. I just stood there, physically drained but aching for more.

When Zeus was down for the night and I was in my pajamas, I looked at the photos again, pulled out the noisemaker, closed my bedroom door to avoid disturbing dog and parents, and blew it on every second and third beat as I waltzed in my room, to music that wasn't there, with a boy who wasn't either.

I fell backward onto my bed, phone in hand. "We waltzed tonight!" I texted to Jack and Nikki, and sent them the photo. "Fun details later, plus useful New Year's resolution data."

34

Opposition

I AWOKE AT 8:30 the next morning, so I could text Troy before his 9:00 a.m. church meetings. Then I remembered the Pullmans were going out of town to hear a cousin speak before she left on her mission to Spain.

"Good morning!" I wrote. "Where are you? What are your thoughts?"

"Good morning. Almost there. Left 7, starts 9."

"And my second question?"

"Ladies first."

"Okay, this: Last night is a beautiful memory. Thank you!"

Nothing coy about me this morning.

"I waltzed with an angel," he wrote. "How cool is that?"

I sent him a heart emoji and imagined the look in his eyes, if he could see my smile.

"Have another dream I can work on?" he asked. "Want to get started. Also, Mom, Dad, Nan, and Lily say hi. Lily sends Zeus a hug."

I had dreams enough with Troy's name on them, but I couldn't bring myself to list them for him. It took a minute to come up with something I could send. "Just be my boyfriend, and my dreams will take care of themselves." My face was hot. I was pretty obvious—but we already knew we were serious about each other.

"Also, tell everyone hi. Zeus sends a nuzzle and a tail wag for Lily."

"Done. You'll tell me if I'm missing a dream, right?"

"I promise. I was thinking, a great boyfriend is like a superhero."

"You don't like superheroes."

"I like my own. When are you back?"

"Midyear interview with the bishop at 3:30, so before then. We're here. Gotta run. Skype tonight? Maybe 8-ish?"

"It's a date," I wrote.

—◦—

I thought I was making small talk later on Skype, when I asked how his interview went, but his smile faded.

"Sucked. Made me angry."

"Uh-oh. Something you can tell your girlfriend?"

"Tell you the whole thing. No secrets."

I'd had similar interviews every six months since I turned twelve, with my bishop or one of his counselors—every bishop had two assistants called counselors—but every interview was different. Bishops were different too, and I already had my doubts about Troy's. I recalled him not laughing at a pretty good joke.

Troy said it started okay. His bishop thanked him again for speaking a few weeks earlier and said he'd done well. Then he asked about school and summer plans, and whether Troy still planned to serve a mission after high school.

"Yes, sir," Troy said. "It's mostly paid for already."

"Excellent. You couldn't have a better goal."

"Thank you, sir. I have some good goals after that, too."

I suppressed my giddy hope for a leading role in those post-mission goals and focused on listening to Troy.

"Glad to hear it," said his bishop. "Of course, there are obstacles to serving a mission other than money."

"I'm in excellent health, sir."

"Good. As you know, worthiness is also an obstacle."

Troy reported that to me with a straight face, but I giggled. His bishop must have been tired.

Troy replied, "Bishop, don't you mean *un*worthiness is an obstacle?"

"Sorry. Long day. How are things in that department?"

"So far, so good, sir."

They talked about commandments ranging from tithing and honesty to avoiding alcohol, tobacco, and drugs. Then his bishop said, "Sexual temptations are everywhere. I'm sure you realize the Lord gives us effective ways to avoid them."

They read together from *For the Strength of Youth*—about waiting to date until age sixteen, which Troy had done, and going with other couples when you first start dating, which he'd also done. When they came to avoiding frequent dates with the same person, Troy asked if that was a commandment or just counsel. He got a familiar answer.

"This is official counsel from the inspired leaders of the Lord's Church, so you'd be safe to consider it a commandment."

Troy was blunt. "I don't consider it a commandment, Bishop. If I did, some things would be different."

His bishop was blunt too. "Does this involve the girl you danced with last night?"

"I danced with several girls last night, Bishop, including Mom and my sisters. But mostly with my girlfriend, yes."

They read about the danger of having serious relationships too early in life, which the booklet said could limit acquaintances with other people and possibly "lead to immorality."

I only blushed a little when Troy recounted that. It wasn't new.

"Bishop," he said, "there's no immorality going on, and there won't be. And I meet lots of girls."

"These are powerful temptations."

"Yes, sir. But if I really care about someone, I won't hurt her. And we won't do anything together that would be a problem for either of us."

"That's easy to say," said his bishop. "I worry that you're flirting with danger."

Danger, thy name is Jenny. I felt slightly insulted and playfully naughty at the same time, but that quickly faded to worry or even fear, except I wasn't sure what to worry about or to fear. I kept listening.

Troy said, "Maybe I'll do better on the next thing, sir."

He did. It was about getting your parents acquainted with your dates. After that was dating only people with high moral standards.

Troy told him my moral standards were fine. Then he said, "Found out that's not true of some other girls I've dated, but I didn't do anything wrong with them either, even when they wanted to."

"That's good. That's very good," his bishop said. "I think I'd worry less, if I'd ever seen you two walking together without your arm around her, or if I hadn't seen how you were dancing last night."

He might have seen some hugging too, I thought. I didn't feel guilty about that. I didn't interrupt Troy's story to mention it either. Had Troy explained why he always had his arm around me, and why we danced only slow dances?

"What really matters, sir," Troy replied, "is that we know the commandments, and we're obeying them. We know the counsel too, and we're following most of it. If you think I'll jeopardize my future or hers, because I can't keep my hands where they belong and my pants zipped, you're wrong, sir."

I wondered if such graphic detail was further proof of my dangerous influence. Either way, I approved.

"And Bishop," he said, "she wouldn't do anything like that either."

So I wasn't dangerous after all. Which I already knew.

"I'm not breaking up with her. Sir."

Troy's non-dangerous girlfriend wanted time to melt over that declaration, but Troy was already reporting what his bishop said next.

"Troy, prophetic counsel on these topics is given to help us keep some crucial commandments, and ultimately to lead us to the celestial kingdom. I hope you'll consider its wisdom and choose your behavior accordingly."

"That was about it," Troy told me.

"At least we all agree on the importance of commandments," I said. "I wonder how many other people talk to him like that."

"Don't know," Troy said. "What really ticked me off was what he didn't say. Didn't ask me your name or anything about you. You're not a person to him, just a problem that might affect someone he's supposed to worry about. Maybe I'm just a problem too."

"Maybe he's not a people person," I said, wondering why I would defend the man. "Maybe he had a bad day, talking to people who actually do the things he worries about."

"Maybe. I'm sure he's a good man. But now I either want to avoid him as much as possible or schedule another interview and take you with me. Let him see you as a person, not a problem."

"I'm with you either way."

"You're a very good girlfriend. The Bible says we have to love everyone, but it doesn't say we have to like them, right?"

My vague worries survived our conversation, but I still couldn't pin them on anything. Besides, there was a happier thought, and it wasn't vague at all: Troy and I were firmly, stubbornly together on this.

———◆———

The next day, it was my turn. I wasn't expecting it, but I was ready for it, in the sense that I still didn't like what Troy's bishop had said.

I lingered in the classroom after seminary to proofread a worksheet that was due. My teacher, Brother Stickinger, was feeling talkative.

"I've seen you with Troy Pullman," he said. "Are you boyfriend and girlfriend?"

Just that quickly, I was frustrated and defensive. How long had he waited for this opportunity to pounce?

"Yes, we are. I'm the girlfriend." In my frustration I was trying for disrespect, not humor.

"I hope you'll be cautious in your relationship with him. He needs to serve a mission."

"That's the plan."

"There are risks, Jenny. They're not small."

"So I've heard," I said. "May I ask you something?"

"Of course."

I unloaded on him.

"You tell us we should date and get to know lots of people, and have fun and develop our social skills. What do you expect me to do when I meet a really good guy while I'm doing that, and we really like each other? Should I just move on and ignore him, until he comes up again in the rotation? If there even is a rotation?

"Everyone's always listing things we shouldn't do. What should we do? Should I date boys who might have lower standards, so I don't spend too much time with a boy I know has high standards?"

I assumed that his look, pursed lips and all, was disapproval. I kept talking.

"Everyone says we're an especially strong generation, sent by God for a time that requires special strength. So why don't you believe that a lot of us actually want to be good? Why don't you try to help us with that, instead of trying to scare us into not being bad? Why do you assume we're looking for ways to sin and get away with it?"

"I can see you're upset," he said, ignoring my questions.

"I'm not exactly hiding that." I was still disrespectful. Troy would have done better. And he wouldn't have felt like crying.

"You know, it's pretty common for people to think they're exceptions to rules they don't want to obey," Brother Stickinger said. "I would just urge you to take the counsel seriously and avoid unnecessary risks."

"We take it seriously. We think two pieces of it aren't helpful for us, but we're careful about the rest." He looked like he wanted to speak, but I pressed ahead. "I trust Troy. Maybe you think that makes me a fool. My parents trust him too, and they're not fools. So do his parents. They're not fools either. They trust us to behave, and we do. Not that it's any of your business."

He nodded his bald head slightly—I doubted he was agreeing with me—and I thought I saw some extra color. "That's easy to say now, Jenny, but in the heat of passion—"

I cut him off. "I don't know much about the heat of passion, but if I did, I'm pretty sure I wouldn't discuss it with my seminary teacher. I'm late for lunch. Please excuse us." I looked down. "Come on, Zeus."

I waited until Zeus and I had turned a corner before wiping a tear from each eye. At least they hadn't escaped, and there weren't any more behind them.

After school, when I told Troy what had happened, he was frustrated. "You'd think they'd have a better reason for girls to be chaste than just keeping boys chaste so we can go on missions," he said. "How sexist is that? It's like you only matter because you can influence me."

"Can he really believe that?" I asked.

"If you asked him, probably not. So he should think before he talks. He's giving impressionable kids like us the wrong impression."

"I may transfer at the end of the term," I said. "I want a different teacher."

"He'll probably think you're doing it out of guilt. But I love what you said: 'I'm pretty sure I wouldn't discuss it with my seminary teacher.' You're spectacular."

I thought it was a good line too. Even if I had been unkind.

In the gym on Thursday, after school, I let Troy persuade me that it didn't make sense for me to dress down once a week and rebound for him, but never shoot the ball myself. After his shoot-around he spent 10 or 15 minutes trying to teach me layups. I was clumsy, but he didn't mind, and I managed to laugh at myself a few times and even forget my uneasy truce with the law of gravity.

When he reached around me from behind for the third or fourth time, to help me get my arms in the right shooting position, I leaned my head back and rested it on his shoulder.

"Mm. I like basketball," I cooed.

He laughed and put his arms around my waist. "Does this mean we're done for today?"

"We should go see Grandpa. But let's do this again next week. Especially this part."

35

Accusation, Invitation

Aᴌᴌ ᴡᴇᴇᴋ ᴛʜᴇ ʜᴀᴛᴇʀꜱ had ignored me. It felt like an improvement, but it turned out they'd just changed tactics.

When Troy met me after school on Friday, before rehearsal, his cheeks were flushed and his lips were a thin line. He barely smiled. I asked him what was wrong.

"Not here," he said.

"Are you angry with me?"

"Not with you."

We found a quiet corner near the auditorium. He said he'd just met with the assistant principal and the resource officer, the police sergeant assigned to the high school. The officer had heard a rumor that Troy had hit Brooke, one of the toxic cheerleaders, in the face that day, when she'd resisted his attempt to grope her. She had a nasty bruise.

Fortunately, the assistant principal already knew Brooke had fallen badly in cheerleading practice and bruised her face. She'd even been checked for a concussion. When he and the officer compared notes, they made the connection.

Just to be sure, they talked to Brooke. Then they pulled Troy in to tell him the matter was closed. It was the first he'd heard of it.

I would never have believed the rumor, but it upset me anyway. I was angry at girls—I assumed it was girls—who would do such a thing to my boyfriend. Any girl's boyfriend.

Still, I tried to be positive. "It's nice of them to tell you you're cleared. I'm glad Brooke was honest."

"Yeah," he said. "But what's wrong with people? This is stupid."

"I wish I knew what to do about it," I said.

"So do I. Ought to be some way to get them off our backs without breaking up."

The words "breaking up" turned me cold. My voice quivered. "Even that might not stop it. And let's not find out."

He gave me a long squeeze. "Can we find a happier topic?"

"You know I'm not a unicorns, rainbows, cotton candy sort of girl."

"Thank heaven for that," he said with feeling. His voice brightened. "Would you go to prom with me?"

"Yes, I'd love to," I said. "Wait a minute!"

"What?"

I had to smile, so I tried for a mischievous grin. "Aren't you supposed to find some way to ask me without talking to me or making eye contact? Icing on a cake you baked yourself? Messengers in gorilla suits? A scavenger hunt? A word game with the names of candy bars? Maybe a waterproof note in a huge block of ice, so I have to melt the ice to read it? Or a male quartet singing lines you composed yourself? Is just opening your mouth and asking me even allowed?"

He smiled through my whole speech. "That what you want?"

"No." I finally gave him the full smile he deserved. "Of course I'll go with you. Thanks for asking."

"Wanted to ask without all the drama."

"I like it. Simple, direct. I didn't have encode my reply in crop circles on your lawn or have the drum line beat it out in Morse code."

He chuckled. "I know Zeus doesn't like dances, but we should think up a day date he'll like. Unless you don't like those either."

"Day dates are Troy time for me. Make me an offer."

⊷◆⊶

At dinner I was tempted to tell Mom and Dad about the afternoon's rumor, but I didn't want the larger conversation that would invite, about what was going on at school. Besides, I had other news to report. I told them I had a date for prom.

"Anyone we know?" Mom asked blankly. It was a challenge.

My poker face worked sometimes too. "I'm not sure," I said. "Have I told you about Hank? He's a wrestler. There's no way his IQ hits triple digits, but he's hot. He and Troy arm-wrestled today, to see who would take me. Apparently, wrestlers are stronger than basketball players." I sighed and tried to sound giddy. "I like strong. I doubt he's much of a dancer, but dancing isn't necessarily what I want most from a boy on prom night. You're not buying this, are you?"

Dad was grinning. "No, but it was fun. I was starting to worry what your mom would say. She's very competitive."

I looked to see if she'd pick up Dad's gauntlet. Or mine.

She smiled. "Not this time. I had a response that would give us all nightmares, including me, so I'll pass. How about this? Thanks for reminding us what a fine young man Troy is. We're eager to hear how he asked you to prom."

"He just asked me. I said yes."

"That's old-fashioned," Dad said.

"I teased him about that, but I like direct. Promposals are stupid."

"Some girls expect them," Mom said.

"I want him to be man enough to ask in person, or at least talk to me on his phone. I want to be woman enough to answer the same way."

"Maybe a boy just wants a girl to feel special," Mom said.

"I feel special when a great guy likes me enough to ask me to prom without playing games."

"Not every boy is secure in the knowledge that a girl is that sensible and already adores him," Dad said. "Or even that she'll say yes."

I saw his point, but I still thought the extra drama was stupid.

Later I ate in silence, while Mom and Dad discussed something else. My thoughts had moved on from prom—but not from Troy.

Dad asked, "Jenny, are you sad, worried, or just tired?"

I swallowed. "What do you mean?" As if I didn't know.

"You just told us your boyfriend is taking you to prom. Isn't that worth ten minutes of happiness?"

"I'm happy about prom. I'm very happy about Troy. It's something else."

"Care to share?" he asked.

I thought for a moment. "Okay." I put down my fork. "Seminary was boring today, so I reread *For the Strength of Youth* instead of listening. They like us to review it, right?

"I counted the things it tells us to do and not do. It's about 200, which seems like a lot, but quite a few of them repeat. I agree with almost all of them. I believe in them. What I really wanted was to see how many things I'm not doing that it says I should, and vice versa."

"It could be worse," Dad said. "There are something like 613 rules in the Torah. How did you do?"

"Some don't apply, because I'm not old enough or I don't have brothers or sisters to be kind to. Some are hard to measure, like being humble. Besides those, the only two things I clearly don't do by the little book are the ones we've talked about before. I keep going out with the same guy, and we're serious. At least serious for high school.

"But we're being careful. We're not breaking any commandments. We're not even breaking any other rules. And we don't sit around moping because we're not allowed to go biological."

Dad snorted at that. Mom looked bemused.

"That's what Jack calls it now. Anyway, all four parents think we're okay. You'd tell me if you didn't, right?"

Mom nodded. Dad said, "Definitely."

"Thank you. I mean it. Even Bishop Savage is okay with us, I think. So here's what bugs me.

"It's not like everyone has to agree. If our seminary teacher and Troy's bishop think we're foolish or rebellious, maybe even wicked, why should I care? I don't want to care, but I do. So does Troy. I guess my real question is, how can we stop caring what they think?"

Mom and Dad said nothing. They didn't smile, but they didn't frown either. They looked thoughtful.

"They're not rhetorical questions," I said after a moment.

Mom finally spoke. "We're used to thinking of Church leaders and teachers as God's messengers—which they are, and we are too, when we're in those roles. When God's messengers disapprove, we worry that God himself disapproves."

"Do you think God disapproves of you and Troy?" Dad asked.

"Not even close. There's nothing to feel guilty about, except that I just dangled a preposition. And I don't think guilt is what we're feeling. So why does two men's bad opinion have to bother us?"

"I'm not sure this is the answer," Dad said, "but see what you think. Ever since you were small, you've always been the good girl, and Troy has always been the good boy, I think. You've had everyone's approval, both of you—at least your leaders' and teachers' approval."

"That's not unanimous anymore, and some of the dissenters are in positions which incline us to care what they think. Life just got more difficult. It does that."

"We must be such a disappointment to them," I said. "Where's that scripture about even the very elect being deceived? If they thought we were the good ones before, they probably think that's about us now."

"Matthew 24," Mom said. "You haven't disappointed us. Either of you."

"Thanks, seriously. But I want us to stop caring what they think."

"Keep behaving," Mom said. "Maybe they'll figure it out. If not, they won't be Troy's bishop and your seminary teacher forever. You won't be in high school forever."

"You wish they'd see the good in you, right?" Dad asked. "What if you try to see the good in them? I'm sure there's plenty."

"I'm sure there is, but I don't want to look for it. The more good we see in them, the harder it will be not to care what they think."

"Fair point." Dad was stern. "What if you try to see the good in them anyway—not for your sake, but because it's the right thing to do? Mom's right. You may have to live with their disapproval."

What I heard in Dad's words was a rebuke. He really didn't want me trying not to see the good in people. And he was right. And talking with him and Mom probably helped somehow. It just didn't help me stop caring what two authority figures thought about my boyfriend and me.

I nodded. "I can do that. I guess we'll be okay."

⋅◆⋅

After that, for a while, preparing for prom and working on *Fiddler* mostly distracted me from the haters at school, and from the people at church and seminary who knew exactly how all their little rules applied to everyone else's life.

36

Staging

"OKAY, CUT!" CALLED THE drama teacher, Mr. Otteson. He walked down toward the stage from his seat in the sixth row. "I know we're all tired and getting nervous, but relax a minute and listen up."

He ran his fingers back through his dark brown hair, then massaged his neck. He was thirty-something and handsome. Some of the girls wished he were closer to our age and single. I wondered if he knew that.

Probably not. He wasn't preening. He was focused—and he was tired too.

"We have to nail this," he said as he reached the stage. "We're two days from dress rehearsals, and I know these last scenes feel like we're just tying up loose ends. But if we play them that way, we kill them—as in dead, not the way you guys use that word. We're going for, 'Wow, incredible show!' Instead we'll get—he switched to a feminine voice with a refined British accent—'Oh, aren't they simply charming when they try to put on a play?'"

He didn't smile, and there was less snickering than I expected.

"I have to go handle a situation," he said in his normal voice. "Jenny's the director for a while."

He might as well have dropped a brick on my head. My knees went weak—even though I was sitting—and my stomach twirled.

"Pay attention. Do what she says. Bring this to life," he said. "They won't feel what you don't feel. If I'm not back, she'll turn you loose on time, not early."

I was front row center as usual, and now I was wide-eyed and speechless. He approached, speaking softly. "Sorry for the surprise, but this can't wait. Try to create some feeling. They'll listen. You'll be great."

"Mr. Ott—"

He held up his hand, not letting me protest that I had no idea what I was doing. That I was just the prompter. That he must be having a psychological emergency in addition to whatever else was going on. "Sorry, gotta run. You'll be fine. Don't show fear."

He hurried away, and I tried to tame my thoughts. He wanted feeling. That was a start. Maybe I wouldn't panic yet.

I stood up, looked at the cast, and tried to appear thoughtful. Most were watching me—some looking bored or tired, others attentive and expectant. I had to say something intelligent, and soon. My eyes found Troy. He was at full twinkle, either enjoying my predicament or trying to be encouraging.

"Okay," I said. "I've been watching the script, not the scene. Let's run it again from the same place." Mr. Otteson always said that. "This time I'll watch you."

I watched for a couple of minutes, and it really was flat. I didn't know how to fix it, but seeing the problem helped me focus.

"Cut!" I called, not waiting to see the whole scene. "Reset, please. Then we'll talk."

When they were in position, I looked at their faces. They were still serious—except Troy. He was enjoying this too much.

"Thanks for doing that so quickly," I said. "I'm just the prompter, right? But here's what I'm thinking. We look like bored people loading junk into a cart. But we're not bored. We're exhausted. We're scared for the future. And it's not junk."

I was making it up as I went along.

"They're forcing us to leave our homes, because we're Jews. We're taking what we can, but it's not much. We're leaving behind the lives we know, leaving Russia for a new country we've only heard about. It'll take a long time to get there, if we ever do.

"Maybe we wonder why God doesn't intervene to protect us, like the Bible says he's done before. Maybe we wonder if there's a god at all. If there is, we're supposedly his chosen people, but that doesn't seem to be helping right now. What if he's decided to choose someone else and be done with us?

"Either way, we'll never see this place or most of our friends again. This may be the last time we see some of our family. We're saying goodbye forever to practically everything and everyone we've ever known. We're grieving and we're scared. How would you feel if you and your family suddenly had to pack whatever would fit in the wheelbarrow and start walking to Argentina before Saturday?"

I was thinking aloud, but they listened, even nodded, some of them—not because I was the one talking, I thought, but because they wanted this to be good. It made me proud. And more nervous. I needed to step up and actually help somehow.

I had an idea.

"Every time we put something in the cart, let's relive a memory and face a fear. Think about Golde's candlesticks. They've been part of every Sabbath in our home for years. We're taking them with us, but how long will it be before we have a home again? Or a proper Sabbath? Maybe we'll have to sell them to get where we're going.

"I don't know much about acting. But what if you somehow pretend that everything you carry is a few pounds heavier than it really is, and try to remember the times you've had with it over the years? Try to wonder if those times will ever come again. And when you hug someone or shake someone's hand, remember it may have to last us for the rest of our lives.

"The edict gave us three days to leave town. We have to hurry, but we can't hurry this part. We have to slow down and feel."

I finally stopped talking and we ran it again. I could see they were doing what I asked, but it wasn't enough. I didn't stop them, because I didn't know what else to say, except it was a little better, and we should try again. That could wait.

I watched Tevye quietly say goodbye to some of the minor characters, and I felt something. I didn't know why. He lingered with each person, but they were all doing that now, and it wasn't enough. What was working for him?

Then he came to Lazar Wolf, the butcher, who'd spent much of the play furious with him for breaking his word and letting Tzeitel marry Motel instead of him. The silly, jealous part of my brain was firmly on Lazar Wolf's side on that one. He could have Tzeitel. Motel was mine.

They'd had a lot to say before, in friendship and anger, but now they said only two or three words each. For a few seconds before they spoke, and several seconds after, they held each other's gaze.

That's what was working for me.

"Cut!" I called. "Listen while you reset, please. You're doing exactly what I asked. Thank you. But it's not enough.

"I think Tevye and Lazar figured it out for us. This time, do everything you just did, and we'll add what they did. When you say goodbye, don't say more than a few words, if you say anything at all. Just hold each other's gaze a lot longer. You're already emotionally exhausted. We don't need dramatic expressions of worry or sadness. Think about that, and we'll run it again. Thank you, Lazar and Tevye!"

It. Worked. Beautifully.

I knew what they were doing, but I still felt a bundle of emotions grow as the scene progressed. They were mostly negative, all confused and intertwined. I tried to understand why. Maybe, if the actors gave them a chance, the audience's minds and hearts filled in the emotion and the unspoken thoughts. Dad and Mrs. Tornow both said writing worked that way with readers.

There were tears in my eyes. The scene itself had moved me, but I was also relieved that we'd fixed it—and I hadn't ruined it.

I opened my mouth to tell them about it, but Mr. Otteson beat me to it. He must have returned in time to watch from the back. "Yes! Bravo! You nailed it!" he yelled, walking down the aisle. "Two more times, exactly like that. Then we'll go home."

The whole mood of our rehearsal had changed, I thought later as the cast left. There was life in their steps and energy in their chatter. A few of them caught my eye and gave me a thumbs-up—and I blinked back tears again. They'd taken me seriously. I was part of the team.

When Mr. Otteson asked me what I'd done, I tried to give Tevye and Lazar the credit. He wasn't surprised they'd figured it out. "But you got them started. Then you noticed what they did and described it for everyone. That's exactly what we needed from you. You just worked yourself into a job, if you want it. Assistant director next year?"

I was stunned. "I don't know anything about theater."

"That's clearly not true. You're learning. You have good instincts. They did what you told them. You were fairly good on stage yourself in Troy's audition. Did I tell you that? And aren't you some sort of writer?"

"I'm trying to be. Are you sure?"

"It's yours if you want it, so think about it. I'd want you in drama class next year. You can do some acting and directing in class, even some writing, if you want. It's been years since I had a serious writer. That could be fun."

I nodded meekly. "I'll think about it. Thanks for asking."

By then Troy had collected his things and joined me. He was much taller than Mr. Otteson. I didn't remember noticing that before.

Mr. Otteson stepped away to shut down the auditorium, and Troy gave me a squeeze. "Nice job!"

On our way to the parking lot, he said, "You looked nervous at first, but you were great."

"I was nervous the whole time."

"When you explained everything, I was thinking it's good to have a writer for a prompter. What'd Mr. O say?"

"He offered me assistant director next year."

He grinned. "Wow! You want it?"

"I don't know. Maybe. I never imagined doing something like that."

"You like working with him?"

"I do. Look what he can do with high school kids. Plus I'm just the prompter, and I'm a novice, but he's never talked down to me."

Troy chuckled. "Can't talk down to you. Same height."

"He's a little taller. But I'll bet he weighs less than me, unless classy goatees are heavier than they look."

"Wouldn't know about that," Troy said.

"Good choice," I said with a little smile.

"You like his goatee better than my . . . whatever this is?" Troy stroked his beard.

"Yes. Sorry. Yours is getting better, though."

"I like his better too. Anyway, you should do it, if you want. We could take drama together. Might be good experience for a writer."

"Let's see if it fits my schedule—after the show's over. I might hate the idea by then."

"Doubt it."

"I still can't believe they listened and did what I said."

"You're surprised we listened?"

"Surprised. Puzzled. Grateful."

In his car, before he started the engine, he turned to me. "Here's why you shouldn't be surprised. Speaking for the cast as a whole, we respect our director, and he told us to listen to you. When we did, you made sense and said please and thank you. You've always been ready when we needed you, and you're always kind. You never sound like you want to scold us when we forget something. And one more thing. You treat Mr. O with respect, and he treats you with respect, like when he stops to discuss cuts with you. Coach says that's infectious."

"Wow," I said.

"Face it. Jenny Miller's amazing. It's an increasingly well-known fact."

Prom would be one week after closing night. Jack and Nikki had dates too, so we worked together to find just the right dresses and hairstyles. Our moms helped with things like credit cards and doing our hair.

I wanted a simple, elegant dress, nothing too big or fancy, so I could dance comfortably and wear it for other nice things someday. Just once, as we looked at dresses, I asked Mom the wrong question. "Do you think Troy would like me in burgundy?"

She was gentle. "He'd like you in burlap too. Dress for yourself. Do you like you in burgundy?"

"I like my hair and my face with a darker dress. I look a lot like you, and you're gorgeous in your burgundy."

"Thank you. It's one of your dad's favorites."

"You don't dress for him, do you?" I grinned. "Someone told me that would be wrong."

Her tone was serious, but her eyes sparkled. "Sometimes I do."

"So . . . do as you say, not as you do?"

She smiled warmly. "I'm married to the guy. But I still mostly dress for myself. He likes me in a lot of things."

A few minutes later, I was at the mirrors, studying a navy gown I almost loved but not quite, when my dear, wise mother tried to embarrass me to death.

I asked her how she liked the gown.

"It's beautiful," she said. "You're beautiful in it. You fill out a dress quite nicely, these days."

"Mom!" I cried in horror. But quietly, because we were in a store.

"It's a compliment. It's also true."

"What if somebody heard you?" I hissed through clenched teeth.

"On the women's floor? Everyone here understands how the female body develops."

"That's not—"

"You're standing in front of three mirrors. Look at yourself. I'm right."

"That is so not the point," I said, still clenching my teeth. My eyes darted to one of the mirrors. My face was scarlet. So was my neck. I didn't look any lower.

"I understand your point," she said. "My point is, those of us fortunate enough to have it may as well enjoy it."

"Mom! Do you want me never to go shopping with you again?"

"Relax. And before I forget, depending on what you do with your hair, you might add a pair of my diamond earrings."

I began to settle down. "That would be perfect. Thank you."

I chose a floor-length, burgundy evening gown. It was narrower and less ornate than some—I wanted beautiful girl, not fairy-tale princess—but it wasn't one of those form-fitting things a girl can barely walk in. It was subtly accented and gathered a little at the waist, flattering without being overtly sexy. It was modest enough that Troy wouldn't be embarrassed to look at me, but elegant enough that I wanted to look at myself. In it *I* was elegant.

The neckline was a shallow, asymmetrical "v" in front and back. I loved the asymmetry. It felt exotic, like my combination of black hair and blue eyes. It had long bell sleeves; that's what the sales lady called them. They were removable, with tiny, hidden zippers, and I went back and forth on whether to wear them or not. I liked both ways.

In the spirit of asymmetry, I even tried wearing just one sleeve, but that looked weird and costumey, not exotic. So both sleeves or neither. On an April evening, probably both.

It all took more time and more of my parent's money than I usually devoted to my appearance, but it was my first prom, and I enjoyed the preparations. So did Mom. And no matter what she said, to me it was at least partly for Troy.

37

Triumph

OUR FIRST DRESS REHEARSALS for *Fiddler* were on Friday evening and Saturday afternoon. They were long and rough. Things we'd polished barely worked at all. Most of the actors missed cues and dropped lines where they never had before. Four costumes and one of the sets had major problems. And we kept stopping to fix things between the singers and the orchestra.

Mr. Otteson wasn't worried. He said that's why we had dress rehearsals.

The last one, on the following Tuesday with a partial audience, went much better. After that we did a sold-out show every night, from Wednesday through Saturday.

I was nervous every night—more nervous than Troy, and I was just the prompter. The audience wouldn't see me dance or hear me talk or sing.

In costume Troy looked more or less like a young Jewish man with a beard. He was fun to watch. His Motel was awkward and nervous, even weak—until the father of the girl he loved announced that she would marry Lazar Wolf. Even after Motel manned up enough to get the girl, Troy was still a convincing wimp. I was biased, but he may have stolen a scene or two.

Our Tevye, a dark-haired senior named Hunter, had been solid and fun to watch in rehearsals. With an audience he was mesmerizing. A few scenes into opening night, I realized his extra energy and emotion were infecting the whole cast. They were less nervous and more in character when he was onstage—and soon enough, when he wasn't.

Mr. Otteson had told me he usually chose the musical to fit his strongest cast members. This year he had a Tevye, so we did *Fiddler*.

Wow, did we have a Tevye.

There wasn't much work for me the first three nights, but Saturday I was busy. Everyone was tired, including me, and a few kids were sick. I almost missed one of the times they needed me.

That night I left my post for the final scene—my scene. I watched from just inside a door at the front of the auditorium. The action was in front of the orchestra pit, where I couldn't have helped from backstage anyway.

A few yards from me, Tevye and his family finished packing their cart and said goodbye to their neighbors. Somber faces and prolonged, wordless gazes worked their magic. My heart supplied five kinds of emotion that went unspoken. When I saw tears on Tzeitel's face, my own eyes filled.

Others trudged up the aisles on the far side of the auditorium, carrying bundles and pushing carts. Tevye and his family crossed in front of the stage and followed them. As they looked back at their home for the last time, my chin began to quiver, and my tears overflowed. We had created this beautiful thing, and I was a part of it, and it was about to end.

When the last refugees were halfway up the aisle, with spotlights following them, the fiddler began to play in front of the stage. Another spot illuminated her, and Tevye turned around. She stopped playing and looked at him, her arms spread in a silent question. He gestured with his head for her to follow.

The curtain had closed while everyone watched the action in the aisles. When the fiddler reached the rear of the auditorium and the last spotlight went out, the orchestra started up again, and I joined the audience's ovation. I knew Troy and everyone else had left their props and were racing through a hallway back to the stage, so they wouldn't be late for curtain calls.

I'd mostly avoided being jealous of Jordyn through dress rehearsals and performances, but once every night—especially on closing night—I couldn't help myself. She and Troy took their curtain call together, holding hands as they walked to the front of the stage and bowed. They were in character and doing what they were told, and I loved how every night the applause got louder when they appeared. But when I saw Tzeitel holding Motel's hand, I wanted to be holding Troy's.

Tevye was the last cast member to take a bow. The audience roared. The house lights were partway up, so we could see them. What I saw was, anyone who wasn't already standing stood for Tevye.

On closing night Mr. Otteson let Tevye's ovation go extra long. Then he appeared and quickly took his bow. He pointed to the orchestra and its conductor. Then he beckoned for the stage crew and me, and we joined the cast on stage.

I'd been on stages with choirs. I'd had solo parts in a few songs, and the director had singled me out for applause. But until *Fiddler*, I'd never been on stage for a standing ovation from a packed house. I knew the applause was for all of us—far less for me than for others—but it hit me in almost palpable waves, amid the whoops and whistles.

On opening night I was so dazzled that I'd have forgotten to bow, if we hadn't all been holding hands and bowing together. By closing night I felt like a veteran, even if I was in tears like most of the cast.

Every night, the entire cast and crew made one last bow together and waved to the audience as the curtain closed. But the cheering and applause didn't stop, so they opened the curtain again, and we all bowed and waved again.

On closing night Mr. Otteson had Tevye step forward alone again and take another bow. The applause seemed to go on forever. The cast and crew cheered as enthusiastically as the audience.

When the curtain finally closed for the last time on our *Fiddler*, Troy found me for a long backstage hug.

His smile softened. "You're crying."

I couldn't talk, so I nodded.

"You're crying and smiling."

I shrugged.

"Think I understand."

He held me tightly. When I could speak again, I told him he was wonderful. The whole show was wonderful. The whole experience was wonderful.

For half an hour each night, the cast greeted audience members and posed for pictures with friends, family, classmates, and other adoring fans. Troy was in lots of photos with Jordyn, which I understood but didn't love. He and I were in a few together, mostly for our families. On closing night, after all the hugs and photos, when the costumes and props were put away and the stage makeup removed, the cast party began in the drama room.

Near the beginning, I sat, as usual, while Troy went for drinks. I saw Jordyn walk up to him, say something, and give him a hug. He smiled and hugged her back, and I told myself not to be a jealous girlfriend. Again. Then he led her right to me, and I stood.

He handed me my drink. "Jordyn has something to tell you."

I spoke before she could. "Jordyn, you were wonderful. You're so talented." I could be sincere and jealous at the same time.

She smiled broadly. "Thank you for helping me so much."

"You needed one line, about a month ago."

"I was just telling Troy, I've been onstage since I was four, and I knew he wasn't that experienced, and we had a lot of scenes together. I was worried at first. Sounds awful, doesn't it? But he was easy to work with, and he came so well prepared that he could focus on the hard things, like how to run like a dorky tailor instead of an athlete."

Troy was watching me, not her. We traded smiles, and I forced my attention back to her.

"He says you were his dialogue coach, practice dance partner, and everything else, all rolled up into one amazing girlfriend. And you talked him into trying out in the first place."

"Couldn't have said it better myself," Troy announced. He gave me a squeeze and excused himself.

"He gives me too much credit," I said.

"I don't know. I was there when Otteson had to leave. You're good."

"Thanks. But if I had thought for two seconds about you being on the stage since you were four, I couldn't have said a word."

"I hear he offered you assistant director. Think you'll do it?"

"I think I might, but I really don't know what I'm doing."

"Nobody expects you to be the director, just to help him. You'll learn. That's what I love about the theater," she said. "We try new things. We get to be people we've never been. And usually something wonderful happens. You should do it."

"Thanks for encouraging me."

"I hope I didn't make you too jealous," she said. "I was your boyfriend's fiancée, then his wife." She giggled. "I even had his baby."

It was the giggle that made me want to strangle her. I smiled instead, more or less. "I tried not to be jealous. I mostly succeeded." I turned my voice surly and glared. "I want a paternity test. Now. Tonight."

She clapped her hands. "You are so funny!"

"He really liked working with you," I confessed. "He told me more than once."

"You two must have an awesome relationship, if he can tell you that about another girl."

"We talk all the time about everything."

"The perfect couple," she said.

"You must not be listening to the cheerleaders," I said. "They think I'm the wrong species for him."

"Why would I listen to them? Why would you?"

"My boyfriend's a basketball player. I go places where there are cheerleaders."

"Yeah, okay. But obviously he wants you, not them. He adores you."

My insides got all fluttery, and I might have blushed. "He kind of does, doesn't he?"

"I could have used a boyfriend to adore me this year. I'd never steal yours, but you know, one of my own."

"How does a girl like you not have an adoring boyfriend?" I asked seriously.

"I don't know. Maybe I'm too much of a diva. Maybe there's something wrong with the universe. But at this point I can wait for college."

"Theater?"

"Music Dance Theater. MDT, that's me."

"I'd love to see you in something else someday," I said.

"I'll be a small fish in a huge pond, I think. But I'm doing some fun things over the summer. Let's connect online. Then you'll know where and when, if you want to come. And I'll come see what you can do as assistant director next year. I told Troy he'd make a great lead. Did Otteson tell you what he wants to do?"

"He hasn't said anything to me."

"I'm sure it'll be fun. Always is." She pouted. "My last show here is over, and I'm about to cry again. Could you distract me somehow? Please?"

"Tell me about summer."

"Good idea. Another *Fiddler*, Tzeitel again. And drama camp for a month. Two plays, not sure which. One Shakespeare."

"That sounds fun," I said. "Hey, there's a boy coming this way. He might be aimed at you."

She didn't look. "Is it Chad?" He was our rabbi.

"Still with the fake beard."

"He's not boyfriend material, but he's decent company," she said. "May as well enjoy him. Can I hug you first?"

As she wandered away with Chad, I enjoyed the thought of making a new friend of a girl who'd made me jealous five days a week for the past month.

Troy came back and asked what we talked about.

"Theater, boyfriends, summer plans, that sort of thing."

"She has a boyfriend?"

"Unbelievably, no. But she said she'd never steal mine. You adore me too much."

"She's very perceptive." He was suppressing a smile.

"She is a senior. But seriously, you two were great together."

"Thanks. You helped a lot."

"I'm so proud of you, Troy."

We pulled each other into a hug that lasted more than a moment and less than forever. Then we just stood a few inches apart, face to face and holding both hands.

"I was always glad you were there," he said, "so we could hang out between scenes, and I could take you home. And just see you."

"Jordyn said we're the perfect couple." I glowed at him. "She's really nice. I thought she was a diva."

"Sometimes she is. I like that she tries not to be."

"She says you might be lead material next year."

"Think she's right?"

"We should find out."

When the mountains of pizza, snacks, and soft drinks had shrunk by about half, the reenactments of favorite scenes began. Troy joined in, and they pulled me in too.

"Jenny, what's the next line?" someone would ask. Mostly I could remember. Once when I couldn't, a girl said, "Just make something up!" So I did, and they liked it. They kept asking for new lines, and things got sillier.

Then they wanted Tevye, but Hunter was out in the hall talking to some family member on his cell phone. Someone called out, "Who wants to be Tevye?"

Troy grinned at me. "Jenny does. She wanted to audition for Tevye."

So I became Tevye in a bizarre reprise of the scene where Tzeitel pleads with him, and he yells at Motel and the world in general, and Motel finally yells back that even he deserves to be happy—which is where the scene fell apart. Troy was laughing too much to continue. Jordyn said Motel really wanted Tevye, not his daughter, and we laughed even harder.

When our star returned, I yielded the role like a good understudy and took my seat. I looked around, hoping everyone was obeying the rule Mr. O had imposed from the beginning: no video recordings. He said it was a copyright thing, but I could think of other reasons.

We left before the party ended. Troy had a headache and was eager to shave off his beard, and I was exhausted, or I'd have wanted to stay. More than ever, I felt like I belonged, like I deserved to be there, though still I mostly sat. I'd never felt that way at a big party before.

Lots of kids hugged us on our way out.

As I got ready for bed, I tried to think of prom, which was only a week away, but my thoughts kept returning to *Fiddler*, and how much I loved being part of it. And how I loved being in it with Troy.

And how long and how tightly he hugged me, when I said I was proud of him.

Prom

38

The Big Day

TROY CALLED THE NIGHT before prom to change plans for our day date. The guys had been watching the weather forecast. We were moving outdoors.

By 11:00 a.m. it was sunny and warm. We met Will, two of Troy's other teammates, and their dates at a park with a pretty lake. We started with a round of disc golf on the park's course. I was bad at throwing the discs, but I wasn't the only one, and it was still fun. Playing on the grass was safe for me. I even ran around some.

Zeus would have loved it, but he was at the vet with Dad. We suspected he was reacting to his new medication. I worried about him. He was ten, and the average lifespan of a German shepherd was eleven.

After disc golf, we chose a spot on a grassy slope by the lake. Troy and Will passed out water bottles, while the other guys left to pick up lunch from a nearby Italian place.

Water wasn't the only beverage they'd brought. Soon we girls were sipping sparkling cider from plastic champagne flutes, while Troy and Will spread out five small picnic blankets, one for each couple and one for the food. They wouldn't let us lift a finger, even to freshen our drinks.

Soon the others were back and we were filling our plates. It was a small feast. I was glad I'd skipped breakfast.

"Everything smells amazing," said Will's date, Bridget. She was tall and athletic, with long blonde hair. She was a goalkeeper on the varsity girls soccer team, and she'd beaten all of us at disc golf, including the guys.

"Don't save room for dessert," Will said. "We didn't order any. Some of us have to fit into tuxes later."

"Thanks for sharing our concern for your figures," said Kaycee, a trim brunette, as she arranged her plate in her lap. "Oh, I forgot breadsticks."

One of the guys flipped a breadstick at her. It was off target, but she caught it in midair and took a bite, while Bridget said something about soccer reflexes. Kaycee was the other goalkeeper.

"These are too good for boys," Kaycee moaned. "Throw me one for my other hand, please." She caught it too.

I turned to the only other person in our group who wasn't an athlete and smiled in mock chagrin. Imani was on the next blanket. I knew her a little from junior high, but now she went to the other high school in town. "I don't have soccer reflexes," I said. "I barely have normal reflexes."

"I hear you," she said with a smile. "She's right about the breadsticks, though. Too good for boys."

After lunch the others went to play another round of disc golf, while Troy and I took a walk by the lake. The gorgeous setting, the beautiful day, the afterglow of a delicious lunch, and the boy whose arm was firmly around my waist had me in heaven. I set aside my concern for Zeus for a while. I forgot about being the girl who had seizures. I even put off my worries about my hair and everything else that could go wrong later.

"They're so cute!" I said, as a duck led her family across the water near the rocky shore.

"So tiny," Troy said. "I think they're getting out."

The mama duck stepped out of the water a few yards from us. Her ducklings struggled to follow her on the sand between the rocks.

Troy stood behind me as we watched, his arms around my waist. His chest expanded and contracted against my back, and his breath was warm on the top of my head.

"You've done it again," I said. "You created a perfect day for me, just like the day of my first waltz lesson."

He held me more tightly, and it was better than perfect. "Expect some flaws tonight," he said reasonably. "It's guys making dinner."

"Okay, but it's perfect so far. The weather's gorgeous. Lunch was amazing. I even had fun being bad at disc golf. And strolling around the lake with you is the perfect combination of ev—"

I didn't finish my sentence or even the word.

I had a seizure.

I'd had hundreds of them, often enough when I was standing up, but I was always surprised when I found myself falling. I never lost consciousness from the seizure itself, so usually I was just starting to worry about hitting the ground, when I actually did.

This time I didn't. Troy was already holding me, and he somehow kept his balance when I went limp. He was strong enough to keep me from falling and ease us away from the rocks.

After maybe ten seconds, I was okay again. But nothing was okay. It was my first seizure in almost a month. I'd begun to hope they were gone for good. It was also Troy's first time seeing me like that. It didn't make sense to be embarrassed and ashamed, but I was. Worst of all, prom day wasn't perfect anymore, thanks to me.

Even after I could stand on my own again, he still breathed heavily and held me tightly. His arms shook—or I did.

His voice was husky. "You okay now? That was scary."

I nodded but couldn't bear to look at him.

"Let's sit," he said. "If you don't need it, I do." He guided me to the nearest bench, with one arm tightly around me, as if I might collapse again. His arm definitely shook.

Neither of us spoke. I stewed in shame and disappointment, which merged into anger—not at Troy personally, but he was there.

"You sure you're okay?" he asked after a minute.

I nodded stiffly. I didn't feel okay. A storm was building inside me. I felt like I was inside it, and it was about to break.

"Because you don't seem okay yet," he said.

The storm broke angrily. I pushed his arm away. He resisted for an instant, then let me go.

My meltdowns, as Mom and Dad called them, didn't happen very often anymore. They weren't part of my epilepsy, and my seizures weren't the cause, except that sometimes I reacted to a seizure with a childish, self-indulgent tantrum. I knew better, but I still couldn't stop this one. Maybe I was too busy feeling sorry for myself to try hard enough.

I put two feet of empty bench between us and snapped at him. "Just stop, okay? The seizure comes. It goes. You caught me. I didn't hit my head on a rock. Everything's fine. I'm sitting over here for a while."

"Everything?" he asked quietly after several seconds. He sounded concerned, not angry.

I kept melting down. "Yes, everything. Everything except the fact that I'm a freak, and I always will be. I should stop wishing and hoping and praying that someday I'll no longer be a freak."

"Jenny, you're not—"

"Don't say it," I hissed. "Just don't."

I still hadn't looked at him. If I did, I knew I'd see worry. Maybe pain too—which I caused. But the storm overwhelmed such thoughts.

I'd been facing straight ahead; now I turned slightly away, in case I was tempted to look at him. "That was the first one in almost a month," I said bitterly. "I don't remember the last time I went that long. I was hoping they were gone."

I paused for a deep breath. "It's not fair. What if I can never drive a car? Or hold a baby? I'm a freak, and I always will be. Why did I ever think I might be normal someday?"

When he still didn't speak, I wondered if he was angry. If so, I knew he'd try to be silent, to avoid saying angry things. Maybe he had turned away from me too.

I stole a glance. He was staring at the grass in front of his feet, not at me. So I took a longer look. The eye I could see was big and sad, and his lips were slightly parted, not pinched at the corners. He wasn't angry.

He didn't look like he was about to say anything. Which was good, because my storm raged on. I looked away.

"I wanted this to be perfect for you too," I whined. "I wanted to be normal for you today. You deserve normal. Instead you get me."

I took another deep breath. Something warm and unpleasant washed over me like a sheet of wind-driven rain. It felt like self-pity. Like I wasn't drenched in that already.

I looked down and complained more softly. "It's who I am. I should just accept it. But it's not fair. Today was perfect."

We were both silent after that. I waited to see if I was finished. He was probably waiting to see that too.

Eventually he said, "Jenny, any day with you is perfect enough for me. Sorry about the seizure. New experience for me. Kind of terrifying. But we know it happens, and it's no one's fault. I'm very glad you're not hurt."

He was wrong about that. I was so hurt. Just not physically. The storm blew stronger.

"Troy, please shut up." I instantly regretted that, but it was too late. "I know you're right, but please stop being the perfect boyfriend for a few minutes. You're not helping."

We sat silently again, and farther apart than we'd sat in a long time, even when there was a gear shift lever between us. Part of me wanted to be alone, to disappear somewhere for a while. But if I got up and walked away, where would I go to feel better? And I couldn't ask him to leave.

Anger blew hot. Despair blew cold. Shame, self-pity, sadness, and disappointment intertwined, and now they were joined by disgust with myself at how I was treating Troy.

Whole minutes passed, and he said softly, "If I were the perfect boyfriend, I'd know what to say and what not to say. Sorry I made things worse. And if I'm making things worse now."

Maybe the storm was waning, because I didn't lash out again. I still didn't look at him.

He was patient.

"It's my fault I'm having a meltdown, not yours," I said, when I felt I could control myself. "Could we just sit a while longer and not talk?"

"Sure. May I put my arm around you while we sit?"

I considered that. "If you like. As long as it's not to hold me up."

"It's not," he said with feeling.

So we sat in silence again, but not apart. I had no eyes for the beautiful lake in front of me and scarcely a thought for Troy. I focused on the turmoil inside, wanting to stop feeding it, willing it to pass quickly.

Gradually it spent itself, leaving me strangely empty of feeling. My mind seemed mostly numb, and the few thoughts still in it were slippery. I clung to one of them: I needed to fix things with the faithful boyfriend beside me, before I made them even worse.

I looked out over the lake, which looked blue but felt gray. When I spoke, there was a tremor in my voice. It was exhaustion, I thought, not emotion. Meltdowns were exhausting.

"I'm sorry I got angry and told you to shut up. I should have been thanking you for catching me." I finally looked at him. "That was really good. First try." I attempted a smile. "Thank you for catching me."

He nodded soberly. "You're welcome. Glad it actually worked." I heard relief and concern in his voice, but I didn't feel them. At least the storm was over.

We sat quietly again.

"I was so disappointed," I said after another minute. "I still am." Now I could feel that, at least.

"Because of the month, almost?"

"And wanting to be a normal girl for you today."

I began to slip back inside myself, but I thought of the arm around my waist and the boy who liked it there, and I managed to keep talking. "And being weak little Jenny and needing to be rescued."

It was his right arm that was around me. I reached for his left hand and held it tightly. "You were gentle and kind," I said. "You told me why I shouldn't feel that way."

A long moment passed. He said, "Which didn't help, because you did feel that way?"

"Being rational with me doesn't always help, even if it should."

"Is there anything I could have said to make things better instead of worse?"

"Like what? I was even embarrassed to have your arm around me. That is not the girlfriend we both know and love." I tried again to smile. Only then did I realize I'd sort of just said that he loved me. He'd still never said it in so many words. Not that there was room for doubt.

"Okay, but my arm wasn't here to hold you up. I like it here." He gave me a long squeeze. "I like you here."

"So do I," I said. "Except when I'm the angry, freaked out version of me, I guess."

"I'm fine with whatever version I can reach. But you're not 'weak little Jenny.' You're strong. You just have a seizure sometimes."

It was a kind, forgiving thing to say, I thought, still without really feeling it. So I tried smiling at him again, and it went a little better.

He pulled me closer. "What if I'd held you like this, and said something like this?" He pushed my hair aside and spoke softly in my ear.

"Jenny, I'm sorry you're disappointed. I hope you're not embarrassed. I know you wanted today to be perfect, and I'm sorry it's not. But it's still going to be a very good day."

My head liked it. My heart should have liked it. "That was good, but what if I'd asked you, 'What makes you think it's still going to be a very good day?'"

"I'd have said, 'Because for me it already is.'"

"And what if I were snotty, like the night we met, and I asked you, 'Why, because you get to be the hero and save the damsel in distress?'"

"I'd have said no." He hesitated. "I like being your hero." There was a catch in his voice. "But the reason is, I love you, and I get to spend today with you."

The only sounds were ducks quacking, seagulls calling, and little waves lapping at the shore. My mind went blank again, except the inner voice telling me I should be feeling a lot more than I was. Then I realized I felt surprise. Did that even make sense?

I looked up. "You love me?"

It wasn't how I'd imagined answering, if he said it first. But I had daydreamed of a tender, romantic moment, not the grisly aftermath of a childish emotional train wreck.

"Yup."

"Are you sure?"

"I'm new to this, but yeah, I'm sure."

"Why?"

"Why what?"

"Why do you love me?"

"What do you mean why?" He sounded worried again, not angry. "Is it unbelievable?"

"I believe you. I believe you. But I'm not lovable today. And I'm just Jenny. I sit and—"

"Stop!" he said. "Please."

I stopped, stunned by his frustrated tone, and just looked at him.

"I don't want to hear another list of reasons why you think you're not lovable," he said. "I could give you a pretty long list of reasons why you are, but that's not the point either. I love being with you. I like myself better when I am. I want to be good for you. I love you. That's the point."

It was more than I could take in. I really was starting to feel again—at the moment, a confused mix of things, including shame and regret. We just stared at each other, not smiling, not frowning either, really.

Finally I could speak, and I had to. "Tell me again that you love me. Please? I need a second chance at my part. It went so much better in my daydreams. Not that reality was all bad. Your part was amazing. I liked what you—"

He touched two fingers to my lips and held them there. "Jenny, I love you. In reality, not just your daydreams."

My heart may still have been partly numb, but my smile knew what to do.

He moved his fingers. "I love you too," I said. "I really do. You're my favorite reality and my favorite daydream."

He pressed my head to his shoulder, and I nuzzled his neck. I still wasn't feeling everything I should have, but I desperately wanted to.

"You're right. That was better," he murmured.

"I suppose you don't want the long list of reasons why I love you."

"No," he said ardently. "Maybe someday. Don't erase it from your memory."

I clung to him. "No worries there."

If he'd held me any more tightly then, I'd have struggled to breathe. So it was perfect. But I needed to say something more.

"Thank you for staying with me today, even when I pushed you away. And catching me, so my skull didn't crack on a rock."

"You already thanked me," he said seriously. "But you're welcome."

I had to look up. "I hurt you, didn't I? I'm so sorry."

He shrugged, and I thought I saw a flash of pain. "I'll be okay."

"I'm so sorry." I attempted a wan smile. "So you wondered if those things you might have said would have helped before."

"And?"

"I don't know. Maybe not." I sighed. "They're really working now."

He stroked my hair with gentle, unhurried fingers, and I purred.

Desperate as I was for both of us to forget Mean, Childish Jenny, he hadn't forgotten her yet. He spoke cautiously. "May I ask a question that got me in trouble before?"

I nodded. "I'll try to be civil."

"You sure you're okay?"

"Yes."

"Is prom one of your dreams too, like waltzing?"

"Definitely."

"There will be another prom next year, if you'd rather stay home tonight and do something quiet. With or without me. But with me, I hope."

"We'll be fine. It almost never happens twice in one day. Besides, you just proved you can catch me, and you're strong enough to hold me up." Then I added, "Thanks for caring more about me than all the plans you've made."

"Thanks for noticing," he said. "Do you tell your parents you had one? Will they still be okay with prom?"

"Yes, and I think so, especially with you." I made a mental note to tell him later about his fictional rival, Hank the Wrestler. "Let's find out."

I let go of him long enough to retrieve my phone and text Mom and Dad. "Seizure at the park. Troy caught me. First try. No harm done. Please tell Zeus I'm okay and hope he is too. No changes to plans."

Mom replied: "Are you sure you're okay? Thank Troy for us."

Dad sent, "Good man. He shall live another day. Zeus too."

We finished our circuit of the lake, then sat on a blanket, nibbling cookies one of the guys had baked and watching ducks on the water. The others weren't back, so we had our picnic spot to ourselves.

"I'm sorry," I said, after my third enormous yawn.

"You okay?"

"Just tired." My smile felt half-sad, half-embarrassed. "Tantrums are exhausting."

"I'll find you something for a pillow."

"I should stay awake. This is prime Troy time for me."

He smiled. "We have all evening. Could I be your pillow for a while?"

"Are you sure?"

"A nap now might help you later. And I love you, remember?"

I looked into his eyes, trying to be sure he really didn't mind. Then I nestled comfortably against him, and closed my eyes. He wrapped his arms around me.

"Love you too," I said sleepily.

The next thing I knew, he was trying to wake me. I couldn't be sure, but he might have been trying for a while.

"Wake up, pretty Jenny."

"Mmmm. Do I have to?"

"Sorry. I need to help with dinner, and you have important girl stuff. Heard there's a big dance tonight."

I agreed to cooperate, if he would help me up.

The others had already packed up almost everything. As we left the park, I apologized for sleeping.

"I liked it," he said. "Liked watching you sleep."

I checked my phone. "Is that all you did for almost an hour?"

"Watched the ducks too. Had a couple more cookies. Tried not to leave crumbs in your hair. Deflected a stray Frisbee before it hit you. Then the others came back, and we all tried not to wake you."

I rubbed my eyes. Then I closed them again and slept for the rest of the half-hour drive. As we pulled into my driveway, I woke and apologized again.

39

Elegance

A FTER SPENDING THE DAY with Troy's friends, we planned to dress and dine at my house with Jack and Nikki and their dates, Colin and Ty.

While the boys were downstairs, preparing dinner with Mom's help, Jack, Nikki, their moms, and I turned my parents' master suite upstairs into our dressing room. We banned everyone with a Y-chromosome, except Zeus, and went to work.

For my hair I'd chosen a low, messy bun with a teased crown and a twist on the sides. My hair was just long enough, we knew from practicing, and Jack's mom did it to perfection.

My burgundy gown was perfect too. No buyer's remorse there.

I assumed Mom's offer of diamond earrings meant studs. She had three pair. When I texted her to ask which one, she came upstairs and brought out something else, a pair of diamond and white gold chandeliers I'd hardly ever seen her wear.

"Really, Mom? Thank you!" I hugged her.

"You're welcome. They need to get out more, and they'll enjoy prom."

"Thank you!"

She nodded. "This much beauty cries out for diamonds. But I have to get back to the boys. All those open flames and sharp, pointy things."

The earrings were Mom's, so they were modest for chandeliers. They dangled a little and sparkled a lot. I put them on, looked in the mirror, and decided I didn't need a necklace.

I couldn't stop looking in the mirror, and I could hardly wait for Troy to see me—even if I was only the third most beautiful girl in our trio.

Nikki was gorgeous. Her long, mint-green satin gown tastefully flattered her dancer's build, and she wore her brown hair up in a classy ponytail, with the ends lightly curled. Everything about her was graceful, as always.

Jack rarely wore her red hair down anymore. Tonight was the exception. It fell in big, loose curls over a royal blue gown with three-quarter lace sleeves—and that wasn't even the best part. She was cute with her glasses, which she almost always wore, but tonight she wore contacts. Her eyes were bewitching. Colin might forget his own name, or worse. Did boys ever swoon?

Dad texted me to announce that our dates were handsome, ready on time, and looking nervous. Rock-paper-scissors determined I would go downstairs last. Stairs were dangerous, but I'd had my seizure for the day.

Troy waited at the bottom of the stairs, his face lit up even more than usual. He'd never seen me so elegant. He'd never seen me elegant at all.

I smiled and started down. I'd never felt so radiant. Maybe it was Mom's diamonds. Maybe it was the I-love-you's.

As I reached the last step, he took my hand, shaking his head slightly. "You look amazing. Jack and Nikki too, but wow, Jenny! I love your hair. What do you call it?"

"Black," I said innocently.

His eyes twinkled.

"It's a messy bun," I said. "And thank you. You look great too." He looked even better in a tux than a regular suit, and his bow tie and cummerbund matched my dress.

He grinned. "Thanks."

I was still beaming. "So I look okay?" I wanted to hear it again—and I whispered, so it could be just between us.

"If I didn't already love you, I'd be smitten now. I am smitten now."

I giggled. "I can't stop smiling."

"Must have looked in a mirror."

"A few dozen times. Such a good mirror! I admit it. I'm vain. I'm proud. I'm beautiful. Also my date is very handsome. We look classy."

"At first I thought I looked like a penguin. But I never saw a penguin with a bow tie, a cummerbund, or a stunning human girlfriend in burgundy and diamonds."

I was about to ask how long he'd spent preparing that lovely speech, when he steered us away from the others. "Brought you something.

Don't want to give it to you in front of everybody, and you don't have to wear it tonight." He handed me a small jewelry box.

"You didn't have to," I said with the same eagerness I felt on Christmas morning.

"Wanted to."

I tried for patient, ladylike dignity, but my hands shook too much for dignity, and my heart fluttered too wildly for patience. When I saw what was inside, I gave him a huge smile. "This is beautiful. Thank you!"

It was a small silver pendant on a simple silver chain, a stylized heart with a small, ruby-red stone in the center. I loved that it was from him, and I loved that it was a heart. I loved that we'd already said to each other what we both knew the heart meant.

"Glad you like it," he said, after I set it on the windowsill and pulled him into a careful hug.

"I more than like it. Plus it's a gift from my boyfriend on the day he said he loves me. Let's see how it works with my dress and Mom's earrings." I let go and turned my back to him. "Help me put it on, and we'll see what she thinks."

"Practiced on Lily," he said. "But I'm not good at this."

It took a couple of tries. A dozen would have been nice. Every time his fingers brushed my neck, I got chills. Or whatever is the opposite of chills. Then we found Mom.

"Mom, see if you think this matches my dress and your earrings."

"Very nice. I can guess where it came from. It's beautiful, Troy." She smiled at him.

"Thank you, ma'am." He stood perfectly straight and nodded, and he might as well have clicked his heels. He spoke in a lofty tone. "But if you'll excuse me, ladies, I must check on dinner." He took Ty and Colin with him. Mom followed with a restrained smile.

I found Jack and Nikki. "I thought you decided against a necklace," Jack said, before I could explain.

"It's new." I imagined my eyes sparkling like Mom's earrings.

"In, like, the last five minutes?" Nikki asked. "Can we just clone your boyfriend next time?"

"Oh, do you think he likes me?"

"He buys you jewelry," Jack said. "Who cares if he likes you?"

We giggled.

Ty and Colin returned, and a moment later Troy rejoined us too. He seemed mostly to want to look at me with what Mom would have called a twitter-pated grin. I lost track of the rest of the world, including Jack and Nikki and their dates—and the parents and the cameras and anything and everything except Troy.

I bounced from one blissful thought to another. I was going to prom with this boy who loved me! He was gentle, handsome, generous, amazing! I loved the boy who loved me! We were elegant tonight, and we had the entire evening to spend together!

The smell of food overwhelmed me, and fluttery things turned rumbly. I whispered to Troy, "Dinner smells irresistible. I'm so hungry!"

"Your timing, my lady, is perfect." He turned to the others. "Ladies, gentlemen, won't you please join us in the dining room? I believe they're ready to seat us."

We sat across from our dates, with boys on one side of our long table and girls on the other. When I wasn't admiring Troy, I was thinking that Colin, who was lean and dark-haired, looked like he should have been Nikki's date, not Jack's. Nikki's date, Ty, was blond and a bit freckled, with a solider build. He looked like he should have been Jack's.

The blinds were down, and we ate by candlelight, with Troy's little sisters as our servers. They wore cute black dresses, with their hair in matching buns. They moved with the grace of dancers, which they were, and the confidence, I thought, of girls who knew they looked great.

The beautifully printed menu listed six courses, and the food was pretty fancy for boys' cooking. It was also easy to eat without messing up prom dresses and tuxes. Troy said Mom insisted on that. He also said she made the cooking fun.

The only course they hadn't made was the seven-layer chocolate mousse cake, which came from a bakery. Mom had declared the day too busy for baking and frosting a fancy cake.

After dinner it was time for flowers. Jack and Nikki had wrist corsages, but I'd told Troy I preferred a pin-on. Mine was a white orchid with tiny, deep-red spray roses that matched my dress.

"It's lovely," I said. "Oh, wait, I think we have another little imperfection in our day. Mom, do we have corsage pins? This otherwise perfect creation doesn't have any."

Troy was embarrassed and apologetic. Mom told him not to worry—twice—then went next door. She was back in five minutes. She picked up the corsage and ceremoniously handed it and two long pins to Troy. He just stood for a moment, holding them and looking concerned. I tried to look expectant, not amused.

Mom smiled knowingly. "Is something wrong?"

"Ma'am, I kind of hoped you would do this. Don't want to ruin prom night with, you know, bloodshed."

She laughed, but I managed not to. Then she said firmly, "It's a gentleman's duty to pin on the corsage. I'll tell you how, but I won't do it for you. If it helps, you're more likely to stab yourself than your date."

She showed him what to do and told him what not to do.

"I think I understand why people like wrist corsages," he said.

"And burgundy dresses?" I asked impishly. "So the bloodstains won't show?" Mom laughed. Troy smiled faintly but still looked worried.

I put my hand on his arm. "Sir, I forgive you in advance for any pinpricks you may accidentally inflict during the pinning-on of the corsage on prom night. Or any other time you give me a corsage." I grinned. "Come on, boyfriend. New experience."

It was a new experience for me too. His hands shook slightly as he pinned it on, but I wasn't nervous. I was too busy resisting the temptation to tease him. It went smoothly, and no one was wounded.

"Thank you," I said, when he stepped back to inspect his work. "It really is perfect. Thanks for getting the pins, Mom."

Pinning on his boutonniere was routine. My hands were steady, but I didn't gloat. Not on the outside.

We were still at the house when his phone made the parent sound. It was a text message telling him to call home ASAP, so he excused himself for a minute. When he returned, he said, "I'm afraid there's another small imperfection in our evening."

"Oh?"

"My uncle's driving to the Bay Area on two hours' notice, and my parents want him to take my car, for the gas mileage. He'll save about

200 bucks. He's leaving us his pickup. It's not new, but he takes good care of it. It's almost a classic. He'll have it here in about ten minutes."

"That sounds perfect enough," I said.

We girls had told the guys not to spend money on a limo. Troy's car and Ty's small SUV would be fine for the six of us. When I saw the pickup, it had a nice extra feature. Troy's Honda Civic was fine for holding hands, but it had bucket seats with an annoying console and gear shift lever between them. The truck had a bench seat.

He opened the passenger door and helped me climb in, making sure my dress was all the way inside before he closed the door. Then he went around and got behind the wheel.

"Hope it's okay," he said.

"To be honest, it could be better."

"Sorry."

"No worries. Let's fix it." I slid to the middle, next to him, fastened my seat belt, and put his arm around my shoulders. "Now I'm comfortable. You may have your arm back long enough to shift."

He shook his head and smiled. "Never really liked pickups. Now I think I want one."

Dad told me later that there was an unofficial front seat etiquette, when he was a teenager and bench seats were more common. Polite guys always let the girl in and out the passenger side, and she choose the middle or not. Other guys just assumed and let her in the driver's side. Troy got it right every time, and I slid to the middle every time.

We took nearly an hour driving around in our two-vehicle caravan, so everyone's family could see us all dolled up and take pictures—which had sounded boring when we were making plans. But we had plenty of time, and it was fun.

At the last home, just before we pulled away from the curb, Troy squeezed my hand. "How's prom day going for you now?"

"Funny thing," I said. "It feels perfect after all."

40

Grand Elegance

Prom was in the grand ballroom of the nicest hotel in town. The walls were hung with ornate curtains, and the gleaming mahogany under our feet might have been the most beautiful floor I'd ever seen. The chandeliers sort of matched Mom's earrings.

I could see from the few couples who were already there that the room would soon be a kaleidoscope of color. The lights were brighter than usual for a dance, and I hoped they'd stay that way. So much color and beauty would have been wasted in low light.

Two ornate, matching signs on easels flanked the entrance and announced the theme. "Grand Elegance," I read aloud. "That's how I voted. The other one might have had us crashing some other school's prom."

"What was that one again?" he asked. "Unicorns and Rainbows?" His eyes twinkled.

I grimaced. "Candyscape."

"Unicorns and Rainbows would have been better than that."

I pulled something out of the air. "Big City Morgue would not have been worse."

He laughed. "Don't let the prom committee hear you, or we'll be voting on that next year."

We took advantage of the short picture line, then danced every slow dance for the next couple of hours. In the first hour we traded partners with my friends and his a few times. It was all elegant and amazing.

After that, we might have been alone on the dance floor, despite the growing crowd—still elegant and maybe even graceful, but only for each other.

Later we filled two little plates with fancy refreshments, sat at a small round table, and talked and watched people, even through the slow songs. Most of the boys were handsome, all dressed up, and most of the girls were beautiful. Which got me thinking. Which led to Troy asking what I was thinking. I was almost ready to put it into words. I decided to try.

"So much beauty," I said. "Here tonight, I mean."

He didn't take his eyes off me. I couldn't help giving him a happy smile. "Not just me," I said almost nervously, but also a little boldly. A new thought was taking me places I'd scarcely imagined.

"True," he said, his eyes still on me.

"I looked at myself in the mirror so many times tonight, when we were getting ready. I couldn't stop looking."

"Now you know how I feel. Wait," he said. "Did you just admit you're beautiful? You said that before dinner too."

I felt my cheeks flush. "I think I've made a decision."

"To love me would be an excellent decision."

"I decided that a long time ago. I don't even know when, exactly."

That made him smile. "What did you decide just now?"

Our plates were empty, so stacked I them. "Let's clean this up and go back to our seats."

Which we did. It was better for snuggling, and it gave my mind an extra minute or two to prepare my thoughts.

"First, I want to tell you what I decided not to do," I said.

"Okay."

"Part of me wanted, and please note the past tense, to point to one girl after another here, ask you if you think she's beautiful, and if so, why."

"Not sure I'd do that, even for you," he said. "I hate it when guys do that to girls. Or vice versa."

"I decided not to ask you that—and not to want to. I also decided not to point out that my feet might be too long and my legs are a little heavy, and at least hint at a few more parts after that, so you'd have to tell me you like my figure."

He looked at me seriously. "Like it a lot. Not just tonight. I should have someone sneak into your bedroom, since I'm not allowed, and etch a warning on your mirror, like there is on the right side mirror on cars: 'Warning: Girls viewed in this mirror are more beautiful than they appear to themselves.'"

"I used to look in that mirror and imagine I was a willowy, green-eyed blonde."

"I could love you as one of those. But don't mess with success. Blue eyes. Raven hair. Curves. It really works."

"Ooh, raven! Not black?" I asked in a token effort not to think about him thinking about my curves. Much as I wanted to.

"I may only know twelve colors, but I know more than one word for some of them. What did you decide to do?"

"Will you let me try again if I make a mess of it? Explaining, I mean."

"Do you have to ask?"

"No." My face flared. "Here it is. I hope." I took a deep breath. "I've decided to believe in beauty I don't see, beauty I haven't learned to see yet. Not just in girls or people generally." I hesitated. "In me."

He watched me intently.

"For example," I continued, "you thought I was beautiful that night at my concert, and lots of times since then, apparently. Once I learned to trust you, I could believe you really thought that's what you saw. Now I've decided to believe it's real and you do see it, even when I don't. And a lot of other beauty in other people, not just at prom."

I could see him still getting his head around my sudden declaration. When he finally spoke, it was only four words.

"Is it working already?"

"It's easy to believe in my beauty tonight. I even feel kind of sexy too. Is that wrong to say?"

Bold Jenny should have clapped her hand over Prom Jenny's mouth already, but now Prom Jenny wanted to hear the word *sexy* from Troy's lips, not just my own. The vixen.

He didn't actually say the word, but if he was shocked, he also seemed pleased. "Don't know if it's wrong," he said slowly. "Maybe. But you are, and it's not just prom. Been noticing that about you for a long time."

Now we were both partially in shock, but I couldn't doubt he meant it. I took his free hand and held it firmly with both of mine.

"Maybe it sounds dumb to think I can just decide to believe something, but I think I'm ready. I think it'll make me a better girlfriend. Probably a better human too."

"I love it," he said. I knew he was still in shock when he asked, "When did you decide I was handsome?"

I couldn't tease him. Not now. "As soon as I was sure you weren't a figment of my imagination. That took about half a second."

"You thought you were imagining me?"

"I was trying to stay cheerful at the dance that night by writing a story in my head about a girl who waltzed with a tall, handsome, well-mannered boy. Then I saw you."

"You were smiling a little," he said.

"It was a good story. Ours is better."

A thought arrived just then, wrapped in emotions, and I tried to put it into words. "Being in love is more difficult in more ways than I ever imagined, and I don't feel like I'm very good at it yet. But it's also so much better than I ever dreamed." I was almost in tears. "Thank you." I half-smiled. "Sorry, I kind of changed the subject there."

He nodded pensively. "May I tell you part of today's story I really like?"

"Of course."

"At the park, even when you were upset and didn't want me to touch you for a while, you didn't tell me to go away. That was a huge relief, because you needed someone, and I wanted it to be me. I kind of always want it to be me."

"Thank you," I murmured. He deserved a better reply, but I couldn't think about the beautiful thing he'd just said without remembering the whole ugly scene. I changed the subject again. "Could you come help me with something for a minute?" I asked.

"Sure. What?"

"It's getting warm in here," I said. "You can help me take off part of my dress."

He looked at me, then away, then back at me. "Sorry. I can what?"

"Just the sleeves. They come off, but I can't do it myself, when I'm wearing them. I almost didn't wear them at all, and now they're too warm."

"Yeah, I feel warmer too," he said.

We found a relatively private corner. He fumbled nervously with the tiny, hidden zippers, but we got the sleeves off. It was an instant relief.

"What do you think?" I held out my arm for inspection. "Better with sleeves or without?"

"Love you either way," he said.

"This way you see more of your girlfriend." Somewhere in my head, Bold Jenny's eyes bugged out, watching Prom Jenny work.

Troy's eyes didn't bug out, but I had his attention. "Yeah, I like that," he said. "Which way do you like?"

I studied my shoulders and arms. "Either way. But this is cooler, temperature-wise." I looked up at him. "If your arm were around my shoulders right now, sleeveless would win by a mile."

He didn't make me imagine how right I was.

The next dance was a slow song, so we took the floor. I was already deeply, ridiculously happy, and Troy didn't stop smiling. "A penny for the thoughts behind your happy smile," I said.

"It's a pretty big day for me," he said.

"Oh?" I asked innocently.

"I told you I love you, and you said you love me."

"Eventually. After I argued. Sorry about that."

"It's okay. Now I'm dancing with an angel. And you finally believe you're beautiful. Wasn't expecting that one tonight. Pretty amazing."

"I've been working on it. The Sunday morning after we danced the first time, I was brushing my hair before church, and you texted me. I saw my smiling self in the mirror and thought, 'Maybe I really am beautiful.'"

His smile grew.

"Another penny for the thought behind that smile," I said.

"You're good for me. Love that I'm good for you sometimes."

"It's more than sometimes. Thanks for always listening, and always letting me be . . . all the things I am sometimes."

"Be whatever you want, long as it's with me," he said soberly.

Swooning would look too much like another seizure, I decided. Melting would have to be enough. "Does that include curious?" I asked after a moment.

"Curious Jenny is one of my favorites. What would you like to know?"

Will came by just then, carrying a small water bottle in each hand. "How's it going?" he asked.

"You tell me," said Troy. "Is my date beautiful or what?"

"Yeah," he said with an appreciative smile. "And the guy she's with isn't a complete embarrassment." He held up a water bottle. "My date is beautiful and thirsty. Catch you later."

As Will walked away, I remembered a new safety precaution they'd announced that week for all of our school dances. Except for a bottle or can that was still sealed when you opened it, you weren't supposed to accept a drink from anyone but an adult behind the refreshment table. And you shouldn't return to your drink, if it was open and out of your sight for even a few seconds. We'd had an assembly about guys at other schools spiking girls' drinks with date rape drugs.

Troy said the new rule was routine where he came from, but just remembering the stories they told us made me queasy.

Guys like Troy and Will would never do that. I put it out of my mind.

"I think Curious Jenny was about to ask me something, before Will came by," Troy said.

"She was. Ready for more of my thoughts? Actually, I want more of yours."

"Okay."

"It's about beauty. Promise to believe I'm not thinking about myself?"

"If you believe you're beautiful, I can believe that." He beamed.

"I'm serious. What do guys see in girls that makes them decide they're beautiful? I mean, obviously, certain . . . prominent . . . physical features play a role, right?"

"Yeah."

"Let me put it this way. Two girls with approximately the same figure. What is there that makes one more beautiful than another? Not just superficially. To guys that get to know them. And I'm really not trying to get you to talk about me."

He thought for a moment. "A lot of things, I guess. But I think, if there's one thing a lot of us want in a girl, it's being real."

"Meaning?"

"Being who they are, not hiding who they are. Not pretending to be someone they're not, that they think someone else might like. Appearance, partly, but also what they think and like and don't like, everything. I'm not saying girls shouldn't dress well or even elegantly, or have nice hair and makeup, or use good manners or try to be the best version of themselves. I'm not even saying they shouldn't edit their photos a little for social media or whatever. I'm saying they shouldn't try so hard to be someone else. Remember when I told you Mom liked that you're genuine?"

"And I took it badly? Sorry."

"Not that. Hadn't really described it to myself that way before, but I realized she was right. I went out with about a dozen girls here before before I met you, and one of the big things I noticed about you right away was that you were genuine in a way some of them weren't." He smiled. "That, and talking with you is kind of a different world, compared to them. I mean, some of them are nice, and they're all pretty, but you know. You're real. It's not just that, but you're real.

"Think about Nikki," he continued. "Just on the outside, before you know her, she's pretty. I know some girls don't like their freckles, and she has a few. If she masked them—is that the right word?—she might look like a magazine cover or something. But she doesn't, and if you look at her for five extra seconds, you can't . . . you can't not see that she's beautiful. Same with Jack. They're unique. They're themselves. How do you improve on that?"

"How many guys actually think this way?" I asked.

"Not some of Beth's dates, from what I hear. But I think a lot of us are learning to—from bad experience, partly." He shook his head. "I had kind of a head start. Want to hear a really weird story? Just between you and me, please?"

41

Girl Lessons

I NESTLED AGAINST TROY as best I could without messing up my hair. "It's just between you and me," I said. "Are you in this weird story?"

"I'm the male lead," he said. "Here goes.

"I was thirteen, and Beth was eighteen. She finished high school and started college that summer. It was a Friday night, probably July. Nan and Lily were already in bed, but Mom and Dad and I were doing some yard work late, when it wasn't quite so hot. Then we got out the ice cream. Meanwhile, Beth was on a date with some guy from college.

"Mom and Dad were putting their bowls in the dishwasher. I was still at the table, taking my time with my ice cream, because after that I had to go to bed. We heard Beth come home, apparently a lot earlier than Mom and Dad were expecting.

"She stormed into the kitchen, stomped up to Mom and Dad, and before they could even ask, she said, 'Why is every man I know who's not my father a complete lowlife?'

"Dad asked her if something went wrong on her date, and she said, 'Something *is* wrong with my date.' I don't think she saw me at the table, because then she said, 'We were having a pretty nice dinner, and while we're waiting for dessert, he tells me I could be really attractive to men like him if I got breast implants, some collagen treatments for poutier lips, and I don't even remember what else he said about my face. I left before dessert, which was going in his face or maybe his lap, if I stayed.'

"Mom said she was sorry and there were other fish in sea. Beth said, 'A lot of trash fish. He's the third date just this summer who said I need a boob job. Without actually seeing what I have here, you'll be pleased to know.'"

Troy shrugged. "That's what she said. So Mom says something about 13-year-old ears, but I don't think Beth heard her, because then she's asking, 'Who taught all these guys that I'm just a sex object? Don't they have mothers or fathers or parole officers or something?'

"Then Mom says, 'Can we do this later, when your little brother isn't listening?' But Beth doesn't back down.

"She practically yells my name, so I have to look up. Mom looks concerned. Dad looks something between shocked and amused, and Beth looks really, really angry. Scary angry. She marches over to the table, folds her arms, and says, 'Troy, are you going turn into lowlife pond scum over the next few years, like every other man I know except Dad?'

"You'd have loved my high-pitched little squeak. I think I said no, because she said, 'Damn right you're not.' Sorry. 'If I do one good thing in my life,' she said, 'I'm keeping you from becoming one of those scumbags.'

"Then she suddenly calmed down a lot. She turned to Mom and Dad and said, 'I know he's your job, generally speaking. But I can do this one, and I'm going to. I won't do anything bad, including murder, though that would prevent the problem.'

"Dad asked, 'What do you propose to do to him?'

"'With him,' she said. 'I'll let you know. I'm sure I'll have to bribe him with pizza or something.'"

"You're enjoying this," I said. I was enjoying him.

"I guess. So far."

"Foreshadowing a dark turn," I said appreciatively. "Nicely done."

"I don't know about dark. Pretty weird."

"I can hardly wait. I like the main characters a lot."

"Yeah. I don't know if she ever told Mom and Dad what she planned. Maybe. She woke me the next morning, said we were going to the mall, and I was going to do what she said, and she wouldn't embarrass me in front of strangers, and then we'd have whatever kind of pizza I wanted, and plenty of it."

"She took you shopping? For what?"

"Not shopping. Girl-watching."

"What?"

"Told you it was weird."

"Does she . . . like . . . girl-watching?" I asked carefully.

"It was for me."

"I'm all ears." He wasn't smiling anymore, but I was.

"Beth said, if I'm going to be handsome like Dad, and athletic and popular, so girls want to be around me—sorry for the little ego trip—then she had to make sure I'm thoroughly taught to use my powers for good, not evil. Then she asked me straight out, 'Are you interested in girls yet? You are, right?'

"Apparently, it's hard to hide. Anyway, we spent a whole hour watching girls and talking about them. Girls and women. She'd point out a girl and ask if I thought she was pretty, and then, whatever I said, she'd make me find something specific that was pretty about her."

"That sounds too familiar," I said. "I'm sorry I even thought of having you do something like that tonight."

"We're okay. Anyway, it wasn't just junior high girls. Sometimes it was a frazzled mom with two screaming kids. Did that two Saturdays in a row at different malls. Ended up telling her things I'd never tell Mom and Dad. Or you. Ate a lot of good pizza.

"She took me to a picnic with a lot of her friends. Kind of lied to them and said Mom and Dad were out of town and I was her responsibility. They mostly ignored me. After the food, they sat around drinking beer or Diet Coke and swapping stories. She took me off to the side and started pointing out her girlfriends, one by one. After I told her what I saw on the outside, she told me about the person inside. Nothing too personal, I guess, but of course she knew things about them that I couldn't guess from just looking at them. Mostly good things. She told me about some of the guys too.

"The next Saturday, Mom and Dad really were out of town, at least for the day, and Nan and Lily must have been with them. She ordered pizza to pay me for going to her picnic, plus one more thing she said we were doing that day at home. Handed me a pen and a notepad. Then she got up and stood a few feet away.

"Said to look at her carefully and list anything I thought was beautiful and anything that wasn't, including her figure. For example, she said, if her hips were too big or she'd be prettier with . . . with a bigger chest—not how she said it—then I should list that. You can imagine the color of my face the whole time."

"That's borderline sibling abuse," I said. "By her."

"Maybe not borderline. Anyway, she promised not to be offended, as long as I was candid. Think she had to explain candid. For a few minutes I should see her as a stranger in the mall or the new girl at school."

"I hope your good list was a lot longer than your bad list," I said.

"Wasn't going to write anything bad, but she said, if there weren't some convincing negatives, I'd have to do it all over again with one of her friends. So I listed stuff like her eyes looking tired, and I liked her hair better when it wasn't crimped. Said maybe she'd look hotter with more curves. I actually didn't think that way about my sister, and I don't call girls hot, but I needed material, and sometimes I overheard guys talking about her at church.

"Didn't make up the good things. Pretty eyes and hair, and she has this little smile I love, when she's happy and doesn't know anyone's looking. Other stuff."

He reached for his phone, pulled up a photo, and handed it to me. "My favorite picture of her. Took it last summer, when she didn't know I was there. Showed her later, so I wasn't completely sneaky. She likes it too. Had me send it to her."

Beth sat on a boulder by a wooded lake, with the first hues of sunset in the sky. She had Troy's features, but the contours were softer, with a few cute freckles like Nikki's, when I zoomed in. Her hair was lighter than his. It fell in casual disarray around her shoulders, except a few strands blowing in the breeze. She seemed to be smiling to herself.

I handed back the phone. "That's a treasure."

"Is to me. After my list, she pulled out her own list. Said she'd made it that morning. I thought it would be about me, but it was about her. She said it was real, not just stuff she'd listed to make a point.

"Her positive list was really short. Her negative list was long, and it overlapped a lot of my positive list. Took her a while to convince me she was serious. I actually accused her of not being candid, now that I knew what that meant.

"I can still hear her saying, 'Stop arguing and listen to me. Most of the time, this is what I see. Part of me knows it's not completely true, but this is how girls think. This is how we feel about ourselves—at least most of us, most of the time. And I think it's how a lot of scumbag guys want us to feel.'

"I thought she was upset with me, so naturally I got upset with her. Thirteen, right? Told her she was an idiot and her bad list was almost a hundred percent crap, and if guys or other girls couldn't see she was pretty, their eyes must be full of crap too. Told her my friends thought she was pretty, which was kind of an understatement. Did I mention her list was crap?" He smiled wryly. "Had a smaller vocabulary back then."

I laughed softly but said nothing.

"Thought she'd chew me out, but she didn't. She hugged me and said I was her favorite little brother ever. I said pretty soon I'd be bigger than she was. She said, 'Only if I let you live. Which I probably will now.'"

His smile was distant. "Can you tell I miss her? Haven't seen her since Christmas, except online. Hair's shorter now.

"She said she was going to be the voice in my head, and if that ever stopped working, we'd have more training, possibly with a blunt instrument.

"Said anything I thought wasn't pretty about a girl, the girl already knew about and probably agreed. And most of what I thought was pretty, she had serious doubts about or worse. If I ever said anything negative about a girl's appearance or personality, she'd remember that ten times longer—maybe a thousand times longer—than anything good I could say."

He stared at her picture on his phone and blew out a breath. "Still have her voice in my head. 'Troy, you need to remember, that's how I'm wired. That's how Nan and Lily are wired—and they listen to you. You didn't cause it, and you can't fix it, and you don't have to. But you're going to be one of the good guys, and I'm sure you won't want to make things worse for the girls you know—especially the girls you love.'"

"Which now includes me," I murmured.

He smiled. "Yeah." Then his smile faded. "Never told Beth, but making those lists about her, even if she told me to, and looking at her that way, that was the first time—maybe it doesn't make sense, and I don't know if she planned it—that was the first time I had this sick, dark feeling that I was a scumbag for looking at a person like a piece of meat. Didn't know how to tell her that. Wanted to say maybe she was looking at herself that way, and it was wrong."

He'd been facing the dance floor, but now he turned to me. "Should have felt that way sooner, when the girls weren't my sister."

"You had to learn," I said. "We all do. I still do."

"I don't want . . . I never want to see you as just a . . ."

When he didn't continue, I helped him, though it set my face aflame. "A collection of interesting body parts?"

"Yeah. Anyway, she said we were done and gave me a hug. And a kiss on the forehead. Still not sure how I feel about that one.

"Weird as it all sounds, it made sense to me. I was only thirteen, but I saw how much those guys she dated hurt her. Even if I hadn't, I really would rather focus on what's beautiful. She made sure that got to be a habit a lot sooner than it might have. That's my weird story."

"Thanks for telling me all that. I don't have to mention it when I do, but I want to meet her."

"She wants to meet you. But tell me the truth. How weird does it sound?"

"Not weird," I said. "Maybe unusual. Did she ever find a guy who wasn't a scumbag?"

"I met a couple of boyfriends after that. Didn't hear her say they were scumbags." He hesitated. "What do you see?"

"When I look at guys?"

"When you look at girls."

"All the ways they're prettier than me. Then I look for flaws to prove they're actually not. The flaws I find aren't always convincing. Or real." I looked up at him earnestly. "Thank you for always being so good to me."

He didn't actually tell me he loved me then, but that's what I saw in his eyes. I leaned my head on his shoulder.

This was it. This was how I thought I'd feel the first time he said he loved me. Only it really was better than I ever imagined. It was a cool summer breeze and a downy pillow and a warm blanket. It was biting into a perfect, tree-ripened Bartlett pear and feeling the juice trickle down my chin, or letting a piece of Swiss milk chocolate melt on my tongue, or savoring a large bowl of homemade lemon ice cream with fresh raspberries on top. It was curling up by the fire for a warm, lazy evening with a new book, or an old one, with something passionate and classical on the stereo.

I didn't feel giddy or dizzy, and I wasn't about to burst. I was happy, confident, comfortable, content. I loved a very real, very good boy who loved the actual me, who wanted me despite my flaws. He even loved my quirks. Well, some of those he probably just endured—but willingly, patiently, gracefully.

My amazing feeling wasn't because we were elegant for prom, but that made everything even better.

The thumping beat of a song faded away, and a soft ballad began. I could almost whisper, and he'd still hear me. "Troy, I need to hug you now. Then we need to dance."

What I thought but didn't say was, When we get to my front porch tonight, if not sooner, we need to kiss.

He grinned. "I'm in."

We stood, and I hugged him almost fiercely for . . . not more than several seconds, probably. We didn't want chaperone trouble.

My mind wasn't on the dance floor, as we danced. It was on my front porch.

42

The Perfect Ending

I T WAS WARM ENOUGH on my front porch, which was good, since my removable sleeves were in my purse. Troy's arms were around me, and my head was on his chest. He gently stroked my hair, taking care not to mess it up, I thought.

He spoke softly. "Thanks for going to prom with me. Had an amazing day with you."

"Thanks for asking me," I said. "And . . . everything." I wanted to look into his eyes, but I was warm and comfortable where I was. "Do you know what would be the perfect ending?"

"Fine chocolate?" he asked.

"Excellent but not perfect."

"I give up," he said, but something in his voice gave me confidence.

"You could kiss me, if you want to." I should have been nervous, but I wasn't. And I still didn't look up.

He pressed me to his chest, and I thought I heard his heart beating over mine. "Been wanting that for a long time."

I glowed. "Long, as in hours? Or long, as in weeks or months?"

"Both."

"Are you too shy, like your girlfriend? Because I've been wanting to kiss you too."

"Didn't want to be one of those guys who tries to go too far, too fast. It's not too far. Just didn't want to go too fast."

"You're not one of those guys. I think your reputation is safe by now."

"What if I'm bad at it?" he asked. He sounded playful, not concerned.

"Maybe I'm bad at it too," I said. "Jack says we should practice together until we're both good at it. I know you're good at practicing things."

"Jack's pretty smart," he said.

"She's brilliant." I finally looked up with my longing eyes and asked something else I'd prepared in advance. "Why are we still talking?"

His big, gentle hands moved to my shoulders, then slipped down to my bare upper arms. For one silly instant I was glad we'd been keeping his hands warm, but I kept that to myself.

He bent down, and I reached up, and his lips met mine.

Our first kiss was shy and hesitant. Our second was less so. Both were over almost before they began. I wanted more.

His arms slipped down around my waist, and mine reached around his neck. Our third kiss wasn't shy or hesitant at all, and we lingered at it a while.

More than time stopped for me. Even the part of my writer's brain that compulsively sought words for everything was overwhelmed. Kissing Troy was beyond words.

When that kiss ended, I felt a warm, longing, hopeful sort of emptiness I'd never felt before, which I knew only our next kiss could fill. But instead of kissing me again, he rested his forehead on mine. His breath on my face felt nearly as intimate. He breathed deeply a few times, then said, almost whispering, "Don't want to worry your parents too much."

"They wouldn't watch us," I murmured.

"They have ears. If we're not talking out here, they might get ideas."

"I'm sure they already have ideas." I pulled away slightly, so I could see his face clearly, and tried to act upset. "This is what you think about when you kiss me for the first time? How can you have logical thoughts at a time like this? I thought you loved me."

He didn't miss a beat. "What's logical? It's pure survival instinct. It's ancient. Prehistoric. Primordial. We must survive to kiss another day. I see that clearly now. To perpetuate the species and all that."

I grinned. "You know what would really freak them out? Hearing you talk to me about perpetuating the species."

Then we both laughed—maybe a little more loudly, so Mom and Dad would be sure to hear.

"Troy, you're cute. In the first ten minutes after we met, you told me I'm beautiful. Then you wanted to kiss me for months—months?—before you ever did."

"Kissing you was worth wanting for a while," he said.

"How many months?"

"January."

"Our first date?"

He nodded. "Among others."

"We should try it again soon," I said. "We're already improving." I reached up slightly, in case my fourth kiss ever was about to arrive.

It didn't. He just smiled. "Definitely soon." He was teasing me, and I liked that too. "Okay if I just look at you for a minute? Want to remember how you look tonight."

"Until the photos are done?"

"They'll just be photos," he said. "This is you."

I melted inside. "Okay, but I get to look at you too."

We each took a step back, because you can't see much of the person who's in your arms. Letting him go even that far made my heart ache.

"Shall I pose for you?" I already knew the answer.

He shook his head. "Just be you."

I smiled self-consciously. "How can I, with you staring at me?"

"Not staring. Admiring the girl I love."

I forgot to be self-conscious.

After a minute of just standing there, watching him watch me, I turned toward the door, looked back at him, and nodded for him to follow. Before I'd taken two steps, he put his hands on my waist from behind—and I felt more attractive than I had ever felt in my life.

"Mmmm." I gently shivered, and not from the cool night air. His hands met in front, and I put my hands over them.

"Was kissing one of your dreams?" he asked. His breath was warm on my ear, and I melted a little more.

"Yes."

"Two dreams in one day. Boyfriends have done worse."

I looked back at him. "It was at least three dreams."

"Three?"

I turned and slipped my arms around his neck. His hands still held my waist. "You said you love me. Maybe four dreams, or at least three and a half, because later you kind of said I'm sexy."

He blushed. "You are sexy."

He'd actually said the word. A thrill raced through me, and I beamed. "I'm sorry, did you say something? Please just be quiet and don't interrupt my speech."

That's when I learned that I enjoyed feeling him laugh even more than hearing him laugh.

I spoke more softly. "You didn't run away or throw up or anything when I told you I love you. And meant it." I took a deep, happy breath. "I guess you really do love me."

"Yeah, I kind of do."

I rested my head and arms against his chest. He enveloped me and held me tight. I was speechless—and my parents, if they were listening for conversation on the porch, could think whatever they wanted.

Finally I asked, "Isn't prom supposed to be a disaster? It is on TV and in the movies. But what a perfect day! Thank you for making approximately 3.5 of my dreams come true in one day."

He laughed again. It felt intimate and alive.

"What?" I asked.

"Approximately 3.5 of your dreams?"

"Yes," I said slowly. "What's so funny?" I smiled in anticipation.

"I'm used to you being a total language geek, but obviously you're a math geek too. It tickles." He brushed a few strands of hair from my face, touching my cheek as he did so. "It's adorable."

"Mmm. I feel adored, but I'm not done thanking you. Thank you for not freaking out when I did today, or before that, when, you know."

"You can say it," he said. "When you had a seizure."

"When I had a seizure. Thanks for catching me."

"You're welcome. May I kiss you again, before I go?"

"I really wish you would. But come in and say good night to my parents first." Teasing was a two-way street. "And thanks for being so careful with my hair. I don't mind them knowing we kissed, but I don't want to look like we got carried away—which we didn't."

"Didn't want to mess it up. It's so pretty. Shall we go in?"

"In a minute."

Our wonderful day was almost over, and so was one of my happiest moments ever. I made a conscious effort to remember everything about it. About him. I consulted all five senses, one by one, like we did some-times in writing classes.

My eyes were closed, but I wouldn't soon forget how handsome he was tonight in the splendor of the ballroom and the soft light of my porch—or how he looked at me so many times and smiled so fondly.

We were both silent now, like my whole neighborhood, except the traffic on the busy street a few blocks away. But I could still hear him telling me he loved me and I was beautiful and he'd wanted to kiss me for a long time.

My sense of touch was almost overwhelmed. Besides his warmth against the cool night air, I was close enough to feel him laugh. And his arms around me weren't just gentle. They were strong enough to catch me when I collapsed at the park. I was safe in them, as safe as I had ever been.

I inhaled deeply. Troy, plus a hint of some intriguing cologne I couldn't identify—not that there was any cologne on the planet that I could identify, except Dad's.

I recalled how, just a few years ago, if we girls had to talk about boys at all, they were "yucky, smelly boys." Now I liked how a certain boy smelled. I liked it more than the mingled fragrances of the flowers Mom had planted around the porch a couple of weeks earlier than usual, because we'd be hosting my prom dinner.

Taste made five, and my heart fluttered, but I couldn't actually re-member the taste of his kisses. I'd need frequent reminders.

Unfortunately, my sense of passing time was working too. "What time is it?" I whispered. We'd promised my parents I'd be home—inside—by midnight.

"Three minutes."

"I wish it were longer."

"I don't want to let go," he said. "I . . . Remember when I told you I never met a girl like you?"

"Mm-hm."

"I never even imagined an actual girl could be as amazing as you."

My heart skipped a beat or two. "I never thought a boy like you would fall in love with me, but here we are." I added some mischief to my smile. "If you keep saying sweet things, I'll have to stay right here in your arms and listen, and I may die of happiness, and we'll never go inside, and you'll never get to kiss me again." The mischief fell away, leaving only wonder. "It would almost be worth it."

We went inside at 11:59 p.m. Zeus met us at the door. Mom was already upstairs. Dad was still downstairs, but he was reading a book at the dining room table, far enough from the front door that he might not have known whether we were talking or not talking on the porch.

We chatted with him for a couple of minutes, as usual, before I walked Troy to the door.

What happened next was the most wonderful goodbye I'd ever had, complete with I-love-you's and two more kisses. I watched with longing from the doorway, as he pulled away in his uncle's truck. It would be 38 hours and 22 minutes before I could see him again, on Monday after school. Maybe a minute or two less, if I was lucky.

43

Dad

I SAT WITH DAD for a while in the dining room. He asked, "How was your evening, really?"

"Wonderful."

"I'm glad. Weren't you wearing sleeves when you left?"

"It was pretty warm toward the end."

"Nice option to have. How's Troy? He looked good."

"Troy is very well indeed. He has a beautiful, smart, funny girlfriend, and he just dined and danced and talked the night away with her. So far, by the way, he's a lot like the man of my dreams."

He took my provocation calmly but seriously. "We must speak of your dreams sometime, and more particularly the men in them and their great good fortune."

"Don't worry. When the time comes, the actual man of my dreams will have already served his mission. I'm a good Latter-day Saint girl in that way, among others."

"There's that. Did you dance a lot?"

"Quite a bit. We traded partners a few times. I danced with some of his friends and Jack and Nikki's dates, and I made sure they all knew not to drop me, on penalty of death. We sat and talked a lot too. That was almost my favorite part. He's easy to talk to, like you."

"You flatter me, but I am undistracted. Did he kiss you?" The question wasn't stern and fatherly. It was casual and dad-like, and he smiled like he already knew.

"Can you tell?"

"Besides some recent foreshadowing, I heard car doors long before the front door opened. Truck doors, I suppose. And you both had a certain happy energy when you finally came in. It seemed more consistent with a first kiss than, say, midnight at the end of a long, busy day."

I glowed. "He kissed me. For the first time. That was my favorite thing tonight, and you know what else?"

"There's more?"

"I kissed him back. But kissing is as far as we went."

"So you two are still being careful? With two hearts and two futures, among other things? Even on prom night?"

His asking shouldn't have bothered me anyway, but I flared a little. "I think I just said that." I forced myself to relax. "We're being careful. There are some pretty firm lines just past those goodnight kisses."

"Good girl," he said. "Kisses in the plural?" He raised an eyebrow, and the corners of his mouth turned up a little.

I smiled. "We needed the practice."

"Must have gone well," he said.

"It was amazing. I want more."

His other eyebrow joined the first.

"More kisses." I held up my left hand. "I won't be crossing those lines with Troy or anyone else until there's a ring here. Technically, two rings."

Dad used his best technique for keeping me talking: he nodded and kept listening.

"I won't deny the . . . mutual . . . attraction. But I expect Troy to be a gentleman, and he is. Might be a Texas thing. Or a brother-with-a-smart-older-sister thing."

"As long as it's a thing," he said.

"Some other girls see how he treats me, and I think they want boys to treat them that well too."

"Interesting. Tell me more," he said.

For some reason I blushed. "First of all, we dance without draping ourselves all over each other.

"He thinks I'm beautiful, even though I'm not one of the gorgeous, popular girls.

"He doesn't expect me to get too physical, just to have him as my boyfriend. Or more and more physical, if I want to keep him.

"Some couples sit and make out, but we sit and talk. I think a lot of girls would prefer that. Probably some boys, too, at least the ones who can keep up a conversation."

Dad just kept listening.

"From what I hear, he never says disrespectful things about me in the locker room. And if they saw how friendly he is with my parents and how welcome I am with his family, some girls would want that too."

Dad nodded. "Maybe someone will learn from you liking all that too, and from how you treat him. He sounds like a keeper."

"He is for now, but we're way too young for big decisions."

"Yes, you are. You know your parents worry some?"

"It's your job, right?"

"Also our hobby." He smiled.

"If it helps, he tries to avoid worrying you—more than I try, sometimes."

"Respect for one's elders," Dad mused. "That could be a Texas thing. Helps us trust him with our daughter. May I ask a very personal question?"

"More personal than whether we kissed, and how many times? That was five, by the way."

It was more personal.

"Do you love him?"

I'd been telling Dad all sorts of personal things, as usual, but I shyly dodged this question. "I'm sixteen. What do I know about that kind of love?"

"Evasive, but nicely played," he said. "You sound like a woman who's in love but also smart enough to realize she has a lot to learn about love."

A woman, he said. Not a girl.

I nodded. "Before, I just liked him a lot. I still do, but now it's more. Not just more of the same feeling. It's different. I feel like I love him, and at the same time, like you said, I'm just starting to love him." With that, I ran out of crazy boldness, even for Dad. I couldn't tell him I really did feel like a woman—a very young woman—instead of a girl.

"Do you think he loves me?" I asked.

"He does. Has he told you?"

"This afternoon, for the first time."

"Did you tell him?"

"Shortly after he told me."

"It's been obvious for a while," Dad said. "He cares about you, not just himself. Pretty grown up for seventeen."

"If this is love, I like it. My first love . . . What?"

He looked past me with a faint, distant smile. I wondered if his thoughts were about his past or my future.

"Nothing."

"No, really, Dad. What?"

He didn't answer immediately, and when he did, he started slowly. "First loves . . . are . . . wonderful . . . assuming you stay inbounds, but this isn't a lecture about that. Most of them end eventually, even if you get it right, and that's painful for a while. But if it's really love, you learn a lot, you grow up a lot, and you end up wanting each other to be happy, whether that's together or apart. If it's not together, it makes you better at loving someone else later."

I was certain he had a story I wanted to hear. "What was her name?"

"Katie. Kate."

"Will you tell me about her?"

His eyes focused on me again. "Someday. But for now you tell me something." He stood and offered his hand to help me up. "My last, best love helped some high school students have a great prom day. She wouldn't have missed it for the world, but now she's asleep upstairs, and I should join her. Is my little girl too grown up to kiss her dad good night?"

I took his hand, stood, kissed him on the cheek, and embraced him. "Never too grown up for that. I love you, Daddy. If she wakes up at all, tell her I said thanks. I'll tell her again tomorrow."

He kissed me on the forehead. His voice had a gruff edge. "I'm not saying it's tomorrow or next year, but dads don't look forward to giving up their daughters, even to the men of their daughters' dreams. No, actually we do look forward to it—with dread and sorrow. And grief. And despair."

He was overdoing it. "Relax, Dad. I will always be your little girl."

"I guess a dad can sleep on that. But Jenny?"

"Daddy?"

"Mom and I are endlessly proud of you. And tonight I don't know how any guy at the dance could take his eyes off you and look at his own date."

"Thank you." I blushed. "But you didn't see all the other girls. And you're totally biased. I look a lot like Mom, right? Besides having your eyes?"

"Spitting image, almost."

"I'm completely okay with that. But I don't spit." I looked down at my gown. "Not when I'm dressed up as polite company."

He chuckled, and we said good night again. I kissed him on the other cheek and hugged him, and he hugged me back. "I will always love you," I said.

He went upstairs, and I went to my room. Zeus tagged along with me, as usual. I told him Dad had treated me lately like more of a grownup than I really was. And he should remind me to ask Dad about Kate sometime.

I pulled up short. "Wait! What?" I looked down at Zeus. "Dad's first love ended. They often do."

Zeus looked at me in silence.

"I don't want this to end," I said, "even if we are too young to plan a future together. Obviously it could."

That cold thought prowled the borders of my amazing day but came no closer. For once there was no room for fear.

"You're right," I told Zeus. "We won't think about that now. He loves me, and I love him. We kissed tonight. I hope you don't mind. Maybe it will end someday." I smiled. "Maybe it will last forever."

I took my time letting my hair down, getting out of my gown, and preparing both of us for bed. I still didn't want the day to end. To prolong it, I sat and narrated the highlights for Zeus.

Finally my eyelids drooped, my head craved my pillow, and the warm glow of prom day wrapped itself around me like a blanket. I hugged Zeus and sent him off to bed.

Just in time, I remembered a solemn obligation of girl friendship. I woke up enough to send Nikki and Jack a message: "I love you's. Goodnight kisses. Even told Dad, when he asked, and he doesn't want to ground me or kill Troy or anything. Jack, we took your advice and practiced some. Brilliant! Hope you both had fun too. Details tomorrow. Make that later today. Very, very, very happy."

I'd be in trouble with them later for waiting so many hours to report the I-love-you's. But they'd forgive that, when I described the kissing. Maybe by then I could find some words for that, but it wouldn't be tonight. The memory was too vivid and alive, and my heart still drowned out my brain.

Troy kissed me! I kissed him! It was—

The writer in me would find the words eventually.

It was after 1:00 a.m., but Jack and Nikki were still awake. Nikki replied, "Yay! Handshake and nervous smiles here. But lots of fun. You were gorgeous tonight. We all were."

Jack replied, "About time! Fun prom day! I made Colin hug me. He didn't actually resist, but he turned burgundy like your dress. No new jewelry, I'm sorry to report."

I thought about my new necklace. It was made to be worn close to my heart. The silver heart was Troy's. I was the red stone inside, and it was a solemn thing when a boy gave me his heart. I resolved to take the best possible care of it—for as long as it had me in it.

For a long, long, long, long time, I hoped.

Forever would be nice.

44

About Those Kisses

I AWOKE EARLY FOR a Sunday, put on my new necklace—I liked it with my baby blue pajamas too—sat in my favorite chair, and texted Troy. I hoped he'd have time to chat before he went to church.

"Good morning! Yesterday was wonderful, rather like yourself. I'm wearing my new necklace. I love you. Thanks for so many things."

He replied immediately. "I love you too. That's fun to write. And you're welcome. And thank *you*. Tired?"

"Maybe later. Dad detected our happy glow, assumed kissing. He's okay with it, already figured out that you love me. Obvious for a while, he said. I told Zeus the highlights, to prolong our amazing day."

"Lucky Zeus," he replied. "I could only remember, but that was good."

"The ending was perfect."

"Yup," he replied. "Kind of aching to hug you, etc."

"Now that you mention it, I'm aching to be hugged." I hesitated, thinking twice, then sent what I was thinking. "As for etc., I feel increasingly unkissed. Eight whole hours now. Wish you could help before tomorrow. You know, if you want to."

We'd decided to show our parents how wise and responsible we were by not seeing each other at all on Sunday, after spending so much of Saturday together. My mind still saw the sense in that. My heart simply wanted him.

I put down my phone and pulled on my fuzzy blue slippers—and smiled at my cold feet. They'd been cold on the front porch last night too. I'd had literal cold feet when I was as far from figurative cold feet as I had ever been.

My phone announced his reply. "If? There's no if. Only want."

Something inside me stirred. If we'd been talking in person, I couldn't have spoken as calmly as I wrote. If I'd been writing with a pen, my penmanship would have suffered. In electronic print I seemed calm enough. "Happy Jenny," I wrote. "I'm glad we understand each other. What will we do with ourselves today?"

"Thought I'd try pining for a while," he replied. "Then longing. Then I'll languish for a few hours. After that I'll need a thesaurus."

"Well said, literate boyfriend! But poor you! I'm sending you a photo Jack took. Hope it helps." It was just a random candid of Troy and me before dinner, but I liked it.

Two minutes later, he replied. "You're beautiful. Handsome date looks happy too. Tell Jack I owe her."

"Do you love the picture that much, or are you just desperate?"

"I think both," he wrote. "Sorry, have to go to church now."

"Points for the movie quote. Try to concentrate on God, not some girl you love."

"Right. Like that will happen today."

After his church meetings and before mine, he texted me again. "I rationed. Looked at the photo 10x exactly, plus some daydreaming. Didn't do so well at concentrating on God."

I sent a smiley and a heart. "It's 12 hours now."

"Counting just makes it seem longer," he wrote. "Think you can do better?"

"With the photo? No. If I wanted to try, which I don't, I might keep it to 9x."

"Been thinking about something," he said.

"Besides me?"

"Not exactly. We need a song."

"As in our song?" I wrote. "Do you have one?"

"Not yet."

"Maybe a waltz?"

"Probably. Something we've already waltzed to?"

"'Three Times a Lady' and 'Moon River' are nice," I wrote. "That country song was all right, but I liked the words better than the music."

You know—I couldn't possibly have said—*the song about dancing with you for the rest of my life?* I was blushing all over my bedroom.

"None of them seems like our song," I concluded.

"Agreed," he wrote. "Not saying we have to pick something now."

"This will be fun. As Dad says, food for thought."

Mom knocked softly, then poked her head in to tell me it was time to leave. I quickly sent, "Leaving for church. Bye."

"Lucky church. Bye."

⸺◦○◦⸺

All day, off and on, I thought about our kisses and tried to find words to describe them to myself and to Jack and Nikki. They were coming over after dinner. Apparently kissing meant I owed them ice cream, not just details. It wouldn't be kissing and telling, we reasoned, at least not in a bad way, if it was just my two closest friends.

Meanwhile, dinner was Mom's first chance to hear about prom. I narrated the highlights, not including our talk about beauty. Just as I wondered how much to say about kissing on the front porch, she said, "I don't need details, because you deserve some privacy, but I trust your first kisses were worth the wait."

I smiled, nodded, and only blushed a little.

She smiled too. "I'm a girl too, so maybe one detail. Where did it finally happen?"

"Where I wanted it. On my lips. His too."

She laughed softly.

"On the front porch," I added. "After the dance."

She nodded. "There's a memory."

"Yup," I said in an obvious tribute to the boy who kissed me.

"When did you finally get to sleep?" she asked. I could have hugged her for changing the subject—for respecting our privacy.

"About 2:00, I think."

"Sounds about right. What a fine day you had! Shall we clean up?"

After that, I started to find the words. Our first two kisses weren't like all those Disney films, where the prince and princess kiss for the first time, and the sky explodes with fireworks. Not that I wasn't thrilled. We were about to kiss! We were kissing! We'd just kissed! It was electric and sweet and awkward and uncertain.

The third time was different. The thrill was still there, but the awkwardness and uncertainty were mostly gone. It wasn't as if we'd lit a passionate fire that might consume us. What I felt most, as we sampled and began to explore each other's lips, was an overwhelming sense that I was home. Not because we were on my front porch. I was in his arms; it didn't matter where. In that long, delicious moment, even more than before, I thought and felt and knew that we belonged together.

"That's the oxytocin," Jack said, when I described everything to her and Nikki over ice cream, after Mom and Dad had excused themselves. "The hypothalamus makes it. The pituitary releases it. It does fun things."

"Which you're not telling me now, right? Maybe not ever?" Don't ruin my kissing with your biochemistry, I thought.

"Not if you don't want me to. But ask me what tells your brain to release the oxytocin."

"Okay, what?"

"Love."

"Is that the real answer?"

"Pretty much. It makes you feel more attached to each other and less interested in anyone else—but only if you're already attached. There's actual research. In your case, Troy's all about you, so it makes him even less interested in cheerleaders and actresses and other places a charming hunk of boy could park his lips."

"And his heart," Nikki said.

"And his heart," Jack echoed.

"So you're not saying the best moments of my whole life were just chemistry or biology or whatever?"

She shook her head. "Nope. Love and trust. Like I said, oxytocin only does the fun stuff if you're already attached. It happens with mothers nursing babies too, so it's not just romantic love. And there's another fun discussion to have about dopamine, but not maybe tonight."

"My friend Jack, the science geek," I said with genuine admiration. But we were so not going to think about mothers nursing babies. Not for years yet. Then I realized that thinking about not thinking about them was actually thinking about them, and I forced my mind to listen to Jack, not my girlish, romantic, very biological hopes for the distant future.

"I should do less reading and more of my own field research," she said with a rueful smile.

My blush was more excited than embarrassed. "I can hardly wait for more of mine. I missed that boy today!"

"This is so cool!" Jack and Nikki exclaimed in unison, then laughed.

"Your first kiss!" Nikki added.

"First kisses," Jack said. "With lots more to come."

That was a girlish, romantic thought I was willing to think.

⸻ ❖ ⸻

I thought about songs for a few days without inspiration. On Thursday, on our way to Grandpa's, Troy said he had some music for me.

"A suggestion?" I asked. We traded smiles.

"Could be. First it's all the songs we've waltzed to at actual dances, to get us into a nice 3/4 mood. And for the memories."

Those got us to Grandpa's parking lot, so we left Troy's suggestion for the ride home.

Grandpa was pleased to see us, as always. We talked about prom and showed him pictures. He told us how pretty I was and how handsome Troy was about four times. He asked if we were treating each other well, and we said yes.

For all that, it was a sadder visit than usual. He had more trouble staying focused on the conversation, and he was weaker. He could still stand when we arrived, but with more difficulty, and his arms shook when he hugged me goodbye.

His frailty tore at my heart. As little as was left of his mind, and as hard as that must have been for him for the past few years, I wasn't ready to live without my grandpa. It was all I could do not to burst into tears as he hugged me.

Troy must have noticed the same frailty when they shook hands. He gave me a concerned look. Then he insisted on helping Grandpa sit down, even after Grandpa politely declined his help.

I made it to the elevator before any tears escaped. Troy wrapped me in his arms until we reached the ground floor. Then we walked slowly out to his car.

As we left the lot, I tried to be happy. "You have a song for me?"

"If you don't feel like it now, it'll wait."

"I can use the distraction. I'll be okay."

"You sure? Wouldn't want to ruin a first impression here."

I managed to smile. "You think you've found our song. Is it a waltz? Have I heard it before?"

"Yes, yes, and I don't know. Probably. But we can talk about the weather instead," he teased, "or listen to the news or traffic reports or sports talk radio or something."

"Play the song already!"

"Your wish is my command. And vice versa." He'd picked up using "vice versa" in odd places from my dad.

"Dad's a bad influence on you. And vice versa."

"Thanks." He grinned. "Here goes."

I had heard it before, and I should have thought of it myself. It was "Ten Minutes Ago," from Rodgers and Hammerstein's *Cinderella*. A man sang of finding and dancing with an angel, and a woman sang of finding him.

I remembered the first time Troy sat with me at a dance, and the first time we danced, and how he said at the end of the evening that he was glad he met me. How he visited Grandpa with me for the first time, then told Dad I was like an angel. Our first waltz lesson, our first official waltz—and how I hugged him between dances and knew that I loved him, even if we didn't say it yet. How he texted me the next morning about dancing with an angel.

I remembered how he caught me when I had a seizure at the park. How he stayed by my side and endured my self-indulgent meltdown, then pulled me out of it and restored my perfect day. He was my angel too.

We'd happened so quickly. Not in the first ten minutes, but they were a good start. In a hundred days, give or take, we'd gone from being complete strangers to I-love-you's and kissing on my porch.

"What do you think?" he asked, when the song ended.

"Tell me what you think," I said.

"I think it's our song. Could hardly wait to play it for you. Happy to keep looking, if you're not convinced."

"I'll tell you in a minute," I said.

We finally got the red light we needed.

"Here's what I think." I pulled him toward me and kissed him until the light turned green, which happened a lot sooner than a boy and a girl might have hoped for.

Then I let him drive. Neither of us said anything right away. To the extent that I could think at all, I rejoiced at a new way to communicate things I couldn't say with words. Writer or not, there were more of those things lately.

"I see," he said, after we'd driven a block or two. "How would you put that into words?"

I scrambled for words after all. "It's perfect. It's our song. I love you. And it seems pretty fast, but we'll waltz to it, right?"

"About 168, almost twice as fast as our other waltzes. The Hills say it's a Viennese Waltz tempo. They're happy to help."

"They're so kind," I said. "You went back and measured the tempos of all those songs, didn't you?"

"Took longer than I expected."

"Why? You count for ten or fifteen seconds and multiply."

"Think about it," he said.

"It's counting plus some basic arithmetic," I said.

"Yeah, counting was the hard part. Think about sitting and listening to the songs we've waltzed to."

I closed my eyes for a minute, then opened them and smiled. "You had trouble counting, because you kept thinking of me."

"Took me half an hour for four songs."

"I like having that effect on you. And nice work! You found our song and another great excuse to waltz. Play it again?"

As the music started again, he said, "Actually, Nan found it. She watched *Cinderella* last night with Lily, and she told me it sounded like our song." He smiled. "She didn't know we were looking."

"Tell her I said thanks, okay? Next chance I get, she gets a hug."

Mom was having a good week too. I was out when Troy, Colin, and Ty brought her a bouquet and a thank-you note. They thanked her again for letting them use our home for prom dinner and supervising the cooking—and helping with with corsage pins, Troy added.

They even thanked her for planting her flower beds early, so the front yard would be especially pretty. She'd been finishing that, when Troy and I pulled into the driveway after visiting Grandpa on the Thursday before prom. We'd helped her clean up.

"They didn't have to bring me flowers," she said later, as I admired the bouquet. She was smiling, but her eyes were damp. She didn't usually tear up over stuff. "Just the note would have been plenty."

She'd told them that, and Troy had replied, "No, ma'am. Wouldn't have been the same without you."

Now she asked me, "Why didn't boys like that come to my door when I was in high school?"

I grinned. "You found a good one eventually."

"Not until grad school. I was starting to wonder. My parents had been wondering for years. They were quite relieved when your Dad came along and chased me until I caught him." She smiled. "And vice versa."

"It just took a while to find someone good enough for you," I said. It wasn't flattery. I meant it. "Was Dad your first love?"

"Not my first crush. Not even close. But he was my first real love, and he still is. Before him no one I really liked wanted the job, and the few guys who liked me, well . . ."

"You could have just said 'vice versa' again. In honor of Dad."

She smiled and nodded. "He had to work at it more than he should have. By then I was bitter about men in general, not to mention discouraged. And suspicious, when he came along."

I chuckled. "You could be suspicious of Dad?"

"Not for long. Four or five dates, not more than a couple of months. Less and less, as we got acquainted. He was obviously a good guy, but I didn't exactly know him as your Dad then."

"No kidding. How long did it take to start liking him a lot?"

"Not long. It was just right. Like y—" She looked at me with an expression I couldn't read. I was instantly on pins and needles, delighted at what she'd begun to say but wondering why she'd stopped.

After a few seconds I asked, "Were you about to say, like me and Troy?"

"Yes."

"Why did you stop?"

Wrinkles deepened between her eyebrows, and she seemed to look past me, before she focused again. "Two reasons, I think. I don't want to pressure you about the future. We don't know the future, and it's only partly within our control. And it's a little scary to see you in love the way you are, and so young."

I remembered Dad telling me they worried. That and scaring Mom a little caused a pang of regret—for troubling them, not for being with Troy. "I'm sorry. I mean, I'm not, but I see your point."

"I'm not complaining. You're behaving yourselves, and it's generally fun to watch. But it makes us nervous sometimes. Do you talk about the future?"

"Mostly that we shouldn't mess it up. We're in high school."

"That's wise," she said.

"So you don't hate Troy for kissing your only daughter?" I thought it was a safe question.

She smiled. "If your dad can handle it, I can. I'm glad you two waited a while to go there, but I don't hate him, and I'm not disappointed."

For a few minutes Mom and I talked about what was and wasn't too much kissing. I'd heard it all before. The difference this time was, I wanted to listen.

There was one other difference. This time, I hardly blushed at all.

The haters at school spent the week after prom alternately glaring at me in silence and repeating the project theme. I didn't let it bother me. I loved a boy who loved me, and they couldn't change that.

Rules

45

It Seemed Like a Good Idea

T HE NEXT MONDAY MORNING, Troy texted me a full hour before my alarm. I wouldn't have heard the alert, but I was half-awake for a minute from the sounds of Mom leaving early for work.

"Good morning, beautiful. Up yet?"

"Good morning. Does it have to be morning already?"

"Sorry. May I pick you up for school this morning? Early, about 7:00? Zeus too. We need to talk before we get there."

Dad planned to drive me, but he wouldn't mind. "Sure. What's up?"

"Better in person."

"For you I can do 7:00."

Dad was on an early conference call in his study, so he said Troy didn't need to come in. Zeus and I waited on the front porch. When Troy arrived, I collected a hug and kiss before he opened the car doors for Zeus and me. My week was off to an unusually good start.

I noticed Troy's frown as we backed out of the driveway. His eyes looked stricken. Had I only imagined him smiling a moment earlier? The instant he was done shifting gears, I took his hand. "What's wrong?"

He kept his eyes on the road. "Need to tell you what I did. You're going to hate me."

My head and stomach were instantly in turmoil. I tried to speak calmly. "I can't imagine hating you. What's wrong?"

I waited half an eternity, or at least a few seconds. When he spoke, his voice was higher-pitched. "I screwed up. Big time."

I couldn't get my head around the thought that he'd done something really bad. "What happened?"

He shook his head slowly, his eyes still on the road. I tried to imagine possible boyfriend-related horrors, but I couldn't think clearly.

"Saw Maddi in the foyer after church yesterday. Without her minions. She was coming out of a missionary farewell in the sacrament meeting after ours. Thought I'd try to be friendly and ask her to stop being mean to you. Should've known better. That girl's messed up."

"Thank you for trying," I said. "I don't hate you yet." I was trying to be cheerful.

I'd never seen him frown so deeply. His lips were pressed together, and his knuckles were white on the steering wheel. He took a deep breath and blew it out. "Now . . ."—several seconds passed—"now she's saying I told . . . that . . . that I told her you're a good lay. Sorry for the language."

"Did you?" I asked too calmly, before it sank in.

"No!" His anguish broke my heart.

"I didn't think so."

He said Maddi invited him to walk her to her car, and he asked if she and her friends could do him a favor and stop being unkind to his girlfriend.

"Who's your girlfriend?" she asked, as if she didn't know.

"Jenny Miller," he said.

She pretended to be surprised. "I heard you were trying to date Brooke. Well, until you tried to grope her, and she wouldn't let you, and you hit her, and somebody reported you. But never mind. You've moved on to this Jenny? Is she the one with the dog? She has seizures, right? She'd have to put out to be worth your trouble."

Troy had stayed focused—heroically, I thought. "Maddi, you and your friends say mean things to her in the halls at school. Please stop."

She feigned surprise. "She told you that? She must be confused. But we should be compassionate. Epilepsy is like brain damage, right?"

"She's not confused," Troy said. "It's you and your friends."

"Do you think she's afraid of losing you to some other girl? It must really bother her that she's not the healthy, beautiful girl a handsome athlete like you deserves. She can't even dance much, can she? I know you love to dance."

Troy's patience failed him. "Maddi, you're a messed-up little girl. Please stop bullying Jenny. She's a lot less sick than you. More beautiful too, inside and out."

I shook my head. "Not good. Calling her a little girl and less beautiful, and telling her she's sick."

"Yeah," Troy said gruffly. "I'm the one with brain damage. Notice the other problem?"

He was miserable. I wished we were in his uncle's pickup. Stupid bucket seats. "What am I missing?"

His voice rose half an octave. "Here's where it gets really hard for your idiot boyfriend."

I slipped toward panic. "Troy," I said too sharply, "be nice to my boyfriend!"

He signaled, pulled over, and parked the car in front of a house. "Safer this way."

He let go of my hand to shift into Park, and he kept both hands on the wheel after that. I was afraid to wonder what that meant. It felt like a bad time to be disconnected. He looked at me out of the corners of his eyes. His face was pale and wretched.

"Don't want to say this, but it happened." He stared at his hands. "After I said 'inside and out,' Maddi said, 'So you've been inside already? Everything seems to work? Good for her. But you should confess to your bishop. I know boys will be boys, but you're not supposed to go that far. You couldn't leave the poor girl even a little self-respect?'"

His eyes darted to me, then away—too quickly, I thought, to take in my distressed eyes and quivering chin.

"I finally just told her to leave you alone. She said, 'It sounds like you should leave her alone.' Then she smiled really big and said, 'Nice talking to you!' and got into her car."

He hung his head. When he spoke again, his voice was still high. "Last night she texted her friends. Told them I said . . . you know."

His chin was quivering too, which had me ready to fall apart. And he still wasn't holding my hand.

"One of the guys saw it late last night and told me. I'm sorry, Jenny. I'm so sorry. I thought I was helping us."

I stared at him. It was all just words, but I felt violated—by her casual talk about my anatomy and by the lie she was spreading. I wanted to lash out at her—or cower in a corner or hide under a rock. Or just cling to Troy. But I couldn't even do that, thanks to seat belts and other inconvenient car parts.

"Jenny?" Troy finally said.

"Is she insane?" I demanded. "She must be insane."

"I must be, to try talking to her."

I reached for his wrist and pulled gently. He looked over at me, then down at my hand. His knuckles were still white. It took a few seconds, but he relaxed and let go of the wheel. I pulled his hand toward me and laced my fingers through his. His eyes met mine, but then he turned away and faced forward again.

"I can't hate you for trying to help me," I said.

His mouth barely moved. "Trying to imagine how this makes you feel. Don't know the word."

"Violated."

He hung his head again. "That's why you're the writer. Violated. And it's my fault." His voice broke.

I tried to sound firm. "No. It's Maddi's fault."

He shrugged.

This time I was firm. "Troy, this is not your fault."

He wiped his eyes with the back of the hand I wasn't holding and leaned back against the headrest. His face slowly relaxed, not completely, but enough that he didn't look utterly miserable.

I held his hand in both of mine. He squeezed it firmly, then sat up and mumbled, "Better go." He gently extracted his hand from mine.

He pulled us back into traffic, then gave me back his hand. I watched him and wondered how to help him feel better. Neither of us spoke again until we came to a red light.

I tried pretending there was a bright side. "It's probably better to be known as a good lay than a bad one."

He jerked his head around and snapped at me. "Don't do that! Don't make a joke out of it, or try to find a silver lining or whatever. There isn't one. I just helped her do this to you."

"*You* didn't do it. She did," I said. "To us, not just me."

"To us, then. Be angry with me. I deserve it."

I ached for him, and I wanted to dissolve into tears, but that would have made him feel worse. So maybe there was one thing I could do for him: not cry.

A polite honk announced the light was green, and he turned his attention to the road. I stared out the window and worked on the one thing I could do.

Usually, when we arrived somewhere, he'd hop out to open my door. This time he didn't. I was still staring out my window. I didn't realize his hand was missing from mine until it came back.

"Jenny?"

I couldn't look away anymore, but I'd crumble if I saw his face. So I stared at our hands and hoped in vain that my voice wouldn't tremble. "You said I should be angry with you, but that's not possible."

"Of course it's possible."

"I can't be angry with you."

"If I ever gave you a good reason . . ."

"Troy, listen to me. I can't do it. Not for this."

"Why not?" he asked loudly enough that I recoiled. "Look what I just did to your reputation."

Biting my lip helped me not to cry. So did my frustration with what he said. I raised my eyes to his. "It's what Maddi's doing to our reputations, not what you did to mine. You did something brave and . . . and unpleasant, and you did it to help me, not hurt me. You love me, and you know I love you. I can't be angry with you for this, and I won't."

"Love feels like it should change everything, but it doesn't," he said. His resentful tone stung. "Doesn't make everything all better."

I wanted to snap at him for doubting us, for letting Maddi make him doubt us. And I still wanted to cry. "It changes enough," I said, not calmly at all. "It changes this."

The first bell rang, and we shared a desperate look. He started to get out of the car, and I didn't wait for him. I opened my own door, climbed out, and opened the back door for Zeus. Troy was there to take my hand after I shut the doors.

He didn't ask why I didn't wait for him to open my door, as I always did, and I couldn't have told him, because I didn't know.

We walked together as far as we could toward our first period classes. Neither of us spoke, and I barely noticed the crowded halls. When we had to separate, he turned to me. He looked like he might never smile again. "I'm so sorry about this. I love you."

I reached up and kissed him on the cheek. "I know you do. And I love you. It'll be okay."

I saw it in his eyes and face, then his walk, as he turned away and trudged toward his class. He didn't believe it would be okay.

I wasn't sure I believed it either.

Through most of first period I ignored the lecture and searched for the right word to describe Troy, because a writer finds words for things. Maybe it should have been obvious right away.

He was ashamed. I'd never seen him ashamed. But at least it hadn't come from doing something bad. He'd done something good, and Maddi had turned it bad.

My next thought hurt worse: I didn't know how to help ashamed, let alone fix it.

I worried about not waiting for him to open my door. Did he feel rejected? Or punished? Was I punishing him? No, I'd just been thoughtless, because we had to get to class. But that was bad enough. It was a small thing he liked to do for me, and I should have thought to let him.

⸺◆⸺

There were gestures from the haters in the hall that day—including one I didn't recognize, but I assumed it was crude. I worried that their "little project" greetings would have a new word or two, but they just whispered and laughed quietly among themselves. It was enough to keep the knot in my stomach from going away.

Troy and I checked on each other by text message after every class. We couldn't get together after school, because he had another dentist appointment.

In the evening we Skyped, and he apologized again. I didn't want him to, but I didn't object. He sounded exhausted. His face was drawn and somber, and something about his eyes made me think even listening required unusual effort.

I did my best to explain the car door thing, but maybe I didn't need to. He'd just thought we had to hurry.

"I have good news," he said. "Texted Will after school, and he hadn't heard the rumor. Said he overheard some prom night rumors about other couples, but not us. You'd think it would have spread by now, if it was going to. He says most kids wouldn't believe it about us anyway, especially if it came from Maddi. Hope he's right."

"That is good news," I said. "I guess, if our reputations couldn't survive Maddi gossip, they wouldn't be much of a loss."

We talked for a while about whether to tell our parents about the rumor and risk encouraging even the slightest suspicion. We finally decided we had to, so they wouldn't hear it somewhere else first. But we wouldn't tell them Maddi's name. We didn't want them contacting her parents. She'd be just "a jealous girl at school."

We talked about happier things at the end. I felt a little better, and he smiled faintly once or twice. At 10:00 p.m. we said goodbye. I closed my laptop and began the long, short walk to Mom and Dad.

46

Courage

M Y PARENTS DIDN'T YELL, curse, threaten, or throw things when they were angry, but Maddi's rumor obviously angered them. They pursed their lips and frowned. Mom's cheeks flushed and Dad's ears turned red, and his jaw was firmly set. Their eyes flashed, and I was glad they weren't angry with me.

They guessed immediately why I didn't tell them Maddi's name, and that didn't please them either. At least they believed me when I said the rumor wasn't even almost true.

"We need to chat with her parents," Dad said, when I declined to name her for the third time. "That's one of the things we're here for."

"If that gets her in trouble," I said, "she and her friends will probably just be worse."

"Is there more going on at school than you've told us?" Mom asked.

I knew my parents. This was about to escalate. And I couldn't lie to them. I thought quickly and very carefully before answering.

"She says mean things in the halls, but if it were a big deal, Zeus and I would have told you already."

Dad gave me a knowing look. "Nicely done. A bit of humor to lighten the mood and distract. But this is more than unkind words in the halls."

"We should speak with her parents," Mom said. "Things will almost certainly get worse if we don't."

I thought about that.

Actually I didn't. I thought about how to get them to back down.

"Is it one of the kids who upset you a few months ago, when you had that spat with Troy?" Dad asked. "When you were ill?"

I didn't remember mentioning names, so I nodded. "Yes."

"Has it been happening ever since?" Mom asked.

"Off and on. But I have thicker skin now, and I still have the boyfriend. What if I don't tell you her name now, but if it gets worse, I'll tell you right away, and you can do what you have to do. Please?"

They shared a wordless frown.

"Okay," Mom said. "That's a reasonable compromise. If it gets worse, you will promptly tell us, and we'll take it from there."

✦

As I got ready for bed, I thought of Troy. He must have had a miserable, sleepless night after seeing Maddi's text. He must have spent the night angry with Maddi and himself, worried that the news would hurt me, and thinking I might blame him as much as he blamed himself. Which I didn't.

Suddenly I wasn't so tired after all. My angry face in the mirror looked a lot like Mom's.

Maddi had no right to spread lies about us. And she was hurting Troy. Somebody needed to do something. I needed to do something. It was my turn to defend us.

If life were a TV show, I'd attack her physically. But it wasn't, and I wasn't like that. I didn't want to get expelled, and I wouldn't win a fight anyway. My only weapon was words.

I wouldn't use them to spread lies behind her back. And tattling to a school counselor or principal, or her parents, whom I'd never met, seemed childish and weak. It had to be face to face.

I could stand up to her. I wasn't a delicate little flower other people had to shield from being stepped on. At least she'd see that her behavior was under protest.

I wondered if I shouldn't just turn the other cheek, as usual. Wasn't that the Christian thing to do? It probably was, when they insulted me in the halls. But defending someone else was different from defending just myself. Besides, with Maddi I'd run out of cheeks.

Was I making sense? I slipped under the covers and walked through my thinking again, trying to imagine what Mom and Dad would say, if and when I explained it to them.

It made enough sense. I could stand up to Maddi without Troy or anyone else. And I would. Tomorrow. Then I'd tell Troy, and we'd both be proud of me.

My mind started to drift, and I let it go. I could find the right words for Maddi tomorrow.

⸻◆⸻

During lunch break the next day, I stopped by the office to get Maddi's schedule, so I'd know where to find her before fourth period. I waited in the hall until the secretary was on the phone, then walked in. The student aide, Kellie, asked if she could help me. A big, white button on her bright orange t-shirt asked the same question.

I knew she wasn't supposed to give student schedules to just anyone. I didn't tell her I was asking for a teacher, but she assumed I was, and I didn't correct her. If I wasn't dishonest, I was close.

As an afterthought I asked for Maddi's locker number too. Kellie helpfully pulled up a map on the screen and showed me where to find it. I thanked her and left the office. The secretary was still on the phone.

Maddi's locker was near her last class, so she'd probably stop there. That's where I'd meet her. Jack and Nikki wanted to go with me, but I told them I had to go alone. I even left Zeus with them.

I reached her locker three minutes before the bell, which gave me time to review what I planned to say. I was getting nervous, and I'd just realized she might have friends with her. I hadn't planned for that.

She came early and alone. She didn't see me at first, though I was only a few feet from her locker and we had the short hallway to ourselves.

While she dialed her combination, I noticed that our outfits were oddly alike. Our sneakers and jeans nearly matched, except her jeans were skinnier and ankle-length. We were both wearing magenta tees, though hers was a v-neck with ruffled sleeves. It was tighter than mine, which worked for her. Her platinum hair was usually up somehow, but it was down today, and a few inches longer than my hair.

At least I could look slightly down on her, when she wasn't in heels.

"Maddi, may I speak with you?" I didn't sound nervous or weak. Or calm. I sounded ticked off. So far, so good.

She started and looked up. "What?" She wrinkled her nose. "Oh, it's you. Where's your boyfriend?"

"On his way to seminary," I said.

"Isn't there usually a dog too?"

"Usually."

She turned away long enough to open her locker, then looked at me impatiently. Her brown eyes were cold. "I have to get to class. Say what you came to say."

Fortunately, my mind went only partially blank. "I was about to ask you to stop spreading lies about Troy and me, but that wouldn't do any good, would it?"

I sounded condescending. This was still going well. "Troy was right about you. You're one messed-up little girl."

She scowled, and her eyes flashed.

"So I'll just say this. We won't let you ruin what we have, no matter how many lies you tell about us. Sorry to disappoint you."

Her scowl became a sarcastic smile. "You done?"

"With you? Yes." I held her gaze. I felt especially proud of that.

"You know, just because you're having second thoughts about doing it with Troy doesn't make what he told me a lie."

I hadn't expected her to defend herself so smoothly. She was quick. Maybe even smart. But still evil.

"What he told you?" I used my best I'll-never-believe-you tone.

"We talk sometimes. That probably bothers you, but whatever. He said you were pretty good. And he would know. I hope you used protection." She turned back to her open locker.

"You're sick," I hissed. "And we already knew you're a liar."

She turned back to me, speaking calmly. "One of us is sick. I don't think it's me. So was Troy good? Was he worth it?" She smiled nastily. "Speaking of sick, can I give you some friendly advice? It might still be too soon after prom night for a pregnancy test. I don't know. But when you get it, or even if you don't, you should get some other tests too. You never know what little gifts your boyfriend might have brought with him from all those skanky Texas girls."

Just that quickly, I was past anger. Beyond it lay not violence—fortunately—but disbelief, mixed with confidence and sarcasm. "This is incredible," I said. "You really believe your own lies? That's talent."

She answered with a quick, cold laugh. "My lies? Troy got caught bragging about his latest conquest—not that you're much of a conquest—and he's blaming me so you won't blame him for telling, well, pretty much everybody."

Whatever she saw in my face just then, it wasn't me doubting Troy.

"He probably said you were his first. And you believed him. And those lingerie shots you sent him?" She shook her head. "You probably thought they were sexy. By the way, they never keep those to themselves, no matter what they promise."

The bell rang. The hall got crowded, and some of her friends approached.

"This was really fun," she sneered, "but I have class. Good luck with those tests. Don't ever talk to me again."

I tried for a baleful glare.

As she joined her friends, I heard one of the girls say, "Gross! Why were you talking to *that*? What did it want?"

"Not sure," Maddi replied. "It was upset about something, but it made no sense when it talked."

I hadn't expected remorse or an apology, and I got neither. But this was a win—because I was brave, and my part had gone well enough.

By the time I'd met Jack and Nikki, retrieved Zeus, and arrived at my next class two minutes late—my teachers rarely marked me tardy, even when I deserved it—I was thinking I might have mistaken stupid for brave. Maybe I'd just made things worse for Troy and me.

When the teacher turned her back to walk a student through something in our homework, I sneaked out my phone and sent Troy a quick text. "Might have been really stupid just now. Got brave, confronted Maddi. Details when we Skype. Your angry girlfriend (not angry with you) loves you."

When I turned my phone on again after school, there was a message. "Young Men tonight. Skype after 9:00. Can hardly wait to hear this. I love my angry (not with me) girlfriend."

47

Complications

IT WAS ALMOST 9:30 p.m. when Troy Skyped me. At first I thought he couldn't see me, because his face didn't light up.

"Hi, Jenny," he said quietly.

"Hi. You sound tired."

"Think I just made our lives worse again. Twice in three days, if you're counting." He seemed defeated, not just tired.

"I'm not counting. You didn't talk to Maddi again, did you?"

"My bishop."

I was instantly relieved. His bishop wasn't my favorite person, but how bad could it be?

"You talked to Maddi," he said. "Tell me about that first."

I told him what I'd done, and by the end he was smiling a little. Which made one of us.

"What if I made things worse?" I asked. "It felt like courage, but now I feel like a reckless fool. I shouldn't make decisions when I'm angry and exhausted. Or, you know, talk."

"I think you were brave," he said. "Haven't been here that long, but I never saw a girl stand up to Maddi like that. Guess I didn't see you either, but I'm not sorry you did it."

"I hope you're not sorry eventually. Now tell me your thing."

His smile faded. "Bishop Waldron's worried about me," he said. "So tonight, after Young Men, he wanted to talk."

"How did that make things worse?"

"I told him I love you enough to behave myself with you. Enough not to dump you to please some people at church, including him. Said I was sorry if that bothered him."

"I already like your story better than mine," I said. "What did he say?"

"He's worried about my future, including my mission. And he's just trying to help.

"I said I know that, but it feels like it's just more of what we get at school. Told him about Maddi's rumor, which started down the hall from his office, in a way.

"He said that's terrible, and no one deserves to be treated that way. You won't believe what he said next."

"Uh-oh."

"Yeah. Exact quote: 'In general life is easier when we obey inspired counsel, and harder when we disobey.'"

I digested that for a few seconds. "He actually said that? He thinks the haters at school are God's punishment for our disobedience?"

"That's what I heard."

"That's cold."

"Yup. If he's going to say things like that, I'm done talking with him. I thanked him for his time, because I couldn't be totally rude. I'm from Texas. Then I swallowed all the things I wanted to say and left. Didn't shake his hand. Didn't look back. Didn't slam his office door, but I wanted to. May I come to your ward this Sunday?"

"Of course." I studied his troubled eyes. "I wish this terrible week you're having weren't all about me. And us. How can I help?"

"Listening helps. Talking helps. Seeing you on my screen helps."

"How do I send you a hug on this thing?"

"Don't think there's a button for that."

"What do you think he'll do?" I asked.

"That's what worries me. He can't talk about confidential interviews, but I'm sure he'll share some general concerns with Mom and Dad. They'll want to know what we talked about, because I can tell them, even if he can't.

"Then they'll worry, because he's worried and he's the bishop. They'll be disappointed that I was a little rude to him. They really like you, but you know. They're my parents and I'm their son, and he's the bishop, and we're in high school, and I'm in love with you."

I really needed to hug him.

"They'll sit me down for a talk," he said. "That'll be tense. But they'll probably be okay in the end. I hope. They're trying to trust us. They mostly do, I think."

"Maybe we should talk to them together. Don't know what we'd say."

"Might be good," he said. "I know Bishop Waldron's not a bad guy. And my parents didn't raise me to be disrespectful, especially to him. But you're the happiest part of my life, and he thinks that's wrong—and it's not!"

He almost yelled. "We are not wrong!"

The image on my screen shook, and I thought I heard him hit something twice. I couldn't see his hands, but I imagined him pounding his desk to emphasize *not wrong*.

I was stunned, but in a happy way. This passion was for us. For me!

"Why can't he see that?" he asked gruffly. "Why won't he see that?"

"I don't know," I said.

What I did know was that I had an urgent, overwhelming, physical need to hold him, but we were connected only by wires or radio waves or whatever. I wrestled with my own frustration and my sense of his despair. I asked quietly, "I'm the happiest part of your life?"

"Yeah."

"I love you. I wish I were hugging you."

"Wish you were too."

We stared silently at our screens. I wanted to say something to make him feel better, but I didn't know what. I wanted to say unkind things about his bishop, but I couldn't put words to any of them. What I finally said surprised me.

"Tell me something good about your bishop."

Wherever that came from—I thought when I heard myself say it—it was a good thing to say. It was positive, when we were negative. It was optimistic and hopeful, when we were morose. And it was kinder than saying bad things about him, even if he deserved them.

"Okay," Troy said. He thought for a moment. "You know I'm his second assistant in the priests quorum presidency."

I did know. We girls had our Young Women classes at church, which met for an hour on Sundays and one evening during the week. The Young Men met at the same times, but their groups were called quorums, because they were ordained to the lower offices in the Church's lay priesthood. That difference in roles bothered some people, and maybe someday it would bother me, but it hadn't yet.

Boys who were worthy—who behaved themselves—were ordained priests when they turned sixteen. They could bless the bread and water of the sacrament and baptize people.

We had plenty of adult advisors, but the actual leaders in our quorums and classes—the presidencies—were youth, except that for some reason the bishop himself was always president of the priests quorum. He chose—"called"—two boys to be his assistants in that role, and Troy was one of those.

"I think you know I'm in charge of assigning priests to bless the sacrament every Sunday, among other things," he said. "I may not be his assistant much longer, though. He didn't say anything, but . . ."

"Will you be disappointed if he releases you? Or hurt?"

"Maybe embarrassed, because I'll know why. Leaders are supposed to be good examples, and I kind of want to be okay at that."

"You are a good example, whether he thinks so or not."

"Thanks. You know Rodney, right?"

"Rodney Grant? Senior? Tall, dark, and less handsome than my boyfriend? Everyone knows him."

Rodney was unusually kind and polite. He smiled at the shy kids in the halls, held doors open, and picked up litter. When some bully pushed him around or called him names, which I'd witnessed a few times, he looked hurt, and he seemed to want to say something in response, but he never did. He just shrugged it off and kept being helpful and kind.

They picked on him for the same reason he hardly ever talked—because he stuttered.

"He's in my quorum," Troy said. "He struggles with the sacrament prayer, but he gets through it, as long as the other priest at the table helps him in the right way when he needs it. We've worked on that. I make sure he blesses the water, because the prayer's shorter, and it doesn't come first, so he's less nervous.

"So one Sunday I screw up and assign a brand new priest who doesn't know any of this to bless the sacrament with him. The new guy's terrified, so he insists on blessing the water.

"Rodney's terrified too, but he agrees, which is pretty brave. Then he gets stuck about two lines into the prayer. Starts over and gets stuck in the same place. So he starts over again, and he gets stuck again.

"By this time I feel like a total loser, because it's my fault, and I'm wondering if we'll ever get him to the sacrament table again. Or if I should walk up to the front and help him. He tries to get past it again, but he can't. And the new guy doesn't know how to help.

"I can't see Rodney's face, because he's kneeling and his head is bowed, and I'm at the back of the chapel on the other side. But I know how he looks when he starts to panic. His jaw goes slack and his eyes get big. When Mr. Grover read a poem to us in English the other day and told us to imagine a look of existential despair, Rodney's the closest I could get.

"So I hand my scriptures to Nan and head for the front. I'm partway there when I see the bishop on his way to the sacrament table too. He's closer, so I slip into a pew, where there's space on the aisle.

"From there I can see Rodney's face, and it's exactly what I expected. I feel like crap. The new guy has this wide-eyed, helpless look. He doesn't see the bishop coming, but he sees me stop and sit, so he's about to panic.

"Bishop Waldron sits next to Rodney on the priests' bench and puts a hand on his shoulder. Rodney doesn't even look at him. He's still kneeling and staring at the card we use with the prayer on it. Meanwhile, everyone in the chapel is trying not to look. It's getting more awkward by the second.

"The bishop whispers to him for a minute, then helps him start the prayer. He whispers two or three words at a time, and Rodney repeats them. It's slow and awkward, and he has to correct himself a few times, but he gets it right.

"The next thing we do is stand up and hand the trays to the deacons. After that, the bishop gives him a fist bump and a big smile. Rodney even smiles a little. The priests' bench has room for three, and the bishop stays there while the deacons pass the bread."

Deacons were even younger boys, ordained when they turned twelve—as Dad liked to say, if they would sit still long enough to be ordained.

"He helps the new guy a little too, when he blesses the water, because now he's a bundle of nerves.

"I thought the bishop was really cool about everything, including the fist bump. He could have told Rodney to have a seat and said the prayer himself, but he didn't. Never said a word to me about screwing up the assignments either. Not that he could've made me feel worse. I apologized to Rodney, but he was actually okay. Said the bishop told him about a time when he was a priest and had to say the whole prayer five times to get it right."

"That sounds like something my bishop would do," I said.

"He's not a bad guy," Troy said. "He's just completely wrong about us."

48

Good Works of Omission

O N Wednesday evening in Young Women, they told us our planned activity had to be postponed, so we were having a lesson. Sister Alberson was our teacher again. Her face seemed rounder and a little flushed, and she was perkier than usual. I half-expected her to announce she was pregnant, but she just launched into her lesson.

Our topic was Integrity, one of our eight "Young Women values." We talked about them a lot. The values themselves were fine—and a lot more substantial than some of our discussions of them.

I knew I should try to listen patiently and say very little, if anything. She tried hard, and she was friendly and kind, even if some of her lessons were short on clarity and logic.

Sister A didn't know it, but she had her own definition of integrity. It was different from the real one. "You can always spot a young woman with integrity," she said. "She'll be the one, when you see her, who's always doing what you know is right."

I let it go the first three times, and no one else objected. After the fourth time I raised my hand. When she called on me, I said, "It seems to me that if someone has integrity, she's always doing what *she* thinks is right, not what *I* think is right."

"Aren't those the same?" Her tone said we all should know that.

"Only if she and I understand each other perfectly, share exactly the same values, and apply them in precisely the same way to each other's lives." I said. "Which isn't very likely."

"Actually," she said, "we will think alike, if we all know the simple principles of the gospel, and if we follow the prophet and have strong testimonies."

"The prophet" was the President of the Church—sort of like the pope, only for Latter-day Saints. We understood him to have a unique connection with God, so we took his teachings especially seriously. We had hymns and children's songs about following the prophet and not going astray.

"So good, faithful people who follow the prophet never disagree?" I asked.

"Not on the important things. Not if they have strong testimonies," she said.

"So if we both understand the gospel and have strong testimonies, and if you have integrity, I will agree with all the important decisions you make in your life?"

"Of course, eventually. For now you need to remember that us adult leaders are older and wiser. That's why we're your teachers. When you know what we know and have grown-up testimonies like us, then yes, you'll see people living their lives the way you know they should, and you'll know that means they have integrity."

I tried one more time. "So if you have a strong testimony, and you disagree with my decisions, then it's not because you're wrong, or because my beliefs are a little different, or because it's none of your business." I said that part as gently as I could. "It's because I lack integrity?"

"Exactly," she said—not as if she'd won an argument, but as if she could barely contain her joy that one of her slower students had seen the light.

I tried not to sound sarcastic. "Thanks for clarifying that, Sister A. I think I understand now."

I kept my hand down and my mouth shut after that, which was easy, because I pretty much tuned her out. I amused myself by looking up the word *testimony* on my phone. A dictionary said it was a public statement of a person's religious experience or conversion. That worked. The Church's website said it was a spiritual witness of truth given by the Holy Ghost—the conviction itself, not just the expression of it. That worked too. I didn't find anything anywhere, I thought grouchily, that said a testimony was my burning conviction that someone else should live her life according to my beliefs instead of her own.

It got worse after the meeting.

After we all put away the folding chairs, Sister A came to me and thanked me for asking my questions, because questions and discussion are important parts of a lesson. She told me again how wonderful it is when everyone can see that you have integrity, because they see that your life and your decisions match the truth they know.

I politely bit my tongue. Good Works were a Young Women value too, and being kind when you'd rather not was a Good Work. And sometimes it was kinder not to tell people they weren't making sense.

Next came our class president, Britney. I was one of the youngest girls in the class, which started at sixteen. She was two years older and several inches taller. She'd been captain of the girls' volleyball team at school, and she was about to graduate. She was all jeans and pretty sweaters and medium-brown curls, and she just knew she was the right girl to help guide us lesser, shorter girls to new heights of spiritual goodness.

She put her arm around me. I wanted to say something caustic and wriggle away, but I was meek. That was another Good Work. She probably meant well, like everybody else at church. Except Maddi.

"Jenny, I hope you don't feel like that wonderful lesson was aimed only at you. We know you're struggling to follow the prophet right now, and us leaders are praying for you, but we all needed that lesson, not just you."

I felt hollow when she said that, sick of being judged for sins I wasn't committing, devastated that even church meetings weren't a refuge anymore. Then anger began to fill the void—but I didn't correct Britney's grammar, and I didn't strangle her with Zeus's leash. If there were sins of omission, I thought, there must be good works of omission too, and not killing my Laurel class president was probably a big one.

"Thanks for saying that," I said, but I didn't mean it.

Zeus and I escaped down the hall, away from the Young Women room and around the corner. I was more tired and sad than homicidal. I should be happy to be at church. But lately what should bring me comfort often brought pain instead, and what was supposed to make sense often didn't—and that was okay with lots of people, apparently. Had something gone wrong at church? Or was something wrong with me after all?

Around the next corner we ran into my bishop. He was often there on Wednesdays, attending youth activities or meeting with ward members in his office. His pale green, paisley necktie was loose, and the top button of his white dress shirt was undone, so his meetings and interviews were probably over for the evening.

"Hello, Jenny. How are you?" His voice was warm and deep.

"Hi, Bishop." I offered a poor excuse for a smile and didn't answer his question.

He knitted his brow. "Could you use some good chocolate and a comfortable chair for a few minutes? I have something for Zeus too."

I nodded, and we followed him into his office.

49

Trust and Chocolate

Lots of kids—adults too—were nervous in the bishop's office, and you could hardly blame them. One of his roles was to hear confessions of serious sins and help people get past them. Some people said a bishop could look into your soul and see the sins you weren't confessing too.

More often he had an assignment for you, like speaking in sacrament meeting, or a job—a "calling"—in the ward organization, which you were expected to accept if you could. But to me Bishop Savage was mostly a friend, as he'd been before he was called as bishop. He and his wife were older than my parents, but they'd been friends of the family for as long as I could remember. His daughters were my favorite babysitters when I was younger, and Zeus and I had spent a lot of time at their home.

He closed his office door, and we sat in matching, comfortable wing chairs. Mom and Dad said he was the only bishop they ever saw who didn't have a desk in his office. They said he didn't want a big piece of furniture walling him off from people who came for his help.

"What troubles you tonight, my friend?"

"Not what you worry about when a girl with a boyfriend wants to see you after prom."

"I'm glad but not surprised. Should we leave the door open, so nobody thinks this is a confession?"

"I'm trying not to care what they think."

"Okay." He swung the door shut. "Milk, dark mint, or both? It's domestic, but it's Dove."

I attempted a smile. "It's a milk chocolate kind of week."

"Excellent choice." He opened a small black canister filled with Dove Promises wrapped in blue foil, took two or three for himself, and passed it to me. "Keep this handy. Sounds like you may need a few."

He turned to Zeus. "Zeus, PB&J or apple cobbler? Both from Bark and Wag, of course. I'm thinking apple cobbler. You know what to say."

This had happened enough over the years that Zeus did know what to say. He gave a single bark and waited alertly. He didn't have to wait long—just long enough for me to wonder whether any other dogs visited the bishop's office. Maybe he stocked gourmet dog treats just for Zeus.

"Now, how can I help?"

I tried to speak intelligibly with a small, thick square of heaven on my tongue. "Good chocolate helps. Listening is good."

"Sounds about right." He unwrapped a square and popped it into his mouth.

I told him what the kids at school were doing, and what Britney said after class. Then I told him about our seminary teacher and Troy's bishop. "Why can't his bishop be more like mine?" I asked. "You want to listen and help. Bishop Waldron wants to preach and judge."

"I'm sure he wants to help, and your seminary teacher too."

"Let's say you're right, Bishop. Why are you so much better at it than they are?" I put another chocolate in my mouth with less enthusiasm than it deserved. Then I remembered my manners, sort of, and squeezed a few syllables past it. "These are perfect, thank you."

A corner of his mouth turned upward. "You're welcome. I don't know about better, but I've known you and your parents longer than your seminary teacher has, and longer than Troy's bishop has known the Pullmans. And I think I have a few more years at this job than Bishop Waldron. What I'm trying to say is, bishops are just men. You know that. No matter how much help we get from other people or from heaven, and there's plenty of both, or how much we care about our people, in some ways there's no substitute for experience."

"How does experience help with this?"

"We learn to listen more and talk less. We learn not to judge any more or any sooner than we have to. Ideally, we learn to look for what's most important, beyond all the little rules we use to measure ourselves and each other. Rules are important—commandments are tremendously important—but we learn to recognize when good-hearted people are being good."

"Is that what Troy and I are doing?"

"Isn't it? And as long as you keep doing it—carefully, please—I have the luxury of worrying less about two exceptional young people."

"Thank you. What makes you think we're exceptional?" When the words were out, more chocolate went in.

"I know you. And the fact that you'll have Troy for your boyfriend tells me most of what I need to know about him. The fact that your parents are comfortable with him tells me the rest."

I nodded, and tears rolled down my cheeks. I'd been close to tears all week, and now my defenses were melting away faster than the chocolate.

I sniffled. "The kids at school are just being stupid and mean, but why do some adults at church have to make it hurt even more?"

"Well, causing you pain isn't the point, of course, but we see youth—and plenty of adults—get into serious trouble all the time without realizing how quickly it can happen. So we worry about people. Sometimes we worry too much, because we're afraid to worry too little. We're all just doing our best to help people." He balled up a wrapper and tossed it into the wastebasket. "Sometimes we're not wonderful at it."

"I guess it doesn't have to be easy." I spoke softly and carefully, trying not to whine. "But this is already a really hard week, especially for Troy, and it's only Wednesday, and I don't know how to make it better for him. It's like the adults—some of them—are convinced he's evil for loving me. Not for doing anything evil or wanting to, just for loving me. Some of the kids at school want to punish him too. Punish both of us. He thinks that's partly his fault, but it's not."

"Your parents are still comfortable with things, aren't they?" he asked.

"They love him almost as much as I do. They trust him. He works hard at that. They trust me too. Which isn't to say they aren't vigilant. And we don't hide things from them."

"How about his parents?"

"More or less the same, so far, but Troy's afraid his bishop will make them worry after yesterday." I picked the foil from another chocolate. "I'm afraid of that too."

"I like that you talk to your parents."

"We're trying to be good," I said. "We've never done this before, and we know we could use some help. Right now, though, I just wish I knew how to make Troy's week a little better. You don't have to know either, but if you have any ideas, I'd love to hear them."

In went the chocolate.

He thought for a moment, then spoke carefully. "In Troy's shoes . . . if I knew you loved me . . . if I knew you'd still love me and stick with me even when things are difficult . . . that would count for a lot."

I knew a good idea when I heard it. I even smiled a little. "Finally something I can do. I'll make sure he doesn't forget. But I won't do anything to worry my bishop or my parents. Or his."

"Atta girl. Want me to talk to Brother Stickinger? Seminary teachers usually take bishops seriously, given that we have actual authority in the Church, and they don't."

"If you think it'll help, that would be great. I'm surprised he hasn't called you with grave concerns about the welfare of my eternal soul."

He smiled. "How do you think I remember his name?"

"Oh, no. Really? May I ask what you told him? I think I know what he told you." I picked up one more chocolate.

"I thanked him for his concern. I said I've known you and your family a long time, and you and I talk a lot, and I'm keeping an eye on you. I told him I trust your goodness, your strength, your intelligence, your judgment, and your parents."

I began to sob—with relief and gratitude and probably some other things. My writer's brain searched for a way to describe the feeling.

His trust was a tall glass of ice-cold lemonade for a girl baking in the desert heat. It was a thick, soft blanket to relieve my hypothermia. It was the warm, gentle summer rain after the thundering bluster of the arriving storm.

That one, I thought wryly. The one with water dripping.

He pushed a box of tissues toward me on the accent table between our chairs. "I didn't mean to make you cry." He smiled gently.

It took me a minute to compose myself, but he was patient. The wrapped chocolate stayed in my hand.

When I could, I said, "Thanks for trusting me. That's what made me cry." I took a deep, unsteady breath. "What will you tell Brother Stickinger this time?"

"How about sending me a copy of your talk from the other Sunday? I've been wanting one anyway, and I'll forward it to him, maybe tell him he might be underestimating you. You should unwrap that before it melts. Maybe he'll start to understand you. It was powerful."

I nodded. "I'll send it tonight. Thank you."

He smiled. "Don't expect too much. He'll probably still think I'm naïve and not zealous enough in protecting my youth. That was pretty obvious between the lines when we talked before. But he can think what he wants. I don't answer to him. Neither do you. Not for this."

I put the chocolate in my mouth, and he ate another piece too. We sat in chocolatey silence for a minute.

"He's not a bad teacher," I said. "He's pretty good. He's just wrong about Troy and me, and I don't think he's capable of realizing that."

The bishop grinned. "I should tell him about calling you that Friday night to ask you to speak. That was classic. But he'd probably just worry more—about both of us. Ready for another one, Zeus?"

He tossed Zeus the treat which had somehow appeared in his hand.

"How come I can talk to you like that, and you still believe I'm a good person, and I'm going to behave myself?"

"I don't know. But talk to me any way you want, as long as you talk to me."

I remembered Troy saying I should be whatever I wanted, as long as it was with him, and I wanted to cry again. I managed to hold back my tears for the moment.

I took one more chocolate, then pushed the container toward him. "You should keep these away from me until next time."

He grinned again. "I'm glad we're friends enough to talk without standing on ceremony. It's nice for a bishop to have people around who still do that. And you know what? You'll figure out how to help Troy."

"What makes you so sure?"

"Because you love him, and that's what love does."

That started the tears again. "I know it really wants to."

He just nodded.

"I'm sorry I'm such a mess," I said. "I'm using all your tissues."

"Have you heard my standard response to that?" he asked.

"Have I ever cried in here before?"

"Maybe not. Anyway, the box isn't here for me. I'm a cold-hearted, dry-eyed bishop."

"No, you're not. But you are generous. Thanks for letting me eat too much of your chocolate."

"You're not feeling ill from it, are you?" he asked.

"No."

"Then it wasn't too much. And you're welcome."

We both stood. "Thanks for listening," I said. "And talking. And trusting me. And us. You're not allowed to hug me, are you?"

"It's discouraged," he said.

"But sometimes you can't avoid people hugging you?"

"That's true. Last week, it was in a grocery store, and I don't think that sister's fiancé was too pleased. Not that he had anything to worry about."

"I don't have a fiancé, just a really good bishop." I hugged him quickly and said good night.

"Tell Troy I said hello. Tell him thanks for being so good to our Jenny," he said. "I want to meet him."

At home I texted Troy. "My bishop isn't like yours. Sorry if I'm gloating. He reminds me of you. He saw me looking sad tonight, and we talked in his office, while he fed us chocolate and gourmet dog treats. Chocolate for him and me, dog treats for Zeus.

"The big thing is, I love you. Especially this week. Next week too, and so on. Also, my bishop sends his best and thanks you for 'being so good to our Jenny.' Your Jenny thanks you too, with additional punctuation. At least the desire for additional, in-person punctuation."

It was just before 10:00 p.m. when he replied. He sent back "<3"—which was supposed to be a heart, I knew, but I always thought it looked like puckered lips. That worked too.

"Are you okay?" I asked.

"I have you."

"Yes, you do."

We said good night.

50

Storm Warning

Our last high school choir concert of the year was Thursday evening. Mom and Dad went to a meeting late, so they could hear my women's choir and the first piece or two by Troy's men's choir.

On another evening they might have sat with Troy's family near the front, and that might have been good. Instead they sat where they could slip out easily. From the brightly lit stage I couldn't tell which dark, parental shapes near the back belonged to me, but I saw Nan and Lily waving enthusiastically from the third row. I smiled but didn't wave. We weren't supposed to do that on stage.

Nikki was somewhere in the audience too. Jack was in the choir room with Zeus, warming up her oboe to accompany one of the men's numbers. After my choir finished, I picked him up and took a minute to check my phone. I had eight text messages.

Mom and Dad both said my choir was excellent. Also, would I please make sure all the windows were closed when I got home? A storm was coming.

A message from Nan had more emojis than words, plus a fond hello from Lily to Zeus.

One message was from Nikki. "Your choir was great, but the guys should sing every week. I'm halfway to Zany Fangirl, and they're not even on the stage yet."

Jack's text warned that my boyfriend was backstage, e-flirting with some cute second soprano he knew.

It was true. I had three flirty messages from him. Which pretty much made it my favorite concert intermission ever.

"I hope someone back there flirted with Jack," I whispered to Zeus as I turned off my phone. "She deserves it."

Troy and I left the school together well before 9:00 p.m. I hoped to go out somewhere, but his parents needed him at home. They hadn't said for what.

"You're due for a happy surprise," I said as we drove out of the lot.

"Hope you're right," he said. "Rather spend the next 74 minutes with you."

It hurt to ask, but I did anyway. "Are they trying to keep us apart?"

"They're fine with me taking you home. They said 9:15 is soon enough to be back."

"Okay. Still want to go to the dance tomorrow?"

He kept his eyes on the road. "Tell you what. I'll take you to the dance, if I can kiss you good night in a minute."

"In a minute, for a minute—but you have to kiss me tomorrow too. And you can't come in tonight, unless Mom and Dad are already home."

"Have to get home anyway. For my happy surprise," he said drily.

"Here's a happy thought for you. Mom and Dad went to their literacy committee meeting late, so they could hear my choir. That's parents being parents. But they went even later, so they could hear some of your choir too. I think they like you."

We were stopped at a red light when the storm front arrived. A wall of dust and litter blew toward the car, then surrounded it. I felt the wind rocking us.

In my driveway Troy let Zeus out of the back before he opened my door, because Zeus had fur and I had bare arms and a knee-length skirt. Then he wrapped me in his suitcoat for the short walk to the shelter of my front porch. He insisted I keep it on while we said goodbye. I insisted his arms go around me inside the coat, not outside. There was plenty of room.

"There's something else you could do for me tonight," I said.

"Name it."

"Before our phones turn into pumpkins at 10:00, send me a text or two. I'm sure you can find something to say."

"If my happy surprise is still going at 9:45, I'll take a break and tell you about it."

"Perfect. I'll wait by the smart phone."

It wasn't happy, and it wasn't that much of a surprise. His parents sat him down for a serious chat—about us. They were officially worried.

They said they didn't want to forbid him to see me, because they thought highly of me, and they knew we liked each other. I wanted to roll my eyes at that, when he told me. They knew we were well beyond just liking each other, or they wouldn't have worried.

Troy decided he had to be forceful, in case their talk about not breaking us up was intended to make what they'd say next look reasonable and lenient by comparison. When they said they were growing concerned about how much time we spent together, but they didn't think we were doing anything physical that we shouldn't, he went on the offensive.

"So you're worried that I spend too much time doing nothing wrong with a very good girl?" He should have stopped there, he told me, but then he asked them too heatedly, "How does that even make sense? Look around. You're the smart parents."

Troy's dad said he didn't care for the tone or the attitude. His mom said, if he'd talked to Bishop Waldron that way, they didn't like that either.

Troy apologized. He told them he was having a rotten week and asked if they could talk about things in a few days. He promised not to misbehave with me in the meantime.

They agreed to postpone the discussion, which I thought was kind of them.

I learned all this in a string of long, painful messages, which Troy started early but ended obediently at 10 p.m. I knew he didn't mean the last message to upset me, but it did.

"Out of time. I love you. I'm sorry people are like this about us, especially my parents now, and I'm sorry it's partly my fault. I'm so sick of this. Anyway, good night, beautiful Jenny. I'll try to be happier tomorrow. Sleep usually helps."

I couldn't sleep after that. I sat in my favorite chair and tried to figure out how two high school kids could love each other and behave themselves and not turn people against them. The question was too big for my tired brain.

I tried not to think about how being my boyfriend had become such a miserable experience for Troy. I failed at that too. Five words echoed in my mind: "I'm so sick of this."

I finally went to bed, but I still didn't sleep.

It was so unfair. I thought of the feud in *Romeo and Juliet*, and the ending. Our plight wasn't that grim. Was that why we studied that play in junior high? For later, when we'd need perspective? We weren't tragic yet, but it was bad enough. What if we really were out of time, not just for one evening?

What were we supposed to do? Never meet in the first place? The same church whose leaders and teachers thought we were flirting with evil had also sponsored the dance where we met the second time—and danced for the first time, and started to get seriously attached to each other.

Should we have run in opposite directions as soon as we knew we liked each other, to avoid the risk of falling in love?

I could never have run from Troy, not just because he was an athlete and I wasn't. Besides, it didn't make sense to avoid a boy I liked just because I liked him, or date only boys I didn't like, or date them only until I liked them. But wasn't that what their rules added up to? At least for girls like me?

They kept saying dating was important, so we could get to know people and develop our social skills. But liking someone enough to date him more than once or twice? That was reckless. Foolish. Disobedient. Selfish. Wrong. It was Not Following the Prophet—even if the prophet didn't know me personally or my social life.

And whose bishop was right? Mine or Troy's? I knew which one we liked, but weren't they supposed to be guided by the same God?

And what about Troy's parents? We'd done nothing to betray their trust. Now they worried that we weren't safe together? That was even less fair to him than to me, because they knew him better.

Would they tell him to stop seeing me? Parents sometimes told you they didn't want to do something, right before they did it.

What would he do then? Obey them, no matter how much he didn't want to? That would be right, wouldn't it? "Children, obey your parents, for this is right." That's what the Bible said. It sounded a lot like a commandment.

Would we try to see each other secretly? How long could we keep that from our parents? A month? A week? Half an hour? And how much worse would everything be when they caught us? Did they think it was wise to leave sneaking around as the most attractive alternative to having our hearts ripped out?

If his parents tried to break us up, my parents—and my bishop, if I asked him—would tell me I should respect that, and so should Troy. They'd have to say that. Would I have to do it?

What if his parents allowed us to see each other, say, once a month, if we each went out with someone else in between?

That wouldn't be fair to our other dates, and besides, I would just die. Probably not literally, but what could I do?

I could spend half my time trying not to cry and the other half trying to stop crying. That's what I could do.

51

Not Breaking Up

I SHOULD BE CRYING a lot, I reasoned, if I wanted to do things right. Because I was taught to be good. Allowed to be good. Expected to be good. I was bad if I wasn't good. I just wasn't allowed to be happy—not if it involved falling in love and behaving myself with a boy. Being happy was evil in some way I couldn't comprehend, and crying my eyes out was good. That was what the Church's rules added up to.

Which pretty much made Maddi the Arm of the Lord. She was doing God's work by punishing us for being together. That wasn't quite what Troy's bishop had said, but almost.

If that was true, then the people who were supposed to help us learn about God and follow him, who should know more about God than we did, because they were called to be our leaders and teachers—many of them were on Maddi's side, and she was on theirs.

She was a dirty-minded, vicious, lying . . . I wouldn't use that word, even alone in my room . . . who laughed when her friend flipped me off.

If it weren't for my parents and my bishop . . .

And Troy. If it weren't for Troy . . .

Was I overreacting? Was I too defensive?

Maybe not. I wasn't just defending myself. I was defending him and our relationship. Maybe our future. I was defending something good against people who thought it was evil and wanted it to go away.

Happiness was supposed to be the blessing God sent you for being good, not something you couldn't have, because you were good.

The angels God sent to help push your handcart weren't supposed to knock you down when you tried to inch forward, and drag you backward and call you wicked, then chop up your handcart with an ax and build a bonfire from the pieces. Unless they weren't angels after all.

Maddi was no angel. She was the opposite.

Troy's parents were more like angels, but which way would they go, when they had their serious talk with their son?

I'd forgotten to pray before getting in bed, to thank God for lots of blessings and ask for a few I really wanted, like I usually did at both ends of the day. Good girls prayed every morning and night and sometimes in between. And I was a good girl. Except for loving Troy.

"So, Father in Heaven," I said softly in God's general direction—because you didn't have to kneel to pray, and you certainly didn't have to be loud. "This is a big, painful mess. Is this the part where I'm supposed to be grateful? If so, thanks a lot." God wanted sincere prayers, after all, and he had to understand sarcasm. And my sarcasm was nothing if not sincere.

I fell silent, while I decided how snarky to get with the Lord God of the Whole Fouled-up Universe. I wanted to say, "You're going to fix this, because it really is good. You can do that if you want to, right? Because you're God? Do it soon."

"Because thou art God," I said aloud, correcting my prayer grammar in a caustic tone my earthly parents wouldn't have liked. "Thou canst, if thou wilt." I liked how harsh I could make the consonants in "canst" and "wilt." I was practically snarling.

I wanted to fire off some acid thoughts about a universe where being good was supposed to make us happy, but being happy was somehow wrong. And about God's Church, where people who were supposed to represent him took sides with lying weasels like Maddi.

"Okay," I continued aloud. "Let's pretend thou knowest not what I've been thinking and feeling, so I actually need to ask this. Do you get—*dost thou get*—that I'm trying to be good? That Troy and I are behaving ourselves? That we make each other happy? That my reward for obedience is that I, a supposedly beloved daughter of God, am lying here, crying my eyes out in the middle of a school night? And Troy's reward is to be miserable too, but probably drier?

"You're omniscient, right? I mean, thou art omniscient. So tell me, please: what's wrong with this picture?"

I gave up on my prayer after that. Then I gave up on thinking altogether and just cried. I didn't notice God sending any comfort—not that

I deserved or expected any, after what I'd said. I hadn't asked for any. But that was okay. I eventually fell asleep anyway.

⸺◦⸺

I was so tired and so late when I awoke the next morning that I forgot to say my morning prayer. I threw on some clothes, took my meds, brushed my teeth for half a minute and my hair for less than that, and presented myself at the front door just in time for Mom to take me to school on her way to work. She'd helpfully fed and watered Zeus for me.

I tried to concentrate in my classes, but I could barely stay awake. Even worrying was difficult, but I managed. My evening with Troy couldn't come soon enough.

When evening finally came, our dance was at the church where Troy's ward met, but his bishop was nowhere to be seen. That was probably good.

It wasn't a couples' dance, but we stuck together. I wondered silently whether we could have done that, if Troy's parents had already finished their discussion with him and settled on new ways to keep us safe from each other and ease their troubled minds.

He was tired too, and the music was too loud. We talked less than usual. We danced a few times, but mostly we were just together. It was harder for me to be sad and discouraged when I was with him. I hoped that worked both ways.

We got through the first hour before my worries took over. After a slow dance I said, "I really just want to sit with you and talk. I wish they'd turn down the music."

He nodded. "Maybe there's someplace quieter."

Soon we were at the other end of the building, where there were padded chairs in a small foyer outside Troy's bishop's office. No one else had wandered that far, or if they had, the chaperones had herded them back to the dance.

Troy went out the nearest door into the wind to check for a light in the bishop's window. No light, no bishop, so we pulled two chairs together. Maybe, if the patrolling chaperones saw we weren't making out, they wouldn't mind us sitting for a while.

His arm was firm around me, my head was on his shoulder, and he leaned his head on mine. It should have been comforting, but he was tense, and I was nervous. I knew how this conversation would start, because I was about to start it, but not how it would end. It didn't have to end happily.

"You know how I said I wanted to dance, but not like everyone else?" I sounded grave. "And thanks to you, we've actually waltzed?"

"Yeah." I felt him nod.

"May I tell you what I want now?"

"Please."

That one strained, anxious word made me want to stop and find out what was going on in his head, but I needed to tell him what was happening in mine. I snuggled closer.

"I want to have a relationship with you. Keep having one. I want to spend lots of time with you, and talk and listen and hold hands, and kiss you sometimes. More than sometimes, but you know. I want to tell you I love you, because I do. And I don't want it to end."

"I want that too. But?" He sounded more resigned than curious.

"I don't want to be possessive and suspicious, or flirt with other boys to make you jealous. I don't want either of us thinking we have to prove our love by doing something wrong and stupid. We won't do that, I know.

"I don't want to worry or scare or deceive our parents. I want people at church to trust us too, but I don't know how much that's even possible.

"I don't want to mess up your mission or your life, or my life, by making really big mistakes with you. I don't want to set a bad example for your little sisters or anyone else. I want us to be safe, and I want us to behave, even when we're weak or tired or just really attracted to each other." I took a deep breath. "I know I can't always have everything I want, but that's what I want."

He was silent. And still tense. And maybe athletes didn't need to breathe as much as the rest of us.

"You're a wonderful listener, but I can listen too."

"Okay," he said. His voice was higher-pitched than usual. "I love you, and I want everything you just said, and I don't want the same things you don't want. You know that, right?"

"I do know that."

Then he told me what was going on in his head.

"Jenny, are you breaking up with me?"

His words turned me cold. "No! How could . . . I just . . . No!" I reached for his free hand. "I just want us to figure out how this will work, because it's not working very well this week."

He gently pulled his hand from mine, which frightened me, but then he pulled me close and wrapped me in both arms instead of one. He let out a long breath, while I tried to remember anything I'd said or done that could have been the prelude to a breakup.

"Jenny, I was af—"

He stopped. I pulled away just enough to see his eyes.

They were wide with distress. "I was so . . ." Finally he relaxed and pressed my head to his shoulder.

"It's a bad week," he said. He took another deep breath, and his voice sounded steadier. "You got it from Young Women again. I got it from my bishop again, then my parents." Another pause. "And we won't talk about Maddi, even if I just did. Sorry. I'm sure your parents are—"

"Vigilant?" I said.

"Yeah."

"Yet here we are, after all that," I said. "Still together. I still love you, and I'm pretty sure you still love me."

"I do."

"I know."

We sat in silence, but it was more comfortable now. Being in his arms was enough to calm my frazzled mind for a minute.

Then a thought struck—without warning and with devastating clarity. It wasn't all that different from what I'd thought the night before, but it stunned me.

It was simple. *If we lose our parents, this is over.*

52

Scared

"**J**ENNY, ARE YOU OKAY?"

I wasn't. If Troy's parents decided we shouldn't see each other, we were done. The thought was unbearable.

"I'm sorry. I have to think a minute."

"Think about what?" Troy asked.

"Please, I have to think." Tears were pooling, and I sounded distraught, even to myself.

He started to say something, then stopped. I pushed myself upright and moved forward in my chair. Only one of his arms could reach me there. That one slipped down to my waist.

I closed my eyes, clasped my hands tightly in my lap, and tried to convince myself that our peril might not be as dire or immediate as it felt. All I could think—I wanted to scream it down the empty hall—was that this was completely unfair. We didn't deserve this pain.

He took his hand from my waist and reached for my hand, but I instinctively grabbed his wrist and held it away. I needed to focus.

In the instant I felt his arm relax, I realized what I'd done to him. I had to undo it. I let go of his wrist, interlaced my fingers with his, pulled his hand to my lap, clung to it with both my hands—and then tried to focus. I still couldn't.

I opened my eyes and found his. I needed to see strength or at least clarity. I saw worry and confusion turning to fear, but I couldn't blame him. My own eyes had nothing good to offer him, just exhaustion, distress, and hot tears.

He shifted in his chair, turning toward me, and brushed a few tears from my cheek with the hand I wasn't squeezing. "What just happened?" he whispered hoarsely. "Please tell me."

I hesitated, then nodded quickly and swiped at the next few tears. "I'll try." I reached for his free hand and clung to it too.

"Are we okay?" he asked cautiously.

"I don't know. I want us to be okay."

He seemed to deflate. "Whatever it is, please just tell me." The resignation in his voice nearly broke my heart.

I sniffed, sniffed again, and began. "Last night, after we texted, I was tired and upset, a lot like I am now. My thoughts about us were all over the place. They didn't all make sense, and I wasn't connecting things very well. What just happened, I think, is . . . I finally connected some things."

"I don't understand," he said softly.

"I love you, but I'm scared."

"So am I, but what could you be thinking that's so terrible?"

"It adds up to this," I said in a high-pitched voice that upset me even more, when I heard it, and probably didn't do him any good. "We can't do this without our parents. If they're against us. Yours or mine. Without them we're done."

"That's it?" He sounded puzzled and wary—which I preferred to hopeless resignation, at least.

"Think it through for me. Please? Aloud? See if you come to the same conclusion."

"Okay."

He just stared at me, saying nothing.

"You're not thinking out loud."

"Sorry. Um . . . we mostly worry about keeping one commandment, the obvious one, but there are others. We can't disobey our parents, and we can't lie, especially to them."

He took a deep breath. "So if our parents—probably mine—insist that we stop seeing each other, that's it, isn't it? Done. Over."

"I think so," I said. "Maybe not forever, but . . ."

"What would we do?" he asked. "Break up and try to forget? I couldn't forget you. Wait until we're both eighteen and they can't stop us, or they change their minds or give in? That would be torture. We could try to sneak around, or maybe just rebel, but it couldn't work for very long." He reached up and brushed away a few more of my tears. "Don't know what that leaves that we could do."

I couldn't stop weeping, and I didn't try. "I don't either. What if they—"

I couldn't say it.

He pulled me close again, but I was too upset to enjoy it.

"You scared me half to death," he said. "First I thought you were having some new kind of seizure. Then you . . . Do you have any idea what happens to me, when I see you cry? Then I was afraid you were breaking up with me after all. I'm still not entirely sure you're not."

"I'm not." I sniffled. "Please believe me."

"Okay, I believe you. But you're right. This doesn't work without our parents."

I felt him take another long, deep breath. When he spoke, his voice was almost normal.

"So we can't lose my parents. Or yours. And maybe we don't have to. I think they want to trust us, as much as they can."

"You know your mom and dad better than I do. What can we do?"

"If I had an idea about that this week, it would probably be a disaster like all the rest."

"I have the beginning of a thought," I said after a moment. "I'm not sure where it leads. I can't think calmly about this." I looked up at him. "I'm not . . . I can't be objective about you. Or dispassionate, or whatever the word is. Not that you ever wanted that."

Troy's mild, slightly crooked smile made me feel a little better. "Nope. Just tell me when you're ready. In the meantime we're safe, at least for now. For tonight."

He kissed me on the forehead, then guided my head back to his shoulder and held it there, while his other arm tightened around my waist. It took a minute, but I really did start to feel safer.

He kissed the top of my head.

"I like that," I murmured. "Here's what I think I'm thinking. Obviously it's not enough anymore that we've always been the good boy and the good girl. It's not enough that they know we know the rules, or that they believe we want to be good. It's not enough that you're serious about a mission, or that I want it for you too, which I do. Right now I'm not sure why. But they know me well enough to believe we both want that, right?"

"Think so. What would be enough?"

"That's the question, isn't it? They're not worried about us not knowing what we shouldn't do. Did I say that right? Thinking is really hard right now. They're worried that we'll do things we already know are wrong. So we have to help them be confident that we'll make the right decisions, when only God is watching. Am I making any sense?"

"Yeah. Am I holding you tightly enough?"

He couldn't see it, but I smiled weakly. "Almost."

He held me a little more tightly. I felt a little safer.

"Thank you," I said. "There's . . . there's a connection they have to trust us to make, between what we know and what we do. So how can we help them trust us? Actually, there's another connection, between what we do and what we want."

"Okay, I get the first one," he said. "Maybe we sit down with them and talk about commandments and rules, so they can see that we get it. Then we turn that into our own set of, I don't know, not too many rules, but enough. We have most of them already, and maybe we add a few. We put it all in writing, because they'll like that. Then we agree to obey the rules, and they agree to trust us."

"I like it," I said. "And we do whatever else we can to help them trust us together."

"Yeah. What was the second thing? What we want and . . . what?"

For once my thoughts fell neatly in line. "They have to know what we want, and how much we want it. Maybe they already do. They also have to know that we see the connection between our choices and getting what we want, and we don't expect the blessings from making good decisions unless we actually make good decisions.

"Sorry. Say that last part again?"

"I'll try different words. They have to believe we're grown up enough not to think it's okay to fool around now and repent later."

My tears had stopped. My voice and my heart were calmer. There was something about trying to solve a problem that was less scary than just knowing it was there and realizing how bad it could get. There was something about having Troy wrapped around me too.

"You're a very smart girlfriend," he said.

I looked up. "I'm a very motivated girlfriend."

My calm was thin and fragile, and it didn't last. I was still looking up at him when my chin began to tremble. What if it didn't work? What if nothing worked? What could we do?

He took my face in his hands. He wiped new tears from my cheeks with his thumbs, then leaned toward me, bent my head gently toward him, and kissed me lightly on the forehead. Then we were eye to eye again, and his were full of tenderness, which now seemed mixed with strength. He watched patiently while I drank it in. At least that's how it felt to me. At just the right moment he reached down and forward, until his lips barely touched mine—and he stopped. Only his breath on my skin marked the passing moments.

His lips moved ever so slightly to kiss mine. Mine answered reflexively.

It was like no kiss we'd every shared, and none I'd ever imagined. It lasted only an instant. It was barely a kiss at all—but it planted a seed of peace and sparked a new flicker of hope.

Then we were eye to eye again, and he moved his hands to my shoulders. He didn't smile or frown, but his expression wasn't neutral, and his quiet voice was everything I needed it to be.

"We'll tell them what we want. How much we want it. We'll tell them we know we have to do it right, and we're not looking for shortcuts."

I took a long, unsteady breath. My cheeks wanted his hands back, but my shoulders liked them too. Why couldn't the boy have four hands?

"It might work," he said.

I found myself nodding. "It has to work."

He pulled me to him and wrapped me in his arms again, and for a while we just breathed.

When I was calmer, I nuzzled his neck, took a deep breath, and resumed thinking out loud. "We've done really well at being in love without getting in trouble," I said. "Now we have to convince them we'll keep doing well, so they don't have to worry so much, even when some busybody Church leaders do. They'll probably worry anyway. They're parents. But if we talk through it with them, and it makes sense, and they see that we're serious, and our actions match our words, maybe they won't think we've just gotten lucky so far." I smiled sheepishly into his shirt collar. "That's probably the wrong way to say it."

He chuckled. "You think? Okay, we have work to do. Dad's back Monday, so we have at least a couple of days. I can probably put them off until next weekend, if we have to. Should we start preparing tonight?"

He sounded eager, but I was too tired for eager. I snuggled closer, and he held me more tightly.

"Tonight," I murmured, "could we just sit a while longer and maybe dance a couple more times, then go home early? I'm exhausted. Oh, and you should do your wallflower project."

"That's a team sport, and I'm the only one here. But the rest of it sounds good." He hesitated. "Maybe it doesn't make sense, but I really was afraid you were breaking up with me."

Hearing about a breakup again, even if it wasn't happening, started me unraveling again.

"Troy, no! I've just never done this before. I wasn't sure I ever would. I mean, I wanted to, but what boy wants to fall in love with a girl who sits all the time and has to have a seizure dog? I'm not fishing for a compliment. That's what I thought sometimes."

"I know it's a rhetorical question," he said. "May I answer anyway?"

"You are the answer. And I'm mostly past that now. But I'm also sixteen, which used to sound old, and now it feels very, very young."

"Yeah. Seventeen too." He kissed the top of my head. "We'll figure it out. Thanks for giving me hope."

"I give you hope?"

"Yup. Kind of been needing that. Want to go back to the dance?"

"This is nice."

"You're very tired."

"Last night was so bad. I tried to cry myself to sleep, but the sleep part didn't work very well."

He reached up and stroked my cheek with the back of his fingers. I turned and kissed them. He held them there, and I kissed them again, then turned back, so he could continue with my cheek. I moaned softly and closed my eyes.

"Honey?" I said after minute. I'd never called him that before.

After the slightest pause, he said, "Yeah?" It was more a sigh than a word.

"Thank you."

"For what?"

"Everything."

"You're welcome," he said. "You cried yourself to sleep last night?"

"Cried, yes. To sleep, not so much. Not right away."

"That's on me. I'm sorry."

"You're not the one I blamed. Can you imagine me getting outrageously snarky in my prayer last night, about how unfair everything has been lately?"

"No. Really?"

"I owe God an apology."

He chuckled.

"I'm not joking. I was obnoxious and sarcastic. I was mean."

"I believe you."

"You laughed."

"That's because most people see you and think you're quiet and shy, but I get to know the Jenny who rails on God—then apologizes next time, because you're just good, and he doesn't have to send a lightning bolt or anything."

I couldn't process all that. I was having a different thought about God.

"Honey?" I said. "Is it okay if I call you that?"

"I like it."

"Honey . . . do you think God sent me you?"

He was silent and still.

"I've been thanking him like he did," I added.

"I've been thanking him for sending you," he said.

Something clicked inside, and I started to believe, not just hope, that this was more than an everyday high school romance we really liked. There was something special about Troy and me together.

I didn't know the future, whether we would last or for how long, or what we'd choose, if someday we could choose forever together. Just because God sent us to bless each other's lives for a while didn't mean forever would happen for us. I wasn't sure what it all meant, except that we should do all the good we could for each other, while we could.

And one other obvious thing.

"I need to be stop being snarky with God," I said. "I need to be more grateful."

"Might be less entertaining for God. But yeah, grateful beats snarky."

"Would you tell me your answer? To my rhetorical question? You wanted to answer."

"Ask me again."

I opened my eyes and looked up. "Who wants to fall in love with a girl who sits all the time and has to have a seizure dog?"

He smiled, and it was a big one. "Any guy who ever looks into her eyes and sees her smile will want to fall in love with her."

Which is what happened to Troy right then—looking into my eyes and seeing me smile. That other thing had already happened.

"I have another question, if you don't mind," I said. "I was afraid to ask it before, but I think I can bear the answer now. At some point this week, did you consider breaking up with me?"

He was silent and his eyes looked pained. I wondered if that was my answer. If so, it still felt okay—which was practically a miracle.

"Is that a yes?" I asked.

53

Still Not Breaking Up

"**I**T'S NOT THAT SIMPLE," Troy said. "I never wanted to break up with you. That's the last thing I want. This week, and a long time before this week."

"What part isn't simple?" I asked.

"I kept thinking about everything I did to you. Opened my big mouth and made Maddi want to spread an ugly rumor about us. Sort of gave her the idea for the rumor. Got angry and tripped some alarms in my bishop's head, so he got my parents worried too. I don't even know which of those is worse. You deserve better than I've been this week."

Before I could find a loving way to tell him how ridiculous that last part was, he continued. "Wednesday, while you were at Young Women and talking to your bishop, I was wondering if I should offer to break up with you. In case you were tired of suffering for my mistakes."

I should have been bitter and hurt, or at least puzzled and concerned. An hour earlier I might have been devastated. But now it really was okay—which he needed to feel, not just hear. I pulled him to me and took care to speak gently, almost casually.

"Did you think that would be noble or chivalrous or something? Did you think I wanted to break up? Was I going to have a choice?"

"Sounds pretty stupid now," he said, "but yeah, for a while I was afraid you might want that. Pretty grim for an hour or two. Sorry I doubted you."

"You doubted yourself, and some of it splashed on me. It's okay, honey."

"I'm still sorry. I love you."

"That better be two sentences, not one," I quipped darkly.

"What? Oh. Definitely two."

"I know. I was trying to be clever. What made you decide not to offer heroically to break both our hearts?"

He just breathed.

"It's okay," I said. "It really is. I just want to understand. I know you love me. It's okay."

"I couldn't do it. Can't imagine tomorrow without you, let alone next week or next year. When you texted me that night, you said you love me—especially this week. That helped a lot. Thought maybe you weren't as upset with me as I was, so maybe I hadn't hurt you as much as I thought. Thanks for saying that. Really needed it that night."

I began to weep. They were completely different tears, but he didn't know that yet.

"I'm sorry," he said, and his voice broke.

Then I was kissing him, and it wasn't gentle or fleeting. It was a good thing there were no chaperones watching.

I pulled away just far enough to talk. "This isn't a thing to be sorry about," I said. "Let me explain."

I told him how Bishop Savage gave me the idea to tell him what I texted him that night. Then I said, "So maybe that was God blessing me with you again. Or still."

He leaned forward, so our foreheads were touching.

"It was God blessing me with you," he whispered.

I still needed to explain. "What you need to know is, these are happy tears now."

For a while he just held me. The front of his shirt didn't get completely soaked. And I enjoyed feeling him breathe.

Then I was waking, sort of, to hear my name.

"Jenny?" He seemed distant, though we hadn't moved. "Pretty Jenny, you awake?"

"Uh, what? Um . . . yes. I don't know. What was the question?"

He chuckled. "You awake now?"

"Oh, right. Was I snoring?"

"Honest answer?"

"Only if it's no."

"You were a beautiful, non-snoring angel."

"That's nice." I took a deep breath and tried to be conscious. "Sorry I fell asleep on you again. You're not boring. You're very comfortable. My very comfortable boyfriend."

"Best words in that speech are 'my' and 'boyfriend.' What if we don't go back to the dance?"

"Whatever you want is fine."

He read my mind. "We'll have other dances," he said. "Let's get you home. If you get any less conscious, I'll have to carry you. Which I could do."

"Didn't you offer that, the night we met?"

"Yeah, but carrying you onto the dance floor is easier than carrying you down the hall, out the door, down the steps, and across the parking lot. Mostly afraid I'd hurt you, stuffing you into the car. And it wouldn't look good."

We were both enjoying this. "I'll try to walk. But you steer. I may have my eyes closed. And I need a minute."

While I inched toward wakefulness, he said, "We had company. Didn't want to wake you."

"Friends, enemies, chaperones?"

"Chaperones."

"Good thing they didn't see us sooner. They didn't insist we go back to the dance?"

"No. It was the Langers. Pretty cool for being in their seventies. They live around the corner from me. Dad and I are their home teachers. They caught me shoveling their walk a few times this winter, and they say they like my lessons, when it's my turn to teach every other month."

I covered a yawn. "Friends, then. Excuse me. What did they say?"

"They were told not to let kids wander around the building or sit in dark corners and make out. But we weren't wandering, and this corner isn't dark, and we weren't making out, so they figured we were okay."

"We like the Langers."

"Told them we were escaping the volume in there, and we'll probably go home soon. They said to drive safely."

"Okay, if they insist." I yawned mightily and stretched—elbows up, back arched, fingers laced behind my head. At first I had my eyes closed, which was easier than keeping them open.

I was still stretching when I opened them and saw him watching me. He wasn't looking me in the eye.

The fog in my head lifted a little. I realized I was displaying my figure in all its questionable glory—while he watched with an appreciative smile.

I slowly relaxed and lowered my arms. My cheeks only warmed a little—and not from embarrassment. I was thrilled that he liked what he saw.

His eyes met mine. "You're beautiful," he whispered.

My smile felt intimate, not shy. For a moment, neither of us said a word.

My eyes left his for an instant to look past him, down the hall. "I guess we should go."

He nodded, then stood and offered me his hand. On the way out we stopped inside the doors to watch the blowing snow. We'd left our coats in the car. He stood behind me with his arms around me.

"I'll pull the car up and bring your coat in. In a minute or two."

A thought filled my mind, not about cars or coats. "I'll walk out with you. But thank you."

"Bit of a hike, and it's nasty out there."

I turned, put my arms around him below his shoulders, and rested my head on his chest. "Here's what I need you to remember. I'd rather face a lot more of the storm beside you than a lot less of it anywhere else."

His arms tightened around me. "Jenny, I think that's my favorite thing you ever said to me."

I couldn't hold him any more tightly, which was kind of a pity, but I tried.

"And I really do like it when you call me honey," he said.

"Not too old-fashioned?"

"Nope. From Texas, remember? In the South everybody's honey."

"We're in the West," I said.

"Where we save it for the ones we love?"

I loosened my grip and leaned away, so I could look into his eyes and put my arms around his neck. "Troy's my honey. Life is sweet." I stood on tiptoe and pulled him down to me. It was all I could do to stop at one short kiss.

I fell asleep again on the way home. He woke me with another kiss.

Our early arrival worried my parents. We'd been sitting in the living room for only a minute, when they came downstairs.

"Is everything okay, you two? Jenny, are you all right?" Mom asked in the calm voice she used when everything wasn't all right. "Troy?"

I nodded—without moving my head from his shoulder or opening my eyes, but I nodded.

He said, "We're fine, ma'am. Just left early. She's exhausted. Not much sleep last night, I think."

"As long as you're both okay," Dad said. "How was the dance, Troy?"

"Too loud, but no complaints about the company, sir."

"Glad to hear it. Thanks for bringing her home." I heard a smile in his voice. "First time you've put her to sleep?"

"I'm not asleep, Daddy. I'm listening with my eyes closed." I sat up slowly, then stood. Slowly.

I reached for Troy. "I'll walk you out. We won't be hurrying."

He said goodnight to my parents, and they left us alone. At the door I kissed him, but by then I really wanted another hug. That was next.

"Thank you for tonight," I said. "I really do love you."

"I love you too."

"Especially this week?" I asked hopefully.

"More than last week. Less than next week."

"Happy Jenny."

"Best kind."

I looked at him seriously. "This has to work. Whatever we do has to work."

He nodded silently.

"I'm going to pray it will work," I said. "I'll pray for us to figure out how to make it work, and I'll try to have a little faith."

"I will too," he said. "If our first try doesn't persuade them, we'll keep trying, until we either figure it out or wear them down. I'm not giving you up."

"Now you're giving me hope," I said.

He smiled gently. "Been thinking something else too. Don't want you to be self-conscious, but I like how you get all cuddly and sweet when you're tired. Not that you aren't those things anyway. I like cuddling with you. Guess you already knew that."

"I like how I can trust you," I murmured, "even when I'm tired and cuddly."

What I couldn't tell him was that maybe he shouldn't trust me just then, even if I trusted him. I saw clearly in that moment why they taught us not to be out too late, too tired, and with nothing specific to do but cuddle somewhere. My willpower was exhausted like the rest of me, and I wanted things I shouldn't want, things we shouldn't do.

And Troy waking me with a kiss? I would totally sign up for a lifetime of that, effective immediately.

I needed a distraction, and he'd just offered one. I gathered the remnants of my mental strength. "Are boys even allowed to say they like cuddling?" I was afraid to attempt a mischievous smile. It might come out completely wrong, under the circumstances.

He grinned. "Only to our girlfriends. Keep my secret?"

"Sure. But be careful where you point that plural. You might hurt somebody." Banter was a good diversion too.

"'Girlfriends'?" he asked. "One's the perfect number for me. Her name's Jenny. This you know. Good night, sleepy beauty."

"Good night, honey."

A smile and another quick kiss, and he was gone. I stood for a while in the entry, pondering how much of his presence seemed to survive his departure. And how much didn't.

I found my parents, gave them each a tired hug, and said goodnight. Zeus got the same. Then I took my meds and went to bed—but not before slipping an apology into my bedtime prayer for last night, and being thankful for an evening which began in fear but ended in hope. And began and ended with Troy.

And not before asking the God I'd railed on the night before to help us figure out what to do and how to do it, so we could stay together.

54

Negotiations

I SLEPT THROUGH ALMOST all of Saturday morning. Troy came over for the afternoon, and we put our heads together—literally, a couple of times, but mostly we worked on our plan to convince our parents, especially his, that we could safely stay together.

We were optimistic. We'd passed through a difficult week and found hope on the other side. And if our first try wasn't enough, we'd keep trying. We weren't giving up on us.

First we listed three relevant commandments: no sexual activity outside of marriage, honoring our parents, and not bearing false witness—in this case not deceiving or lying to our parents. Then we listed the dating rules they taught at church, plus our parents' rules and a few of our own.

We reduced that list to one page of clear, specific rules for ourselves. We were obeying almost all of them already. We didn't sneak in any loopholes—they'd never get past our parents—but we left ourselves enough room to kiss, hug, cuddle, dance, hold hands, and spend plenty of time together, in person and electronically.

On Sunday evening we Skyped for almost two hours, planning exactly what to say to his parents and how to say it.

Monday night, after our respective family home evenings, we sat with his parents in their family room. Troy didn't seem nervous at first, but I was. I tried to treat it like a choir performance and focus on what we'd prepared, instead of imagining all the ways it could end badly. It helped a little that his mom and dad seemed ill at ease too.

We thanked them for agreeing to let me join the discussion. Troy said we had some things to suggest, but we'd be happy to listen first.

His mom began. "Jenny, I'm sure you know my husband and I worry about your relationship's potential to lead to problems eventually. Please understand, you're the kind of girl we want Troy to date, and we don't think you two are misbehaving. We're very fond of you, and it's easy to see why our son is too."

"Thank you," I said.

Troy's Dad said, "We're not accusing you two of anything. It's just that, when parents see children falling in love so young, it scares us. There are dangers, only some of which you know. We're each older than both of you combined. We've seen where things can lead, and how quickly and how far, even with good people who mean well—which you certainly do."

Troy asked, "Have you ever seen two people fall in love in high school and stay together without getting in trouble?"

His mom said, "I think we have, but that's not the point. The stakes are very high here, and the risks are real."

"Mom, I think it is the point," Troy said. I could hear him trying not to sound frustrated. "The stakes are high whether we love each other or not, whether we date each other or someone else. In fact, aren't the risks greater if we don't love each other but hook up anyway?"

He didn't give them a chance to respond. "But here's the real question. Is it possible to behave ourselves in spite of the risks, or not? We think we want the right kind of future badly enough to behave ourselves. Is that so hard to believe?"

His parents said they believed it. They knew we wanted that. But the perils were greater than we could know. Troy and I had already compared our frustrations with adult appeals to things we couldn't know yet, but obviously there were such things.

I knew they'd covered this ground a few times without me. But I hadn't heard everything directly from his parents before. There were things I wanted to say to them, but I listened and tried not to fear the worst—for maybe ten minutes, but it seemed longer.

The discussion went in circles, but I began to be encouraged. Yes, they cared about their son and wanted the best for him. But they weren't treating me as an intruder. They cared about me too. Still, we weren't really getting anywhere, and Troy's frustration was growing. His cheeks were slightly flushed and the pitch of his voice was subtly higher. He finished a thought and turned to me. I squeezed his hand and started talking.

"Mr. and Mrs. Pullman, when Troy and I met, he did everything he could to help my parents not to worry about me or him, and to help them feel comfortable with things like my dancing in spite of my condition, or going on a date without my dog. He still does those things. They trust him, and he's earned it. Sometimes he's more respectful of them than I am."

I wanted to say that, if he were my son, I'd be proud. But that was too much like telling them how to be parents.

"I know I'm only sixteen. The fact that I love your son and he loves me scares me too. Not as much as it thrills me, but a little. We're just starting to learn what love means. We know that. And Troy says seventeen doesn't feel that much older."

I didn't say what occurred to me just then. I was only sixteen, but I could be surprisingly bold in things that really mattered to me. I could tell two concerned parents how much I loved their son.

"I didn't plan to fall in love like this in high school," I said. "I didn't expect to meet Troy. I never expected him to love me. But here's what I know: I feel safe with him. I trust him to act well all the time, not just most of the time, and not just when people are watching. That makes him pretty special."

I decided to say something we hadn't prepared. "He has good friends, guys who treat girls with respect. They treat each other with respect too."

They were still listening, and I was still speaking coherently, even with Troy squeezing my hand, which I loved. I wanted to turn and see his face, especially his eyes, but I had to focus.

"Troy and his friends don't behave themselves just because they lack opportunities to misbehave. They're popular and handsome. Plenty of girls would misbehave with them, if that's what they wanted. They behave because they choose to. They're the best examples I know."

I returned to our plan. "As long as I love your son, I want the same future for him that you do. My dad says you never stop loving your first love, if it's really love, or wanting him to be happy. Well, her, in his case. So whatever happens down the road, I don't see myself ever wanting less than the best possible future for your son."

Concentrating on what we'd prepared helped me not to worry about his parents' expressions, which seemed serious but not hostile, or their body language, which I was bad at reading anyway. But when I talked about Troy's future, they both nodded slightly and seemed to relax. Mr. Pullman had his arm around his wife's shoulders, and he drew her gently toward him. There was a hint of a smile on her lips, but I didn't know whether she was smiling at my words or his squeeze.

I finally turned to Troy. He regarded me with what looked for all the world like admiration. I couldn't stop to dwell on it—we still had work to do—but we were doing a difficult thing, and that might have been admirable. Plus he could probably read his parents better than I could.

I tried to transmit an entire smile through my eyes alone. Then I turned back to his parents before I got completely distracted.

"I want you to be able to trust me as much as my parents trust your son. If we can do things to help you worry less, we want to do them. We've talked about this a lot. We're prepared to tell you what we're thinking in detail, if that's okay."

They said it was.

Troy was calm again. He mentioned the three commandments we'd considered, then began to list the rules we'd prepared, some of which our parents had imposed for dates or activities in general, before we ever met. We wanted to manage the risks intelligently, he said.

The first part of our list was about when we'd see each other and how often, and curfews for school nights and other nights, including our electronic curfew. The next part was rules about what we could and couldn't do when we were together, and places we wouldn't go. I presented that.

We included a few rules we were willing to obey but didn't think we needed, and some that were stricter than we preferred them to be. We didn't want his parents even starting to make changes—but we didn't tell them that.

When we came to our rules about physical contact, I turned to Troy. "Do you want to make us all squirm, or shall I?"

He smiled a little and rescued me. "I'll man up and start, at least.

"Okay, physical contact," he said. "We hold hands a lot—about as much when we're not around our parents as when we are. That's a fact, not a rule, and so's this. I often have my arm around Jenny, or vice versa, not just when I'm subbing for Zeus. We don't think we need to change that.

"Back to rules." He glanced at the paper in his hand. "We don't touch each other anywhere we shouldn't, or ask for that or allow it. Like the little book says, we don't lie on top of each other anywhere. Also, no massages, no back rubs.

"You know there's been kissing. We'll limit ourselves to kissing hello and goodbye, and rarely in between." He glanced at me. "Actually, rarely isn't enough. Let's say 'occasionally in between.'"

I smiled—but so did his parents.

"Occasionally is good," Mr. Pullman said, "but there are kisses and there are kisses. Where do you draw the line?"

"The little book says no passionate kissing. That feels safe—whatever it means. How much detail do you want, Dad?"

"How much is there?"

Troy turned to me. "I think they'd enjoy hearing you answer that."

He must have been pretty confident of the outcome to say that. I tried to be calm. "Okay, but if they send you off to boarding school in Vermont tomorrow morning to get you away from me, it's only mostly my fault."

Troy grinned. His parents smiled too.

"Okay, kissing," I said. I must have been blushing already, because my face didn't get any warmer. I knew what our list said, but I checked it anyway. "Nothing on the neck or anywhere below the neck, except on my hand, when your son is feeling particularly gallant or French or whatever. Or I might kiss his hand. I did that Friday, actually.

"And speaking of French," I said—then tried to hide my horror at having said it aloud—"when we kiss, we keep our tongues to ourselves. Also, we try to be candid with our parents, even about this stuff."

So my face could get warmer after all. Had I just made boarding school a real possibility? I couldn't look at Troy.

"We can see that," said Mr. Pullman. He was smiling and shaking his head. "Does your list actually say all that?"

"Pretty much," Troy said.

Mrs. Pullman's cheeks had reddened a bit, but she didn't say anything. She was hard to read, but I thought she looked more surprised than amused.

We walked them through the rest of our list, then gave them each a copy, after we used a pen to change "rarely" to "occasionally." We'd waited to give them the list, so they couldn't read ahead.

Troy said, "Mom and Dad, we're trying to be as wise as we can, and still be together."

"And in high school," I added.

"We all know we're ignoring some counsel we hear a lot," he said. "But we think, if we keep obeying these rules, we'll be okay. We hope you'll keep trusting us to do that."

Part of our plan was to emphasize that we weren't asking for anything new or different, just to continue what was already working. So Troy was careful to say "keep obeying" and "keep trusting us" instead of suggesting they start trusting us more.

"If you want us to add or change something, we'll listen," he said. "If you want to check in regularly with me or both of us and go down the list rule by rule, we can do that. We'll have this talk with Jenny's parents, and we won't object to you comparing notes with them whenever you want."

I said, "When all six of us agree on the list, we might share it with our bishops. Maybe they'll worry less. Anyway, if you're uncomfortable with any of this now or later, please tell us. If you start to think we need some new rules, or if you're ever uncomfortable with our behavior, please tell us that too. Troy and I will review the list together once a month and report that to you, if you like."

Troy asked, "Mom, Dad, what do you think? Will you keep trusting us together, if we keep obeying these rules?"

"Jenny, Troy, I think my husband and I should talk about this privately," said his mom. She held up our document. "This is thorough, intelligent work."

"We're trying to be good, Mom," Troy said. "And intelligent."

"We know that," said his dad, "and we don't want to force you apart. But we want you safe."

"That's what we want too," Troy said. "If Jenny and I get the ice cream, will that give you enough time to talk?"

His mom raised her eyebrows. "Let's start with that and see if it's enough."

I could hardly wait to get Troy alone. I thought things had gone well, and he seemed pleased, but I wanted to be sure. The instant we got to kitchen, I said, "You know your parents. How's it going?"

He smiled. "I think it's working. Maybe we'll know in a minute. You were amazing." His smile got even warmer.

I wished I could see my own eyes. They felt happy and hopeful, and he seemed drawn to them.

"Better get the ice cream," he said after several blissful seconds, but his eyes didn't leave mine.

"Yup," I said. My eyes didn't leave his.

"Before they wonder what we're doing," he added.

"Yup," I said.

Finally he turned away. "I'll get spoons and dishes, and the scoop. Napkins are right here. You pick the ice cream. We like everything in there, so pick what you want."

There were three flavors. I settled on huckleberry, which I'd never tasted. I didn't even know what a huckleberry was, but it seemed like a flavor a book-loving future writer should enjoy.

We must have given his parents long enough to talk. While we all ate, his dad held up his copy of our list. "If we agree to trust you on these terms, will you two obey all these rules all the time, and report slip-ups promptly to both sets of parents? Even small ones? Not that there should be any."

"Yes, sir," we both said at once. Then Troy added, "We'll add that one to the list and reprint it."

"We can write it in. Where do we sign?"

"Do we need to sign?" Troy asked.

"Just an expression. Good work, you two." He turned to his wife. "Didn't we promise the girls they could come down for ice cream?"

"We'll get the ice cream," Troy said. "Want me to get them too?"

"I'll sneak upstairs and get them," said his dad. "I want to see if they're studying or just goofing off."

We disappeared into the kitchen again. "First things first," we said in unison, then laughed quietly. Our hug was happy but too short.

"We did it," said one of us, with joy and relief.

"We did it," said the other, with barely-contained glee.

The "occasionally in between" kiss that followed was hurried. We needed to start sounding busy.

"We never defined occasionally," Troy said, as he noisily opened the silverware drawer. "What do you think?"

"Less often than we want to. Probably a lot less." My pout was exaggerated, but there was real regret behind it.

"The times we kiss between hello and goodbye should probably be fewer than the times we don't," he said, matching my pout. It was adorable. I wanted to kiss him again, but I didn't.

"I agree," I said, as I scooped a generous portion into the second bowl. I sounded much too responsible. "'Occasionally' has to be less than 'often.'"

"Probably a lot less," he said.

"Words have meanings," I said.

I returned the ice cream to the freezer, and he picked up the bowls. He looked at me, set them down again, and pulled me into a hug that ended with another kiss.

"Hello," he said.

I giggled.

"Have to check with Landon," he said, when our foreheads were touching and our noses were about an eighth of an inch apart. "But I think 'occasionally' gets us an infinite quantity of kisses, if we extend it for an infinite time."

"I could swoon right now."

"Let's deliver the ice cream instead."

As we returned to the living room, I wondered if anyone would notice that our feet weren't touching the floor.

55

What Impressed Her

Troy and his dad went to the garage to finish installing a light fixture, while his mom and I took care of the dessert dishes—not because we were women and they were men, she said, but because they were taller, and it was a ceiling light. I liked that, even if I didn't quite believe it.

"Parenting is scary sometimes," she said. "We're just trying to be cautious and wise."

"Are you comfortable with our agreement?" I asked.

"Comfortable enough." She held out the wood-handled ice cream scoop she'd just dried. "This isn't dishwasher-safe. Second drawer down, to your right, please. With the others."

I put it away. "We can change something."

"No, you did well. Let's leave it alone for now."

"Okay." I started to wipe down the sink. "May I ask you something?"

"Of course."

"Are you just humoring us, until you see us making small mistakes that aren't dangerous in themselves, but might prove we can't handle this after all? Then we'll see for ourselves that we have to break up, before the mistakes get more serious?"

When she didn't answer immediately, I worried. I finished the sink and turned to face her.

She closed the dishwasher, pushed some buttons, and leaned against the counter. "We're not using reverse psychology or giving you just enough rope or expecting you to fail. We think you can do this, or tonight would have gone differently. The rules allow a generous safety margin, but that's just being smart."

"Thanks for thinking that," I said. "And telling me."

She smiled. "Come sit with me."

We sat in the alcove where we'd first talked a few months ago. "Do you have any more questions?" she asked.

I had one, and I was less nervous when I asked it. "Wouldn't it be easier for you, if your son and some girl weren't trying to have a relationship while they're still in high school?"

She smiled even more warmly. "Great question. For a while I thought so, but I may have been wrong. He's happy, and that's important. It's increasingly obvious that you're good for him. I hope that goes both ways."

This evening, I thought with relief, was turning out far better than it could have. "It does," I said. "It all works beautifully and makes perfect sense, as long as Troy and I behave."

She smiled again. "There are challenges this way, but I'm not sure they're more difficult. Just different."

"You're welcome to check up on us," I said. "He wants a mission, and I want it for him. I may serve one too, if things change enough that it's possible. Both my parents did."

"Thank you, Jenny. Whatever you decide, I hope those things change."

"Thank you."

"What kind of future do you see after that? If you don't mind my asking."

Blushing was inevitable. "You mean together? We're not there yet. Not even close. We'll just have to see."

"That's wise." She chuckled and shook her head. "Nan and Lily are less patient. Tonight over dinner they announced their intentions for his future. So he mentioned arranging marriages for them and started naming names. They retreated in a hurry."

I threw caution to the wind. I wanted her to trust me, and she deserved my candor. "I love the thought of having a future together," I said, "but we don't talk about it much. We both have a lot to do before we get there. If we get there." I smiled. "I hope we get there."

She smiled too, again, but the best part was, she didn't look worried.

"I hope I wasn't too graphic about kissing," I said more soberly. "Sometimes I can't believe what I just said."

She laughed. "You were very quotable."

"Oh, boy."

"Your wit was the one of the first things we noticed," she said. "That and your shoes. And how Troy lights up when you're in the room. He told us what you said to your bishop, when he called and asked you to speak. 'I'm sitting exactly zero inches from the nearest boy. I think he likes me.'" She chuckled. "Did you really call my pies 'carnal, sensuous, and devilish'?"

"I did. The scripture says 'sensual,' but that adjective is for people, not pies."

"My point is that I'm flattered. Which is your favorite? I'll send you home with one on Friday."

"Thank you. I love all your pies. Mom might prefer the French silk."

"French silk it is. That's my favorite."

"You're so kind. I hope you don't judge your son's girlfriends by their baking skills. I can barely bake a cake from a mix, and the only thing I can do with pie crust is eat it. But you said something about my shoes?"

"Even when you dress up, you wear lovely but sensible shoes, with small heels at most, usually flats. I think it says something about the kind of person you are."

"Afraid of heights?"

She laughed again. "Sensible. Responsible. Comfortable with yourself and your real beauty, so you don't have to try to be glamorous."

"I never saw glamorous as a possibility."

"Glamour's okay," she said. "Your beauty doesn't need it."

"Thank you. I wish that really explained my shoes. I just hate high heels. And I don't need any farther to fall."

"Lots of us torture ourselves anyway, especially with tall men," she said. "I've done it. Not recently."

I finally changed the subject. Shoes? Really? "Troy got pretty candid with your bishop this week. I guess you heard. I hope it won't be a problem. He's been defending me, and us, a lot more than he should have to."

"He was pretty upset when he came home the other night. You probably heard more details than we did. He said the bishop all but told him to break up with you, and hinted that the trouble at school might be your punishment for breaking some rules."

"Those were the highlights," I said.

"I assume it's worse at school than he says."

"It's bad enough, but it's just words. We're okay."

"You'll let us know if it gets worse? Or if we can help?"

"If you're comfortable with what we discussed tonight, that'll help him more than anything. Lately he feels like your bishop's against us, our seminary teacher's against us, and you and his dad might be against us soon, thanks to your bishop. Plus the nasty kids at school."

She reached for my hand. "We were never against you two. We were for you, and we still are."

She had me close to tears. I put my other hand on hers. "Ma'am, I think we both—Troy and I—understand that a lot better now. I don't know the words to tell you how grateful I am." I looked into her eyes and chose candor again. "Or how relieved."

She nodded, smiling gently, and I pressed ahead, before I started to cry. "He thinks the stuff at school is partly his fault, which it's not, and he wants to protect me, not just physically. I love that about him. Last week was pretty hard for him, but we got through it. Tonight helps a lot."

"It was a hard week for both of you," she said.

I nodded.

⸻◆⸻

On the way home Troy said, "You were amazing. Dad's still smiling about the kissing. 'Speaking of French.'"

I smiled and blushed a bit. "Your mom threatened to quote me."

"Not a threat. Pretty soon, whenever you meet one of her friends, or especially her sisters, you'll find you're already famous."

"Infamous," I groused, but I was mostly kidding. "She says your dad's okay with us, and so's she. We had a good talk while you worked. We even talked about shoes, which apparently say more about a girl than I realized."

"I've heard that speech. I'm glad you talked. Something you said impressed her. She says you obviously love me and want the best for me, and you don't just care about yourself. Might have been about the stuff at school. What did you say?"

I told him.

"That was it," he said.

"I don't see it."

"She said, let us know if we can help, and you talked about making things better for me, not for yourself or even for both of us."

"Wow. Maybe I do love you."

He grinned. "That is not news. But I like it."

"Do you think we worried too much?" I asked.

"About Mom and Dad? Wondered that too. But I think if we hadn't taken them seriously, tonight would have been more difficult. I'm glad we prepared enough to show them we're serious, not just defiant or rebellious. Or starry-eyed and love-struck."

"I'm pretty love-struck," I confessed. "But I understand. What did your dad say?"

"Not much about us. Said we did well, and you're completely adorable, which also isn't news. Mostly we concentrated on not getting electrocuted or starting a fire. When do we talk with your parents?"

"Soon," I said. "I'll work on that tonight."

It was sooner than I expected. When we arrived, Mom and Dad were in the living room. I had told them what we were doing at Troy's home, what we worked on all weekend, and why I hadn't slept much Thursday night. When we reported success, they suggested we have our talk with them right then. Troy texted his parents to say he might be late and why, and we got started.

My reward for being brave with his parents—that's how I saw it—was hearing him tell Mom and Dad that he loved me, which melted me so thoroughly that he had to do most of our talking.

In the end they didn't want to change anything, and it went so quickly that Troy left on time after all.

—◆—

Later Dad said, "I wonder how I got such a great daughter."

I was relieved and feeling silly, so I took the bait. "Do we need to talk about where daughters come from?"

He smiled broadly. "Hey, I gave you a pretty good straight line. By accident too. Must be late."

I didn't mean what I said next to be another straight line. I just wasn't thinking. "How'd I get such a good dad?"

I knew what I'd done the instant he began to speak. "Jenny, when my parents decided they loved each other very much, they got married. Then they gave each other a very special hug. And because a little seed from my dad collided in just the right way with a bigger seed from—"

"Stop!" I commanded. "Or I'll tell you what it's like to kiss my boyfriend. I'm a decent writer, so you may feel like you're kissing him yourself. You'll especially love the part where you feel like he's kissing you."

"Oh, Jenny." He smiled but sounded serious.

"What, Dad?"

"You used to be grossed out when we talked about this stuff. My little girl is growing up."

"That's hard for a dad," I said.

"Yes, but you made parenting easier tonight."

"We want to be good. And together. If our parents believe we can be both at the same time, I guess we'll be okay if other people don't."

"You be good, and we'll have your backs as much as we can. We'll worry, but we're learning to, you know." He smiled expectantly.

I knew my cue. "To trust the daughter? And the dog?"

"Yes. And the boyfriend, strangely enough."

56

Allies

Later that week, after school, Brother Stickinger called Mom. She was marking papers at one end of the dining room table, and I was doing math homework at the other end. When he identified himself, she smiled slightly, raised her eyebrows, put one finger to her lips, set her phone down—and put him on speaker.

She didn't tell him I was there, which wasn't like her. The only sense I could make of it was that Mom was awesome.

He said he'd tried to reach Dad without success, so he thought he'd call her. She rolled her eyes at that—which I couldn't remember seeing her do ever. I usually got in trouble when I did it.

"The reason I called," he said, "is a rather troubling conversation I had with Jenny a while back, and how she seems to have changed since then. I thought I should speak with you, in case there's a problem developing that you're not aware of. The short version is, I'm worried about her relationship with Troy Pullman."

If Mom hadn't already gone out of her way to take my side, I might have boiled over. I simmered quietly instead.

"What worries you specifically?" Mom asked, as if I hadn't reported that episode and my new resolve to participate as little as possible in his class.

"We discussed the desirability of avoiding steady dating until they're older, so as not to jeopardize his mission. That is, I mentioned it. She objected rather heatedly, then left instead of staying to discuss it. Since then she's been in class, but she seems withdrawn. She participates only when I ask her a direct question, which is a conspicuous change. Her participation grade will be fine; the bar for that is fairly low. But I hope everything's okay."

"I appreciate your concern," Mom said. "For what it's worth, I find she's much harder to offend when I hear and consider what she has to say before I tell her what to think."

My eyes might have bugged out a little. Mom had just sliced up my seminary teacher and made it sound diplomatic.

"Well," he said after a moment, "I wanted you to know."

"Thanks for your call, Brother Stack . . . Stuck . . . Stock . . . I'm sorry, what's your name again?" Mom sounded just a bit like the airhead she totally wasn't. Her smile lit up her eyes, and it was all I could do not to laugh out loud.

"Stickinger. Heber Stickinger."

"I'll try to remember next time," Mom said. "Thanks again for your call, Brother Stickinger. We'll be sure to discuss it here. Good day."

So much for the airhead shtick, I thought. She should have said, "Have a great rest of the day." With appropriately excessive perkiness.

When the call ended, she tried for a straight face but failed. What burst from me was part joy, part admiration for her, and part indignation at him.

"Best. Mom. Ever. He's such a jerk. And a busybody."

She just smiled.

"Thanks for letting me eavesdrop," I said. "And rolling your eyes at him. So much for those rules, right? And that little airhead thing with his name was pretty good. I almost laughed and gave us up."

"You deserved all of that. So did he."

I was the cat that swallowed the bird. "And in the future, as I've noted before, I should do as you say, not as you just did?"

"Well said. You know, if there were a problem that he was seeing and we weren't, that call could have been a very good thing."

"You told him we'd discuss it. Shall we wait for Dad or discuss it now?"

"I think we just did. Best mom ever, huh?"

"Pretty much."

— ◦ —

Meanwhile, Childish Jenny had invented a nickname for a certain seminary teacher: Brother Stick-Up-His-Butt. I probably wasn't the first to call him that during his career, but it was unkind. I quickly realized I didn't want it to spread beyond Troy, Jack, and Nikki, and I didn't enjoy hearing it from them either.

I wondered if he'd heard Maddi's nastiest rumor. I was glad we'd told our parents when we did.

———◆◇◆———

The next plot twist belonged in one of those Shakespeare plays from ninth-grade English, where characters eavesdrop the old-fashioned way, from behind a curtain.

Nan was a youth speaker in the Pullmans' ward the next Sunday, so I went to church with them. She did well. I struggled not to glare at their bishop, especially when he stood at the pulpit to conduct the meeting.

We stayed for Sunday school, but I excused myself after several minutes. I had enough of a headache to want a quiet place to sit alone for a while. Troy wanted to come with me, but I insisted he stay in class. We didn't need any more trouble with Bishop Waldron.

I found a small, unused classroom with no window, left the light off, swung the door almost shut, sat on a folding chair, and closed my eyes.

A few minutes later, I heard soft voices in the hall. They must have been near the door. A woman addressed someone as "Bishop," and I sort of recognized his voice. They talked about filling an empty adult role in the Young Women organization, so I figured she was the ward Young Women president.

They obviously didn't know I was listening—and I tried not to, at first. They mentioned specific women, but I didn't recognize the names. Then he said, "That girl I keep seeing with Troy Pullman—do you know her?"

How could "that girl" not listen?

"Mostly by reputation," she said. "She's stayed for Young Women once or twice, but I've never had much of a conversation with her."

"I don't know her either," he said. "I wish I knew how to discourage him from being so serious about her."

"Why would you want to do that?" She sounded stern.

"What do you mean?"

"From what I hear, they're good kids, very good kids, and they're setting a good example at school, along with their friends. That school could use some good examples."

"From what you hear?" Which was my question too, but it sounded bad when he asked it.

"Some of my girls go there, of course. I sub occasionally, and I know some teachers. I've heard some of the popular kids don't like them together and aren't shy about showing it. But these are kids who can help some things change at that school. From what my girls say, it's already started."

I wanted to open the door and ask her how we were changing our school. And did she know any of my teachers?

He wasn't buying it. "They're kids, Sister. They're playing with fire."

"Sounds to me like they're fighting fire. And you want to stop them why? They're the ones showing other kids how not to do the things you're afraid they'll do."

She continued in a gentler tone. "Besides, if Troy tried anything, Zeus would probably take him out."

"Sister—President—I don't want to argue with you."

What I heard was, he didn't want her to argue with him.

"Who is Zeus?" he asked.

"Have you ever seen Jenny without Troy?" she asked.

"No."

"Zeus is her service dog. She's epileptic. Troy walks with his arm around her in case she has a seizure, so she's less likely to fall and hurt herself, and so she won't have to sit so much. I'm sure those aren't the only reasons, but she had one on prom day, and he caught her. That's also why they dance only slow dances. It's safer."

"Troy never mentioned any of this. Does it happen often?"

"The seizures? Often enough, I guess. Think what it means to a high school girl just to dance, after sitting and watching for years."

She was right about that.

"I saw them at our ward dance," he said.

"So did I," she said. "Did you know he took her to waltz lessons with the Hills, because she dreamed of waltzing? Paid for them with yard work and snow shoveling. That night was the first time they waltzed at an actual dance. Troy bribed the DJ to play a song in 3/4. Ten dollars, I heard."

Whoever she was, she had great sources.

"I saw them on the dance floor," he said. "I had some concerns."

"We probably saw the same thing. Bishop, if a boy who liked me had made it safe for me to dance, then arranged for waltz lessons at his expense, then bribed a DJ to play a song we could waltz to, I'd have snogged him until someone ran for a fire extinguisher."

I suppressed a laugh.

"He says he loves her," said the bishop.

"I'm sure it's mutual. So?"

I'm sure too, I thought, all melty and fluttery.

"Shouldn't that worry us?" he asked.

"They all worry us, no matter what they do, right? You should ask his parents what they think."

"I gather you've done that?"

"I sat with Bobbie Tuesday evening at the dinner. She and Kevin think Troy and Jenny are grown up enough—and good enough and strong enough—not to mess up each other's lives. They love her. They trust her. She says Jenny's parents trust him. Even the dog trusts him. Maybe you could try to trust them both."

"We can't just pretend we don't have the counsel we have. The counsel is—"

"I know the counsel," she said. "So do they. Deciding what counsel fits our circumstances, and how, is a pretty important adult skill. We'll keep an eye on them, but they'll be okay. I think they'll be spectacular."

I shouldn't have listened to any of that, but I was glad I did. A new adult ally was good medicine for my headache. And I owed Troy's mom a hug. I owed her son more than that. When the hallway was quiet again, I rejoined Troy in his class and tried not to smile too broadly.

"You okay?" he whispered.

"Better than okay," I whispered back. "I'll tell you later. I think I'll stay for Young Women."

When we were finally alone and he was about to drive me home, I said, "Honey, it's time for one of those occasionally-in-betweens." It had been a few days.

He grinned. "I'm in. What's up?"

"First things first. " I kissed him. Then I kissed him again. "That's because your bishop didn't know I'm epileptic. You never used it as an excuse with him for having your arm around me or dancing only slow dances."

"Didn't think he needed to know," Troy said. "What are you talking about?"

"Here's the thing," I said. "You make me feel normal. I'm kissing you again."

When I told him about the conversation in the hall, he understood.

———◦———

A few days later, Troy brought Lily to my children's choir concert at a local junior high. Several of us were "graduating," in the sense that we were too old to be in the choir next year. They gave us each a rose before the final number. They'd already added most of us to a large plaque with the names of everyone who'd ever been in the choir for at least three years.

Our spring concerts always ended with a lush, six-part arrangement of "Sometimes," an old Carpenters song. It was our musical thank-you to parents and families. Choir alumni in the audience were always invited to come up and sing with us. This time, more than a dozen did, including some boys I knew, who'd left the choir when their voices changed. I liked what their deeper voices added to our sound.

I managed to sing a line here and there, amid my tears. We had techniques for singing funny things without laughing and poignant things without crying, but they didn't work for the last song in the last concert of my seven years in the choir. I didn't really expect them to.

Afterward I held Troy's hand, while I showed Lily my name on the plaque and let her smell my rose and inspect my purple choir robe. Then, while she had a heart-to-heart chat with Zeus, Troy told me why they'd come late.

Bishop Waldron had dropped by the house to make peace. He called me by name, which meant he'd taken the trouble to remember my name, once he heard it. Troy's Mom said something to him about every story having at least two sides. She could carve up an authority figure diplomatically too.

Before he left, he told Troy, "I'm not completely comfortable, but maybe that's okay. Some good people trust you, and I'm trying to be one of them. I apologize again for overreacting. I hope I didn't cause too much grief."

Troy said to me, "I let him off the hook. Didn't tell him how much grief he caused. Thanked him. Told him he should meet you."

It was kind of Bishop Waldron to apologize. It showed humility. We decided that, if he was trying to trust us, we could help him by giving him a copy of our rules. Bishop Savage too. We wouldn't bother explaining anything to Brother Stick. The school year was almost over, and he'd soon be irrelevant.

—◆—

Troy and I were finally able to relax. We started to think everything would be okay.

We thought that for about a week.

Trial

57

#TRISP

A s the school year wound down, signs appeared in the halls with only a hashtag: #TRISP. We saw it on marker boards and sidewalks too. Student body elections were a few days away, so perhaps it was from someone's campaign.

Will was running for student body president, and Troy and I helped. We made fliers to distribute, but we were lucky to get five seconds of attention from kids in the halls. We told them Will was a good guy and wasn't all about being popular. We got a lot of nods, and some kids took the fliers.

What we couldn't explain quickly enough was that Will didn't let all our little circles affect how he treated people. You didn't have to be popular for him to notice you and treat you kindly.

We enlisted Jack and Nikki, who actually used social media, for some electronic campaigning. They drafted two of their favorite geeks, and before we knew it, "Vote for Will" posts and tweets were going out automatically every day, right up to the class period when everyone voted.

When the voting passed with no explanation of the mysterious hashtag, we thought the senior class officers might be using it, with SP for Senior Party.

Two days after the election, #TRISP appeared in new places. If it was about the senior party at first, it wasn't anymore.

———◆———

The day started happily, with news during first period that Will had won the election in a landslide.

In third period, just before late lunch, we had a practice test in Mr. Cain's sophomore English class. He said the other English teachers were giving their sophomores the same test that afternoon. He'd created it himself and refined it over several years.

"I hope you enjoy it," he said with a beatific smile. He seemed pleased when several students groaned, but I expected to enjoy it. It was on grammar and vocabulary, and I always did well on those tests. I also did them quickly. I hoped he'd let me leave class early, once I finished. I wanted some Troy time before his team meeting about shoes near the end of early lunch.

I was probably the first student in my class—maybe any class—to see question 23.

> 23. What is the meaning of the acronym TRISP?
> A. Troy's Revolting Interspecies Service Project
> B. Texan's Romance Isn't Seizure-Proof
> C. Troy's Ridiculously Inexpensive Sex Provider
> D. All of the above.

I stared in disbelief. It couldn't have said what I thought it said. I read it again.

Maybe it was because Troy's name was on the paper and mine wasn't, or maybe these things just happen when you love someone, but I first thought of Troy and how this would hurt him.

I got a good start on my own pain too. Half-dazed, half-something—I didn't know what—I walked with Zeus up to Mr. Cain's desk.

He looked up from his book, saw my face, and instantly looked concerned. "Is something wrong?" he whispered.

I stared at him for few seconds.

"Are you okay?" he asked. "You look pale."

"I'm sorry. I have to go."

"Okay. Can I help you somehow?"

Half-angry. That's what I was. I shook my head and said softly, "You suck, Mr. Cain." My voice shook. "You totally suck." I dropped my practice test on his desk, and Zeus and I headed for the door.

Most of my stunned brain focused on escaping the classroom. But part of it noted a girl bursting into laughter behind me, and a boy saying, "Good one, Mr. Cain." They must have seen question 23.

As the door swung shut behind us, Mr. Cain snapped at the class, "No talking! Keep your eyes on—!"

The door latched with a click that echoed in the empty hallway.

Jack and Nikki told me later that they saw me leave but thought I'd finished and gone to see Troy. When Jack saw the question a minute later, she showed Nikki. They marched up to Mr. Cain's desk, slapped their papers down in front of him, and told him there was a problem with question 23.

Nikki said, "If you wrote this, you're sick."

Jack said, "We're leaving to find our friend."

They grabbed both hall passes and left.

There was a quiet room next to the nurse's office, where Zeus and I had gone before, when I was banged up after a seizure, to be alone and rest. No one was around to see us go in and shut the door. If the English wing had been further from the nurse's office, or if I'd gone past the cafeteria, I'd have found out sooner how much worse things were than I knew.

What I knew was bad enough.

I wanted Troy, but I couldn't bear to go looking for him. I sat down, put my arms around Zeus, and sobbed.

Sometime later I heard the door open and realized I'd heard a gentle knock just before that. When I looked up, Troy was quietly closing the door behind him. Zeus slipped out of my grasp and stood between us.

"Hi, Jenny." He was pale, and his eyes were big and troubled.

"Hi, Troy." It wasn't my voice. It was a shaky, small, high-pitched, little girl's voice. I talked in bursts between sobs. "I knew you . . . would find me."

He started toward me. Zeus growled and barked. It wasn't playful or friendly. It was a warning.

"Zeus, stop," I said. That wasn't a command he knew, but I couldn't remember any commands he knew.

Troy started toward me again, and Zeus growled and barked again.

"Okay," Troy said. "I'll sit over here." He sat on the floor near the door.

"I'm so up— . . . upset he . . . probably . . . thinks every— . . . everyone's . . . a threat." I swallowed and brushed away some of my tears. "Guess you know . . . why I'm . . . here."

He looked exactly as I felt, but without the sobs. His eyes didn't leave me as he spoke. "Coach saw the flier before our meeting. Blew a gasket. Hardly ever heard him swear before. Then Mr. Cain brought him your English test, because Coach is the acting principal today. The principal and all the vice principals went to some meeting. Mr. Cain already collected that page from all the English classrooms. Coach sent the rest of the team to pick up all the fliers and told me to find you. Didn't really need to be told."

Watching Troy and hugging Zeus while I sobbed didn't leave much brain power for thinking. Mostly I thought Troy and I were too far apart—but I couldn't think of solution. At least he was here.

"Jack and Nikki looked for you too," he said. "We tried outside, but then they remembered this room. They went to tell Coach we found you, so I could come in alone. They'll be back. Sorry, I'm just babbling. Don't know what else to do."

"I knew . . . you would . . . find me," I repeated.

"Texted you to ask where you were."

I pulled my phone from my pocket and stared at it. "Forgot to . . . turn on. . . . Should have . . . texted you. . . . Thanks for . . . finding anyway." I left it turned off.

I didn't think I could feel worse, but then I saw what he had in his hand, and something he'd said finally registered. My insides turned to lead, and I wanted to vomit. Which mostly stopped my sobbing.

"A flier too?" I moaned. "Not just the practice test?"

He looked at the paper in his hand as if he'd forgotten it. His eyes got even bigger, and he looked up at me again. "All over the cafeteria. Hundreds of them."

"It's worse," I said. It wasn't a question.

"Yeah. TV screens too."

The thought of TV screens didn't make me feel worse, so it was official. This was rock bottom. "How bad?"

He wasn't sobbing, but he spoke with pauses too. He sounded crushed, which hurt me that much more. So I really could feel worse, if it was for him.

"I swore too. More than once. Shouldn't have." He looked at his right hand, flexing it. "Punched a locker. Don't know how many times. Shouldn't have done that either. Will stopped me, I think."

I stared at the paper. "May I see it? Please?"

"You shouldn't read this."

"I have to. Please?" It still didn't sound like my voice.

The pain on his face overwhelmed me, but I held myself together. I had to be strong, because there was a place below rock bottom, and a place below that, and . . . "Please, Troy? I have to. I wish you could protect me from this, and I know you want to, but you can't."

I sobbed again, and Troy waited a minute or two for me to stop. He looked completely miserable.

He slowly extended the flier. Zeus growled and barked again.

He pulled it back. "Zeus is right. Don't read this." He was grasping at straws, but I loved him for it.

"Please. I have to. Zeus, lie down!" That was a command he knew.

Troy stared at me in obvious torment, then slowly handed me the paper.

On one side, in letters an inch tall, it said,

> Troy's
> Ridiculously
> Inexpensive
> Sex
> Provider
> #TRISP

There was a close-up photo of Troy handing me a dollar bill in the hall a few days earlier. I remembered him doing it. It was his share of our cookies at some club's bake sale.

On the other side was a photo of me and Zeus, with two bystanders Photoshopped into the background. They each had a speech bubble.

One asked, "When Troy makes love to his cripple, what does the dog do?"

The other answered, "Which one is the dog?"

What happened inside me was beyond disbelief and horror, beyond a lead weight in my stomach, beyond wanting to vomit. The pain came in waves.

I had to get to Troy. He looked like he needed to cry too, but I needed him to hold me. I slid off the couch and sat by him on the floor for all of one second before I dove into his arms, closed my eyes, and shook with more sobs. Neither of us talked for a while.

We were both hurt, but I had something he didn't: two strong arms holding me together.

Holding us together.

58

Damage Control

T HE AGONY GRADUALLY RECEDED. When it was just below breathtaking and I thought I could talk, I looked up at Troy. I wanted to help him, even if the best I could do was a lot less than he was doing for me.

He wasn't pale anymore. Rather the opposite. His eyes were narrower, and his lips were compressed. When he saw me looking, his expression softened.

I took a long, ragged breath. "It's amazing how much this hurts," I squeaked.

He nodded.

"Are you more hurt or more angry now?" I asked.

"Both," he said after a long look. "Angry."

"If you feel like talking, I want to listen." I held his gaze until he nodded slightly. Then my head found his shoulder, and I waited.

He finally spoke. "They're not just saying you're my project now. They're saying you're my . . . Know what? Can't say that word. Not about you."

"I think I know what you mean."

"They're treating something good . . . beautiful . . . like it's cheap and dirty. Maybe you expect crap like this from the jerks in the hall, but now it's in places that were safe before—fliers and screens and a practice English final. You don't think Mr. Cain—"

"I was rude when I left, but he'd never do this. There's another thing," I said. "For me." I took a deep breath and tried not to crumble. "Remember how I decided to believe in beauty I don't always see? In myself? They just called me a dog in front of the whole school." I started to weep. It was all I could do not to break down into sobs again.

"You are beautiful," Troy said earnestly. Then his voice turned cold. "They're ugly. Whoever they are."

"How could a person do this to somebody?"

"That's easy," he growled. "People suck. Almost all of them suck."

We were silent for a minute, until he said, "Coach is furious. He wants some serious punishment for somebody."

"Coach is not one of the people who suck," I said.

We heard a quiet knock. "Neither are Jack and Nikki," he said. "Was pretty hard for them not to come in when I did. Or push me out of the way and come in first."

Someone tried to turn the knob but couldn't. I hadn't noticed, but Troy must have locked the door. "Just a minute!" he called.

I escaped myself long enough to think that a girl was lucky to have friends who run toward the trouble. Then I sank back into the pain of being the trouble they were running to. Troy stood and coaxed me onto one of the couches. Not being in his arms was unbearable. I reached for his hand and squeezed it.

The next knock was louder.

"Think Zeus is up to more company?" he asked.

I had to concentrate to make sense of his question. "I think he's okay now. My falling apart must have scared him."

I stood and followed Troy to the door, so I wouldn't have to let go of his hand. He let Nikki and Jack in, then stood back and let them surround me, and I did have to let go.

There weren't many words. Eventually they turned to Troy and gave him a quick hug. Then they sat on one of the sofas, while Troy and I sat across from them and clung to each other, and Zeus put his head in my lap.

My insides were still a mass of lead, but I thought I was mostly finished crying. For the moment. And I hadn't vomited yet. And the waves of pain hadn't actually drowned me.

Troy asked them, "What's going on out there? Did Coach break anything?"

"We didn't overhear everything," Jack said. "But we saw that disgusting flier, and I think your moms and dads are on the way. Coach was on the phone. Sounds like he and the resource officer will investigate, and there might be criminal charges, not just school discipline. We heard him mention littering, criminal mischief, some kind of cybercrime."

"Who do you think did this?" Nikki asked.

"We'll destroy them for you," Jack said.

"We have a pretty good idea," Troy said.

I nodded.

"Did you tell Coach?" Nikki asked.

"Not yet," Troy said.

"Troy," I said, "let's let them figure it out, so we don't have to accuse anybody."

"Seriously? We should name names right now."

"Tell him if you want. But I wouldn't want to name four names, if only three of them are guilty, or something like that."

After a long silence, he said, "Just want to do something to somebody."

"You deserve to do something to somebody," I said.

"It's what they did to you that makes me want to punch the someone."

"Like a certain cheerleader?" Nikki asked.

There was a knock, and the door opened. Coach looked angry but sounded tired and concerned. "Troy, Jenny, are you still in one piece?"

Troy shrugged. I nodded half-heartedly.

"Your parents will be here soon. I called them. Would you please come to the principal's office in, say, five minutes? Nikki and Jack, isn't it? I'm glad you're here, but you don't need to be in that meeting. Were you properly excused from class?"

"Yes and no," Jack said. "We took Mr. Cain's hall passes." They held up well-worn pieces of board with the words "Hall Pass" burned into them. "But we didn't ask for them."

"Okay. Give them to me, and I'll get them back to him and handle your excuse, if he hasn't already. It's late lunch in a minute anyway."

"Thanks, Coach," said Nikki.

He turned to Troy and me. "On second thought, don't come in five minutes. I'll get you when we're ready." He closed the door.

That was when Troy thought to check his text messages. His phone had vibrated a few times, and he had a bunch.

One was from his mom: "We'll be there soon. Are you and Jenny okay?"

Five were from Will. The first one asked if he'd found me, and how I was doing. The second one said the team had picked up all the fliers they could find, and they were working on all the #TRISP signs, including the chalk on the sidewalks.

The third message was about Coach telling the team to figure out how to make the school a place decent people might want to attend next week. That might have been Coach just blowing off steam, I thought, not giving them an assignment, but Will said they had some ideas.

"That's so cool," Nikki said to Jack. "We should find a way to help."

The fourth message said, "BTW Coach had the video announcement system turned off." The last was my favorite: "We've got your back. Jenny's too. Tell her a lot of us love her, not just you."

"Tell him thanks for me, please," I said. What I didn't say, and I felt ungrateful even thinking it, was that I wished someone had had our backs a little earlier.

Jack almost yelled. "I've got it!"

"Got what?" Nikki asked in a scolding tone.

"I hate to say this, but this has to have hit social media, right?"

Troy scolded her too. "Not what we need to hear right now."

"She's right," I said. "What are you thinking, Jack?"

"Someone has to clean that up too. If the guys do the paper and chalk, we can help with the electrons."

"How does that work?" Troy asked.

"You know our two star hackers, Matt and Chris? They have crushes on me and Nikki. Big crushes. We can use that."

For a moment I felt like myself again. "Why didn't I know that?"

Jack smiled broadly. "We only found out this week, and you've had other things on your mind. Boyfriend, kissing, politics."

I should have smiled, but I couldn't. "Which one has a crush on which of you? Are they desirables?"

"Desirables, yes. Which one of them is crushing on which one of us, we're not sure," Jack said. "Maybe they're not sure. They might be interchangeable."

"Maybe we're interchangeable," Nikki said, and they both giggled.

"Sorry," they said in unison, but it was okay.

"So anyway, they can help us watch for anything that pops up," Jack said. "Then we'll arrange for it to disappear."

"How?" Troy asked.

"We start with friendly requests, then peer pressure. Or threats. If that doesn't work, we file complaints. If that doesn't work, Matt and Chris hack them back to the Stone Age. If even that doesn't work, we'll get the legal team of Mom and Mom to send some threatening letters. There ought to be some advantage in having lawyers for moms."

"My best friends are amazing," I said. My voice sounded tired.

"Yes, we are." It was a very Jack thing to say, and it cheered me a little.

"One request?" I didn't know where it had come from, but it filled my mind.

"Anything," Jack said.

"No revenge, okay? Clean up whatever you find, and our undying thanks for that, but no revenge. No rumors or accusations. No hack attacks. No destroying anybody. Right now the distinction between the good guys and the bad guys feels pretty clear. Let's keep it that way."

Jack looked disappointed. "Are you sure? Because there are other ways to do this. Hackers are like magic, almost, and boy hackers will bend to our geek feminine will."

She deserved another smile, but I still couldn't. "No revenge. Please."

59

Aftermath

W HEN COACH ASKED US to join him in the principal's office, he had already briefed our parents and shown them the flier and the practice test.

Mom got to me first. Her damp, searching eyes told me I looked as traumatized as I felt. She wrapped me in a hug. "Honey, I'm so sorry this happened. But you're both strong. We'll all get through this together."

She was steady, unshakeable. I needed that—especially when Troy let go of my hand and turned to hug his mom.

"You could turn on your phone when bad things happen," Mom said gently.

"Sorry," I said.

"It's okay. We're here. And we knew you weren't alone."

Dad and Mr. Pullman looked a lot alike: jaws set, cheeks flushed, eyes watchful and alert, veins bulging in their necks. They didn't quite look dangerous—maybe I knew them too well—but they looked like they wanted to be dangerous. Just seeing them made me feel safer, though I couldn't have said from what.

Then Troy's mom was squeezing my hand and sounding just as concerned as mine. "How are you, Jenny?"

"I don't know." I shrugged. "I've been better. I've been a lot better."

She gave a me a big hug, and maybe it helped a little. Then Troy and I sat together between two sets of parents. He took my hand, and I studied his face. He looked a little bit traumatized and a lot like our dads. I wondered if he was recovering more quickly than I was, or if he just didn't want to look vulnerable. I had a wry thought about guys and machismo—but I didn't want to look vulnerable either.

We got started. I should at least have been curious to hear what Coach would say, but I wasn't. I had to force myself to listen. Coach mentioned an investigation, some possible consequences for the whole student body, and school discipline for the perpetrators—and criminal charges, he hoped.

His tone was grim. "When these things happen to kids who are less strong or less stable, at least one kid sometimes ends up dead. We're not playing games with this."

Mom said, "Thank you, Mr. Witt."

He asked if we knew who did it. Troy told him we weren't sure, and we didn't want to guess. I was proud of him.

"I can appreciate that," Coach said. "We probably have enough leads. But later, if you can do more than guess, I want you to tell me, okay?"

We agreed.

He promised to tell us what they found. He was concerned about social media, so we told him Jack and Nikki's idea. He was grateful and complimentary, and he said good things about us too—which was nice but didn't reduce the pain at all.

After the meeting, Troy asked my parents if he could drive me home, and they agreed. "Don't be too long," Mom said.

Zeus didn't want to leave me, but I sent him with Mom and Dad, after hugging him and telling him I'd be okay, and I'd be home soon, and he'd been a big help.

As we left the school in Troy's car, I said, "Coach is very kind, but I don't think we're as good as he thinks we are."

"I'm not," Troy said. "I want to hurt people."

"I want to watch you hurt them. No, I want to help you hurt them."

"You were right," he said. "No revenge."

"I pick a heck of a time to be right."

"Yeah." Some of the pain left his face for a moment. "Did you say heck? What's next? Dang and fetch?"

"My vocabulary cracked under the stress. Next time I'll say hell."

"Bet you won't." I watched the pain return to his eyes. "Jenny, giving you that flier was one of the hardest things I've ever done."

I slowly lifted his hand and kissed it. "I believe you." I kissed it again. "Thanks for doing it anyway."

He nodded but kept his eyes on the road.

There was a welcome normalcy in driving a familiar route in a familiar car, but the drive wouldn't be long enough. I took a cue from Mom telling us not to be too long. "Honey, could we stop somewhere and talk?" Before he could ask the obvious question, I added, "We'll text our parents. I don't think they assumed we'd be right behind them anyway. They'll understand."

"Where shall we go?"

"Somewhere with no gear shift between us."

The park where we'd once taken a Sunday afternoon walk was nearly empty, and there were enough trees to keep us from feeling we were on public display. We sat on a bench by the lake and held each other.

Troy finally spoke. "I got you into this. I'm sorry. You know who did it, and you know it's because at least one of them is jealous of you and me. If I'd been a little friendlier to them a lot sooner, or ignored them less, maybe this wouldn't have happened."

"Being friendly didn't work," I said. "You can't feel guilty for this. I probably made things worse by confronting Maddi, but nothing we've done justifies anything like this. Nobody should do such terrible things because someone else is happy. Besides—"

A thought struck me, and I fell silent.

"Besides what?"

"Two things, maybe. I wouldn't trade you—or us—to avoid today. Or next week, because that'll be awful too. And maybe that's the answer to the next question."

"What answer to what question?"

"Sooner or later," I said, "we have to decide whether we can bear to go back to school next week. Coach said they'll arrange things, if we can't."

"What's the answer?"

"We have to. And when we see the people who did this, we think, we have to act like it's just another day."

"Or punch them in the eye," he said.

"You would never hit a girl."

"I'm kidding, but I don't want to be."

"I know, right? And if anyone else laughs or says anything, we just walk away and try to be happy."

"I can take what they do to me," he said. "But when they hurt you, the one guy I don't want to be is the nice, polite, forgiving boy from Texas."

"The angry, noble, protective boy from Texas still won't punch a queen bee in the eye," I said.

"Might be guys to punch. You could scratch the girls' eyes out."

"I'd rather punch them too," I said. "In the eye, the throat, wherever. Can you teach me to throw a punch like a boy?"

"Said the polite, gentle girl who's not from Texas. What should we really do?"

I spoke slowly, because I was making it up as I went along. "We stick together as much as we can. I wish it could be more. We restrain each other if necessary. We show them we're not ashamed or destroyed, and they can't keep us from being happy or together or anything else we want to be."

"Might be harder than handing you that flier," he said.

"No." I turned his face toward mine and kissed him gently, then looked him in the eyes. "That one you had to do alone. This one we do together." I kissed him less gently, then put my head on his shoulder.

For me it was a comfortable silence, but when he spoke again, his voice was higher-pitched and trembling. I knew what that meant in my voice. "Do you ever want to stop being brave and just lock yourself in your room and cry?"

"I sort of did that today. Different room."

"I didn't, and I think I want to."

"Just tell me when and where. You can take a few minutes by yourself, if you want, and then Zeus and I will come and sit on the floor with you, and you can cry on our shoulders. In a tough, properly masculine way." I hugged him tightly. "And it can't be your bedroom. We have a rule."

A moment passed. "Just tell you when?"

"Yup." I tried to sound light-hearted.

"Does Zeus have to be there?"

"No, but he loves you too."

"How about now?" he asked. I felt, not just heard, the catch in his voice. His face was distorted and miserable.

I pulled him to me and held him. "We'll skip the part where you're alone."

He shook with sobs. I just kept holding him—and getting more and more angry at the people who hurt him. Hurt us. Gradually he settled down.

"Sorry," he said. My shirt muffled his voice. "Guys are supposed to be stronger than this."

"You're always strong for me, you big, handsome, wonderful, chauvinist boyfriend. Like you were today. Don't I get to be strong for you?"

"Guess so."

"You don't sound convinced."

He sniffed. "Sound embarrassed, I think."

"Troy, we girls take a while to learn this, but guys are people too. You get to be human. You get to cry on our shoulders when you need to."

"Still embarrassed. Don't cry much."

"Yes, well, I cry enough for both of us. But I understand you better now. I'm ready to hurt just about anyone among the countless multitudes who suck. Because they hurt you."

"You were still right. No revenge."

"Sucks to be right."

He exhaled loudly. "This is hard." He took a deep, almost steady breath, then a few more.

"Are you okay now?" I asked.

"For now. You?"

"For now, thanks to you. We should go home to our four anxious parents and my one anxious dog."

"Can I tell you something first? May I?"

"Anything."

"It's pretty amazing that your parents let you ride with me today. We couldn't have blamed them for saying no."

"They trust you."

"Hope they don't blame me for this," he said quietly.

"They won't. They might worry about you blaming yourself. I'm worried about that too. So don't."

He nodded somberly. "Let's go home."

60

You Love Me

I T TOOK A WARM, gentle breeze in our faces to get me to notice what was around us, as we walked back to the car. There was snow on the mountain peaks, but in the valley it was spring. The grass had turned from grayish brown to green, and most of the trees had their leaves or were getting them. Soon it would be summer.

What caught my gaze was a tree which hadn't started to bud yet. If it wasn't dead, it was dormant and barren, still stuck in the winter the rest of creation had just escaped. In that tree spring was still just a promise.

Inside I felt like spring had come, then retreated under winter's devastating counterattack. My blissful life of hours ago was a faint memory; returning to it was an impossibly distant hope. I shivered and clung more tightly to Troy. Maybe I was further from being okay than I knew.

Mom, Dad, and Zeus were waiting in the living room. Troy didn't stay long. He thanked my parents for letting him bring me home and not minding too much that we stopped to talk. Mom hugged him and, for the first time, kissed him on the cheek.

Then he knelt and thanked Zeus too—to please me, I knew, and it did. We kissed goodbye at the front door and promised to text each other later, by which we meant sooner.

Back in the living room, Mom put her arms around me and squeezed. I didn't cry, but only because I was cried out. Dad stood back and watched. He still looked like he wanted to be dangerous in my defense. But the dad I knew and loved was a writer, not a fighter.

"Honey, will it help more to talk about it or not to talk about it?" Mom asked.

"Not."

"Then we'll ask you only two questions right now, and we won't ask any more tonight. After that, if you feel up to it, you can help me make dinner. It's comfort food from scratch tonight: chicken noodle soup with homemade noodles, rolls, and chocolate cake."

"That sounds good."

"Do you think the person who did this is the one who harassed you in the halls, whose name you never told us?"

"Probably."

I thought Mom would ask for Maddi's name, but she didn't. "Okay. Do you think she could have done everything herself?"

"No."

To that she just said, "We'll see what they turn up."

It was time to honor our compromise. "Her name is Maddi Burke. She's a cheerleader. And a junior."

Neither parent reached for a phone. Mom just nodded. "Then we'll see if it turns out to be Maddi Burke."

"I thought she was just jealous of me over Troy, but now she's hurting him too, so I don't know." I hoped it was Maddi. The possibility that it was someone we didn't even suspect was more unsettling. No, it had to be Maddi.

We made dinner together and talked about other things. It didn't make me feel worse. I answered Jack and Nikki's solicitous text messages with fewer words than usual, and later I Skyped with Troy. We didn't talk about our day, except Will's election victory.

After I went to bed, when my body had surrendered but my mind hadn't yet, I recalled Coach mentioning possible criminal charges. I envisioned Maddi in a jail cell, looking amazing even in a prison jumpsuit. I doubted she'd have what she needed to do fancy things with her hair, but it would look great anyway.

I didn't expect them to put her in jail, but I thought sleepily that I might enjoy visiting her if they did. Troy and I could go together. We wouldn't talk to her. We'd just stare at her through the bars, then leave and go out for ice cream—because we could and she couldn't.

Which was just weird, said one part of my brain to another. Inaccurate too, if television meant anything. We'd only see her through a thick window in a visiting area, and we'd never see her cell. And they wouldn't really lock her up.

Still, a girl could dream.

My hair would be fine in prison, I thought, since I rarely did much with it anyway. And I might look okay in a jumpsuit. But Troy and I couldn't share a cell. They wouldn't let us, plus we had a rule. So we should probably stay out of prison.

It was getting weirder, said that same part of my brain.

***

Troy invited me to lunch and a video at his home on Saturday. He said it was his mom's idea. Nan and Lily made it an event. They prepared a nice lunch, then watched an old, fun, romantic movie with us.

The sofa in their family room was almost long enough for the four of us. We huddled comfortably together, like I was just another member of the family. I leaned on Troy, and he held my hand. Nan leaned on me and held my other hand, like the little sister I never had. Lily claimed Troy's lap and the shoulder I wasn't using.

All day I avoided trying to make sense of Friday. I wondered how I could feel so numb when it was so painful, and vice versa, but I wasn't ready to analyze it. Troy wasn't either. Every time our conversation wandered toward anything connected with Friday, we pulled up short and changed the subject.

***

On Sunday I woke up early—for me on a Sunday—and tried to figure out why Troy and I had become such a lightning rod for abuse. Not lightning *rods*, I thought in a short burst of happiness. We were one lightning rod. At least there was that.

I thought I understood the stuff at church, much as I didn't like it. But what made a few kids at school so hostile? I'd been picked on before for being different, mostly because I was epileptic, but that hadn't happened in a while, and this wasn't that. Could jealousy be so malevolent, so dark?

Shakespeare and scripture said it could. But in ordinary teenagers? Was someone—probably Maddi—jealous enough to do all that?

She couldn't have done it all herself. Were others jealous too? Or so devoted to her that they'd do whatever awful thing she asked? Did she want Troy that badly? She'd hurt him too.

Why didn't she just choose to be a decent human being?

Did hatred just happen, or did it have to come from somewhere? Did she hate me for some reason independent of Troy? She hadn't seemed to care that I existed until he came along.

I smiled at the thought of Troy discovering my existence. Maybe I was recovering, if happy thoughts kept invading my reflections on ugly things.

Was Maddi actually evil, so she hated our efforts to be good? At church they taught us to expect darkness to oppose light. "For it must needs be, that there is an opposition in all things," said the scriptures. Dad liked to quote an old Russian author about God and the devil fighting, and the battlefield is the human heart. I wondered about that, but I didn't blame Satan for Maddi's sins.

I blamed Maddi. If she'd done it. But I still didn't understand how things could get so bad. Maybe I never would. Maybe I didn't want to.

Discussing all this with my parents might have helped, but it would have involved painful details I hadn't told them yet, about what Maddi and her friends had been doing—and they'd probably remind me that we didn't know all the facts yet. We weren't even sure it was Maddi.

When it was official, maybe I'd ask Mom and Dad my questions.

Sunday dinner at home was nice, and dessert was nicer. Troy arrived with a big apple pie at just the right time. His assignment from his parents was to stay and help us eat it, he said, and not come home until we kicked him out.

We all ate pie, talked about anything but school, and watched an amazing film about Abraham Lincoln. By 9:45 p.m. the pie pan was empty and washed, all four of us were stuffed, and I'd been held and cuddled a lot. We had a few extra minutes to say goodbye.

We still hadn't talked about tomorrow. I planned to procrastinate until morning, when my routine could take over. But Troy said, as I walked him to his car, "I know we don't want to think about tomorrow, but I need to tell you one thing. When your dad drops you and Zeus off at school, I'll be waiting for you at the curb. We'll walk in together, okay?"

I looked up and nodded. I started to thank him and say I loved him, but a more pressing thought came out.

"You love me."

"Yup. And you love me. Good night." He held his index finger to his lips, kissed it audibly, and pressed it gently to my lips. I smiled and kissed it. Then we tried it without the finger.

Later, as the glow of our goodbye faded, I felt guilty. I loved him, but I hadn't loved him well enough to do for him what he'd done for me. I hadn't faced the unbearable before I had to and looked for ways to make it bearable for him.

Maybe it wasn't too late. I could at least be cheerful and grateful in the morning, so he'd worry about me less. I could try not to let anything hurt me—because that would hurt him too. I could look for opportunities to think of him instead of me, even when it was difficult.

Meanwhile, it was amazingly, impossibly true. He loved me.

Before bed my parents asked if I'd be going to school tomorrow, and was I ready to face it again?

For the first time I thought I might be, and I knew whom to thank.

61

Monday, Tuesday

I AWOKE HALF AN hour before my alarm and couldn't go back to sleep. Troy's magic was already working. Instead of dreading my arrival at school, I could look forward to seeing him. I made two important decisions.

First, I put on the heart necklace he gave me on prom day. Maybe I'd wear it all week.

Second, when we met on the sidewalk, as Dad drove away, our hello would flout the school's rule against PDA on school grounds. This morning, Troy mattered more than their rule, and he deserved a Public Display of (My) Affection. Their rule was strict enough, despite what we sometimes saw in the halls, that we could break it without bending our own rules. If we were caught, the worst we'd get for our first offense would be a warning.

He was there as promised, looking adorable and not terribly worried. I did my best to hug the stuffing out of him. Then I kissed him until we were both a little breathless. If a teacher or principal had seen us, we might have been reprimanded. On an ordinary morning, or if we were anyone else, we'd have heard some whistles, and someone would have called out, "Get a room already!" But none of those things happened when we kissed.

"There," I said softly. "We can think about that today, when we're tempted to think about something unpleasant."

He gave me one of his warmest smiles. I'd be remembering that too.

"Good thinking," he said. "Nice day for the necklace. Looks good on you."

"The way I see it, the heart's yours, and I'm the red stone inside it."

"I like it," he said. "Ready?"

I nodded.

We turned and headed resolutely for the front doors. On our way he told me that, for at least the next two days, he had permission from all his teachers to leave class early and arrive late, so he could walk me to all my classes.

I had a lot to learn about love.

Walking through the halls wasn't awful. No one was mean, and no one laughed at us. Our friends were solicitous, and the haters we saw kept to themselves. Most kids didn't know what to say, except hi, but I wouldn't have known either.

His locker was a happy sight. The door was covered with dark blue paper hearts—a "heart attack." I told him I wished I'd been part of it.

Our next stop was my locker, and I'd been heart attacked too, but with red hearts. He said he knew nothing about it.

During the day, light-blue hearts appeared over the dark ones on his locker door, and pink hearts covered most of the red ones on mine. The darker ones were all the same size and arranged in orderly rows and columns. The lighter ones were different sizes, with smiles or hearts drawn on them or short messages written in different hands. My favorites on both locker doors said "Troy + Jenny" or "Jenny + Troy"—which Nikki sagely called "a textbook example of the commutative property."

The notes made our day go better. So did some extra nods and waves. Nobody really smiled at us—to me it wasn't a day for smiling—but the kind attention helped.

We heard rumors of kids being called to the principal's office for questioning, but lots of kids might have seen something, so we avoided jumping to conclusions.

After school I told Troy I wanted to see Mr. Cain, and he was welcome to join me. "I have to apologize," I said.

We found him at his desk, grading papers—and looking older, I thought, or at least tired. His door was open, but we knocked anyway.

He looked up. "Yes? Oh, hello, Jenny—and you must be Troy."

"May we talk for a minute?" I asked.

"Of course. Come in. Sit if you like."

We stood in front of his desk.

"Mr. Cain, I owe you a huge apology for what I said Friday. You would never do such a thing. I'm very sorry."

"Thank you. But I didn't blame you." He shook his head. "How could you not be upset? Besides, you said it so softly that no one else heard it. That was classy."

He put down his red pen. "I apologize for letting someone sneak that horrible question into my practice test. I know they did other things too, but that one has me mortified."

"I'm sure it's not your fault," I said. "And you don't suck. You're actually kind of cool."

He smiled faintly. "Thank you. How are you two holding up?"

"We haven't collapsed yet, sir," said Troy.

"Was your weekend awful too?" I asked.

He nodded. "The difference is, I arguably deserved it. Anyway, I'm glad you came to school today. That's courage."

"Thanks," I said. "We should leave you to your work."

"Before you do, I want to tell you something." He rose and stepped out from behind his desk. He was almost as tall as Troy. "We can't undo what happened. I wish we could. But we will fix the culture of this school."

"Thanks, Mr. Cain," I said. "Maybe we can help somehow."

He nodded. "I'm quite sure you will. Thanks for stopping by. Hang in there." His handshake was firm.

On our way home, Troy and I speculated about what they'd do to Maddi, when she turned out to be guilty. Suspension, definitely. Expulsion, maybe. Probation, probably, if they were serious about criminal charges. Jail time, probably not, but I still liked the idea.

—◆—

Tuesday was a lot like Monday. More paper hearts appeared on our locker doors. There were more rumors of students being questioned. I wore my heart necklace again. And the boy I loved walked me to my classes.

I had Mr. Cain's class for the first time since Friday. None of our suspects was in the class, but he had stern words for us anyway. "Some of you saw cruelty happen," he said, "and you laughed." He publicly apologized to me.

He returned the practice exams with one page removed. I tried to concentrate on our discussion of each question, especially the ones I hadn't seen, but the only thing keeping my thoughts out of painful places was my memory of kissing Troy before school, which worked so well on Monday that we repeated it.

I asked Troy not to escort me to fourth period, after lunch, because I wanted to be ten minutes early. Mrs. Tornow was an amazing teacher. Advanced Writing was my favorite class ever. I'd missed class on Friday. And next week it would be over.

I was lucky to be in the class as a sophomore. According to Mr. Cain, the class had been full every year for two decades, and there was always a waiting list of seniors. Fifteen was the official maximum, but Mrs. T would sometimes approve one extra student, if she was sufficiently impressed. This year, she chose fifteen seniors and me.

We wrote a lot, and every few days we read each other's work and critiqued it. It was anguish sometimes, but you couldn't improve as a writer if comments and critiques paralyzed or upset you, or if you couldn't bear to read your work aloud before you thought it was finished.

My worries about fitting in had ended on the second day of class, when the seniors took my first two-page essay seriously and welcomed my feedback on theirs. They probably assumed I had talent, because Mrs. T let me in two years early.

With only three class meetings left, we still had plenty of work to do. Most teachers backed off in May, especially with seniors, but no one complained when she didn't. It felt like she took us seriously.

For most of the month she'd led us through another unit on writing fiction. We'd had three already, scattered through the year, each with a different emphasis. This time we worked on ways to make characters and plots more interesting. We did lots of exercises, individually and together, and worked on our own projects.

She was generous with praise but never stopped pushing us. Over and over, in our group work on characters, for example, she'd reject an obvious motive or trait we proposed, or insist that we also find and incorporate its opposite. If our heroine was the kind of person who did this, under what circumstances would she do that? If she was known to be selfish, what chain of events could move her to stunning self-sacrifice—and vice versa?

She kept insisting we put ourselves in someone else's—even an object's—place to examine motives and experiences from the inside. "When you write a scene," she said, "no matter how you write it, you should be in every head in the room."

It wasn't easy. It was sometimes frustrating and frequently intense. "Writing is work," Dad often said. "Don't expect otherwise." He was right—but I loved almost every minute of it. I was born to be a writer. I'd even begun to think that maybe, when I became a real writer, I'd also want to teach like Mrs. T.

Our final project was fiction, a short story of 3,000 to 6,000 words. It was due the following Tuesday at the beginning of our last class. Mine wasn't finished yet, but I already liked it. It was about an old man with Alzheimer's receiving visitors one afternoon, written from his perspective. Mrs. T had praised my latest draft, then given me two pages of notes on how to improve it. Other class members had helped with their critiques. I'd given Troy a draft too, since he knew Grandpa. He'd thanked me for letting me read it, even if it wasn't finished yet, then praised it and offered two helpful notes.

But that wasn't due until next week. For now, Advanced Writing was the eye of the storm. I was relieved, not just glad, to go there, even while I mourned our nearness to the end.

Mrs. T was alone, sitting at her desk, writing on the little laptop she used for her own work. Zeus and I waited at the edge of her peripheral vision. She'd notice us soon enough.

She was older than Mom, with gold wire-rim glasses and short, low-maintenance blonde hair fading to gray. She pursed her lips, shook her head slowly, and glared at the screen. She resembled the scary elementary school librarian whose look alone had kept students out of the library, when we had a choice. But I knew Mrs. T. She was passionate about writing, hers and ours, but not scary.

She sat back, exhaled loudly, closed her laptop, and gazed out the window.

"Excuse me, Mrs. Tornow," I said. "I'm sorry to interrupt."

She turned. "Hi, Jenny. It's no interruption. I was trying a different ending for something, but it doesn't work." She made a sour face.

I wondered if she'd show the class what she was writing. She was the only English teacher I knew who routinely asked her students to critique her own writing. It was all about respect and better writing, not power or fragile egos, she said.

"I'm sorry," I said.

She smiled. "I'll figure it out eventually. How long were you standing there?"

"Two minutes, maybe."

"See, you really didn't interrupt. I had no idea." Her smile disappeared. "How are you?"

I shrugged. "I'm here. Thanks for asking. I'm sorry for missing class Friday. I came to find out what I missed."

"I can't tell you how much I wish Friday had been a normal afternoon, with you here in class, as usual." She looked at me so sadly that I wanted to cry. "I'm glad you came early. I wanted to talk to you. We'll review the essentials from Friday at the beginning today, and you'll be fine. Nothing to make up. Then there's an exercise you should consider not doing."

Advanced Writing had never felt like gym class before. "What is it?"

"The timing is an unfortunate coincidence. The exercise is to put yourself in the mind and heart of someone who's recently hurt you, and write from that perspective instead of your own."

My stomach flipped. "I see the problem."

She nodded. "I can only imagine what you've been through. You could choose someone else, but anything you choose may be too painful."

"You keep telling us our best writing will hurt," I said.

"True, but this is just an exercise. If it's too painful, don't do it. Work on your final project. Write nothing. Or less than nothing. Eight stanzas of iambic pentameter on unicorns and rainbows."

I had to smile. "I'll see how it goes. But don't expect unicorns and rainbows. I'm not that kind of girl."

She smiled too. "You could put yourself into the mind and heart of such a girl."

"That would be painful," I declared.

Her eyes twinkled. "I'm glad you're here today."

I didn't want to skip the exercise entirely, so I wrote from the perspective of Troy's kindergarten classmate who started The Club of Kids Who Are Saved by Jesus and Don't Worship Satan. It wasn't my best work, and Mrs. T was right to worry that it would hurt. Questions about Friday kept distracting me. Someone must have helped Maddi. But why? What had Troy or I ever done to turn them into The Club of People Who Hate Troy and Jenny?

When the bell rang, Zeus and I waited for traffic to clear, as usual. Then I went to Mrs. T and thanked her for thinking of me.

"I've been trying to find something to say that would help," she said.

"Anything you want say, I want to hear."

"All I have is this," she said. "You'll get through this. You're already getting through it. Things will get better. If there's anything I can do to help, anytime, I'd love for you to tell me. For example, if you ever want to talk, I'm pretty good at listening. If you ever want to listen, I'm even better at talking."

"Thank you," I said earnestly. "I might take you up on that."

"Speaking of things getting better, see that boy in the doorway? You should go, before we both cry in front of him."

I managed a wry smile. "I've done that before."

"I haven't. See you Thursday."

On our way to his car, Troy and I found Nikki alone on a bench, head in hands and with Jack nowhere in sight. Her shoulders subtly shook.

Troy beat me to the question. "Nikki, what's wrong?"

She couldn't talk at first. We sat beside her, and I put my arm around her. "What's wrong?"

Finally she said, "I just need to calm down before I meet Jack at the car."

"What happened?" I asked.

She looked at us with distressed eyes. "They called me to the office about Friday. They offered to wait until my parents could get here, which I thought was a bad sign, but I said I'd be okay. I have nothing to hide."

I was baffled, and part of Friday's lead weight was back. "Why would they question you?"

"They said they have evidence that I was part of it. They wanted me to confess." Her brown eyes were enormous. "I was not part of it!"

"Why would they think you were?" I asked. "That's crazy."

"It's actually not. When they checked the PowerPoint presentation that replaced the real announcements and showed that awful stuff on the screens, the file properties said I was the author. So did the PDF file of the test review they used on the copier. But I would never do that to you!"

Her face crumpled, and I held her tightly.

"We believe you. Did they believe you?"

She wiped her eyes and visibly fought for control. "They said I'm more than good enough with computers to pull it off. I guess that's true. I told them I'd have been smart enough not to leave my name all over it.

"Then I thought, sometimes I forget to log out of a computer in the lab. I get in trouble for that sometimes. I could have forgotten, and somebody could have done something after I left. I think they're checking on that. What if they don't believe me?"

"What do they think your motive was?" Troy asked. "You've been best friends forever."

She looked at him. "They thought maybe I was jealous of Jenny over you. And you know what? I am. I'm about one percent jealous of my best friend, and about ninety-nine percent really, really happy for her. I didn't just not do it. I couldn't do it. Not to you two. Not to anybody, I hope."

I pulled her into a hug. She cried quietly, while I tried to focus on the ninety-nine percent.

Troy looked somber. "One percent doesn't seem like enough of a motive for this," he said.

Nikki took a deep breath and looked up. "That's what they said."

"You told them?" I asked.

"It's the truth."

I shook my head. "Maybe it'll help. But you make a lousy criminal."

She frowned deeply. "I'm not a criminal."

"Want us to talk to Coach or the principal?" Troy asked.

"I don't know. I mean, thanks, but let's see if they figure out what really happened, and that gets me off the hook."

"Okay," he said. "Say the word."

"Thanks for believing me. Both of you. I should go. Jack's in the car." She turned to me. "Give Troy an extra hug for me, okay?"

"Just one percent?" I asked.

"Maybe two percent at the moment." She managed a wan smile. "You should hug him yourself."

Which she did.

On the way home, I did a foolish thing. I began to treat my best friend as a writing exercise. I tried to imagine a scenario in which Nikki would do what someone had done to Troy and me. I couldn't—because she wouldn't. But I thought through it far enough to wonder which would have hurt me more, learning of her betrayal or witnessing her punishment?

Note to self, I thought. Don't turn people I love into writing exercises. I'd just done it twice in one afternoon.

I had nearly imagined my way to actual tears, but Troy rescued me in time. "Are you back to believing in beauty you don't see?" he asked at a red light.

I considered that for a moment. "It's strange. I haven't really thought about that since Friday." I looked into the eyes I loved. "You still see it. I believe in you."

He brushed back a few strands of my hair, then ran the back of his fingers slowly down my cheek.

I loved long stoplights.

62

Who Did What

On Wednesday Jack and Nikki reported on their social media cleanup. They wouldn't tell Troy and me what they'd seen, and we hadn't looked. They said it was a lot less than they expected, and everyone they asked to remove something did so without argument.

We thanked them, and Troy added, "Thank your hackers for us, please. We will too, when we see them."

That prompted Jack's trademark mischievous grin. "We'll thank them. Again."

Nikki blushed. "This time, maybe dinner and a movie."

I wondered what that meant, but it could wait for just the three of us.

❖

Troy and I went out for hamburgers that evening. We picked up our food, then drove to a park to eat. When we returned, Nikki's car was parked in front of my house, and Nikki was sitting on the front step.

"Mom and Dad are home," I said as we hugged. "You could have waited inside."

"That's what they said, but I wanted to wait out here." She was somber, maybe even morose.

"We'll sit with you," I said. The step was wide enough for three of us. I sat in the middle. "What's the bad news?"

"It's not bad," she said quietly. "It's not wonderful either, but it's not bad." She looked at Troy, then at me. "I'm not a suspect anymore."

"That's great news!" Troy said, and I nodded vigorously, but she still looked unhappy.

"I'm not a suspect, but it was partly my fault anyway, for not logging out when I should. I'm so sorry. They'll explain everything tomorrow, I think, but they already told me that much. I just wanted to tell you." She began to sob, and I wrapped her in a hug.

"Please don't blame yourself," I said, when she was calmer.

Troy reached for her hand and squeezed it. "What she said."

When Nikki finally drove away, after parting hugs from both of us, I retreated to Troy's embrace. "Thanks for being kind to my friend," I said.

"You don't blame her, do you?" He sounded as if he thought I might.

"No," I said. "Do you?"

"No, and she shouldn't blame herself."

"But she does," I said. "This has been hard on her too."

"Maybe tomorrow will help," he said.

"I hope it helps somebody," I said.

⎯⎯◆⎯⎯

By Thursday afternoon, six days after the horror, I thought less about the trauma than about the school year ending—and with it, Mrs. Tornow's class. I had to push that thought away too, so I could concentrate on her final exam.

The first part was supposed to take only five minutes. "Your boyfriend or girlfriend just kissed your best friend on the mouth—right in front of you. It didn't look platonic. List three scenarios in which this would *not* be a betrayal. If your first thought is, he or she is drunk and thought it was you, don't go with that."

I wrote, "(1) They're rehearsing a play, and they're decent actors. (2) I begged him to kiss her. She's helpless with nerves about a possible first kiss tomorrow with the boy she likes, and we're preparing her. (3) Terrorists say they'll blow up his mother, if he doesn't kiss my friend."

The second part was supposed to take the remaining hour. I turned the page and read the prompt.

"It's five days before Christmas. You're male, and until recently you were a college junior, headed for a top law school, but things have gone terribly wrong. You're in court, where you've just pled guilty to felony battery. You tinkered with a fellow student's wheelchair, because he had someone let the air out of your car's tires after a heated political debate. The outcome was worse than you intended. He lost control on a hill and crashed into the side of a parked bus, breaking his jaw, his nose, and both arms, and suffering a concussion.

"Your parents hired a good lawyer, hoping to get you the shortest possible sentence. The prosecutor refused to reduce the charge to a misdemeanor, even though it's your first offense. It's a well-publicized case, and he's running for reelection.

"Even before the judge announces your sentence, you've lost a lot. Your dream of a legal career is gone, your fiancée has dumped you, and you're being kicked out of school. Your best hope is a one-year minimum sentence. Perhaps the fact that it's almost Christmas will move the judge.

"The sentencing hearing moved quickly. The victim declined to make a statement. The prosecutor said simply that in the state's opinion your crime and your guilty plea speak for themselves. You apologized briefly, when it was your turn to speak, but you didn't beg for leniency. Your attorney told the court you've never been charged with a crime before, let alone convicted, not even a misdemeanor. He argued for the minimum sentence, so you can finish learning your lesson and be home with your family by the following Christmas. Now the judge is watching you and leaning toward his microphone.

"Write the moment. Describe four people's thoughts and feelings about you in this moment. Consider the victim, one of your parents, a member of the victim's family, and one other person. In the process, show us your own perspective as the convicted criminal. Try to avoid head-hopping. Use description, interior monologue, recollection, etc., whatever you need to help us feel what they're feeling—except contemporaneous dialogue. Everyone is waiting silently for the judge to speak.

"Remember, you hurt a guy in a wheelchair, and you could have killed him, so you probably can't persuade us you don't deserve punishment. But maybe you can make us regret your fate.

"As ever, three good pages beat five rough pages.

"Finally, be advised: if your work is technically perfect but completely predictable, I reserve the right to sentence to you a C for having learned nothing this past month."

I grinned. Mrs. T was awesome.

We did our in-class writing on computers, to make the most of our class time, then printed hard copies to turn in. I wrote and rewrote quickly, coaxing my thoughts into sentences and paragraphs which mostly flowed smoothly and showed more than they told, I hoped.

As the defendant, I probed my own mind enough to discover shame and dread for the future. Then I took each character's obvious thoughts and emotions and complicated or even inverted them.

My best invention was that the victim's sister had known and loved me since junior high, though I'd never given her the time of day. When she looked at me, I expected to see anger or indifference, but her eyes mirrored my own fear and shame. She cared about me, not just her brother. That realization wrenched my fictional heart in a completely new way.

Ten minutes before the bell, I printed a draft for a quick final edit. I fixed a few typos, moved two paragraphs, cut some unnecessary words, and pared down a key emotional beat to make things more subtle. Dad always said to leave room for the reader's mind to help tell the story, and Mrs. Tornow urged us to avoid writing a lot of words where a few would do, if they were just the right words.

My three and a half double-spaced pages were pretty good for an hour's work. I loved being a writer. I waited after the bell, so I could be the last to reach Mrs. Tornow's desk with my exam.

"Would you like me to read this now, while you wait?" she asked.

"Sure, if you like."

"I like."

She smiled at the first section. "I've asked variations of this before. I don't get a lot of terrorists demanding two people kiss. Nice touch, making his mother the stakes, not himself or the whole cosmos."

Sometimes the emotions I wrote spilled into the real world. Sometimes vice versa. "I love his mother," I said. "Him too. The cosmos in general can suck it."

All four of our eyebrows shot up at my language, but there was a mischievous glint in her eye. "Amen. I'll read now."

Half-nervous, half-hopeful, and more shocked at myself than embarrassed, I watched her read. She seemed engaged. Whether she was reader-engaged or just teacher-engaged, I couldn't tell.

Finally she looked up. "At first reading, there's human feeling here. It's unpredictable, it feels genuine, and for the most part you didn't overplay it. Well done!"

"Thanks. It was a great class, Mrs. T. I miss it already."

She nodded. "I miss it every summer. And thank you." She added my exam to her pile. "I've been meaning to ask, would you like to take this class again next year? You can spend part of your time being my TA and helping the others. That'll make you a better writer too."

I beamed. "I'd love that! Thank you!"

"I want to see how much you improve with another year of serious work in here." She spoke more soberly. "I'm proud of the way you've handled the last few days. A lot of us are. I said it before, but things will get better. Sometimes we really do get what we deserve in the end, even if the middle's pretty ugly."

—◦—

Troy, Nikki, and I were scheduled to meet with the principal and our parents half an hour after school. We found a place to sit and wait. I told them about Mrs. T's invitation, but after that we didn't talk much.

My thoughts wandered off on their own. I reimagined my courtroom scene, with Maddi as the convicted criminal and the principal as the judge. I was the victim. In real life I'd been rolled around in a wheelchair at the hospital a few times, and I'd had concussions, but all I needed was gravity for those. I'd never been in danger of colliding with a bus.

Would I feel better in a few minutes, if I heard what Maddi's—someone's—punishment would be? Would Troy? Would any of us feel sorry for Maddi's—someone's—sad but self-inflicted fate?

Earlier in the week, for a few minutes at a time, I'd been eager to learn who did what and how they'd be punished. But if the price of knowing was reliving that afternoon, it might not be worth it. We already knew they considered Nikki a victim, not a perp, and that felt like enough.

I looked at Troy and Nikki in turn. "I don't think learning everyone's punishments will fill me with joy. Or learning their names." They murmured their agreement.

Coach met us outside the principal's office, while the principal finished a phone call. Our parents were waiting too.

"Coach, I'm so glad you're here," I said.

He frowned. "I have a detailed report for all of you—whether you want it or not, I guess."

"Mostly I just want it to be over," I said. "With all the wreckage magically swept away, so we can forget it ever happened."

"I don't have a magic wand or a time machine," he said gently, "but I hope it helps."

The door opened, and the principal invited us in. The resource officer was already there. Standing next to each other, they looked like Laurel and Hardy. But I didn't feel like smiling, and they weren't doing comedy. Principal Simmons was shorter than the other men in the room, with a thin face and dark hair. His red power tie was perfectly straight, even at the end of the day. Sergeant Ramirez, the resource officer, was round-faced and much more solidly built. He was in civilian clothes, a navy polo shirt and khakis, but he had a badge and gun on his belt. He greeted everyone, but he didn't smile like he usually did in the halls.

When we were seated, Principal Simmons began. "Thank you all for coming. As we said when we invited you, this is not just a status report. We now have a clear picture of what happened. It involves a number of students. We have everyone's written permission and the district legal office's blessing to tell you privately who did what. We have full confessions from everyone involved. We told the perpetrators that, in exchange for complete cooperation, there will in most cases be no criminal charges filed, and if there are, the charges will be reduced."

We were about to know everything. I hoped that was good. But the thought of criminal charges put a knot in my stomach.

"We'll tell you what we know and answer any questions we can. Coach?"

Coach had several pages of notes. "The hashtag #TRISP," he said. "The student council invented it to promote the senior party, SP. T was for Totally. What R and I meant depends on who you ask. They met in Mrs. England's room, as usual.

"Maddi Burke, a junior and one of our varsity cheerleaders, was there. Two other cheerleaders, Brooke Richardson and Katie Strong, met her there afterward. At that point they were alone in the room, except for one student I'll mention in a moment.

"The girls started playing with other possible meanings for the acronym, related to you and Troy. They didn't go quite as far as what we all saw later, but they thought it might be fun to spread around. That led to the fliers. They considered using social media too, but they didn't want their names on anything.

"The other person there was Norbert Pratt, one of our gifted computer students. He was working on something in the back, but also eavesdropping on their conversation. Apparently he's had a crush on one of the girls for a long time—from a considerable distance—and he'd have done just about anything to please her. He had a moment of courage and offered his help.

"Specifically, he hacked the announcement screens. He also had the idea to hack the sophomore English practice test. He's on duty in the computer lab a lot, and he knew Nikki often forgets to log out. The announcement loop on the video system is a looping PowerPoint presentation, and the test review prints from a PDF file, so one day he used Nikki's abandoned session to create his own versions with the offensive material. That's why the files showed Nikki as the author. By the way, Mr. Cain makes a new test every year, but he always uses the same review."

Coach paused to turn a page. I looked at Nikki. She stared sadly at the floor, and her chin trembled. I put my arm around her waist. She glanced at me with desolate eyes and looked down again.

Coach continued. "Apparently, Norbert doesn't dislike any of you. He just wanted to please a girl, and his instinct was to hide their tracks. Maddi and the others liked the idea of framing Jenny's friend.

"He slipped the PDF into the copier queue in place of the real file. Nobody noticed the change in one question before it was printed, delivered to the teachers, and passed out to students.

"He could be in the worst legal trouble. Our student data's on the same network as the announcement system, and unauthorized access to a government computer network containing confidential records can be charged as a felony. He could be charged as an adult."

The knot in my stomach tightened, and my thoughts began to fray.

"I asked him if he knows how to spread things on social media, using fake names or by hacking other students' accounts. He said he does. So I asked him why he didn't suggest that to Maddi or just do it for them."

Coach shook his head. "Maybe it's the difference between a teenager and a criminal sociopath. He said what they did was contained—he used that word—so it wouldn't go beyond the school, and he would never turn something like that loose on social media, not even for a girl. What he actually said was, he wouldn't go nuclear, even for her."

So it could have been worse. I didn't feel better.

"Meanwhile," he continued, "Brooke and Katie went to Kellie, our student aide. The cheerleaders are always having her copy things. This time, they asked to make their own copies. She's not supposed to let students do that, but they were friendly, and she was so happy and flustered that she agreed. She never even saw the flier until we showed it to her. I think she's been crying ever since."

This was still getting worse. I had used Kellie too, a couple of weeks earlier, to get Maddi's class schedule and locker number. That wasn't as bad, but it wasn't good. Kellie wasn't the brightest bulb in the chandelier, but she was helpful, cheerful, and kind. I had taken advantage of her innocence and her trust. I'd let her believe something that wasn't true, so she'd do something for me that she shouldn't.

I forced myself to keep listening, but I needed to think about apologizing to Kellie. Soon.

"One of the girls heard that the principal and assistant principals would be away on Friday at a district meeting. They decided to combine all their attacks into the same day.

"Norbert hacked the server and set it up to show his presentation for a while during first lunch, then go back to normal, then show it again for part of last lunch, then put things back to normal again and erase most of the evidence. When I had the secretary unplug the computer, it was before his program—he called it a script—before his script could destroy the evidence."

"On the low-tech side of the operation, the girls arranged for someone to drop a tray and start a loud argument in the cafeteria, to distract everyone while stacks of fliers appeared on tables and in the school newspaper racks. The guys involved in the argument didn't know why they were doing it. They said they owed the girls a favor." He scowled.

"Maddi, Brooke, and Katie recruited four other girls to help them put out the fliers. All seven were strategically located when the fight started. They pulled the fliers out of their backpacks, set them out, and went their separate ways. It almost worked. Only a couple of students saw them do it. Everyone else was watching the show.

"So there were seven girls and one boy who knew what happening, at least to some degree, and participated. The office aide and the two boys who did the fighting were also involved, but didn't know what was going on.

"Mr. Cain wasn't involved at all, of course, but he was helpful in the investigation. He has good computer skills and a cunning, suspicious mind. He also felt terrible that his practice test was involved, not to mention that this happened at all. Jenny and Troy, he was grateful for your visit on Monday."

Coach put down his notes and looked at Troy, Nikki, and me for a moment. "One more thing I want to tell you. We talked to a lot of kids, just looking for eyewitnesses from the cafeteria. I asked most of them how they reacted to the flier and the announcement screen, and how the students around them reacted. A lot of them said it wasn't funny, and I mostly believed they were sincere. Hardly anyone believed what it said about you, Jenny, and you, Troy. I confess I was pleasantly surprised that two students' good reputations are stronger than that sort of attack."

He smiled faintly. "I don't know if that helps. I hope it does."

It did. It also fit how we'd been treated since Monday, including the heart attacks at our lockers.

Coach turned to the principal.

63

Consequences

Principal Simmons took over. "This feels like a minor league terrorist operation," he said. "The masterminds timed it for maximum chaos, framed someone else, limited their operatives to what they needed to know, and carried out multiple coordinated attacks. It grew out of three girls persuading themselves to hate two fellow students, and a hacker who was intellectually inspired and morally paralyzed by his unrequited passion for a cheerleader. They used an innocent girl who was just glad to be treated with civility by the queen bees, plus four girls with more loyalty to their friends than to any recognizable moral principles, and two boys who didn't know what they were abetting, but might have helped even if they had.

"We'll talk about consequences for all of them, but first, does anyone have any questions about what happened?"

Others did, but I didn't. I was thinking about Kellie, and I didn't want to dwell on the rest of it. The last question came from Nikki's mom. She asked what measures were being taken to prevent similar attacks in the future.

"I'm glad you asked," said the principal. "We've scheduled outside audits of our office procedures and network security. We'll fill whatever holes we find. The building was already scheduled for new video surveillance in the halls and other common areas. That would have sped up our investigation and possibly had some deterrent effect. We'll see what else develops. I'm also expecting good things from our student leadership. But let's talk consequences. They're primarily my decision, but we think you all have a right to have some input."

He wanted input from us, not just our parents? Despite our fantasies about punching people, and my weird, sleepy thoughts of visiting Maddi in jail, I wasn't eager to influence actual punishments.

The principal stood. "Before that, I'm sorry, but I've been stuck in this office for hours, and I need to excuse myself for a few minutes. Let's take a five-minute break."

He left, and I turned to Troy. "She had a lot of help."

"You okay?" he asked.

"Not really. You?"

"Don't know. But I should visit the little Troy's room myself."

I winced. "Thanks for the pun. I'll miss you a little less while you're gone."

Nikki left too, for water and air, she said. I wordlessly answered concerned parental looks, then ignored our parents' quiet conversation and landed back in my writing exam. I was about to hear Maddi's punishments and the others'. How would Maddi and her parents feel when they heard? How would the others feel?

I'd feel rotten, if the knot in my stomach was any indication.

If I were the guilty one—the guiltiest, the ringleader—what would my parents think and feel? Would they make excuses, blame others, and try to get me off with the lightest possible punishment? Would they wash their hands of me?

No, they'd act like parents. They'd try to figure out what would be best for me. They'd wonder if my character was as bad as my behavior and needed drastic measures. They'd hope it was an aberration and I'd grow up into a decent human being.

Could I ever look them in the eye again?

Was Maddi capable of shame?

Troy, Nikki, and the principal returned, and I pulled myself back to reality. The principal asked if we had any more questions about what happened. No one did.

Okay, consequences," he said. "We could file charges of criminal mischief, theft of school property, the unauthorized network access charge Coach mentioned, even littering. However, we agreed to back off most of that in exchange for their full cooperation and candor. We think we got it.

"Here's Plan A. The three who didn't know what was happening on get a stern lecture—another one—and one day of suspension next week."

One of those was Kellie. She didn't deserve suspension. Did I? My frayed thoughts began to unravel and my stomach churned ominously. I checked the location of the nearest wastebasket, just in case. It was in the corner, next to the coat rack.

"The four girls who only placed the fliers get a week of suspension. Their punishment is more severe, because they could look at the flier and know they were being cruel. As a result of their suspensions, some of them will be in summer school. They're also banned from extracurricular activities through the first quarter of next year.

"Maddi, Brooke, Katie, and Norbert face misdemeanor versions of the criminal charges I mentioned and will likely spend some time on probation. They are expelled for the remainder of this year and next year. They'll have to find other schools. We can't charge them under the new bullying statute, which the legislature passed last session, because it goes into effect July 1."

Maybe I was still stuck in my writing exercise, because his list of punishments for them felt like body blows to me—not just because I felt guilty for using Kellie. Once I began to imagine how the kids being punished more severely would feel, I couldn't stop. I clung to hope for a Plan B—because he'd called this Plan A.

My hands trembled. Troy was holding one, and he looked at me with concern. I looked at him but said nothing.

The principal continued. "Here's Plan B. Everyone makes a personal apology to Jenny, Troy, Nikki, and Mr. Cain. Norbert and the three cheerleaders make a public apology to the student body and faculty. No criminal charges, and the suspensions end with this school year. No one is expelled for next year. However, the three cheerleaders are banned from extracurricular activities for their entire senior year, including cheer, dances, games, and everything else that isn't during the school day or part of their regular classwork."

Plan B was much less severe. Why didn't I feel better?

"Norbert forfeits access to school computer systems and the school Wi-Fi for the duration of the coming year," said the principal. "All four of them do a hundred hours of service in the school or community before they graduate." He looked up from his notes. "Any thoughts?"

"Sounds about right to me," said Troy's dad, and the other parents nodded. "Do you think they'll make the apologies?"

"I think so. They're scared of the consequences otherwise, and in hindsight they scared themselves by what they were willing to do. If possible, we'd like all of you to meet with them tomorrow morning before school for the private apologies. We'll have an assembly Tuesday morning, because Monday is Memorial Day. They can make the public apologies then.

"Now, Jenny, Nikki, Troy, I wasn't kidding when I said we want your input. What do you think? Nikki, let's start with you."

She looked at me, then at Troy, then turned to Principal Simmons. "I don't know what I think yet. Could you come back to me in a minute, please?"

"Of course." He studied her face, while I considered my own sorry state. My head was muddled, the knot in my stomach kept getting tighter, and my heart was pounding like it was in an Edgar Allen Poe story. I'd have to say something, but I didn't know what.

"Jenny, what are your thoughts?"

I tried to have thoughts. But I had only one simple thing to say, and I wasn't sure it came from thinking. I glanced at Troy, then Nikki, then Mom and Dad and the other parents. I looked at Coach, the principal, and Officer Ramirez, then back at the principal. They were all watching me. "It's too much."

The principal considered that for a moment, then asked, "Do you mean Plan B is too much?"

His question helped me order my thoughts. "Plan A is far too much. You take away a year of their lives—for four of them—and it's their senior year. Plan B isn't that much different."

"It seems a lot different to me," he said.

"If the only thing they can do during senior year is go to class, you might as well expel them, because they'll have to find another school anyway, or they'll be miserable. And I'm sorry, Mr. Simmons, but the idea of publicly humiliating them is making me sick to my stomach."

"You mean public apologies for a public offense? What would you prefer?"

My answer wasn't an answer. "Some time to get my thoughts straight?"

When I had nothing to say after that, he nodded. "Thank you for your candor. Troy, what are your thoughts?"

He didn't hesitate. "Sir, I have to go with Jenny on this one."

The principal frowned. "I'm genuinely sorry to ask this, but is that because she's your girlfriend or because you really think that?"

Nikki glared, but I didn't mind his question. I might have asked Troy the same thing.

"Good question, sir." Troy looked at me, and I realized it didn't matter what he said. He either agreed with me, or he wanted something because I wanted it. Either way, the boy loved me.

"Not sure how to say this, sir. Part of me wants their punishment to be as severe as possible. I want it to hurt them. A year from now I still want to see the pain in their eyes. But I trust that part of me to do . . . to know what's right . . . a lot less than I trust Jenny."

He looked at me again. Tears pooled in my eyes—because of his words and because the silly boyfriend was putting his trust in a basket case. He turned back to the principal. "It's not because she's my girlfriend, sir. It's because I know what kind of person she is. I'd like some time to think about it too. How soon do you have to decide?"

"Before our 6:30 a.m. meeting tomorrow, at least."

"Pardon my frankness, sir, but were you serious when you said you want to consider our input?"

"Absolutely." He smiled. "I'll pardon your frankness if you'll pardon mine."

"Thank you, sir. What if Jenny, Nikki, and I get together tonight and figure out what we're thinking? We could meet here again in the morning, before the other meeting, and tell you whatever we have, if that's soon enough."

The principal nodded slowly. "Okay. Any objections to 6:00 a.m.?" He scanned the room. "So be it. I guess that's everything from me. Anyone else?"

After a few seconds he continued. "We'll adjourn until 6:00 a.m. Thank you, everyone. I'll see you then."

The abrupt end left me reeling. I probably looked dazed.

Mom extended her hand to the principal. "Thank you, Mr. Simmons. We appreciate how you're handling this."

"Thank you, Dr. Miller." He said something about parents who raise great kids, and we took our leave.

There was only one thing wrong with the hug I gave Troy outside the building. It had to end, so he could take me home.

64

The Right Question

I HELPED WITH DINNER cleanup, then sat on the living room sofa and slipped off my shoes. That was Zeus's cue to lie down across my feet. He'd done that for years, since I grew tall enough that my feet reached the floor when I sat. I didn't know whether it was protective, affectionate, or both, but I liked it.

"Such a good dog," I told him. "Help me think, okay?" I put my elbow on the arm of the sofa and leaned my head on my hand. "Any suggestions?"

If he had any, he kept them to himself.

Troy and I hadn't talked much on the way home about the elephant in the car. Mom, Dad, and I had ignored it when it stayed for dinner, except that I apologized for getting them into an even earlier meeting, which they said was okay. But I couldn't avoid it any longer. Troy, Nikki, and Jack—we wanted her too—would arrive in less than half an hour.

"I don't understand myself, Zeus. Why does it feel so wrong? Why shouldn't it cost them something they love? They deserve Plan B at the very least. Especially Maddi."

I leaned forward to pet him, then resumed my useless thinking pose. "So why do I feel sick? She was evil. She organized them to hurt us. They *worked at it*."

I had no trouble remembering how awful we'd felt that day, especially when I considered how many kids had helped them. Any more lenient punishment I could imagine was clearly less than they deserved. But Plan B still felt like too much. I looked down at the warm, furry mass of canine silence. "You'll tell me if I'm not thinking straight, right?"

Because dogs always talk to sane girls. "Here's a weird thought, Zeus," I finally said. "This feels like Mrs. T's writing exam. Which I'm failing this time, by the way."

I finally put into words the growing weight of something Troy had said in the meeting. "If I had the moral compass Troy thinks I have, I could figure this out. I wouldn't be so hurt and so confused."

Zeus happened to look up just then.

"I'm not the kind of person he thinks I am," I told him. "Or the kind I thought I was, I guess."

Zeus put his head back down.

"Am I the girl you thought I was?"

He didn't answer. There was no answer. I gave up thinking and just sat.

When they arrived, Jack and Nikki took the armchairs. Troy joined me on the sofa, and I leaned on him. Nikki had told Jack what we'd learned in the principal's office—"in absolutely infuriating detail," Jack said, just before we appointed her moderator. Nikki volunteered to take notes.

"First, a disclaimer," Jack said. "I'm not a neutral moderator. They should all be drawn and quartered, then burned in the public square, if we have one, in flames fueled by the dung of unclean beasts. I understand if some of that seems impractical."

We had to smile at Jack being Jack, no matter how rotten life was at the moment.

She allowed herself a faint smile. "Seriously, let's concentrate on Maddi first, since, big surprise, she was the ringleader. Whatever the others deserve, it's no more than she deserves. So without considering specific punishments yet, do we all agree she deserves some punishment?"

We agreed.

"Do we agree that everyone who helped her deserves some punishment?"

Troy and Nikki nodded. I said, "Except Kellie."

"Good thought," said Jack.

"Everyone . . . except . . . Kellie," Nikki echoed, writing it down.

It was a good start, but then two things happened. We reviewed Plans A and B, which made me feel sick again. And we tried to figure out how anything less than Plan B made sense, given what Maddi and the others had done to us. Like a rolling fog, the muddle in my head expanded to swallow the room and everyone in it, until I was ready to give up and just cry.

Jack must have seen it in my face, and maybe she felt it too. "We're nowhere," she said quietly. "Maybe you need a better moderator."

My eyes started to drip.

Troy gave me a squeeze. "Jack," he said tenderly, and she shifted her gaze to him. "We're a lot more likely to figure this out with your help. Let's just keep working, okay?"

Her smile was unguarded and sweet. Then it turned the tiniest bit wicked, and she was Jack again.

"If you make me cry too, I'm going home, and Maddi and those other awful people can just get what they deserve."

"Sorry," he said, but I knew he wasn't sorry for being kind. "So how do we figure this out?"

"It's no wonder we're stuck," said Nikki. "I don't know what anybody deserves, or what they don't."

"I don't either," I said.

Jack looked up sharply. I could see that wheels were turning. Finally she asked, "What if what they deserve is the wrong question?"

Her words hung in the air. I tried to think but couldn't.

"That's it!" Troy exclaimed. I looked up and saw him smiling. "Way to go, Jack!" He turned to me. "You and Nikki have an awesome friend, and I'm going to kiss you for it." Which he did. "I'd kiss them too, but I can't reach from here."

I liked the kiss well enough, but it was an odd burst of enthusiasm. I looked at him, then the others. Jack's eyebrows had climbed her forehead, and Nikki was bright red.

I turned back to him. "What's the right question?"

He pointed a finger at Jack. "She's the one with the light bulb over her head. She's a genius, you know." Jack's face turned redder than Nikki's.

"We know. What's the right question, Jack?"

She spoke quietly and methodically, as she often did when she worked through something complicated. Just hearing her talk that way gave me hope.

"We've been asking ourselves what they deserve, but we don't know that. We don't know completely why they did what they did, or everything they were thinking or feeling, or what someone might have done to provoke or hurt them somehow. We don't know if this is their first serious offense or just their latest. Maddi and some of the others have been nasty to you two for a while, but I'll bet she hasn't been in serious trouble before. And we can't be sure that any given punishment—except my idea—will keep them from doing something equally awful in the future."

She was on the edge of her seat. "What if we change the question? What if we stop trying to be all-knowing judges who understand what everybody deserves?"

"We all want better than we deserve," Troy said.

"Exactly," said Jack. "So we make that the question."

"Sorry," Nikki said. "What's the question?"

"I'll explain," said Jack. "Jenny, you and Troy already think the principal's being too severe."

"So do I," said Nikki.

"What if you dial back their punishments until you're sure they're getting better than they deserve? If we would want that for ourselves, maybe we should want it for them."

"Sounds promising," I said. It felt promising too. It was calming my inner turmoil.

Jack shrugged. "I'm still partial to drawing and quartering and flaming heaps of dung. But this way it won't feel like revenge, like you're part of them getting worse than they deserve."

"We end up helping people, not hurting them," Troy said.

"Exactly," said Jack. "But they still get punished."

"So what do we call this in the meeting tomorrow?" Nikki asked. "Forgiveness? At least partial forgiveness? Jenny, you're the writer-in-residence. What's the word?"

I produced a wan smile. "The writer-in-residence is too addled to know the word. Sorry."

"I don't think it's forgiveness," Jack said. "That's separate from punishment. We have to forgive them even if there's no punishment. Even if forgiveness seems impossible. That's how I read the scriptures."

I liked her bringing the scriptures into it.

"Amnesty?" Nikki asked.

"Not if there's punishment," Jack said. "Amnesty's like saying, we know you broke a rule, but it's okay. I don't think we're saying that."

"Commuting their sentence comes after sentencing," Nikki said. "A pardon too, I think."

"It's not justice," Jack said. "Justice was the wrong question."

No, it wasn't justice. But that led me to something else. Maybe the fog was lifting. "I think I know the word," I said quietly. Maybe even calmly.

They all looked at me.

"Mercy. The word is mercy."

"'Blessed are the merciful,'" said Nikki with a shy smile.

"Mercy tempers justice," Troy said.

"Mercy is better than we deserve," I said. "By definition."

Jack grinned. "How about that? We all listened in seminary. Who knew we'd ever use it in real life?"

We worked quickly after that, agreeing on measures we thought were less than they deserved and preparing for the adults' likely objections. Jack was a godsend for that, partly because she still wanted something worse.

Nikki wrote it all in her notes. After we reviewed them and tweaked a few things, Jack leaned back in her chair. "I think we figured it out. Who's saying what tomorrow?"

We decided Troy would start, and I would take a turn. Nikki said she'd jump in if we missed anything, but she'd be happy just to listen. Jack volunteered to sleep in, since she wasn't invited anyway.

"Okay, it's 9:45," she announced. You two can't say goodbye to each other in less than ten minutes, so Nikki and I should go. Good luck tomorrow. You'll be awesome."

"We'll walk you to the door," Troy said.

"Such a gentleman," Jack teased, "and it's not even your house."

"I have something for you outside," he said.

On the porch I thanked them both, and they hugged me.

"Do you think we're getting this right?" Nikki asked.

"All I know is, I feel better," I said, "and I think it makes sense now. Troy's right. You're both awesome."

Jack glanced at Nikki. "Obviously they're right," she deadpanned.

"Come here, you two," Troy said. "Jenny, watch at your own risk."

He took them both by the hand. "Nikki, I owe you something from earlier tonight." He reached down and kissed her lightly on the cheek. She reddened instantly.

"Jack, we couldn't have done this without you." He kissed her too, and she outblushed Nikki again.

"Now go home already." He guided them toward the steps. "Other people need kissing, and we're short on time."

Before they reached Jack's car in the driveway, he and I were sharing a gentle kiss, and not on anybody's cheek. Then we just held each other while they drove away.

"You're so good to my friends," I said. "Thank you. They're practically my sisters."

"I'm not in trouble for that?" He didn't sound worried.

"Just don't kiss them like they're your girlfriends. Or me like I'm your sister."

Our phones beeped. We had one minute. He led me to the edge of the porch and stood on the first step, so we were eye to eye. When we leaned in, our foreheads touched.

"I promise never to mistake you for my sister."

When he kissed me, I certainly didn't feel like his sister.

Later, as I got ready for bed, I wondered whether we'd have thought differently about punishment, if the principal had just told us what would happen, rather than asking what we thought. When he did that, suddenly the question became, what we were willing to do to them?

I drifted toward sleep, still thinking of tomorrow, hoping the principal would take at least some of our suggestions. If he didn't like everything, our asking for a lot less might get them a little less. If he took none of them, at least we'd have tried.

I didn't feel sick anymore. There was just a fuzzy, tired fringe around my thoughts, and a fresh, almost physical memory of Troy holding me in his arms.

65

Plan C

A T 5:30 A.M. Nikki, Troy, and I exchanged text messages, to make sure we all still agreed, which we did. At 6:00 we and our parents crowded into the principal's office again, along with Coach and Officer Ramirez. This time, Mr. Cain was there too.

After welcoming us and thanking us for coming, Principal Simmons said, "First I'll quickly review Plans A and B. I'll consider something more lenient, but you'll have to persuade me." He glanced at Troy, Nikki, and me in turn. "I'm sorry to be so blunt, and I really am open to alternatives, but time is short, and I need to be sure we're making disciplinary decisions based on something more substantial than the squeamish feelings of three high school students."

Nikki and I shared a worried look, but Troy had his game face on. "We understand, sir," he said. "Thank you."

The principal summarized Plans A and B, which made me queasy again. Then he said, "Now tell us your Plan C."

Our parents watched expectantly. We hadn't told them the details, just that we agreed. We thought our best chance of persuading them was to make our case together in the meeting.

Troy consulted Nikki's notes and began. "Sir, we'll tell you what we're thinking, then why. We'd like private apologies from everyone who knew what was going on. We also think Maddi, Brooke, Katie, and Norbert should have to apologize privately to the people they used and to Mr. Cain."

I knew my voice would shake, and it did, but I added, "If you want the other two guys and Kellie to apologize privately too, that probably makes sense. But please don't punish Kellie any more than that. She wouldn't intentionally hurt anyone. She made an innocent mistake. I'm sure she feels awful already."

There. I'd said it. I felt a little less guilt.

"We don't want public apologies from anyone," said Troy. "Maybe the whole school deserves one, but what good does it do to humiliate them again in front of everyone, just because we can?"

The principal raised his eyebrows but said nothing.

"You don't even need to announce their names," Troy said. "Everyone will find out who they are without anyone here saying a word."

I said, "Also, no expulsions. No suspensions beyond this school year. And no ban from activities next year. For anyone. But we love your idea of a hundred service hours each, for the four of them. That should keep their attention for a while, and they'll actually do some good."

"We're not network security experts," Troy said, "so we have no recommendation about Norbert and the school computers."

"I'll stop you there," said the principal. "I'll be glad to hear the rest, if there's more. But these students—except for Kellie; you're right about her—these students deserve much worse than you're describing, and it's for what they did, not 'just because we can.' Parents, any thoughts before we continue?"

Troy's mother spoke. "You three remember how it hurt. Don't you think they've earned serious punishment?"

Troy answered quietly. "I remember, Mom. It still hurts. But I also remember that, when I was angry and wanted to hurt people, Jenny persuaded me that revenge would be a bad thing."

"Then he persuaded me," I said.

"This isn't revenge," said Nikki's mom. Nikki resembled her as much as I resembled Mom. "It's punishment."

"We don't think we should make recommendations based on our desire to hurt them," Troy said. "That feels like revenge, ma'am."

"Son," his dad said, "we're talking about serious, premeditated bullying. They deserve some major consequences."

"Maybe so, Dad, but hurting them more won't help us. We thought it would at first, but we were wrong. Besides, we're all just stupid kids. We overreact to stuff, and we do dumb things and misjudge the consequences."

I squeezed his hand. I couldn't have said it better. Maybe I couldn't have said it at all.

Nikki's dad joined the discussion. "Don't you think severity now will make other kids less likely to do similar things in the future?"

Jack had prepared us for this one.

"No, sir." Troy turned to the principal. "Mr. Simmons, you've used the same punishments for serious things for years, right?"

"More or less."

"It still happened to us, sir."

"I see your point," said the principal. "But it's what there is. I guess I need to understand why you want us to be so lenient."

Nikki sounded a lot calmer than me. "Mr. Simmons, last night we talked in circles, trying to figure out what they deserve for what they did. Maybe that's the right question for you, but it wasn't for us. We thought we wanted justice, but we don't know what justice would be."

She glanced at me, then Troy, as if to confirm that she should continue. Troy looked thoughtful. I tried to look encouraging.

She turned back to the principal. "We do think they should be punished. But we all hope for better than we deserve, in lots of ways. So we stopped trying to figure out what they deserve, and we looked for punishments that are less than they deserve. That way, we don't have to wonder if our motive is revenge, and they don't have to quit what they're best at, and they don't lose their senior year.

"Troy's right," she said more quietly. "We're all just stupid kids. We do things without calculating the consequences, and sometimes we hurt people. And we all want second chances, even when we maybe don't deserve them."

I reached for her hand and squeezed it. Her eyes darted to mine, and she flashed a little smile.

"If it's okay, sir," Troy said, "if you end up taking any of our suggestions, we'd like you to tell them a little mercy was our idea."

"This is more than a little mercy," said his mom. "I think these kids should be punished severely—for their own good."

"Mom, a hundred hours of community service is a lot, and private apologies are humiliating enough."

She quietly shook her head, and my thoughts got muddled again. We weren't even persuading our parents, let alone the principal.

"Jenny, what do you think?" Dad asked.

What I thought was that maybe, if I spoke quietly and squeezed Troy's hand, my voice would be steadier, and I wouldn't seem weak, while I gave the explanation I'd rehearsed in my head since last night.

"Dad, first, if they'd shown us a little mercy when they were angry or jealous or whatever, none of this would have happened. We want them to learn how mercy feels. If they don't like it, that's their problem. We'll have given them a chance.

"Second, Mr. Simmons, nothing you do to them will make us feel better. We thought—" My voice caught, and it was about to get worse. I paused to regain my composure, if I could. "We thought it would, but it won't." A deep breath by me and a squeeze from Troy helped me continue.

"Third, what we're suggesting will get their attention. If they want to change or grow up or whatever, maybe they will. If not, maybe they'll think about the consequences before they gang up on someone else. So I guess we're hoping for deterrence after all.

"What we get out of being merciful is this. We get to stop thinking about hurting them, and we get to feel better about ourselves and them, because, when they hurt us, we tried to help them." I looked at Mom and Dad, then Principal Simmons, and a couple of tears escaped. "I really want that."

"We all really want that," Nikki said.

Mom's voice was gentle. "Are you three sure you're not doing this so they'll like you, when all this is over? Sometimes people hate the person who's generous or merciful to them even more."

"Ma'am, are you saying mercy is wrong here?" Troy asked.

"No, Troy, I'm not." She didn't elaborate.

Nikki said, "We don't care whether they like us or not. This way we get to think about something else."

Then the only sound was my sniffling. The principal's hands were clasped in front of him, on his desk, and his gaze was fixed on them. I could have tried to explain how every punishment he'd listed felt somehow like it was for me, but I didn't understand that, and I didn't think it would help, and I didn't want this to be about just me.

I told myself we'd made our best case—but I hung my head. We hadn't convinced anyone but ourselves.

Finally the principal looked up. "That was well said. All of you. Thank you. Parents, what are your thoughts now?"

They looked at each other. I saw raised eyebrows and a few shrugs. Then it struck me: they weren't shaking their heads. They weren't saying no.

Troy's Mom spoke first. "I'm for Plan C, if that's what they want."

The others quickly agreed.

Troy and Nikki looked as stunned as I felt.

The principal's neutral expression hadn't changed. "Coach?"

Coach had been staring at the floor. Now he nodded slowly and looked up. "What we have here is three young people who actually care about the welfare of others, even when it's difficult." He looked at us. "I'm convinced. Mercy is as likely to help everyone as anything else we could do. Probably more." He turned to our parents. "As a teacher, I'm impressed. As a fellow parent, I think you must be bursting with pride."

"We're taking bursting under advisement," said Nikki's mom, sounding like the lawyer she was. "It could happen."

The principal smiled. "Don't do it here, okay? The taxpayers just gave me this nice new carpet."

That's when I knew we'd persuaded him after all. The adults laughed, but Troy, Nikki, and I were still in shock.

"Are you three sure you want this?" asked the principal.

My voice was steady now. "It's most of what we want."

"What else?" he asked hesitantly.

"We want to get our friends involved in something right away."

I turned to Troy. He said, "Coach, thanks again for sending the team out to clean up the mess that day. Jenny's friends did the same with social media. We want to put the same people to work on keeping kids from abusing the perps, now that we know who they are. Like I said, even if nobody here names them, it can't stay secret very long."

The principal tapped his fingertips on his desk. "You don't need my approval for that, but you have it." He turned to Mr. Cain. "Lewis, you've kept your own counsel. What are your thoughts?"

"If you'll indulge me," said Mr. Cain, "I'm thinking about history. In Plato's Seventh Letter, which may or may not really be Plato's, he says that, if peace is to be achieved and maintained after a conflict, the victors—'those who have for a time gained the upper hand,' as he puts it—must treat the conquered with mercy and as equals, rather than exacting vengeance or heavy tribute. Some believe this, if we'd done it after World War I, might have prevented World War II, at least the European part. We did it after World War II, more or less, and Germany and Japan have been our friends and allies ever since."

I'd have bet money that, by dinnertime, Mom and Dad would have looked up Plato's Seventh Letter, read it carefully, and either sent me a link or handed me a copy, possibly highlighted, so I could read it too. Then we could discuss it, not just in the context of what Maddi and her minions had done. Which was fine with me. I liked that they included me.

But Mr. Cain was talking about world history all the way back to World War I. How long would it be before we knew if it worked for us? A month? A year? A decade? In any case, now I wanted him to teach a history class, not just English.

My parents' new favorite high school teacher concluded, "I suspect mercy is the likeliest road to lasting peace here as well. It is certainly an admirable road." He smiled at us and nodded. "Well done."

I thanked him with a smile, while another tear rolled down each cheek and onto my shirt.

"Thank you, Lewis," said the principal. "Does everyone now prefer Plan C? Do you really feel good about this?"

It was unbelievable.

Then he said, "One more thing. Maddi was named cheer captain for next year. That won't happen now. We don't want her in a position of leadership."

We hadn't prepared for this one, but I thought I could handle it. "Sir," I said, sounding like Troy, "maybe you could leave that question open for a while, and decide later whether she's earned it?"

"How would she earn it?"

Troy said, "She has the skills, sir, or she wouldn't have been picked in the first place. So showing some leadership? Positive leadership. Maybe leadership outside of cheerleading."

"And good progress on her service hours," I added.

The principal looked at us, drummed his fingertips softly on his desk again, then nodded. "I'll call Coach Palladino and see what she thinks. Or Coach, maybe you would do it?"

Coach excused himself to make the call.

"So mercy it is," said the principal. "But first I will describe to them what they've escaped, to help them appreciate the gift. Shall we move next door for sentencing?"

66

Mercy

OUR MEETING WITH THE perps and their parents in the principal's conference room began with a surprise.

"Miss Adams, why are you here?" asked the principal. "As far as we know, you did nothing."

He was talking to Audrey. I was puzzled too. And disappointed. No one had said she was involved, and we wouldn't have suspected her.

"Mr. Simmons, I didn't know exactly what my friends were planning, but I knew it wasn't good. You're right about me doing nothing. I did nothing to stop them. So I'm here, if that's okay."

"I can't punish you for doing nothing," he said.

"I wanted to be here."

He nodded. "Thank you."

He walked them through Plan A, saying it fit what they'd done. Then he reviewed Plan B, calling it the plea bargain. "With this in mind," he asked, "would you care to apologize to these fellow students of yours?"

He called on them one by one.

I barely even cared what the minor perps said, but I was disappointed when Brooke and Katie just said they were sorry. They sounded remorseful enough, but I wanted to know why they helped Maddi do such things and didn't try to stop her. I couldn't bring myself to ask them.

At least we had Audrey as a reminder that someone could have stopped it, but no one did. Her presence had a visual effect too. She didn't quite look her best, but she looked nice in mint green capris and a white top with a colorful Aztec design on the front. Next to her, Brooke and Katie, who were beauties on most days, looked pale and plain in jeans and random faded t-shirts. They usually dressed better for school. Then again, they wouldn't be staying for school.

When it was her turn, Kellie could barely talk between sobs. We heard the word "sorry" once or twice, and the principal thanked her and moved on. She sniffled quietly, and I felt like dirt. Her orange sweatshirt mocked me. It had "I like you" printed across the front in big block letters.

He called on Maddi next. She looked at the floor. "We didn't mean to hurt you," she said. Then she stopped and looked at Troy and me.

She was suspended too, but dressed for a normal day, in white, knee-length shorts and a patterned top in just the right shade of red, which the cheerleaders often wore. Her platinum blonde hair fell sleek and straight, almost to her waist. On another girl I might have admired it.

Her eyes turned me cold. From seeing her in the halls I was accustomed to cruel delight, but now I thought I saw mostly emptiness, as if she'd turned her poison on herself, and most of herself was destroyed. I thought I must be reading too much into a look, but I felt a shiver.

There was only slightly more life in her voice than her eyes. "Yes, we did. We were trying to hurt you. We wanted—"

She looked down again, then back up at us. "*I* wanted to hurt you. When somebody asked me what I thought you'd do, I said maybe you'd take a whole bottle of pills together and die. I was stupid and cruel. I'm sorry."

She hadn't shed a tear, and talk of our possible suicide left me too stunned for tears. I wondered silently whether mercy was exactly the right response for such people or exactly the wrong one.

Norbert was next. I didn't know him well, so I studied him as he spoke. He was a stocky Hispanic boy, dressed in new blue jeans and a white dress shirt. It was clean and freshly ironed but slightly dingy with age, and the collar was worn. He apologized to all of us, but especially to Nikki. She looked hurt but nodded.

Audrey was last. She glanced at her fellow cheerleaders, then looked at us. "I knew it was wrong to do nothing. Maybe, if I'd done something, things would have turned out better for everybody. I'm sorry. I hope you'll forgive all of us someday."

I felt like I should admire Audrey's loyalty to her friends and the courage it took to show up and share the blame. Later, maybe I would.

But I really wished she'd been courageous a lot sooner and found a way to stop everything before it hurt us.

The principal turned to us. "Jenny, Nikki, Troy, Mr. Cain, parents, anything you want to say?"

We just thanked them for their apologies.

"Okay, moving on," said the principal. "There's an assembly at 10:00 a.m. Tuesday. All you offenders will be there, as part of your plea bargain. Troy, Jenny, and Nikki, you don't have to be there, but I'd like you to be. Parents are welcome, as always."

I knew our parents would only attend if we asked them to. They were cool that way. And we wouldn't ask.

He turned to the offenders and their parents. "Do you all remember those public apologies I mentioned?"

There were nods, a few tearful, some just sober. Maddi stared with lifeless eyes. I was glad I knew what they didn't, that it was about to get better.

"They will not happen," he said, "and we will not announce your names at the assembly. We met last night and this morning with Troy, Jenny, and Nikki. Their parents were there too. These three argued for reducing your punishment to a lot less than I think you deserve. After some discussion and careful consideration, I've decided to honor their wishes.

Some of the perps and their parents had been staring at the floor. Now every eye was on the principal.

"They don't want to humiliate you or damage your future. Think about that. They refuse to do to you what you tried to do to them, even though you deserve it. They've advocated mercy you haven't earned. Please learn from that and show some mercy yourselves in the future, when opportunities arise."

He looked down at his notes. "Here's what mercy looks like today. None of you will be expelled or banned from all activities next year. Four of you were already suspended, beginning yesterday. That suspension will end at two days, and we'll see you back in school on Tuesday, not just for the assembly. Officer Ramirez will not file formal criminal charges against any of you, though God knows some of you deserve them."

His voice softened. "Kellie, I'd like you to return to work this afternoon. We'll be glad to have to you back, if you'll come."

Her teary face brightened, and she nodded eagerly. Her mom was weeping.

"Thank you," he said. "The rest of you—actually, just the four of you—are on conduct probation for the remainder of your time at Lakeside High. You've used up all the slack you can expect from me. You four will each do one hundred hours of supervised community service, subject to my approval, or you won't graduate from this school. Coach?"

Coach turned to Maddi. "Miss Burke, in a sense you're doubly on probation. As you know, you were selected to be head cheerleader next year. Since you're not expelled or banned from all activities, and since the word of the day is mercy, I spoke with Coach Palladino this morning. Your appointment as head cheerleader is rescinded for now, but you may remain on the squad. She and I, because I'm Athletic Director, will review your conduct and attitude regularly. If you show positive leadership outside of cheerleading and good progress toward your hundred hours of service, you may be reinstated as head cheerleader in July. That's not a guarantee. Otherwise, someone else will be appointed."

He smiled faintly and shook his head. "Sorry, I keep forgetting the title is cheer captain now. You can thank Troy, Jenny, and Nikki for this second chance too. It was their idea, not ours. They argued your cause eloquently."

Maddi turned her empty eyes on us but said nothing.

The principal said, "Now we'll excuse Jenny, Nikki, Troy, their parents, and Mr. Cain. Kellie, you and your mom are welcome to go. Thank you for coming this morning. Coach and I need maybe three more minutes with the rest of you."

Audrey found us later that day and apologized again. She told us Coach tore into the offenders after we left. "We took it," she said. "We deserved it." He said he'd seen students at other schools commit suicide over less, even homicide once. He told them to ponder how lucky they were that no one was dead because of what they'd done. Some of the girls cried.

I wanted to ask if Maddi had cried—or said anything—but I didn't.

So far, I was glad we'd argued for mercy and the principal had finally agreed. But I couldn't forget the emptiness in Maddi's eyes.

Troy and I spent part of that evening reading to Grandpa. Mom sent a book with us, called *One Minute Mysteries*. He liked trying to follow some of the mysteries, which were only a couple of pages long, and he seemed a little stronger. We read aloud from the scriptures too, which he always enjoyed.

On the way out I asked Troy, "Do you think we got it right this morning?"

"Hope so. What do you think?"

"We did our best," I said.

"And?"

"How do you know there's an 'and'?"

He grinned. "Usually is. Like that about you."

I suppressed a laugh. "*And* I think our best was good, *and* I'd rather wonder if we helped her—them—get off too easily than wonder if we were too harsh."

"So would I," he said. "Think she's getting off too easy?"

"I guess I want to see what she's like after this. So maybe that's up to her. You?"

"I want Maddi to be like the weather in Siberia. Might be stormy, and it's probably cold, but it doesn't matter, because it's the other side of the planet."

In his car I said what popped into my head. "What if we'd done what she did?"

He looked at me seriously. "We wouldn't."

"What if we did?"

"Well . . . I probably couldn't go back to school or ever look you in the eye again. Be a long time before Mom and Dad trusted me for two minutes out of their sight. Couldn't blame them. How 'bout you?"

"Pretty much the same, unless I just ran away to keep from seeing my parents' disappointment all the time. I'd be too ashamed to look in the mirror."

"I'd feel pretty bad disappointing your parents too," he said.

"What a good boyfriend! Any more thoughts I might like?"

"We left a scripture out of our discussion last night. Thought of it today in seminary. Looked it up and memorized the whole passage instead of listening to the lesson."

"You're such a rebel."

"I know, right? 'Ye have heard that it hath been said, Thou shalt love thy neighbour, and hate thine enemy. I say unto you, Love your enemies, bless them that curse you, do good to them that hate you, and pray for them which despitefully use you, and persecute you; That ye may be the children of your Father which is in heaven: for he maketh his sun to rise on the evil and on the good, and sendeth rain on the just and on the unjust.'

"Think we'd have done anything different if we'd read that last night?" he asked.

I pondered for a moment. "No. We did the 'bless them that curse you, do good to them that hate you' part anyway. Now I feel even better about that. But I'm not ready to love Maddi in any way I can think of. That may haunt me for a while."

"Me too," he said. "But the weather in Siberia, you know?" He started the car. "Want to hear what else I've been thinking?"

"Always."

"No one, including Maddi, told us why she hates us."

I reviewed some painful memories. "She said she wanted to hurt us. Maybe we should have asked her why. We could ask Coach. Why do you think she did it?"

"Jealousy, I guess. That's what the principal said."

I nodded. "I just assumed that. We should have asked."

On Memorial Day Mom, Dad, Zeus, and I checked Grandpa out of his place just after lunch and took him to the cemetery to visit Grandma's grave. I saw no hint that he remembered her. He loved being outside, though, and he loved the flowers that filled the cemetery, and he loved being with us. I pushed his wheelchair some, but Mom and Dad had to do all the hills, in case I had a seizure at a critical moment and sent his wheelchair careening down the hill, like the one in my writing test, but accidentally.

Sometimes just seeing Grandpa outdoors in his trademark flannel shirt and baseball cap made it seem as if we'd turned back time. He seemed less frail and more himself. Then I'd look into his face and watch his eyes and listen to him talk, and my heart would ache, because it was all an illusion. He was more frail and less himself.

We took him on a scenic mountain drive, then ate with him in his dining hall. Dinner wasn't bad, but it wasn't the outdoor barbecue Troy was enjoying with his family, somewhere out of town with his uncle, aunt, and cousins.

After dinner Zeus and I offered to stay with Grandpa, instead of going with Mom and Dad to a movie they wanted to see. Mom handed me some papers before they left. "Read this tonight, to yourself or Grandpa. You'll like it."

Grandma had kept a journal in her impossibly precise penmanship, and Mom had recently unearthed it in some boxes. She'd spent a lot of time reading it lately. The parts she'd copied for me were about me on the morning I was born, then off and on through the next few years. Grandpa quickly fell asleep, so I read silently.

From the beginning Grandma loved my blue eyes. She said they were wide open, attentive, and intelligent. When I was four, she wondered how long it would be before some man was completely captivated by them—besides Grandpa and Dad, who already were. "I hope she'll be at least sixteen," she wrote, "or whatever age is old enough to be a woman about it, not a giddy little girl. I hope she'll be wise enough not to fall for a cad or a twit, even when some of those fall for her. She wouldn't have to be as old as her mother was, but if she's to do as well in the end, she'd best get it right from the beginning.

"This will be fun to watch!" she wrote, ending that day's entry.

She didn't get to watch, I thought, but she got part of her wish. Sixteen years and three months. I was a little giddy, but I was also getting it right so far.

I wished she could meet the boy. I was sure she'd like him. I wondered if they let the spirits of the dead watch the lives of the families they left behind. If so, she knew who I'd become—so far—and she probably knew enough about the boy to love him too.

I wondered if she was able visit Grandpa at all. I hoped she visited often.

"It was a good weekend," I texted to Troy, just before 10 p.m. "I love you. I missed you today. Mom gave me some pages from Grandma's journal to read tonight, and I think she'd love you too. I suspect she actually does, from the other side. It helps that you're not 'a cad or a twit.' Her words."

I got his reply just in time. "I love you. I'll love you tomorrow too. At least we can sit together at the assembly."

I wished he hadn't mentioned tomorrow.

The truth I'd been trying to ignore was that, underneath all the genuinely good and happy things we'd done over the weekend, there was an empty ache that never stopped—and hadn't since the day we were attacked. I thought it might gradually go away with time. Maybe a lot of time. But I was pretty sure tomorrow's assembly wouldn't help with that at all.

67

Hearts Together, Eyes with Pride

I'D HAVE BEEN FINE without an assembly, I thought on Tuesday morning, as my two best friends, my boyfriend, my dog, and I took our places together in the main gym. Principal Simmons had reserved space for us on the front row, near the center. The bleachers behind us were nearly full, including the upper level.

He waited behind a podium, while some stragglers found seats. We'd seen a lot of his thin-lipped frown lately.

I distracted myself from the reason we were there by studying him. He had to be in his forties, and he was a high school principal. Shouldn't his brown hair have some gray in it by now? Maybe he dyed it.

"There will be consequences," he said, after welcoming us and telling us what the assembly was about, which everyone seemed to know already. "But they will not be public consequences, and no year-end activities will be cancelled. We considered that option.

"Several students were involved in varying degrees. I will not give you names or other details, but there have already been suspensions and private apologies, and the worst offenders will be doing a substantial amount of community service this summer, among other consequences."

He paused for a sip of water.

"You may have heard rumors to the contrary, but there will be only one public apology today. It's mine.

"The fact that such a thing happened here means that the students, teachers, and administrators of Lakeside High have failed to learn and teach some of the most crucial lessons. As a result, in this incident two of you were publicly persecuted, and one of you was falsely accused of being responsible. I ask you three to accept my personal apology and the apology of everyone at this school."

When he left the podium and came to shake our hands, which was too much of a show for my taste, there was scattered applause. It didn't make the moment any less embarrassing. Even Troy blushed.

Back at the podium the principal said, "I'm aware that smaller cruelties are common here, as in most schools, and I don't wish to dismiss them in speaking of larger ones. To everyone else who may have suffered here, I say, please accept my personal apology and the apology of us all. We have failed you. We have hurt you. We are so very, very sorry. We will work harder to be a school which civilized people can be proud to attend and remember. We thank you for giving us all another chance.

"With the blessing of our outgoing student body president, Alli Ford," he said, "I've asked our student body president-elect, Will Marlowe, to chair a committee himself, to recommend some co-chairs, and to recruit a full committee to work on changing the culture of this school. He recommended, and I have approved and hereby announce, the appointment of Jack Nieder, Nikki Abbott, Audrey Adams, and Micah Robbins to serve as co-chairs."

I didn't know Micah Robbins—but Will knew everybody. I turned to Jack and Nikki. "You've been keeping secrets from me."

They both smiled. "Only since Friday," Nikki said.

"It gets better," Jack added, nodding toward the principal.

"I asked them not to wait for school to resume in the fall. We'll have weekly activities and projects during the summer, starting next week, for all of you who wish to participate. We hope you will. There will be lots of food and plenty of fun.

"I won't belabor the details, but since things fell apart here the other day, four of these five have shown excellent leadership in helping us put them back together. Applause is a small token of gratitude for such service, and their larger work is only beginning, but I'd like Will, Jack, Nikki, and Audrey to stand, and let's applaud them now."

Jack and Nikki stood and half-turned toward the crowd of students. Nikki offered a self-conscious little wave. Jack smiled and nodded once. Will was further down the row. He towered over Audrey, who was next to him.

"Thank you," said the principal, and they took their seats. "You may not know Micah Robbins. He'll be a sophomore next year. He was unable to join us this morning.

"These five took me seriously. They had their second meeting early this morning. At their suggestion, we'll call this the Tiger Committee. Any of you who want to join it and work hard will be welcome. You'll hear more in the morning announcements tomorrow, and also in the last e-mail newsletter of the semester.

"That's all I have to say, but Will wants to speak to you. Please pay attention and participate when he asks you to. When he's finished, your day will go better, because all the teachers will be happier, if you return to class without delay. Thank you for being here and taking this seriously."

My deep, empty ache was still alive and well, I reflected, but at least the principal was finished, and Will would probably be good.

He had dressed up a bit. He looked sharp in khakis and a navy blue, long-sleeve dress shirt with a light blue necktie. He wore a wireless mic and ignored the podium. He moved closer to the front row and roamed nearly from one end of the bleachers to the other as he spoke. I knew that technique. It helped him keep everyone's attention.

His speech felt like a conversation, and it didn't seem masterly at first. But I changed my mind as I listened. It was brilliant.

He talked about some good things at our school. He described his own experience moving to town and starting school at one of our junior highs. He told us how hard it was at first, and how much it still meant to him that a few students had reached out and befriended the new kid.

"A week and a half ago, something awful happened," he said, "partly because nobody who could have stopped it did. Since then, we've been talking about ways to make things better here. We wanted the students we hurt to come back to school and give us a second chance, and we never want things like that to happen here again."

When he mentioned Troy and me, I was glad he was in front of a different section of the bleachers. That way, if kids looked at him, they didn't see us too.

His choice of words struck me: "students *we* hurt" and "give *us* a second chance." I didn't think he was saying the whole student body was as guilty as the perps. He was saying we were all responsible for the kind of school we had. We were watching a lesson in leadership. Maybe two lessons, because the principal had said the same thing in his own way, by the way he apologized.

Will continued. "Those students we hurt are friends of mine. It was hard for them to come back, but you did little things that helped, even when you didn't know what to say. Thanks for that. By Friday I even saw a certain couple smiling again—at someone besides each other."

Quiet laughter behind us accompanied a welcome squeeze for me.

"We also talked about not hurting the people who hurt them. People deserve second chances, even when we think they don't. We're all just stupid kids sometimes, trying to decide what we want and what we're willing to do to each other to get it. The ones who hurt our friends—they're our friends too. It was hard for them to come back to school too, and face what they did. But they're here.

"Look, they screwed up. They screwed up so bad that some of them were about to be expelled. But the people they attacked convinced the principal to give them another chance here.

"We all screwed up, by letting this happen here. We all get another chance."

He looked at the notes on his phone.

"I mentioned some really good things about you and us and this school. From today on, through next year, which is my senior year, and for the rest of my life, when I remember us and this school, here's what I want. I want the first, best thing on my list of memories to be this: We looked out for each other. No exceptions. We had each other's backs. No exceptions. We didn't hurt people, not intentionally. No exceptions, no excuses. When there were screw-ups, we gave each other and ourselves another chance. But we didn't screw up because we were reckless or jealous or cruel. We only screwed up because we're human and we make mistakes, and we sometimes fail at things, even when we really try.

"That's the school I want to remember. Maybe we're closer to it now than we were a week and a half ago."

He glanced at his phone again.

"I want to remember a school full of good people, doing good things for each other without waiting to be told, and not caring if there's any applause.

"So today I'm asking all of us to take one big, loud step together toward being that kind of school. I'll explain in a minute. I'm asking you to find other steps to take yourselves, tomorrow and every day after that.

"I don't know what all those steps will be. Most of them will be quiet, probably, and some will go unnoticed. They won't be the same for everybody, but you'll figure them out. Most of the time, we don't need anyone to tell us what to do when someone needs help, or what not to do because it could hurt somebody.

"I just told you what kind of school I want this to be. So now you tell me. Do you want that kind of school?"

I nodded. Others must have nodded too, because Will said, "Yeah, here's the thing. We can't hear you nodding. We will hear you if you clap. Do you want that kind of school?"

The clapping started slowly but grew. It didn't feel like the first applause, which was awkward and strange and made me even more self-conscious. It felt like hope, and I could join in, because it was about more than just me, Troy, and Nikki. It was about the future, everyone's future—because the past was the past, Will was saying, and we could all decide together what came next.

"Thanks, everybody. Seriously, thanks. Let's talk about that big first step. Then we'll take it. This one isn't quiet. You might think it's symbolic, and it is, but I think it's more than that.

"There's a bad kind of pride, like if I thought I was better than you, or if I had something good, and it made me really happy that you didn't have it too. We need less of that kind.

"There's also a good kind of pride, like when your parents are proud of your hard work on a paper, or you're proud of your little cousin for doing her best at her first piano recital, even though she was nervous and scared and missed some notes. Or when we're proud to be part of this school—not because we're better than other schools, but because we try to do good things here, together, and we try to be good to people.

"We need more of that pride, but we have to earn it. I've been thinking, what some of us did the week before last isn't what you do if you want to be proud of your school. It didn't make anyone else proud of us either.

"So anyway, when you say the word *pride* in a minute, we're talking about the good kind, okay?"

Now Will was directly in front of me, but he looked further up into the stands. He took a few seconds to scan the crowd from end to end. Close up, I could see there were dark circles under his eyes, and talking seemed to require extra effort.

"My brother was a drum major in the high school marching band in our old city. After a long day of summer rehearsal, the band always did something really cool. I heard them do it a few times, and it gave me goosebumps. I called him last night, and he told me about it. Even sent me a video. I showed it to Nikki, Jack, Audrey, Micah, Principal Simmons, and Mr. Cain this morning, and they liked it. We changed a few words to fit us.

"We're not a marching band, and we're not an athletic team. But I think it might help. So try it with me, okay? We'll learn it now and practice it a few times before we go back to class. It'll be really awkward at first, but when we're good at it, we'll see if we like it. If we do, we'll call it the Tiger Yell, and we'll do it when we're together.

"Here's how it works. You can see this on the scoreboard screen behind me."

He turned toward the screen, and I looked too. It was blank.

He smiled faintly. "Let's try that again. You can see this on the scoreboard screen behind me."

The screen flashed, and some words appeared.

"Thank you. I say, 'Tigers, stand ready!' All of you who can will stand up and face forward, and shut up so you can listen. Then I yell, 'Attention!' You yell, 'Hype!' When we get that together, we'll shake the roof.

"Then I ask some questions, and you yell the answers. Where are your feet? On the ground! Shoulders? Straight! Hands? Ready! Minds? Awake! Hearts? Together! Eyes? With pride! Eyes? With pride! We do the pride one twice."

"Then you're silent and you stand at attention until I say, 'Fall out!' Then you can relax and make as much noise as you want. So let's do it. Tigers! Stand ready!"

The first time was ragged and weak, and it felt reluctant. The second was a little better. Will urged us on, and I overheard students encouraging each other behind us. We gradually got louder and more together, and by about the eighth time, we were into it. Our yells were thunderous, with near-total silence in between. Even Zeus joined in by the end. His timing was pretty good.

The last time, Will took off the mic and just yelled. I'd never heard him so loud or seen him so animated, except on a basketball floor—where he was standing at the moment, actually, toward one end of the bleachers.

The effect in the gym was electric. When he finally yelled, "Thank you! Fall out!" a thousand students headed back to class, buzzing with new energy.

68

More Mercy

Troy and I worked our way upstream through the departing crowd, toward Will. Troy exchanged fist bumps with a few kids on the way, with the hand I wasn't using. My other hand held Zeus's leash, so I just smiled. Some of the fist-bumpers bumped my shoulder instead, but gently enough that it didn't hurt.

When we reached the place where we'd last seen Will, he wasn't there. We found him sitting on a chair, past the end of the bleachers and hidden from the throng. His head and shoulders were against the wall, and his eyes were closed.

"Great speech, man," said Troy as we approached.

Will opened his eyes and smiled faintly. "Thanks."

"It was brilliant," I said. "Are you okay?"

"Feels like I played quadruple overtime."

Troy chuckled. "If it helps, I think you won."

"It helps." He groaned. "What doesn't help is not sleeping. Hardly slept at all last night. Or the night before."

"Tell her what you told me," Troy said.

Will looked down and closed his eyes. I saw two deep breaths before opened them again and spoke. "I was gonna resign. I have better things to do next year than be student body president at a school where crap like this happens. I thought about it all week, and Friday morning I was gonna text the principal and Mr. Cain and tell them I was done."

I was stunned. "What made you change your mind?"

"Thursday night I talked to Mom and Dad. They said they'd support me either way, but they wanted me to do one more thing before I sent my resignation." He looked at Troy, then at me. "Pray. Which I did. Then

Friday morning, instead of resigning, I asked to speak at the assembly. I spent the whole weekend figuring out what to say."

"You seem sad," I murmured. "Sad?"

He shook his head. "No, I think it was good. I'm just really, really tired." His voice quivered.

So did mine. "Are you standing up and going to class anytime soon?"

One side of his mouth twitched upward. "I'll walk out with you." He sighed, leaned forward, and slowly raised himself from the chair.

I let go of Troy and Zeus, and before Will could take a single step, I wrapped him in a brief but earnest hug. I barely came to his chest.

He squeezed me back. "What's this for?"

"Sleepless nights preparing a brilliant speech," I said. "Instead of re-signing. You're amazing."

After I let go, there was a quick man-hug. All Troy said was, "Yeah, what she said."

Will set a slow pace across the gym and out into the hall.

———◆———

I thought a lot about our new Tiger Yell. If a teacher or principal had tried to get us to do it, we might have laughed him out of the gym. If anyone had tried a few weeks earlier, it wouldn't have worked. But it was a serious time, and good things really had happened after our horrible day. And the principal's speech helped. And maybe most people didn't suck.

But only Will could have pulled it off. He was friendly and charis-matic. He had a strong, deep voice. He made sense when he talked. He didn't talk down to people. He didn't try to help just his friends, while he hurt or ignored everyone else. And when he was in, he was all in, and you wanted to be in too. He was the only person I knew who could both come up with the idea in the first place and get us all past our self-consciousness and everything else, so the Tiger Yell became moving and powerful for us—so it united us, instead of being weird.

———◆———

I picked at my lunch that day, while Zeus drank from his water dish under the table. Then I returned my tray, and he and I headed for my locker.

I'd told Jack and Nikki that I needed to apologize to Kellie, and why, and we'd gone shopping for a small gift. Half the school, including us, knew her favorite color was orange, so I'd settled on a bouquet of orange tulips from a flower shop. I retrieved it from my locker and walked toward the office.

Mrs. Almond, the fifty-something secretary, had straw-colored hair that was fading to gray. Her pixie cut made her seem taller than she was. I asked timidly if Kellie was there, and if I could talk to her. I was never timid with Mrs. A.

"She's in the copy room, but I can finish for her. I'll send her out." She looked at the bouquet. "Are those for her?"

I nodded.

"Good. Maybe they'll help. It's understandable, but she's not herself. Are you okay? And Troy?"

"Yes, thank you." Except for the reason I'm here, I thought.

"Interesting approach, what you talked them into. Unexpected. I hope it works. I'll get Kellie." She disappeared into the copy room. I heard her tell Kellie there was someone to see her, and she'd finish the copying job while Kellie went out front.

Kellie insisted it was her job, and she should finish. She sounded upset, and I was afraid the most cheerful girl in school was getting angry just when I'd come to apologize. Finally she appeared in the copy room doorway. She saw me and froze.

"Hi, Kellie." I tried to sound friendly and cheerful.

"Hi, Jenny," she said after a moment. Her speech impediment was evident in her first two words.

I held up the flowers. "These are for you. Could we sit together? I was hoping we could talk for a minute."

She shook her head and disappeared into the copy room. I wondered if I should follow her, but I heard Mrs. Almond speaking gently.

Kellie reappeared. "You can talk to me. The flowers are pretty."

"They're for you. Come sit by me. I need to tell you something."

There were chairs in the corner. I sat in one and gestured toward another. She came reluctantly and sat.

She looked at the floor when she spoke. "I'm sorry I helped the bad cheerleaders hurt you and Troy. I was bad."

"Thank you, Kellie. But we don't blame you, and you're not bad. That's not why I'm here."

She looked at the bouquet. "Are you here to bring me flowers?"

"Partly." I handed them to her. She held them to her nose and drew in a long breath.

"They smell pretty." She turned to me. "I like almost all the colors, but orange is my favoritest."

"I'm glad you like them." I tried to smile, then took a deep breath. "I came to say I'm sorry for something I did."

"Not you," she said. "The bad cheerleaders."

"Not for that."

"What did you do? Were you bad?"

"I was a little bit bad." It was my turn to look at the floor. "I was bad."

I lifted my gaze. She'd pursed her lips and cocked her head.

"Remember when I asked you for a girl's class schedule and locker number?"

"That's not bad. We tell teachers all the time."

"I wasn't asking for a teacher. You just thought I was, because I didn't tell you I was asking for myself. I'm sorry I deceived you."

"Deceived?"

"I let you think something that wasn't true, so you would do something for me that you shouldn't. I didn't exactly tell a lie, but it was bad, and I'm sorry."

She thought for a moment. "Do I have to tell the principal I was bad, 'cuz I told you bad Maddi Burke's classes and said her locker is G19, but you're not a teacher?"

"I don't think so. I just wanted to find Maddi, so I could talk to her. Anyway, I came to tell you what I did and say I'm sorry."

"Because you deceived."

I nodded. "Because I deceived you. I won't do it again."

"I forgive you. Nobody's perfect," she said seriously. "My mom said that after the meeting. Before it too."

"Thank you." I smiled, and she smiled in response.

"Is Zeus a very nice dog?"

I looked at him and smiled. "He is."

She started to reach for him, then pulled her hand back. "Is it okay to pet him?"

"Yes. Thanks for asking."

She reached out again, brushed the side of his neck a few times, then pulled away.

"Watch this," I said. "Zeus, this is Kellie. She's very nice. Shake her hand?"

He held up a paw. Her hand darted out again. She took his paw for a fraction of second, then pulled her hand away. She turned to me and grinned.

The bell rang. "I have to go to class," I said.

We both stood.

"I have to do my job," she said. "My classes are morning classes."

"Thanks, Kellie."

"Okay. Have a nice day. 'Bye, Zeus!" She almost bounced toward the copy room, hugging the flowers.

That's when I saw Mrs. A, standing and watching from behind her desk. I might have been projecting my guilt onto her stern expression, but I gathered she'd heard my apology. I was partly alarmed and partly relieved—because I wasn't sure apologizing to Kellie was enough.

"I'm sorry," I said. "Am I in trouble?"

"No. Don't do it again."

"I won't. Please don't blame Kellie."

"I don't." I'd seen her use the same stony look on misbehaving students, but never on me. Until now.

I looked down. "Thanks."

She didn't say anything more until I looked up again. Her gaze had softened. "As Kellie and her mom say, nobody's perfect."

"I'll understand if you don't trust me after this."

"What if I trust you to admit your mistakes, even when no one else knows you've made them, and you might get in trouble if you do? That's a fairly high level of trust."

I'd expected something completely different, so it took me a few seconds to process her words. I nodded slowly. "You're very kind."

"Thanks for caring about Kellie," she said. "I'll help her find a vase." She smiled. "As soon as I can get her to let go of them for a minute. You go to class, before you're tardy and have to come back here in real trouble."

"Thanks, Mrs. A."

"You're welcome. Go to class."

⸺◆◇◆⸺

Graduation was Thursday evening. I went to see some of my senior friends from Mrs. Tornow's class graduate, and because the Tiger Committee spread the word about a surprise for the end of the ceremony. A lot of sophomores and juniors were there.

The gym floor had rows and rows of graduates, and the bleachers on both sides of the gym were filled. After the speeches, and after the graduates went through the diploma line, the principal asked the graduates to stand. He formally presented them to the district superintendent and the school board. The superintendent formally accepted them and congratulated them, their parents, the faculty, the principal, the school board, and everyone else he could think of.

A lot of cheering and other bedlam usually came next, including throwing caps in the air, which Mom told me they always said not to do, because someone might get hurt. This time, something else happened first. There was nothing in the printed program about it, and it hadn't been announced.

Will, Nikki, Jack, Audrey, and the rest of the Tiger Committee quickly lined up in front of the podium and faced the crowd. The dignitaries on the stand looked puzzled. The principal smiled and nodded.

They didn't use microphones. They yelled in almost perfect unison, "Tigers! Stand ready!"

Every student stood—the graduates on the floor and the rest of us in the stands, the choir seats, the orchestra, and everywhere else. We were silent, and a hush fell over the rest of the crowd.

"Attention!" yelled the committee.

Our "hype" was enormous and mostly together. They let it echo for a couple of seconds.

"Where are your feet?"

"On the ground!"

"Shoulders?"

"Straight!"

"Hands?"

"Ready!"

"Minds?"

"Awake!"

"Hearts?"

"Together!"

"Eyes?"

"With pride!"

"Eyes?"

"With pride!"

Our first "with pride" was amazingly loud. Our second was even louder. Then there was silence for maybe three seconds—but it felt like ten.

"Tigers! Graduates! Fall out!"

Hats flew into the air, people clapped and cheered, and graduates hugged. Sophomores and juniors gave each other high fives and fist bumps. I saw adults wiping away tears, and it wasn't just women.

<hr>

Friday was a short day at school for sophomores and juniors, just long enough, the teachers said, to count as one of the 180 school days state law required. We were out by mid-morning.

I'd envisioned myself marching out the front doors with Troy and not looking back, with my eyes or my thoughts, for most of the summer, at least. Except for missing Mrs. Tornow's class.

I was wrong. I felt like I was leaving for an extra-long weekend, from a place to which I wouldn't mind going back, when it was time. My deep, empty ache was less than it had been, which was a good sign. Attending graduation had helped—especially the thrill at the end—but, looking back, I thought Will's speech and what he said afterward had helped most. I'd already written him a thank-you note he could see for years to come, in his yearbook.

On Wednesday they'd excused us from fourth period to pick up our yearbooks. Zeus and I were just in front of Will in the "M" line. He was the first to sign my yearbook, and I was the first to sign his. I already knew what to write.

> Will—This year isn't just ending better than it began for me. Thanks to you, it's ending more happily than I imagined it could just a week ago. You're more than a dear friend. You're already the best student body president ever. Love, Jenny

I'd have hugged him longer than I did, when I handed him his yearbook, but we didn't need any new rumors.

We walked together toward the corner where we'd arranged to meet Troy. He'd been in the faster-moving "N thru P" line. On the way I mentally polished my message for his yearbook. I wanted it to be romantic but muted enough that it wouldn't be talked about by everyone who signed his yearbook after me.

That's when I collided with another girl. We both dropped our pens but not our yearbooks.

Will was built a lot farther from the floor, but he was down, picking up our pens, almost before they landed at our feet. I started apologizing before I even saw who the girl was. So did she.

"I'm so sorry, I wasn't—"

"No, I was—"

It was Maddi. She looked at me with sober, guarded eyes. "Somewhere else," she said. "Sorry, Jenny."

"Are you okay?" I asked.

She nodded, and we held each other's gaze for an instant. Then we both thanked Will for retrieving our pens—I with an embarrassed smile and she with the same serious look—and went our separate ways.

While my mind reeled, Will mused, "If I were Maddi, I think I'd pick up my yearbook and leave." He stopped. "You know what? Tell Troy I'll find you in a few minutes. I should catch up to her and sign her yearbook."

I watched him go, wondering if I should feel betrayed, which I mostly didn't, or admire his good heart, which I did mostly out of habit, at first. Later, when we asked him what he wrote, he said, "Nothing special. Good thing I caught her when I did, though. She was on her way out the door. Wished her a great summer, senior year will be awesome, stuff like that."

Because the past was the past, I thought, and the future could be different. My boyfriend's best friend was amazing.

Summer

69

Unopened

I N ONE BIG WAY I didn't look forward to summer. Troy and I would spend a lot of it missing each other, mostly from different time zones.

Everything was at the wrong time. He'd spend the first two weeks at a basketball camp in Texas. Just before he returned, I'd leave for a week at a church girls camp in the mountains. Then we'd have a few days together before I left on a month-long trip with Mom and Dad to a writers retreat they ran every summer at a college in Maine. The day before we returned, he'd leave for two more weeks of basketball camps. When we were finally together again, our summer break would be almost over.

I believed our relationship could survive. We'd work at it. And if absence really did make the heart grow fonder, that would be good. We'd have Skype and text messages, and the Tiger Committee's weekly activities could help distract whichever of us was home. The only one of those we could attend together would be the last one.

On the Sunday morning after school ended, Troy left for the airport at 4:15 a.m. We'd said our goodbyes the night before. I thought the first day of my three Troyless weeks might go better if it was shorter, so I slept as late as I could. It was almost noon when I awoke.

My first conscious act was not my morning prayer. It was checking my phone. I had two text messages from him. They were hours old.

"Jenny, I'm at the airport, about to board, thinking I'm an idiot. Later you'll know why. No big deal, just a missed opportunity. I love you. Check your front porch."

My new dull ache wasn't from what happened at school. It was from our goodbyes. He wouldn't be telling me he loved me in person again for weeks.

The second message said, "Just landed in San Antonio. Doesn't quite feel like home anymore. Wish you were here."

So did I.

I threw on sweat pants and a t-shirt and hurried to the front porch. I found nothing. I hadn't seen Mom or Dad, so I stood right there and texted them. "Good morning. Was there something for me on the front porch?"

Dad replied immediately, "Good morning. Kitchen counter." I probably would have looked there next.

It was a perfect red rose in a baby blue vase, and a slightly darker blue envelope that felt like a thick letter. I was about to rip it open, when I saw what he'd written across the flap. "Open on Monday night of girls camp."

The dull ache sharpened, and I stared. The boy I loved was far away. His long letter was in my hand—but not to be read for more than two weeks.

I carried it slowly to my room, set it on my desk next to his picture, and stared at it some more. He'd printed my name on the front, in his neat but spartan hand. I picked it up, thinking I'd put it out of sight in a drawer, but I didn't. I kissed it and returned it to my desk, with the back facing up. I'd need the reminder.

"Open on Monday night of girls camp."

⸻◦⸻

The rose helped. It went next to his picture too, and it lasted for days. I started every day by looking at it, breathing in its fragrance, and reminding myself that, when evening came, Troy and I could Skype again. Sometimes I came back to it in the middle of the day. If my heart already ached, it ached a little less. If it didn't, it would start.

Jack and Nikki were insanely busy during the first week of summer break, as the Tiger Committee worked to organize our weekly activities. There would be one every Thursday, starting immediately. I didn't join the committee, because I'd be gone for half the summer, but I wanted to help when I could.

The first activity was a massive cleanup project at school. I spent the morning sitting safely at a laptop in the faculty room, helping Jack, Nikki, and some adults keep track of which projects were complete and who should do what next.

There were 43 teams of ten kids each. They washed windows, lockers, and desks; picked up trash outside; repaired textbooks; moved things into storage; planted flowers; and even did some painting. Every minute or two a team leader would call or text with a question or need, to request an inspection of completed work, or to report the team was ready for its next assignment.

Jack said our headquarters team wasn't as efficient as air traffic control, which her dad had taken her to watch a few times, but it felt about the same. Her eyes twinkled. "We're harnessing the forces of destruction. It'll be a miracle if we don't collapse into chaos."

To me it felt like chaos from the beginning, but an enormous amount of work got done. In the process there were scattered water fights but no paint fights or actual fights. Morale seemed high, and by noon the school and the grounds felt renewed.

Pizzas arrived—120 of them—and we gathered in a gym. Will took a minute to thank everyone. Then he led the Tiger Yell and turned us loose on the pizza. Twenty minutes later, a pizza and a half remained, most of the kids had left, and the rest were cheering on some sophomores from the cleanup crew, as they tried to build a tower 118 pizza boxes tall. They failed spectacularly, which might have been their goal.

"Look who's in charge of lunch cleanup," Nikki said, when the crew gave up on their tower and started clearing away the rubble.

No one was standing around, giving orders or holding a clipboard or anything. "I give up. Who?"

"Maddi."

I followed Nikki's gaze. Maddi was wiping down a table. "Is she on the committee?"

"She asked if she could join. Said she wanted to help, and she didn't care how. We thought it would be okay."

"Looks like it's working," I said.

"I think she's trying to be different."

"Anything different is good," I said, then wondered if that was un-kind.

Nikki smiled. "Bonus points for the movie quote. She asked for in-coming sophomores, and then she volunteered them to clean up after lunch."

"Maybe she's more comfortable around kids who weren't here to see what happened."

"Bet you're right. Anyway, they seem to like her. I like that she's working as hard as they are, not just bossing them around. Kind of looks like leadership."

—◇—

After relaxing for a week, I planned to spend half of every summer day writing. I had some ideas for short stories and essays, but I couldn't con-centrate for more than an hour at a time. I kept thinking of Troy—miss-ing him, of course, but happy thoughts too. So I kept myself busy with things I could do with him filling my mind: extra cooking and housework, some yard work, helping my Young Women leaders with preparations for girls camp—and putting something together for Troy that made me more than a little nervous, no matter how much I loved him.

Our second Thursday activity was in the evening, with ice cream and an outdoor movie, *The Princess Bride*, at the football field after dark. A local grocery store donated an unbelievable amount of ice cream. Another store donated paper bowls, napkins, and plastic spoons. A local company set up some projectors, and thirty kids came early to build two huge screens from PVC pipe and old white bedsheets.

Nikki, Jack, and I sat on the front row of the bleachers, in case I needed to be close to the ground. There was no Troy to snuggle, but there was some unplanned entertainment. A gust of wind toppled one screen just as Inigo and Fezzik were about to find the secret door to the Pit of Despair. The setup crew had weighed down the screens' bases with sandbags, but they didn't have enough. Large volunteers from the football team became human sandbags for the rest of the movie. They almost let both screens blow over, while they bowed and waved to the crowd before taking their positions.

Nikki and I went for more ice cream for ourselves and Jack, while Jack saved our seats. I didn't notice until we reached the front of the line that our server was Maddi. I was glad she spoke first, because I couldn't. It was too awkward.

"What can I get you?" she asked softly. "We're out of cookies and cream."

"One scoop of Neapolitan, please."

"A popular choice," she said.

"It's a lot like avoiding a choice," I said, trying to lighten my own mood, at least.

She didn't smile. "I see what you mean." She put an extra-large scoop in my bowl. "Here you go."

"Thank you." At least I remembered to say that.

"You're welcome."

Nikki and I had one of the toppings tables to ourselves. Between the hot fudge and the caramel sauce, I said quietly, "Not exactly the toxic Maddi we used to know."

"Yeah, no kidding," Nikki said. "Yesterday Will heard some kids joking that she must be on a new medication. She wasn't there to hear it, but he invited them never to say anything like that about anyone ever again."

I smiled. "Invited them?"

"Commanded them."

I thought about that for the rest of the movie. I wasn't close enough to Maddi to know what was going on with her, but I couldn't imagine a medication that could turn a girl from what she'd been into what we were seeing now.

Whatever was happening, there was life in her eyes, where I had once seen emptiness.

⸺◆⸺

The next day was sunny but not windy or too hot, a perfect Friday for a picnic. We took our picnic lunch to the park where Troy and I had spent the afternoon on prom day. That was my idea. I assured Jack and Nikki I'd be happy there, not sad from missing Troy.

We strolled around the lake after lunch, avoiding the more rugged parts of the shoreline. We tried to skip rocks from little beaches here and there, when we could find flat rocks to skip.

For two hours no one mentioned my favorite subject, and I wasn't sad. I finally said, "You should see Troy skip rocks. He makes it look so easy, it's embarrassing."

"Quite a catch, that boy," said Jack. "Have you been thinking about him the whole time?"

"Only a little. This is fun. It's a gorgeous day."

They both looked skeptical.

"Seriously," I said. "I still love hanging out with my girlfriends and my dog. I haven't changed that much." Which was true, except that I felt like a different version of myself. My world seemed mostly familiar, but larger, and my place in it had shifted.

"You're happier than you were before Troy," Nikki said.

"And bolder," Jack said. She was an expert at boldness. It was one of my favorite things about her. It was her way of not being paralyzed by her own shyness.

"How much of that is because of Troy, do you think?" I knew some of it was.

"The happiness or the boldness?" Jack asked.

"Both."

"What do you think?" Nikki asked.

"I might not have danced without him, let alone waltzed. I wouldn't have gone to basketball games or rebounded for his shoot-arounds. I doubt anyone else would have kissed me. I probably wouldn't have been in *Fiddler*. Some bad stuff wouldn't have happened. And no one would have asked me to prom." I knelt and stroked the fur on Zeus's neck. I wondered if I was subconsciously trying to distract myself, so the dull ache of missing Troy wouldn't return.

"You're wrong about prom," Nikki said.

I took in her reserved smile and the twinkle in her eyes. "What do you know that I don't?"

"We're sworn to secrecy," Jack said. "Let's just say we're not talking about losers who have to look up to see the bottom rung of the social ladder."

"I had no idea."

"That's what secrecy means," Jack said. "But you're cute, fun, talented, and smart, a lot like your amazing girlfriends, and some boys are just barely bright enough to like that. Troy got to you first, so he might be a little brighter than the rest. Or just lucky."

"Not first by much," Nikki said, but she didn't explain. "Lots of changes since that New Year's breakfast. We weren't outcasts before, exactly—neither were you—but you being with him boosted our social status."

"I'm glad I could help you for once," I said. "I owe you a few. Both of you. A lot more than a few." I skipped a rock, but badly. One skip, then plunk. Maybe Troy could give me rock-skipping lessons. Hours and hours of them. I smiled. Then my heart went plunk with the next rock, and the dull ache was back.

Nikki skipped a rock just as poorly. "Is all this talk about Troy okay? Are you okay? Did you have a miserable week without him, and we weren't around very much to comfort and distract you, but you're too polite to complain?"

"I miss him. I've been too distracted to write very much, but I'm not miserable. Not even unhappy. He'll be back one week from tonight."

We resumed walking.

"I feel like the same person, only different," I said. "Older, I guess. And the world feels bigger or something."

"I feel that way without a boyfriend," Jack said.

"So do I," said Nikki. "You don't think we're growing up, do you?" She grinned.

I smiled. "All I know is, you're the sisters I never had."

"Don't be silly," Nikki said. "You've had us for years. Your parents secretly adopted us about a month into seventh grade. But you didn't hear that secret from us either."

Jack led us out onto a gravel bar.

"You know, I couldn't be luckier if that story were true," I said.

"You're not the only lucky one," Jack said soberly, as she skipped another rock. It skipped across the water, bouncing at least ten times before it sank. "Look at that!"

We climbed back up toward the path but waited just below it, while a slow-moving old man with three matching white poodles passed by in the other direction.

"Since we're practically sisters," Nikki said, "Troy will make a perfect brother-in-law for us. Your babies will be like our very own nieces and nephews."

"Please don't make me blush," I said, but it was far too late.

"Tell me you don't daydream about that," Nikki said.

I looked at her silently and kept blushing.

"That's what I thought," she said. "I know I would."

"It's years away, if it ever happens," I said. "And I try not to think about making babies with anyone for a while, thank you very much."

Jack grinned. "We'll wait."

"So will I."

70

Her Fears, My Fears

W E STEPPED ONTO THE path that circled the lake.

"Troy's been good for us too," Nikki said. "Besides making you so happy and helping us meet desirables."

I looked at her quizzically.

"Lately guys have been trying to act like him, when they're around us. It's nice. It was almost comical on prom day, but you were too distracted to notice."

"What'd I miss?"

"You know we've gone out a couple of times with Matt and Chris. Ty and Colin again too. They've all started calling our parents 'ma'am' and 'sir.' It's all about gallantry and good manners now, not just video games."

Someone I hardly knew had said Troy and I and our friends were changing our school for the better. Was this what she meant?

"They talk about starting their own wallflower project," said Jack, "which I'll believe when I see it. And they claim we're not wallflowers. Tell me that doesn't sound familiar. I mean, *they're* practically wallflowers, and I'm not sure boys can even do that. Anyway, it's not just Troy and his jock friends anymore."

"They want to learn to dance," Nikki said. "Which is good."

"I don't think we like them quite the way you like Troy," Jack said. "But the quality of dates and potential boyfriends around here is way up. So's the quantity. Ya done good, Miller."

"Glad I could help," I murmured.

"There's more," Nikki said. "It's common knowledge that Troy went three whole months before he tried to kiss you, even if you were both totally smitten within a week."

"Common knowledge?" I asked. Would Troy kiss and tell? Or not-kiss and tell, before that? Maybe he told Will. I couldn't blame him; I told Jack and Nikki. Then maybe Will told someone . . .

"And before you wonder if Troy likes to kiss and tell," Jack said, "he just likes to kiss you. We're the ones who told."

"We thought some people should know," Nikki said.

Jack said, "It takes some pressure off them and us. We get more good conversation and fewer sweaty palms and awkward silences. But it's good for you too. It counters the rumors Maddi spread for a while."

The afternoon passed quickly. We paused for a photo in the middle of a footbridge across a narrow part of the lake, then headed for Jack's car. Jack and Nikki had a double date that evening, and Nikki wanted extra time to prepare.

They lived on the same block, about a mile from me, but we dropped off Nikki first. She insisted on sitting in the back with Zeus, since she'd be the first out, so I rode shotgun. Before I knew it, we were pulling into my driveway.

I hadn't really looked at Jack since we left the lake. When I turned to thank her for the ride, my happy thoughts scattered like startled sparrows. Her face was slack, with no trace of her usual smile. She stared straight ahead and didn't speak. I realized Nikki had done most of the talking since we left the park, and Jack hadn't said much at all.

"What's wrong?" I asked.

"Nothing I know of," she said.

"Okay. What are you thinking?"

She closed her eyes for a few seconds, then opened them. "You don't want to know."

"If it makes you sad, I want to know."

"You've had such a happy day. I don't want to ruin it."

I hesitated. "I thought *we* had a happy day."

"We did."

"But now you're sad. Sad?"

She shrugged.

"What happened to 'we're practically sisters'?" I was starting to feel hurt.

She looked at me, still expressionless, then looked away. "Absence doesn't always make the heart grow fonder. Sometimes hearts grow apart."

I digested that for a moment—in the sense that I swallowed it and started to feel nauseous. "Is this about Troy and me? Do you know something I don't?"

"Only theoretically, and no, respectively."

"I don't understand. What are you not telling me?" I took her arm. "Please!"

"I'll just say it. You love Troy. He loves you. I love seeing you so happy. You'd think I'd be jealous, but I'm not. I want to be just as happy for myself at some point, but I don't want you less happy in the meantime."

"Okay, you're not jealous. I'm really glad about that. Are we talking about Troy and me?"

"Not entirely. It's complicated."

"Does that mean you don't want to tell me?"

She shook her head. "I can try." She leaned back in her seat. "Where do I start? When we lived in Minnesota, and I was about nine, Brent took me for a walk at a park by a lake. We skipped rocks and asked a stranger to take our picture on a little bridge.

"We took a lot of walks. He's fourteen years older than me, but for some reason he'd tell his kid sister what was on his mind, when he wouldn't tell anyone else. I guess he needed to talk to someone, and he trusted me to keep his secrets. I loved that. I felt important.

"Anyway, he was leaving for a semester in London. I knew I'd miss him a lot. I hoped his girlfriend would still come over while he was gone, because I liked her too. I'll come back to that.

"You know we talk on Friday morning sometimes, because it's Friday afternoon for him, and he's working, but he has time to talk. I rang him before our committee meeting this morning, told him about the activities and all that. He was pretty enthusiastic. When I asked him how he was doing, he changed the subject. A little later, when I asked him again, he dodged again. I tried to insist, but all he would say was that he's okay, and so are Joan and the kids.

"Thing is, by then he didn't sound okay. He said he was just tired, but the way he said it made me think he was lying. It's never been like that before. I've always felt like he was open with me. So now I'm worried that he's sick, or there's something wrong with one of the kids, or with Joan or the latest pregnancy. Or something else.

"I forgot about him for a while today, but then the bridge and the photos . . . Something's wrong over there, and he won't tell me what."

She met my eyes for moment, then continued. "So that day, before he went to London, after pictures on the bridge, he took my hand, and we walked toward his car. He said that, before he left, he was asking Rachel to marry him when he got back, and would I be okay with that?

"It was win-win for me. I wanted him to be happy, and I wanted Rachel for a sister. He swore me to secrecy."

"Okay," I said cautiously, "I see why that memory would come back today. I understand why you're worried. I hope they're okay. But how does this relate to Troy and me?"

"Because when I worry about one thing, I worry about everything. And because, when Brent came home from London at Christmas that year, he was in love with an English girl named Joan. And Rachel didn't tell him this until he was breaking up with her, but her heart wandered too. Her wedding was a week before he married Joan.

"I love Joan. She's wonderful. But they only visit once a year, and I've been over there to see them less than that."

"Just enough to enrich your vocabulary," I said. I would have smiled, but I couldn't. Just then my insides turned sharply, and I thought I understood. "Are you afraid Troy and I won't make it through the summer?"

She looked at me and nodded. "Sorry. I mean, I hope absence doesn't make the heart go wander. You're so happy lately, and I really like Troy. But things happen sometimes, even if nobody wants them to. Like I said, I'm kind of afraid of everything right now."

My insides tightened another quarter-turn. "Do you know something I don't? About Troy?"

"You already asked me that, and no. I just know he's practically irresistible, and you're not so resistible yourself. Two months is a long time to be apart—look who I'm telling—even with three days together in between. Hearts do . . . unexpected things sometimes, even when they're not far apart."

I wasn't sure my heart was still beating.

"I'm sorry," she said. "If I weren't worried about Brent, I probably wouldn't worry about you and Troy, all of a sudden. And I wouldn't be making you worry. You don't need this from me."

I attempted a smile, but I was too upset. "You're right. I can conjure dark thoughts without anyone's help. Troy and I aren't engaged. We're not married. I don't have any official claim on him. I know there are pretty girl athletes at that basketball camp. He's known some of them for years, and he has things in common with them that he'll never have with me. There are probably some gorgeous Latter-day Saint girls in the ward he attends on Sundays down there. I can't even say it would be wrong if he . . . if I . . ."

"Okay, stop," Jack said. "You're making both of us feel worse. And yeah, I know I started it."

I didn't stop. "Who knows? Maybe I'll meet one of those boys you told me about, when I go to a dance without Troy. Or maybe there will be some smoldering demigod of a young writer for me in Maine, and I'll be tragically torn between—"

"Stop it! It's not funny." There were tears on her cheeks.

We stared at each other. It was like looking into a distraught emotional mirror, with red hair and freckles.

"Did I sound like I was joking?" I finally asked.

"You sounded frantic." She swiped at her tears with the back of her hand. "Why are we sitting here making each other cry?"

I took a long, deep breath. "Because sisters do that sometimes?"

I saw her try to smile—and fail.

"I'm sorry, Jenny. I want you to be happy. And I'm worried about Brent."

I reached for her hand. "I hope they're okay. Do you think I should worry about Troy and me?"

"I think you should ignore me, and you two should be inseparable. And unconscionably happy. In perpetuity."

I tried to smile. "Nice use of big words. You know, the night I met Troy, I was talking to Dad, after you and Nikki went home. I asked him something like, 'What if Troy turns out to be a jerk who just happens to be good at charming a lonely girl at a dance?'"

Her smile was slightly more successful. "That turned out not to be a problem."

"True. But my point is that Dad quoted Stonewall Jackson."

"'Never take counsel of your fears'?" she asked.

"I don't remember telling you about that."

"He's quoted it to me a few times. You know Stonewall Jackson was a slaveowner, right?"

"I know. But I think Dad was right."

"Then you definitely shouldn't take counsel of my stupid fears."

"Or my own. But that doesn't make them stupid. You need to go, right?"

"Yeah. Wish it could be a triple date. When are you Skyping him?"

"The usual," I said. "About 9:30. Maybe a little later. He has a tournament."

We hugged, and I got out of the car. I felt a little better. For the moment.

71

Connections

MOM AND DAD WERE out. I puttered around the house with Zeus, thinking too much and waiting for the hours to pass. What if Jack's fears came true? What if Troy and I wilted like the rose he'd given me before he left? It had lasted more than a week, but by now I should have thrown it away. I just didn't want to.

I'd welcomed it as a symbol of us. What if it still was?

What should I say to him? Were there clues I should watch for? Would he see my fears? Should I tell him what Jack said? He and I talked about everything too. Would he think I was childish or petty, or would he take my worries as more evidence that I loved him?

I wandered into the living room and sat in a chair, as the antique clock chimed the half-hour. Our call was still at least an hour away. If I told him my fears, would he think I didn't trust him? Or worry that my heart was wandering, or wanted to? It didn't.

I sat up straight. I knew what he'd say. He'd already said it, before he went home on the eve of his trip. I hadn't been in great shape that night either. Anxiously, hungrily, I replayed the memory in my mind.

"Here's why you shouldn't worry," he'd said that night, resting his forehead on mine.

⊰⊙⊱

We stood on my front porch. It was mostly dark. The air was cool, and his breath was warm on my face. It smelled minty from the ice cream we'd just devoured.

"Here's why you shouldn't worry: I don't plan on asking for my heart back. It's much happier with you. So unless you bring it to visit me, no one's getting anywhere near it in San Antonio." He wrapped me in his arms. "It's like we belong together. Can't imagine feeling this way with anyone else."

My happiness at his words temporarily overwhelmed my sadness that he was leaving. "My man waxes eloquent tonight," I murmured. "And very romantic. You should kiss me now."

He kissed me gently on the mouth, then kissed away each tear, as it appeared on my cheek. "Happy or sad tears?"

"Yes," I said pathetically, and he hugged me tightly. It was nearly time for him to go home, so he could fly to Texas in the wee hours of the morning.

"I'm sorry," I said. "It's only three weeks. I'll probably survive."

"Hope so," he said with a twinkle.

"Why do you look happy?" I whined. "What is there to be happy about?"

He broke into a grin. "Actually, I'm very happy."

I pouted. "I don't understand."

"That's because from where you are, you can't see the beautiful, amazing girl who's coming home to me from camp three weeks from yesterday afternoon."

"That'll be wonderful," I conceded. "For three and a half days. I'm glad it makes you happy"—I didn't sound glad—"but I'm feeling really sorry for myself right now." He was still beaming, and it still wasn't contagious.

"That's because you're not the one who gets to come home to you six weeks after that."

Our phones beeped their one-minute warning. My face contorted. My tears were about to turn into sobs. He pursed his lips, leaving only a hint of a smile at the corners. It was better—until I saw his eyes. They were just as happy as before. And not very concerned for my feelings, I thought. I cried, and he was happy. It wasn't right.

He took my face gently in his hands. My hands moved instinctively to press against his. His look was a caress. I responded with wide, earnest, soggy eyes. "I will miss you every day," he said. "But I love you, and you love me, and I'll see you in, oh, 475 hours, give or take."

He didn't wait for me to say anything, and I couldn't speak anyway. He kissed me harder than usual on the lips, which took my breath away. He kissed me again, gently and sweetly. Then he glowed at me, told me he loved me and he'd see me soon, and jogged down the sidewalk to his car.

He smiled and waved as he pulled away. I weakly lifted a hand.

By the time he turned the corner at the end of the block, I was almost smiling.

Almost. A little. I watched for a while after he was gone, then went inside.

Mom met me in the entryway. "Are you okay?"

I produced a wan smile. "There's something seriously wrong with that boy." I closed my eyes and shook my head.

"I know what it is," she said.

I opened my eyes. She was smiling too.

"He loves my daughter."

***

After replaying that night's goodbye twice in my head, I felt a little better. There was a good chance my world wouldn't end anytime soon. But I was still frazzled. Then we had trouble with Skype, and by the time we connected, most of our time together was gone. I was near tears again.

He smiled when he finally saw me on his screen, which made me smile, sort of. "Hi, beautiful. How was your day?"

"Long, busy, and Troyless. Yours?"

He grinned. "We won the tournament. You're looking at one big, exhausted ache right now, but it was totally worth it."

"Congratulations! That's amazing! While you did that, Jack, Nikki, and I went for a picnic at our lake from prom day. Zeus went this time."

"Did you miss me?" he asked.

"I did, but it was okay. We have happy memories there. Can you teach me to skip rocks? I'll need long lessons and lots of encouragement. And frequent rewards." My smile felt shy.

"Works for me," he said.

"So why you aren't you out celebrating with your team?"

"They went somewhere with the winning girls team, but I'd rather talk to you. Plus I'm really tired."

"You talk to me every night." Was I testing him? I wasn't sure.

"Wish I could fly home tomorrow instead of Monday."

"I do too. So you miss me sometimes?"

"Pretty much whenever I'm awake and not busy with something."

"What do you do?" I asked.

"When I miss you?"

"When you miss me a lot." My voice broke.

"Jenny, are you okay?"

I was crumbling again. That's how I was. "Not really," I said. "The park was good, but since then I've been missing you so much I've kind of been useless. I didn't know whether to tell you. It's so childish or needy or something. Do you ever feel like that? What do you do?"

"When I miss you so much I can barely breathe? I remember my favorite times with you, and I think about the times we'll have together when we're both home. What do you do?"

"Mostly the first one. Do you ever worry that I'll meet somebody while you're gone, and you'll come home and find out we're not a couple anymore, and I was too much of a coward to tell you?"

He scowled. "Not until you said that. Should I worry?"

"No!"

"Then I won't."

"Should I?"

"Not for a second," he said firmly.

I managed half a smile. "Then I won't."

"Good. Been saving kisses for you."

"I can't wait to take delivery." I paused to enjoy a wave of relief. "Did you play well?"

"Shot well, passed well, hardly any turnovers, a few steals. Our defense was suffocating, especially in the championship. Did I tell you there's a guy on my team this week that's the same size as Will? Plays like him too. So this camp has probably been extra helpful."

"You were already my champion. Sappy but true."

"Winning my tournament is almost as good as Skyping you. No sap, only truth."

We said hasty goodbyes and signed off. It was 10:00 p.m. in my time zone, but I was suddenly so exhilarated—and relieved—that there was no point in trying to sleep. Not for hours yet. So I sat in my favorite chair with my sappy smile and thought about Troy and me.

Half an hour later, I felt happy and secure enough to think back a few hours. Jack's worries about her brother and his family had turned into concern for me and Troy, and her little meltdown had triggered mine. Maybe I'd tried so hard to be happy and positive without Troy that my doubts and worries finally had to push back.

It helped to know Troy missed me a lot, that he knew what I was feeling. Maybe growing together while we were far apart wasn't just a nice thing to say. Maybe this was how it worked.

After Jack, Nikki, and I had checked in with each other and said good night by text message, I still wasn't sleepy. My thoughts skipped all the way back to January, then wandered forward through all my weeks with Troy. I'd remembered this way before, but this time things seemed more solid, more settled. I was watching a stretch of rapids we'd already run, from the safety of the bank.

I'd learned something since school ended and Troy flew to Texas. Now that I was having adventures, it was good to have a break from them. The last few months of school had been mostly wonderful, partly horrible, and totally intense. I needed to unwind, process everything, and learn what I could, before jumping into the next thing—in this case, girls camp.

I thought about my future too—not the fears Jack and I had shared, but what I wanted to do and where Troy might fit in. I wanted at least one college degree. I wanted to be a writer—I didn't know what kind, maybe several kinds—and maybe I wanted to teach. I wanted a good husband and a happy marriage and children of my own. I couldn't imagine Troy not being part of that. Well, I could, but I didn't want to. We'd have to wait for each other for years, but I could totally do that. We could keep growing together, even at a distance.

If we grew apart—shredding at least one heart, probably two—and discovered that his future happiness and mine didn't necessarily involve each other, I could probably recover eventually. I could probably find someone else who was smart, interesting, and good. I could love him, and he could be almost as good as Troy at finding things to love about me that I didn't see in myself.

For now, my heart was far away in Texas, in the care of a boy I hoped would never surrender it or ask for his own heart back. I could be happy just waiting for him to come back to me, which he would. I'd try to wait just as happily while he was away for two years on his mission, with a lot less communication. Then he'd come back to me again, and we could start our forever together.

His two-year mission was only a year away. I consoled myself with two thoughts. I could try really hard to put off thinking about our two-year separation. And when I finally had to face it, I could remember that other women had waited far longer, without knowing whether their men were alive or dead, when they sent them off to war or other things.

I felt a lot more collected after two weeks of summer and my talk with Troy. Saner too. Some of the confidence I'd thought I was faking felt real now. I thought I knew why, but I hadn't quite put it into words yet.

It was almost midnight. Mom and Dad had long since said good night. I moved to my desk and opened my laptop. I'd try to put it—most of it—into words for Troy. If it worked, I could e-mail it to him tomorrow.

72

Distance

Dear Charming, Hunky, Distant Troy,

    "Hunky" is silly, but Jack and Nikki called you that today, and I liked it. They're not wrong.

    I love you. I miss your actual self, but Skyping helps.

    I've been thinking some thoughts, since we talked tonight. I'll try to write them for you. For me too, because I'm still figuring them out, and writing helps. I'll send this tomorrow, maybe. It's too late tonight. But you knew that.

    (Don't worry that this note will end badly. It may not end a masterpiece, but it's not going anywhere sad. Did I mention that I love you?)

    I've had a little time, now that school's out, to think about the last few months. When I haven't thought about you, I've thought about me.

    I used to wear a helmet—thick padding to keep anything from hurting my head. Then I got Zeus, grew up a little, and stopped wearing the helmet. But maybe I kept a thick layer of . . . something . . . around me after that, so as few things as possible could hurt my heart. That was because I knew I was a freak, though I didn't want to be, and attempting any extended contact with normal life would only hurt me in the end. It didn't help that people treated me like a freak—not cruelly, usually, but not expecting very much normal life from me either, and going out of their ways to protect me.

    Along came a boy who didn't see me as a freak and didn't treat me like one. Not that everyone did. Jack and Nikki have always treated me like a normal person, as much as they could, and Mom and Dad have done their best. Then your friends and family treated me like a normal girl too.

Lately, even when some jealous kids were hostile and cruel, it wasn't because I, as a freak, was somehow your special project. They hated me as a normal girl who had the boyfriend at least one of them wanted. I'm not saying they were kind, just that they treated me like a normal girl when they were vicious.

When Mr. O had to leave our Fiddler *rehearsal, he didn't stop to ask solicitously if I was able to take over for the last fifteen minutes. He told the cast I was in charge. Then they—you—listened when I talked. Later, when Jordyn and I talked at the cast party, it was normal girl to normal girl.*

The emotional roller coaster of dressing in gym clothes (prior bad memories!) to help you rebound was pretty normal too.

Even harsh judgments from your bishop and our seminary teacher, among others, were based on my being a normal high school girl with a boyfriend.

So lately I've been feeling more like a person and less like a case. I'm better at seeing others do well at things—you playing basketball, Will giving a stunning speech, kids doing wonderful things on the stage—without feeling sad and jealous because I can't do all those things. I can do other things. A decent speech too, I think.

I wouldn't have been jealous of basketball itself, just your prowess in it and the joy it gives you. I'm still Jenny.

I've been feeling like I can be myself, without the bubble wrap, and there are places for me in the world. Not every place I might want—nobody gets that—but places where I can be a person and do good things with good people.

Some of this, maybe all of it, might have happened without you, at least eventually. I realize that. Not as quickly, I'm almost certain. I absolutely love that it's happened with you. I'm happy and grateful. "With you" is my favorite place, and that's more than geography.

Here's the real revelation, I think. The biggest, happiest change for me is not that more people treat me like a normal girl instead of a freak. It's bigger than that. Maybe not bigger than us, but big. It's this: I don't see myself as a freak anymore. I'm a person. I can do things, and I get to have a life. Maybe I sit more than most people, but sitting is no longer who I am.

True, I'm sitting now. I'm sitting and thinking of you. I can almost feel your arms around me, almost taste your kiss, almost hear you whisper that you love me.

Almost.

Almost comes with a dull ache sometimes, but right now I'm more than almost fluttery. I hope you can almost see that in my eyes and my smile as you read this, and almost hear it in my words, and almost feel my hand in yours, and almost taste my kiss.

I want to know your thoughts about all this, so tell me, please, when we get the chance.

Good night again. I love you. I am ...

Your Jenny

***

I left for girls camp early on Monday morning, mere hours before Troy returned from San Antonio. Missing him sucked, but girls camp was always fun. Zeus and I had gone every summer since I was twelve. Mom went with me the first two years, which was partly an embarrassment but mostly a relief.

Every year, the young women in my ward and our adult leaders went for a week to a sprawling camp in the mountains, with girls from lots of other wards in separate campsites. We slept in cabins with bunks and mattresses, took hot showers, even had refrigerators—but we left our personal electronics at home. That meant no contact with Troy from Monday morning until Friday afternoon. We hadn't gone that long since the night we first danced.

It was a church camp, so religion was a theme, especially in the evenings. Sometimes they made it too cute or worked too hard to make us cry, but it was mostly okay. We had lots of outdoor activities during the day, often things Zeus and I could do, if I was careful.

By late afternoon we'd all be sitting around in our camp, exhausted, talking about whatever and experimenting with each other's hair. That was more for fun than for looks. For five days nobody worried much about makeup or perfect hair or dressing fashionably. I wondered if that was why our social circles seemed to disappear by the second day. For me, it also helped that Britney wasn't my class president anymore, and she wasn't around to worry about the state of my eternal soul. She'd just finished high school, so she had aged out of the Young Women program.

On Monday, Tuesday, and Wednesday evenings we had big meetings in an outdoor amphitheater with girls from other campsites. They were an hour long and partly fun, partly religious. Afterward we sat around the fire in our own camp, until the leaders shooed us into our cabins, well after dark.

A lot of the girl talk was about boys, and this time I was a bit of a celebrity. It wasn't just the boyfriend. Everybody knew what had happened at school, and some wanted to know more. So on Monday I answered their questions. It wasn't too painful, but the end of another day without Troy made my heart ache—until I remembered what was under my pillow on my bunk. I went to bed a little early, so I'd have time before lights out for the pretty blue envelope I'd yearned to open for two weeks.

I opened it carefully and pulled out a long, handwritten letter on matching blue paper. It was dated the day he left.

⸺⊹⸺

Dearest, Beautiful, Amazing Jenny,

Remember how I was packed for camp before I came over last night, so I could stay with you as long as possible? I overdid it. I woke up at 2:45 a.m. and couldn't go back to sleep. (I hope you're still asleep.) I got dressed and made breakfast, and now there's nothing I have to do for the next hour, until it's time to leave. So I'm doing what I want. This.

I'm writing on paper, so you can take it to camp. I'm using Nan's stationery, because it's almost the color of your eyes. She's asleep now, but she keeps saying I should use it anytime I want to write you "a love letter." She sounds very serious when she says that.

This really is a love letter, because I love you. Thanks for being my friend and girlfriend these last few months. I can hardly wait to see you again.

Right now I'm thinking of kissing you. Sometimes I wish for "often" or "constantly" instead "occasionally in between." It's a smart rule.

This summer, we'll have too many weeks in a row with no kisses at all. Starting today. Sigh.

Anyway, what I'm thinking now is:

I'd like to kiss your forehead, because it's easy to reach and it's yours.

I'd like to kiss the place between your eyebrows that wrinkles when you concentrate. Watching you is one of my favorite things. You know that, right?

I'd like to kiss your eyes, because they sparkle when you look at me. And they're yours.

I'd like to kiss your cheeks, because they're cute, and they turn fun colors sometimes. Like now, maybe.

I'd like to kiss your nose. It's cute, it's on my way to your lips, and it's yours.

I'd like to kiss your lips—because they're yours, and I love how you smile with them, and I love it when you use them to kiss me.

I'm thinking about kissing your chin. I like it too.

If we didn't have a rule, I wouldn't stop there. I'm not getting bored, and I don't think we should do more than we do. The rules are fine. It's you I love, not just kissing you or holding your hand. So I'm content to reverse direction. Now I'm back to thinking about kissing your lips, which is pretty much paradise. Doing it is paradise. Thinking about it is nice.

I hope you enjoy my helping you think about me kissing you. Also, I enjoy thinking about you thinking about me thinking about kissing you. Remember "that Scout Law thing"? A Scout is trustworthy, loyal, <u>helpful, friendly</u> . . ." I feel like I'm doing okay with some of those this morning.

Dad and I have a quick errand. Then I'll leave this at your door on our way to the airport, along with a rose I picked out. If I miss you this much at 4:08 a.m., it's probably a good thing I'm usually asleep at this hour.

. . .

It's a little later now. We're about to make my delivery, but I'm not finished writing yet. So dad's pumping gas (on the Sabbath, I know, but we forgot yesterday) and checking the oil—usually my job—and grabbing a couple of snacks, since we're already here buying gas. I just want to say, I'm an idiot.

Riding to the airport with Dad makes sense, since he's flying this morning. But he just told me Mom doesn't have her usual early Sunday morn-

ing meeting today. It was cancelled yesterday, but she didn't think to tell me. She could have driven me a little later, and you could have come to the airport with us, and she could have taken you home. I should have found this out sooner, somehow. We could have ridden to the airport together. I could have kissed you this morning.

Beelzebubble!

I'm an idiot, but I'm your idiot. I adore you. I already miss you. I'll text you from the airport.

Here comes Dad. I'm sealing this with many actual kisses right on the envelope. I'll mark the locations with tiny x's.

Have a great week with Smokey Bear. He doesn't love you like I love you.

<u>*Yours,*</u>

Troy

Before lights-out I had time to read his letter twice, read the kissing part two more times, enjoy how he underlined "yours," and kiss each of the places where his lips had been—but discretely, in case other girls were watching.

There were seventeen *x*'s.

Tomorrow, probably, he'd get the letter I sent him before I left for camp, where I described sixteen times I'd thought of him while he was gone—one for each day he was gone. I told him where I was, what I was doing, what made me think of him, and what I thought. Some of it was trivial, like wishing he were with me to see a fun bumper sticker or a bad typo on a store's marquee. The mushiest one was my attempt to describe how it felt to be loved, wanted, and wrapped in his arms.

I kissed the blue envelope a few more times after lights-out.

A letter from Troy is warmer than an extra blanket, I thought, and it quells the ache for a while. And maybe if I fall asleep thinking about him kissing me, I'll dream about him kissing me.

When I awoke the next morning, I was still smiling. Or smiling again. I couldn't tell which. I didn't remember dreaming, but it could have happened.

73

Girl Talk by the Fire

I N OUR BIG CAMP meeting Wednesday evening, the main speaker spent twenty minutes outfitting a white-robed mannequin with the sword of the Spirit, the shield of faith, and the rest of the Apostle Paul's armor of God, explaining each piece in detail. She assured us that God wanted us to be like our fake warrior-princess—not her exact words—and we were already like that on the inside. We just didn't know it yet.

She probably had a point—at least Paul had a point—but I desperately wanted to whisper to one of the girls next to me that God wanted us all to have vacant stares, buns of plastic, dirty-blonde wigs with dark roots, and no soul. Everyone around me was paying attention, and none of them was Jack or Nikki, so I didn't distract anyone.

After the meeting I lingered at rim of the amphitheater, admiring a bald eagle soaring above us. Its graceful orbit took it out over the small lake that shimmered in the valley below, then back toward me, until it was almost overhead. I hoped to see it dive on some prey—maybe a fish—but I was content to watch it fly.

"Is that a hawk or an eagle? I can never tell."

The voice was familiar, so I didn't turn to look. Amy was a quiet, pretty girl from my ward. She was a year older than me, and she was our new Laurel class president—but she wasn't annoying and judgmental like the last one.

"Keep watching," I said.

She stood quietly beside me until it flew nearer again, and the light and angle were just right. "Oh! It's a bald eagle! It's beautiful!"

We watched a few more orbits. Neither of us made a sound until something rustled in the dry grass a few yards away. Amy grabbed my arm with a high-pitched whimper.

A chipmunk darted toward a large pine tree, then stopped and looked around before scampering out of sight.

She let go of my arm. "Sorry. I worry about snakes."

"I would too," I said, "but I've never seen one up here."

"Neither have I. If we do, will Zeus protect us?"

"Definitely."

The eagle flew into the distance. We waited for it to turn back, but it didn't, so we started up the trail to our campsite. The first part was steeply uphill, which discouraged chatter. Zeus and I kept to the center of the wide trail, because the edges were lined with rocks.

Halfway there, when we weren't quite so winded, she broke the silence. "Can I talk to you about something?"

"Sure."

"The last few guys I've gone out with have treated me like crap. All in different ways. They're rude, and they're so full of themselves. Does Troy really treat you as well as it looks like?"

I smiled warmly. "He really does."

"Not just when other people are watching?"

"All the time."

"Does he always have to talk about himself?"

"He listens more than he talks. But I like that he talks."

She shook her head. "Do you know any other guys like that? They don't have to be seniors."

"I don't know that many guys, but there's Troy's best friend, Will."

"Will, the student body president? I'm five-foot-three-and-a-half, and I'm lying about the half. I'd need a stepladder."

I chuckled. "I'll try to think of someone shorter."

We wandered into camp and sat on an empty log near the crackling fire. I was glad someone had restarted it already. Twilight was turning to darkness, and darkness in the mountains came with a chill.

"Everybody's shorter than Will," Amy said. "But you know what? I could totally do the stepladder."

"He'd be worth it," I said.

Two more of the older girls joined us. "Who'd be worth it? Worth what?"

We sat together and stretched blankets across our shoulders and laps. Amy and the others told stories about boys—mostly boys I knew—who'd treated them badly, on and after dates.

I couldn't see Troy starring in any of their stories. I couldn't imagine him sitting in his car outside my house, honking for me to come out. Or begging me to take off my shirt and send him a selfie. Or stomping away angrily if I beat him at mini golf (which wouldn't happen anyway). Or wanting me to get drunk or high with him. Or paying more attention to his phone than to me. Or trying to turn me against my parents. Or making angst-filled speeches about how his love for me would drive him to madness, unless I yielded my body to his all-consuming male needs.

I wondered aloud if boys knew that girls shared details and named names. Did they realize how they treated us affected their reputations a lot more than the white shirts most of them wore to church on Sunday, or the pious things they said when it was their turn to give the spiritual thought at the beginning of a seminary class? If they did, they'd behave better, we all agreed.

From halfway around the fire, someone asked me if my parents and Troy's were okay with us being together, and how we convinced them to trust us that much. Other conversations died away, and I tried not to be nervous. I didn't tell the whole story, but they kept wanting more, and I told them enough.

Even the twelve year olds listened. I remembered being twelve and being fascinated with boys—older ones, because my male classmates were still children. I'd been in awe of girls who were old enough to date, and who could talk about it without blushing and stammering. For a heartbeat or two I relived the pangs of sitting and wondering, then and more recently, if I was such a freak that no boy I wanted would ever want me.

Troy had pretty much resolved that concern. For a moment I felt happy and grateful. But I hadn't kissed him in almost forever. For weeks after prom night, I hadn't gone two days in a row without a kiss.

I'd be back from camp Friday afternoon, and he'd pick me up at 6:00 p.m., so in 45 hours I could see and kiss and hold him. That was better than 46 hours, but it seemed distant. I'd already grown used to the dull ache of missing him, underneath whatever else I felt. But it was late, and I was tired. The ache didn't stay dull, and it didn't stay underneath.

I tuned back in as Ashton Bigler asked me a question. She was the youngest girl in our camp. She'd turned twelve just in time to qualify. "Do you miss Troy a lot?"

I wasn't ready for that. I nodded sadly and blinked back tears.

Despite our age difference, Ashton wasn't shy with me. We'd been back-fence neighbors all her life. She'd been a tomboy, with her blonde hair cut short, until a few months ago, when she confided that she now preferred the "girl clothes" she'd mostly avoided before, and she was growing her hair long. She wanted boys to like her.

When she saw my sad eyes, she got up, worked her way carefully around the fire, and gave me a hug.

"Thanks, Ash," I said. "Here, sit by me." We made room on our log and shared our blankets. She beamed.

A few minutes later, she asked softly, "Do you think a boy will ever look at me the way Troy looks at you? We've all seen it. We practically swoon when you bring him to church." Her voice was full of longing. "I want a boy to look at me that way."

A few of the girls overheard. I saw smiles, but no one teased her.

"Let's think for a minute," I said. "You're smart, you're kind, and you're fun, so that's good. You're already cute, and you're starting to look like your Mom. She's really pretty. So when the boys your age get old enough to see how amazing you are, I think you'll be fighting them off with a stick."

Her face brightened. "How soon will that be?"

"High school at the latest," I prophesied.

"Better say high school at the soonest. So far, the boys my age are pretty dumb. They'll need a few years."

I suppressed a laugh. "High school's soon enough, right?"

"I guess so, but I may not fight them all off. All but one, maybe. The one that's as good as Troy."

Troy would love this, I thought. I would love telling him. "I don't know, Ash. There may not be any others as good as Troy. You may have to settle for almost as good."

"No way," she said. "No settling. I want one just as good."

"Okay. When you find him, I want to meet him. I promise I won't steal your boyfriend."

She looked as if I'd said something foolish. "Duh! By then you'll be married to Troy and having babies together, and you won't need a boyfriend, because he'll be your husband."

Some girls giggled, and I wondered why my face wasn't instantly warmer. Maybe it was already warm from the fire. Maybe it was the not-so-dull ache.

Ashton scowled. "Sorry. Too loud."

"No worries. You didn't say anything bad, did you?"

"No." She spoke more loudly. "They pretty much all love Troy like I do, even if they're smirking right now. I hear them talk when you bring him to church." She put her mouth to my ear and whispered, "Do you have to sing a hymn now, because I made you think about marrying Troy and having babies?"

I suppressed another laugh. Sometimes we joked about singing a hymn to help us banish impure thoughts. Sometimes we weren't joking. It usually worked. I replied in an even softer whisper. "If you hear me singing a hymn, you'll know."

One of the adults announced that it was time to go to our cabins, and the leaders would put out the fire. Zeus and I lingered, while the other girls left. I wanted to talk to my Young Women president.

Unlike our class presidents, the leader of the whole organization was an adult. She was a petite, energetic woman about Mom's age. She took time off from her medical practice to spend the week with us. As usual, she'd listened to our discussion around the fire without saying a word. Now she put her arm around me. "Beautiful evening. I love the stars up here."

"I do too," I said. "I hope I didn't say anything wrong. I don't want to be a bad influence."

"You didn't, and you're not. I hope what you said sinks in."

"Really?"

"If they'll communicate like you and Troy do with your parents, and insist that boys treat them well, a long list of bad things will happen a lot less. What you said about risks and safety and commandments was pretty smart too. Nice bit of teaching. They don't always listen to us that way."

"Sometimes I don't listen," I confessed. "But I wasn't trying to teach. I was just talking."

"You don't know this yet, but you're a natural leader. You were teaching and leading."

"I was just being one of the girls. More than before, I think."

"Fitting in is good," she said, "but this was more."

"I don't feel like a leader. Most of the time I feel like an outsider."

"They watch you more than most, to see how a girl should talk and act. They also watch how you and Troy treat each other. It's not just the younger ones." I looked up and saw her smiling. "It's almost lights-out. You go. I'll douse the fire."

74

Belonging

EVERY YEAR, ON THE last evening of camp, we met in our own campsites with just the girls from our ward, instead of having a big, combined meeting. By tradition our bishop would join us for the evening. Bishop Savage arrived before dinner, wearing jeans, a red polo shirt, and a baseball cap, instead of his usual coat and tie.

I overheard him asking the adult leaders what he could do to help, but they said he was our guest. He should sit and relax.

"There must be something I can do," he said.

"Look around," said our camp director. "Everything that needs doing already has girls doing it."

We all had jobs before dinner. Mine were to update the white board with our schedule for the evening and the next day, and to get Zeus's dinner. Our dinnertime was easier for him if he'd already eaten. My job later would be to introduce the bishop as our fireside speaker. They told me to take a few minutes, so I needed material. When we could, Zeus and I joined him by the fire. Zeus could eat there as well as anywhere.

He gave Zeus a pawshake and a treat. Then I asked him for some fun and interesting things about his life that the girls weren't likely to know.

Our fireside meeting began after sundown with five silly camp songs, four of which were about girls and boys; a hymn; a prayer; and some announcements. I gave my introduction, using some of what the bishop had told me. I also mentioned how he and his wife had visited me often when I was in the hospital for a few weeks, to cheer me up and give my parents a break. I wanted them to see that he wasn't just our bishop. He was a good man, a good friend, and he cared about us.

I took my seat, and he stood. "Thank you, Jenny. I'd be content to introduce you and have you talk to us tonight."

Ashton spoke up. "We listened to her last night. Monday night too."

"I wish I'd been here," he said.

"No, Bishop," she replied. "We talked about boyfriends and stuff. We couldn't have asked our questions with you here."

He chuckled. "I've never known Jenny to be shy about saying what she thinks, just because her bishop is listening." He gave me a knowing smile. "But maybe you're right."

I could tell some of the girls were impatient with Ashton's interruptions, but the bishop didn't seem that way. "Ladies," he said, "I do lots of things as bishop. I wouldn't call most of them fun, but some of them are. I love escaping to the mountains for an evening with you. Dinner's always better here than at Scout camp. And this is the only place I ever eat where they love me enough to put plastic worms in my food. They were plastic, right?"

He waited for the laughter to subside. "I made a resolution tonight. Next year, when I come, I'll find a way to show you that I love you that much too."

An adult leader called from the back, "Tough talk, bishop!"

He nodded. "Next year, on the last night of camp, let's compare notes and see how we did."

He scanned his audience for a few seconds. "Here's what I came to say. We talk a lot about standards, I know. Sometimes it seems like standards are just lists of things that sound fun, so we're not supposed to do them. They're more than that, and you know they're important. But tonight I want to talk about our Standard, with a capital *S*. Jesus Christ himself is our Standard. You know that too. So let's consider how he talked and acted, and how he treated people."

Quoting scripture from memory, he walked us through Jesus' temptations in the wilderness, explaining what they meant, how big they were, and how they resembled our own temptations. He showed us how Jesus kept pointing people to his Father, not craving the fame or credit he could have claimed for the wonderful things he did.

He had us list people who were usually shunned, hated, or ignored, but whom Jesus noticed and treated kindly—lepers, Samaritans, poor people, sick people, children, Romans, tax collectors, and others whom the Scribes and Pharisees considered unworthy or unclean. He described how kind and gentle Jesus was with people who'd yielded to temptations much smaller than the ones he'd resisted. Then he said, "We adults think it's important to emphasize his sacrifice, so you'll never forget we can repent and be forgiven. That's true. It's an infinite gift. We can never repay him. But there are other good reasons to talk about him.

"We need to see that he treats us the same way he treated people when he was here on earth. We need to know how able and committed he is to help us in all of our trials, not just when we've sinned. We need to understand that the only way for us to become better than we are, to be more like him, is by his power and grace. And we need to be so well acquainted with him that simply knowing him helps us to love others and want to be like him."

I loved listening to Bishop Savage. He talked like he knew the Savior in ways that I wanted to know him. Best of all, when he taught the gospel, it made sense and felt good, and it didn't hurt in ways I felt it shouldn't. I wished Troy were listening with me. I made notes by firelight, when I wasn't listening so intently that I forgot, to share with him later.

If I hadn't been paying close attention, I'd have been trying to figure out what to say in the last part of our meeting, because we always ended our last evening at camp with testimonies. Girls and leaders would each take a couple of minutes to share their thoughts and feelings about God, the Church, their families, and each other. Girls who never said anything like that anywhere else would do it at camp once a year. When girls who weren't members of the Church came to camp with us, they were welcome to say something too, and they usually did.

This time the bishop solved that problem for me. "I didn't ask Jenny's permission earlier, so I'll ask now," he said. "She gave me a copy of her sacrament meeting talk from a few months ago, and I brought it with me tonight. Most of you heard it then, but I want to read some of it to you. If that's okay, Jenny."

Like I would say no to him, of all people. I nodded.

He started at the beginning, reading by flashlight. He stopped in the middle and said, "After I'm done, we'll have testimonies, as always. Jenny may have something else she wants to say then, but for now I'd like her to read the rest of her talk to us. It's one of my favorite testimonies ever. Then I'll finish up."

I picked up where he'd left off, with the part about the Savior's suffering. Then I made a mistake. As I read about the people God had sent to bless my life—my angels—I let myself think about the people who'd been good to me since I'd first said those words, when other people sometimes weren't. It wasn't just Troy or even mostly Troy. It was also our parents, some old and new friends, some teachers, a coach who wasn't even mine, my bishop, and a lot of kids at school.

When I got to the last part, about wanting to thank God more and love him more and so on, I had to stop. I couldn't read through my tears, and I couldn't continue from memory, because my mind went blank. I wiped my eyes, composed myself, started that part over again, and made it to the end without crumbling.

I turned and handed Bishop Savage the flashlight and his copy of my talk. He took them and squeezed my hand. "Beautiful," he whispered. "Thank you, my friend."

I took my seat, while he turned to everyone else and thanked me again. Then he said, "Last thought, ladies." His voice was a little gruff, and he stopped for a sip of water.

"I know you sometimes feel discouraged or even broken. Maybe you feel that way right now. I feel that way too, some days and nights a lot more than others. It's okay to feel that way. We are broken. All of us are broken—including the ones we compare ourselves to, the ones who look like they have it all together. The good news is, we're broken in ways that a Savior can fix. He will fix us, if we'll let him, if we'll give him time and patience and try not to push him away. He's already working on us.

"Someday we'll look back, like those pioneers who couldn't pull their handcarts up another rocky, snowy hill, and like Jenny, when she thinks about the people who've blessed her life and the loving God who sent them. Someday we'll look back on our darkest hours, when things were nearly unbearable for us. We'll see that he was marking our path, nudging us forward, holding us together, gradually making us better and stronger. We'll realize that he actively cared for us, when we thought he was angry or indifferent or absent; that he prepared and protected us, when we thought he was standing back and letting things tear us apart.

"We'll look back and understand that our joy here on earth was real, when we tasted it, and it was a gift from him, the smallest sample of what he plans for us when we're finally ready to return home.

"We'll see that, when we didn't know who we were, or who we should try to be, or even who we could be that wouldn't be a waste of skin, he knew who we were, and who we'd been when we lived with him as spirits before our birth, and who we could become here and hereafter with his help. Then we'll see that all the pain and heartache and doubt and confusion here were temporary—and somehow, miraculously, they were worth it.

"I want to borrow some wise and beautiful words from a dear friend and say this. When I look back and see the hand of God in my life and the lives of the people I love, 'I want to thank him, and love him, and praise him, and obey him, and serve him even more.'"

I heard sniffles. When I glanced stealthily at the girls nearest me, there was firelight enough to see tears shining on their cheeks, which meant anyone who cared to could see plenty on mine. I didn't wipe them away.

Then it was time for our own testimonies. I often disliked testimony meetings, especially the small ones, where I felt pressured to take a turn because everyone else did. This one didn't feel like that. I'd already said something, and it was enough. And the warmth and peace I'd felt while the bishop spoke lingered.

The testimonies went on for more than an hour, but that was okay. After the closing prayer there was lots of hugging, as always—and more hugs and kind words for me than ever before, by far. Maybe something I'd done or said that week had meant something to someone, but it felt bigger than that. I—myself, as a person—meant something to them.

Happy thoughts of belonging competed with thoughts of Troy, as I settled into my bunk with paper and pen. I wished I could tell him right then that maybe we weren't bad examples after all, and sometimes at church meetings we got it right, and it didn't hurt, and it made sense and felt wonderful. Maybe those times made up for other times.

The best I could do before tomorrow evening was write him a letter, but there wasn't time before lights-out. I scribbled enough notes that I could write it out for him in the morning.

75

Summer Weekend

F OR THREE AND A half days after camp, until Mom, Dad, and I left
for Maine, Troy and I were both in town.

On Friday evening we went to a neighboring city to watch Jordyn in
a community theater production of *Fiddler*. It was easier to enjoy her
performance when I wasn't tempted to be jealous, and when I wasn't
mostly watching Troy instead. I noticed lots of ways the same play was
different with a different director.

On Saturday morning Jack, Nikki, and I went to breakfast at a little
German bakery downtown, where the *plunderschnecken* were to die for.
We skirted the fringes of a group pastry coma, eating slowly and getting
silly while we talked about boys and camp. Their camp would be later in
the summer, but they'd been before.

They told me about the Thursday activity I'd missed, a dance with a
live local band that was starting to go regional. It drew a huge crowd.
What Troy hadn't already told me—maybe Will hadn't told him—was
how we'd scored a band like that for a school dance.

"Mr. Cain, of all people, has a nephew in the band," Jack said. "He
told his nephew what we're doing this summer and asked if they could
play for one of our activities. They wanted to, and the timing worked
out for this week."

"Why did you say, 'Mr. Cain, of all people'?" I asked.

Jack's eyes twinkled. She'd set me up, and I was happy to play along.
"Because he's a teacher, he mostly teaches English grammar, and he's old,
like fifty. He shouldn't be cool enough for something like this."

"Jaqueline," Nikki said mock-soberly, "you need to remember there
are people who think grammar is one of the coolest things in the universe. They often descend from writers and English teachers."

"How many of those people are currently sitting at this table, Veronica?" Jack asked.

Nikki couldn't contain her laughter. "Exactly . . . one," she sputtered.

We laughed at her, which only made her laugh harder. She was practically convulsing, and she began to fall off her chair.

She caught herself and mostly stopped laughing. "Wow. It wasn't that funny. Must be the sugar." She took a deep breath. "I'll stipulate to awarding Mr. Cain fifty honorary coolness points."

"Coolness points are a rhetorical device," Jack explained. "Rhetorical devices are a frequent subject of dinner conversation at the Miller home."

"And pillow talk between Miller parents," Nikki said, "when they're feeling especially, um, romantic." She started shaking again. Tiny snorts punctuated her laughter, which set off the giggles in Jack and me.

We were silly more than loud, but people at other tables were glancing at us. They looked amused, so I didn't worry, but Jack said, "Okay, ladies. Public faces."

We tried, but we kept looking at each other and slipping back into mirth.

Jack slowly blew out a breath. "Okay. Well. Wait 'til you hear—" She stared at me. "What?"

My smile felt nearly as happy as yesterday's, when I saw Troy for the first time in 474.9 hours. "I missed you two this week."

"Aww," Nikki crooned, sounding syrupy.

Jack pulled Nikki's plate away. "No more *plunder*-thingies for you."

"Aww," she repeated, then pushed her lower lip into an exaggerated pout.

I swallowed a laugh so big it actually hurt. "You were telling me about the dance."

"Wait 'til you hear about the next school dance you're going to miss. It's three weeks—No!" She slapped Nikki's hand, which was inching toward the confiscated plate. "It's three weeks—"

Nikki hung her head dramatically, faking sobs.

"Oh, all right. Just don't fall out of your chair." She pushed Nikki's plate across the table. Nikki grinned triumphantly.

Jack pursed her lips, but her eyes twinkled. "It's three weeks away. We did most of the planning in our meeting yesterday."

Nikki jumped in, talking around a bite of pastry. "Maddi's doing her community service at that place"—she paused to swallow—"that place we go once a year to wheel handicapped people to their Sunday church meetings and Wednesday night activities."

I was never allowed to help when it was my ward's turn, because seizures.

"Maddi's idea," Jack said, "is to have our next dance there. We'll decorate their outdoor pavilion, have great refreshments, and dance with the residents. Or sit and talk with them, or whatever they can do. We're bringing someone to our activity the week before to tell us how to make it fun for them and teach us to dance with people in wheelchairs."

"Maddi came up with this?" I asked. "Our Maddi?"

"Yep."

"When she told us her idea," Nikki said, "one of the new guys on the committee asked why we'd ever do something so lame. Will said, 'I think the word you wanted was *creative*.' His voice was so cold, the guy just wilted. We asked Maddi how it would work, and by the time we were done, we had most of a plan. We're decorating a long pathway too, for taking them on walks."

"Will told Maddi she was the obvious one to be in charge," Jack said, "but she said she'd rather not. She wouldn't say why, but after the meeting he got her to tell a few of us that she wants to spend her time dancing and sitting with everybody. She knows a lot of them now, and they know her, and she thinks it'll make them more comfortable. So Will's taking charge of this one, which frees Maddi to be a one-woman extreme wallflower project."

"What is up with Maddi?" I asked.

"You mean, has her excellent body been taken over by friendly aliens from the Magical Planet of Unusual Kindness?" Jack asked.

"And Humility?" Nikki added.

"That's the rest of its official name," Jack said. "Whatever this is, I'm not complaining."

"Maybe it really is medication," Nikki mused.

"I talked to my Young Women president about that," I said. "She's a doctor, right? She says there's no drug or combination of drugs that changes a person from what Maddi was last month to what she is this month."

Jack looked thoughtful. "You mean from a devil to a saint?"

"Something like that. She said therapy can help, with time, and medication too, but mostly this is what happens when someone decides to be good and finally means it. Well, unless they're addicted to something. Then it takes more than just deciding, no matter how determined they are.

"She said the good Maddi was probably locked up inside the whole time, hurt and ashamed and wishing for an opportunity to come out. She finally had to decide who she was going to be, and I guess she decided right. Maybe that part's more of a Church leader's view than a medical one. She says there's light in every human soul. We just have to find it. Or they do."

"So far, so good," Nikki said.

"So far, very good," Jack said. "We'll see."

<hr>

While we were at breakfast, Mom, Dad, and Troy prepared for the rest of our Saturday. Mom and Dad had rented a boat, so the seven of us, including Zeus, could go fishing on a gorgeous reservoir an hour up into the mountains.

Zeus didn't fish, but we humans each caught our limit. For bait we alternated between crawfish and nightcrawlers, neither of which I cared to touch. So Troy baited my hook, and I paid him with a little kiss each time. Maybe that wasn't exactly "infrequently in between," but kisses would be rare enough for the rest of the summer.

Back on shore, I paid Troy with a bigger kiss, after he cleaned my four rainbow trout and washed the blood and fish guts off his hands.

When we'd stowed everything for the trip home, there was still time for a leisurely walk along the lake. Mom and Dad went off on their own, and Jack and Nikki volunteered to walk Zeus, since I had Troy.

I wanted to talk about Maddi. Which made one of us.

"What happened to the weather in Siberia?" he asked.

"I think it's changing."

I mostly talked, and he mostly listened. I told him I thought Maddi really was changing. Then it got weird. I wondered aloud if I'd be strong enough to change so much for the better, and so quickly, or if I'd even know how. Maybe knowing how took some counseling or something, but still.

Then it got weirder. "It's like she's starting to resemble Will," I said.

Troy's eyebrows arched, but he said nothing, so I explained. From what I'd heard and seen, she didn't favor the popular kids at all anymore. If anything, she was more attentive to the shy, awkward kids, especially the lonely ones. "Maybe Will's rubbing off on her," I said as we ambled along the asphalt path. "Maybe he's rubbing off on all of us, because I want to be like him. I know how bizarre this sounds, but now I want to be like Maddi too. They both act like the circles don't exist."

"That's backwards," he said.

"What do you mean?"

"Anybody being more like Will is good. But she should want to be more like you, not vice versa." He sighed, and it sounded like giving in. "I guess I could notice the weather in Siberia, if it's changing that much. But I have better things to notice." He pulled me into a hug.

I wrinkled my nose. "I notice you smell a bit like a fishing trawler. I suppose you're worth it."

I didn't know much else just then. Finding something to admire in Maddi, of all people? That was disorienting.

76

Maddi

MOM AND DAD URGED me to have friends over on Monday evening, instead of our usual family home evening. I planned homemade pizza and a video. Troy came early to help with the food, after a full day of work at his summer job in a warehouse. The first two pizzas were almost ready for the oven when the doorbell rang. We didn't expect anyone yet—and it wasn't someone we expected.

It was Maddi. I was surprised, intrigued, and a bit disoriented again.

Her navy top, knee-length denim shorts, and sandals seemed conservative for her, and she looked and sounded nervous. "Hi, Jenny. I know you're not expecting me. Could I talk to you for a few minutes? Troy too, if he's here. Unless this is bad time." She glanced toward the driveway. "I thought that might be his car."

Automatically I invited her in. But if she wanted my help with her dance, I'd have to tell her I was leaving town. "Troy's in the kitchen," I said. "I'll text him."

At first I just stared at my phone, too rattled to process what I wanted to tell him. Then it came to me. "Need you in living room. You'll never believe who's here."

He didn't reply. He just came. The next thing I knew, he was saying, "Hi, Maddi." His tone wasn't glacial, but it wasn't warm.

I invited her to sit. It was easier to be gracious than I might have expected. Before I could ask what on earth she was doing in my living room—but more politely than that—she spoke instead.

"Thanks for inviting me in. Sorry to intrude." Her eyes got bigger. "I'm really nervous."

"Don't be," Troy said calmly. "We're pretty harmless."

She nodded, and her lower lip trembled.

"What can we do for you?" I asked.

She looked down at her hands. They were clasped so tightly in her lap that her knuckles were white. Then she looked back up at us. "Tomorrow morning I have a meeting with the principal, the athletic director, and Coach P about whether I'll be cheer captain or not. It was going to be July, but we added a workshop, and they need to decide now."

"What do you think they'll say?" I asked.

"I don't know. Maybe it doesn't matter. At least I'm doing cheer. That's why I came—to thank you for that, and for not hating me like I hated you. If you hadn't persuaded them to let me stay . . . I still can't believe you did that, after what I did. I'm really, really sorry."

"Thank you," I said. Somehow I wanted to help her, and I had an idea. "We could go with you. We might get a chance to tell Coach Witt something nice about you. At least they'd see us."

She stared at me. "You would do that?"

I had the same question. The answer turned out to be, "I think we would."

"Why?" Her eyes darted to Troy and back. "Why would you help me?"

Which was another good question. I looked at Troy, but he just watched expectantly.

"I'm not sure how to say this," I said. "I don't want to hurt you."

"Don't let that stop you," she said. "Anything bad you could say, I probably already agree with."

"Okay," I said. "The old Maddi hated people. Hurt people. Went out of her way to hurt people." The last few words came out shaky.

I quickly composed myself, so I could sound happy for the happy part. "But nobody's seen her lately. The new Maddi helps people. You're kind and unselfish, even humble. Why wouldn't we help you?" There were still some good reasons, but I was trying to be better than that, even if part of me wanted her to acknowledge them.

"Because . . ." She gave me a pleading look. "Because I lied about you . . . both of you . . . abused you . . . humiliated you in front of the whole school. Because I . . . wanted to destroy you."

It was her remorse, not my remembered pain, that overwhelmed me. From that moment I was convinced the new Maddi was real. And pretty amazing. "We haven't forgotten," I said softly. "But you're obviously not that person anymore."

"Obviously?"

"Pretty hard to miss," I said.

"I've been trying not to be evil."

I had another crazy idea. "Do you have other plans tonight?"

She shook her head. "Too nervous about tomorrow. And this. I sat in my car for twenty minutes before I could walk up to your door and ring the bell."

"We have friends coming for pizza, salad, and a video," I said. "Want to join us? Right now you could help us in the kitchen."

"I only meant to stay a few minutes," she said. "Do you really want me to? Both of you? I don't want to intrude." She bit her lower lip for a second, then turned to Troy. "You haven't said anything for a while."

"Not much to say," he said. "Jenny pretty much nailed it."

She looked at me, then him, then me again. "I'll stay if you want me to. Thank you."

"I want more than that," I said.

"Okay," she said tentatively.

"The friends are Will, Jack, and Nikki—big surprise—and they might bring dates. I'm thinking, the student body president and most of the Tiger Committee leadership carry some weight, and under the circumstances Troy and I probably do too. Maybe we could write a letter and all sign it, telling them you've been a fine leader so far this summer."

In the silence that followed, we heard a beep from the kitchen, but I couldn't remember what we were timing. We didn't have pizza in the oven yet.

Troy jumped up. "I'll get it." He left for the kitchen but quickly reappeared. "Jenny, could I borrow you for a minute?"

I looked at Maddi and shrugged. "Sorry. I'll be right back."

By the time we reached the kitchen, I'd figured out the beeping. The oven was done preheating.

"What are you thinking?" Troy asked.

"If the pizza's a little late, it's not a big deal."

"I mean out there. Maddi."

I studied his serious face. "I don't know. I just want to help her."

"Why?"

"That's what I don't know. I just do."

He was silent.

"We helped her before," I added. "And you already have tomorrow morning off work for me. If you don't want to, I'll understand."

His gaze grew distant.

"Are you remembering the pain?" I asked.

He nodded. "Anger too."

"You don't have to do this," I said, trying not to remember the pain and anger myself. "I should have asked you first."

He sighed, breathed deeply, sighed again, and seemed to return to the present. He smiled faintly. "You're more forgiving than I am."

"Not more." I took a chance. "Maybe a few minutes faster in some cases."

He pulled me into a hug. I felt a few more deep breaths. Then he asked, "How can I help? Besides going with you in the morning?"

I leaned away enough to look up. "Are you sure?"

"I'm with you."

"Let's go back to Maddi, and I'll explain." I hesitated. "Unless you want to hear it first, in case you . . . you know."

"I trust you," he said.

Maddi was sitting straight, at the edge of her chair, hands clasped in her lap. Her whole posture seemed poised and composed, but her eyes were anxious.

"Here's what we're thinking," I began. "We're running a little late, but that's okay. If you'll help me finish the pizza, we can put Troy to work on my laptop writing a letter, which I'll bet we'll all sign."

She looked at Troy—and so did I. He looked at me and smiled a little. I smiled a little more and turned back to Maddi.

For the first time ever, I saw tears gather in her eyes. She stared at her hands in her lap for what felt like minutes. Finally she said, "I can't believe you'd do that, after what I did to you."

"We'll have to ask them," Troy said. "But Will says you've been great on the committee, especially with the sophomores. Sounds like leadership to me. If you ladies will excuse me . . . Great idea, Jenny. Laptop in the study?"

I nodded. He leaned down to kiss my cheek as he left, and I blushed, because Maddi was there. We both watched him leave.

"I had no idea how good a guy he is, when I started hating you because he liked you," she said. "But look who I'm telling."

"He's pretty amazing," I said.

"You looked so happy together, from the very beginning. I hated that." Her voice dropped nearly to a whisper. "I thought you were nobody. I was so wrong. I'm glad you're still together, no thanks to me."

We stood, and somehow she ended up hugging me tightly. After a second I hugged her back.

She spoke quietly. "I'm sorry for everything I did and everything I said. And everything everybody else said or did because of me. And every time anyone laughed or said something rude when they saw . . ." Her voice caught. "When they saw those last things I did to you."

Some of the old pain returned, but it was easy to suppress, when the girl who'd caused it was hugging me and apologizing again. And when I believed her.

"I wanted to say all that on my own once," she said, "when they weren't offering me a lot less punishment if I apologized."

If I hadn't already been convinced the new Maddi was real, that might have done it. "Thank you," I said. "But now you really never have to say it again."

On our way to the kitchen she asked, "Do you think you two and Nikki will ever completely forgive me? I know it's too soon, but eventually?"

It was yet another good question. I thought before I spoke. "I think we're getting there. The new Maddi makes it a lot easier. Do you think she'll ever completely forgive herself?"

She looked at me with damp, sad eyes. "I don't know. Maybe." The corners of her mouth trembled, and she looked away. "Not soon."

"May I tell you something?" I asked.

She nodded.

"When you first started saying things to me in the halls, I thought your eyes were full of cruelty and maybe hatred, like you said. But at least there was life in them. In the meeting that morning, the one with all the apologies, your eyes looked empty and lifeless. It was scary."

She nodded somberly, and I continued. "I can't imagine how bad that week must have been for you. Lately, though, like tonight, your eyes are sad, but there's life in them again. That's a good thing, right?"

A faint smile appeared, then disappeared. "Sometime, not tonight," she said, "I should tell you about that week and maybe some other stuff. You and Troy. If you want. Maybe Nikki too."

"Okay," I said. "For now, we're about to have starving basketball players on our hands. Let's get to work."

"I hope I have friends like all of you someday."

"We'll see how it goes when they get here," I said breezily. "Maybe you already do."

I shouldn't have said it. She started to weep.

Jack and Nikki soon appeared with Ty and Colin. Everyone was surprised to see Maddi, and it was awkward at first, but they were gracious. Will came alone, which I thought made Maddi more comfortable, because she wasn't the odd girl out.

While everyone ate, I invented an excuse to pull Nikki and Jack into my room for a minute, to tell them the latest. Nikki said Maddi had already found a moment to apologize to her again.

Maddi nervously excused herself before we told the others about our idea for the letter. Will was immediately in, and the others didn't take much longer.

I found her puttering with dirty dishes in the kitchen and invited her back. She didn't move. I knew what she wanted to ask, and I was eager to tell her. "We'll all sign the letter, and we'll all go with you in the morning, not just Troy and I. If that's okay. They were easy to persuade."

I handed her another tissue. This time, she smiled through her tears.

When we were back with the group, she said, "I didn't join the Tiger Committee so you would do something like this for me. I just wanted to help for a change."

"We know," Will said gently. "You are helping."

"I'm not even counting it as part of my community service. They said I could, but I'm not."

"So it's okay if we come?" Will asked.

She looked at him for a few seconds. "Thank you. Yes. All of you. Thank you."

After that, we watched an old, dumb movie that was Troy's idea. It was a lot of fun. Maddi relaxed a little, but she barely said a word.

The party broke up about 9:15, because we suddenly had an early morning meeting, and I still had to pack for Maine. I'd planned to procrastinate that until morning, but now I couldn't.

As she left, Maddi started to apologize again, but I stopped her. "Remember? You never have to say that again."

"Okay." She nodded. "Thanks for everything tonight. And tomorrow."

"I'm glad you came," I said, and it was the truth. "See you at 6:45. Those doors near the locker rooms, right?"

"I still can't believe you're doing this. Thank you." She hugged me again, and we said good night.

Troy left last, and delightfully slowly, but earlier than usual. Later, just before our texting curfew, he wrote, "Good party. Love you madly. You were so kind to Maddi tonight. I tried to keep up."

I sent him a heart.

He replied, "Trying not to miss you until you leave."

I sent four more hearts. And tried not to miss him.

77

Reunion

Early the next morning, we met at the school and delivered our letter, then waited outside Coach's office. While Maddi was in the meeting, we attacked the donuts and juice Will brought for everyone.

Audrey was there too. After some small talk which got gradually less awkward, she said to me, "It's amazing how kind everyone has been to Maddi and the others. You and Troy started it, right?"

"It wasn't just us. Will did a lot, and Jack and Nikki, among others."

"She said this morning was your idea."

"I guess it started that way. As hard as it was to like her before, it's a lot easier now."

"She was pretty awful for a while," Audrey said. "I didn't realize how awful. But the Maddi I've known since preschool would never have done some of those things. I get that New Maddi is better, but the one I used to know wasn't so bad."

"I didn't know her before I met Troy," I said. "I mean, I knew her name. Now I'm glad I know her. May I ask you something?"

"Sure."

"Who will be cheer captain, if she isn't?"

She shrugged. "Probably me."

"So by helping her, we're making it less likely that you'll be cheer captain?"

"It's okay. I'll do it if I have to, but she's the only senior who really wants it. She's more of a leader than any of us. That's what I told Coach P. So I'm glad you're doing this, if that's what you wanted to know."

"It was," I confessed.

She hesitated. "Maybe I shouldn't tell you this, but I guess she won't mind, since you seem to be a fan of the new Maddi."

"I kind of am."

"She called me last night, pretty late. She was going to come today, thank them for considering her, and tell them she doesn't deserve to be captain and I do. We actually argued for a while. She really wants it, but I think she wanted to give it up to prove she's a different person now. Plus she still feels bad that I apologized too, when . . . you know."

"Who won?" I asked.

"The argument? I did, but I wasn't sure until this morning. I told her everyone can already see she's different, and the fact that she's different means she deserves it even more. Which is true, I think. Told her I wouldn't want it anyway." She looked up at me. "Which is mostly true."

They sent Maddi out while they deliberated. We sat with her and said encouraging things. Audrey tried to get her to eat a donut, but she was too nervous to eat more than a bite or two, and she didn't say much.

She didn't just want to be captain, I thought. She wanted to deserve it. And maybe Coach had chewed on her some more about what she'd done to lose it in the first place.

They invited her back into the office. When she came out a few minutes later, she was smiling through tears, just like the night before at my house. They were reinstating her. They'd said our letter and Audrey's recommendation had helped.

"A lot," she said, and her smile quivered. "They helped a lot."

She wouldn't let any of us leave without a hug and a tearful thank-you. Audrey was right beside her, hugging everyone and thanking us for helping her friend.

On the way home, to distract ourselves from what was next, Troy and I joked about how Ty and Colin couldn't walk straight or even breathe normally after two gorgeous cheerleaders hugged them. We were exaggerating, but only slightly.

⚬

An hour and a half later at my house, Jack and Nikki hugged me, kissed me ceremoniously on the cheek, promised not to steal my boyfriend while I was gone, said goodbye, and left. Unlike past summers, it wasn't the saddest part of leaving for Maine.

Before I got to the sad part with Troy, there was the nervous part. I handed him a thick manila envelope. "This is for you to read while I'm gone," I said as calmly as I could. "Or when you want to. If you want to. Don't open it now."

He grinned. "Okay, but what is it?"

I blushed. "I made copies for you. Some things I've written. The ones that might suck less than the rest." I'd spent hours and a lot of emotion choosing things and copying them—and telling myself to be brave—but I didn't tell him that.

"Thank you," he said as earnestly as if he had known what it cost. By the time he said, "This will be fun," he'd already wrapped me tightly in his arms.

After that came the sad part. We tried to be happy that there was so much to be sad about, and we stocked up a little on kisses—only three or four days' worth, but it was nice. Then we said goodbye for a month and a half, which totally, completely, and in all other ways sucked. I'd be gone for a month, and he'd leave for his second basketball camp the day before I returned. Our timing was terrible. Again.

I managed not to cry until he drove away. Then I turned to Mom, who had quietly appeared behind me. She hugged me, dried my tears, and applied a few comforting words which didn't work at all. Soon the three of us and Zeus were on our way to the Eastern Time Zone—but my heart wasn't.

———◆———

After four and a half days, more than 40 hours of driving, several little sightseeing detours, and hundreds of text messages between Troy and me—and hundreds more among Nikki, Jack, and me—we arrived at the lakeside cottage we always rented during the conference.

I was missing Troy too much to appreciate the lovely town, the gorgeous campus, the stunning tree-lined lake, or every beautiful mile of our drive through New England, but I broke into a huge smile when we walked through the front door. On a little table just inside, next to the gift basket the college's English Department always sent, were a dozen roses. There were three in each of the colors Troy had used in my Valentine's Day bouquet: red, white, pink, and lavender. My favorite parts of his note were at the end: "Jack and Nikki said to tell you I know what all these colors mean.—Your Troy."

The two-week writing workshop was intense, but I loved it. I was pretty tired for my nightly Skype dates with Troy, but they were a treat. Most nights, after we signed off, I connected with Jack or Nikki or both.

They were busy with more than the Tiger Committee. Jack was taking a summer term chemistry class at the university, besides having extra oboe lessons and practicing a lot. Nikki was attending a couple of dance camps for high school dancers and staffing camps for younger ones. In a way I was jealous of both. If my adventures had been close to home, I could have spent a lot more time with Troy, despite his summer job.

———◆◇◆———

People who knew about such things said it was mostly a normal high school summer. There was girl drama, and Will and Troy said there was boy drama too. There were breakups and makeups; some totaled cars, but no grave injuries or fatalities; and scattered rumors of a few arrests and an unplanned pregnancy or two.

What I thought might not be typical was that we all absorbed the drama and stuck together. School didn't feel fragile or threatening anymore, at least not to me—especially when we all did the Tiger Yell together, as we did at every school activity with at least a hundred kids, except dances. We got really good at it.

Hearts together, I kept thinking. Will was amazing.

———◆◇◆———

On a cloudy mid-August morning, Mrs. Pullman took Lily and me with her to the airport to pick up Troy. I texted him on the way, telling him he should hug his Mom and Lily first for two reasons: we'd win some points, and when he got to me, we wouldn't have to hurry.

That's what he did. And we didn't hurry.

On the way home his mom won some points too. Troy offered to drive, but she said no. Then she kept Lily busy with conversation in the front, so she wouldn't bother us in the back.

"I read everything while you were gone, then I read it again while I was gone," he said. "You're so talented."

"Thank you," I murmured. He'd mentioned some of it in the last month and a half, always kindly.

"Like how you wrote your age on every piece."

"So you wouldn't expect too much."

He chuckled. "Yeah. Got that."

"Thanks for reading, especially twice."

"Thanks for letting me."

We didn't talk much after that, and we didn't kiss at all after the airport. I put my head on his shoulder, and he put one arm around me, and I held his other hand in both of mine. It was forty full minutes of perfection.

I was so focused on Troy himself that I struggled later to remember what he was wearing, so I could rerun the airport scene properly in my mind. Probably the jeans he usually wore. I seemed to remember feeling the texture of denim when we were in the car, with our hands knit together and resting on his leg. But it might have been my leg. I also remembered two nice upper arms with black sleeves, so he was probably in one of the San Antonio Spurs t-shirts he liked, maybe even a new one.

What I remembered best was his touch, his eyes, and his smile.

⎯⎯⎯◆⎯⎯⎯

He took me to the last summer activity at school. He was definitely wearing jeans and a Spurs shirt that night—but so was I. He'd bought a nice shirt for me, and I was happy to wear it. We hardly let go of each other's hand the whole evening.

All the local junior high kids were invited to our end-of-summer bash, and hundreds of them came. We had mountains of food, some games, the school jazz band, a few local celebrities, and another outdoor movie.

We even taught the younger kids the Tiger Yell. It only took one demonstration and a couple of practice runs before they were all in. We were outdoors, and I imagined people hearing us all across town.

At the end, as Troy and I tossed some of the last bags of trash into the dumpsters behind the school, Maddi appeared, carrying another bag. Troy took it from her and tossed it in.

"Thanks," she said. "That's the last one." She removed her rubber gloves. "Could I talk to you two for a minute?"

We all discarded our gloves and walked a few yards away, to escape the dumpster odor. I hadn't seen her in almost two months. She looked different. Her hair was in a simple pony tail, and she wasn't wearing much makeup. Her face and her Tiger Committee t-shirt were a little dirty from the cleanup, and she looked tired. And older.

Her eyes were big, serious, and alive. She was beautiful. She said, "Could I come talk to you sometime before school starts? Just the two of you?"

"Sure," I said. "But you don't need to apologize again."

"I need to tell you some other things."

Troy and I had plans, but they were easily adjusted. "How about tomorrow at my place?" I suggested. "About 8:00?"

78

Joy

WHEN THE DOORBELL RANG, my parents disappeared upstairs. Before we opened the door, Troy said, "If we're together on the sofa and she's in a chair, it looks like it's us against her. What if you sit with her on the sofa? I'll take a chair. If you don't mind."

So Maddi sat at one end of the sofa, and I sat at the other. Troy sat in the nearest wing chair. Maddi could see both of us at once, which was good, and if I needed to hold Troy's hand at some point, he was within reach.

After a few pleasantries, we moved on to awkward silence and nervous half-smiles. "So what did you want to tell us?" I finally said.

Her cheeks flushed. "I've been talking to people I hurt and people I used, trying to fix what I can before school starts. I don't want to make excuses, and I still don't know what to say to you two, but summer's almost over. So here I am."

She smiled faintly, then looked down at her hands. "I've been seeing a good therapist this summer. She's helping me understand some things about myself, and other people too. It's kind of a new experience, trying to care what other people are going through. I started listening at church too. Hadn't done much of that for a while."

She looked up. "This is a long story. I hope you don't mind."

"Okay," I said, and she looked down again.

"My mom was the first person I tried to understand. She's so messed up. She married the wrong guy and got hurt, then stayed and let him keep hurting her, because she loved him. That was Dad. He's a lowlife. She divorced him eventually, and it was ugly. Then she married my stepdad—my ex-stepdad—who was worse. Either that or I understood what was going on a little better.

"Things with Evil Stepdad were bad off and on for about four years. Then last summer he tried to do some things to me, and Mom caught him. I guess she was afraid to blame him, so she blamed me. I'd have run away, if I could've thought of anywhere to go. I don't know why I didn't think of Audrey's or Brooke's or maybe Katie's. Their families would have taken me in. Anyway, I barricaded myself in my room every night, so nothing else would happen. Then he came home drunk on their anniversary, and, long story short, she finally threw him out. That happened last August, on the last day of summer break.

"I'm leaving out a lot of ugly stuff, and I'm not saying any of this to make excuses. It's so you'll understand, well, you'll see." She took a deep breath. Troy and I waited silently.

"The speaker at the seminary fireside that morning talked about fresh starts and second chances. I was pretty hungry for that. Something she said really stuck. 'Be the friend you want to have. Be the good person you want to become. Be the joy you want to feel.'"

She shrugged. "That sounded really good. I thought about it all day. Decided it was time for me to change what I could change. I went to the dance that night with simpler hair and makeup than usual. I wore a nice blouse and some pants that weren't skintight, which you know was unusual for me. I was surprised how much I liked the look.

"My therapist says I liked it because something inside me was telling me I'm more than how I look, more than just a body." She smiled wryly. "It was a long time before I listened to that little voice again. That's another lesson I've been trying to learn.

"Anyway, at the dance we did a mixer. They taught us a step, and we changed partners every minute or two, so I danced with a bunch of different guys. I'll show you a picture in a minute."

She looked up at me. "Were you there?"

I nodded. "I sat and watched, as usual." Or tried not to watch. I couldn't remember for sure.

"It was fun," she said. "I sort of forgot my miserable life for a while. Somewhere in the middle of the mixer, I danced with this guy I thought was cute. He was nice too. He asked me my name, and I thought, new school year, new start, maybe I needed a new name. So I said my name was—"

"Joy," Troy said. He looked at me. "She said her name was Joy." He turned to Maddi, looking pensive. "That was you."

I looked back and forth between them.

She nodded. "Not very original. 'Be the joy you want.' Plus it's actually my middle name. First time I can remember not hating it." She tapped at her smart phone for a moment, then handed it to me. "One of my leaders sent me this."

It was a picture of Troy dancing with Maddi, who looked like a different person from the one we'd known at school. If I hadn't already seen her simple look, I might not have recognized her.

I didn't care for pictures of Troy dancing with other girls, but I tried not to worry or judge. I passed her phone to Troy, and he stared at it.

"You were beautiful that night, Maddi," he said. "Kind of shy, but friendly enough. Everybody was new to me, and by the end all the faces were just a blur. Maybe that's why I didn't recognize you until now. I remembered your name." He shrugged. "Thought you must have been visiting, or maybe you went to a charter school or something."

"That's what I get for changing my name." She smiled ruefully and turned to me. "I won't be stealing your boyfriend, not that I could."

I smiled weakly. I didn't know what else to do.

"Things went bad before the dance was over," she said. "A couple of the girls came late and saw me looking different. I hadn't told them what I was doing. They accused me of thinking I was better than them and trying to make them look bad, when I was worse than they were. You can probably imagine what they called me. A lot of it wasn't true, but whatever. Some friends, right?

"I remember exactly what Mom said, when I got home and she saw me looking different. 'So now you think you're too good for me? Maybe you can fool yourself for a little while, but you don't fool me. You're evil and sick, even if you suddenly look like you belong at church.'"

Three tears rolled down Maddi's cheeks, seemingly unnoticed, and dripped onto her shirt. Her voice shook. "Even if I maybe wasn't as bad as they said, Mom and my friends were right about one thing. Changing my appearance didn't change who I was.

"Evil Stepdad hit her pretty hard while I was gone, before he finally left, maybe twenty minutes before I got home from the dance. She was in a lot of pain, and for a while she blamed me for ending her second marriage.

"The next day at school, I was back to my old self. My friends liked me again, and, Troy, you didn't recognize me at all. After that, when I tried to get you interested, you weren't interested. Then you two got together, and I hated you, Jenny. I made sure you knew it, too. When you both just ignored me—which was smart, and I don't blame you anymore—I told myself you thought you were too good for me."

She looked up at Troy. "By then I kind of hated you too."

I hadn't realized how high-pitched her voice had become, until she continued at her normal pitch. "It's not like I was a nice person before that. I wasn't. Except to my friends, most of the time. And I'm not trying to make excuses. I guess I said that already. I did what I did, and I said what I said, and it was horrible." Her voice was ascending again, and weaker. "It was my choice to be evil. And I know you said no more apologies, but I am so, so sorry."

More tears spilled down her cheeks—and mine.

Troy said quietly, "Maddi, I did think we were better than you. I'm sorry."

When he said that, a thought that had tried to form in my head finally did. I was guilty too. We were guilty—at least for judging Maddi without really knowing her. There was comfort in remembering we'd tried to be merciful eventually, and we'd helped her after she hurt us. But that wasn't enough to stop the guilt.

"I thought that too," I said, "and I'm sorry." I dabbed at my eyes with a tissue. Then I took another one and dried some of her tears. "And I'm sorry for what I said in the hall that day."

Troy started to say something, but Maddi smiled faintly and held up her hand to stop him. "Don't apologize to me. Somebody had to tell me the truth. I didn't like it, and I didn't think it was true, but it was."

Troy said, "I'm sorry I didn't recognize you after that dance."

She turned to him. "The girl you met that night wasn't real. Besides, what would you have thought if you had?"

"Probably that I liked Joy a lot better than Maddi."

"Yeah." She smiled ruefully. "So did I. If only Joy had been the real me. I wouldn't have done . . . a lot of things."

In my mind I saw Maddi as she'd looked the night before, after the school activity. I squeezed her hand. "What if she was the real you, and you just didn't know it?"

Her eyes met mine. "You two are so good together. I can't believe I hated you. No, actually that's why I hated you. Pretty stupid." Her hands began to shake again, and her voice trembled. "There's more I have to tell you."

I glanced at Troy and wondered what awful thing was coming.

Her voice was husky and soft. "Last spring, when they were going to expel me, or at least not let me do cheer anymore, I had a plan. I was serious. And I'm pretty good with plans, as you've seen. Cheer was the only thing in my life where I was worth anything. If they took that away, which I knew they would, there'd be nothing left of me."

She looked at Troy, then back at me. "Nothing to live for. My plan was to go home after that meeting, wait for Mom to leave for work, and take a whole bottle of her worst pills. I did some research to see which ones would make the most lethal overdose. Then I was going to lock myself in my room and barricade the door with my dresser and just be done."

She fell silent, but I was too stunned to speak. So was Troy, apparently. I watched tears roll down her cheeks and remembered what Coach had told us about kids ending up dead. For all my imagining, I hadn't imagined Maddi killing herself.

"I deserved everything they were going to do to me at school," she said. "I knew I did. But you convinced them to let me stay and . . . and you gave me my life back . . . after what I did to you. You even talked them out of the public apologies, which you really deserved. You didn't know you saved my life that morning, but you did."

She wiped her eyes a couple of times, and I wiped mine. Troy looked as shocked as I felt.

"By then I think I hated myself more than I hated you. Maybe you hated me too, but you saved me anyway. Thanking you doesn't seem like enough, but I don't know what else there is. So . . . thank you."

We were still too stunned to reply.

Her voice was steadier. "Mom took me home after the meeting. She didn't say much. Then she left for work. I tore up the note I wrote, and

I didn't go near any pills. I eventually cried myself to sleep. Didn't wake up until the next morning."

She breathed deeply. "You've saved me in another way since then, you and your friends. Thanks for letting me be part of things this summer. You've been telling people to forget the past and give me another chance, haven't you?"

"Will and some of the other guys were in charge of that," Troy said. "But yes."

"Thank you for that too. I hope I deserve it someday."

She let go of my hands and stood up. "I should go. I know you haven't had much time together this summer. I like that you're still together. Thanks for letting me say all that."

I didn't want her to leave. "Thanks for telling us," I said. "Even the ugly parts. But don't go yet. Could we talk a little more?"

"Okay." She slowly sat down.

Troy's voice was quiet. "We didn't know what you were going through. We just thought you were evil and we were good. Maybe if we hadn't been so full of ourselves . . ."

I said, "Maybe if people had let you change that first time, when you wanted to . . ."

"I made my own choices," she said. "I didn't see why you should be happy, if I wasn't. I really was evil."

"You're not evil anymore," I said.

We looked at each other without another word for a long moment. I began to smile. It was a friendly, genuine smile. It felt good. She tried to smile too, but she was still pretty upset.

"I'm starting to admire your courage," I said, sounding slightly nervous, because I was.

"*My* courage?"

"It must take a huge amount of courage to face everything and everybody, and change and move on. It might be the most beautiful thing about you, and that's saying something."

"You really think that?"

"I do now. It's kind of a new thought."

"Thank you."

"I really am glad you told us what you did," I said, "but we don't need to tell anyone else."

"You should tell your parents," she said. "They should know what a good thing you did. Nikki too. And Jack, if you want. They're kind of a matched set, right?"

⚊⚊⚊◆⚊⚊⚊

Before bed that night, I told Mom and Dad the scary part of Maddi's story. Even Dad's eyes got damp. Mom said they should never have doubted that mercy for Maddi was a good thing, when we insisted on it. I said I had doubted too.

I lay awake for quite a while that night, thinking about what Maddi almost did to herself. But there was another persistent thought, a happier one: Our new Maddi Joy had the kind of outward beauty I wished I had, and Troy thought I had. Now it was beauty we could admire and enjoy, because it wasn't just on the outside anymore. It was real.

Last Day

79

Not Again

FOR SEMINARY STUDENTS THE last day of summer break typically began too early, with the annual school-starts-tomorrow-so-we-want-you-feeling-super-spiritual sunrise fireside. At the other end of the day was a church dance which ended early, because it was a school night. This time was different. The fireside was in the evening, and there was no dance—but I was still walking on air, because I was dressing up for an evening with Troy.

I loved my new dress. The fabric resembled tiny stonework, with robin's egg blue shapes for stones and white for mortar. It was knee-length, light, and summery but with sleeves. I knew Troy would like me in it, and we'd look good together.

When he asked me if he should wear a necktie, I went a little overboard and suggested one of my favorite Troy looks: his pale yellow, subtly checked, long-sleeve dress shirt; off-white khakis; and a beautiful, understated blue necktie with more subtle shades than I could count.

I was considering asking Mom for her favorite string of small pearls when my phone vibrated. Jack was texting me. "Worried about the fireside?"

"Why? Am I speaking?" I wasn't, but I was dressed for it and feeling radiant.

"That would be excellent. You really don't know?"

"I know I'm wearing a new dress I like and going with the boy I love. And meeting my friends there. Kermit the Frog can speak for all I care."

"It's not Kermit. Ringing you now."

An actual phone call could be serious—but this felt like one of Jack's fun little comedies, so I didn't worry. When my phone buzzed again, I tapped the green button. "Hi, Jack!"

"Here's the thing. It's not just our fireside. It's a Church-wide broadcast for youth, and the speaker is the prophet. They've been announcing it at church for a couple of weeks. Where were you?"

"Not paying attention, I guess. I wondered why there's no dance. But we've had broadcasts before. What's the big deal?"

"You haven't heard the rumors?"

"What rumors?" Maybe this wasn't one of her comedies. Tiny creatures began to stretch their tiny wings in my stomach.

"Big changes. One of the neighbors works at Church headquarters. She heard it's a new edition of *For the Strength of Youth* they've been working on, with stricter standards for dating, not to mention banning caffeinated sodas, energy drinks, and some other things. The Church website says he's talking about relationships . . . hang on, here it is . . . about 'pleasing the Lord in all our relationships.'

"Anyway, I thought you might worry. I know you're not doing anything wrong, but what if he says something that makes the local Pharisees decide it's their duty to make you and Troy miserable again?"

Whole flocks of inner creatures took flight.

"There's more. In my ward they told all the youth to read a *New Era* article from last month as preparation for tonight. Supposedly that little assignment came from way up the food chain. I forget who wrote the article, but whoever it was doesn't get your counsel-or-commandment thing at all. It's weird how they can act like every last bit of counsel in some booklet ought to be considered a universal commandment, when they're about to announce major revisions to that very booklet, if that's what they're doing, but . . . If you didn't hear who was speaking, you didn't hear about the homework either, right?"

The miniature flying hordes landed hard and began to march around in their big heavy boots. I collapsed into my favorite chair and tried to think clearly.

"Still there?" she asked. "Did my stupid phone drop another one?"

"I'm here. I'm just imagining. I haven't read it. Is that wrong?"

"What are you imagining?"

After last spring, putting my fear into words was too easy. I wondered why I wasn't in tears already—and how a sudden empty feeling everywhere else could coexist with the parade in my stomach. "I'm imagining the President of the Church looking straight into the camera and saying, 'My dear young brothers and sisters, the love between a man and a woman is a splendid, sacred thing. It's meant to be eternal. But you must all be stricter than many of you have been, in the matter of delaying serious attachments until you're a few years older, when at least one of you has likely served a mission and you're both of an age to consider potential marriage partners.'"

"Ouch," Jack said.

"I'm not finished. 'I plead with you not to consider yourself an exception, not to think that this call to higher obedience is for everyone else but you. By taking this lightly you will forfeit essential blessings. We ask every parent and all others who lead or teach the wonderful youth of the Church to renew their efforts to teach these principles to each young man"—I took a quick breath—"and each young woman. Please reach out to them individually and help them to have the strength, desire, and understanding to choose the right.'"

Now Jack sounded morose. "You should be a speech writer. You don't think he'll say that, do you?"

I still wasn't crying, which was still strange, considering I was verging on panic. "I don't know what he'll say. But Troy and I are getting it right!"

"I know," she said. "And I'm sorry. I did it to you again. You weren't worried, and now you are. I'm really sorry."

"It's okay," I said—but nothing felt okay. I imagined Troy and me, facing each other with yearning, woeful, desperate eyes, then turning slowly and trudging off in opposite directions. Because the Lord's prophet had said we couldn't be together anymore until after Troy's mission, and we wanted to be good. Which meant obeying the Lord. Which meant following his prophet. Which meant walking away.

Ten minutes earlier, my life had been wonderful.

"We'll find you and sit with you," Jack said. "Probably a few minutes late, as usual."

"I will love that, as usual," I murmured, wondering if I still wanted to go.

"He probably won't say anything to cause you grief. He never has before. We usually like his talks."

"From your mouth to God's ears," I said.

"And God's mouth to the prophet's ears," she added. "And the prophet's ears to the prophet's mouth."

When we ended the call, I sent Troy a text. "Could you come early, please? I need some extra Troy time, and I need it soon. If you can."

He replied instantly. "Sure. What's up?"

"I need actual you, not virtual you."

"Leaving now. I love you."

"Thanks. I love you too."

Mom appeared in my bedroom doorway. "Remember, dinner's late tonight. Want a snack before—" She cocked her head and frowned. "What's wrong?"

"What do you mean?" I answered instinctively, as if I wanted to hide my fears, which I didn't. I wanted her to make them go away.

"You look like you're wearing the wrong dress to a funeral. Something you can tell me?"

Then I was in her arms, telling her what I was afraid to hear at the fireside. "I'm not even crying," I concluded. "I just feel empty and tired, and a little nauseous. I was so happy a few minutes ago."

"Honey, I'm pretty sure this is one of those things you shouldn't worry about unless it actually happens. Maybe not even then."

"What if it does? What if he says the counsel we've been ignoring is now an actual commandment? Prophets can do that, right?"

"The Word of Wisdom comes to mind. But I'm not too concerned in this case."

"That makes one of us," I grumbled.

"What will you choose if he does that?" she asked.

"Between breaking up and getting kicked out of the Church?"

"Your relationship with Troy won't jeopardize your Church membership. At your age you'd have to go very far astray, which you won't. Probably persistently, which you also won't."

"Between staying with Troy and making some Church leaders happy?"

"That's more like it," she said.

I took a deep, ragged breath, then another. "I'm more sure now than I was six months ago, when we talked about it in family home evening. I was pretty sure then."

"This is my point," she said.

"I don't want to go through all that again, or worse. Or longer. I want us to be glad to go to church and seminary."

"I want that too, and I still think it's too soon to worry. Besides, you can love God and the scriptures and the gospel, and worship and serve him, no matter what other people think. Is Troy worried?"

"He's on his way. All I said was, I need some extra Troy time. So he's probably worried. He just doesn't know why."

I heard the smile in her voice. "Maybe he can cheer you up. When he says you're beautiful, you should believe him. I love the dress. I was about to suggest a string of my pearls, but you don't need them. If you want them anyway, I'll get them."

I thanked her, but I wasn't ready to be distracted yet. "Has it ever been hard for you to go to church?"

"You know it has, and we can talk about that again sometime. But for now, please stop worrying about things that may never happen. Try to enjoy listening to the prophet. Later you can tell Dad and me all about it."

Another slow, deep breath, still slightly ragged. "You're really good at this, Mom."

"Good at hugging you? Or multiplying words to help you feel better?"

"The whole Mom thing."

"Thank you. I do what I can. Does any of it help right now?"

"Yes, but I don't know how much yet, or how long."

"One more thing. When you've been at this a little longer, you'll learn to read the rumors. Most are false. The few that have some basis in truth are almost always off the mark and wildly exaggerated. And for some reason, in the Church local decisions and instructions tend to be attributed—by others—to the First Presidency."

"You mean like what Jack said about reading that article to prepare for tonight?"

"Exactly," she said. "I think it's usually an innocent mistake."

"So there are actual reasons for me not to worry? Not just that it's too terrible to contemplate?" My voice broke.

She let go, stepped back, and put her hands on my shoulders. "This will not be a disaster. You'll see."

"I hope you're right. I'm still scared."

"A little or a lot?"

I finally crumbled. "Terrified."

She held me for another minute, while I cried on her shirt. Then she took my head in her hands and kissed my forehead. "You two will be okay. Was that a car door? I'll let him in."

I went to my dresser and picked up my heart necklace. I started to put it on but stopped. I wanted Troy to do it.

On a whim I retrieved the old, green noisemaker from the gray skirt in my closet, for a good luck charm—but that was just silly. I left it on my dresser.

A few minutes later, wearing my necklace and on my way out the door with Troy, I told Mom, "See you by 10:00." My voice sounded almost normal. I was faking it as hard as I could.

"Make it 11:00," Mom said.

"It's a school night. The fireside will be over by 9:00."

"It's the last evening of summer vacation," she said. "You're dressed up. Maybe you'll want to go somewhere nice afterward. Two sets of parents want you to take the extra hour." She grinned. "And you really should obey your parents, even when it's fun."

I turned to Troy, "Where will we want to go?"

"You'll see."

The instant the front door latched behind us, the lingering effect of Mom's comforting words slipped away, and I stopped pretending. We stood in the driveway for a few minutes, while I talked and he listened. His face darkened with concern. Finally he opened the car door for me, and I got in. He walked slowly around the back, opened his door, took his place behind the wheel, and looked at me for a long moment.

His voice was quiet and strained. "I don't know what to say."

"Sorry for the nasty surprise," I said.

"It's okay. Do you think he'll say something like that?"

"Mom doesn't think so. She says not to worry about things like that until—unless—they actually happen."

He nodded. "Makes sense, but it's not working for me right now."

"Me neither."

"Guess I better drive," he said. "Opposite direction?"

"I'm with you," I said. "But . . . you know."

"Not our style?"

"It's really not."

He reached over and brushed my latest tears away, then started the car. We drove toward the fireside, not away from it. I told myself that driving in that direction wasn't the same as going in and sitting down. But we'd eventually do that too, unless we had the good fortune to get a flat tire or something.

Unlike our evening meetings at girls camp, most of our so-called firesides were indoors, with no actual fire. This one was in a big church near the school. We held hands all the way there, but neither of us said another word.

We arrived twenty-two minutes early, by the dashboard clock. He let go of my hand to shift into Park, then took it again. We didn't get out of the car.

He gave me a wan smile, then leaned back in his seat and exhaled. "You've had longer to think about this, but may I tell you what I think?"

"I'm over here practically dying to hear what you think."

He tried to smile again, and I tried to smile in response.

"If he tells us the Lord now commands teenage couples to stop kissing, we could probably do that. Might be torture sometimes. I plan to kiss you before we go inside, just in case. If you don't want that, tell me now."

I didn't even breathe.

"Cool," he said. "Seriously, if he says sixteen and seventeen are too young to fall in love, I'll have to say that ship has sailed."

This boy was my rock.

My rock's voice trembled, but somehow seemed even stronger. "I will live the gospel the best I can," he said. "Worship God however I can. He's real, and he's good.

"What I won't do is let half a churchful of imperfect, well-meaning, meddling humans push me away from you or from God. If we have to endure another year of zealots and Pharisees telling us we're foolish or reckless or wicked because we're together—don't want to do that again, but I'd pay a lot higher price than that to be with you."

My heart wanted to expand, wrap itself around him, and never let go.

"If you feel the same way," he concluded. He sounded pretty confident that I did.

I looked into his eyes as warmly as my heart knew how, and he looked into mine. It didn't feel like silence to me, but maybe it did to him. "Please say something," he finally said.

I should have smiled, but I couldn't, and my voice shook. "Honey, you really should have borrowed your uncle's pickup for tonight."

That got me the smile I needed, and somehow my voice stopped shaking. "I decided long ago not to let anyone—and I think I have to mean *anyone*—at church push me away from you. Yes, I want to please God. I want to live the gospel. I want you—and if the Church has to fuss about that last one, it can just get over itself. Oh, and Mom and Dad are still on our side."

I started to wonder about his parents. I was reading his mind or vice versa.

"My parents adore you," he said. "I think we have enough credibility with them now. If there's something to figure out, we'll figure it out. Let's go hear what he has to say. Maybe he'll talk about tithing."

"Kiss first," I said quietly. "More than one, just in case."

80

The Prophet

A s Troy and I walked into the chapel, the phrase "lambs to the slaughter" flitted through my mind. When he asked what I was thinking, that's what I told him.

"Hope it's not that bad," he said, as we found a pew with room for Nikki and Jack.

"I know we won't die," I said. "But he can make the next year a lot harder for us, if he wants to."

Before I settled in for a good snuggle, I looked up at him and forgot what I was going to say next.

"Why are you smiling?" I asked. It was a strange time for a smile, even a small one.

He gave me a squeeze. "Remember when we looked out at a winter storm one night, and you said you'd rather face a lot more of the storm beside me than a lot less of it anywhere else?"

Now I had to smile too.

"Seems like a long time ago," he said. "But it's still my favorite thing you ever said to me."

I commenced snuggling as the broadcast began from the Conference Center at Temple Square in Salt Lake City. The Young Women General President was announcing the program when Nikki slipped into our pew.

"Jack's right behind me," she whispered. "Restroom. You okay? She feels awful for scaring you."

I nodded and smiled. It was a real smile, and she knew the difference.

"Good," she said, and turned toward the screen. When Jack joined us, I had a real smile for her too.

Soon it was the prophet's turn to speak. He had too much energy for a ninety-year-old man, but about the right amount of hair, which wasn't much. He stood at the pulpit, smiling warmly. Then he greeted us and said it was an honor and a joy to meet with the youth of the Church throughout the world. He thanked God for the technology which made such meetings possible. "You've grown up with smart phones and the Internet, but AM radio was still a wonder when I was your age." He shook his head slowly. "There are other wonders for me now. For example, my three children are senior citizens, and I wonder how they got so old." He paused for a ripple of laughter.

"We're given so much in this glorious time," he said. "So many marvelous blessings. So many ways to bless others. But blessings come with expectations." He quoted a line from the scriptures, "For unto whomsoever much is given, of him shall much be required."

The broadcast was supposed to be only an hour. We were twenty-two minutes in when he stood up, so he'd probably speak for about half an hour, I thought, and leave time for a hymn and a prayer. So two minutes down, twenty-eight to go. We were okay so far.

He told true stories from around the world, of youth finding ways to serve people. I liked them all, but it was the crippled boy in Africa who made me cry. The boys in his priests quorum took turns going a mile out of their way to wheel him in his wheelchair to school or church and home again—and they didn't have paved roads or concrete sidewalks. When his wheelchair broke, they carried him on their backs until it was fixed. That's when my tears started to pool.

He was a grateful and talented student, and he wanted to give back, so he started free evening classes in his village. Six nights a week, after the sun went down, he taught reading and arithmetic. Some of his students were children who had to work during the day instead of attending school. Some were adults who never went to school.

My tears overflowed. I brushed them away and checked the clock. Ten minutes to go, maybe, and Troy and I were still okay. Our hands might have been glued together.

"If you want to please the Lord," the prophet said, "and I know you do, keep up the good work. You're already pleasing him. So many of you do so wonderfully well. Turn to heaven often for guidance, power, and whatever forgiveness you need from day to day. Then reach out and take care of others in whatever ways they need, in whatever ways you can. Bring to every relationship, to every life you touch, the love of the Lord—the love he feels for you, the love you feel for him, the love he can help you feel for each person you are blessed to meet and know here on earth. There is no power in the universe to equal Christlike love."

Eight minutes to go, maybe, and our world still hadn't ended. I basked in a warm, joyful, comfortable feeling, which my parents and teachers often said was the Holy Spirit confirming that I was where I should be and doing okay for now, and what I was hearing was true. I'd almost forgotten my fears.

Then he said, "Before I sit down, we need to talk for a few minutes about commandments. This is important. You know that some of our relationships are more exciting than others. Some bring greater temptations and greater potential to harm others and ourselves."

I was a bundle of nerves again. My hand began to ache from squeezing Troy's so hard, but not enough to make me stop. Seven minutes was plenty of time to destroy our world.

I glanced up at Troy. He looked somber. His eyes were riveted on the screen.

"In all your relationships, if you would please the Lord, keep his commandments. You know them. Keep all the commandments all the time. Don't make excuses. Help each other to obey. If you haven't been doing very well at that, resolve to do better, starting tonight. Turn humbly for help to the Lord, your parents, even your bishop, all of whom live to help you.

"Please understand: Simply obeying the commandments which tell us what not to do is not enough, not in our friendships or families, not in our romances, when they come. We must do more. Where much is given, much is required."

Six minutes, maybe, and my nerves were doing more. So were Troy's, judging by his wide eyes and firmer grip on my hand.

"What I want to say about that is what I've been saying for the last half hour. It wasn't new to you when I began. Jesus said the first commandment is to love God with all our heart, might, mind, and strength, and to serve him. He said the second great commandment is to love our neighbors as ourselves, and he taught us that everyone is our neighbor. Tonight I've given you a dozen everyday examples, among millions from around the world, of you doing exactly that.

"That friend of yours is a child of God, just like you. That shy classmate or neighbor who stays home or keeps to the edge of the crowd is a child of God, just like me. So is that parent or sibling you can barely tolerate sometimes. If you're with a friend or family member or even a stranger, as you watch this fireside, you're both sitting with a beloved child of God.

"In all these relationships—in all our relationships—we please our Father in Heaven by trying not to focus on what others can do for us. We please God by imitating him, by focusing on what we can give—wisely and always within the proper bounds—and by struggling to see and know how best to lift others."

In the next moment he reminded me of Will.

"How can you and I bless their lives?" he asked. "There are a million different answers today. There will be a million more tomorrow, because everyone is different. Every day is different. But God will help each of us, if we ask him humbly and with real intent, to find the answer that applies to a specific person we can serve today. Usually it will be a small thing. It may be at home. Often it will employ the unique set of gifts he's given each of us to bless others. He will magnify and multiply those gifts, as we use them to serve him and others instead of ourselves.

"Blessing others' lives blesses our own, of course, but don't think very much about that. When you see an opportunity to be completely unselfish, to help someone who can offer nothing you want in return, don't let it pass you by. Embrace it for what it is: a blesséd opportunity to be the hands of God."

After that, I could tell he was concluding. I was weak with relief. Troy and I were still okay. He hadn't told us and everyone who knew us that our relationship was wrong. He'd told us how to improve it and every other relationship. I began to think all our trauma before the fireside was for nothing, but it wasn't. What Troy had said to me wasn't nothing. What I had said to him was something too.

The prophet turned carefully away from the pulpit, and someone took his arm to help him to his seat. Then he stopped, turned slowly back to the microphone, and smiled. "You can do this, when you're in charge of the meeting. If our fine organist and conductor will indulge an old man, I'd like us to sing a different hymn than we planned. I want to sing 'I Know That My Redeemer Lives,' and I want to sing it with you—because he does live, and we know it, you and I. God bless you, my dear friends."

I cried as much as I sang, but my tears were sweet. Then it was time for the closing prayer. I'd been taught since before I could frame a sentence to close my eyes and listen to the prayer, but this time I didn't. My wandering eyes found an amazing distraction.

A row or two ahead of us, on the far side of the wide chapel, Will and Maddi were sitting together. I'd seen Will earlier; he was hard to miss. But someone between us had shifted, and now I saw Maddi too. His arm was around her shoulders, and she was leaning on him.

I'd never seen him pay much attention to the old, toxic Maddi. He wasn't unkind, just uninterested. This was our new Maddi Joy, but it was still practically a miracle. She was practically a miracle. It was almost another miracle that I felt happy for both of them, not betrayed by Will. No, that one was definitely a miracle.

I didn't wait for the prayer to end. I tapped Troy's knee and pointed. He opened his eyes, saw them, and smiled.

After the prayer, Troy said we had to leave for our reservation right away. We said goodbye to Jack and Nikki and slipped out before refreshments and mingling, without talking to Will and Maddi.

In the parking lot he opened my door for me. I thanked him but reached for him instead, for a long, relieved, grateful hug.

"Think this is how church meetings are supposed to make us feel," said Troy after a minute. "Think I love that man."

"So do I," I said. "How could we not?"

"Pretty sure some people will still think we're getting it wrong," Troy said. "But I don't think he encouraged them tonight."

"I'm sure they will." I looked him in the eye and spoke earnestly. "I think he encouraged us."

Troy grinned. "Yeah."

<h1 style="text-align:center">81</h1>

Ending and Beginning

THE RESTAURANT WAS OUTSIDE of town, on a bluff overlooking a lake. The sign on the door said it was open until 11:00 p.m. The host led us to an outside table on a balcony.

The sun had set across the water, and the moon was close behind. The fiery clouds that streaked the evening sky were rapidly cooling to purples and blues, and the dwindling heat of the August day was just right for sitting outside.

I turned to Troy. "This is stunning! What's the occasion?"

He grinned. "This is for all the times you wished I was with you this summer, and vice versa, before we get busy with school again."

"I love it. But this is expensive. Dessert will be plenty."

"It's on Mom and Dad. I'm supposed to tell you they'll be disappointed if we order the cheapest things on the menu or skip dessert."

"Good thing I missed dinner at home," I said.

"Yeah. Whose idea was that?"

"I'm guessing you talked to Mom. This is really sweet of your parents."

"They love you," he said. "They think you're good for me, which means they trust us. Pretty good way to start a school year."

There was that word again. "Trust," I echoed. "Do you want me to cry again?"

He smiled gently. "No."

"Then you'd better change the subject."

"Okay. How about Will and Maddi? Looks like we'll be seeing more of her."

"Is that good or bad?" I asked.

"Might be okay. Hard to believe."

"Might be fun to watch," I said. "And not because he's sixteen inches taller. If he asks, tell him we approve."

"Good thought, girlfriend. But tonight's about us."

I beamed. "I love us."

He chuckled. "So do I."

We ate under the stars and talked, danced to the live piano, and ate and talked some more. We talked about us, but not in a breathless-for-the-future way. Mostly we remembered together—and it was the good things we remembered. The bad things didn't seem to matter as much. I wasn't sure what that meant, but it felt like it meant something.

Before we left, Troy excused himself to use the restroom. While I waited, I leaned on the balcony railing and watched the lake shimmer in the lights along the shore.

I heard him returning and recognized his step, so I wasn't startled when I felt two hands on my waist. I stood up straight and pulled his arms around me.

"What were you thinking about?" he asked softly.

"You first," I said.

"I saw you here, and I thought, your boyfriend is the luckiest guy in the world."

I squeezed the arms that squeezed me.

"Your turn," he said.

"Now I'm thinking my boyfriend is the luckiest guy in the world." I wanted him to laugh, and he did. "Before that, I was thinking about something the prophet said. Sometimes we get a chance to do something completely unselfish, and we shouldn't miss the opportunity. I was looking for anything I've done lately that was completely unselfish."

"You found some things, right?"

"I found two."

"I can list more than that," he said.

"You list. I'll listen."

"I've seen you with your grandpa. You're an angel. That's one thing every week. Sometimes more."

"I didn't count that. Doing things for my family feels a lot like doing them for myself."

"It's a good thing," he said. "I know you don't always do it for fun."

"I'm not saying it's fun or easy, and I know it helps him. I'm just saying it's partly for me. When you're there, it's even more for me."

"What about rebounding for me? You never wanted to do that."

"That was totally for me. It was one more way to be part of your life."

"I'm for that. How about insisting on mercy for Maddi and the others? We did that together, but you started it. Did a lot more good than we knew."

"I'm still reeling," I said. "It may be the best thing I've ever done, and I'm glad we did it together. But my main motive wasn't helping her. The punishment they were planning was making me ill. Plus I knew I'd run into her somewhere, someday, even if she was expelled, and I didn't want to be the one who got her kicked out of school and then some. I wanted to feel better about myself than that."

"So if the best, kindest, bravest thing you did all year—besides falling in love with me—was partly selfish too, how did you come up with anything that wasn't?"

"Here's one. It's a little thing, but see what you think. You know Ashton, my back fence neighbor?"

"The little girl who wants a boy to look at her the way I look at you?"

"The very one. We older girls were sitting together around the fire at camp one night, and I invited her to sit with us. I think it made her day, maybe her week. I didn't do it because I wanted her there. I kind of didn't. I just knew it would make her happy."

"Nice," he said. "What's the other one?"

"The time we invited Maddi to stay for pizza and a video, then delivered that letter the next morning. I didn't want anything for myself. I just wanted to help her. It was a sacrifice too, because it cost me some alone time with you, when I was about to leave for Maine."

"Good one," he said. "I'll put it on my list too."

"What else is on your list?"

"Just that," he said. "Everything else I can think of has you in it. When I do things for you, I feel like I'm doing them for myself. Bringing you a drink at the dance where we met, arranging for waltz lessons, giving you flowers, bringing you here tonight, everything."

If I hadn't loved the way he was holding me quite so much, I'd have turned and kissed him. "Mmm. Sounds like you love me."

"Yup," he said. "That's exactly what it sounds like."

I love you too.

I meant to say it aloud. Then I realized I hadn't. Then I realized I didn't have to. He'd heard me say it before, and I'd say it again and again, including later tonight. In the meantime, he absolutely knew.

We were quiet for a while, until I had to talk, because I had more thoughts. "At the New Year's Eve dance, a week or two before we met—were you there?"

"Beth was only here a couple of days, and she was flying out the next morning, so—"

"So you chose her over a dance. What a nice brother!"

"Her word was *loser*, but I think she was glad. Maybe I should have gone anyway. Could have met you sooner."

"You'd have been the only boy who even said hi to me that night. I just sat there and wished for things I couldn't have. Four things."

"Four? Let's see. You wanted to dance. You told me that one."

"I also wanted a boyfriend. What I told Jack and Nikki was, I wanted to be in love with a good boy who was in love with me. Most girls want that, I guess."

He kissed the top of my head. "Turns out, those are things you can have. What were the others?"

"You can probably guess."

"You more or less told me that second time that you want to be good, and it's been pretty obvious ever since. I love that about you."

"Happy Jenny. Can you guess the fourth thing?"

"Not really guessing. You wanted to be normal. Who wouldn't?"

"First try," I said.

"Eventually," he continued, "I learned to see the need behind all those. A very normal need. Pretty sure I need it too."

I spoke softly. "What is this need you saw in me?"

"You hate feeling like an outsider. You need to belong, not just with your parents and your two best friends. If you ask the boy who loves you, you need to realize you already belong. Think of all the things you've been part of since then. *Fiddler* and prom and girls camp and helping Maddi and dancing and going to basketball games, for example."

The memories parading through my mind stopped short when he spoke again.

"Been trying to help with that, when I could. Like you helped me from the first ten minutes."

"What did I do for you from the first ten minutes?" I asked. "What did you need from me? Because I didn't really think about that. I've mostly just been trying to be a good girlfriend so you'll keep wanting me."

"You're thinking about it now. What do you see?"

I forced my frazzled mind to engage. "If you just wanted a girlfriend, there were eager candidates. Gorgeous candidates. But you wanted me, not them."

"Not exactly news," he said. "Sorry, still listening."

"What happened from the very beginning is, we connected. We talked a lot. We listened a lot, laughed a lot. We made a connection we didn't have with other people. I mostly saw my side of that, but maybe you needed it in a way I didn't. They'd just uprooted you and moved you to Utah. That has to be really bad for feeling connected."

"You know me," he said.

"I also love you, but I have a confession."

"Okay."

"You've been thinking about what I need for a long time, obviously. We both thought a lot about what we need together. But I never thought very much about what you need individually, and how I could be a part of that."

He kissed the top of my head again. "Pretty sure what I needed was exactly what you just said, and there you were. Here you are."

"I just don't remember thinking about it like this before. I should have. I will, after this."

He squeezed. "I have a theory which might explain both our observations."

"Theory and observations? Jack will be so proud."

"Maybe your head is just catching up with what your heart saw all along, and answered without mentioning it to your head."

"I like that. I'm sorry about that day I was sick."

"We did okay," he said. "I think I learned to be less selfish on the way to the game that day."

"You were selfish before?"

"After that, I thought more about helping you, not just enjoying being with you. Good thing to learn."

"For later? Like prom day? After lunch, by the lake, to be specific?"

"Yeah, but don't do this."

"Don't do what?"

"Don't recite all the moments that were less than perfect." After a moment he continued. "Pretty sure I love the real you, not just . . . not just the filtered version of you."

My phone beeped softly. It was almost time to go.

"Now what are you thinking?" I asked.

"I am the luckiest guy in the world. You?"

"I'm the luckiest girl in the world, and I want another kiss before you take me home."

I got what I wanted.

On our way out we passed the open doors to a private room. A large, loud party ahead of us had just left, and the long table hadn't been cleared. "Wait here," Troy said.

He slipped into the room, looked around, and took something from the table. A plastic bag, maybe. "Show you in the car," he said when he returned.

In the car he showed me an opened bag which still had two noisemakers in it. "They left these. Must be for us." He handed me one and took one for himself. "They're not historical artifacts."

"Give them a minute," I said. "What are we celebrating?"

"Us," he said. "Together."

"Perfect," I said, and blew my noisemaker so the paper rolled out and hit his cheek.

We did that to each other until his tangled with mine enough that just blowing them again didn't separate them.

"I'll fix this," he said. His eyes sparkled in the parking lot's lights.

"Don't," I said. "Let them stay together."

"Yeah," he said, and suddenly he was serious. "May I tell you what else I've been thinking, not just tonight?"

I must have looked worried, because then he said, "It's not bad. I promise."

"Tell me."

"Remember when you said—I think it was at prom—that being in love was more difficult than you ever imagined?"

"And still better than I ever dreamed," I said. "It got a lot harder after that. Sorry, I'm interrupting."

"No, that's what I was going to say. Got a lot harder. But it's better than I ever dreamed too. Thanks, Jenny. I love you."

"And I love you." I could barely say it, I felt it so deeply.

⸻ ◆ ⸻

I lay awake that night, holding my heart necklace in my hand and thinking thoughts born at the restaurant and the fireside. I remembered the wintry Saturday night when we met. I thought of the January version of me, sitting at dances, trying not to wallow in self-pity.

Seven months had passed, and I had danced. I had waltzed. I had the boy, and not just any boy. I'd done more things that normal girls did, and I'd been treated—and mistreated—as a normal person more than before. I still had my illness, sat a lot, and needed my wonderful dog. But I was starting to feel normal or at least normal-adjacent.

Being good was more complicated. I hadn't just wanted to be good. I'd wanted people to think I was good—so it hurt when they didn't trust me.

In the sense of not doing what Troy and I shouldn't do together, we'd been good. And I'd helped people in some ways.

I prayed, read scripture, and attended church, but church was often painful, and some of my prayers were beyond snarky. My occasional tantrums were bad and selfish when I directed them at mortals too.

I generally told the truth and followed the rules, but I hadn't even hesitated before deceiving Kellie, to get some information she wasn't supposed to give me.

I obeyed and even talked to my parents—but the real reason I hadn't seriously considered seeing Troy secretly, when I thought that was all his parents might leave us, wasn't to honor anyone's parents. It just wouldn't work, especially for a girl who couldn't drive and wasn't used to hiding Troy-sized things from her parents.

I'd been a part of doing good things for Maddi, but mostly out of self-interest. Even her revelation that we'd helped her more than we imagined came with a sobering thought. For years, since long before I knew the word *stereotype*, I'd hated people looking at me and seeing a case, not a person. But I'd done that to her for months without a second thought. I'd looked at a struggling human soul and seen a villainous caricature.

So I was good sometimes, not always. In some ways, not others. I wasn't nearly as good as I'd thought, or as good as I might have been.

I could keep working on all that. Meanwhile, I had the boy. I yawned and stretched and smiled in the darkness of my room.

Oh, the boy, the boy, the boy, I thought, as I drifted toward sleep. The boy was amazing. The boy made me happy. The boy loved me, and I loved him. The boy and I would have lunch and some classes together every school day this year, starting tomorrow.

I opened my eyes just enough to see the clock on my nightstand.

Starting today, actually.

THE END

Afterword

To enjoy even realistic fiction, we must suspend our disbelief. We do this willingly, eagerly—as long as the author doesn't make it too difficult.

Some readers will think I've made it too difficult. They'll think the most unbelievable things in this story are how hard some young people try to be good and how well they succeed. I'll understand if you're unconvinced, but the quality of many youth I've known is almost literally unbelievable.

This book is not about any of those real youth in particular, or the real adults in their lives. The characters, settings, and specific situations are invented. But in a sense it's about all of them, at least in its optimism about youth and therefore about humanity in general. Hence this book's dedication.

I thank them, all of them, for making me believe.

DR

Acknowledgements

I don't know the names of everyone who helped as I wrote and rewrote this novel. Some were contest judges, who liked early and later versions of the first chapter well enough, apparently, but also suggested important improvements. And I may be forgetting some whose names I do know. Earnest apologies if that's you. The momentary limitations of memory do not diminish my enduring gratitude.

I especially thank my Irish alpha reader, Silvia O'Dwyer, who was as enthusiastic about this story as her notes on every chapter were meticulous. Beta readers Gayelynn Watson, Rebekah Walker, Shannon Devenport, Cassandra Carlson, and Lisa Kaye Johnson were diligent, insightful, and, given the length of the manuscript, quite generous. Sterling Johnson, Rachel Johnson, Chelsea Davis, and several of the Good AF Writers (AF is for American Fork) read portions of the story and provided useful feedback.

You might expect, as I certainly did until I learned better, that writers would be a competitive lot, perhaps even vindictive. After all, publication opportunities, shelf space in bookstores, book-buying dollars, and book-reading hours all are finite resources. But the writers I've met in the past several years, in Utah, Colorado, and elsewhere are not like that. They're helpful and endlessly encouraging, and I thank them.

Finally, my thoughts turn to James Odell, the sort of high school English teacher I wish everyone could have. I never imagined, through two years of his demanding classes at Snake River High School, that I would ever write fiction. But even then I had thoughts that needed to be written somehow. He taught us to see and believe in the power of just the right words, and, day after day and week after week, he showed us how to seek and find them.

"New and full of surprises."
—2025 Utah Book Awards

a 2025 Utah Book Awards Notable Read
winner of a 2024 Silver Quill Award

The Dad Who Stayed (a novella) is a child's view of family, friends, church, school, and a progressive 1970s university town. Then twelve unrelated short stories explore friendship, family, and romance in the lives of characters from seventh grade to old age.

"Every emotional payoff, whether flash-of-lightning funny or tearfully joyful, is earned through a rich depth of honesty that is the polar opposite of sentimentalism."

—Darrin McGraw, co-author of *Animal Future*

"Utterly charming . . . clever and kind."
—2025 Utah Book Awards

a 2025 Utah Book Awards Notable Read
winner of a 2024 Bronze Quill Award

In *Poor As I Am* (a novella) two grad students meet in a story of five Christmas Eves. Will the money he doesn't have or the money she doesn't want get in the way? Or does love conquer all, especially at Christmas? Then, in eight short stories, two eleven-year-old detectives investigate a Christmas mystery, a girl in a reindeer costume craves a Christmas kiss from Santa, and more.

About the Author

David Rodeback spent his childhood in urban Colorado, his youth in rural Idaho, and lived for a decade in upstate New York before moving to American Fork, Utah, where he has lived since 1998. Along the way he served a two-year proselyting mission in western Pennsylvania and New York for the Church of Jesus Christ of Latter-day Saints, completed degrees at Brigham Young University and Cornell University, and studied at the Pushkin Russian Language Institute in Moscow, USSR. He is Chief Marketing Technology Officer at a Utah manufacturing company.

He has worked as a speech writer, editor, translator, and college writing instructor; has won four Telly Awards for commercial video; has managed and advised political campaigns; has spent more than 30 years in lay leadership in his church (but prefers to teach); has blogged off and on for two decades on topics from politics to faith; and has seen exactly 66 words of his writing carved in stone. His two collections of short fiction have won Silver and Bronze Quill Awards and were named Notable Reads by the 2025 Utah Book Awards. He is the League of Utah Writers 2025 Writer of the Year.

He and his wife have four children and two grandchildren.

Let's Connect!

David is easy to find on Facebook (authorDavidRodeback), and at Medium, Simily, Goodreads, and Amazon, or you can connect more directly here:

Author website: DavidRodeback.com
Blog: BendableLight.com
E-mail: author@davidrodeback.com

Want to bring David to your classroom, writing group, or other venue, in person or virtually? Use the e-mail address above.

Sign up for David's quarterly e-mail **newsletter** with the QR code. (It points to DavidRodeback.com.)